PARALYSED SOULS

A M DHARMA

NEW GENERATION PUBLSIHING

Published in 2009 by New Generation Publishing

Published by New Generation Publishing

For more information regarding the author and his work go to

go to http://arbackyard.com

Dedicated to Dexter James....

PROLOGUE

As darkness began to quickly descend upon Rachel, the dark clouds rolled across the sky in what looked almost like time lapse photography. The silver streaks billowed across the sky in the opposite direction to her destination, almost as if they were running scared from what it was that she was approaching. To Rachel, it felt as though they knew the condemned depravity to the secrets in which she despairingly searched.

Continuing her journey, the silhouettes from the trees became haunting in their appearance. The long branches stretched out as far they could reach. It was almost as if, *they too*, were searching for the forbidden answers that they longed so dearly for. Their limbs doing all they could to retain the last of the leaves. Leaves which they had worn throughout the spring and summer and which would soon shed themselves as winter fast approached. When they would be mercifully stripped bare for the coldest duration of the year.

It was like the sick joke that nature had decided to play on them each year throughout their existence. She watched silently, thinking quietly to herself, as the woodland passed her by into another yet another province. As Rachel drove past the open fields, where livestock bared the harsh realities of the world within which we lived each day, she thought about how we all did our best to conquer all the shit that the world decided to throw at us.

The trees on opposite sides of the road came together as one and formed what appeared to be a gateway for her. As the head lights brightly illuminated the black tunnel throughout the deep foliage, Rachel felt somewhat compelled to stare at them as they entwined with one another. They seemed like shameless lovers...

or the devil's minions, engaging in sordid acts of depraved lust, as they observed Rachel travelling alone from high above the road.

Every now and then, the headlights from an oncoming vehicle would enlighten them. The branches seemed to scurry away from the exposure to the light that glared upon them. It was like scared, trapped rats.

As she tackled the winding country roads, which were covered with saturated leaves, Rachel knew that the eerie activity of the branches was merely from the harsh volatile winds that she could blatantly hear whistling loudly outside. The same wind that was trying its best of efforts to penetrate into the confines of the vehicle.

There were much quicker and easier ways to get to where she was going. But she liked the animosity of the country roads and lanes, as she glided her midnight blue Ford Explorer up from the steep climax through Alderley Edge. Sliding the gears of her four wheel drive with ease, she tackled the cold, wet road, whilst taking in her surroundings as the memories flooded back to her.

She couldn't believe that it was autumn already. She had always loved this time of year, especially places like where she was driving through at present. She and Becky, her daughter, had always loved coming up here in the autumn. The leaves throughout the woodland would shimmer with sheer intensity, as the rays of sunlight tried to rupture through the trees red and golden exterior. All the while, enhancing their colours, and making the woods appear almost as magical as all of the old folk tales, which went hand in hand with the areas history.

As thoughts of young Becky clouded her mind, she could feel a single tear escaping, trickling down the left hand side of her face and obscuring the image she'd been taking in. But she knew, that no matter how many tears she shed, they would never prosper in obscuring the image she held tightly in her mind of her precious little girl. Her precious little princess as she had always referred to her, always making her giggle bashfully.

As her eyes opened, Rachel suddenly lost all sense of space and time as she witnessed the image precisely before her, as if the road no longer existed, and she bore all the sensations of freedom finely being granted to her. It was as if her prayers, which she no longer believed in, had finally been answered at long last.

Rachel perceived the clear vision before her, as the two of them ran wildly, susceptible of the forest that engulfed them. Screaming and laughing without a care in the world as they both

headed towards her husband Peter, with Becky shrieking out in utter joy for her father, as he scooped her up into his arms lovingly.

She was lost in the euphoria of it all, grasping at it, never wanting it to end, when suddenly the flashing headlights coming straight at her and the squealing of the horn, brought her crashing violently down into reality.

As she swerved wildly from the wrong side of road, to avoid colliding with the oncoming vehicle, she crashed straight into the grassy, mud soaked embankment.

Breathing both hard and uncontrolled as sweat stung her eyes, the sound of the screeching horn from the driver of the oncoming car pierced through her ear drums.

As the driver sped past, she noticed that he continued screaming obscenities towards her. His face deranged with the anger he felt for Rachel, as he flipped two fingers rudely at her, and continued his journey without any thought given to her well being.

Whilst the image had dissipated from her perceivable outlook, she closed her eyes tightly to try and relinquish the beautiful sight that had been before her only seconds earlier. Only now, catching the ever fading representation, which she found herself reaching out for so desperately. As her little girl, her Becky danced away, tauntingly so, towards the bright light, that engulfed the entire veneer of what she so longed to hold onto.

Her daughter's laughter, also becoming increasingly abatement, as she opened her eyes to the scattering clouds that were dispersing all around her. It felt as if they were desperately trying to escape away from her, *as if it was she*, herself, was the one to be truly feared.

Falling forward, with her arms placed against the steering wheel, her head lodged against them. She sobbed out loud, as she thought back to the nightmare, that was twelve months ago to this very night. The night when all the contented laughter ceased to exist, and only, the perplexed affliction of deranged screams, relating to the unconditional anguish remained…

As Rachel had sat there on the large yellow settee, that had been recently purchased and was now tarnished with the dark crimson colouring that covered both her hands and face. She was filled with unconditional impassivity, as she gazed out of the smoky window panes. The yellow street lights were all but a haze to Rachel through her blurred vision.

Feeling the weight of the room around her. As all of its consequences had followed her back down the stairs, as the police officer had guided her away from the scene that she had already been tainted by holding Becky so tightly in her arms. So tightly in fact, that she swore she could still feel the little girl's body against her. Could still smell her lost innocence against her skin. She was almost sure of it and yet at the same time, she knew that it couldn't be so.

Not at that very moment, not at any other moments. The conviction hit her like a thunderbolt.

'Rachel,' said the familiar voice she recognised immediately. Her voice calling out with the sheer urgency it deserved, as her friend and associate entered the room.

Rachel looked up and saw the face of her friend, belonging to Detective Inspector Susan Hunter.

'Oh Jesus Christ Rachel, come here,' said Hunter, taking Rachel in her arms and holding her close. 'What the hell has happened?' She asked observing the police officer who stood beside the window. She immediately realised that his oppressive face told her the answer to which she searched.

Rachel began sobbing uncontrollably, as she clung onto her friend with absolute despondency. She began to fall to her knees, taking Hunter with her. The uniformed police officer turned and looked away, out of the window, uncertain where else he should look. Hunter soothed Rachel, as a mother would comfort a child, stroking her hair, holding her close and tenaciously - all the while, whispering, reassuringly to her.

Hunter's partner, Detective Inspector Mike Andrews suddenly appeared in the doorway to the living room. The lights from the hallway glistening behind him, as he looked down at the floor where Hunter was still kneeling with Rachel's head cradled against her breast. As Hunter glanced to her partner, she witnessed for the first time since she'd known him - that all colour had drained from his face, as he merely shook his head at her. Hunter closed her eyes, and held onto her friend all that much tighter, continuing to soothe her as best as she could. All the while, whispering reassuringly into her ear.

As Hunter opened her eyes and looked to Mike, he could see that for the first time since he had known her in all these years that her tough exterior had finally been broken. As he watched her cry openly. And all the while, he was thinking, that the worst part of it, was that she still hadn't seen the bedroom that awaited her upstairs.

Rachel and Hunter had known each other, more professionally than socially for several years now. In fact, it had been Hunter who had introduced her to her husband, Peter. Rachel had often tried to break through Hunter's external facade of toughness. And had tried on numerous occasions to get to know her more personally. But she had never succeeded in doing so. So had come to except, that although she considered Hunter to be a true friend, she also considered her to be, the most distant of her friends.

She was the only person she knew, who seemed content in living within a dark and depraved world of sadistic criminals. Their mere existence seemed to feed her the salvation that she had come to depend on so much as she had become so entangled within the dark world which she worked on a day to day basis.

Soon after Rachel started her postgraduate work, she became an unpaid trainee clinical psychologist with Salford Health Authority. Her long term goal had been to gain enough experience within the clinical field, so that she could go into the private sector. Allowing her to also work as a criminal psychologist.

The criminal interest had stemmed from her life as a child, and the family including the environment that she had grown up in and around. That's not to say, that by the studying of criminals, she felt that she was going to be able to understand her own family and their background better. That had never been her goal at all. But Rachel had figured, that with her families background being what it was, that she would already have an exceptional comprehension of how their minds already worked.

She hadn't been born with a silver spoon in her mouth, and she hadn't come from a particular nice part of town for that matter.

In fact, Rachel had grown up as the youngest of three children, with her two elder brothers on Ordsall housing estate in Salford, just outside of Manchester's city centre. By saying this though, it didn't mean that she had come from a poor family, and that they didn't have money, because they did. Only, it was money gained through her Irish father's many criminal activities that provided the family with the necessary security that they had needed.

Thomas Henessy, had arrived from Belfast like a whirlwind that wasn't about to be stopped. As he wreaked havoc and mayhem throughout the streets of both Salford and Manchester, he struck fear through the hearts of its residences. Things were beginning to tumble out of control, and it wouldn't have been long before Tommy's incarceration would have been inevitable.

Then to the delight of everybody, he met Katherine Coppershaw, who soon became his wife and bore his their first child Anthony. Tommy suddenly, almost as if overnight, began to calm down. He still had his wild streak of course, and he still engaged in many criminal activities. Only now, with a family before him, he'd become more careful, and a lot more calculating as to which activities he became involved within. Usually, only the kind of activities with high risk and a good return, money wise were his doings. But it was also to be his downfall.

It had been his so called activities, which led to rival family members, not only from the same estate, but also surrounding areas of the city, to become more and more distressed with his apparent rise throughout the years as he began to take over and operate one of the town's most notorious crews.

Therefore, before things became worse as rival factions perceived them to be, they had gunned down Tommy, their father and Kate, their mother with severe consequences. Rachel had only been eleven years old at the time. It had left her eldest brother, Tony, who had only been twenty-one at the time, to look after both her, and her fifteen year old brother Christopher.

Rachel had helped Hunter, both officially and also unofficially over the years. Breaking down crime scenes and evidence with a psychological approach. Working with the police force as a criminal psychologist whenever she was needed. Taking the necessary time out from her private practise, to help profiling a suspect. Assisting, so to narrow down the suspect field somewhat.

Hunter had reluctantly discovered, that a psychological approach to analyse an investigation, narrows down the potential subjects. Helping the police effectively focus their resources. It gave them a clearer indication of what they were looking for, even though it wouldn't supply them with a name or an address.

Rachel had helped with many investigations. Always trying to provide a clearer indication, to just how the suspects mind worked towards motivation in the crimes that they had committed.

'I need to go take a look upstairs now Rachel.' Hunter told her, as she held her at arms length. Rachel merely nodded acknowledgement.

Easing the Explorer over to pavement, just outside the small florist, beside the even smaller roundabout in the village of

Prestbury. Rachel sat there for a moment, watching silently observing, as the lady whom she assumed to be the proprietor of the establishment went about taking in her display from outside. Preparing to shut up shop for the night.

Climbing down from the vehicle, she stepped onto the cold wet pavement and shuddered as the nights air sent a chill through to the bone.

She quickly entered the small shop in order to avoid any eye contact with the few pedestrians remaining on the street. All of whom looked hassled and more than a little pissed off with the British weather that was doing its best to make them feel that way.

The strong aroma of different scents that progressed from the array of her colourful environment hit her as she entered the small surroundings. The cool air-conditioning, which was kept running, for the sake of preserving the many plants and flowers, didn't help combat the cold chill that had followed her into the shop.

'Evening,' said the florist, who was now placed behind the counter, dressed in an old heavy looking grey jacket to keep the warmth held tightly within.

Rachel nodded acknowledgement at the woman who looked to be in her early thirties, that was, if it hadn't been for the shock of grey hair upon her head. She was obviously more than comfortable enough with the colour of her hair, because she obviously hadn't bothered trying to dye the colour away.

Her skin was smooth, and she was very attractive. Only her clothes and wild hair made her look older than she was. Her cheeks were a rosy shade as she smiled pleasantly at her, probably more from the cold than anything else. Placing her hands on the counter, Rachel saw that her finger nails had been painted immaculately bright red and looked out of place, sticking through an old battered, woollen pair of fingerless gloves.

The woman noticed Rachel observing her fingers and laughed, 'My niece Leanne,' she said, holding up her hands for Rachel to see. 'She's studying to be a beautician and guess who gets to be the one she practises on.'

'They look nice.' Rachel told her, as she tried to avoid eye contact, and keeping conversation to the minimum.

'Takes after her mother that one,' she shook her head, at whatever thought she'd just had, then smiled brightly at Rachel again.

'Do you have any white roses please?' Rachel asked, changing the subject and trying to smile as best as she could. She swept her mame of gold red hair away from her face and instantly regretted it as the woman's eyes narrowed slightly, almost in recognition.

'Don't I know you from somewhere?' she asked cocking an eyebrow at her.

'No,' Rachel answered a little too quickly, looking to the black bucket containing the white roses, 'I wouldn't have thought so, I'm not from around here.'

'Still,' the florist pondered for a moment, 'you sure look familiar.'

'Could I get two dozen of those roses please?' Rachel ignored her last comment, as she felt the florist's eyes, piercing through her, trying to find some form of recognition.

'Of Course,' she said suddenly, breaking away from the stare and suddenly busying herself with the roses.

Turning away from the woman's inquisitive eyes, Rachel found herself staring out of the window. The condensation, fighting with air conditioner, for control of the glass pane before her. As she stared vacantly at the headlights that kept enlightening the shops interior as they made their way around the insignificant roundabout.

'Got yourself a date for tonight?' She heard the woman call out from the counter, still trying to make small talk. 'I remember when it used to be, that the man bought us women the flowers.' She cackled from the counter at her own humour.

Rachel didn't even acknowledge her, as she continued to stare aimlessly at the rain as it began to pour down hard. The drops bouncing from the road in quick successions as the few remaining people left on the street started to run for shelter. Drenched useless newspapers held in place of forgotten umbrellas. She observed a child, infuriating her mother, as she splashed into puddles, screaming with joy, as the water soaked her mother some more.

The young girl's mother, scolding her as she grabbed the little girl, half dragging her along the pavement. Her only thoughts were to escape the downpour, the little girl still screaming as if her mother was playing a game with her.

Rachel realised that the mother would never appreciate times like these. Not unless they were suddenly torn from her, just as they had been severed away from Rachel's life without any remorse from the one who took it all away.

'Here you go. Cash or credit card love?'

'Cash,' Rachel replied, turning from the window towards the counter. Breaking all thoughts of the little girl enjoying the rain, as only children can truly enjoy such a simple act of nature to its fullest. The flowers looked beautiful, the florist's years of experience shining through her display, as she handed them over.

As Rachel handed the money over to her she smiled at the woman, and thanked her for the roses, 'So you never told me,' the florist said. 'Is it a big date that you've got yourself tonight? Pretty young lady like yourself.'

As she smiled warmly, Rachel simply said, 'No, they were my daughter's favourite flowers.'

Just as she was turning, she saw the florist's curiosity click into place, as she completed the small confusing puzzle within her mind. But by then, she was already walking hurriedly out of the shop and back into her the privacy and warmth of the jeep...

When she thinks back, to both that day and night, a year ago now, back in 2001, she remembers every detail like the recurring nightmare that haunts her sleepless nights.

It hadn't been any different really. There wasn't anything different about that day that she could pick out as something that she should have picked up on. Both Becky and her had spent Saturday daytime running themselves silly around Alderley Edge. Exploring the dark damp caves with the enthusiasm that only a six year old could have. Becky continually asking questions and demanding answers from her mother. So inquisitive and so full of passion for the nature emcapturing her. Rachel had never known the child to have had a bad day when they had gone there. Everyday up here was a glorious day out, to be enjoyed to the utmost.

But that night, things at home hadn't been so glorious to say the least. The arguments with Peter had once again erupted. Arguments this time around, about her wanting to visit Tony that evening. She knew that her husband despised her eldest brother Tony, because of his background. And in a way she didn't blame him. After all, he had been one of Manchester's leading Crown Prosecutors. But because Tony Henessy was not only known to him, but to most of the law enforcement establishments throughout Manchester and its surrounding areas, he felt uneasy about Rachel wanting to spend time with him.

But what did he expect, Tony was not only her brother, he was the one who had acted as both a father and mother figure when she had needed it most in her life. At the time when both her

parents had been brutally killed and viciously taken from this world all them years before. Yes it was quite true that Tony had stepped into their father's shoes and taken over his business, much to the dismay of their rivals. Tony had hit back hard at the ones responsible for the deaths of their parents. Only to open up a bigger can of criminals, all of them wanting a piece of the action.

Although she was close to Christopher, the same couldn't be said for Tony and Christopher. They had never been that close. And that had been proven, when only a year after the burying their parents, Chris had completed his last year at school, and headed straight off into the army.

But what had really put an end to their relationship, was that, from leaving the army, Chris had headed straight off to Hong Kong to join the police force. Far out from his brothers reach.

Tony had fought long and hard to achieve what he had, and had, at the same time looked out for Rachel. Seeing her through some personal rough spots. Like when she started to dabble with heroin with the other kids from the estate. He'd been the one to step in, and send her away to university. She owed a lot to him, and knew that no matter what the two brothers felt for one another, both would always be there for her.

Therefore, the argument had once again erupted into a screaming match between the two of them that night. With little Becky storming off to her room, and locking herself away from the yelling and shouting. It also led to Rachel storming from their home in Wilmslow, heading straight towards the one the place in the world, that she felt truly safe. Her brother's house that, despite all of his money, still remained on the council estate in Ordsall.

The two of them had headed into the city centre and gotten themselves into a drunken state by one o'clock in the morning. Rachel had decided that it would be best if she got a taxi home.

Feeling like she didn't have a care in the world, she couldn't even remember what the argument from earlier that evening had been about as she climbed from the taxi into the cool night. Feeling the breeze stroke against her cheeks as she paid and thanked the driver.

She found that the cold air turned her on somewhat, and she suddenly, shamelessly, longed to be held in her husband's arms. To feel his hands exploring her body and his fingers tease her inner warmth, as their naked bodies tangled against one another.

But as she walked through the front door, she felt a chill run through her as she entered her domain. The air conditioner had been left on in replace of the heating. As she shivered, wrapping her arms around herself, she called out Peter's name to no response.

Spotting lights on upstairs, Rachel had presumed that is where her husband must have been. Therefore she headed towards the stairs. Something didn't feel right though, but she put it down to all the alcohol she'd consumed.

Edging the door ajar slightly to Becky's room, she loved to watch her daughter sleep. Sleep that was untainted, by the day to day struggles of every day life. Rachel was more than a little surprised to see that Becky's bed was empty. The bed sheets had been yanked back carelessly. She simply thought that their daughter had gone to join her father in their bed, maybe for comfort, after witnessing the fight earlier.

She then stepped towards their own bedroom, but as she was about to reach for the handle, something more than a mere chill ran through her, and she knew in that instant, that it wasn't anything to do with the temperature of their home. Pushing the door open she took her first step through the gates of hell.

She continued her drive up towards Macclesfield, there were no street lights in this part of the village. In fact, come to think of it, she couldn't recall ever seeing street lights in Prestbury. Which considering the money that went hand in hand with the residents of the area you'd have thought that street lights would be a deterrent to burglars, instead of the invite they imposed by not having them.

Then again, the tastes of the rich and somewhat famous, could sometimes, more often than not, never be explained. It was as if they thought of street lights, as something for the more common population that they wanted no part of.

The only light that she had, was from her headlights that kept switching from high beam and back again, as another vehicle approached. She glanced at the roses sitting next to her on the seat, remembering happier times. Thinking back to one Valentines Day when her husband, not one for convention with the usual red roses, had instead, sent her a dozen white roses not that long after the birth of Becky.

She remembered her daughter's eyes coming alive with the fascination. Staring wildly at these simple white rose buds. Remembering the way she kept reaching for them from her high chair. Rachel could still see the look on her face, as she handed

the white bud to her daughter, who rather than trying to eat it like just about everything else that she tried to eat, had become completely mesmerised by the flowers beauty and aroma.

She recalled that night, also being the first time, since the birth of Becky, that they had made love again. She remembered how they had fit together seemingly so perfectly physically. They'd been going through some rocky patches towards the end, but no matter what, physically they'd always matched. The sex, no matter how infrequent towards the end, had always been good with the two of them. And that's all that seemed to have mattered for some time.

She could see the gates up ahead, as she steered her way towards them, and the memories flooded back once again...

The walls were covered with dark red scrawlings and deranged illustrations. Words that she couldn't make out, the only certainty was that it had been composed in blood. Rachel stood there, her eyes wide in complete shock at the horrific scene before her.

Their bed had been moved into an upright position, its mattress had been removed and lay strewn across the floor, the sheets drenched in blood. The dark heavy oak frame had been placed against the wall in an up right position. Strapped with blood soaked white bandages at his wrists and ankles, hung her husband naked. It was as if somebody had crucified him. She let out piercing scream, as she stepped towards him.

She couldn't believe the sight before her, it was like a bad dream as she shook her head to rid itself of the image and screamed out his name, then the name of Becky in the same succession.

As she opened her eyes she couldn't believe what she was staring at, the image was almost surreal to her. His entire torso had been torn open, and his rib cage had been broken away - exposing his internal organs for the world to see - like some sick perverted display that was regarded as artistry.

Whoever had done this, had taken their time creating the scene. She had been to many crime scenes in the past, but had never witnessed something as graphic or as precise in all her years working with the police.

As Rachel went towards her husband, she found herself screaming her daughters name over and over. Becky had been placed at the feet of her father, and had been positioned on her knees, her small hands clasped together as if in prayer for their dying souls that had been stripped from them.

Reaching out for her daughter, Rachel collapsed to floor, her own screams falling obstinately onto her own ears as she grasped like a mad woman at the carpet. Pulling herself towards them both, the floor, seemingly holding her back like some unknown force, as her tears blinded the way.

Becky fell backwards from her kneeling position into her mother's arms, as Rachel wrapped her protective arms, around the body of her only child. She suddenly felt her whole world collapsing, imploding in on itself, as her little girl, had also had her chest torn open.

Rocking back and forth, with Becky held tightly in her arms, she was mumbling pointless apologies and telling her over and over, just how much she loved her.

As she held Becky in he arms, cradling her limp form, she noticed something that wasn't supposed to be there. Not relinquishing her grip, she moved Becky's long golden curls away from her face and looked down into the emptiness that had occupied her daughter's small yet most precious lifeline, and in that instant, she realised, that Becky's heart had been removed.

As more tears flowed, she looked closer, perceiving something white and realised in that precise moment, that in its place was what appeared to be a white dove. As she gazed up towards her husband's body, see realised that he too had, had his heart removed. And there also, she could see the stained white feathers sticking from inside the cavity of his existence.

As she finally began to take in her surroundings. She could now clearly see the wings that had been drawn crudely in blood. Sprouting gloriously, as if they were part of her husband, as if, Peter was an angel.

There was other scrawlings that filled the walls that she couldn't quite make out. But her eyes kept coming back to the wings, as if it was all some kind of a sick perverted joke someone had played. But this wasn't any kind of a joke or some sick game that someone played, this was for real, someone had taken the lives of the two people she loved more than anything else.

As she held tightly to her daughter's body she cried like she'd never cried before, and was still in that same position when the police arrived on the scene.

Rachel sat there staring at the gates to the enclosed surroundings. She could hear the low hum of her motor ticking over keeping the heating alive. She knew that at this time of the year when darkness fell so quickly, they locked all the entrances. Fully aware, that beyond the gates, would be deserted. Nobody

16

was around; nobody wanted to be around a place like this when nightfall descended.

But she preferred it like this, when darkness had succumbed, and everybody had gone home. Nightfall gave her the secrecy, and obscurity that she truly appreciated. Especially after all the publicity of the previous year that the case had attracted.

She remembered back to Peter bringing her here when they had first started dating. He'd brought her to meet his parents for the first time that had always lived in Macclesfield where Peter had grown up. He'd walked her through from the far entrance into what was known as West Park. At the time that Peter brought her here, it was in full bloom. The park was divided into two sections. The upper part where the children played on the climbing frames and swings, and where the pensioners played bowls in the summer time.

And then the lower half, where Rachel now sat. The darker existence of the park, where the children didn't play and the pensioners tried best not to think about.

Peter had been different from anybody else that she had ever met. He wasn't like anybody that she'd known growing up. At the time that they had met, he had been working a case against a serial rapist that Rachel had profiled for Hunter. She'd had to give evidence to her role in the investigation, and it had been Hunter who had introduced the two of them.

She'd been attracted to him immediately, although she had refused to go out with him for fear of rejection once he learnt of her family background. Hunter had encouraged her, saying that Tony shouldn't be a factor in the issue if she liked the guy, which she certainly did do. He had persisted, until eventually she had agreed to go out for a meal. She planned on telling him all about Tony, and her family's background that night at the meal. But there had been no need, as he'd already known.

Peter had told her that he'd done some checking, and that it didn't matter, as it was her that he was interested in, and not her family. But that had all changed, as both their relationship and careers began to grow to greater heights. Things had gotten a little better after the birth of Becky. But despite what he'd said in the beginning, it hadn't been enough for Peter to be able to forget about Tony's existence – and the world within which he lived.

It hadn't helped that Tony had felt the same way about Peter. And it also didn't help that Peter, had put some of Tony's closest friends away, as guests of Her Majesty in places like Strangeways or remanded to Walton in Liverpool. In a way, she

thought the biggest problem had been that her husband was afraid of the day, that he may have to be the one to put his own criminal of a brother-in-law away.

Tony though, had been especially close to Becky, and was always spoiling her. He'd never had children, which when Rachel had seen the way that he was with Becky, had surprised her. Although he'd always brushed her off with comments about the estate being no place to bring a kid up in.

She suspected that it was more to do with the fact he couldn't find any girl that he felt comfortable enough with to have a child. And that wasn't to say that girls were hard to find for him, as there was always more than enough interested in him at any one time.

But saying that, Rachel also knew that Tony had been the closest one out of the family to their father. And knew that deep down, he was worried, that he one day may face the same comeuppance that had ended their parent's existence. And she knew that for all his tough exterior, the one thing he feared, was not his own safety, but the safety of those around him, who he both cared and loved for.

She shook her head at the thought of her brother and climbed down from the Explorer. Sliding the roses gently through the frozen wrought iron gates, she then proceeded to climb over the gates...

Hunter and Mike Andrews had driven Rachel to the station in silence. In all her years in the police force, she knew that Rachel had never witnessed what she had in that bedroom. She and Rachel had worked some nasty, gruesome crime scenes in the past. But she knew that no matter what, nothing had prepared Rachel for the confrontation that she received, as she walked into that room tonight.

Rachel stared out of the window at the traffic, and dull grey buildings, passing her by as they made their way through the near deserted streets.

At the station, the other detectives thought that maybe it were best if they questioned Rachel, especially with Hunter's acknowledgement as her friend. Thinking that possibly Rachel would hold back. She didn't argue, as she needed time to get to grips with her own thoughts on just how the investigation would proceed. Needing to sort them into some sort of workable order. Besides which, all the detectives knew that it would be Hunter heading the investigation, as she one, was their superior and two, was the best detective that Manchester had. They all knew

that if anybody was going to catch this sick bastard, then it would be Hunter.

Rachel had told the doctor, that she was all right to answer any of the questions that they wanted to ask. Against his best wishes, before she reminded him, that she was also a doctor and that she wanted this part over with as soon as she could.

So that she could grieve for her lost ones in her own way, and that way, she thought to herself, was to track down this sick deranged fuck and kill him with her bare hands. Although she kept that part to herself.

Feeling numb throughout her entire body, she knew that their questions needed answering. Aware that the sooner they did it, the better her mind would be to recall everything about that night in question. The detectives questioned her, as to her whereabouts that night. They wanted to know everything about the night in question. All of which would be confirmed by the witnesses that had seen her and Tony, drinking all night in Henry's wine bar, around the back of Deansgate that night. There was also the taxi driver who would confirm dropping her off at home.

Why had they argued? What frame of mind had she been in when she left the house? The raised eyebrows at the mere mention of her brothers name. All the same shit she'd heard them use time and time again with suspects that she'd heard them question... Only this time, it was her being questioned.

They'd kept her there until morning before releasing her. It had been Hunter that had been there, waiting for her outside. in her car away from all the mayhem inside the station. She'd been there from the beginning and had waited. She had told Rachel that she was ready to take her back to her own home, for as long as she needed. Until they caught the sick bastard that had been responsible for the killings, if that's what it took.

Rachel thanked her, but told her it wouldn't be necessary. As there was only one place that she longed for now. Back home to Tony and the estate, she needed time alone, she needed to sort her head out, as she planned what it was that she was to do.

The only certain thing that she was sure of, was that no matter what her decision was, Tony would back her one-hundred percent, no questions asked, no answers required, and that is exactly what she needed at the present time.

Finding her way through the darkness with ease, she been here before and even if she hadn't been, then she would still have found them in the darkness. This part of West Park held the

small church and crematorium where the service had been held at the request of Peter's parents. The haunting surroundings of the mausoleum, gave Rachel nothing but comfort. Knowing that they resided here gave her a warm feeling inside, despite the torrential downpour that she was oblivious too.

As she stood over the gravestone of her husband and child, that was situated by the cemetery's far wall, she let the tears fall freely down her face without any shame for them being there. Her only shame is that they still hadn't caught the killer responsible for their deaths. That, and the fact, that she still refused to help Hunter in any official capacity.

Though she felt no shame in the verity, that both her, and her brother had taken the liberty of the hunt themselves. They may have even been close at one point. But the one thing that she was certain of, was that she wouldn't rest peacefully until the killer was brought to justice, and it was her own kind of justice that she sought out.

Bending low to the gravestone, placing the white roses on top the grave, she felt the night air brush her cheek. Closing her eyes, and for that moment she let herself believe that the breeze was that of Becky caressing her face. As the intrepidity stroked through her, battling with her coat, she then allowed the breeze to work its way through her and she then allowed herself to now shamelessly think, that it had been Peter stood there touching her with the passion that she missed so dearly.

Through the sensation she felt and the rain drowning out all viable sound. She thought she could hear the sounds of what seemed to be an owl cooing in the way that owls did. But as she opened her eyes she saw the bright white feathers as they began to fluster frantically from the cemetery's wall. As though, by opening her eyes, she had somehow scared the doves from the perch as they observed her. She strained to see them, as they sailed wildly off into the dark sky. Circling with one another as they rose higher and higher.

Struggling through the rain to envision them, they disappeared from her view, leaving her motionless and wondering if she had in fact seen anything at all. Or whether it was simply her mind playing more tricks on her.

Once again she was all alone. Although deep down, she was certain that she wasn't alone in spirit. She truly believed that until she carried out the promise she had made to herself twelve months ago to the night. That both her husband's and her daughter's souls remained suspended in waiting for justice to be carried out, before they could truly rest in peace for all eternity.

Finally, she made the silent promise once again to the gravestone before her that bore the names of Peter and Becky Murphy. An unforgotten promise, that she would not quit searching out their killer for the vengeance that they deserved. And in seeking vengeance, she knew that she could finally set free their *paralysed souls*.

ONE

'**J**ust how old was this kid that you took there Tommy? He asked the arrogant teenager. The teenager who'd been asking around town about the two of them, and who was now slouched in back of his silver Mercedes. The lad was constantly sniffing away, as if he was full of a cold.

However, both he and his close friend sat next to him knew better than that. He was obviously one of the many rent boys that worked this area of Kings Cross railway station. Working to feed his habit, rather than feed himself. The lad was constantly looking out of the window, his eyes invariably darting in one direction, then another. He shook his head at the lad without turning to look round at him. He knew that his actions were associated to his paranoid nature, parallel with always having to keep an eye out for the police.

Finally turning to look at the scruffy lad, who was visibly shaking, probably more from whatever drugs he was strung out on, than the cold weather. None the less, he smiled at him, to try and calm him down somewhat, as he took in the boys clothing he wore. It was an array of miss matched attire. But from what he could see, they were all brand name clothing. His filthy Nike sweatshirt, that he presumed, must have been white at one time, and his oversized baggy denim jeans, probably designer also, that hung loosely around his waist. So much so in fact, that the kids Calvin Klein boxer shorts were showing though at the top.

As he glanced at the lad's trainers, he noticed that they were the one brand new thing that the kid appeared to be wearing. They also looked to be the new range of Nike Cortez; the ones with the metallic silver swoosh. In fact they were the same that he'd recently bought for his nephew in Manchester. Considering that

this kid was living on the streets, and despite his scruffy appearance, he sure wore some expensive clothes.

Besides, he could have been wrong in thinking that the kid was scruffy. For all he knew, this could be the fashion these days. He shook the thought away and nodded at the kid.

'Come on, tell us how old she was?' the big one suddenly asked, who was sat in the passenger seat. The one whose voice was so deep, it sounded almost as if it was fitted with one of those super woofers he'd seen in the electrical shops that he nicked from.

'She, she was only, nine, nine years old,' he finally answered them, although looking away at the same time. They weren't sure whether it was from the shame of what he'd been doing, or that he was just incapable of holding eye-contact with either of them.

'We need to be sure of all the details,' the driver continued. 'Are you sure that you saw him with other kids from the estate?'

The lad stared at him and nodded slowly, 'I never seen him with them kids, but I just know this is the guy you're looking for. When I heard about those kids going missing from the estate, I just knew it was him that was taking them, Believe me mister, this guy's a complete sick fuck.'

As Tommy watched the two in front of the vehicle curiously, he silently observed as they continued to look to one another. It was as if they were trying their best to fathom him out. But he was cool with that, for now anyway. Besides, he'd heard the stories, or more to the point, had heard the rumours that were associated with the two of them sat in the front of the vehicle.

The one who had spoke to him first, the slick looking driver, was known simply as Sleeper, whatever that was supposed to mean. It was the same with his counterpart, the one he kept referring to as Eazy, with a 'z'.

All he kept thinking to himself, was where the hell had these two guys got their names from. Then in that same thought, thought that it was best if he never found out where they're names had derived from.

As he perceived them both, he was convinced that Sleeper was definitely black, although his colouring was a shade lighter than his friends. He also had a slight Oriental look to his features. Bestowing him the appearance, of a shady cat-like figure, that was up to no good.

As for the other one, well he was at least twice as large as this Sleeper character. And it was safe to say, that they both scared the shit out of him. Although, if push came to shove, then he just

knew by looking at the slicker of the two guys, that you never fucked with him or anybody he knew.

Sleeper's feline eyes held no life to them. It was as if they'd lived a lifetime already, and now they had returned, to seek vengeance upon those who had wronged him in the past life.

'How long ago was this again?' It was Eazy that spoke to him now. Only he was looking at him through the sun shields window mirror, rather than turning around. 'When you took that girl to him?'

Tommy viewed the apparent look of disgust in the big mans eyes that he felt towards him. But he was used to shit like that, so just ignored it. Living on the streets like he did, you did whatever you had to. Merely to make it through to the next day. There were no morals to living on the street. The only reason he was sat here with these two now, spilling his guts to them, breaking the code of so called silence that went hand in hand with the street was that he had heard, that these two, would pay top dollar for any information on those kids that had gone missing from that estate in Lewisham.

'Just over a month ago was the last time I saw him,' he finally replied. 'I haven't seen him since then. He's not been around since then. And I've tried to stay out of sight after what happened last time with him.'

Tommy could see the back of Eazy's head, it was shining like polished marble, resembling a huge black bowling ball. Tommy didn't think that he'd ever seen anybody so big in real life before. The guy was huge, although it was still his friend, the one driving. He was the one that scared him more. He knew that the big one could probably kill you with his bare hands. But he reckoned, it would be how the slick one dealt with you, which scared him more so. He didn't want to even comprehend the consequences at the hands of Sleeper.

Neither of them said anything, not even to each other, as they waited for him to continue. 'It, it, was just supplying him at first,' he finally spoke up again.

'What do mean supplying him?' asked Eazy, who still hadn't turned around.

Tommy suspected that he was way too big to even manage it. 'With the younger kids that he wanted.'

'How young are we talking?' Eazy wanted to know.

'He liked them the younger the better,' he looked away again, in shame, or was it. 'The kids always came back alright though, I never thought anything of it, honest.'

'How old they were, I asked.'

'As, as, they, as young as four, or five,' he stammered, trying to hold eye contact and failing miserably.

'Where the fuck did you get kids that old from?' Sleeper snapped at him, then shook his head, 'What the fuck are kids that young doing out here.'

'It's not the kids on their own you know. It's them mother's, father's even. You'll be surprised what these smack heads will do for money mister,' he replied defiantly. 'It's all kinds of drugs nowadays. Gear from crack to smack to whatever else they can get off on. Shit, you guys know that. Like I said, them strung out bitches are even bringing their own kids with them nowadays. Shit, I bet the kids can make more money for them than even they can in this day and age. They're so fucking messed up on all that shit,' he paused, sniffing loudly in recognition of the habits they all kept. 'This ain't exactly the fucking Ritz or Mayfair they're working. This ain't some jumped up hookers pad in Chelsea... This is the streets, and we all do what we have to do in order to fucking survive the day to fucking day nightmares.' He had an impertinent look upon his face, as if challenging them both to put up an argument.

Sleeper looked to his friend shaking his head, at what the kid had just told them both. He was glad that they'd both pulled out of the drug business several years before. He hadn't been and wasn't blind to what depraved acts people resorted to. But if what the kid had just told him was true, then they were reaching an all time low. To sell your own body for your fix was one thing. But to sell your own child, *Jesus fucking Christ*, just what the fuck was the country, no, in fact, what was the world coming to.

They'd both been legit for a number of years now. The only occasional illegal activity that he still engaged in nowadays was the disposal business as he preferred to refer to it. Paid contracts, *hitman*, whatever the hell people wanted to call it. That had always been his main speciality. Although, he now had his own set of strong morals, as to the contracts that he would or wouldn't take. And they were usually only personal ethics that allowed him to get involved theses days. Jobs like this that they were doing at the present time. Searching for missing children, or at least, searching for the one responsible for taking the children.

The kids had been going missing from their old estate in Lewisham over the past few months and the police seemed to be doing absolutely nothing about it. They knew that the police looked down on the ones from the estate. Knowing that they

weren't giving it their one-hundred percent where the kids were involved. Believing that they had all come from broken homes to begin with. But no matter whether that was the truth or not. The families deserved more than the police were offering them. Besides which, they had both grown up down there, and still kept in contact with their friends from the estate. Many of whom still resided there.

Although this wasn't a paid contract as there wasn't any money involved. The people on the estate had asked him to look into things because they knew of his past. They knew that even though he wasn't involved illegally anymore, that he still retained all of his old contacts. They knew that he could probably discover more than the police. Other families from the area were frightened for the safety of their children. Therefore, they had all scraped together what money they could between them, in order to ask for his help.

He'd accepted the offer, but refused their money. This was more personal for him, for both of them, they both had nephews and nieces and the thought of something happening to them, scared the shit out of them.

Neither of them needed the money. Between the two of them, they had profited well from all of the earlier illegal activities, and there had been many of them. But they had both invested the money wisely. Owning several legal enterprises, based both here in London, and further up North, in Manchester also.

'He made me do it, he said he'd kill me if I didn't do it,' said Tommy, breaking the silence that had hung so dryly in the confines of the vehicle, before once again falling silent on them.

'Come on Tommy,' said Sleeper sighing deeply, his patience starting to tether slightly with the lads nonchalant attitude to what he'd done. 'It'll be better if you tell us what happened, Come on now you don't want to tell the police about this shit do you now?'

'They can't know about this,' he snapped, as his eyes were suddenly wide with shock, as he looked back and fourth between the two of them. 'They can't ever know, they'll throw the key away. They'll, they'll, they'll lock me up with the sex cases, and they'll think that I'm some sick nonce or something.'

'Let's start again Tommy.' Sleeper said in a sombre tone, as he bent a little lower so to look into his eyes, and was shocked to see absolutely no guilt there. Shaking his head he continued, 'Just what the hell happened if you was only supplying him with the kids.'

26

'He never hurt them before,' he said shrugging as if that made it all okay. Wiping his nose on the back of his sleeve, he then rubbed his bloodshot eyes with the palm of his hand, all the while sniffing constantly. 'He always brought the kids back, and paid me to pay mothers whatever they wanted...and I always got my cut. Things were good, but, but, this one week night he turns up and doesn't want a kid. He just wants to talk with me, so I climb into this real nice motor, a lot like this one, but it was a darker colour, not sure of the exact colour.'

'Go on,' Eazy said impatiently, as Sleeper nodded at him to ease off a little for the time being.

Staring at Eazy with cold eyes for the interruption, he continued, 'He tells me that he wants me to get him a kid that won't be missed for a least a couple of days. He also says that he wants me to come along that night. You know, so that I know the kid will be alright like... But, he's says that he wants to keep the kid for the whole weekend. Says he'll pay me real good. The only thing is that I can't tell the mother about what we're doing.'

'Just how much was he going to pay you Tommy?' Sleeper asked, curious to know just how much it would cost for such an act of absolute depravity.

'A grand,' he replied, as his eyes lit up at the mere thought of it. Then suddenly dropped again at the thought of what had happened. 'He told me that I could do what I wanted with the money. But that the mother just wasn't to know. So I agreed. There's this homeless bitch that lives down in the underground. I'd used her kids before, and she was always so strung out that she never realised. So I figured that I'd just grab one of her kids that weekend.'

'Then what happened at the weekend?' Sleeper wanted to know, as Tommy went all quiet again.

'He drove me and Katie, that was the little girl. He wasn't bothered if they were girls or boys. Anyway, he drove us out into the countryside. Or at least that's what it looked like... there were fields and shit, not like you see here in the city. He took us to this real nice house.'

'Where was the house at Tommy?' Eazy asked, looking directly at him.

'That'll cost you,' he sneered greedily at them. 'Why do think that I've asking around for you guys. I knew that you were willing to pay for the information. Shit, ain't nothing for free in this world lads.'

Sleeper produced a wad of notes and watched as his eyes illuminated at the sight before him, 'But we need to know everything first kid.'

'Alright, alright, I'll tell you the story first.' He kept eye contact with Sleeper for a few moments then said, 'Then it'll be up to you what you do to the sick fucks.'

'What do you mean, fucks, Tommy?' Sleeper asked curiously, 'You said fucks, as in plural. You mean there was more than one of them?'

'That's the bit I'm getting to,' he groaned deeply, blowing the air out in a restless manner. 'When we got to his house, he tells us that he's got a treat for us in the basement. Now I'm not stupid, I know he's saying all this for the sake of Katie to make her feel more comfortable. But when we get down there, well, it, it was scary you know. There was all these bright lights, and I mean real bright. And I knows is that there is someone else there. He didn't say it. But I just knew that there was someone else there watching us. I could see camera equipment set up everywhere as well. There was this man that was sat behind the equipment and the lights. That's when it happened, it, it was, it was so fucking sick man.' He suddenly let out a loud sob, taking the two of them by surprise.

'What did they do?' Eazy reached out a lifted the kid's tear filled face to his.

'Jesus, it was so fucked up. I kept saying that I'd wait upstairs. But he said that I had to stay and watch, I kept saying that I didn't want to, but, but he just wouldn't listen. And I was scared about the other man that was there. I knew he was there and he knew that I knew and that scared me man. It was real weird, it wasn't fucking normal,' he said.

As if any of this story, was at all normal, Sleeper thought to himself. 'Are you sure about this other man Tommy,' Sleeper asked. 'I mean are you certain it was a man?'

'I seen his silhouette later on when they made me do it.' Wiping his nose on his sleeve again, he continued, 'He didn't even try to be nice with Katie. The sick fuck just started tearing at her clothes and... well you know what I mean right?' He suddenly snorted loudly, then rolling the window down spat the contents of the thick green flem out onto the street, 'She was so scared and I kept blaming myself.' He stared at them, as if he wanted them to believe him so much, 'Then he made her put this white dress on for him. All the while he kept giving her instructions on how he wanted her to pose for him. He, he then, then he made her.... it, it was, it was so fucking sick and it was

all my fault. But by that time, I couldn't do anything. I just, well I just thought about the money I'd get.' He suddenly stopped talking and began staring out of the window.

'Go on then kid, what happened next?' said Eazy, in almost a whisper, with his head bowed low.

'But then when he finished that awful shit with her, then, then, it got even worse.' He stopped talking and shuddered at the next thought.

'What happened?' Sleeper asked, feeling completely repulsed.

'He, he, the sick, he fucking made her…me…her,' he suddenly sobbed like the child he was, his entire attitude suddenly dissolved in a single moment. 'I didn't want to… but they made me, and, then, then, then he fucking …'

'Alright, alright Tommy enough,' yelled Eazy stopping him. 'Just give us the address.'

'There's more,' he said, as Sleeper looked to Eazy, not sure that they really wanted to know more of the horrific story. 'It was when I was there on the floor that I seen that he was a man, the other one who was there. I couldn't see his face or nothing, but he was naked and he was jerking off whilst he watched us... he was...'

'*I don't want to hear no more Tommy,*' shouted Eazy, as the confines of he vehicle literally shook at the bass of his voice.

'But I've got to tell you this bit,' he said, shaking as he sniffed and wiped his nose again on his sleeve, 'Afterwards, that fucking bastard that had fu... done that to me... well he dragged me upstairs and locked me in one of the bedrooms. That's where I escaped from, I just had to get out of there man. I managed to force the window open and get the fuck out of there. But just before I did, I heard the screams. I could hear Katie screaming, it must have been the other one that was there. He got off on hurting them. He must of, 'cause he didn't touch either of us whilst I was down there. But those screams man. Jeez, it wasn't like anything that I would want to ever, and I mean ever, hear again. I still hear the screams man, inside my head man. Whatever they did to that little girl afterwards, well I don't know. All I knows, is that they hurt her real bad. You see now, you see what I'm telling you. He has to be the guy you're looking for.'

'Hang on a minute Tommy, wait one fucking second. What do you mean you escaped from the house?' Eazy asked him, as he realised what he'd just told them. 'Where's the kid, where the hell is Katie now?'

'She never came back man, it's, it's all my fau...' He never finished, as Eazy took him by the throat.

'You took that poor child there and you fucking left her there? What kind of sick fuck are you? How the fuck could you do what you did? What the fuck is wrong with you people?' Sleeper took his friends arm and eased it away from Tommy's throat as the lad had already begun to go a shade of purple.

'The address Tommy,' said Sleeper without even looking at him, as the lad coughed and spluttered loudly.

'The money first,' Tommy spat the words out at them, through his coughing spasm. 'I want the grand I should have got that nigh...' He was cut short, before he could finish, as Sleeper had suddenly produced a hand gun as if by sheer magic. He had pressed the suppressed Glock model 21 .45 ACP semi-automatic, right into Tommy's now, extremely scared face. The purple colouring draining to a mask of whiteness.

'The address Tommy,' he said once more, not losing his cool, his eyes burning right through into Tommy's. 'If you even think about lying Tommy, the pain I'll put you through, will make what happened that night, seem like a walk in the park.'

'But I though...'

'You thought wrong you sick little prick,' interjected Eazy. 'Jesus, what the fuck did you expect us to do? You're lucky that my man doesn't shoot you where you sit, you sick fuck. You only feel sorry for what happened to you, not what you put that poor little girl, or what you put all those other poor kids through.' He grabbed for the lad again in anger, as Sleeper grabbed his arm before he reached him.

'The address Tommy... Now,' said Sleeper, not taking his eyes from the lad.

Tommy suddenly spilled the address out for them, as Eazy piled out of the car and opened the back door. 'No... No, leave me alone,' Tommy cried out loud backing away from his huge hands, as Eazy grabbed hold of him and threw him from the car to the roadside as hard as he possibly could do.

They left him lying there in the road, as he began vomiting all over himself, as the two of them drove away towards their next destination.

TWO

She'd received the phone call late last night, as she walked through the front door to her new apartment in Salford Quays, wet, cold and feeling more than a little anxious to just be able to climb into a hot relaxing bath and soak for as long as possible. Both the drive, and the time spent in the graveyard, had taken its toll on Rachel, and the last thing that she really wanted, was to end up speaking to Hunter.

Although she suspected, that this hadn't been the first call that Hunter had put through to her that evening. She returned the call, relenting slightly to the sound of apprehension in her friend's voice, telling her that she'd been thinking about her, saying that she'd planned on coming to see her. But well, because of work, and, well you know... as she'd put it, of course, hadn't done so.

Once Hunter had got the formalities out of the way, she got straight down to business. That was so like her in every way, Rachel thought as she listened. Feeling both, a little confused, and also a little curious to the request, that had led to her being sat in Hunter's office at Police headquarters in Manchester's city centre that very, rainy afternoon.

As she stared out of the window on the fifth floor of the building, whilst waiting patiently for Hunter to arrive, her mind wandered back to the last time that she was sat in this very office...

As Rachel had been directly involved with the victims, of what had become known as the Dark Angel case. She obviously, hadn't been allowed any involvement as a criminal or forensic psychologist. She knew that in one way, it made sense. She also realised, that if things had been on the other foot for somebody

31

else in her position, then she'd have been telling that very same person, those exact same words.

But, as she had discovered so painfully, once it actually happened to you, then all that you wanted in the world, was to have some active involvement in the case. Just to feel that you were doing your bit. No matter how small, or irrelevant it appeared. Just to be doing something, so that you didn't feel so helpless.

Rachel had begged Hunter, to at least, let her be present when Brendan McCarthy, the criminal psychologist gave his report. She called in favours, favours that she knew, she was blatantly out of order for throwing back in Hunter's face so shamelessly, in order to gain entrance to that meeting. Hunter finally relented, fore warning Rachel of what she already knew. That this wasn't going to be nice in anyway whatsoever.

She knew of course, because she had studied the way these people operated in such a clinical way over the years. But it had always been with no personal attachment to any of the cases. But that was in the past, and this was the present. She had to face the realities of what had happened, although deep down, she wasn't sure, whether or not, she was in fact, ready for it.

Rachel had heard of Brendan many times before. Mainly because, he worked in the same field that she had. But for whatever reason, their paths had never crossed. And because of that, she actually knew very little of his background...

As she had sat there, gazing inattentively around her surroundings at the immense, yet very slender and extensive office, she realised that it had changed very little since the previous year. Then again, there wasn't a whole lot of stuff that Hunter could have changed in her domain. From the sparse furnishings of her polished bureau, to the uncomfortable chairs and several filing cabinets that seemed to take up most of the room in the large office space.

Rachel had often wondered, that if by mistake, they had in fact placed Hunter directly in the filing room itself, as there were that many cabinets stored with her.

There weren't any personal photographs in the office. Hunter had no husband or children herself. Although, Rachel knew that men weren't short coming to her friend, who was gorgeous at six foot-one, with natural shoulder length blonde hair, that was often pulled back and either clipped or held in place using pencils in a casual demeanour.

Her hair was pulled away from her face, showing off the features of her hard looking, yet beautiful face. It often reminded Rachel of the actress, *Robin Wright Penn*, from the movie, *State of Grace*.

Hunter, with her flawless deep blue eyes, captivated the many men who she engaged in with relentlessly, with an array of sexual encounters.

Rachel had always been in awe at Hunter's natural beauty. Yet in more recent years, had witnessed how much the job had been taking more and more out of her. Plucking away a little more with each case she undertook with such temperament, as if it was her very first and very possibly going to be her last one.

The pressure of her work itself, was enough to drive anyone to an early grave. Only her friend seemed to thrive on the investigations. In its perverse way, it seemed to be, her only salvation in life…

Brendan hadn't been at all what she had expected. First off, she'd always imagined him to be much older than her thirty-one years. So she had been surprised to see that he wasn't much older than she was. He was also very attractive, yet another label, for whatever reason she hadn't attached to him.

At well over six-foot five, with long thick jet black curls set upon his head, hanging spontaneously around his shoulders. With piercing blue eyes that were almost inappropriate against his dark seasoned colouring. Yet, they were one of his most attractive features.

Rachel noticed that the other females in the room, Hunter included, were also taking all of this in. And she felt a rush of mortification, at even looking at another man in such a way. Quickly dropping her eyes to the floor, so to stop herself from gawking so candidly at his immense physique, as she twisted her daughter's small gold necklace, the one that Tony had bought her for her christening, that was nowadays always wrapped her left wrist as a constant reminder.

He had been the first to speak that day, breaking through the silence that had hung so heavily in the confined space of the crowded office. There were many detectives and uniformed officers, all of which had been brought into the case to help with the investigation. Some seated, the rest standing, all filling every conceivable space.

The conference room that would normally have been used, was at that time undergoing renovations. And it had been Hunter's office, rather than Chief Mackenzie's office that had been

selected. The stifling heat getting to all of them, as the buildings air conditioning had gone down at the time.

'First of all, I'd like to say that, and no disrespect here to Rachel. It is alright that I call you Rachel?' he asked very abruptly, with a hint of a Scottish or possibly even Irish accent, as she gave a quick nod. 'Anyway, I wish to point out, that I don't think that it is right, that you be here today. Please...' He held up his hands defensively at her as she was about to protest. 'You and I work within the same jurisdiction. You know that from I've seen, and what I've come up with today is going to be direct. I know that you've dealt with this kind of thing before, but, well, you have no involvement in this case and I therefore feel...'

'No involvement,' Rachel had snapped, as Hunter placed her hand on her arm to calm her down. 'Jesus, that's a little below the belt isn't it McCarthy. How much more involved would you have liked for me to have been?'

Now she had taken a sudden dislike to the man before her, and couldn't believe his attitude. She then immediately realised that she hadn't even given him a chance yet. But no matter, there was something about him she didn't like. And despite his rugged good looks that she felt a censurable attraction towards, she didn't feel it towards his obvious lack of diplomacy.

'Now that's exactly the kind of thing I'm talking about, and I've not even started yet.'

'Why don't we just press on Brendan,' Hunter said.

'That would be an excellent idea Mr McCarthy,' said Chief Superintendent Tom Mackenzie who was Hunter's direct boss at the station. 'Make sure you take down the necessary notes Stephen,' he added to the Detective Inspector sat next to him.

'Of course,' replied Detective Inspector Stephen Halenbrook, already scribbling in his spiral bound note book. He was the chief's right hand man, and Rachel knew that because of that, not many people at the station liked the man.

'Very well then,' said Brendan sighing deeply, and staring coldly at Rachel. 'I have to say firstly, that this isn't any ordinary kind of killer that we are dealing with.'

'You're telling us,' Mark Andrews, Hunter's partner said to a few nods of agreement from around the room.

'As there hasn't been any other murders that we know about, then we can't label the killer to be prolific murderer, or more commonly known these days to you people, is what we'd call a serial killer. However, in my opinion, if this killer is not found and incarcerated soon, then he will kill again.' He glanced at

the notes before him, and took a deep breath, 'The crime itself was very organised, and a psychological approach to this case will help to analyse the crime itself. It will narrow down the potential subject, to help you people here today, narrow down your resources. Breaking down what information we have so far, and should give you a clearer indication to what it is you should be looking for in this killer. For example, the fact that he used a knife to commit the actual killings of the victims may bare reference to the type of work he does. Maybe the killer works with knives, and is therefore comfortable in using them as his preferred method of execution.'

'That's not exactly much use,' said one of the detectives from the back of the room.

'I'm not here to give you a name or an address,' said Brendan, staring at the detective.

'I'm only here to give you a clearer indication about how maybe the killer lives or possibly, how his mind works towards the motivation, behind the crime he has committed.'

'So what about motivation behind the crime itself?' asked Hunter trying to get things moving.

'The killer knew exactly what he was doing, and what he wanted, was to create the impact that he achieved. First off... by Rachel entering the bedroom. After he had finished using the victims, and positioning them in such way, he therefore, created the level of shock, shock that he would have set out for in the beginning. This would have been part of the killer's motivation; part of his fantasy would be the continued anguish of suffering that he created on the night in question.

'But that would have been only part of his motivation. The other part of his motivation, is that he is clearly a sexual predator of sorts. As indicated by the sexual abuse by which the two victims perceived. That is the second part of the motivation, and is very relevant to the case. Because people's sexual functioning, can be tied and crossed as they have been here with other things, In this case, it is tied directly to the murder itself, the third part of his motivation. Maybe this killer has a partner who he doesn't feel can experience the same kind of sexual intimacy that he fantasises about. Maybe through this, he has developed certain fantasies and quite possibly, certain fetishes which may have led to him losing the ability or possibly sustain, or enjoy sex... that is, until he begins to imagine or act out his fantasy.'

'So the fantasy part of this is a big factor?' asked Andrews.

'Oh yes,' he spoke enthusiastically. 'People sometimes become so preoccupied with their fantasies that their masturbatory thoughts turn increasingly towards their main fantasy and fetishes. The use of drugs, such as cocaine, crack or LSD, or any other drugs, both legal and illegal that can stimulate and heighten their fantasies more visually within their own minds, and can often be found to have used at some point. But not necessarily at the time of the killings themselves. Such a person has a enormously powerful visual fantasy system. A system that even with today's technology, scientists and computer programmer's have a long way to go, if they are to even come close to matching it.

'Also another factor that should be recognised here, is the fact he had clear sexual interests in both sexes and is obviously not restricted to women, but also men, and even a fascination... sexually that is, with children. Possibly, he could be only interested in men. Seeing as he only had sex with them both anally. But I seriously doubt this. I think that if the woman had been present, he would have wasted no time in raping her too.'

Rachel realised in that moment that Brendan was probably right on both counts. One, his profile, and two, she shouldn't have been here. The way he talked about her husband and daughter so coldly as the victims, really brought it home to Rachel. His intrepidity to the case was unnerving. And Rachel found herself wondering, if she came across so cold to the other people in the room, with whom she had worked with in the past. Just to hear someone else talk about them, as she herself would have spoke about other victims in a related crime made her realise that she shouldn't have been sat in that very room at that moment in time.

'Eventually the fantasy won't be enough for him,' he said looking around the room, his eyes dropping to Rachel's. 'He will feel the need to go out and act out these fantasies in the real world as the vividness and the pleasure both start to fade within his mind. There is a process that the killer may have gone through before the night in question. Everything from following the victims to watching their movements late at night from his own hiding place. Possibly even breaking into the victims home before hand. Rachel herself could have very well been part of his plan. The killings themselves could possibly have been an act of vengeance to her betrayal for not being there herself.'

He stared at Rachel, as Hunter butted in, 'Now we don't know that McCarthy,' she interjected. 'Shall we continue.'

'I'm sorry,' he shrugged casually, 'I didn't mean it to quite come out the way it did,' he added looking back down to his notes. 'This sado-sexual, and even sadomasochistic fantasy that the killer carried out, has a number of different domains to it. However, in reality, the band of domains can be narrowed down somewhat. The killer in this case may have resorted and quite possibly did do, to verbal interaction and possibly degradation, but we don't know that for sure. The one thing we are sure of, is the bindings he used as constraints with the male victim. Now that is a common factor of sado-sexual fantasies. Also we have the use of the knife, which was used at the time of death in a particular manner. Both of which, would suggest that the creator of his own fantasy, who is the killer in this case, and used it to maximise his sexual release.'

'Do you think that the sexual abuse bares significance to the actual murder itself?' asked Hunter.

'Both the victims were sodomised. Even the little girl had been successfully raped anally. Showing that the killer was aroused enough by the act itself, in order to be able to maintain an erection to carry out the act. He probably raped the little girl in front of the father who was bound to the frame at the time. He gained extra pleasure from the father having to witness the depraved act that he brought upon his daughter. The post-mortem showed that the girl died from knife wound, and the pathologist thinks quite possibly right up until the point of her heart being cut out. It is more than likely, that the killer did this whilst he was still raping her. However we'll come back to that. It's all part of his act. He was probably so excited by the father having to watch, that he wasn't gratified enough by the act itself. Therefore, by then taking it one step further, and repeating the act with him also.' He sighed deeply, and then looked to Rachel again, almost, as if on purpose she thought to herself.

'The killer probably only ever fantasised this part of the murder before, and the exhilaration that he would have felt by slicing open the little girl would have been an enormous arousal to him. The energy that he would have used in the past, in order to hold the images within his mind, would have suddenly became real that night. Not only has he got the image suddenly before him, but also he can see the blood, and smell it on his hands, on his flesh... feeling the power of the knife that he holds in his hands, the hands that caused the death before him. I would imagine that he actually gained increased amounts of pleasure from raping the male victim, as the exhilaration began to decrease from the first killing, he needed the second victim to

gain the arousal again. He knows now, that he has changed himself in such a way that he had never predicted before. He knows now, that he has crossed the threshold. The one separating him from mankind, and that whatever happens from now on... he will always be a sexual murderer.'

'What about that with the heart?' asked Chief Mackenzie, 'What do the doves that were left behind indicate to you?'

'Yes,' added Halenbrook, 'what about the doves?'

'The fact that he brought both the knife, and the doves, is further evidence, that the killer shows a great deal of planning and deliberation to his act. Also the fact that he didn't leave the knife would show that he may have forensic awareness to the crime itself.' Shuffling through the paper on the desk he continued, 'This is also heightened by the fact that at the scene you found no evidence of the killer's semen. Indicating that he wore a condom. There wasn't even hair samples or mismatching fibres discovered at the crime scene, which is very rare as you all know with any crimes scenes. In fact, am I correct in believing that apart from the way the bedroom had been left, it appeared to have been cleaned first?' he asked Hunter.

'We found traces of cleaning powder and also indication that possibly the room had been vacuumed by possibly a small hand held vacuum cleaner of some kind.'

'That indicates that this killer does not plan on being caught,' he said. 'Like I said before, he will kill again, mark my words on that.'

'What about the doves?' asked Mackenzie again impatiently.

'The idea of trophy taking is...'

'What's trophy taking?' asked Halenbrook, putting his head down as Chief Mackenzie stared at him.

'Trophy taking, is when the killer takes part of the body or belonging from the victim away with him. As in, a trophy of sorts for his accomplishment,' he told the detective then looking back to chief. 'The idea of trophy taking and sexual mutilation is still quite uncommon for you murder investigators and pathologists. Usually the most important thing is to establish the cause of death and the murder weapon used.

'The fact he left the doves in replacement of the hearts, is a clue to that we're all going to have to find the answer to,' he said pausing for a moment. 'The doves are a major clue here to the way he was thinking. The only thing I've come up with so far is that some people relate doves to being God's angels here on earth.'

'Which is further indication to the illustration of the wings used,' said Hunter.

'The wings and the way that the male victim were portrayed do indicate a strong resemblance to him being an angel, yes that is correct Susan. Also on the walls were words like Rekulla, an old Hebrew word. And there were other scriptures written in the victims blood. I am looking into what the scriptures actually relate to at the moment. Either way though, they were all indication, that the killer possibly thinks he is an angel of some kind.'

'A dark angel, like the press have named him you mean?' asked Andrews.

'Possibly, The Dark Angel or Angel of Death as I've also read in some of the newspapers. This could actually play a big part in his fantasies from here on. That is, if it hadn't been part of his goal in the first place,' he answered.

'So then, we just wait for Halloween. Then we're looking for guy walking around, knife in hand, with black wings attached to him,' laughed one of the detectives, and everybody else laughed also, breaking the tension around the room slightly.

'The victims themselves could help,' Brendan said, ignoring the comment and breaking the laughter, 'We should look to their personal lifestyle. Also their jobs. As you all know the more information that we have, the better equipped we'll be. I want everything on the backgrounds, education, medical history, any personal dairies.' He looked to Rachel who shook her head in response to the personal diary request. 'I want drug and alcohol history, friends and enemies, family background, I want you look at maybe grudges at work that the victim may have had.'

'Can you be more specific?' asked one of the other detectives. 'You've been pretty vague up to now you know.'

'As I said to you at the start of this session, profiling the crimes, is not supposed to solve the crimes for you,' he said sharply. 'It's only supposed to assist you in the investigation. You're only supposed to take what I say and make what use of it that you will...'

He had been so right Rachel thought to herself sat there, in those words of, *"make of it what you will."* Although she wasn't officially allowed to work directly with the case, both her, and her brother Tony, had been conducting their own investigation over the past twelve months.

She could hear Hunter's voice arguing with someone outside of the office and recognised the other voice as belonging to the chief of police, Tom Mackenzie.

Although she couldn't make out all of what was being said, she could tell that it was a heated argument all the same, as their voices kept on reaching high points, then lowing as she heard a third party walk by.

She didn't really know Tom Mackenzie, apart from his constant protests to her having any involvement in cases. He didn't believe in profiling. It was part of his elder generations beliefs, that progress through unfamiliar territory, could never amount to anything good.

And despite Rachel's success rate with the cases she had worked with Hunter, he was still a strong non-believer. It was the detectives that solved the crimes he would say, and that was also true. But it was also true, that people like Rachel did help, and she wasn't bothered what the small minded ones like Tom Mackenzie believed.

She'd always thought that Tom Mackenzie was a funny looking individual, almost resembling a bird of prey, possibly a kestrel, with his large hooked nose and beady eyes, that always appeared to be inquisitive of everything going on around of him at all times. His full head of grey hair was perpetually, immaculately groomed to perfection, giving it the appearance of a hair piece that had been placed there, although she was almost certain that it was indeed his own natural hair. His entire semblance, and temperament, incessantly reminded Rachel of one of her patients that was a paranoid schizophrenic, and whom was invariably wound way too tightly.

Rachel knew that he'd made Chief through kissing a lot of arse along the way as Hunter had put it. Saying that he was incompetent at the job, and the likes of her, and the other detectives, because of their dedication to the work that they produced, carried him along very nicely. Rachel had never doubted her one bit in her evaluation of Mackenzie, but refused to be judgmental, despite his feelings towards what her were.

'The victim has traditionally been ignored as one of the main components of a crime,' Brendan said as he dimmed the lights to the room switching the projector on. 'What you are about to see you have already bared witness to. But I'd just like talk through the scene with you again to try and give a different perspective on things.'

As the first crime scene photograph projected onto the white screen, it was a shot just outside of the bedroom.

'This is just one of the area establishing shots,' said Brendan clicking the picture over.

The next picture had been taken from the doorway, looking into the room itself. Rachel shook her head at the image in all its full horrific glory, Rachel found that she had to look away as Hunter once again found her arm and squeezed it slightly.

'Now as you can all see,' began Brendan pointing to the picture. 'This is where everything took place. This was the husband and wif... well it was the main bedroom anyway. I think something that needs pointing out here is the fact that there was absolutely no sign of forced entry to the house that night. Did the victim know the killer? Also here if you look,' he clicked the picture. The picture was of her husband Peter, hung there as dramatically as she had discovered him. Only the photograph brought all the memories flooding back to her. 'If we look here at the victims wrist where it has been bound, we can see the strap of his watch.'

'So?' said Halenbrook.

'Further indication to us that this was not robbery motivated,' he told him. 'It's just that I should point out that money and jewellery was left behind on show I might add. Further indication that this was not a robbery motivated crime.'

'I think we know that,' said Hunter.

'Yes, of course,' he nodded. 'But maybe the killer wants us to know this also. Wants us to have clear knowledge that he's not interested in the victims personal belongings. He wants for us to know that his main goal here is to take the hearts. But why?'

'That's what we all want to know,' said Andrews. 'Maybe he's just some complete fruitcake that doesn't know the answers himself to these questions.'

'Do not make that mistake detective, people tend to rationalise killer's intelligence to his cognitive functioning rather than his mental state or possible personality dysfunction. I repeat, do not make the mistake of thinking that this killer is mentally ill. As I for one, don't believe that he is. Not to have carried out the acts he has done here. You see, as this killer reached his controlled plateau of excitement, he would have begun the mutilation. It's all part of his act to get to know the corpse more intimately, heightening the pleasure so that has now transcended the actual act of sexual violation that took place. The removing of the hearts could indicate that he was trying to reach them on a more personal level, by getting to know them with the intimate

exploration shown here. Possibly it was a way of perverted exploration that led to punishing them.' He pointed once again to the photograph. 'The incisions were made from left to right. You can see the arc here. This would indicate that the killer is right handed, 95% of people are anyway. But this necessarily isn't correct. From what I can make out with both the victims, is that he was stood behind them. Raping them. Then as he began to reach the point of ejaculation, he would have began to slice open the chests, using a large hunting or possibly even industrial kitchen knife of sorts.' As he described all of this, he subconsciously allowed his arms to create the actions.

'Why a kitchen or hunting knife?' asked Halenbrook.

'Because the slice is extremely clean on both the victims,' he answered. 'So much so, that on the child he actually broke through the rib cage. The knife would have to have been extremely sharp in order to carry out such an act. Also the depth of the incisions is further indication towards this, rather than a small surgical blade.'

'What about the writing?' asked Andrews.

'I'll come to that,' he sighed. 'First though, The other thing here we have to take notice of is,' he pointed to the torso that had been torn open. 'The fact that he took their hearts would indicate the killer required some sort of trophy from his act. I explained what a trophy to the killer is. Although, I think he took their hearts as the one true part of their bodies that were their lifelines. I think that in some sick way, he will possibly use these for his own self gratification at a later date.'

'You think that he still has the hearts?' asked Andrews.

'Most definitely,' he answered switching the slide to the next frame. 'I also think that any suspects that you come up with, you should do all you can, to gain a search warrant in order to check out their premises. The hearts may be stored in kind of a cooler or fridge freezer. Possibly he has some kind of medical knowledge, although from the crudeness of the way the torso have been torn open, I seriously doubt it. But that's not say he doesn't know medical procedures, and maybe he has their hearts stored in jars of some kind of preserving liquid, you know, as a medical examiner would store them in formaldehyde.'

'And the wings?' asked Mackenzie.

'You can see here the wings that I spoke of earlier,' said Brendan bringing the picture out further, pointing out the large wings that spread lavishly, illustrated with their own blood. 'I'm not quite sure yet, but I think that the wings that you see here are recognition of the killer in some perverted way trying to

rationalise his own crime. I think that maybe the guilt that he was feeling after he'd committed the sexual abuse and slaying of his victims is in his mind was possibly rationalised by the use of the representation of the angel that we see here. He may have done so as part of a sick joke in his own perverted way, he feels that he is in fact, helping them onto the next life, with the child begging for the father to take her with him.'

'What about that there?' asked Hunter pointing to the screen.

'Ah, yes,' he sighed as he pointed to the crime scene photograph showing the white dove that had been placed within the chest where the heart had been removed. 'This, I think that this is further indication of the killer pre-organising the murder by bringing the doves in with him. There is also a belief among some people as I told you before, that doves are fact, God's angels here on earth that have been sent here to look over us. They were also placed inside the victims once the bleeding stopped to preserve them as best as the killer possibly could. There is also the possibility that there was in the killers mind a trade that took place of some kind. The fact he swapped the hearts for the pure white doves is some indication that the killer had possible feelings towards the victims. You need to check out people who possibly breed the birds or collect them, or the availability of obtaining the birds themselves.'

'Already being checked,' Hunter said looking up from her notes.

'What about how the child victim had been placed?' asked Andrews, 'Do you think with all these angelic references and the way Rachel described the victim as have being placed in a position of prayer bares some reference that we are indeed dealing with some religious nut of some kind?'

'Well I never got to see how she was positioned did I now,' he said, staring annoyingly at Rachel.

Rachel didn't even respond to his remark that blatantly referred to her messing with the crime scene.

'But yes,' he added, 'That... could bare significantly towards uncovering a connection between the them. Another possibility could be that it was some kind of ceremonial murder.'

'We've got someone working that angle also,' Hunter told him.

'Good, very good,' he smiled at Hunter, and Rachel was surprised at how much the smile transformed his obnoxious, cold exterior. 'Keep me posted on that will you. I'd be interested to know what you find.'

'What was used to write, or draw even, on the walls?' asked a detective from the back of the room. 'And have we confirmed the blood types?'

'Both of blood types that were discovered at the scene belonged to both of the victims,' replied Brendan glancing back down at his notes. 'We have also discovered that the hearts were used as the tool in which he drew onto the walls with. Hence, the lines you see here. Both on the wings, and with the writing also. The uneven lines were created by the fact the hearts were dipped into the victim's blood and then applied to the wall, very much like a brush would be. Further indication to what I just said about the way the killer's mind worked, this in my mind is not the work of someone mentally ill.'

He switched the slides over again to a photograph showing the walls and began pointing again to the wings, 'The writing around the wings is very hard to make out. Some of it was impossible. Maybe not even English. But I know that you've got someone working on that. But the one thing I'd like to go back to, is this,' he said, bringing up a close up of what appeared to be a name of some kind, although it was smeared badly and looked like the lettering used in a Ralph Steadman cartoon.

The lettering was both thick and thin with no consistency to the lettering, almost as if a child had tried to paint their name onto the wall. As they stared at the name before them they realised that it could possibly be the name of the killer, or more than likely the pseudonym that the killer used. Only it wasn't clear enough, for any of them to make out what it said.

'It's the position in which this has been signed, if indeed it is supposed to be a name,' he said bringing the photograph out into its full gory detail. 'This is what intrigues me. As I said before, I think that to the killer, this represents some kind of art form to him.

'I think that by him signing the wall here, he possibly felt that he was signing his work of art. Very much like an artist would sign a painting that he has created on a piece of canvas. The wall became his very own piece of canvas. His mind may be working in a way that an art collector's may work. In saying that, I'm referring to the fact, that he may be creating his own works of art. In a place that offers him quiet pleasure, and a deep fulfilment that none of us can truly comprehend.'

Rachel saw Hunter whispering to one of the detectives who began jotting down notes in reference to whatever it was she had told him.

'When he had finished with the victims and positioned them in the way the he did, you have to understand, that the vivid images of this will remain in the killers mind for quite some time. He will replay them over and over like you would a favourite movie,' he said looking around to make sure he had everybody's attention. *'Playing them over and over in his mind is for his own masturbating fantasies in the same way all of you here remember a particular enjoyable love-making experience with your partner.'*

'What happens when the images begin to fade as you mentioned earlier?' asked one of the uniformed officers that was present.

'That's when the nightmares will be begin again,' he said, sighing deeply and rubbing his eyes as he did so. *'When the images begin to fade, he will automatically begin to imagine that he could have carried out the crime better than he did do,'* he spoke more quietly now as if the meeting was taking it out of him. *'I would imagine that he will look at the hearts that he took, and think to himself, what he will do next time around. You have to understand that the most unique, pleasurable experience in this man's life from here on now, is the slaying's he has committed and when the urge is strong enough, he will go out and do it again.'*

'You alright there kid?' asked Hunter, as she walked into the office where Rachel had been waiting, and referring to her as she always did, as kid

She often said that Rachel reminded her of a lost child, or a puppy she once owned that pissed everywhere, but had still kept around. Although the thought of Hunter owning a puppy was beyond conceivable to Rachel, just as it seemed inconceivable to Hunter that Rachel was in fact only five years her junior. But Rachel always ignored the remark in all their years working together and had actually become used to it.

'Sorry to keep you waiting,' she said, as she the two of them hugged. 'I was thinking about you last night. I know that this last year has been hard on you.'

'Thanks,' said Rachel, and allowed herself to be hugged a while longer, enjoying the rare show of affection from her friend.

'So what's up then?' she then asked, as they broke the embrace. 'What was all that about out there with the chief?'

'That's actually something that I need to talk over with you later,' she smiled at Rachel, as she sat at the opposite side of the

desk, the view of a not exactly unique drizzly day of Manchester in the foreground. 'It's something that I'd like come over tonight and discuss with you. If you are available of course. I need your help with something. Only it's in an unofficial capacity.'

'What is it?'

'I'll tell you tonight,' she suddenly looked all serious. 'Besides, I think it may do you good to get back to doing something proactive.'

'What makes you think hat I haven't been doing anything proactive already?'

'Well,' she sighed deeply, 'that's actually the other thing that I wanted to discuss with you here today, if that's alright.'

'Sounds serious Hunter,' she replied.

'That's for you to tell me kid,' she said lighting a B&H cigarette and inhaling deeply, with a look of sheer satisfaction as she tossed the packet to Rachel.

'I've quit,' she replied.

'No shit,' she said exhaling the thick stream of bluish smoke. 'Think you'll last?'

'Obviously not,' she laughed, taking a cigarette from the pack, and lighting up as the two of them shook their heads.

'So do you want to stop with the small talk Hunter,' she said, pulling deeply on the cigarette, exhaling the smoke dramatically. 'I know you're hopeless at beating around the bush, even with me.'

Hunter smoked her cigarette silently for a moment, staring at the burning ash, as she blew her smoke at it, 'I heard a rumour the other day.'

'You should know better than to go listening to rumours Hunter.'

'Very funny kid,' she said, but she wasn't smiling. 'The rumour was about you and your Tony, and what you've been up to for the last twelve months Rachel.'

Rachel smiled at her, 'This must be serious Hunter, if you're using my actual name.'

'I just want to know one thing,' she said stubbing out her half smoked cigarette as she immediately lit a fresh one. 'Did you and Tony find him like I heard you did?' She paused and shook her head at Rachel, 'And this is the thing that I really want to know, did you kill him like I've heard you did?'

Rachel had been shocked to hear from Brendan McCarthy a couple of months ago. She hadn't had any contact with him since

that meeting, and he hadn't exactly rubbed off well on her. But she'd agreed to meet with him alone, as he'd requested.

She'd been shocked at how different he seemed upon meeting him, and she once again, couldn't help but take in his good looks censurably.

'First off, I must apologise for the way I acted when we first met Rachel,' he said with a smile, as she sat down in the small coffee shop in St. Ann's Square. He had lost of his entire attitude towards her, and actually came across to her as being quite charming. It was something that she had thought possible of him that day at the meeting.

'It's alright,' Rachel assured him. 'I know that I shouldn't have been there. I kind of guilt tripped Hunter into letting me be there.'

'I know,' he smiled at her, and she liked the smile, a little bit too much she thought to herself.

For the next half hour, the two of them chatted about old cases, making small talk. Rachel enquired about what he was working on at present, and he too, asked about her future plans as he'd heard that since the murders, she hadn't worked at all, and had in fact, closed her private practise down.

Eventually, Brendan said, 'I guess that I got most of it wrong that day eh?'

'I wouldn't say that Brendan,' she told him as she sipped her coffee. 'When I look back on it, I realised that, I would have come up with the same assessment. All the signs indicated that he would strike again. Even though he doesn't have appeared to have, doesn't mean that he hasn't.'

'I know,' he sighed deeply, as if he had the weight of the world upon his shoulders. 'It's also the reason that I am here today. I should really be telling this to Hunter you know, but, well, to be honest... I still feel a little guilty to my attitude towards you that day. I kind of felt somewhat threatened, and was, I suppose a little jealous... if truth be known.'

'Why jealous?' she asked confused.

'By the fact that Hunter had never used me before, and always used you instead.' He shook his head at her, 'I know it sounds juvenile... But I was always in awe of the work you produced with the other cases that you had worked with Hunter.'

Feeling awkward, she didn't know what to say to him as they both sat there now in an uncomfortable silence.

'I have something for you today,' he said breaking the silence. 'But not Hunter or anyone else must know about this you understand.'

'Of course,' she replied not sure what he was going on about.

'I worked in clinical psychology for a number of years, and there was this one patient from right here in Manchester that I used to treat at the psychiatric hospital over in Sheffield where I first worked.' He stared directly at her, and she felt just how powerful his eyes could be. 'Well this could be nothing, and I never thought anything of it before, because the last I'd heard, was that he was in prison. But the more I thought about this guy, the more he seemed to fit the fantasy side personality of the killer. He used to talk of his fantasies always in a third party, as if not acknowledging that it was in fact his own mind creating the fantasy. He would talk endlessly about what his third party thought about doing to his victims, and, and well it was very similar to what took place that night. He claimed that the third party would take their heart to cleanse their soul, if you can believe that.'

'Go on,' said Rachel.

'I know this doesn't make him guilty by a long shot, but I did some digging on my own and was shocked to find that he'd had the conviction overturned. And he was in fact free at the time of the murders.'

'Who the hell is it?'

'There's something else you should know,' he paused and stared at her. 'It seems that your husband sent this guy to prison eight years ago for the murder of the two young women he had apparently sexually abused as well. Although, whilst he claimed to have had, as he said, consensuses sexual encounters with both the women that night, he claimed that their lives were in fact taken by this third party. I had to be there in court at the time, to give evidence about the state of his mind. And although he didn't cut their hearts out, he did in fact take their lives with a knife that was never discovered.'

'Why the hell haven't the police checked this out?'

'He's allegedly been out of the country since his release from prison.'

'Why'd they set him free?'

'Forensic evidence was found to prove that it hadn't been him,' he told her. 'I was never called for again. But his lawyer overturned the evidence produced against his client from a second lot of blood that had been discovered at the scene. A blood type, which the police had conveniently kept from being used as evidence.'

'Why didn't I know about this guy?'

'Because I would imagine that it was just before you met your husband,' he answered. 'Possibly he didn't mention it later on, because he didn't consider the guy a threat to any of you.'

'But he'd wrongly convicted him.'

'The evidence was strong against him, and he had been in contact with both the women. Only it would appear that he wasn't the one who killed them.'

'So where the fuck is he now?' she snapped at him.

He produced an envelope from beneath the table, sliding it casually across the table to her, 'Here,' he said, 'this is by way of an apology to my behaviour that day. Do with it what you will. But just be sure to keep my name out of it.'

'I will do,' she smiled at him as he took her hands in his.

'There is one more thing that you should know Rachel.' He looked deeply into her eyes. 'He called the third party, the one he claimed had these fantasies, the one who he claims was always responsible for the killings, well he said, that...'

'Go on Brendan,' she said, 'what did he call him?'

'Gabriel,' he said. 'He claimed the killers name was Gabriel.'

As he said the name, the significance dawned on her to what Brendan had obviously picked up on himself. It had been right there in front of them, and all of a sudden the scrawling of the name at the bottom of the wall became clear to her, as it must have been to Brendan. If indeed, you'd known what you were looking for that day, any of them would have made out the letters spelling the name of the archangel, Gabriel, scrawled as deranged as it had been to throw them off.

With that he was gone, no good-byes or anything, he just got up and left Rachel staring into the envelope that contained a single photograph, and a torn piece of paper with the name Joseph Reilly scrawled onto it, with an address right here just outside the city centre...

Finally Rachel broke her thoughts and looked at Hunter, 'No Hunter,' she said, staring at her friend directly in the eyes without blinking, 'we never found him.'

THREE

'**I**s this the gaff he was on about Sleeper?' Eazy whistled at his friend in admiration, as they observed the old Victorian style house in Guildford, Surrey. 'You sure we got the right address mate?'

'Positive,' he replied. 'The guy who's registered to this address is a Colin Spencer. I checked it out with my guy at the station in town.' Eazy knew that it, the guy, and the station was one of the many bent coppers that Sleeper still kept on the payroll from the old days.

'He ran a check on the address for us, and it turns out that this guy has got himself a record for all kinds of petty shit that's not worth mentioning, Although the one thing that is worth mentioning, is that he runs the BMW garage right here in Guildford.'

'That'd explain all the different cars that Tommy was on about.' Eazy sighed deeply, obviously remembering some part of the story he'd heard the previous night, 'What've you done about that kid anyway Sleeper?'

Sleeper casually glanced at his gold Rolex, a gift from a friend. 'A couple of the lads are visiting with him right about now.' He smiled knowingly and Eazy knew he didn't have to ask anymore.

'You reckon this could be our guy or what?' he asked, changing the subject.

'You know what Eazy,' Sleeper stared at him. 'After what that kid told us, I don't care whether or not it is him. All I know is that if this guy is as sick as Tommy said he was. Then he's going to have some answers for us. I mean these kind of fucked up perverts seem to sniff one another out. If there was someone else there, like he said there was, then just how the fuck do these

people come into contact with one another. I mean you'd have to be pretty certain that the other person isn't going to freak out about this kind of shit. These sick fucko's somehow find each other. And keep the rest of the world excluded from their sick existence.'

'So what's the plan then,' Eazy nodded towards the house, and looked at the heavy gold Rolex that matched his friends and was also a gift from the same individual. The time was just after nine o'clock. 'The place looks empty to me brother,' he smirked knowingly at Sleeper.

'Best go and take a look for ourselves then eh?'

Although the house was situated along the main road across from Guildford University, it remained secluded from the rest of the row that contained both private homes, and also bed and breakfast establishments. Surrounded by the high wall that kept it enclosed from the rest of the street, Sleeper and Eazy slipped silently through to the rear of the house.

Within moments Eazy had secured the alarm, so that they could gain admittance without attracting any attention. Going to work with the small set of burglar tools that Eazy had owned for a number of years now, and refused to let go. Always stating with a little grin upon his face, that you just never knew the day that you may lock yourself out.

As the two of them entered through into the kitchen, they noticed that the kitchen had a feminine touch to it. It was also very clean and tidy. Sleeper looked to Eazy who merely shrugged as he looked around. 'Maybe he's got himself a cleaner. What did your guy say about him? Did he say whether or not he was married?'

'There wasn't any information to suggest it.' Sleeper walked through the kitchen into the hallway and noticed the wooden door built into the staircase. The door was obviously what would lead you down into the basement. 'Shall we?'

'Be my guest El jefe,' he replied, smirking at him. 'I'll be right behind you.'

'Why the fuck do I always get to go first?' He cocked an eyebrow at him.

'Come on Sleeper,' he said still grinning. 'You know that I'm scared of the dark.'

Sleeper laughed, 'Yeah right, more like the dark is scared of you,' he said flipping the light switch. 'Good job that we got lights then,' he nodded. 'After you mucho hombre grande, seeing as you've taken to speaking Spanish.'

51

Eazy laughed as he pushed Sleeper through the doorway. 'But I insist Sleeper. I know how you always like to go first.'

Sleeper shook his head, as he made his way down the cold stone steps. As they reached the fundamental surroundings of the basement, they both looked at one another again. Nothing was out of place. There were shelves with food stacked neatly in place down one side of the wall. The other wall contained what appeared to garden equipment, with a tool bench on the far wall. There was some old furniture stacked neatly along with what looked like an antique dining room set buried under the actual stairwell. The cellar smelt damp, like old leaves that had been stored inside of a box for a long time, although smell mingled strongly with another scent.

'Like I said before,' Eazy sighed, 'you sure that we got ourselves the right person here.'

Sleeper was walking around the cellar ignoring his friend; suddenly he bent down low to the cold damp slabs that covered the floor. 'You smell that?'

Eazy sighed, 'Cleaning fluid of some kind. I smelt it as we came down the stairs. So what though? From what we've seen so far, the place is spotless.'

'Why would you clean the cellar?' He looked up from the crouching position as he stroked his finger across part of the floor and held his right hand up towards Eazy, pointing with his left at the thin surgical gloves that he was wearing. 'Unless of course, you were trying your best to cover something up that is.' The tips of his fingers were stained thinly with dark crimson streaks.

'Oh shit,' Eazy looked away and back up the stairs. 'Is that what I think it is?

Rubbing the tips of his finger together, Sleeper then smelt the tips of his fingers and nodded. 'Come on, let's check the rest of the house. We'll split up. It'll be a lot quicker.'

Eazy was already heading back out of the cellar, 'I'll take downstairs, you can take the bedrooms upstairs.' He suddenly stopped and looked back down the stairs, 'I'm starting to get a funny feeling about this lot mate,' he breathed deeply, shaking his head as he did so, then walked through the door leaving Sleeper still crouched there smelling his fingertips and thinking the same thoughts.

As Eazy moved from room to room, he professionally went about his work. Neatly replacing everything back into place once they'd finished. If this wasn't their guy, or even the guy that

Tommy had told them about, then the last thing that they wanted, was for the guy to go calling the cops.

Making his way upstairs, Sleeper took in the unpretentious pictures that adorned the walls. Pictures of country cottages and plants hung side by side gracefully giving the house a homely feel to it. He noticed that the first bedroom he came to, appeared to be the guest room, or maybe it actually belonged to someone. Making his way around the room he noticed nothing out of place, and once again noticed that everything was clean and tidy.

Checking the drawers amounted to nothing of interest, as they were stuffed with only paper work. Opening the wardrobe doors, he discovered that they were near empty, apart from a few summer and winter jackets that were hung in there. Further indication, that this was indeed some sort of guest room.

Looking to the base of the wardrobe he noticed some shoes were scattered about. Only on closer inspection he noticed that the base of the wardrobe to be slightly out of place. Sleeper found that the wooden panel at the bottom of the wardrobe was in fact loose. As he pulled the panel away, he shone his maglite into the darkness beneath the wardrobe. There he found a small safe, the kind that you concrete into the floor. This was all good and well, but made no difference to Sleeper, as he had Eazy with him.

Whistling softly for his friend, who appeared moments later in the doorway, his huge frame blocking the any light from the doorway, 'What we got?' he whispered, despite knowing the two of them were all alone.

'I need you to work your magic whilst I continue to take a look around,' he said, then as an afterthought, added. 'Anything down stairs?'

'Clean as a whistle, literally,' he smiled as he looked at the safe. 'This guy's place is cleaner and tidier than my old dear's gaff.' Squinting at the safe, he then said, 'Just give me a few minutes. This shouldn't be any bother.' He winked at Sleeper, who then went about his search.

Sleeper made his way through into the main bedroom, heading straight for the wardrobes. He was surprised to see both men's and women's clothes occupying the space. All the women's clothes appeared to be evening wear of one kind or another. A large array of different coloured high heels filled the bottom of the wardrobes base. He quickly checked to see if the base was in tact, and discovered that there wasn't anything a miss.

Finding nothing of use, he headed into the last room that appeared to some kind of a study. There was an Apple-Mac PC

set up, and Sleeper clicked the computer on. As he watched the computer starting to boot itself up, he looked around what he presumed this guy used as some kind of an office. The floor wasn't carpeted like the rest of the house; instead it was made up of pine floorboards.

'What've we got in here then?' Eazy said, as he walked into the room smiling as he did so, 'You know they shouldn't call them things safes. They're about as safe as tissue paper nappies would be,' he said passing the weighted A4 manila envelope for Sleeper. 'That's all that was in there.'

Emptying the contents onto the floor, several small video cassettes used in digital camcorders, and a small square piece of plastic fell to the ground. As he picked up the piece of plastic, he realised that it was smart card used for storing photographs on with digital cameras.

Looking back to the computer he noticed that the screen was flashing for a password, that wasn't going to be any use Sleeper thought to himself. Cursing silently, and walked towards it in annoyance, he began tapping away the computer's keyboard with no response.

Eazy was crouched to the floor, examining the tapes when he accidentally let one slip from his hands. As the tape hit the floor boards, there was a thud followed by a hollow knock, rather than a solid noise as it bounced a couple of times to the same hollow knock. They both looked at the floor where the tape had dropped, and Eazy pulled a screwdriver from his small black bag of tricks, as Sleeper took it from him.

Upon closer inspection of the floor, they soon realised that the panelling was ever so slightly raised; you wouldn't have noticed if you hadn't been looking. Using the screwdriver, he began lifting three of the panels away. They both looked to one another then to the all the equipment that was stashed away in hiding, including a Pentax digital camera.

As he began to pull the items out, he passed a Dell laptop over to Eazy, 'See if you can into his files, that one is secured,' he said nodding at the PC on the desk. 'Hook this up as well.' he added, tossing the small digital mobile phone to the computer that allowed it to become accessible from anywhere in the world.

As Eazy went about working the computer, Sleeper slotted the smart card into the Pentax digital camera, and brought up the menu on the small screen. Accessing the pictures that were stored on the disk, he suddenly fell backwards to the floor as Eazy stared at him.

'Jesus, this is fucked up,' he stated, as he worked his way quickly through the photographs that were stored on the camera.

But they weren't ordinary photographs. They showed pictures of both young, very young boys and girls in different sexual positions with an older man. A man who was dressed mainly in women's clothes, clothes similar to what he'd seen in the wardrobe. The kids, and not all of them, but most of them, Sleeper recognised from the estate in Lewisham. They had been made up to look older than they were. The little girls wore make-up, and were smiling as if nothing was wrong with what they were being forced to do. Sleeper couldn't bare to look at the pictures, and switched the camera off. He tossed it to the floor, unconsciously rubbing his hands on his jeans, as if he'd just stuck his hands into pure shit.

Sleeper sighed deeply, as Eazy nodded to the Sony digital camcorder, 'Pass that over will you,' he asked.

Hooking the camcorder into the port at the side of the computer, he then slotted the one of tapes into it, and began tapping away at the keys skilfully, 'Oh no, oh shit, Jesus fucking Christ!' He shook his head.

'What is it?' Sleeper asked as he looked up from the computer.

'Believe me,' he said looking away from the small screen on the lap-top, 'you do not want to see this.'

'I believe you,' he said.

'All I'll say, is that this confirms in graphic detail what Tommy told us to be completely true. What the fuck has the world come to Sleeper, when people need to do this kind of shit just to get off sexually?' He passed the lap top over to Sleeper with home movie still running and said, 'Things never used to be this fucked up did they?'

But he didn't answer; his eyes were transfixed to the screen as he quickly hit the stop button, as his head suddenly twisted in the direction of the door. 'You hear that?' he whispered quietly, switching the torch off, closing the screen on the lap-top.

Sleeper had his fingers to his lips to silence Eazy, as they both clearly heard the key turn in the front doors lock. Signalling again to Eazy, he pointed to the door, to say that he was heading out and own the stairs. They could clearly hear someone moving about downstairs as Sleeper walked casually out of the door, stopping at the top of the stairs, he peered down into the hallway and nodded for Eazy to follow him.

The downstairs hall was alight and they could see the man they suspected to be Colin Spencer. He was hitting the keys to his alarm box with utter confusion as to what was wrong with it. He

was still playing with the control pad, as he suddenly felt the piece of metal make contact with the back of his head.

'Not a word,' Sleeper instructed sombrely, as he pressed the Glock's silencer to the back of the man's head. 'Nod very slowly if your name is Spencer.' He watched the back of the mans head move cautiously.

'I've got mone...'

'The man said not a word,' Eazy cut him off, letting him know that there were two of them there.

'Move very slowly and make your way down into the basement,' Sleeper pushed the Glock harder. Moving Spencer towards the cellar door. As the three of them made there way down into the cellar, they could hear Spencer actually laughing. They didn't know whether it was through lack of fear or the shock of having a semi-automatic pistol pressed against the back of his head. Either way, it made Sleeper shake his head in disgust.

'What's so funny you sick bastard.' Sleeper kicked him hard, as they reached the last couple of steps and sent him toppling to the hard floor.

Both of them were shocked to see his face as he struggled to stand up. He was actually smirking at them. He was also a good looking bloke Sleeper thought, with his boyish looks and floppy mess of mousy hair; he almost looked like Hugh Grant. Only they knew that, that face of innocence held a dark, twisted, sick side to it.

'Fucking niggers,' he snarled at the two of them with pure arrogance. 'Do you realise whose house you broken into you black bastards.'

Ignoring the comment, Eazy laughed casually back at him. 'Seeing as my man here asked you your fucking name, I think we know who you are.'

'You can't know who I am, not if you've broke into my house you black fuck.' He stroked his hair away from his face, his eyes darting back and forth. 'Just take the money and run back to your fucking holes you lowlifes.' He tossed his wallet at them, as Sleeper batted it away in disgust, and in the same motion, pistol whipped him to the floor.

Standing over him Sleeper spat his hatred at him, as Eazy dragged the man from the floor, slinging him towards the tool bench, 'You think that we're here for your money, boy?' Eazy yelled at him. Grabbing his face in his huge hand, he began to crush it, his fingers engulfing his entire face and most of his

head. They could both hear his muffled cries of help and Eazy increased the pressure.

'Tape him to the chair.' Sleeper instructed, tossing the thick roll of black duct tape to Eazy. As he pulled to battered wooden chair from the antique dining room set to the middle of the room, Eazy released his hold on the man who yelped like a little dog. His face had turned reddish-purple from the lack of oxygen. His breathing was short and fast, as he gasped for air.

'You... sick... you sick, black bastard's,' Spencer wheezed at them, as he struggled with Eazy, who began taping him to the chair. He seemed to be keeping a close eye on Sleeper, who constantly kept the gun trained on him. As he finished with the taping, Eazy whacked him as hard as he could with his open palm, knocking both him and the chair he was fastened to, straight to floor, just to let him know what was in store.

'There's no two ways about this,' Sleeper said coldly, pulling his chair back into seating position and staring inimically into his dazed eyes. 'I am going to kill you.' He watched as Spencer's eyes came alive at the prospect. 'The only question is just how quickly I'm going to kill you.'

'What've I done to you,' Spencer pleaded, as he suddenly realised that this was for real.

'I've just watched part of the tape with you, Tommy and a little girl you sick fucking bastard,' he spat the hatred he felt into his face. 'Nothing you say, can ever redeem you from what I just saw. But, and this is a big but... If you answer my questions with honesty... then I may help you along to the next life a lot quicker.' Sleeper stood up and pointed the gun straight at his balls. 'What happened to that little girl? What the fuck happened to all the kids that you took from Lewisham? What did you do with them after you were finished using them for your own sick amusement?'

'Fuck you nigger,' he sneered the words back at Sleeper in an act of pure defiance.

'Where the fuck are they?' he snarled viciously at Spencer, ignoring the insult.

'What the fuck do want me to say?' He shook his head at the two of them. 'You saw the film and no doubt, you saw the pictures. So call the cops. You can't touch me, I'm protected. I don't give a fuck about the two of you.'

Sleeper crouched low in front of him, as he remained locked to the chair and started to tap the gun's silencer to his lips. 'No, no, no Spencer. There isn't going to be any police involvement here. No one is going to save you. You are not protected and I will,

this is a promise now, only give you one more chance to answer my question to the whereabouts of the missing children.'

As he looked deeply into Sleeper's lifeless black eyes, he saw the abyss that lay within there and he felt a chill run straight through him. 'I had nothing to do with them after they were here,' he suddenly splurted out. 'Honest... they were here. All of them were here, but I didn't take them from here. It wasn't me.'

'So who the fuck took them?' Eazy batted the back of his head again.

'It wasn't me, I swear it, hon...' He suddenly screamed out in sheer agony as he witnessed the white flash from the silenced handgun, as Sleeper had pulled the trigger and shot him cleanly, straight through his groin.

'One more time,' Sleeper sighed. 'Who the fuck took the kids from here if it wasn't you?'

Tears were flowing freely down his face that was contorted in sheer agony as the blood began to spread like wild-fire across the front of his beige chinos. Sleeper smiled as he watched the crimson river trickled from the bottom of trousers, over his Rockport boating shoes. His teeth were gritted to drive out the pain. His cheeks were turning purple again at the anguish he was now susceptible to, 'I... I... I can't say... he, he'll kill me, you don't understand, he'll...' He was struggling to find the words, but no matter, they weren't the words that they both searching for anyway.

The slight popping sound, almost like that of a crisp packet being burst, echoed again, only slightly, as he screamed out in agony once again, as the second bullet to be discharged, tore through his left shoulder. The air of the cellar quickly filled with the stench of cordite.

'Wake up call for you Spencer,' Sleeper hissed, 'I'm the one who's going to kill you. I just want the name of the one responsible for taking them.'

Eazy grabbed the back of his hair and yanked his head upright. 'The mans speaking to you,' his voice boomed as it echoed off the walls, as things suddenly took a turn for the worse, in what can only be described as sheer confusion to them both.

That's when the most bizarre thing suddenly happened taking them both by surprise, Spencer suddenly began laughing wildly at the two of them in a deranged manner. The laughter taunting them defiantly, as if he'd accepted his fate, and didn't care one way or the other now. The two of them stared at one another in utter disbelief as the wounded man before them with two bullet's shot at him at close range appeared to be oblivious to the pain.

'You'll never catch him, never.' He grimaced extravagantly, as Sleeper pointed the gun to his head. Spencer actually leaned forward, placing his own forehead against the barrel of the suppresser.

'You won't catch him, because none of us want you to catch him. He's too smart for the likes of you. And he's protected from up above. Not even God could strike him down. He's the taker of lost children. They need him, they want him. They all want us. Children from that hell hole of an estate were dying to be taken away from the place. They couldn't wait to get in my car and come with me. Then once I'd broke them in for the Pied Piper. They went gladly with him. Like he was their guardian angel that had come to save them.' He was babbling now and they let him go on, 'They never even realised how good they had it with me, they thought if they followed the Pied Piper he would save them. They fell in love with him, as he played his flute all the way back to Manchester; everyone loves the Pied Piper, until the very end. He will never be caught. You're just too fucking stupid to realise that.' He seemed totally oblivious to the gun shot wounds, as if deliriously high from his accepted fate, as his eyes were ferocious and looked as if they were wired on drugs.

'Who the fuck is the Pied Piper mother fucker?' Sleeper grabbed his jaw, squeezing it tightly, only he seemed to enjoy the pain even more.

'You'll never catch him you black fucks... Never in a million years.' He smirked knowingly and licked his lips teasingly, in a sexual manner as he stared at Sleeper taunting him. 'Go on admit it nigger, you liked it didn't you? You can tell me that you liked the film you watche...' Sleeper pistol whipped him as hard as he could.

The gun tore through his right cheek, smashing his mouth, breaking teeth, as blood sprayed wildly from the laceration. Only he spat the blood from his mouth, and grinned. His teeth coated with the reddish colouring, making him appear mentally deranged as he smiled, licking his lips again, 'Go on admit it nigger, you loved it. You got off on watching me do it with the kids, didn't you? Did it turn you on watching it, just like it turned the Pied Piper on? Did it make your black cock throb with pleasure; I bet it did, didn't it?' He smirked at them both, then stared at Sleeper, who by now, he knew he was getting to. 'You can keep the tape, it's my gift to you, and you know you want to keep it.'

Sleeper's left eye twitched slightly at the corner, as he squeezed the trigger, the Glock exploding as the white flash that

59

extinguished the bullet, tore straight through Spencer's face, ripping the flesh open instantly and blowing the back of head out completely. The back wall was coated in brain matter and his blood had sprayed extravagantly everywhere.

Eazy stared at Spencer's corpse, and then spat his repugnance at the limp form. Glancing to Sleeper, he suddenly became concerned for his friends well being, as for the first time since he'd known him, he looked visibly shaken. 'You alright brother?'

'This doesn't end here,' he said simply, as he let a single tear roll down his face. 'This can't end here. Not tonight. We'll find this son of bitch if it's the last thing that we do, I swear it right here, right now Eazy. We'll find this Pied mother fucking Piper if the last thing we ever do brother.'

Eazy placed his huge hand on his best friends shoulder, and squeezed lightly, 'I know we will brother.'

FOUR

He loved this place, he always had done, ever since being a little kid when his granddad used to bring him here. The ferocious and electrifying fanfare, creating the atmosphere surrounding him, the endless stream of miscellaneous lights, some working, but most smashed and not in use. But it didn't matter any to this place, because he loved this place.

To hear the screams of joy and laughter, to see the happy faces, some caked in the sticky pink and blue candy floss that was sold from the many outlets that were also selling the greasy quarter-pounder's smothered in ketchup served on stale burger baps and the huge red candy dummy's now he really liked those.

He'd always loved the fun-fair. But especially this one here in Knutsford. This one was so special to him, as it didn't only consist of merely one of the large gypsy families running it, but several of them all came together once a year to create this monster of a fair-ground for everybody, from far and wide to travel too for a good time out. The kids loving it and the elder generation of Knutsford driven mad by it all.

As he sat in his car, he watched, as he liked to watch, all the kids, running, skipping and jumping. All of them dressed for the summer in little shorts or better still little summer dresses. Using his Cannon digital camera with the zoom lens, he snapped away at the kids, before exiting the vehicle, smiling at the mother's and father's, who immediately returned his smile, some with nods of hello.

After all, he was known in these parts, like he'd said before, he'd been coming here for years, even as a child with his granddad who was well known around these parts, and before all innocence was lost he thought to himself...

'You enjoyed today, didn't you son?' asked his granddad, his father's father, the one the whole family loved, but the one who showed him the special attention.

He used to only ever take him there, none of the other grandkids, and that made him feel real special as he sat on his granddad's knee in front of the fire place afterwards. Still plucking at the remains of the candy floss, that seemed to have gotten everywhere.

'Not to worry son,' he would say. 'We'll take you upstairs for a hot bath.'

That's the way it had always been, for as long as he could remember. Even his dad, used to play this game with him, when mummy was out of course. He didn't mind of course, because this was a special game they played, and even though it felt a little wrong, he knew that they didn't play it with the other kids.

It was just their own special game.

As the hot water cascaded down into the old iron tub, his granddad would undress him out of his little shorts and tee-shirt and he'd give his granddad a warm hug, Granddad loved to be hugged, even more so since nanny had gone to visit God for a while. He loved to keep him happy as his granddad lifted him into the hot water.

As his granddad soaped him down, he always seemed to be concerned with down below, always telling that it had to be super clean, and his hand was forever there, protecting and cleaning me, he would tell him, and he loved to see his granddad's face happy. It made him happy to see him happy.

Then he used join him in the bath, telling him we had to save the hot water by sharing the bath...

He shook the sick thoughts away of the past and locked the vehicle, making his way across to the fun-fair. Walking through the main entrance, he smiled with sheer arrogance at some of the gypsy lads, or was it travellers these days, he couldn't be sure anymore. They looked at him apprehensively, with the caution he deserved.

He felt somewhat superior to all these people here, he felt that feeling wherever he went these days, because he was superior to them in his mind. He had the knowledge they all wanted, he was their master and they didn't even realise it.

Taking his camera out, he made his way over to the Carousel, one of his favourite rides, even nowadays he loved to join the other kids as they all smiled at him and laughed at what they considered to be a big kid joining in with the fun of the ride.

He loved to take the photographs of their unadulterated naiveté. Watching, smiling, as they glided around on the beautifully decorated wooden horses, with all of the magical colours flashing by as he snapped away enthusiastically. Smiling to the parents, who always smiled back or said hello. After all, they knew him, like he said, he'd been coming here since the beginning. He was known to all of them.

As the ride began to slow down, he zoomed his lens in on an extremely pretty little blonde girl, whose thigh was exposed just enough for him to see the rim of her little white knickers. Casually, so not to draw attention to himself he snapped away at the little girl, feeling aroused as his story came together in his mind.

Then feeling the heat of someone staring at him, he turned to face who could only have been the mother, with the same blonde hair, all tied up above her head. Only her glare wandered as he spoke to her. Just as he always interacted with the parents to soothe over any suspicions of him. But there wasn't any suspicion, was there. Of course not, not him, they knew his face after all, he came here all the time.

Casually stroking the little girl's blonde curls, who was now stood beside them both as he still chatted away with the mother, feeling her flirting with him slightly now, he played along.

But only so he could keep the contact, and feel of the blonde soft curls running through his fingers, as the little girl pulled at her mother's hands to go to the next ride. She finally relented and said her good-byes as they wandered away. With him still taking snaps as the little girl bounced innocently along, her skirt wandering too high, creating the perfect shot for him and the many others out there.

Making his way over to the waltz's he past several people he knew and stopped and chatted openly with them, joking and telling them that he'd be in touch with them. Thinking that, if only they knew. But they didn't and they would never know who he really was. No one would ever find out, and what it made it so much better now was that he gained financially for the love of his work. It was the best thing that had ever happened to the likes of him and others like him.

The internet had opened up a whole new world to them and he'd got himself right in on the act from the very beginning. Although always playing that side of things down as if he didn't really know anything about today's modern technology. Only he'd never imagined that it would have escalated the heights that it had done. And he controlled a big part of it to the knowledge

of only a select few, who were way to scared too ever betray him.

Continuing his journey through the park, he snapped away freely at the kids. Catching what would come across as innocent shots to any other, well any other than the likes of him and his kind, both men and women all yearning for what he could give them. But not just what he could give, but what he could receive in return from them.

He had different needs to the others, his weren't quite so forward as the others. His needs were special needs that when the opportunity or urge was strong enough he acted upon without remorse.

Besides they loved him, they all loved him didn't they, because he knew how to show them the love that they were so desperately in need of after all the abuse they'd received at the hands of the others. If only he'd had someone around when he was growing up, he'd have been so lucky, he was their saviour, yes that was it, he was their saviour. He liked that word almost as much as the name he'd been given by one of them.

The name he loved, had loved so much in fact, that his website productions were named after it...

Why had the special game stopped, he often wondered what he'd done to upset them both so much that both his daddy and granddaddy stopped playing the game with him as he got older.

But he couldn't ask them, he wasn't allowed to ask about the game, that was the rules of the game, never ask and never tell or you'd be a bad boy and he didn't want to be a bad boy.

Maybe he was too old for games, maybe now he was ten he was old enough to play the games himself. But how would he know for sure whether or not it was alright to play the games without asking them both. Maybe this was a test like you took in school, maybe if he did good at the test they would reward him and play the games again.

He didn't mind the pain now, it still hurt, but he wanted to make them happy and the way they never spoke about it to him, made him wonder if it had ever happened. No, that wasn't the case, of course it happened to him, it was their special game afterall.

After much thinking he decided that it was a test and that he should break the rules and show his little sister of five years old the game, and so he did do at every possible opportunity.

They played the game whenever no one was around. With him telling their mother that he could look after his little sister if she

wanted to go to the shops or out to the pub at night-time with their father. And she'd always thought of him as a big boy, so often left the two of them alone.

And it was so good, his little sister had wanted so much to please her big brother in the same fashion he had wanted to please both daddy and granddaddy, that he played the game the same way he'd been taught to play the game. They would have been proud of him. He just wanted to make sure that he got the game right before he told them both about it. He knew that they would both be pleased with him and maybe even play the game with all four of them.

That's was until that one night though, the night when everything seemed to go wrong with the game. His mother and father had gone to the pub that night. So he had decided that he wanted to play the game with his little sister, but she hadn't wanted to play and had started to cry.

He had smacked her, as his mother and father would have smacked him if he'd been a naughty boy and she'd cried louder. But as he smacked her harder, he found that the sensation of this kind of physical abuse aroused him even more. Especially as she screamed and cried out louder... But the noise of her was being drowned out as his mind became more and more productive with an altogether immense sensation of gratitude towards himself.

In fact he'd become so worked up that everything after that became a blur of clothes being ripped and then the screams, it was the screams that he could still hear as his father had dragged him from the bloodied, flaccid flesh of his little sister. His sister, who lay motionlessly below him. Her blood was everywhere, the walls, the floor, all over her, but most of all it covered him. He could smell it and no matter how hard his father belted him, the smell kept the punishing at bay.

There had been no more games after that night. There had been no more little sister to play the games with. And he hadn't made them happy with him, Now they were always angry with him and he didn't like it. He couldn't wait until he got bigger and stronger, so that he could do what he wanted. And that's exactly what he did do.

His thoughts had clouded his mind as he wandered, as they often clouded his mind at this time of the year when he visited the fair-ground, so much so that he hadn't noticed that he had in fact reached the far end of the fun-fair, where all of the caravan's were parked side by side.

He gazed around his surroundings at the lavish caravan's that they owned, some with such splendour that they often beat the many council houses that he had to visit on a regular basis. The thumping bass of all the different music that intermingled behind him was merely echoed bass out here, even the screams of joy were muffled out against the secluded area where he stood.

Realising that the area was deserted, as just about everybody from the camp site was working the fairground itself in some capacity or another. He then began to wander around unhindered.

This part of the site was eerie in its enclosed environment, and he let his mind wander to what it would be like later on that night. He imagined that it would come alive with a festivity of heavy drinking and an assortment of sordid acts once the fair had shut down. Local girls would be enchanted with the mysterious fair ground lads, that travelled the length and breadth of the country. Believing the stories the lads told them in order to win their way into their pants, whilst their real girlfriends or wives looked after the many kids that roamed around the site. All whilst they found themselves new and undiscovered girls to have one night stands with. He knew the whole area would become a mass of depravity. Although sometimes he merely let his mind wander in these ways, he never knew this for sure, but preferred to believe his own imagination.

'Hello mister,' a small voice suddenly called out to him, as he turned to see a young lad of maybe only six or seven years old stood in the doorway of one of the caravans.

His face was covered in dirt, and his whitened teeth looked out of place against his filthy face as he smiled at him. The track-suit he wore was one of those awful black and green shell suits that always looked scruffy no matter what. The boy continued to stand there, unafraid, as they always were, smiling, as they always did.

'What's your name?'

'Billy,' he replied. 'What's yours mister?'

He ignored the question and went to the boy, 'Where's your mummy and daddy Billy?'

'They're working over there,' he said pointing away from the camp site towards the fair-ground.

'Are you here all alone Billy?'

'Yes,' he said looking at the man's clothes with interest. 'I was asleep, they often leave me asleep and then I go find them when I get up.'

'Shall we go find them together Billy?' he asked holding out his hand for the boy, who gladly took it in his gleefully.

'Alright then mister,' he replied, then suddenly stopped. 'But only if you tell me your name first, I'm not supposed to go with strangers, but if you tell me your name first then you won't be stranger, will you mister.'

He couldn't help but smile down at the dirty face that seemed intrigued, as they always did with him, 'You're a clever boy aren't you Billy. Your very right about not going off with strangers, but you know that you can trust me, Don't you?' The little boy nodded and squeezed his hand lovingly, as he reached down and scooped the boy into his arms, who laughed vigorously as he tickled him playfully.

'Everyone knows me Billy, I'm the Pied Piper of course.'

FIVE

'**H**ow's it going Hunter?' asked Rachel, opening the door to her top floor apartment, that was nicely situated, over looking where the old dock site used to be. The entire area had been converted into plush apartments with the city council doing its best to attract as many business's as possible into the region despite its notoriety.

Rachel had moved in there from Tony's house in Ordsall only six months before, after the family home in Wilmslow had finally been sold. It hadn't been that she'd waited for the money, in all honesty she still had money from her private practise, even though she'd shut it down now.

Also, she had been automatically paid out the life insurance from Peter and Becky. That money she was yet to even touch. Although Tony reminded her that it wasn't guilt money, she also reminded him she'd know when the time was right.

Hunter smiled at Rachel, handing her a bottle of Chianti that Rachel hadn't excepted. 'How's it going kid?' she asked, then added, 'thought we might have a drink whilst we chatted.'

'Sounds good,' replied Rachel, heading towards the kitchen. 'Just go through Hunter. I'll bring the glasses.'

Hunter was a little taken back as she walked into the nicely, yet sparsely furnished living room. For stood by the oval window, over looking the canal with his back to her, was Rachel's brother, 'You alright there Tony?' she asked, with Rachel trailing in behind her.

'Not bad Hunter,' he said, grinning at her knowingly through the reflection in the window that was almost as clear as a mirror itself with the dark sky-line as its backing. 'But then again, I suppose you know that already. Don't you now?'

Hunter took in Tony's huge torso from behind, as he pushed himself away from the window frame, and turned slowly to face her, in all of his six foot and six inches of glory. He was in his forties, but he'd always seemed a lot older to her. The grey streaks that had started to come through his short black wavy hair, made him seem more distinguished than he actually was.

He was, as he always was, immaculately dressed in black Armani trousers, that had been obviously fitted to match the suit jacket that hung over the back of the armchair. The trousers hung nicely against his polished, Patrick Cox loafers. His white Dolce & Gabana dress shirt was opened at the neck casually, as she gazed into his dark eyes, grinning as she always did at the out of place busted nose that he refused to have fixed. It gave him the impression of what he was, an old street fighter that had been born and bred on the streets of Manchester.

Apart from the nose, he could have quite easily passed for an investment banker stood there in all of his attire, but not if you knew better she thought to herself.

Although it had to be said, she'd always liked him, both on a personal level and also as far as business went. He may have worked the opposite side of the law, but he'd always been a true professional, and that, even she had to respect.

She knew that after the demise of their mother and father, word had it, that he tracked down the killers, who been contracted to do the job. Throwing both of them into tankers of industrial acid... whilst they were still alive. It had been a host of stories similar to this, and also the early stories of some outrageous bank robberies that took place throughout the country, that were used as capital to fund his other business's in the early years.

That was before his money eventually began finding its way into more legal enterprises such as the Salford Quays development, that she knew not only him, but some other key figures from way back when who used to run things, also had put money into its development.

'So how's the estate then?' she asked sitting herself down on the large cream and white three seater sofa, whilst both Tony and Rachel remained standing as she made herself comfortable, picking at imaginary frivolity from her skirt.

This was the one thing that cracked Hunter up. Tony had a hell of a lot of money and property both here in the United Kingdom, mainland Spain and the Canary Islands, but still refused to move away from the confines of Ordsall housing estate. Albeit that he'd converted three old council houses into one, that suited both him nicely, and no doubt the council who would have profited

nicely from the deal. But no matter, it couldn't hide the fact that the estate remained by far one of the worse in both Salford and Manchester.

'Getting worse everyday,' he said lighting an Embassy number one cigarette, placing the packet and the gold lighter back down on the pine coffee table before Hunter, as she reached over and helped herself without being offered. 'You know how these young kids are these days. They all want to grow up to be *gangstars*,' he purposely misworded 'gangster' as she laughed.

'It must be the example you set for them, living like a king Tony,' she said blowing a trail of smoke into the centre of the room, as he sat down opposite her in the arm chair.

'It's just my money at work nowadays Hunter', he told her smiling knowingly. 'I've got too many legal investments to be involved on any personal level with them lot.'

'Whatever you say Tony,' she said, returning the smile, also knowingly as Rachel handed them both a tall glass of the deep, rich, crimson wine.

It was a well known fact, that he did indeed have a lot of money invested in legal investments if that's what they could be called. It was also a well known fact that it was his firm that ran most of the security on the doors of bars and clubs in the city centre, with close to seven or eight-hundred allegedly on his payroll, and that was just for starters. She also knew first hand, that he worked closely with some of the firms from Newcastle who ran Timeshare operations out of both mainland Spain and the Canary Islands where he happened to own several properties.

Hunter also knew that he still had a lot of money working the streets, with several small firms operating in different boroughs of both Salford and Manchester. Although you'd never find anybody who would dare to take the stand against him. And why not, from what she knew from some of her numerous grasses was that he was about the most fair person that you could work for, even if it was indirectly. When she says fair though, you just had to make sure that you never crossed him in anyway personal.

Hunter had always found Tony and Rachel a strange combination, even though they were family. And despite what Rachel did, and the fact she knew exactly what Tony did for a living, the two of them were tighter than anyone else she actually knew.

'So what was it you wanted to see me about?' asked Rachel, sitting herself in the other armchair, muting the television set as she did so.

'Straight to business eh,' she said.

'You forget how well I know you Hunter,' replied Rachel. 'And I know that you didn't come here to ask Tony pointless questions.'

She laughed, ' I guess not.' She looked to Tony, then Rachel, 'You sure that you want Tony here for this. I know it's not official but...'

'Whatever you tell me,' said Rachel, 'you know that I'll tell him straight away anyway. So you might as well save me the bother, hadn't you.'

'I guess so,' she said. 'No offence Tony.'

'You couldn't offend me if you tried Hunter,' he laughed.

Suddenly Hunter's face became serious, 'You've heard the stories about the kids that have been going missing from the council estates surrounding Manchester, even all the way out to Macclesfield haven't you?'

'Of course,' replied Rachel, now curious to know more. 'Wasn't there one that went missing from Lacey Green in Wilmslow also?' she asked, remembering back to when it happened and the fact she'd still been residing in the same town.

'That's right,' she answered. 'That was some time last year. I was brought onto the case after...' she caught herself. 'Well, you know... anyway, the chief, Mackenzie... he had Halenbrook working the case. Although he wasn't getting anywhere with it. So the higher brass had Mackenzie put me on it. Although I have to say that he's pissed to fuck that his boy Halenbrook was taken off the case.'

'Why?' asked Tony.

'You mean besides the fact that he seems to hate me for whatever reason. No, it's not just that. It's because he's the chief's little weasel. The chief likes to give him jobs that will make him shine and he probably figured that this would be one of them. That is... if wasn't so fucking incompetent that he still has trouble finding his way around the station, never mind a fucking investigation,' she laughed as they both smiled at her. Then catching herself, she sighed deeply and shook her head slightly. 'Anyway, it seems that after all this time working the investigation, I'm more than a little embarrassed to say that we're basically, also getting nowhere really productive with it. That's not to say that me and Andrews haven't got a lot further than Halenbrook did with it. We've found quite a few interesting facts along the way.'

'What have you got then?' asked Rachel.

71

'All the kids were taken in broad daylight, which is still the one main puzzling things about the case. It's as if they simply vanish into thin air. But, well, we all know that just isn't the case in this sick world that we live in. But saying that, the one thing we've somehow managed to keep from the press so far is all the parents were addicts of some sort of another. Some hadn't even noticed their kids missing for days at a time.'

'You're kidding,' said Tony in disgust.

'I'm not,' she sighed deeply. 'Some were already known to social services for child abuse, both physically and sexually.'

'You think that somehow the parents are involved?' asked Rachel.

'It was the first angle that I worked,' she told them both. 'But I came up with nothing positive.'

'What have you come up with?' asked Tony.

'We seem to think that the kids have been abducted as part of some peodophile ring that's being run up and down the country.'

'What kind of ring are we talking about here Hunter?' asked Rachel, who'd done some studying into how peodophile's worked.

'We're not exactly sure.'

'What the hell are you sure of Hunter?' asked Tony in an irritated manner.

'What makes you so certain that the kids have been abducted for this peodophile ring?' asked Rachel lighting a cigarette, exhaling the smoke, 'And what evidence have you got towards believing this. As I understand you haven't even found the bodies yet.'

'One of our computer specialists, Danny, has been working the internet angle at work, only he keeps hitting closed doors,' she stubbed out her cigarette then looked at Rachel. 'It would appear a lot of these sites are protected in one way or another. But with one site, and this goes no further, even the families don't know about this.'

'Go on,' pushed Rachel.

'Danny managed to download part of a live transmission being aired a few months back,' she told them shaking her head as she did. 'This was just after the last kid from Levenshulme went missing. Four year old Carla, she was featured in a live sex show over the internet.'

'Jesus Christ,' exclaimed Tony.

'Believe me, it got worse by the minute before the transmission was cut. Danny tells me that there was that many loops and whatever else it is that they do to avoid being traced that it could

72

have been transmitted from right here in the UK or even Australia for all he knew.'

'Your guess would be right here though, correct ,' said Rachel. 'And what do you think is happening to them afterwards?'

'Let's just say that I'm not holding out much hope in finding them alive.'

'Why would someone be going to so much trouble though.' Rachel stood up and walked to the window, gazing outside into the night. 'I mean the fact that they are abducting the kids in the first place attracts attention to whoever is taking them. Especially with the ongoing case. What about some connection to social services?' she asked.

'I've come up short again,' replied Hunter.

'Any drug rehabilitation courses that they were on together,' she saw Hunter shake her head.

'Dealers,' she suggested. 'The same dealers?'

She looked to Tony, 'You'd probably be able to answer that one better than me Tony. You know the streets better than I do.'

'I'll check it out for you, if you like,' he said without any form of protest, as she smiled and nodded her response.

'And just where do I fit into all of this?' Rachel suddenly asked.

'Have you heard of the Cartwright family, Luther and Anabella Cartwright from over in Prestbury?' she asked. 'They own a stud farm over that way somewhere. They're often in the *Manchester Evening News* for charity events that they throw. Basically they're the type of rich fuckers that Tony here, mingles with all the time.'

They all laughed for the first time, as Tony spoke first, 'Not that I have anything to do with them. But I know who you're on about.'

'Their name does ring a bell,' said Rachel. 'What's your point?'

'Well the thing is, this a bit awkward,' she began, helping herself and lighting another of Tony's cigarettes. 'You see, their little girl Charlotte, if you can call a girl of sixteen, little that is. Well, she has gone on the missing list. But the thing is, is that she wasn't reported by her parents, Luther or Anabella, but rather it was brought to my attention anonymously, through a phone call.'

She observed their confused looks, 'So what has any of this to do with your case?' asked Rachel

'Nothing yet,' she said with again. 'It was what me and Mackenzie were arguing about outside of my office today. It

turns out that after my discreet visit to Sir Luther Cartwright, as he is known after his knighthood, believe it or not. But anyway he contacted the chief himself.'

'So is she missing or not?' asked Tony.

'Oh yeah,' she answered, 'but it seems that she's done this sort of thing before and they're not at all worried about it.'

'So they don't want an investigation into it then?' asked Rachel.

'That's why I'm here,' she told them both. 'The chief doesn't want the Cartwright's to suffer any bad publicity concerning their daughter going missing. He doesn't want the press getting the story wrong, and causing unwanted distress to the Cartwright's. It apparently turns out that they also hold a charity event each year, along with the many other events that they hold. But apparently this one the chief is rather favourable of as it is to raise extra money for the police.'

'As if the government doesn't give you lot enough already,' scoffed Tony.

'Not enough to catch the likes of you Tony,' she winked at him. 'The thing is, the family has agreed that we look into the matter privately just in case the press somehow get a hold of the fact that they're apparently not bothered as to the fact that their daughter is missing. So the chief finally agreed that seeing as I didn't really want any part of it anyhow, that I should look towards gaining some outside help in order to keep the whole matter quiet.'

'These kids aren't even within the same age range as the Cartwright girl,' Rachel pointed out. 'The missing kids have all been under ten years old from what I've read in the papers. I don't see the connection.'

'I haven't told anybody else this,' she looked at them both. 'Not even the chief, that's why I made out that I wasn't that interested in the missing girl. But the reason I followed up the anonymous phone call was that the girl I spoke to... said that if I was to discover the whereabouts of Charlotte, that I would discover the information leading to the missing kids.'

'Surely you're having me at it Hunter,' Rachel said, sipping at her wine, leaning against the window as they looked up at her. 'This could all be some sort of a joke with whoever made that phone call through to you. How do you know that this girl hasn't merely run away like her parents have told you. Why don't you just pass this on to someone else at the station for fuck's sake. Surely it can still be kept quiet.'

'That's why I'm here Rachel,' she responded.

'What the hell do you expect me to do?' she snapped. 'I study the crimes after they've been committed, for Christ sake Hunter. You're not even sure that there's been any crime committed here. I'm not an investigator, am I?'

'Yes you are kid,' said Hunter shaking her head. 'You've worked side by side through enough investigations with me in the past.' She then stared directly at Tony, then let her gaze wander to Rachel. 'And I think the two of you have done a pretty good job by yourselves over the past year or so with your own little private investigation.'

'That's below the belt Hunter,' snapped Rachel.

'Maybe' she replied nonchalantly. 'But either way, I'm hear to ask for help with something. It will do you good Rachel to give your mind a break from what its been going through, and to put it to use in something else.'

'That's true,' said Tony, taking her by surprise.

'I'm not saying to forget about anything Rachel,' she sighed. 'Jesus, that's the last thing I'd ever do. You know that I'm still working your case in my own time and that I am behind you one-hundred percent as your friend. But it's as your friend that I'm here tonight.' She looked pleadingly at her still stood by the window, as Rachel looked to Tony who gave her a little smile, reassuring her that he'd be there no matter what.

'So what is it that you want me to do Hunter?'

'I want you to go and talk to the parents for me kidda,' she said.

'You don't think that they are involved somehow?' she asked in disbelief.

'Not so much that,' she replied. 'But I think that you may be able to find out more about Charlotte herself than I could.' She stubbed out her third cigarette. 'I think that if the kid has run away. Then possibly she somehow found out something that she wasn't supposed too and it spooked her somehow.'

'But how could she know anything?' she asked, 'I mean the likes of the Cartwright's and the families of the missing kids are a million miles apart Hunter.'

'Just give it a shot for me will you kid.'

Rachel finally nodded as Hunter spoke again, 'I've just got a funny feeling that if you do some digging, it may point us in the right direction.'

'So what exactly do you want me to do?'

Hunter smiled, 'I've arranged or you to go and visit with the Cartwright's tomorrow morning. They're expecting you first thing, so don't be late.'

Rachel shook her head at her, 'I never even agreed.'

'I knew you would though.' She smiled warmly at her.

'You've not got a problem with the fact that Tony will be tagging along with me?'

'So be it kid,' she said pushing herself out of the sofa. 'I need your help and if that's how I'm going to get it then so be it.'

'I don't know if I like the sound of working for you guys,' Tony protested with a grin at Hunter.

Hunter shook her head at him, then suddenly laughed. 'And you know what else,' she said looking to the both of them, Rachel now stood behind the arm chair where Tony was seated, her hands placed protectively on his shoulders. 'It sure will piss the hell out of Mackenzie.'

SIX

As Gabriel sat watching the television set, waiting patiently for the local news to follow the news at ten, thinking, no that was wrong, knowing, that after all of this time of living in denial, that the time was right again. Fallen angel's needed to yet, once again, rise from the golden flames, from beneath where they lay buried in anticipation of their true destination.

Or at least, that's the perception of what Gabriel and Michael aimed for in the eyes of others, in order to manipulate all of those clever bastards who thought that they knew better than them. For it had been Michael who had searched out Gabriel's mind on a parallel conviction.

It had kind of been Michael's idea in the first place, well sort of anyway. Michael telling Gabriel that they were two lost fallen angel's who longed to be with one another, side by side on the forbidden earth that God had denied them. And that in order for them be together side by side, Gabriel had to listen to the soothing words that Michael washed over ones mind, as he had put it.

For Michael believed that they had to both seek out the vengeance for which they had been denied. It was only right that they take what belonged to them.

Once Michael learned of the dark secrets that Gabriel had hidden for so long, he finally revealed his true self to Gabriel. Unmasking the cloak from Gabriel's eyes where Michael hidden for so long. Telling Gabriel that he had indeed searched both long and hard for his true Gabriel here on earth. Getting right inside Gabriel's mind, searching through the maze that lay ahead of them. Twisting fantasies and abstractions into reality.

But Michael would only visit after dark, once all light had faded and Gabriel's eyes were finally closed. Then, and only

then would Michael reveal himself to Gabriel. Michael would say that Gabriel had been taken advantage of in more ways than one, and that with precision and planning they would strike vengeance upon those who deserved it most. And Gabriel believed all of Michael's loving words.

It had all been but a fantasy at one point in Gabriel's life, which was until Michael had told Gabriel how good it would feel. Michael said that he couldn't believe that it had taken so long to act upon carrying out vengeance on those who deserved it for what had happened over the years. Some of it, a lot of it, had become a distant memory, locked away, forgotten about. That was until Michael found the dark secrets that he been hidden away from everybody.

And once the soothing voice of Michael discovered the secrets of the past, he had demanded to know what was to be done about them. Gabriel hadn't wanted to at first, the pain and suffering was not long forgotten, but had been placed to one side in order to carry on with present day to day life. But when Michael had preyed further still, opening up the even darker secrets to the fantasies that had been played over and over in Gabriel's mind, but always, only as a fantasy and nothing else. Michael had become aroused at the thoughts, and in turn, so had Gabriel.

Michael had never pressured, merely pointed out how right, and just how good it would be... to at least try it out, to feel what the others felt.... *just once*.

Michael had said the first victim had to be chosen carefully, and when the suggestions had been put forward, Michael had been all in favour of carrying out the act with Gabriel as the tool to work the fantasy into the real world.

It had been so good last year, taking the lives of Peter and Becky. They had been the first, picked for two reasons that Gabriel now knew of, only one of them had been a lot more personal than the next.

In fact they were to be the only ones, *just once*, Michael had said. Saying that they would be the only ones and that they deserved it for what they had done to Gabriel. He had made Gabriel believe that it was the right thing to do, the only thing to do, and that Gabriel possessed the power in order to carry it out and get away with it.

Telling Gabriel that he'd be there in spirit throughout the slayings, and when things became too dark, all that Gabriel had to do was imagine the dark place they visited with each other and that Michael would be there. And he'd been right, when things started to tumble out of control that night, Michael had

indeed been their in spirit watching over everything like the true friend that Michael had become to Gabriel.

He told Gabriel in his soothing way, from up high above as he floated observing the scene below of him as Gabriel held the bloodied hearts in open hands as a gift to Michael; he told Gabriel that they had betrayed the beliefs in which the fallen angels had always paid so dearly for.

But the one thing that Michael's soothing voice had never pointed out, was that the killings themselves would be so intoxicating. That to hold the power of life and death in ones hands as Gabriel had done so that night would have left the longing affect of needing that power one more time.

But that's when Michael had pointed out the other reason for Peter being chosen in the first place, the real desire behind the dark secret that had led to Gabriel revealing the hidden secrets that had been locked away for so long that Gabriel had almost forgotten about them.

But that night changed everything, so much so that Gabriel had begged the soothing voice of Michael to allow another slaying. But Michael had said that the wise thing to do, and they were a lot wiser than the mere mortals in which they sought out their vengeance, but Michael said that they had to wait. That they had to drag it out for as long as possible in order to keep the game alive that they had to use all of their self control.

And Michael had, once again as he always did, and used his soothing voice to teach Gabriel the self control that was needed in order to wait as long as they had done. But it had been so hard at the same time, to wait another twelve months before the next lot of victims that had already been chosen in the first place.

Twelve months had been way too long, but the police investigation into the Dark Angel case as the press had named it, had all but run dry. Making the timing perfect to make the next move against the second family that were the ones who'd suffer at the hands of Gabriel. To feel the pain that they all justifiably deserved in the eyes of Gabriel and the soothing tones of Michael.

The intoxication of the first killings had been so strong that Gabriel had future plans and those plans weren't even conceivable to the effect of ever being incarcerated. Not like the others who had been hunted down and captured, like the animals that they were. Their down falls were that they couldn't control themselves like Gabriel could. That level of control was what would keep you alive and ahead of the game, no matter how strong the impulses, you had to control them.

Michael had taught that well, no matter what Gabriel had felt, his soothing voice had helped the last twelve months to come into perspective within Gabriel's mind. But there would be no more twelve months between victims, because they had planned it out within their minds who the next victims would be. Peter and Becky had merely tested the waters for Gabriel, and with the knowledge of what was conceivable made it all that much better to both Gabriel and the benign indoctrination of Michael.

What had also upped the stakes was the fact that the wife of Peter was still alive, Rachel Murphy hadn't been there that night, and that had all been part of the plan. Gabriel had known the movements of the family so well. Studying the family had taken serious planning and patience. Patience that Gabriel possessed like no other. To become almost as intimate as a man and wife would be without their knowledge, was how Gabriel had always assessed it.

That way their couldn't be mistakes, only the clues left behind and they would never work them out, not even that bitch that had been left to suffer the atrocities of the crime committed.

Gabriel had opened up a new era of terror for the so called experts to try and fathom out. And the plans were to keep it as confusing as possible, with just enough clues to keep the game interesting enough for Gabriel and Michael to play.

Watching, as Rachel arrived home that night, looking a little drunk, not realising what awaited her, totally unaware of her surroundings as Gabriel observed silently from the shadows. Still aroused by the slaughters, feeling the warmth of the hearts that had been placed in clear plastic freezer bags, and were concealed in the jacket pocket worn that night. Watching as she fumbled with the key, giggling slightly, so, so, unaware of what she was to walk into.

What Gabriel would have given to see her face as she walked into that bedroom after the crimes committed in there. Just to have been able to see the look of terror and mortification in her eyes. But that would have been stupid, and the last thing Gabriel was as they were all about to find out for the second time, *was stupid.*

And it hadn't mattered anyway, for Michael had described in detail what Rachel had looked like as he had waited and observed from high above, waiting, watching, taking in details to relay back to Gabriel in their next duration of visitation.

Although the screams had satisfied Gabriel enough that night, waiting, still hiding in the shadows across the street for the house as the shrieks of terror pierced through the quiet

neighbourhood, abandoning all the believes of the world within which we lived.

Bringing the nightmares that people believed only happened to others to this once undisturbed vicinity. Waiting just long enough for the first couple of lights to flick on at the neighbours homes, holding out as long as possible in order to absorb the atrocities from the work of art that had been presented to Rachel that very night.

But with the case lying dormant, and their plan mapped out, a wake up call was in order. The police couldn't become too complacent and it was about time that Gabriel reached out to Rachel once again, to open up her nightmares, tauntingly so, pleading for her to try and seek vengeance for what had happened. They had agreed that Rachel would make for the best adversary; Michael had said that with her intimate knowledge, they could use it to their advantage.

It was true that Rachel had been spared last time round, but that had been part of the challenge to leave her free to do her best to track down the killer of her family. Rachel thought that she was so clever, thinking that she could waltz into crime scenes after they'd been committed and try to read the minds of people like Gabriel, trying to get the better of them.

If she'd been so clever then she and that nefarious brother of hers would have worked it out by now.

But what they didn't seem to realise, was that they would never work it out, that's how good it was going to be. Because their wasn't any as clever as Gabriel and the soothing, commanding presence of Michael. All of this was to be proven in the not too distant future.

The local news was now showing, and Gabriel's next victim was the one being interviewed. Gabriel turned the volume up, thinking – no that was wrong – *knowing,* that this time round it would be the entire family that would be slayed.

No mistakes were to be made with the family, and the same dedication to the surveillance and studying of the victims was parallel to that of the first slaying. The wife this time round was of no concern to either Gabriel or the sheer brilliance of Michael's mind. She was a mere house wife who couldn't set a challenge if you gave her the instructions on how to do so.

No, this time round, the pattern of the first murder was to be broken, they were all going to pay this time round.

The man on the television set was talking to the cameras outside of Manchester Crown Court about his latest case. Gabriel knew that the man was Otis Fairchild, and that he was in

fact one of the partners of Morgan and Fairchild's law firm right here in Manchester's city centre. But not only that, he was also one of the many leading barrister's from the law firm where he worked as a successful defence lawyer.

He was talking about the man he was defending, known as Nigel Collins, who was a suspected, not guilty, as Fairchild pointed out, serial rapist. It was known that he'd been drugging women with a drug called Rohypnol that was completely tasteless and colourless in someone's drink.

He'd been doing this for over a two year period at clubs in and around Manchester. He'd then take the girls back to various hotel rooms, where he'd rape them repeatedly, all the while, knowing what was happening to them. Yet in some eerie, repelling, fallacy state of consciousness, succumbed by their drugged state of mind, not entirely sure of what was reality and what wasn't.

Either blaming themselves or being led to believe by Collins that they had in fact consented to these formidable encounters.

It hadn't been until a couple of girls got together and came after him. It had also been after this that the flood gates had opened, and a string of forty one women looked to press charges against him. He'd obviously denied the rape, saying that he'd slept with all the women and they may have been high on a drug, perhaps even ecstasy at the time, but that it hadn't been him to supply the drug to the women.

But he was guilty as hell and everybody knew it, only he was being represented by Otis Fairchild who was very successful at getting his clients off with a lot less than what he'd gone to court with now. Especially with the likes of Nigel Collins, who Gabriel knew was not only a friend to him, but was also extremely wealthy and respectable with his job in a leading advertising firm based in the city centre.

They were all laughing in the face of the police and the prosecution for the crimes committed. Just as nowadays, if you knew how the law worked, it was quite possible to do so. That's the way things seemed to heading these days, with the police catching the bad guys, with the bad guys finding the necessary loop holes within the law to walk free.

It was in fact, part of Michael's plan, to prove to Gabriel outright, that it wasn't law enforcement that was in control today, but that it was in fact the criminals who were the ones in control nowadays. It would be one of the key issues through Michael to show Gabriel just how it was possible to get away

with the crimes they had already committed, and were about to commit.

After Michael's soothing words of truth, it was in fact Otis, who was the real criminal in Gabriel's eyes now. In fact, knowing a lot more about Otis Fairchild than the recent case he'd taken on. Gabriel had been studying the man and his family as one for quite some time now. In fact, unaware of doing so, Gabriel had been watching all of the victim's carefully over the of years.

Gabriel saw the news article had finished concerning Otis Fairchild, but was still desperate to see more of his face. Going over to the Compaq lap-top computer and switching it on. Gabriel then hooked the Sharp digital camcorder up to it, and began clicking away at the keys, hitting the play button, watching as suddenly Fairchild's face appeared on the screen in all of its full glory.

Only this wasn't a recording from the television set, this was in fact a home video recording of him and his family in Heaton Park. Filmed the weekend before, with the Fairchild's totally unaware of being filmed.

Gabriel watched as the wife, Anita Fairchild pushed the little boy, William Fairchild back and forth, higher and higher on the swings as he cried out in joy. Otis was on his mobile phone, much to the annoyance of his wife who kept shouting for him to get off the phone. He was now, apparently arguing with whomever it was on the phone, his face screwed up, his eyes narrowing as he tried his best not to raise his voice.

The camera zoomed in on the wife's face. She was quite beautiful, Gabriel thought, that was going to make it all the much more better. She looked well pampered, and her make-up had been carefully applied, considering that they were only out visiting the park. Knowing that it was pure vanity, that made the likes of Anita Fairchild worry about being seen out unexpectantly, always wanting to look her best.

Otis had wandered back over now, and he kissed his wife, joking about with his son. They looked like quite the happy family, yet Gabriel also knew from watching them, observing them, that they were both having affairs. Hers was with the Yoga instructor who happened to give private sessions at their family home in Whitefield. And his, was with his personal secretary, a younger bustier version of what his wife had probably looked like at one time.

The little boy was the only innocent one out of them. But his innocence had been tainted by the fact he's been bred by the

likes of the two on the screen. It was only right that the boy be punished along with parents.

Gabriel was becoming aroused watching the film on the small computer screen and longed for something more. Knowing that this would happen around this time of the month, Gabriel had already defrosted the hearts. Just as they were always defrosted at this time of the month, so to keep them preserved nicely. Carrying this act out once a month, helping to keep things in perspective for Gabriel. It was part of the control that was necessary in not being caught and proving that Gabriel's mind couldn't be outsmarted.

Eyes closed tightly, with the hearts placed before Gabriel, touching them delicately, fondling their texture, letting the fingers that had taken them, glide over the surface as Michael's soothing voice played over and over in Gabriel's mind. The thoughts and the voices building and building from deep inside, becoming stronger and stronger as they tried to break through the surface. The arousal becoming stronger and stronger as the feelings became almost electrifying.

It was almost as if Gabriel could feel their hearts come alive once again, as they worked their magic against the aroused inner working of Gabriel, intensifying, becoming stronger, more powerful with each thought of what was to become of the Fairchild family. Gabriel finally moaned out loud, the cries of sheer pleasure reaching out for Michael to hear, as the feeling of self gratification, without even having to touch oneself became as imperious and almost as intoxicating.

Just as the night the angel's fell from the sky, just as the angel's were about to swoop down once again in vengeance for all that was once lost.

SEVEN

Making their way up the long winding driveway in Tony's dark racing green, 5 series BMW, which Tony had pointed out to her, would be more suitable for the area in which they were visiting than her Ford Explorer. Rachel also knew, that from the several cars he owned, he just loved to show this one off more than the others, without a doubt this was his favourite vehicle of choice.

She wouldn't have minded, but this wasn't by far, the nicest car he owned. It was more of a childish gloating issue. All because he'd won it the previous year in a card game from a big gambler from Chinatown, known as Chan, who was actually one of Tony's closest friends, and also the owner of the finest Chinese restaurant in Manchester.

Taking in her surroundings as the gravel crunched boisterously beneath the tyres, she smiled to herself. It was a large farmhouse that had been converted from its original building and had undergone extensive work, resembling the many gracious homes they'd passed along the way into the village. The homes of the rich and famous as Tony had told her, also adding that many of the football player's for Manchester United resided there. Rachel had just shook her head at him at the time, saying, 'trust you to point that out,' as he grinned back at her.

But there was no denying the homes the respect they all deserved. Each abode different from the next one along, all of them exquisitely unique in their own way. Only the Cartwright's appeared to stand out from the rest of the crowd.

For not only had it been converted from its original domain into this lavish home, it was also set so far back for the main road to retain its privacy. It would appear that the Cartwright's resided in what appeared to be pure comfort Rachel thought to herself,

as Tony eased the car around to the rear of the house. As Rachel observed the posterior of the house, she noticed that there was so much wood land, so much in fact, that she thought it resembled Alderley Edge itself, right here in your very own back garden.

Climbing from the passenger seat she breathed in the fresh air, closing her eyes, smelling all of nature around of her. As she opened her eyes, she found herself smiling at two very young looking girls, which were obviously stable hands for the family, dressed in riding gear and busying themselves whilst grooming the horses.

'We've been expecting you,' said the voice from behind them at the backdoor, and to whom Rachel assumed to be Anabella Cartwright. Turning towards her, Rachel returned the woman's smile, as the woman's eyes left hers and went straight to Tony's.

'I hope that you don't mind that I've brought my brother along Mrs. Cartwright,' said Rachel looking to her brother, offering no further explanation to Tony's presence.

'Not at all,' she smiled directly at Tony, and Rachel saw her brother smile back intentionally at her, as the two of them flirted blatantly with one another. The attraction between them was obvious to Rachel as she glared at Tony, then back to Anabella Cartwright, who still hadn't taken her eyes from that of her brothers.

Although Rachel couldn't blame Tony for being attracted the woman stood before them both. She was absolutely beautiful and came from obvious class and money, even Rachel had to admit that. Her hair was of the same natural colouring of Hunter's, only it flowed half way down her back. She was dressed elegantly, as if; in indeed she was off out for the evening and they'd got their times somehow mixed up. Rachel found herself glancing at her watch to make sure it was in fact just before nine o'clock in the morning.

Stood there, Anabella Cartwright was smoking seductively in a black all in one Gucci dress, that enhanced her extremely well toned body. Her face, despite the fact it was only nine o'clock in the morning, was fully made up. Although, as Rachel approached to door, she could see the woman's natural beauty and felt that all make up she wore was unnecessary. For beneath the immaculately painted face, was an extremely beautiful woman, the carefully applied make up, only enhancing this fact further.

'Rachel Murphy,' she said holding out her hand as Anabella Cartwright shook it, but without even looking to her, as she still

only had eye contact for Tony. 'And this is Tony Henessy,' she added abruptly, as Tony took the woman's hand.

'You alright Mrs. Cartwright,' said Tony, both of them allowing their hands to linger a little longer than was appropriate.

'Very pleased to meet you, both that is,' she said, finally making eye contact with Rachel. 'And please it's Anabella.'

'And Luther,' said the man walking through the huge kitchen behind his wife, two golden retrievers tailing along side of him. 'Please come on through Ms or I'm sorry is it Mrs. Murphy.'

'Rachel is fine' she told him, taking in his appearance and following them into the kitchen. He was quite large in his build, at almost six foot in height and appearing as he should, well groomed, with the money they had.

There wasn't a hair out of place upon his head. Each dark brown strand was brushed straight to the back of his head, and she imagined that his hair was in fact quite long in its length. The casual beige linen Valentino suit he wore, was of obvious expense and fitted him well, although emerging to be slightly out of place for the time of year that it was. The Polo, sky blue silk shirt, that was open at the neck casually, gave his overall appearance one of trying its best to hold onto the summertime. That's not to say that it didn't suit him, as it did, but Rachel was a little taken back, having expected someone with a knighthood to be a lot more conservative than he was.

Their age had thrown Rachel also, not expecting the two of them to be quite so young looking. She placed them both to be in their early forties, only they could have passed easily for early thirties.

'Please come through to the living room if you will,' he said taking Rachel's hand, as she felt a chill run through her for no apparent reason and quickly removed it away, with him still smiling at her, apparently unoffended by her response.

As they walked into the living room they were hit with the warmth of an open fireplace, burning away, the flames crackling against the inflamed logs. The living room looked very modern, and was what Rachel would have expected from the exterior of their home. Everything appeared to have been brought up to date, and their home had a real contemporary feel to it.

The larger than life paintings, that adorned all four walls, were originals. Albeit that they were by modern artists that Rachel did not recognise, she doubted that their price tags were far behind those of an original Picasso. The colours from each painting,

complemented the room, enhancing the rooms natural effulgence.

Noticing the white grand piano over by the patio windows, Rachel wandered over to observe the beauty of the contrivance, stroking the smooth panelling admiringly as she paid attention the two young stable girls outside, who were doing their best to try and see into the living room.

Also noticing the girls, was Luther Cartwright, now stood directly behind Rachel, his presence uncomfortable to Rachel as he scowled at the girls outside, before drawing the loose white and cream curtains, turning to face them, annoyance upon his face.

'Please sit,' he said abruptly, as he began pouring himself a large Glenfidich malt whiskey. 'Anybody else care for a drink.'

'Coffee would be nice,' Rachel smiled as both her and Tony sat on the huge cream and white sofa, both sinking into its luxury as Tony smiled.

'Cheers,' he said, gesturing at Luther. 'Don't mind if I do.'

'Don't forget me too, dear,' said Anabella without a hint of politeness, as he handed her a glass of champagne, that in fact, he had already prepared.

Handing the crystal glass, full of the malt whiskey to Tony, without even acknowledging his wife's presence, he said 'Go and get the pot of coffee for Rachel.'

Returning momentarily from the kitchen, a wearied looking Anabella Cartwright handed Rachel a single bone china cup of potent smelling coffee, with the cream and sugar already added, even though she hadn't requested either, but she let it go.

'Before we start Rachel,' said Luther. 'I want to know exactly what it is that you think that you can do here?'

'I've been asked by Detective Hunter to come and talk with the two of you, to try and gain a better insight into Charlotte herself,' she told him, as she absentmindedly played with Becky's gold necklace that Tony had bought her for her christening, and that she now always kept wrapped around her wrist.

'That damn woman,' spat Luther. 'I told her that there is nothing to worry about.'

'But what else do you expect to achieve?' asked Anabella, who was, once again staring at Tony as she spoke to Rachel. 'As we hear it. You are not a detective or any kind of an investigator, are you now?'

'As I believe Mr and Mrs. Cartwright,' said Rachel, placing the cup of coffee down on a coaster next to her and staring at the

two of them. 'You didn't want any police involvement and with your daughter being sixteen there doesn't have to be an investigation. So if you like, I'll be on my way.'

'No, stop,' sighed Luther. 'If the press get onto the fact that we didn't do anything it could backfire on us.' He stared at his wife, who briefly broke her gaze from Tony.

'Do you think that you can trace her whereabouts?' asked Anabella, now smiling unconvincingly at Rachel.

'I've helped Hunt... sorry, Detective Hunter on a number of occasions to track down a variety of people. A psychological approach to get to know Charlotte as a person could help the same way it helps with any kind of information you may think helpful or even unhelpful. It's basically so that we can effectively narrow down our resources. It's true that I usually profile what the police should look for in a potential suspect, but it's also true that my approach here could help us to find out what exactly happened to Charlotte.'

'That rude detective will have no doubt told you that Charlotte has done this kind of thing before you know,' said Luther sipping the malt, as he stared directly at Rachel.

Ignoring his comment, that obviously referred to Hunter, she said, 'Psychology is about understanding the motivation behind the things we do Mr. Cartwright.'

'So what was her motivation then?' asked Anabella.

'That's what I'm here to try and fathom out Mrs. Cartwright,' she said. 'Why did she run away before?'

'Because we wouldn't buy her a certain dress she wanted or we wouldn't give way to letting her stay out late,' answered Anabella.

'You serious?' exclaimed Tony.

'That was the last time she did this kind of thing,' Luther told them savouring the scent of the whiskey as he rolled it around the crystal.

'She's done it three or four other times for various other things just as pathetic as that one,' said Anabella irritably.

'What makes you think that she has done the same thing this time around?' asked Rachel.

'You mean apart from the fact she's done it before,' sighed Luther. 'Because her and that no good tramp of a friend of hers have been staying out later and later each night lately. Both of them are probably up to no good with those boys that they've been hanging around with. I'm not stupid you know. I know what girls get up nowadays. But you have to understand the position that we are in here. We are constantly in the limelight.

And we have an image – not to mention our name that we have to protect. We hold more than a few charity events each year and we don't need any bad publicity from that daughter of ours ruining it, by drawing unnecessary attention indecorously brought upon us.'

'Which girl is this?' asked Rachel, ignoring his ramblings on about himself and his wife. 'And did you tell Detective Hunter about this girl?'

'I didn't tell that detective about it... no,' he snapped. 'Because she was extremely rude and arrogant with me. I explained that she shouldn't even be here and I pointed out that she'd done this kind of thing before. But she stormed in here and practically accused us of having something to do with the disappearance of our own daughter, If you can believe that.'

Actually, Rachel could believe the way Hunter would have stormed in here, as she seen her do it so many times before. Hunter was not the most diplomatic of people at the best of times, so Rachel pressed on. 'What about this girl?'

'Her family moved around here, about two years ago now,' said Anabella sipping her drink as she lit another cigarette, allowing her gaze wander back to Tony. 'They are known as the Massey's from some disreputable part of Manchester. Rumour has it that Caroline's father. Sorry, Caroline is the girl that she's been hanging around with. Anyway, this Paul Massey is said to be some sort of a gangster from over that way.'

Rachel saw Tony become slightly uncomfortable next to her and tried her best to ignore him. 'Were the two of them close?'

'Very close,' said Luther. 'They were like sister's.'

'Have you spoken to her?' asked Tony. 'The girl I mean?'

'She hasn't stopped calling around here,' he said. 'She keeps phoning us, threatening me with her father. Telling me that he'll break my legs or some other so called bully boy tactics these disreputable kinds of people use... Anyway that's if I don't tell her where Charlotte is.'

Rachel noticed that he said this with complete nonchalance towards the entire subject, so said, 'You don't seem at all worried about the fact your daughter is missing.'

'She'll show up,' he replied shrugging. 'Like I said, she's done this kind of thing before.'

'Was there an argument that set all of this into motion?' asked Rachel.

'We told her that we didn't want her hanging around with that Massey girl anymore,' Anabella told her abruptly, Rachel

noticing that she still hadn't taken her eyes away from Tony, as she added. 'Very bad influence that one was.'

'The only reason we agreed to speak with you was that Tom Mackenzie said that whoever that Detective brought in, would look into things quietly. Like I've already said, we don't want any publicity involving our daughter missing.'

'It could help us to find her though,' said Rachel.

'No publicity whatsoever,' snapped Luther, then sighing deeply. 'Look Rachel, we're sure that this is all nothing to worry about. Charlotte has money. Believe me; she won't be living on the streets anywhere. This will just be her way of trying to teach us both a lesson.' As he said this, he slipped his hand into his wives as she tore her stare away from Tony.

'What exactly is it that you want from us?' asked Anabella.

'Please, don't take offence to this. But I get the impression that neither of you are close to your daughter. And I really need to get to know everything I possibly can on your daughter or I won't be able to help. I need to know her history. I need to know of any other events the may have caused her to become depressed? Has she been on medication for anything? How did she do at school last year? Is there anything at all that you feel I should know?'

'Apart from the fact she did shit at school last year. Her results were appalling and she couldn't give a toss either way,' he snapped. 'Her grades had always been good until that little slut of a girl showed up. But apart from that, there is not a lot that I can think of,' shrugged Luther, glancing to his wife who in turn shrugged also.

Rachel wasn't at all surprised by their response, she was finding the two of them to be difficult, but wasn't at all sure whether or not it was just the way these people were, 'I think that it may be best if you let me have a look around Charlotte's bedroom, alone if that's alright.'

'No problem,' said Luther, rising from the sofa. 'I'll show Tony the grounds, whilst you're doing that.'

'What about me?' asked Anabella irritably, Rachel thought more at the prospect of not having Tony within her sights.

'You can start by showing Rachel to Charlotte's bedroom,' he said. 'Come on Tony. I'll show you the stables.'

As the two of them made their way through the door, Anabella pushed herself out of the sofa, 'Come on then,' she sighed, bored by this entire matter. 'But I don't see how it will help you.'

Entering the bedroom, Rachel thought that it probably looked just like a lot of other teenage girl's rooms.

'Thank you Anabella,' said Rachel, making it clear that she wanted to be left alone.

'Whatever,' she replied, taking her cue and turning to leave.

Closing the door quietly behind her, Rachel turned and took the room in more closely. The walls were adorned with posters of boy bands like The Backstreet Boys and Westlife, both of whom Rachel had heard of. Taking in the room around her, she also saw pictures of what looked to be Britney Spears or Christina whatever her name was, Rachel couldn't remember and had always thought the two looked alike anyway.

Sitting herself down on the large dark oak, king-size bed, realising that it was in fact a lot larger than her own bed, she began stroking the white silk duvet covers.

Picking up the framed photograph beside the bed, Rachel saw two girls with their arms around each other, that looked to have been taken in a bar or possibly even a club. She made a mental note of looking into that.

Even though she had yet to see Charlotte, as no photographs had been offered and there was no personal photographs adorning the walls as there were many paintings. It was obvious, which of the two was Charlotte, as she was almost as identical as her mother.

Appearing to be so full of life in the photograph, and not at all a girl of sixteen years old. She and the other girl, who Rachel now presumed to be the Massey girl, could have easily passed for young women, and Rachel realised just how dangerous that could be. They were both wearing low cut tops that seemed to cling to their bodies, both with more than ample breasts fighting to stay within the tops. She could see a group of lads in the background, and even they had become blurred from the shot, she could that they were taking in the girls before them.

'Come on Charlotte,' she said outloud. 'Reveal something more of yourself to me.'

Rachel came to the conclusion that she wasn't going to get anywhere with the parents of this child. All that they seemed concerned about was, keeping any bad publicity towards them out of the press.

She was going to have to find out about the girl herself, starting with this very room and then tracking down this Massey girl, of whom she suspected to be the mystery caller to Hunter, and who could turn out to be the best possible source.

Opening the bedside table draw, she found nothing of interest, but old magazines. Although they all seemed to be for someone a lot older than the girl whose bedroom she was in. They were magazines like Cosmopolitan, Vogue and an assortment of other fashion magazines. Desperate to find some sort of correspondence, letters or a diary, anything that might reveal more of who Charlotte really was to her.

Going to the girl's wardrobes, she was surprised to see them still bulging, the clothes were all brand name and the dresses were very expensive and didn't look as though the belonged in a sixteen year old's wardrobe. 'Didn't plan on going far then Charlotte,' she said to herself.

But saying that, she probably wouldn't have noticed a bag full of clothes missing from this wardrobe, which was over stuffed as it was. All of the shoes were neatly placed side by side, along with several pairs of Adidas and Nike trainers.

Moving over to the matching set of dark oak draws, she began going through them finding further items of clothing and a lot of underwear. Much of which, to her surprise, Rachel owned herself. But still nothing of a personal nature, which she so desperately needed to find.

Sitting herself down at the large office desk, that was slightly out of place with all of the dark wooden surroundings. But had none the less, been set up for use of the I-Mac lap-top computer that sat among an array of different scanners and printers.

Flipping through the disks that were stored in the plastic box, with the key still in the lock, she saw nothing of interest apart from appeared to school projects or games stored onto the disks. As Rachel clicked the computer mouse, the computer screen came to life. The backdrop used the same photo from her bedside table.

Rachel began clicking through files, 'Come on, come on Charlotte,' she said in annoyance as she came to only locked files, unlike the storage box for the disks. The computer had been secured; the girl hadn't wanted anybody nosing around the files she thought to herself.

'What are you keeping from us girl,' she asked out loud. 'Come on now, let me have a little peek.'

Suddenly there was a huge boom, echoing away in the distance, but making Rachel jump all the same, 'Jesus Christ,' she screamed and the noise repeated itself in a quick succession.

'It's just Luther showing off with Tony,' said Anabella, who had suddenly appeared in the doorway startling her.

'What are they doing?' asked Rachel. 'They sounded like gunshots.'

'Clay pigeon shooting at the back of the woods,' she answered. 'You find anything?'

'Nothing of much use,' she said looking to the computer, thinking that she'd love the have a look into what was hidden in the files.

'You want to go outside and join the boys?' asked Anabella, as more shots rang out.

'Sure,' she replied. 'I'll see you downstairs; I'll just shut this thing down.'

'All right,' she said and was gone from the doorway.

Quickly shutting the computer down, Rachel went to the door to make sure Anabella Cartwright had in fact gone downstairs. Seeing that she had she quickly went back to the computer, knowing that it would be near impossible to sneak to computer outside, she flipped the computer upside down, ejecting the hard-drive.

'Everything alright up there?' Anabella's voice called from downstairs as Rachel appeared, closing the door behind her.

'Fine,' she answered, walking down the stairs and finding Anabella by the backdoor where they had entered.

'Come on Rachel,' she said. 'I'll take you to them.'

Walking outside to the where the stables resided, Rachel found herself smiling at the girls she had seen earlier, whilst all the while they looked at with a strange kind of curiousity upon their faces.

'This is a beautiful home that you have,' said Rachel glancing at Anabella who she caught intensively glaring at the girls.

'I know,' she replied, automatically dropping the scowl upon her face as she smiled at Rachel, as they now made their way over to the stables.

'So, this is your stud farm then?'

'Oh dear god, no,' Anabella laughed. 'These are just our personal horses. Both ours and Charlotte's. This one belongs to her in fact.' She began brushing the mane of the large white horse that one of the two girls had been seeing to.

Rachel noticed that the young girl wouldn't make eye contact with her, 'You alright there?'

The girl didn't answer, but smiled nervously and nodded.

'This is Lucy,' offered Anabella. 'You've been working with us for a number of years now. Haven't you Lucy?'

'Yes Mrs. Cartwright,' she replied, almost sheepishly almost as though she was new employee rather than one whom had been around for years as just desribed.

'You're well looked after,' she said. 'Aren't you Lucy?'

'Yes Mrs. Cartwright,' she automatically answered again. 'Me and Heather are almost finished.'

'Good work girls,' she smiled. 'You're pay is in the envelopes in the kitchen.'

'Where is the stud farm then?' asked Rachel, changing the subject.

'Over in Knutsford.'

The made their way through the woodland, that was to the rear of the stables, with Rachel taking in all of the wonderful colours. 'I always loved this time of the year.'

'You said that in past tense, don't you anymore?' asked Anabella stopping in her tracks, looking directly at Rachel.

'A long story,' she offered.

'The one concerning your dead husband and child?' she asked abruptly.

Keeping her composure she replied, 'Something like that, yes Mrs. Cartwright. You could say that it stems from something like that.'

'I'm surprised that with all of your so called skills as a criminal psychologist you didn't see it coming,' she smiled wickedly as she said this – no doubt meaning to offend.

'I'm afraid my skills as a clairvoyant passed me by that week Mrs. Cartwright.'

'Too bad,' she replied without any remorse whatsoever.

'Yes it was Mrs. Cartwright,' she stared at the woman who suddenly seemed to be contemptuous towards her for no apparent reason. 'Especially seeing as I had my family torn away from me that night. It's also the reason that Hunter asked for my involvement in helping you find your daughter. Even though it doesn't seem that you're all that bothered about the fact she'd missing.'

'I'm sorry,' she said abruptly – yet almost seemingly sincerely, taking Rachel by surprise. 'I am worried about Charlotte. It's just that's she's done this before and I'm certain that's all it is this time round.'

'Maybe I should just let the police handle it,' Rachel told her.

'No,' she snapped. 'I've said I'm sorry. But if you are willing to help look into finding our daughter it would be much better than the police conducting an investigation. Please, I am sorry for my earlier comments. My husband had a cheque made out

for five thousand pounds. If you need more than we'll pay you more money.'

'It's not why I agreed to help you Mrs. Cartwright.'

'I know it isn't,' she smiled. 'But it's only right that we pay you what we would have paid a private detective. That would have been what Luther would have ended up doing if Charlotte hadn't shown up.'

Rachel just nodded, still unsure that she actually wanted any part of this.

'There they both are,' said Anabella as they'd reached the opening to the field that resided at the back of the woodland.

Rachel watched, covering her ears, as Luther pulled the handle on the release for the clay pigeons as the two disks flew off high into the air. Tony expertly aiming the shotgun into the sky and pulling the trigger twice as both the clay pigeons exploded into dust.

'Fantastic shooting, once again Tony, I might add,' congratulated Luther, clasping Tony on the back as he removed the headphones.

'You two really are just a couple of big kids, aren't you?' said Anabella, linking arms with her husband as she smiled coyly at Tony.

'You ready Tony?' asked Rachel.

'He's quite a shot you know,' said Luther admiringly.

'So I've heard,' said Rachel, as she smirked back at him. 'Only I don't think you want to know where he learnt how to shoot one of them things.'

EIGHT

The two of them were sat silently on the second floor of Chan's restaurant in Chinatown, situated in Manchester's city centre, Tony staring out onto the street below at the mid afternoon traffic of pedestrians wandering back and forth. The restaurant was quiet, as it was only just gone midday and Tony had insisted that they go there to eat from leaving the Cartwright's.

Rachel noticed a couple being shown to their table at the other end of the restaurant. They were both only young, maybe early twenties. Both were wearing suits, that could mean any number of different jobs that they held right here in the city centre. Rachel observed the intimacy between the two of them, the way they constantly touched each other, the way they constantly smiled at one another. Their feet tapping against one another beneath the table, their declaration of tranquillity radiating from them as the continued to stare into each other's eyes playfully, jokingly as he stroked her cheek tenderly.

Rachel gulped away the tear she felt escaping from the absolute delight she felt for the couple. At that very moment she felt the loneliness of not having someone to share those moments with, no matter how small or insignificant. Wiping her right eye with her finger, she saw that Tony had noticed the couple, observing him smile, as he reached over and placed a protective hand over hers.

'You alright ar'kid?'

'Fine,' she replied, placing her hand over his, squeezing it slightly to let him know everything was all right.

'You find anything of use?' asked Tony, changing the subject, just as he knew how to at times like this.

'You mean, apart from the fact that you and Mrs. Cartwright wanted to strip to your bare bones and fuck each stupid where you both stood.'

Tony blushed slightly, as he always did around his sister when she talked about sex in front of him, 'It wasn't like that at all.'

'Yeah right,' laughed Rachel. 'Who you trying to kid? The way you two were undressing each other with your eyes, could have called for a very expensive law suit against you from Mr. Cartwright or is it Luther, your good buddy now and all that.'

'Fuck you Rachel,' he smirked. 'She was a babe though, wasn't she?'

Rachel nodded, 'Yes she was,' she replied. 'And I think that she was rather smitten with you.'

'You think so?'

'Come off it Tony,' she shook her head at him. 'You know that she couldn't take her eyes off you...'

'But?'

'But nothing,' she said. 'I didn't even say but.'

'You didn't have to ar'kid,' he smiled at her. 'I know you weren't keen on her. Was you kidda?'

'She knew who I was.'

'After last year,' he said staring at her, 'what did you expect. You know that your face was all over the TV. and newspapers back then.'

'I know,' she sighed. 'But there was something else. What did you make of him?'

'Very false,' he shrugged. 'But then you find that a lot these days. People trying to be things that they are not.'

'They are what they are Tony,' she said sipping the water that the waiter had placed on the table, as Tony took a swig from his bottle of Heineken. 'Money.'

'That's not exactly what I meant,' he said. 'But you are right. They are money through and through. So what did you find in the bedroom?' he asked changing the subject.

'Not a lot,' she replied, reaching into her jacket pocket. 'Apart from this, that is.' She produced the small rectangle piece of plastic.

'What the fuck is that?'

'This is the hard-drive to Charlotte's lap top computer,' she handed it to him. 'It's also something that I need your help with.'

'How can I help?'

'The files are locked,' she sighed deeply. 'And seeing as I illegally took the hard-drive I don't think that it'll look too good

asking Hunter for her help. I need you to find me someone who can gain access to the files quietly. Then if we don't find anything of use, you'll just have to use your charm with Mrs. Cart... sorry it's Anabella, isn't it Tony. Well you'll just have to charm your way back inside the house, in order to put it back.'

Tony laughed at her, 'You crazy little fucker Rachel,' he shook his head at her. 'I think my guy here might be able to help us. Also there is something else I can help you with Rachel.'

'Go on,' she pushed.

'The Massey's,' he sighed.

'You know them?' she asked. 'I saw you squirming when they mentioned him. I am right in thinking that the Massey they were referring to is the one from the old estate right?'

'He's alright y'know,' he was nodding his answer to her as he told her defensively. 'In fact we've done a little business over the years.'

'I don't want to know what business,' she shook her head.

'Probably best you don't,' he grinned at her. 'But anyway, I can take you to see him after we've eaten. He owns a club not five minutes from 'ere. He's usually there day and night. It's kind of like his office so to speak.'

'Tony,' said the small wiry man walking to the table. 'How are you Tony? You looking after my car for me?' he asked as Tony rose from his seat and then had to reach down to hug the small Chinese man before him.

'You alright Chan?' asked Tony. 'And it's not your car anymore. How many times have I got to keep telling you that old man? Besides which, you never did learn to drive the damn thing. You just had your waiter's chauffeuring you here, there and everywhere.'

'Beside point,' he protested. 'Still my car. You card cheat at that game.' He laughed making the three of them laugh along.

'You remember ar'kid?' asked Tony.

'Stop asking old man silly questions,' he said bending to kiss Rachel on her cheeks. 'How are doing Rachel? It's been a while since we've seen you. You're looking well.'

Rachel knew Chan, as he'd been a close friend of Tony's for quite a number of years now. Chan was also known around Manchester for his connections to the many unsavoury characters that resided in town.

Although his true connections to his own people, seemed to go unspoken of. She knew that Chan had his fingers in many pies around Manchester, although always appeared to be the unknown third party that stayed just far enough out of the circle

to not be directly involved. Very much like her own brother she thought to herself.

'Hello Chan,' she hugged the old man, and like always was surprised at how solid he actually was beneath his fragile looking exterior.

Chan signalled for a waiter to come over, and then started to talk really fast in his own dialect, 'Chan order special food for you two,' he said sitting himself down. 'Not from the menu.' He smiled at Rachel as she thanked him.

'You know anybody who can do anything with this?' asked Tony showing him the hard-drive.

'I don't know,' he said shaking his head. 'What do you want doing with it?'

'We need to gain access to the files,' he told him, 'so that sis' here can have a nosy around.'

'Are the files locked?'

'Each file requested a password,' Rachel told him.

'I'll call Jonah or Kezlo,' he replied, still studying the box.

'How are those lads?' asked Tony, knowing both of the lads since the early nineties when they used to be part of an old crew that ran the Hulme estate, with an old friend of his known as Prey. 'I've not seen either of them for a while now.'

'Good – good. They both are doing well for themselves,' he smirked. 'Plus they've both got very good connections with some computer kid that they use. He does work for me sometimes, good work, very good work indeed. Also he does so on the quiet and I suspect that is what you're searching for, no?'

'Thanks a lot Chan,' Rachel kissed him on the cheek, making him blush slightly.

'One more thing old man,' said Tony. 'Have you heard anything around town on the kids that have been going missing?'

'No,' he replied rising from his seat, 'but I will ask around for you, if you like me too.'

'That would be great Chan,' said Tony nodding at the old man as he wandered off towards the kitchen.

'That isn't part of what we've been asked to do,' said Rachel.

'I know it isn't,' he told her. 'But Hunter doesn't seem to getting far by herself. The thought of these kids being used in some paedophile ring makes me sick to my stomach. And even if it doesn't have anything to do with Charlotte's disappearance I still want to try help if I can. Plus there is the fact that sometimes the streets are a lot more forthcoming with its information to the

likes of both Chan and me than to the likes of yourself or even Hunter.'

'Ain't that the truth,' she replied.

NINE

'This is the club that he owns?' asked Rachel, cocking an eyebrow at her brother, whilst shaking her head at him. 'What are you lot all like?' she laughed.

The were both stood outside of The Pleasure Rooms, in the Chorlton Street district of Manchester, an area that was reputable for all of its known prostitution. The area, just outside of the Canal Street area, which was referred to as *'The Gay Village'* of Manchester.

Although this wasn't strictly true and had become one of the best areas to attend on a night out. Despite its diversity, some of the best clubs and bars now resided within these few streets. The Pleasure Rooms, as it was known, was one of the premier lap dancing clubs to have seen the areas potential and moved in on it.

'What's with you,' asked Tony. 'This is a legit joint that Paul owns here.'

'Yeah,' she sighed. 'But look what it is. Maybe I should just wait for you out here.'

'Jesus Christ Rachel,' he laughed. 'You're more open about this kind of thing than I am.'

'You're right,' she laughed along, teasing him. The two of them headed through the double doors that were being watched over by two burly black men. They both nodded their acknowledgements to Tony, with a little smirk towards Rachel.

As they walked through the heavy set of black doors into the actual club area, the bright lights startled Rachel who had expected different. *Bad Girls* by the artist *Juliet Roberts*, was pumping out of the sound system as the women gyrated themselves in various states of undress. They were entertaining both, the happy looking men and to her surprise, women as well.

In fact there were probably just as many women in the place, as there were men. All of them enjoying, either their personal lap dances, or the four girls who were stripping seductively in their own personal cages hanging high above the centre stage.

It was as if, it one o'clock in the morning, not just gone two in the afternoon. Rachel was surprised to see that the place was already full of customers.

Rachel had to admit that she was impressed with the standard of the club, not that she frequented such establishments. But it fair to say that she had built up a mental picture within her own mind before walking through the doors, as to just how these places were supposed to appear.

But this was far from her expectations, there was no cheesy DJ playing crap music for starters and rather than looking all seedy, dark and shady it was in fact well lit, showing off all of the girl's full potential. The customers all had their own personal, black leather, easy boy arm chairs to make themselves as comfortable as possible in. And appeared to be taking full advantage of them, putting a smile on Rachel's face.

'You alright Tony?' asked the topless Asian girl, in what can only be described as a pure Mancunian accent, that didn't go with her appearance at all. She was suddenly stood before him; a silver tray perched upon her right hand steadily. 'You want drinks or something more personal?' She then asked, giving a little shake as her diminutive brown breasts that swung from side to side playfully making the small gold hoops that adorned her nipples shake along to the beat of the music.

'Just the boss love,' he smirked at her, as she suddenly noticed Rachel for the first time.

'You sure Tony,' she winked at him. 'I can do the two of you if you like.'

Tony started laughing at her, 'Behave yourself girl,' he said. 'That's me kid sister.'

'Oh shit Tony,' she shook her head apologetically. 'I'm sorry love, I didn't realise,' she said looking to Rachel.

'It's alright.' Rachel smiled at her, 'I may come back for a dance later without ar'kid here looking over my shoulder.' She winked at the girl to let her know that she was joking.

'Rachel,' spat Tony, scowling at her. 'Where's Paul?' he asked changing the subject, no doubt embarrassed by what Rachel had said.

'In the back,' she said, heading for the bar. 'I'll buzz you straight through, it should be alright.'

'Cheers for that,' he smiled at her. 'Come on trouble,' he then added glancing to Rachel.

Making their way through the crowd at the bar, a few of the guys began checking out Rachel. But they soon found themselves looking the other way as Tony glared at them. Finding their way to the silver and pine door situated at the side of the bar, the Asian girl waited until they were finally there, then blew a kiss at Tony as the door gave off an electronic buzzing sound.

'Nice girl,' said Rachel teasingly as they both made their way through the door.

'You behave yourself,' he said, then stopped and stared at her. 'And let me do the talking in here kid.'

'No problem,' she smiled, as he knocked at another silver and pine door.

'Who is it?' the voice called out from behind the door.

'Tony.'

'Shit,' the voice laughed. 'Get the fuck in 'ere then.'

As they walked through the door, Rachel noticed the top of the man's head first. His mousy brown hair was sprouting off in all directions, although she imagined that was supposed to be the style of it. It was no doubt Paul Massey himself, bent over the black desk before him, with loud snorting sounds could be heard as the lines of coke found their way up his nose.

Glancing around the office, Rachel noticed there was only the large desk that Paul Massey was entertaining himself over. The leather chair in which he was perched and two other matching leather chairs this side of the desk. Along the right hand side of the wall was a bank of small close circuit television sets, showing various parts of the club, including the front door. Paul wasn't letting anybody in here that he didn't want to, Rachel thought to herself.

Their was one other man beside the desk. A small wiry looking black man, who appeared to be in his late forties to early fifties even. He was no where as big as the door men outside, but he appeared to be a lot sharper than they were. Rachel immediately knew at first glance that he was a dangerous man and could tell by the way her brother and him nodded at each other silently, that there was mutual respect between them both. His cat like eyes suddenly locked in on Rachel's and he smirked knowingly at her.

'Boss,' he said in hushed tones, which seemed pointless to Rachel as she knew exactly what the guy was doing.

Paul Massey lifted his head, wiping his nose as he did so, and winked at Tony offering him the rolled fifty pound note. His smile faltering slightly at the sight of Rachel. She smiled at him as he grinned back at her. He looked to be a lot younger than Tony.

In fact she had him nearer to her own age, which surprised her. There was a neat scar that ran across the bottom right hand side of his chin, but looked like a very old scar that had healed. His blue eyes looked as they should after what he'd just put up his nose, wired and bloodshot. Although he appeared to be in full control of himself as he suddenly laughed at Tony, throwing the note into the top draw.

'What the fuck is this,' he nodded towards Rachel, still smiling.

'It's alright Paul,' said Tony, pulling one of the leather chairs back and offering it to Rachel. 'She's cool brother. You remember my little sister don't you... Rachel?'

'Shit,' he smirked at her. 'Of course I remember you Rachel. How's it going?'

'Alright,' she smiled pleasantly, taking in what she could of the man before her.

Knowing that the possible way of having people to be open with you was to have them like you so that they wouldn't be all defensive with you. With that thought in mind she started to laugh and pointed to his nose, 'You missed a bit there.'

'Cheers,' he said chuckling along, wiping his nose again with the tip of his thumb. 'There we go, all is sweet.'

Glancing to remains of the white powder on the desk, Tony sat himself down and nodded at the desk, 'You missed some there as well Paul.'

He sniffed his response, and quickly wiped the desk, laughing as he did so, 'Shit Tony, there is plenty more where that came from.'

'You alright Brian?' asked Tony looking to the one behind the desk.

'Sweet Tony,' he nodded. 'How's your shit going?'

'Not too bad,' he smiled, and then looked to Paul Massey. 'The club's looking good Paul. I like what you've done with it. The girls seem to be a lot better than those old slappers that you opened up with.'

This got a laugh out of everybody.

'Sign of the times Tony,' Paul said lighting a B&H cigarette, offering the pack to Rachel who accepted. 'You know what as well. Most of the girls I've got on the payroll are students right

'ere in town itself. They are studying everything from law degrees to psychology degrees.'

'Seriously,' laughed Rachel.

'You better believe it,' he said, blowing the smoke out extravagantly waving his hand about as he did so. 'These babes are earning so much cash you wouldn't believe me if I told you. And they've all got themselves student loans and whatever else the banks are throwing at them these days. I tell you, these birds are minted.'

'They're not all students are they?' asked Tony.

'No, but they're my best workers. They love it mate and I make sure that they are treated double sweet,' Paul went on, 'I let them work whatever shifts they please. Some of them have lectures in the morning, work this gaff in the afternoon then go back for more lectures at night time.

'Beats working at McDonalds I suppose,' said Rachel, amused by the whole scenario.

'Ain't that the truth Rachel.'

'You never had to work at McDonalds in Nottingham,' said Tony defensively, as he'd supported her financially throughout her education.

'No,' she laughed. 'But something like this would have been great for some extra pocket money.'

'Fuck that for a game of soldiers Rachel,' Tony snapped, not seeing the funny side of it as the three of them began laughing at him.

'Still the protective big brother, eh Tony,' said Brian. 'You're forgetting that your Rachel is a big girl now.'

'Yeah, whatever,' said Tony as Paul laughed again at him.

Rachel could see that the other two were enjoying seeing Tony becoming more and more wound up. 'You want to make a little extra cash Rach, then you give me a call.' He tossed a business card over the desk as Tony grabbed it.

'Not fucking likely,' spat Tony.

'Oh I don't know,' she teased him. 'You think that I'd do alright Paul?'

Paul Massey leaned over the desk and took in Rachel's body admiringly, winking at Tony, 'I'd pay for a dance anyway.'

Tony jumped up and pushed him back into his seat as the three of them burst into fits of laughter.

'Calm the fuck down Tony,' said Paul through his laughter.

'We're only winding you up,' said Rachel as Tony sat back down and finally grinned at them.

'So anyway,' said Paul, winking appreciatively at Rachel for the little wind up. 'What can I do for you both. I know that you didn't come down here just to get yourself all worked up.'

'It's about your Caroline,' said Tony.

'Why,' he asked, immediately concerned, leaning himself forward. 'What's she gone and done Tony?'

'Nothing that we know of Paul,' he shook his head. 'It's not directly to do with her.'

'Do you know the Cartwright family?' asked Rachel.

'Sure I do,' he smiled. 'Not personally, or at least not that fruitcake of a mother and father that is.'

'You know Charlotte though?' asked Rachel.

'I know that she's missing, if that's what you're asking.'

'Your Caroline and her were close, right?' asked Tony.

'Yeah, they're close alright.' He laughed, 'Jesus, you can't, or at least I should say couldn't separate the two of them. Charlotte was kind of a God send, to tell you the truth.'

'Why is that?' asked Rachel, ignoring her brother's earlier request of letting him do the talking.

'Basically,' he looked directly at Rachel, 'when I got enough money together to move the hell out of Crumpsall. I was going to buy one of them big gaffs over in Whitefield with all them Jew fucks. But to be honest it was still too close to home. I wanted Caroline to have what we didn't growing up. And to be perfectly honest if we'd stayed in Crumpsall she'd have ended up the same as all the other little scally birds pushing prams to get their free house or flat from the council. But, well, to be honest, Caroline didn't want to leave the area or her mates. Which was understandable.'

'Did she meet up with Charlotte straight away?' asked Rachel.

'Pretty much so, yeah,' he nodded. 'Even enrolled with her at the same private school she attended over in Alderley Edge. That's what I mean by she was a God send. Caroline settled in pretty quickly thanks to her. It made things a hell of a lot easier on me and Jackie like.'

'How's she taking the disappearance of Charlotte?' asked Rachel.

'Not so good if truth be told,' he told them. 'She was like her only true mate over that way.'

'Has she any idea as to where she has gone?'

'She reckons that Charlotte kept going on about the fact that she'd found something out about her parents and ran away.'

'Did she say what it was that she found out?'

'She claims not to know,' he said shrugging. 'And to be honest I believe her. She really misses that kid you know.'

'What did you mean by fruitcake parents Paul?'

'Just that,' he smirked. 'Look, obviously they aren't going to have anything to do with the likes of me. Not with all their wealth and endless charity events they hold.' He suddenly started laughing, shaking his head, 'Although the cheeky bastards asked Charlotte to ask me if I'd like to make a donation to some do they were raising dough for... You know what they were raising the cash for Tony?'

'What?' asked Tony, grinning at his friend exuberance.

'Fucking coppers,' all three of them laughed as Rachel shook her head. 'Cheeky fucker's wanted my cash to give to the police force. And the best bit is, they weren't even going to invite to the do itself. They said that there was already a long enough list and that many people just made donations, even Charlotte told me to tell them to go fuck themselves.'

'And did you?' asked Tony.

'Too fuckin' right I did. Only not in such words,' he shook his head. 'To be honest I didn't and don't want anything to do with them. Don't get me wrong, the kid's a blinder. But the parents are full of shit as far as I'm concerned. Plus me and Brian 'ere lost a bundle on the pony's a couple of months back and guess what Tony?'

'What?' he asked, suspecting he knew what was coming.

'It was the fucking Cartwright's pony that we lost the dough on,' they roared with laughter again.

Once the laughter died down, he stared directly at Rachel, 'I'm sorry Rachel.'

'It's alright,' she told him smiling.

'Just why is it that the two of you are interested in that kid anyhow?'

Rachel took a deep breath and spent the next fifteen minutes explaining exactly what it was that Hunter had asked her to do. She also went as far as telling him about the phone call that Hunter received and what the caller told her.

'You think that it was my Caroline that put the call through to the police?' He looked mystified at the mere thought of his daughter ever phoning the police.

'You obviously don't Paul,' she said.

'It's just that she hates the police just as much as I do,' he said.

'But it is her best friend we're talking about,' Rachel added.

'Then you should talk with her.'

'Will that be alright?' asked Rachel.

'No problem at all,' he said scribbling down his home address on a piece of paper handing it to her. 'I'd rather that she talks with you than any coppers.'

'Thanks alot Paul,' Tony said, reaching over to shake his hand. 'This is a big help.'

'And I'll have Brian 'ere do some checking discreetly, into those missing kids. If you like that is?'

'We'd appreciate it Paul,' said Rachel as she also shook his hand. 'And thank you for this.'

'Glad I could help you,' he winked. 'And Rachel, if you have any second thoughts about coming 'ere to work, my door will always be open to you.'

'Thin ice son,' said Tony staring at him. 'You're treading on very thin ice.'

They all laughed, aside from Tony that is, as the two of them made their way back outside.

TEN

'Yes my boy's are here,' said Chan blissfully, as he opened his front door to the two men who had just pulled into his driveway in the silver Mercedes. 'Come here, come here,' he added, grabbing hold of Sleeper's hand as he exited the vehicle. He then pulled him close and began embracing him tightly.

'You alright old man?' he asked, holding Chan at arms length.

Sleeper took in the grounds of Chan's new home in Worsley. The house was an old Victorian looking house. The type where all the bricks appeared to be different, immediately giving the home character.

Sleeper then found himself smiling at the ornamental fountain place that he'd had to ease the car around. The small ceramic cherubs surrounded the entire display and water was flowing freely from the top of the fountain and back down into the small pool where sparrows had gathered to drink the water.

'What the hell is that thing?' laughed Sleeper. 'What happened to all that beautiful Oriental shit that you had at the other house Chan?'

'That thing came with the house,' he scoffed nodding at the display. 'Bloody Ling, she like, so Chan have to agree to keep it.'

'Still under the old lady's thumb, I see,' laughed Eazy coming around the car. 'How's someone so fucking small,' said Eazy, suddenly grabbing Chan's waist and lifting his small body into the air, 'get to be so fucking solid, you skinny shit.'

'I want to know how someone who makes some of the best food I've ever eaten stay so thin,' laughed Sleeper.

'Put me down you oaf,' said Chan whilst rubbing Eazy's huge bald black head.

As Eazy lowered Chan to the floor, he smiled at him. 'So, how's tricks then old man?'

'Same old shit you know,' he smirked. 'Please come, come inside. Bring your bags. Your rooms are ready for you both.'

'We appreciate this Chan,' said Sleeper, taking the two leather hold-all's from the boot of his car and tossing them both to Eazy. Moving his front seat back, he removed a small electronic screwdriver from his pocket and quickly and efficiently began to unscrew the false panel that resided beneath his seat area.

'What's he up to?' asked Chan.

'Tools,' said Eazy, shaking his head. 'Come on Chan. We'll wait inside.'

'I'm finished,' Sleeper called out, shutting the car door, pressing the electronic lock as the alarm bleeped itself into action. 'You got somewhere safe I can leave this Chan?' he asked, producing a long metallic-silver briefcase. Only this wasn't any normal sized briefcase. In fact it was at least three times the length of anything normal and at least twice as wide in width.

'No problem Sleeper,' said Chan nodding at the case. 'You know that Chan could have supplied you with the necessary tools you would have needed.'

'I know old man,' he said winking at the old man. 'But I felt that I needed my own personal shit for this one.'

'You better come inside and tell Chan all about it then,' he told him, shaking his head at the two of them. 'I didn't realise it was that kind of a visit.'

'That depends of what we find out first,' said Eazy, wrapping his mammoth arm around him. 'And that's where we're going to need your help old man.'

'Well let's eat first. Then we will sit down and talk business. You know that Chan will always help where he can,' he said. 'Now come, Ling has been in the kitchen all day and has prepared us dinner boys. Tonight you boys are in for very special treat. Just wait and see all the dishes she has prepared for you.'

'Now that I like the sound of old man,' Eazy declared happily.

'You would,' laughed Sleeper. 'He hasn't stopped moaning about his belly since we left London.'

Chan laughed along as he stared at Eazy's huge belly, 'I reckon you've got enough stored up in there, to see you through winter time into spring.'

'Always room for more though,' he announced. 'Now quit hanging around you two. I need to sample some of Chan's wife's culinary delights.'

The dinner was a magnificent feast of unbelievable amounts. Chan's wife, Ling Yung, had laid on a real banquet for them all. She had cooked both traditional Chinese and also Japanese dishes for them all to sample.

'To start with,' she said, 'I have prepared spicy butterfly king prawns that are coated in Szechuan peppercorns.'

'Fantastic,' announced Eazy before even laying eyes on the dish.

'Also a basket of steamed pork with water chestnuts,' she said placing the bamboo basket onto the table. 'This is served with a light soya sauce and chilli oil dip.'

'That smells delicious,' said Sleeper leaning over to smell the food.

'There is also this steaming bowl of soup for you here,' she producing yet another dish for the table.' This here is filled with chicken wonton soup and served with fresh prawns.'

'What about these?' asked Eazy pointing to the side plates that were already before them all and filled with a colourful array what appeared to be sushi.

'That Eazy,' said Chan, pulling his face, 'Is a selection of different sushi dishes from simple rolled sushi in yaki-nori filled seaweed to tofo-wrapped sushi.'

'Chan, no like,' his wife said. 'But this is very good. Both are filled with freshest salmon and tuna fish that you will have ever tasted.'

'And it is raw fish boys,' Chan told them. 'So if you not like...'

'Delicious,' announced Eazy tossing the sushi into his mouth as Sleeper laughed.

'It is,' he added, although not as certain as his friend was about it. But smiling all the same at Chan's wife who had gone to so much work.

They all sat chatting about the food they were eating, whilst Ling explained enthusiastically just how she'd prepared each dish for them. Before they knew it, the time was already ten o'clock as Ling began removing the dishes, with Eazy helping out.

As Chan's wife began to bring the main courses through into the dining room, Eazy offered to help once again to her protests. 'I swear Mrs. Yung,' Eazy sighed with utter delight as the dishes

were rolled in on a service trolley. 'If Chan here, hadn't already taken your hand I'd be on my knees right now.'

'For the main courses I have prepared you all two different selections of duck,' she said proudly.

'Now that's more like it,' smiled Chan as she placed the silver platters onto the table, 'This one here, is mandarin sesame duck. And the other is my very own special sweet and sour sauce, it like none other that you will have tasted before and is served with fresh mangoes.'

'Just wait till you try this sauce boys,' Chan smiled reaching over and helping himself to the food with his chop-sticks.

'Also we have a silver platter of baked crabs that are sitting of a bed of springs onion and ginger.' This was placed down the centre of the table and Sleeper shook his head at the amount of food.

'This one is my speciality,' she beamed as she placed the huge pot on the table. 'This, I think you will like very much Eazy. It is braised birthday noodles with hoisin lamb that is so tender that it will melt in your mouth.'

'We're not all as big as Eazy Mrs. Yung,' said Sleeper, becoming worried with the amount of food being placed before him.

'It is Ling, no Mrs. Yung,' she shook her head at him. 'And finally we have these to try.' She placed small side plates before them, 'Now you must try these, they are Japanese yakitori chicken kebabs.'

Sleeper and Eazy looked at each other in wonderment, 'Jesus, I thought we'd already eaten with all of the starters,' said Sleeper.

'Don't be so silly,' she said. 'Now you have to try everything that I prepared for you.'

'That will not be a problem,' Eazy told her taking a mouthful of the yakitori kebab and smiling at them all.

'How the hell do you stay as skinny as you are Chan?' asked Sleeper trying the chicken kebab.

'Just lucky I guess,' he laughed.

'Oh my God, Ling,' Eazy's eyes rolled in his head. 'This is absolutely fantastic.'

'True,' added Sleeper. 'This is delicious. You've done yourself proud, thank you.'

'My pleasure boys,' she told them both. 'Are rooms okay for you both?'

'Absolutely,' he replied. 'We really appreciate this. A hotel would have been fine. I just hope we're not putting you out Ling.'

'I wouldn't have heard of it,' Chan told him, scooping the duck onto his chopsticks.

'We very pleased to have you,' added Ling.

'Oh sweet Jesus,' said Eazy. His huge frame falling to the floor. Crawling onto his knees before Ling, he took her hand. 'I don't care if you're married to Chan or not, I think I've died and gone to heaven. You've just got to marry me girl.'

All four of them burst out laughing. The rest of the meal was thoroughly enjoyed by all, and even Eazy had to knock back the offer of dessert, well, until a little later as he had put it.

'So tell Chan how I can help you boys?' he asked.

The three of them remained seated at the dining room table whilst much to her protesting to them helping clear up in the kitchen; Ling had left them to it.

Sleeper went into details of what had been happening down in London. He also told Chan everything with what had happened with Colin Spencer at the house in Guildford that night.

'The world's already a better place without him,' said Chan lighting a Dunhill cigarette, exhaling the smoke. 'Things are taken care of with the body, no?'

'All sorted Chan,' said Sleeper.

'Of course it is.' He looked slyly at Sleeper, whom he knew was an expert in this field.

'Do you know about any pornographic material, using children that is being pushed up here Chan?' asked Sleeper.

'Nothing at all,' he pulled his face. 'I don't think that I want to know either.'

'Who's got their finger on the porn being controlled up here?' asked Sleeper.

'The O'Leary's are probably your safest bet,' he said. 'But old man O'Leary, that Dominic. He was one of the guys who had the convictions from Anderson overturned after... Well you know after what... Well anyway, not that I know him that well personally, but, I very much doubt he's into child pornography.'

'What sort of stuff is he into?' asked Eazy.

'Don't get wrong boys,' said Chan. 'It's the full hard-core shit that he deals in, but I just don't have him down as being into kids. Plus I think that he's been making a fortune from the internet. From what I hear he's got his fingers into a lot of websites that run the porn straight into you home.'

'Is he worth speaking to?' asked Sleeper.

'You wouldn't even get a meeting with him,' Chan laughed. 'Although saying that, there is one person that may be able to help.'

'Who's that old man?' asked Eazy.

'A friend of mine,' he said.

His face suddenly clouded over as he was deep in thought, the two of them left looking at one another.

'You alright Chan?' asked Sleeper.

'Tell me more about why you are both here?' he said, breaking his concentration.

'The reason we're here Chan, is the last part of this guy's story. He told us that night, that the one responsible was some how connected to Manchester. You see, he claimed that he wasn't responsible for whatever happened to the kids afterwards.'

'And the bodies still haven't been discovered?' Chan stared at them both,

'No Chan,' said Eazy shaking his head.

'You think that bodies are here in Manchester?'

'We're not exactly sure old man,' said Eazy.

'So what did this sick fuck say then, that's brought you both up here then?'

'He said that the one responsible, this will sound a little weird I know,' he sighed. 'But he said that the kids followed him and his magic flute all the way back to Manchester.'

'You what!' Chan looked bemused.

'This is where it gets really strange then,' said Eazy.

'Spencer said that they all loved him,' said Sleeper, 'and that they followed him. He said that his name was the Pied Piper. He said they followed the Pied Piper and his magic flute all the way back here to Manchester.'

'What fuck does that mean?'

'That's what we're here to find out,' Eazy nodded.

'You know what you just say, well it can't be mere coincidence,' he said staring at them both.

'What's that old man?' asked Sleeper.

'Only this morning in restaurant, the same good friend who may be able to help with O'Leary,' he looked at them and shook his head. 'That's when it hit me before. When I mention him, it make Chan remember. But anyway, he came in at dinner time today and he ask me about other kids that have been going missing from right here in Manchester and also other areas close by.'

'You mean that kids are going missing up here as well Chan?' Sleeper looked to Eazy who was shaking his head.

'For over a year now,' he admitted. 'It's a little weird that they haven't connected the two together. You not think?'

'Maybe they have and we don't know about it,' suggested Eazy.

'This just gets more and more fucked up as we go,' Sleeper sighed deeply. 'Who's this friend of yours Chan?' asked Eazy.

'I get to that in a minute Sleeper,' he said sighing deeply. 'Chan no believe in coincidences and this is no coincidence that both you two and my friend seek out Chan for help. He never tell me that the police suspect that the kids are being used in paedophile ring though. But to be honest he just asked me enquire around for him. I also know that the same request was made of Paul Massey who owns a strip club not far from restaurant. Word travels fast here in Manchester. Especially when one wants it to and especially when it's at the request of Tony Henessy.'

'Who's that Chan?' asked Eazy.

'Tony Henessy,' he told him. 'He used to do some business with our old friend Prey. Quite some years back now.'

'I've heard of him you know,' announced Sleeper nodding as he did. 'As soon as you said the name. I knew it sounded familiar. He's a player, right?'

'He was,' Chan smirked at them both. 'But he's gone straight, just like us boys.' They all laughed at this.

'Why's he so interested in the missing kids Chan?' asked Sleeper.

'I'm not exactly sure Sleeper. But there is a very possible good reason though.' Chan sighed deeply and stared at the two of them, with trepidation in his eyes.

'What that then old man?' asked Eazy.

'His sister is a criminal or forensic, I can never remember which one, but a psychologist none the less.' He pulled deeply on his cigarette. 'You both must remember that Dark Angel case, that was in the news around this time last year.'

'That's her?' asked Sleeper shocked as Chan nodded and Eazy shook his head slowly. 'Rachel Murphy, that's her right. That was well fucked up. I remember following the story on Sky news. And the papers were full of it. The killer cut their hearts out, right?'

'Poor, poor child,' said Chan nodding. He had a look of anguish in his eyes. 'It's one thing to have your husband taken from you. But sweet Jesus, to have your only child killed in the same way.'

'They never caught that guy, did they?' asked Eazy.

'You're right, they never came close to catching him,' said Chan. 'The sick fuck is still out there.'

'So why is the sister working the missing child case?' asked Eazy.

'I'm not too sure to be honest,' he said. 'All I know is that they want me to access some lap top's hard-drive for them.'

'You can sort that kind of thing out, eh Chan?' asked Sleeper.

'Jonah or Kezlo should be able to,' he said. 'Why?'

'I've got Spencer's lap top with me and some of the files were locked. I need them accessing.'

'It'll be good to hook up with Kezlo and Jonah anyway,' smiled Eazy. 'I only spoke with Kezlo about some records he needed for his shop last week. So we can sort it out at the same time.'

'Good,' said Chan. 'You can ask them to sort out the hard-drive for me as well.'

'What about hooking us up with Henessy?' asked Sleeper. 'I'd be interested to find out why's he so interested in the missing kids.'

'Shouldn't be a problem,' said Chan. 'He's a good lad. I've known him a little longer than Prey. And I have to say that he's one of the most impartial guys that I know of. You'll find he has a lot of backing in town. To be honest, not a lot happens up here without him knowing about it.'

'Sounds like our kinda guy,' said Sleeper.

'I'll set it up,' he replied. 'Now what else?'

'How about that dessert that your missus was on about, eh Chan,' said Eazy as the other two cracked up. 'What's wrong with that!'

ELEVEN

'**D**id you make that phone call Caroline?' asked Rachel, who was sat beside the girl on her bed.

Tony was sat downstairs in the kitchen with Paul's wife Jackie, with whom he'd known since she was only a kid. Rachel and Caroline had been talking for over an hour now, with Rachel letting the girl tell stories about Charlotte, whilst she casually asked question after question about the girl on a more personal level.

Rachel liked the girl before her, and she had kept things friendly with her to try and win her confidence before approaching more awkward questions. As she glanced around the girls bedroom once again. She noticed that it was very similar to Charlotte's, the same posters adorning the walls, and with the same overall feel to it.

'I won't tell your father Caroline. If that's what you're worried about,' added Rachel, looking at the girl who she found to be extremely attractive. Although the years spent living on estates left her with a rough edge, pretty much the same rough edge that Rachel had always retained. Leaving her with a semblance of oneself, that told people that she wouldn't take shit from anybody. Her dyed, blonde hair was cut into the style of the character Rachel from the series *Friends*, and she wore a Reebok track suit, with matching Reebok classic trainers. Even though her attire was casual, and the girl was so young, Rachel could tell that she already possessed a woman's body beneath it.

'I rang some copper, I don't know whether or not it was that Hunter one that you was going on about,' she finally admitted, staring directly at her. 'But I don't know anything about a

connection to missing kids. I was just worried about Charlotte and I knew that her mam or dad wouldn't have phoned the police, because they really don't give a fuck about Charlotte. Not like I do anyway.'

'Why did you phone the police Caroline?'

'Because Charlotte had been acting weird lately.'

'Weird how?'

'Well, I know that this may sound stupid,' she said sighing. 'But Charlotte was always a little jealous of my old man. It's like she looked up to him because of his background. I suppose it's a little my fault as I blow things up a bit as to what my old man does.'

'What's that got to do with her acting weird?'

'Well she kept making out that her old man was up to no good,' she laughed. 'As if you could ever imagine her old man getting up to no good. Anyway, I just figured that she wanted her dad to be more like mine. And that's just never going to happen, is it? Well anyway, I just thought that she was full of shit to be honest. But well, with her now going missing, maybe she wasn't.' She looked a little sad as Rachel gave her arm a motherly rub to let her know it was all right.

'Do you think that her dad has anything to do with her disappearance?'

'I don't know to be honest,' she sighed. 'If truth be known that is. I mean I know he doesn't like me and all. But I know that's just because me and Charlotte were from different backgrounds. But just before she went missing, she was real secretive about things. But wouldn't tell me exactly what it was all about. She was real funny with both of her parents as well. The last time that we were all together at the house, she told them in front of me, that she knew all about them and that the truth would come out sooner or later.'

'What was that about?'

'She wouldn't tell me,' she sighed. 'She just said that the truth would come out and that they would be finished in the high society circles that they ran with.'

'How did her parents react?'

'They both just laughed at her and told her to grow up.'

Rachel thought about this for a moment. The Cartwright's had obviously kept a lot of information about themselves to themselves. But what if they have had something to do with Charlotte's disappearance. She needed to find out more about the girl. And quite obviously it wasn't going to be with the parent's help.

'You two got along though, right?' she asked, 'I mean that you were both really close. I saw that picture in her room too. They look like happy times. Where was it taken?' Rachel reached over and picked up the framed photograph that was identical to the one she'd already seen.

'That was her sixteenth birthday party at this club in Manchester. It was a good night out.' She sighed deeply, 'You know, we was proper close Rachel, like sisters we were. She always said that me and her were sisters. Even used to tell people when we were out that we was sisters like,' she dropped her eyes again. 'But that's the other weird thing you know.'

'What's that Caroline?'

'I don't know exactly, because she would never talk about it. But, well I found these old photographs one day. When I was going through her draw. And well it was her as a little girl, and I swear to God that the other little girl in photo could have been her twin sister.'

Rachel thought that she hadn't found any such photographs as she had gone through the draws.

'What did Charlotte say?'

'Just that it was a cousin of hers from years ago,' she shrugged. 'But she was kind of weird about it. It's hard to explain, but there was something weird about it, if you know what I mean like.'

'What else can you tell me about her,' said Rachel smiling at her. 'I mean have either of you got boyfriends?'

'Not really,' she shrugged. 'I mean we go out and kop off with lads all the time. But nothing serious.'

'Was she a virgin?'

'Not likely,' laughed Caroline. 'I'd say that she had her cherry popped a long time ago you know.'

'What do you mean by that?'

'Well she was always right up for sex with the lads she met,' she looked away. 'But afterwards it was as if she felt repulsed by what she had done.'

'Why?'

'She never wanted them to be near her afterwards,' she said. 'I mean, a couple of times at parties we've had to leave because she'd turned funny with the lads. Like she really liked the idea of sex but not the actual performance.'

'Did you ever ask her about it?'

'She said that she was using them just like they used us,' she laughed.

'Fair enough,' smiled Rachel, trying to gain more of her confidence. 'What about you?'

'I enjoy sex,' she said matter of factly. 'I'm just not interested in settling down or nothing. I mean I'm only sixteen.'

Rachel knew how things were these days, but to hear the young girl before her, talk so casually about sex made feel a little old for the first time.

'So you'd say that she slept with a lot of lads?'

'Oh yeah,' she smiled. 'Now like I said, I like sex. But Charlotte was in the heavy weight class of getting fucked.'

'Do you not think that it is possible that she has run off with some lad?'

'Nah,' she said, 'that's not her style.'

'What do you think has happened then?'

'I honestly don't know whether it has something to do with her parents or not,' she sighed. 'All that I know is that I just want her back here. I miss her.'

'I know you do,' smiled Rachel, placing her arm around the girl, cuddling her. 'What about her acting weird like you said. Do you think that she was possibly depressed about anything.'

'You'd have to talk to her shrink about that,' she said as Rachel looked at her. 'Marty Williamson over in Wilmslow, I think that's what his name is.'

'She was seeing a shrink?' Rachel was flabbergasted that her parents hadn't told her this.

'Oh yeah.' Caroline stared at her. 'Don't tell me you didn't know that?'

Rachel shook her, both at the fact the Charlotte had been seeing a psychiatrist and also at the fact that she knew Marty Williamson, or more to the point Wank Willie as people within his profession knew him.

How he was still practising was beyond Rachel. He'd messed with more patients' heads than she could think of. Even having patients referred over to her after he'd left them in a worse state than when they'd arrived. He also had several female patients press sexual harassment charges against him, only none of the charges ever stuck. Rachel couldn't believe that the Cartwright's had been sending their daughter to see this joke of a doctor.

'Did Charlotte say why she had to go and see him?'

'Just something about her being disruptive in her early years. When they'd first moved to Prestbury,' she sighed. 'She said that her parents had been advised that she saw shrink because of all the trouble she was getting into, and that this guy was

recommended to them. I suppose her parents thought that a shrink would help her.'

'And did it?' she asked, wondering just who in their right minds would recommend Williamson, unless they were after somebody incompetent in the first place.

'I don't know about that,' she said. 'But Charlotte said that it kept them off her back. They also threatened her with stopping her allowance if she didn't go and see him at least once a week. So I suppose that was the main reason she went there.'

'She ever say anything about Williamson himself?'

'Just that he was a right creep.'

'Did he ever hassle her in any way?'

'Nah,' she shook her head. 'She told me that it was a bag of piss to go and see this guy. She said that it was a lot easier seeing him rather than a proper shrink as she put it. Because at least this one was clueless enough not to prey too deeply into her background.'

'Why would she be bothered about someone preying into her background?'

'Don't know to be honest. All's I know, is that he will probably be your best bet on seeing whether or not she was depressed about anything.'

'I think you could be right,' she said, rising for the bed.

Handing her card to Caroline she said, 'Thanks for today. You've been a big help and if you think of anything else, my mobile number is on the card. Anytime of the day or night.'

She looked a little sad as Rachel got ready to leave, 'Find her Rachel, please find my mate for me.'

TWELVE

'**I**s Marty in please?' asked Rachel, in a friendly tone of voice.

Both she and Tony were stood before the receptionist in Doctor Williamson's office situated in Wilmslow's town centre. The reception area was situated above a wine-bar of all places. It was next to where the old Rex cinema had once stood.

That's not to say that the office was at all bad. In fact it was a lot nicer than Rachel's had been, over at the clinic she used to have in the city centre. The walls were nicely covered was abstract painting, that were no doubt a talking point of Williamson's she thought whilst still stood there smiling at the red headed receptionist.

The red head, looked to be no older than eighteen years old, with an absolutely huge pair of breasts that seemed to be struggling to stay within her top. Trust Williamson, thought Rachel, as she smiled once again at the bubble head before her, wondering whether the simple question of whether or not her boss was in indeed a little to precarious for her to answer.

'Is he in or not love?' asked Tony abruptly, obviously irritated by the girl.

'Yes,' she answered in an awfully slow voice, which made her come across as either extremely stoned or incredibly stupid. Rachel wasn't quite sure which one.

'Now was that yes to him being here?'

'Hello there,' she smiled at them as if they'd just arrived. 'What can I do for you?'

Rachel turned and cocked an eyebrow at Tony.

'Listen, space cadet,' said Tony, as the girl began giggling. 'Jesus, look love we've not got all day. We're here to see the doc, so why don't you just buzz through to him.'

'And your name is?' she asked, clicking away at the mouse.

Rachel peered around at the computer screen. Convinced that the girl wasn't capable of using the computer and that she was in fact playing solitaire instead. She couldn't possibly have appointments on the screen, Rachel thought to herself.

'Just tell him that Rachel Murphy is here to see him will you,' she said, shaking her head in bewilderment as there actually were appointments on the screen.

'Murphy,' she said squinting at the screen. 'No, no there's no Murphy booked in here. Would you like to make an appointment?'

'Fuck this,' said Tony walking around the receptionist's desk to the glass doors.

'Hey, you can't do that,' the girl suddenly protested.

'Watch me love,' said Tony as Rachel followed suit.

The girl was out of her chair extremely quickly, considering that she appeared to be so slow at everything else. Grabbing for Tony's arm, the door before the three of them, suddenly flew open. Marty Williamson stood there glaring at them, the smell of cannabis drifting from the office. Rachel could also see a young woman stretched out on his leather sofa, happily chuffing away without a care in the world on a huge looking spliff pressed between her lips.

'What the fuck,' exclaimed Williamson.

He was only a small man, not even matching Rachel in height at her five foot ten inches. His round glasses and long brown curls, gave him the appearance of John Lennon without all of the charisma. Suddenly noticing Rachel stood there as well, he looked even more confused than he already was.

'Rachel?' he asked, almost as if to confirm it to himself

'We need to talk,' she said.

'They just barged in here Marty,' grumbled the receptionist.

'You're really starting to get on my tits love,' sneered Tony. 'Why don't you go and powder your nose or smoke some more of that shit, you air head.'

The girl looked absolutely shocked to have been spoken to like that.

'I'm with a client Rachel,' protested Williamson.

'If I call this in Marty,' she peered the woman on the sofa, who appeared oblivious to the entire matter. 'You'll have no more clients to be with.'

'Marty,' said Sonya. Looking as if she didn't know whether or not, she was coming or going.

'Sonya,' he snapped, then sighed at the girl. 'Go and take your lunch break, will you.'

'But, but, but it's only ten o'clock in the morning Marty,' she blubbered.

'Just go now,' he snapped at her, making her jump. 'Just come back in an hour Sonya.'

'Whatever,' she mumbled gathering her coat and bag.

'You'd be doing yourself a favour love. By not coming back at all,' said Rachel as the girl pushed by her.

'What would you know,' she snapped back at her.

'I know that if Marty here, hasn't already tried to get into your pants,' she smirked as he grimaced. 'Then it won't be long before he tries to love.'

She stared from Williamson to Rachel back and forth, then sticking her mammoth chest out at him said, 'You'd never have got your hands on these, you dirty old pervert. My mum said that was the only reason you took me on in the first place.' And with that, she turned on her heels and waltzed out the door shaking her backside as she did.

'Cheers for that Rachel,' he sighed.

'I kinda like her now,' smiled Tony. 'She's got character.'

'Who the hell are you?' demanded Williamson.

'This is my brother,' said Rachel. 'Now why don't you cut loose your patient in there and then we can talk more privately.'

'What the hell is this all about?'

'You want me to get rid of her, for you?' asked Tony.

'No, no,' he shook his head and turned back into the office. 'Come on Miss Johnson, your time is up. It's time to leave.'

'Already,' said the woman as she swayed back and forth sitting up. Her eyes were wasted.

'Already Miss Johnson,' he said, helping her to the door. She didn't even seem to notice either, Rachel or Tony stood there.

'Same time next week?' she slurred.

'Same time next week,' he repeated, easing her out the door.

'We did good today, didn't we?' she smiled, completely stoned out of her mind. 'No more demon's right.'

'No more demon's, right Miss Johnson,' he sighed deeply then added. 'Except for these here that is.'

The lady stumbled past the two of them as if they weren't even there. Her eyes glazed over, and rolling around.

'What the hell kind of therapy do you call getting your patients stoned at this time of the morning Martin?' scoffed Rachel as they followed him into the office.

'She was a special case,' he smiled, running his hands through his long hair, then pushing his glasses further up his nose.

'And Sonya?'

'Well she was definitely a special case,' he smirked at the two of them. 'And thanks to you. I've just lost my only bleedin' receptionist.'

'Damn shame that Marty,' said Tony winking.

'Now could you please tell me just what the fuck it is, that you two want?' he sniffed his arrogance at them. 'Then you can both very kindly, get yourselves the fuck out of my office.'

Tony began glaring at him. The same stare that Rachel had seen grown men wet themselves at as Williamson pulled his look away and back to her. Tony walked to the sofa behind Rachel. Sitting down and stretching himself out, he placed his hands behind his head and said. 'Nice sofa.'

'Glad you like it,' he sighed. 'Why don't you just go and make yourselves right at home.'

'Thanks,' replied Tony, lighting an Embassy cigarette, tossing the pack to Rachel.

As Williamson stared in disbelief at the two of them. She sneered at him, just before lighting the cigarette. 'Well it's obviously not a no smoking office, is it now?'

'Whatever,' he sighed in defeat, placing his hands behind his head.

'Charlotte Cartwright,' said Rachel.

'Now you know that I can't talk about any of my patients Rachel.'

'You almost sound as if you've got morals, Wank Willie,' she laughed at him.

'Believe it or not,' he said, totally ignoring the coment, 'I have when it comes to clients.'

'Yeah right,' scoffed Rachel. 'You forget where most of your old patients were referred to, after you finished fucking with their heads.'

'Client – doctor confidentiality,' he said. 'You should know that Rachel.'

'Let's put it this way doc.' She leaned a little closer, pulling deeply on the cigarette allowing the smoke to drift above her head. 'I'd be willing to break the confidentiality law with some

interesting sessions of my own. They are tapes of some of your old clients discussing your methods.'

'So,' he shrugged.

'I imagine that the medical board would be rather interested in some of the juicier tapes on the way you tried to seduce certain patients.' She was actually blagging here, and hoping to hell that he was buying all of this.

He clicked his tongue annoyingly as he pondered over what she'd said.

'Come on Rach,' said Tony. 'We're wasting our time here, fannying about with this dick. Let's just go get them tapes so that you can drop them off. His patients would be better off without him anyway.'

Just as Rachel was climbing from her seat, he looked panicked then said. 'What is it you want to know?'

They both sat back down. 'You know that she is missing right?'

'Only because I phoned her parents last week to find out why she hadn't turned up for her session.'

'I've been asked to look into it,' she told him. 'So I want you to tell me all you can about Charlotte.'

'Like what?'

'Why was she seeing you in the first instance?'

'Are you kidding me,' he laughed. 'Her head was so fucked; even I couldn't have fucked it up anymore than it was.'

'What was up with her?'

'She's been seeing me for almost six years now.'

'You what,' exclaimed Rachel. She hadn't realised that it had quite as long as that. 'You're telling me that they sent her to see you when she was only ten years old.'

'A friend of the families recommended me,' he stated proudly.

'Why?' asked Rachel, still curious as to why anybody would recommend the man before her to somebody else. 'Why you of all people?'

'Because they were told that Charlotte would need to see a psychiatrist when she moved up this way. They didn't know anybody, so like I said, I was recommended to them. It's been a nice little retainer to keep each week over the years,' he smiled at the two of them. 'Anyway... Charlotte's always been a troublesome child. The family had moved her from down in London after the death of her sister.'

'Sister,' she said outloud staring at him. She realised that Caroline had been correct about the photograph she'd discovered. 'And what happened to the sister?'

'Died a few years back. Whilst the family still lived in London, like I said.'

'Were they both close?'

'They were identical twins,' he said. 'Can't get much closer than that I suppose. Only from what I know of Bethany. That was her name was by the way. Anyway, when I say that they were identical twins they were. But they were only identical on the outside to look at. Bethany had always been a sick little child and had not stopped having problems with her health from the day shed been born. Where as Charlotte probably never had a day sick in her life.'

'What was wrong with her?'

'Her heart mainly,' he told her. 'Surly the Cartwright's told you all this?'

She shook her head at him.

'Oh well,' he sighed. 'Basically, the girl died when she was nine years old from a weak heart. There was a hell of a lot of other things wrong with her, medically that is.'

'Why did they move away from London?'

'To make a fresh start I expect,' he told her. 'I imagine that he keeps himself occupied with the horses. And I imagine that she does the same with all of those charity events that she seems to always be in the paper for.'

'How did Charlotte take the death of her sister?'

'She refused to talk about it at first and I never pushed.'

'What did you talk about then?'

'She'd talk about all kinds of bullshit that was going on inside of her head,' he said. 'Everything that is but Bethany. And I was getting paid anyway, because they kept sending her to me. She seemed happy enough to lay there and just spiel bollocks for an hour.'

'Why did you say that she was fucked up then?'

'Because she was a pathological liar,' he smiled. 'That's why. She was unreal. Some of the stories she came out with were so unreal, I couldn't make them up, if I tried to.'

'Stories like what?'

'She used to try and shock me with her sexual escapes.'

'From what age?'

'From when she first began coming here.'

'At ten years old?' asked Rachel shocked.

'I very much doubt that they were true,' he replied. 'Well maybe not back then. I imagine that she definitely ain't no virgin anymore. But I seriously doubt that she was anywhere as experienced as the stories she entertained me with.'

'Stories like what?'

'Sleeping with many more than one lad in a night,' he smiled. 'That progressed to things she claimed she done with her and this friend of hers, Caroline, I think it was. Telling me how they both fucked lads whilst they slept with one another. They were entertaining enough stories. But that's all they were. I think she just liked to babble on sometimes.'

'Did she say that she enjoyed the sex?'

'Oh yeah,' he said. 'In fact that's all she used to go on about. How much she loved it.'

'Didn't you try talking to her about why she told you these stories?'

'Not at all,' he laughed. 'I rather enjoyed them. So I just let her get on with it.'

Rachel shook her head in disbelief at him. 'And they sent their kid to you week after week for six years.'

'Bread and butter,' he said.

'You're a disgrace Williamson.'

'Maybe so,' he said. 'I'll tell you one thing though.'

'What?'

'She got to be a right pain in the arse this last year.'

'Why's that then?'

'Like I told you. She refused to talk about her sister at first. Well that was until about a year ago,' he said. 'Then she finally began telling me about Bethany.'

'What did she tell you?'

'Well, not so much about Bethany as a child or anything like that,' he said twiddling his pen about absentmindedly. 'But she somehow came up with this outrageous tale about how in fact her sister hadn't died from a heart attack. She claims the father was sexually abusing her sister. Saying that's why she had the weak heart in the first place.'

'You what?'

'I know,' he sighed. 'Just more of her lies, I tell you Rachel.'

'What exactly did she tell you?'

'That he'd been abusing her since birth,' he stopped twiddling the pen and stared at her. 'I think that she was even jealous from the way she was going on with herself. Saying that daddy always paid more attention to Bethany than to her. The sexual abuse claims were complete nonsense that this girl fabricated within her own mind. I enjoyed her sexual escapades stories better.'

'What makes you so sure that Luther Cartwright wasn't abusing the child?'

'Have you met him?'

'Of course,' she replied.

'Then you must know that it is a crock of shit,' he laughed. 'I drink with him at the golf club sometimes. And believe me he's gets enough women interested in him, not to go putting where he shouldn't with minors.'

'Did Charlotte ever mention the missing kids that have been disappearing lately?'

'Once, but it was more like some kind of reference to that one that went missing from here in Wilmslow.' He thought about it for a moment. 'It was just something to do with the little girl reminding her of Bethany.'

'Have you any idea where the girl may be?'

'My guess is she ran away again,' he told them. 'This isn't the first time, as you no doubt know. And I'll be right here waiting for her to return back home again with some more glorious tales that her head will be no doubt filled with. All to keep me entertained.'

'She used to tell you about when she ran away?' asked Rachel interested. 'Where did she run off to last time?'

'Oh it's all kinds of magical places that she runs off to Rachel,' he laughed at them both. 'Crazy things she used to tell me. Like the time she'd been whisked off to Paris for the weekend. Or maybe even London, "for the shows of course darling,"' he said mockingly. 'Or even the time she went off on a short cruise. And, it was always with this same dark stranger. This character that she's invented in her mind, who takes her to these wonderful places.' He roared with laughter. 'She never would tell me his name though. She told me, he had warned her not tell his name to anyone, because he was older than her. He said that people would talk. She even told me, that he was the one she was going to marry.' He began sniggering at what he was telling them both.

'Are you sure that she didn't say his name?' asked Rachel.

'Never,' he shook his head at her. 'Oh, oh yeah. There was the last time he took her away' It was to this fancy dress ball, where he was the prince charming of the ball, of course. She said that he was dressed magically, wearing a velvet green and red, long feathered hat. Also had on the matching green and red velvet costume to go with his hat. She had loved being there she told me. She said that he'd dressed her in this ball gown and she'd been his princess. And because she was dressed up. No one knew just how young she was. Such a wild fantasy life this kid lived.'

'How long ago again was it,' asked Rachel. 'When she went missing last time?'

'She was thirteen,' he said. 'I remember it so well, because it had been her birthday when she'd gone missing.'

'Did she describe the stranger to you?'

'Not really,' he said. 'Oh, but I bet that he was always some handsome devil,' he was grinning stupidly at them now.

'But where actually was she, you know,' said Rachel. 'You know afterwards. When she returned home. Where had she actually been?'

'They never knew,' he said. 'But she always came home and was always clean and tidy. So the last place she'd been was on the streets. Which is why they're probably not so worried this time around. Especially seeing as she is now sixteen years old.'

'Surely they must have had some idea,' said Rachel.

'Well, they never told me,' he said, 'if they did know, that is.'

'Do you know why she may have run away this time?'

'The last session I had with her,' he said. 'She was a little upset about the fact that her parents didn't want her hanging around with that Caroline girl. But that is about it. I wouldn't have thought that it was enough to drive her away.'

'Do you think that she could be in danger in any way?'

'Not Charlotte,' he laughed. 'She'll just be out gathering more tales to tell the good doctor when decides that she's had enough.'

Rachel shook her head at him. 'You really are pathetic Williamson.'

He shrugged nonchalantly at her. Then glancing to his watch impatiently, then back at the two of them. 'If there is nothing else,' he said.

Rachel glanced to Tony and nodded. 'No, there is nothing else for the moment,' she told him as they were walking to the door.

'Well it was so nice to see you again Rachel,' he said sarcastically as Tony scowled at him. 'Maybe next time you'd like to make an appointment.'

'You'll have to find yourself a new receptionist Williamson,' she winked at him, 'before I'll be able to do that.'

THIRTEEN

'**W**hat have we got then Mark?' asked Hunter, climbing under the police tape that was supposed to keep people away from disordering the crime scenes.

It had been a typical Saturday night in Manchester's city centre. The ebony sky with the stormy clouds threatened them with the usual torrential rain. As the light drizzle spiralled downwards, its weightless drops twisting in the wind. Deceiving everybody of its potential, as it drenched you totally unaware. Hunter had planned on spending Saturday night in the company of one of her many male associates as she liked to refer to them.

In fact she'd arranged to meet a young paediatrician, with whom she'd recently become acquainted, for a late dinner date, their first date to be precise. He wasn't to finish his shift until ten o'clock. And she'd been sat waiting for him to arrive the Luigi's Italian Restaurant. Her mobile phone had rung at precisely the same time the doctor had walked through the door of the restaurant.

The call had been from her partner Mark Andrews. He explained briefly that there had been murder in Whitefield. He gave her the address telling her that both Tom Mackenzie and the station, for some reason hadn't been able to contact her. Making her apologies to the doctor, she had run from the restaurant.

'I've only just got here,' Andrews told her. 'The victim is Otis Fairchild and his wife... and son too.'

'You're joking,' she exclaimed at the news. 'Otis... the barrister Otis Fairchild.'

'The very same one,' he told her shaking his head.

'Jesus,' she sighed. 'I know that we didn't exactly see eye to eye, but, Jesus Christ. What happened?'

132

'From the information that I've received so far, well... From the sound of what they've witnessed up there. It looks like it could be our same guy from last year. It sounds as if the Dark Angel has returned Hunter.'

'Why's he waited so long to strike again?' she asked, more to herself than her partner. 'Have you got the entire area sealed off Mark?'

'It's already been taken care of,' he told her. 'Forensics and the pathologist have all been notified. There on the way down here now.'

'Good,' she replied, staring off into the crowd.

The front lawn where the two of them stood was covered with the thin film of water. The grass appeared to be almost white beneath its sheen. The large four bedroom, detached house stood silently, awaiting them to enter its nightmare. Hunter began to take in her surroundings as the drizzle began to soak its way through their clothing.

The house was surrounded by fern to act as a fence around the perimeter. And although the home was placed central of a busy residential street, with around eleven or twelve houses that were the same. It seemed their luck that the house the killer had chosen was concealed significantly more than the rest. Glancing to the house, Hunter couldn't help but notice that all of the lights had been left on. Deceiving the overall appearance of immorality remaining undiminished.

All this would have been true, but for the fact that there were uniformed police everywhere. But she didn't recognise any of them, as they were from the Salford area. Lights appeared to be flashing all over the place, and their was people stood around the police tape where Hunter had entered. Some were still in their dressing gowns. All of them curious to know happened within the depths of the house.

'So has every Tom, Dick, Harry and his dog trampled all over my bleedin' crime scene, or what Mark?'

'So far,' he sighed. 'Just the officer by the front door. He was first to arrive on the scene. Also, two CID who arrived shortly afterwards. They were the ones who called us in. They recognised the MO straight off and put the call straight through to Tom Mackenzie. To be quite honest Hunter, who in their right mind would want to take this case on?'

'I know what you're saying,' she sighed. 'But this time round we've got to put a stop to him or there is going to be total outrage from the public. This killer has waited patiently for over

twelve months to strike and I want to know why. There has to be a reason behind it Mark.

'First things first though Mark, I want all those people cleared away from here,' she said shaking her head at the crowd. 'They shouldn't be so damn close to the crime scene. But I want you to put all the uniformed onto each of them. I don't want any of them leaving here without a statement being gathered from them. I want to know everything about why they are here. There is a good possibility that our killer is one of them stood there right now watching us as we speak.'

'I'm on it,' he told her.

Just as he turned to leave, she enquired. 'What other detectives have arrived so far?'

'A Randolph and Pendelton from right here in Salford. They are with the lady who called it in over there,' he said nodding discreetly to one of the squad cars in the driveway.

'Put them onto the crowd also,' she told him. 'I don't want no crap out of them about who's case this is or isn't. And I don't give a damn if they out rank me. I want the whole area canvassed tonight. I want people knocked up. I don't care what time it is. I want as much information as possible by the time we leave here tonight.'

'Got it,' he smiled at her.

'Who called it in again Mark?' she asked.

'She's the neighbour. Woman by the name of Audrey Serdahley,' he said, glancing to the woman sat in the back of the police cars parked in the street. Her legs were hanging from the vehicle, a steaming mug placed between her hands. 'She says that she heard the child screaming around seven o'clock this evening. But she also says that she thought nothing of it.'

'What made her call it in then?'

'She claims to have seen someone climbing over the back wall of this house.'

'Did she get a good look at whomever it was?' she asked him.

He shook his head at her. 'Just saw his silhouette climbing over the fence in the back garden. I've taken a quick look and it's pitch black. I'm surprised that she even saw anything at all. Like I've said, I've got the forensics team on its way down here. So I've got two uniforms guarding the back of the house the area off in case of any footprints.'

Just then the skies opened and the rain tumbled from them. It was as if the good Lord himself had opened up the heavens to add further to their problems. The rain was coming down so hard

that you could literally see the water bouncing from the ground as it hit.

'Shit, fuck, this is all we need right now,' she snapped. 'With this fucking downpour, we'll either get extremely lucky or this fucked up weather is just about to wash all of our evidence away.'

'It seems as if the killers choose his night to perfection.'

'You can say that again. Oh fuck,' she exclaimed, as people began to disperse, escaping the weather. 'Stop them people now. I want statements. Stop them from leaving now.' She screamed at the officers around her who began in turn shouting for people to stop.

'What a fucking night,' she sighed deeply. Then glancing to the witness who had now climbed into the car with the Randolph and Pendelton. 'What time did she see this guy?'

'Around nine o'clockish,' he told her looking at his notes as the rain began to destroy them. She looked at her watch; it was ten-thirty-seven.

'That means if she heard screams around seven,' she shook her head, both of them ignoring the rain. 'Sweet Jesus, the killer could have been in there for quite some time.'

'I know,' he said. 'Creating yet another piece of twisted art for us discover.'

A thought suddenly dawned on Hunter staring up to the front bedroom window then to the car where Audrey Serdahley was crying. 'Tell me she didn't discover the bodies Mark?' She stared at him as his eyes dropped. 'Shit!'

'She says that they both have keys to one another houses,' he told her. Then looking to the crowd. 'Here's Lucy.'

A small dark haired woman approached them. She was smiling, as she always appeared to be smiling, no matter what the situation. She had very petite features and was barely over five-foot tall in height. But that's not to say that she didn't have a commanding presence about her.

A lot of fellow colleagues admired her attention to detail with the work she carried out. And she was always willing, no matter what time of the day or night to attend a crime scene. Lucy was one of the leading pathologists in Manchester and frequently held lectures and seminars relating to her work. She was also the one who would work closely with forensics at both the crime scene and later, when she would be the one to perform the actual autopsy.

She'd known Hunter since she'd began working with the police back in the late eighties and nodded to her as she then winked cheekily at Andrews.

'You been inside yet?' asked Lucy, holding the hood to her Sprayway goretex jacket over her head.

Hunter shook her head. 'I'm going now. Let me get the preliminaries over with. I want to be alone for a moment in there. Just give me five minutes, and then you come and take a look Lucy. I would imagine that the times of the deaths are within the last couple of hours, so you should be able to narrow it down somewhat for us.'

'Fine by me,' she answered checking the contents of her small leather bag. 'Just give me shout. I take a look downstairs before forensics arrive. Might find something of use.'

'Okay,' she replied. 'Good.'

'I'll join you in a minute boss,' said Andrews.

'Fine... make sure that you to sort everything else that I asked for Mark,' she told him. 'Then join me upstairs.'

'No problem,' he replied.

Pulling on the thin plastic gloves over her hands, Hunter looked at them both. 'I don't want a single thing touched. If the bodies have been left positioned in a certain way Lucy. Then I want them left like that. I want a forensic psychologist down here tonight. Whilst the crime scene is still fresh. I want a better profile this time round. And I think that the scene should be witnessed first hand.'

'You want me to call McCarthy?' asked Andrews.

'I don't know yet,' she replied. 'Let me go take a look first.'

As she walked to the open front door. The shaky looking officer, who was no doubt older but the fact of the matter was that he looked no older than twenty years old, with all his bad acne scars that were still prominent across his face. He was stood just inside of the doorway. Just about missing the rain that his fellow officers were now caught in the middle of. He was guarding the door, as if his life depended on it. He nodded nervously at her. 'You the officer that was first on the scene?'

'Yes mam,' he said, a little tenuously.

'So you've seen upstairs?'

He nodded his response, 'Yes mam.'

'You didn't touch anything, did you?'

'No mam.'

'I'll find out if you have, you know.' She stared directly at him. He seemed to be telling the truth but she added. 'Best to tell me now and save any hassle later.'

'I know mam,' he gulped. 'I didn't mam.'

'You feeling alright?'

'It's just so awful what's happened,' he told her.

'I know,' was all the words she found to say to him.

'I knew the male victim, if that's him up there, that is.' He shook his head. 'I knew him through work. Just like you probably did.'

She nodded her response at him.

'I know he made our job a lot harder,' he said, dropping his head. 'But nobody... and I mean nobody deserves to die the way they have.'

'You're right there,' she placed a hand on his shoulder. 'Give my partner a preliminary statement before you leave. Then I want to see you down at the station for a full statement. I need all the information that you can give me. So make sure that you have a good think about it. All the details, remember.'

He nodded sharply at her, as she walked in through the front door. Immediately taking in her surrounding, logging everything within her mind. Knowing that everything, no matter how insignificant now, could be vital to her at a later date. She noticed that there wasn't anything that appeared out of place to the eye. The hall lights had been left on, and from what she'd seen outside, so had the rest of the lights. She could hear the television set still playing in the living room. Its volume had been left just as it had been discovered and was still turned up high.

'Turn that off for me,' she said to the officer, 'will you please?'

Nodding at her, he disappeared through into the living room, leaving Hunter stood there all alone. Heading straight for the stairs, she approached the upper story cautiously aware that Lucy was staring at her from downstairs, still taking everything in. Up to now, there were no clues to there being any sort of an incident ever occurring. The house looked spotless and she could smell the wax polish that had been applied, more than likely that very same day. Stepping onto the landing itself she saw the first sign of the murder, as she glanced down the stairs and noticed Lucy had now disappeared.

Staring at the dark crimson streak of blood ran its way from the front bedroom door, all the way along the flowered wallpaper. Hunter took a closer look and clearly saw that it had been left there by a small hand, possibly a woman's or even a small child's. The tips ran from the thick imprints of the fingers through to fine thin streaks. Almost as if the hand had either

pushed and pulled itself away from the wall. But she knew that more than likely, it had been dragged away in force.

Hunter perceived it as the others surely would, to be the latter. As she was now upon the white bedroom door. Further evidence to what she'd summarised, was that there was more of the same blood covering the gloss paint work. She walked slowly towards it. Inching the door open with the tip of her finger, careful not to touch any of the blood as she took a closer inspection.

She could see blood streaking its way up the outside of the door. Unlike the hand print, this was a lot more solid. She saw clearly the outline of a cheek and partial print of a nose. Examining the area, she just about make out what appeared to be blonde hair strands, covered in blood stuck to the door. It was clear that at least one of the victims had tried to escape. Staring at the bloodied, matted strands of blonde hair, she knew it to be the wife, who had been slammed into the door as she had tried her best to escape the madness beyond this door.

Gently pushing the door open, Hunter let out a little moan. The bedroom was darker than the rest of the house. She knew that the several candles that had been placed around the room and were producing the rooms only visible light and created the desired effect that the killer had hoped for. But the diminished light could not hide the horrific crime scene before her. Hunter saw that the light-bulbs had been removed, making things all that much harder to see. But no means impossible. She pulled her small maglite torch from her pocket, switching it on to create more light.

This had been exactly the effect the killer had gone for. The candles flickering with the night freezing breeze that had followed her up the stairs into hell. But even the winter air couldn't defrost the abyss that they would all bare witness too.

'What've we got?' asked Andrews, stood in the doorway. 'Jesus Christ,' he exclaimed, as his hand went involuntarily to his mouth.

'Not quite,' replied Hunter, with her back to him so he couldn't see her face. 'But I think that whoever did this. Did a fine job of recreating the crucifixion to a tee.'

Hanging before them against the entire wall was the killer's latest creation. His sick work of art displayed to them as if it was indeed a huge piece of canvas that he'd completed his work upon. All furniture had been removed away from the wall, apart from the wardrobe that appeared to have been place strategically to the right hand side of the wall. Used as a prop in his display as

there had been something placed on top of there, that they couldn't quite make out.

The candles flickering gave the entire scene a gothic feel to it as Andrews walked to her side, covering his nose to the smell before them. The flies had already started gather. Almost as if the stench of death had drawn them in seductively from wherever it been that they had been hiding.

Dead centre to the wall hung Otis Fairchild, completely stripped naked. His arms were stretched as wide as they would go, his body weight dragging him down towards the floor. He was held there against the plasterboard walls by his hands. They couldn't be sure how but it looked as if he had in fact been crucified with actual nails holding his destroyed torso in place.

His head was hanging down to the left hand side, just out of view. Although they could both clearly see his bulging eyes, which had remained fixed in that position, when his last breath had been taken.

His entire naked body was soaked in dark dried blood. Streams and streams of the crimson tide seemed to cover his flesh, almost as if he'd been flayed of all his skin. Dried blood continued through Otis Fairchild's arms that spread from him. Spreading all the way through into the wings, that they killer had drawn in the victims own blood. The huge wings spread lavishly out onto the walls, covering a vast area of the wall space.

Although there was further scrawling, writing from what they could make out. More biblical references for them, further clues to decipher as to just how this killer's mind worked.

His upper torso had been ripped open crudely. They could see chunks of the severed flesh, hanging loosely down from his chest area. Parts of his rib cage were protruding through the torn flesh. Bones from his rib cage had been snapped and they saw that the heart had been removed.

In its place white feathers protruded through. The killer's trademark doves left in its place. His intestines had collapsed from his stomach area, as the killer had torn the flesh all the way down into his groin area. The twisted coils, entwined and slithered as if they were snakes fleeing the vicinity of imminent death.

Positioned at the feet of her husband holding onto his legs, as if begging for forgiveness was the naked, deceased anatomy of Claire Fairchild. Her back had been ripped open, in similar fashion to her husband's chest.

The killer, no doubt had cut her open whilst raping her. Her spine was visible to them both and though they could not yet see

whether or not the killer had taken her heart. There were the white feathers to wings that had been lodged in there, visible to them. Almost as if he'd created a pair of wings for the wife in the same fashion that the killer had crudely illustrated the wings that extended in the victims own blood, onto the walls before them.

'How they hell, is he held up there like that?' asked Andrews.

'Nails of some kind,' she replied casually. 'At least that's what it looks like.'

'You seen that?' asked Hunter, flashing her torch to the top of the wardrobe.

'Oh no, please – God no,' he said, as his light bounced from the wardrobe. 'What has he done?'

For placed on top of the wardrobe, his tiny chest torn open, his naked flesh white against the darkness of his insides was William Fairchild. He'd been placed with his legs hanging over the side of the wardrobe. The killer had nailed his hands to the wall; his head drooped down by its own weight, held against the tops of his shoulder blades.

'You see that?' asked Hunter, flashing her light onto the wall.

'This is some twisted, sick fuck that we are dealing with here' he answered, holding his beam at the wall where Hunter's light shone.

'That is some twisted sick sense of humour that he has got,' she said.

For against where the boys arms hung, drawn in the boys own blood was clearly what was supposed to be a bow and arrow aimed at his mother and father. Against the wall where hung his head, had been small horns drawn with a small pair of wings illustrated against the wall as if the boy was in fact a cherub from heaven – or was it indeed from hell.

Arrows from the bow were crudely drawn as if in flight

towards where the boy's father hung and mother was positioned

on the floor. As Hunter flashed the light back onto the wall, they

both witnessed the wings spreading out lavishly from Otis

Fairchild's arms.

Everything appeared to have been drawn with an object that wasn't a brush or even anything that was remotely the same size. Each line that the killer had illustrated was of disproportionate

lines. Some were thick, others thin as each bloodied line presented whatever the killer had fantasised. It looked as though the wings had been drawn onto the walls with the hearts that belonged to the victims. The same way the killer had done, with the first murders.

They both knew that they were dealing with someone whose composure was ambiguous. To create the image before them must have taken the killer some time. Not only to produce what the killer considered to be a work of art to them. But also taking into account, that the killer would have sexually abused the victims as the first part of the motivation to the crime. The image created before them was secondary to that, or possibly even primary to the motivations behind the killer's mind. Flashing her light down into the bottom right hand corner of the wall she wasn't surprised to see the same scrawl of a name in the corner.

'Well if everything before us didn't provide with enough evidence to suggest that it's our killer,' she shone the light at what looked like the same name. 'Then that there just about proves it.'

'You want me to call McCarthy?'

'No,' she said staring at him. 'Get Lucy up here first. Then I want some sort of lighting in here as soon as forensics has photographed it like it is with the candles. They we're both going to go over the crime with the psychologist. This isn't normal in any sort of way. I want to hear it straight off the bat, what the psychologist thinks to what has happened here tonight.'

'I'm on it,' he told her as she took her mobile from her pocket and began punching in numbers. 'So if you don't want McCarthy here for this, who are you calling?'

'Rachel,' she said as he looked at like she was mad. 'I know it sounds crazy Mark, but I know what I'm doing,' she told him.

'I'm glad somebody does,' he frowned walking from the bedroom.

FOURTEEN

The three of them, were sat on the second floor of Chan's restaurant in Chinatown. It had just gone twelve o'clock and the waiters had begun the tedious task of clearing the restaurant for the night. Eazy was staring absentmindedly out of the window, as for the first time that night, they had fallen quiet, and each filled with his own thoughts.

The light shower had finally changed and had begun it cataclysm, not too long before. The last few people remaining on the street, were darting in different directions to evade being soaked through to the bone. The streets of Manchester's city centre had been, as expected for a Saturday evening, extremely busy.

As everybody was out on the town, work completed for yet another week. A night of frolicking around lay ahead of them, only to be momentarily interrupted by Manchester's not so unfamiliar rain.

They'd spent the entire evening sat by that oval window, which was by far the best seat in the house and held a number of memories for the three of them. They had been drinking, and occasionally keeping Chan entertained as they both took his money off him at an array of different card games. Each of them, enjoying one anothers company, as they talked over old times and some of the events that had occurred back there and then. Not only in this very restaurant, but around the city centre itself.

Sleeper smiled over at the old man who merely nodded his response. Both he and Eazy had initially met Chan through one of their old friends, known as Prey. Through Prey, they both had got to know a lot of the main characters around Manchester back in the late eighties and early nineties. Back when Manchester

had been well known for some of the best, and also some of the worst times to ever have evolved in the city.

Around that time had seen the rise of dance music and the entire clubbing scene, which had followed. Clubs back than, like The Hacienda to name but one of them, had been one of the main turning points in what the clubbing scene has achieved today. The clubbing scene had escalated beyond everybody's beliefs and the next generation of kids, who had literally been kids back then, had followed their predecessor's footsteps into that world.

It had also been the time that the designer drugs, like Ecstasy and Crack-Cocaine had found their way into people's lives. It was also one of the reasons they had all been as close as they had been. Although it's to be pointed out, that it led to the troubles that had lay ahead of some of their closest friends. The situation and trouble that had evoked both Sleeper and Eazy to call it a day themselves.

'I know that it rains down in London,' said Eazy finally breaking the silence, watching the catastrophe beyond the glass pane with morbid fascination. 'But I don't think that it ever and I mean ever, rains quite like this down there. It's almost as if the rain originates from this place and we just get the leftovers.'

Chan began laughing at him as Sleeper shook his head. 'You so full of shit Eazy,' he said. 'London is such a shit-hole compared to Manchester now with all of its new developments.'

'Don't talk crap old man,' laughed Eazy. 'We're the capitol remember.'

'Should not be so anymore,' sighed Chan.

'And this place should?' asked Eazy, raising his eyebrows to the view outside.

'Of course,' he replied. 'We are the by far superior in almost every way to that filthy rotten place you two call home.'

'Yeah right,' smirked Eazy.

'Is that him?' asked Sleeper ignoring the friendly bickering between the two of them, as he observed the green 5 series BMW pull up outside the restaurant.

'That my car,' Chan told them pointing to the vehicle. 'Or at least, it was my car.'

'You can't even drive old man,' stated Eazy, watching as the huge guy climbed from the interior of vehicle.

'Still my car,' he insisted.

'Why's he driving it then?' asked Sleeper, who was carefully absorbed all he could on the large physique of the man who was

now running to the door of the restaurant to escape becoming drenched.

'He cheat me at cards last year,' smiled Chan. 'Cheat and take my car off me. I offer to buy back. But he no sell back to me.'

'You forget that we've seen you playing cards at first hand old man,' scoffed Eazy.

'And what you mean to say, is that you gambled your car away fair and square,' laughed Sleeper. 'And you're just gutted that he wants to keep it. I can't say I blame him. It's a nice motor Chan.'

'I know,' he stated flatly, leaving his seat as the guy was now walking over to them.

'He's a big lad,' observed Eazy, staring at Tony as he approached.

'I'd say that he matches you in the height department,' agreed Sleeper, who was equally impressed by Tony's size. 'Although, I'd give you a few extra pounds brother.' He smirked at Eazy, who was not sure if is friend was taking the piss or not.

'You alright Tony,' said Chan, taking hold of his hand.

'Not bad Chan,' he replied, taking in both Sleeper and Eazy curiously.

'This is Sleeper,' said Chan making the introductions as the two of them shook hands. 'And this big lump here is Eazy.'

'You both alright,' he said casually shaking Eazy's huge hand, that didn't look so big in his. Knowing that the man before him was thinking exactly the same thoughts, he couldn't help but smirk at him with a little wink.

'Chan here speaks highly of you,' Sleeper told him as he sat down. 'Drink?' He offered the bottle of Remy Martin congac that was sat before them on the table. He began pouring him one, without him answering.

'And I know Chan must think you two are alright or he wouldn't have called me here like this. So why don't we cut to the chase... cheers,' he said holding his glass up as taking a sip. 'And you lads tell just what it is that I can do for you?'

'Chan tells us that you're interested in the kids that have been going missing lately,' said Sleeper sipping the warm, soothing congac. All the while he was trying to work out what he thought of the man before him.

'Something like that,' he answered. 'Why you lads so interested.' He appeared to be paying particular attention to Sleeper, almost as if trying his best to recall some lost detail.

'Because, there has been kids going missing from down are way too,' said Eazy, as Tony started at him silently.

'No shit,' he finally said, leaning forward. 'Are you lads serious?'

'It's what's brought us all the up here,' replied Eazy.

'I hadn't heard about any kids going missing from London,' he told them. 'This may sound a little weird. But what sort of kids are talking about here. What I mean is, are they from good homes. Or more to the point are they council estate kids that are disappearing?'

Both Sleeper and Eazy looked to one another and nodded. 'So far, all we know of is that they've been going missing from our old estate in Lewisham.'

'That's sounds familiar to what's been happening up here too,' he told them. 'Do you know whether or not the parents were addicts of any kind?'

'I can't be one hundred percent to tell you the truth Tony,' shrugged Sleeper. 'Why do you ask?'

'The kids from around here have all come estates.' He sighed deeply and shook his head. 'Even all the way out in Macclesfield. They still disappeared from council estates. But the one thing that the press haven't got onto is that all the parents were addicts of one form or another.'

'How do you know that?' asked Eazy curiously.

'It came straight from the detective heading the investigation,' he admitted, shrugging as he did so. 'But to be honest we're not supposed to looking into that.'

'What do you mean we're?' asked Sleeper. 'And how come you're looking into anything for the old bill?'

'It ain't like that,' he protested holding up his hands defensively. 'Basically, my sister used to do a lot of work, working as a criminal psychologist. She did a lot of work with this one detective, Hunter. Anyway, this Hunter is alright, as far as coppers go, that is. Don't get me wrong here. She's pure professional and is the one copper who has always refused to take a bribe from anybody that I know. She's also the one copper who respects professionals, whether they are of the criminal element or not.'

'Fair enough,' said Sleeper, nodding at him, but still not looking convinced. 'So what's your interest in the missing kids then?'

He looked to Chan who said. 'Tell us why you're interested Tony. It's just that we may very well be able to help one another out, more so than you think.'

'She asked us to look into this missing rich kid, known as Charlotte Cartwright,' he answered without questioning Chan

further. 'The girl is from Prestbury in Cheshire. Although that's only about fifteen minutes drive, from right here in the city centre. The girl is sixteen so does not fit the profile of all the other missing kids.'

'So why she so interested then?' asked Eazy.

'She claims to have received an anonymous phone call,' he said sipping his drink. 'This mystery caller allegedly claims that, if Hunter finds the missing girl, then she'll find a link to the missing kids.'

'You believe that?' asked Sleeper.

'Not sure whether I do or I don't,' he replied. 'But she claims that these kids that have been going missing are being used in some peodophile ring. And that lads, is the reason that me and ar'kid are willing to look for her.'

Both Sleeper and Eazy were staring at one another, when Sleeper his began nodding his mutual understanding between the two of them. So staring intensely back at Tony he said. 'We got the guy who was taking the kids from Lewisham.' Sleeper was watching for his reaction.

A moments silence passed as Tony absorbed what he'd been told. 'You think that it is the same character whose been taking the kids from up here also?' he asked calmly.

'He was using kids from the Kings Cross area from his own sick, perverse pleasure,' said Eazy. 'We traced, or more to the point. I should say this kid requested a meeting with us. He was one of the rent boys from down that way. He seemed to consider himself quite the entrepreneur. Only his racket was using the hooker's kids as pieces of meat for this sick child molester down in Guildford.'

'We followed up on what the kid told us and hit pay dirt with what we found,' added Sleeper. 'We found a whole array of child pornography. All of what he had made himself with the kids he'd been using, I might add. We also found conclusive evidence that he was the one who'd taken the kids from Lewisham.'

'So did you find the missing kids?' he asked them.

Sleeper shook his head at him. 'No, and the worst part is, we know that he took the kids. But we also know that there was someone else involved. We think that this guy used the kids for his own purposes. We think that after this one guy had finished abusing them, that this other guy was the one to actually take them from him. You see, the ones he was using from Kings Cross. He always returned them after he'd finished with them. Apart from this one kid that is. And when he abused that kid, we

know from what the rent boy told us... that there was somebody else there.'

'And I presume, that he didn't reveal who this person was to you,' said Tony.

'Yes and no,' said Eazy.

'What the hell does that mean?'

'He claims that the one responsible is known as the Pied Piper,' Sleeper told him.

'Are you having me at it, or what, lads?' he looked to Chan who shook his head at them. 'So what happened to this guy then?'

Nobody spoke and it immediately dawned on Tony what they had done to the guy. He suddenly found himself smiling directly at Sleeper as another piece of the puzzle fitted into place.

'I know you. I remember you now,' he said, holding Sleeper's stare. 'I've only just realised who you are Sleeper.'

'What does that mean?' he asked, sipping his drink, holding eye contact with Tony.

'It means that I know what happened to the guy. And it means that I just want to shake your hand,' he smirked, leaning over and holding out his hand to Sleeper. Cautiously taking his hand Sleeper raised an eyebrow. 'I met you once in The Hacienda. You obviously don't remember me. It was way back in the early nineties. You were with Prey and Chopper. I remember getting these funny vibes from you, and believe me. I don't scare easily. But it's fair to say Sleeper, that something about you spooked me. So the next time that I seen Prey, I enquired as to who you were. Prey was discreet, as Prey was always discreet with such matters. But let's just say that I kind of worked it out for myself as to who and what you are.'

'I don't quite know, which way to take that Tony,' said Sleeper, as both Chan and Eazy weren't quite sure what to make of it either.

'Believe me Sleeper,' he smiled, holding his drink up to him. 'It's a compliment. I also know of a couple of other jobs that you've taken care of for associates of mine. Both right here in town, down in London and I'm also extremely grateful for a job you took care of in the Canary Islands. Although I wasn't directly involved with your hiring. Let's just say that me and my firm gained financially. So I thank you.'

Sleeper had known exactly what job he was talking about. It had some years back now. Back when he'd not been as conscientious to the contracts he'd taken on. When the money out weighed the moral context to the job required. He'd been

hired by some Newcastle lads, to take care of one of the main heads from of the London firms who ran one of the main Timeshare operations out in Tenerife. He'd taken the contract and completed it successfully, and it appeared to have been in favour of the man before him.

'Alright then Sleeper,' said Tony leaning back in his chair. Visibly more relaxed now. 'Why don't you tell me why it is that you think that this Pied Piper character is here in Manchester?'

'Because towards the end,' he smiled at Tony also more relaxed. He now knew that there was a mutual respect between the two of them. 'This guy started to babble on. He was in a lot of pain and delirious with the prospect of what was to happen to him. I think in way he accepted his fate. But not enough to spill his guts as to the identity of this sick bastard. He told us both, that the kids followed the Pied Piper and his magic flute all the way back here to Manchester.'

'You reckon that it was straight up?' enquired Tony.

'I'd say so,' said Eazy. 'He was babbling and trying his best to taunt us.'

'He said that he was protected by this guy,' added Sleeper. 'He said that we would never find him because they didn't want him to be found. He said that not even God could strike him down. Like he thought this guy was invincible or something.'

'This is some weird shit that we seem to have got ar'selves mixed up in here lads,' sighed Tony lighting a cigarette, tossing the pack onto the table for anybody to help themselves.

'Chan here, seems to think that possibly the O'Leary's could help us in some way,' said Sleeper. 'What do you think Tony?'

'I wouldn't of had, old Dom down as being into that shit Chan,' he said staring at the old man in disbelief.

'But he is well connected with the porn industry,' stated Chan.

'Two different things all together,' he said. 'Plus you know what Dom is like Chan. He's a really cagey fucker. Ever since he got sent down all them years back. Time doing bird messed with his head big time. He trusts no fucker other than his own son, Vinnie. And that sick fuck is one crazy son of a bitch.'

'You reckon that you could set us up with a meeting?' asked Sleeper.

'You have to understand that old Dominic O'Leary is from the old school Sleeper,' he said. 'Since coming out of prison he's become quite the reclusive type. But that's not to say that he hasn't got power. 'Cause, believe me he has. Plus that son of his and me have had a couple of run ins with one another in the past.

'Dominic runs his own crew. Always has done. He's got himself quite a firm together these days. Back in the days of the Quality Street Boys from Salford he was one of the main lads. But he seems content with his small porn empire that he runs now. I also know of some loan sharking that he deals with and a couple of protection rackets. But that side is ran by Vinnie. The real bread and butter is his porn business. He's got in on the internet side of things early. Makes him an absolute mint from what I've also heard. I seriously doubt he's involved here lads.'

'He might be able to help in some way though,' suggested Eazy.

'He may,' he glanced at Sleeper. 'But there is one thing that you should know first.'

'What's that?' enquired Sleeper.

'He want agree to meet with you two. Not a chance lads. He absolutely hates blacks. He's all for the BNP and other shit like that,' he told them, shaking his head. 'I don't know why. And you know yourself Sleeper, that Manchester is about the one place in the country where we pretty much all get along. Give or take a few of the arseholes that is. O'Leary being one of them.'

'Sounds like a nice guy,' smiled Sleeper.

'Maybe if I just go and talk with him,' suggested Tony. 'I could find out what I can for us.'

'Oh, but I insist on meeting this delightful chap,' smirked Sleeper.

'I can tell,' laughed Tony, 'that you just love to create trouble.'

'Only with arseholes,' he replied smiling. 'I'm only fucking about Tony. I don't want any trouble with the old man... I just want to be there to see his eyes when we speak about this shit to him. Believe me Tony, I have a knack when it comes to sniffing out liars.'

'I bet you do,' he grinned as he sipped his drink.

'So it's agreed then Tony,' Sleeper reached over and held out his hand.

'What is?' asked Tony.

'That we will help one another out here then,' he added.

'I reckon so,' he nodded shaking his hand firmly. 'It would appear that Chan 'ere was right. It seems that we have the same goals to achieve. And that goal is to track down and dispose of whichever sick fuck is heading this operation.'

They all raised their glasses to one another and smiled.

FIFTEEN

'I'm here to see Hunter,' said Rachel, climbing under the crime scene tape, as the officer attempted to stop her from entering.

'It's alright,' shouted Hunter from the front door, where she stood talking with the two detectives from Salford, Randolph and Pendelton. 'She's with me.'

Rachel could hear her name being called out, from the many reporters that had recognised her. They were all waiting impatiently like vultures, ready to strike down upon their prey. Only they waited to swoop down in order to scoop their latest story. Doing her best to ignore them, she strode forward across the saturated front lawn, to the house that awaited her.

She had received the call from Hunter, explaining very briefly about what had happened. Hunter hadn't revealed the identity of the victims. Only explaining that it was the same killer, the one they had named the Dark Angel. She said that she understood fully if Rachel wanted no part of this. But also pointed out in the same breath, that Rachel would be able to produce a clearer profile, from actually visiting the crime scene first hand.

And Rachel knew fully well, that to be precisely there was going to cripple her, but she also knew that she had to be there. To smell the blood that had been spilt, to close her eyes at the crime scene and try to imagine just what it was going through Gabriel's, as she had now named the killer, mind. To try and feel what it was that drove Gabriel to perform such an act of sheer depravity.

'You alright Hunter?' she asked, approaching the front door. She was wearing a light weight navy blue Berghaus goretex jacket to prevent both the wind and the rain penetrating her. Although, she still wore the grey Nike jogging bottoms, which

she'd been bumming around her apartment in. Along with the Nike Humera's that were battered and old, yet she refused to throw them out for comfort reasons.

'You alone?' asked Hunter. 'No Tony trailing along?'

'He had to be somewhere else,' she told him.

In truth, she would have like nothing more than for her brother to be here to act as the rock in which he'd been for her this past year. 'What have we got then Hunter?'

'You best come on through up stairs Rachel,' sighed Hunter, as Andrews appeared walking down the stairs.

Rachel could see that the entire colour had washed itself away from his face. And she knew that it hadn't been the rain to have washed it away. 'That bad eh Mike?'

He nodded at her. 'You best take a look,' he said. 'Forensics is working the rest of the house. We waited for you to arrive before we're going to let them in there. I still don't think that this...'

'It is bad Rachel,' Hunter cut him off. 'But you already know that. There is no doubt that this is our same killer again. It's got his trademark written all over it and I want to know exactly what you think to what we are dealing with. Here, put these on. We don't want to taint the crime scene in anyway.' She handed Rachel the lightweight blue overall that the forensic team was wearing.

Slipping out of her wet jacket, and into the overalls, she then began pulling the clear rubber gloves over her hands as Hunter followed suit.

'You about ready kid?' she asked.

Rachel nodded at her as her eyes suddenly went to the front door.

'What the hell is she doing here?' snapped Chief Superintendent Tom Mackenzie. His face turned red with anger, as he waltzed through the door as they all stared at him. 'She's too close to this thing to be here.'

'That's exactly why I want her here, Mackenzie,' snapped Hunter back at him. 'That and the fact that Rachel is the best forensic psychologist we've got.'

'I still don't think...' he began to say.

'This is my investigation sir,' she said. 'And I think that Rachel is our best bet at cracking it.'

'And I am your superior Hunter,' he stated proudly. 'And I'm telling you that I don't want her here.'

'And I'm telling you sir,' she snapped back at him. 'That she is staying and that is that.'

'Detective Hunter,' he was turning a deeper shade of purple.

'Here,' said Hunter handing her identification to him. 'She leaves, then I leave.'

Mackenzie knew that he was boxed in. Everybody knew, including the two detectives stood there gawking at Chief Mackenzie in disbelief that Hunter was one of the best detective's that Manchester had. If he let her walk, he knew that there would be hell to pay, and that it would come knocking at his door.

'Whatever,' he finally sighed. 'But I want it noted that I'm not at all happy with this Hunter.'

'It's noted,' she told him. Taking Rachel's arm. 'Come on,' she said leading her towards the stairs.

'Thanks for the support Hunter. That's about all I needed on top of everything else. Chief Mackenzie breathing down my neck,' she said.

'Don't mention it kid,' she told her, ignoring the sarcasm as they headed up the stairs.

'Just how bad is it?' she asked as the two were finally alone. But she didn't need an answer as they both made their way onto the landing. 'Oh Jesus.' She saw the streaks of blood coming from the bedroom.

'I won't lie to you Rachel,' she said. 'I never have. But he's taken their hearts like the first murders. Things are very similar. Only this time he's killed the entire family. He left no survivors this time round.'

'Who are the victims Hunter?' She stopped where she was and stared at her friend.

'Before we get to that,' she said, 'why don't you take a look first.'

She took a deep breath and nodded that she understood. 'Let's go and take a look then.'

Hunter rubbed her arm gently, switching the small Dictaphone on as they made their way forward. Rachel closely examined the blood. 'It is clear that this is a hand print here.' She pointed out, following it through to the bedroom door. 'It would appear that one of the victims tried to flee the scene. It is clear that the killer grabbed, and slammed the victim into the door here.' She pointed to Hunter who nodded.

'That's what I had also,' she told her. 'Look here. You can see, what I think is the female victims hair.'

As they walked through into the bedroom, the full force of what was before them hit Rachel like a ton of bricks. She'd psyched herself up for this all the way over here. She almost convinced herself that she was capable of confronting her

demons of the past. She'd almost succeeded as well, that was until they walked through that bedroom door and Rachel involuntarily fell to her knees. 'Oh Jesus Christ,' she shook her head at the image, as Hunter took her arm, helping her up.

'Exactly my first response,' she told her. 'You going to be alright kid? Or do you want me to call in McCarthy. I was wrong to call you kid, sorry. Come on; let's get you the fuck out of here.'

'What the fuck are we dealing with Hunter?'

'That's why I've got you here kid,' she replied.

'I'll be alright Hunter,' she shook her head and began to compose herself sighing deeply. 'Just give me a moment will you?'

'Take as long as you need kid,' she replied, rubbing Rachel's back affectionately. 'You sure that you are up for this?'

Rachel nodded her response. Then she began to get her composure together, taking deep breaths whilst all the while taking everything in about the room and the corpses. Standing centre to the bedroom, Rachel stared at the wall before her. Letting the image, Gabriel's latest creation, imprint itself within her mind.

The stench of death engulfed their surroundings. The stench of discharged blood, that appeared to be all around them crawled its way into their snouts as Rachel let the entire horrendous scene wash itself over her. The heartache of the last twelve months had returned to haunt her in that very moment. But, what she had to keep thinking was that it had also returned to give them a second chance at seeking out the killer.

The low hum of the flies that had gathered was the only sound now to be heard. Closing her eyes, Rachel began to feel the room around her as if they were one.

Slowly opening her eyes she began to take in every detail of the crime before her. 'The killer took his time here. A lot more so than the first murders. He's perfecting his crime. As the intensity of the first murders have by now faded. He would have blamed himself for that fervour declining. Possibly looking for ways to perfect his crime over the time period that we are faced with. I have to admit that I'm surprised he's taken as long as he has. But the patience that we see here is projected in the length of time it has taken for him to strike again. We're dealing with a killer who is in complete control of himself. Someone who has the patience to have possibly watched this family for a very long time. Going totally unnoticed to anyone. He obviously blends in. It could quite literally be anyone. He took all the time he needed

in order to create this entire scene. I imagine that he has taken more than the hearts as trophies. There will be photographs, possibly even a filming of what he did here.

'The male victim would have been the last one to die here,' she said. 'He would have killed the wife and child first. I imagine that he would have taken care of the child first. It was an act of further punishment to the parents to see him to do that.'

Walking to the corpses she examined the female victim's bloated face. There was both swelling and bruising to the face and neck areas. 'The nose has been broken here. She also has swelling to the neck indicating the killer strangled the victim at some point. Quite possibly whilst he was raping her.'

She started to look at the victim's back, which had been sliced down the right hand side. 'The incision had entered above her shoulder blade. The knife that had been used had been pulled downwards aggressively. The open wound was more of a rip than a precise surgical operation. There were jagged tears to the flesh. 'It's hard to say whether the killer is right or left handed here. From the way the flesh is torn it would appear that he is right handed. But then if you look here,' she said pointing to the left hand side of the open wound. 'It possible that the killer swapped hands. The tear to this side is a lot worse than that side, unless...'

Examining the wound closer. 'Yes, I would say that he used his right hand here, dragging the knife in a downwards movement. Although from the way this side is sliced crudely to the other would indicate that he changed hands. Which I have to say is extremely weird in a case like this. As you know we had trouble deciding whether or not he was right or left handed with the first murders, because of the way he cut the hearts out from behind the victims. But now looking at this wound I wouldn't be surprised if the killer performed the first ritual of cutting open the chest both right and left handed.'

'So is he right,' asked Hunter, 'or left handed Rachel.'

'Primarily I would say that he definitely right handed.' She sighed, bending her head to look at Hunter. 'Although he appears to have an uncanny ability to use both if necessary.'

'What about the knife?' she asked. 'What kind of knife would you have thought the killer is using?'

'From the serrated edges here,' she leaned closer. 'I would say the killer used possibly a hunting knife of some kind. Possibly a kitchen knife. But I'd put my money on a hunting knife.'

'What about the wings?' asked Hunter, nodding to the white feathers clearly showing through the gaping laceration.

'It has become part of his creation,' said Rachel touching the feathers lightly. 'It's all to do with his over all profile of how he perceives himself.'

'And just how doe he see himself?'

'We'll get to that,' she answered stretching up from the floor and taking another look around from where she stood over the corpse.

'What about those marks around the neck?' asked Hunter.

'He used some form of bindings around the victim's neck. See here.' She bent down to the victim once again and indicated the marks to Hunter. 'You can see the strap marks both here and on this side here also. I would say that he used a belt or something of a similar nature.

The strangling of the victim would have taken place at the same time that the rape was taking place. It is clear that he raped her anally from the wounds. You can clearly see blood from the victim's anal area here,' she pointed to around the buttocks area. 'There also appears to be stratch marks of some kind here, at the bottom of the victim's spine. Have forensics take a closer look at that would you.'

'You think that he killed her by strangling her?'

'No,' she answered bluntly. 'I think that the victim would have been made to suffer further. Although I should point out that the act of strangling someone, is an act of passion in itself. Through raping them anally he is taking away their spirit and breaking them down piece by piece. He is then trying to gain further intimate knowledge of them by taking things one step further and cutting open their bodies. The dissection of the bodies shows us that he has a morbid fascination with getting to know his victims on a much more personal level. It would appear as if maybe he possibly knows them for what they appear to be. But what he requires is further knowledge that no other has access too. And in gaining that knowledge he won't accept them on face value alone. He therefore feels that he has to get to know what they are like on the inside.'

Staring at the walls she nodded. 'There are further references that the killer has left behind. I'll go into in a minute. The killer, although cold hearted is also conscientious. There is more to these doves being left behind than we know. I have a theory that relates to some of the clues that he has left us here.'

'What clues kid?' asked Hunter, standing over the corpse of the wife.

Ignoring the question, Rachel continued to look around. 'She was not killed here on the floor, not here in this spot anyway.'

Pushing herself up from the floor, she walked over to the bed. The sheeting had been ripped away and the mattress was drenched in the victim's blood. 'He killed the wife here. She lost a lot of blood. You can see where the blood has literally sprayed from the victim here.' Sweeping her arm in an arch against the bedroom wall, to illustrate further the geyser of crimson colouring. It had the appearance of a heavy paint brush swung against the wall filled with red paint. Almost perceiving the impression of a Jackson Pollock painting.

Looking from the bed, back to the main wall, Rachel pointed to the male victim. 'He was made to watch whilst the killer rapes and kills his wife here on the mattress. There is something not quite right here though. If you was to see both your wife and child being sexually violated and murdered before your very own eyes. Then I don't believe that whatever it is holding him against the wall would be strong enough to hold him there. The bindings from the first murder are a lot different. In the first murders he strapped Peter to the bed frame so tightly that it would have been near impossible for him to free himself. But here, I not so convinced that the husband couldn't free himself.'

'You think that maybe he put the husband up there after he'd killed him?'

'Not at all,' she shook her head. 'He was up there alright when the killer raped his wife. It wouldn't have had the same effect for the killer if he hadn't been. What's he held up there with Hunter?'

'From what we can make out,' she said glancing back around at the naked corpse, 'he's held up there with nails. It's one of those new homes so there isn't the solid walls that you find in older homes. So it's only plasterboard walls.'

'Still,' she said walking to the wall and examining his hands. The nails had clearly been put through there whilst the victim was still alive. 'One, hammering nails through someone's hands whilst they are still alive is not going to be easy to say the least. Holding his arms in place. Keeping the victim still. I don't buy it. Plus, there would have been the noise of banging against the wall. Too messy.'

'What then?' asked Hunter.

'There are two theories that I have,' she was still examining the hands. Pressing the bloodied palm of the victim, allowing her finger to trace itself around the nails head, probing, lost in thought. 'The first theory is that he didn't use a hammer to do this. I mean in this day and age, we have modern technology

available to us. And that includes availability to the killer also. It also includes the modern day hammer.'

'Which is?' asked Hunter impatiently.

'I'd give odds on favourite that he used a nail gun.' She made a popping sound with her mouth using her fingers and thumb in the shape of a gun as she did so.

'You could very well be right there kid,' smiled Hunter proudly. 'Now what's this second theory on how he kept him up there?'

'You should have them look for traces of some kind of drug Hunter. I think that the killer for whatever reason this time round may have drugged his victims first.'

'What makes you think that kid?' she asked curiously.

'Firstly, because it would still have been difficult to hold a fully conscious man of this size steadily against the wall. Even with a nail gun handy. But secondly, because he took a lot longer with this crime than he did with the first one,' she said staring directly at Hunter. 'You got any witnesses?'

'The neighbour,' she told her. 'Some poor cow who stumbled acro...'

'What she saying?'

'That she heard the child screaming for a short time around sevenish. Thought nothing of it as the screams did not continue,' she said. 'Then claims to have seen the suspect fleeing the scene from the back of the house at around nine to nine-thirty.'

'You've got loads of time right there,' said Rachel. 'But this took longer to create than that. Possibly he didn't drug the child like he drugged the parents. Possibly that is why the neighbour heard the boy screaming and no other sounds from the parents.'

'Why do you think that he drugged them though?'

'Because this time round he's killed both the wife and child,' she said. 'Look here.'

Pointing to the chair beside the dresser. There was blood on the arms on the chair. But that wasn't what Rachel was pointing at. 'He killed the child here in this seat. Look at the markings here. There were obvious bindings to the seat. The imprint left on the cushion is way too small for either the male or the female victim. He abused the child here on the seat with the male victim watching from there on the wall. The blood here on the mirror is where the killer performed his sadistic ritual of removing the heart. You can clearly see the way the blood sprayed as the heart was removed. It is also clear that with the flow of blood, which the killer performed the act whilst there was still blood pumping through the victim. He carried out this act, as the child was still

living and breathing. And he did so as the wife was lay on the bed and the husband was fixed to the wall like that. He was also his own audience for the performance. He watched himself in the mirror as he cut the heart out of the child. Absorbing every detail of the crime he was committing. The arousal that he would have felt from this depraved act would have been taken to the wife next.

'You can see that there are no marks on the bed frame like the chair here,' she said. 'There is no sign of a struggle on the bed. Although there was clear signs of as we approached the bedroom of the female victim trying to escape from the room. I would say that she tried to escape. Maybe the drug began to wear off slightly. Maybe witnessing her child been brutally raped and murdered brought her out of whatever induced state of mind that she was in. It's quite possible that the killer knocked her unconscious as he smashed her into the door. Then he punished her right there on the mattress. Once again whilst the husband was forced to watch.

'I'd say that the killer strangled her to the point of near death.' She examined the blood that had sprayed violently up the wall by the bed. 'There was clearly life still in her. Her blood must have pumping through her veins in order for the effervescence of it, to be so elaborate here. But look how the blood separates against the wall. The killer was behind her as he cut open her back to gain access to the heart. The killer would have been covered in both the victims blood by now. You need to look into how it is that the killer is leaving the scene of the crime and leaving us no trial of blood.

'Check the bathrooms out. See if the killer has cleaned himself before fleeing. It's also possible that he brought some kind of cleaning material with him. Possibly, paper towels or some other kind of cleaning device that he could take with him.'

'I'll have forensics check over every inch,' said Hunter.

'It's also very possible, that the killer has shaved himself of all bodily hair,' she told Hunter. 'I'm still a baffled as to how he left no hair or fibres at the first murders. Quite possibly he's shaved his pubic hair away to leave no trace. But that wouldn't explain how everything is left so clean. Forensically, I think that our killer has studied our methods. I think that what Brendan said about the killer not planning on being caught was correct. But what I want to know is why he's waited so long before striking out again. We need to look into the victims here Hunter. I want you find out why they were chosen. There has to be a connection.' She saw Hunter face drop slightly. 'What is it?'

'He was a defence barrister Rachel,' she admitted. 'It's Otis Fairchild.'

'Jesus,' she exclaimed staring at back at the corpse hanging there. It was clearly visible to her now who the victim was. She hadn't known him personally. But her husband had gone up against him several times before.

'There has got to be some sort of a connection there Hunter. They both worked with one another. I know it was for the opposite side on both accounts. But this can't be mere coincidence, can it? You need to look into that angle,' she told her bluntly.

'Mark is already looking in to it as we speak,' she answered her. 'Did you know what case he was working on at the present time?'

'No,' she replied. 'Is it relevant?'

'It's why I was interested to know about your theory on them being drugged,' she told her.

'Why's that Hunter?'

'Because the guy he was defending Nigel Collins,' she watched for the recognition to kick in. 'you have heard about that case?'

Rachel nodded. 'He's the one who was accused of using that GHB drug on the women – Rohypnol right? I've seen bits and pieces on the trial. Serial rapist, right?'

'That's the one,' she said.

'You think that this could be our guy?'

'After what you've said about them being drugged,' she said. 'I'm going to have the pathologist check the drug angle when she does the autopsy later. If it checks out then I'll issue the warrant against him.'

'Why would he kill the guy who is defending him though?'

'Who knows why people do what they do these days kid.'

'I reckon that there could a good connection,' said Rachel staring at Otis Fairchild's corpse hanging there, all surreal. 'But I will be very surprised if he's the guy. Possibly check his victims. If anything, I'd possibly buy, one of them or their boyfriend's doing it as an act of revenge against Fairchild for defending him in the first place. But then were losing our way. How would that possibly tie in with the murder of Peter and Becky?'

'I don't know,' she admitted. 'Let's get finished here first though. Before we start bouncing things back and fourth.'

Rachel nodded her agreement. 'Now, he dragged the wife across the floor from the mattress. Placing her at the feet of her husband. So that, even though he'd taken her life she would still,

in his own mind have to witness what he was going to do to the male victim. The boy would have also been placed up there before hand. In fact he would have been placed up there as he raped the wife. Again as if the killer feels that he was being made to watch everything from his perch. The boy was then placed up there as if to watch over the two of them as he then carried out his act with the husband.'

Taking a closer look at the male victim, she examined his open torso. Following her way down to his groin area. 'Now this is interesting Hunter. It is clear that the killer raped the husband. But look here at the blood around this area.' She was pointing her finger at the man's buttocks and scrotum.

'He's been raped anally,' she said. 'But how the killer managed it would have been extremely difficult. See the bruising against the scrotum and the pubic area surrounding it. Well that would indicate that he raped the man from here. Stood in front of his victim like this.' She was stood in front of the naked corpse, her legs spread around the corpse of the wife.

'I think he must have raped him before he placed him against the wall. There are markings around the neck once again. But you can see finger marks. Look. There is clear red finger marks here and here on both sides of his neck. He was strangling the victim as he was raping him. It's weird it's almost like he raped him whilst he was against the wall. The only thing is it wouldn't be possible to gain penetration from standing in front of him. Unless...'

'Unless what?'

Rachel ignored the question simply because she couldn't work out how he did. 'He wanted to see the victim's eyes as he took his life away from him. Like I've already said. He wants to get as personal as possible with each victim. But Otis Fairchild was the main prize here. He wanted all of the details to store in his mind, for a later date.'

'What about all of the markings, which he left behind?'

'Now this, I would say is the main part of his motivation,' she sighed stepping back to observe at the wall. 'This is his work of art. Only I fear that he's got a lot more art yet to create.

'The wings are symbols of angels,' she said looking at Hunter. 'That is very clear. I think that our killer has some perverse way of considering himself to be one of these angels. Now that's not just the wings that indicate this. But some of the scrawling last time round, were brief biblical references to certain scriptures.'

Walking to the bottom right hand side of the wall, she wasn't disappointed to see the same markings that indicated the name.

'Now Hunter,' she turned her head to look at her. 'Would you like to know just who our killer considers himself to be?'

'So that is a name then?'

'Look at the way the lines flow,' she moved her finger around the lettering, careful not to touch to wall. 'That's a G, this is an A, into B, that represents an R, and this here is the letter I. That's what this dot here refers too. Although hard to make out, that is an E and the last letter is an L.'

'Gabriel,' said Hunter opened mouthed. 'He thinks that he is the archangel Gabriel.'

'The very one,' she sighed deeply, as she stood up. 'He was considered to be one of the first angels to fall from grace. He is also considered to be the angel of communication. He allegedly was the angel to inform Mary of the virgin birth of Christ. He can also be found through different references. Like the one where Joan of Arc claims that it was in fact Gabriel that gave her the inspiration to challenge the king of France.'

'Is he considered the angel of death?' asked Hunter.

'No, in fact he is considered to be the angel of mercy,' she said. 'Michael was considered to be the angel of judgement. There was also Rapheal, another of these angels. But the three are supposed to be part of the first group to have fallen from the heavens, according to the legend that is. There is supposed to have been seven of these angels who worked side by side with God. But because God created mankind to be the dominion of earth. The angels, of whom he'd created when he in fact created Heaven felt cheated that they were to be refused the fruits of what mankind had been offered. They say that by giving into temptation, the angels fell from grace.'

'Jesus,' she shook her head. 'So they are like the devil himself.'

Rachel pointed to the wall. 'Oh believe me; Satan plays his part in all of this. You can clearly see that our killer, Gabriel, has used the child's heart to write with here. Host of heaven worships you, morning stars there, guardian cherub, disgrace from the mount of God. All of them we'll discover are brief references from scriptures. Ah, there, that's what I was referring to earlier about the doves.' Rachel was stood next to male victim. Pointing to the wall.

'Now I know that this is hard to read,' she said. 'But look here. I noticed it at the first lot of murders, but could never work out what word it was or if indeed it was a word at all.'

'And now?'

'It reads rekullatekha,' she said. 'Although it read rekulla at the first murders.'

'What the hell does that mean kid?'

'It's Hebrew for trade,' she replied. 'There are variations like widespread trade or merchandise or even traffic. It's as if he believes conscientiously, that he trading the hearts of the victims for the doves that he leaves in their place.'

'Are you having me at it or what?'

'Not at all,' she replied. 'It is said that the scriptures imply, that Satan peddled his slander to one third of the angelic host against God himself. You see that after God banished Satan, who by the way was also an angel to begin with. But that he wanted to be the ruler of earth. Therefore he obviously tried to build support for his contention with the angels. He turned them against God and tempted them. Telling them that they were far better qualified to run the earth than mankind was. He was filled with hate and violence towards humanity. And I think that what we are witnessing here is someone who believes that he is one of those fallen angels here on earth to carry out Satan's work for him.'

'How the hell do you know all this shit Rachel?'

'What do you think I've been doing this last twelve months Hunter,' she said.

'Well at least you're officially back on the case now,' smiled Hunter. 'You and Tony can stop working as a couple of vigilantes now. I know it'll piss Mackenzie off to hell. But fuck him. I want you back and you've proven here tonight that you're the best one qualified for the job.'

'Who says that I want back in?' Rachel stared at her.

'Me.'

'I don't think so Hunter,' she sighed. 'I'll continue to look into Charlotte Cartwright for you. But I'm not coming back to work on this case with you Hunter.'

'Then what the hell was all that about then?' she snapped.

'As hard as it's been,' she looked back at the wall. 'It was a lot better for me to have seen all this first hand. Thank you Hunter.'

'Thank you,' she snapped. 'That's all you've got to say. You know if you and Tony go after this Gabriel or whatever the fuck his name is. If you go after him yourselves, then I can't stop what ever force will stand in your way.'

'I wouldn't expect you too,' she smiled. 'It's just something that I've got to do myself.'

Hunter finally sighed deeply shaking her head at Rachel. 'So be it kid. But all of that shit you just told me about archangels and Satan. That's a bit far fetched isn't it,' said Hunter. 'Come on now kid. You don't really believe that do you?'

'I don't believe it,' she cocked an eyebrow at Hunter. 'But it's not my beliefs that we have to worry about, is it Hunter. It's our killer, Gabriel, as he wants to be known to the world. That's who's believes we have to worry about Hunter.'

The two of them stood there silently as Rachel stared at the atrocity before her, and Hunter shook hers at what Rachel had just told her.

SIXTEEN

'**N**ice pad,' said Sleeper, as they walked up to the large vintage wrought iron gates, belonging to the huge house beyond them.

Sunday morning had dawned upon them. They hadn't left Chan's the night before. Instead, agreeing to more card games with the old man. A few of which Tony had let him win, so not to damage his pride too much. In fact, they'd played so many games, that they had set straight off from the restaurant not half an hour before. It wasn't even nine o'clock in the morning yet, but Tony had agreed to take Sleeper, but only Sleeper, to see Dominic O'Leary at the house he owned in Hale, just outside of Altrincham.

He'd said that if they'd taken Eazy along, there was no possible way that they'd have got into the house. Pointing out that he was one hell of a huge lump, as he he'd put it smirking away.

Sleeper had to admit at being impressed with the guy's home. There appeared to be acres and acres of land that was confined, almost like a prison behind the solid looking, brick wall that kept intruders from entering. Sleeper's eyes never kept still, as they made their approach. He saw that they needed to use the intercom in order to request whether or not they could enter the house in order to meet with Dominic O'Leary.

Above the pillars, where the gates hung, were two security cameras. Running concurrent, along the tops of the walls was a trail of barbed wire, that didn't look to be normal barbed wire. It appeared to be the razor sharp type that prisons actually used themselves.

'Considering that he's so paranoid since coming out of prison,' nodded Sleeper at all of the security surrounding the house. 'He sure seems to have confined himself to one.'

'It is a nice gaff though, in'it,' said Tony as they reached the gate, 'But you are right though. It does resemble Strangeways a little. But something happened to him on the inside. I'm not quite sure what it was. But whatever it was, was enough for him to have turned into the recluse that he has. But don't be fooled by any of this recluse business Sleeper. Like I said last night. He used to be one of the main heads, years back. He still carries a lot of pull from back then. Me and him had our run ins, as I was getting started in the business. This was whilst Vinnie was still too young to have gotten personally involved himself. I'm not quite sure how things would have worked out if he'd been actively involved back then.'

'What do you mean by that?'

'Basically, I took over my old man's business in Ordsall,' he sighed then stared at Sleeper. This was twenty years ago now. But my old man would have been running this city within a couple of years back then. Everybody knew this. Only he worked independent to the other firms. He ran his own crew of lads. They were into mainly puling off extremely hard scores. Top line burglaries and arm blags was his speciality. He'd started to invest the money carefully and some of the older heads had soon realised that he was their one true adversary. Including O'Leary.'

'So what happened?'

'They shot gun blasted, both my parents dead, as they pulled up outside the house in Ordsall.'

'Was it O'Leary behind it?'

'I found the two who had taken the contract,' he said pushing the intercom's button. 'It was O'Leary's name that was one of the first to come up and I guess I took it upon myself to judge him on that alone. I took my old man's crew to war against his. Only it wasn't good for business, anybody's business. So O'Leary called for a meeting with me. Sat me down and basically explained to me, that him and my old man had hated each other for years. Said that there was no denying it. But said that it was because of him being jealous over my old dear. Who apparently he'd been seeing just before my old man turned up from Ireland.'

'So was he responsible or not then?'

'Who is it?' called the voice of the intercom as Sleeper noticed the camera above the gate begin to move.

'Tony Henessy,' he said into the small electronic box.

'What do you want Henessy?'

Tony recognised the voice of Vincent or Vinnie as he preferred to be known. 'Just tell your old man that I want to see him Vinnie.'

'Who the fuck's that you got with you?'

'He's safe Vinnie,' he said smiling at the camera. 'Just tell your old man I'm here.'

'You realise, just how fucking early it is?'

'Sorry to disturb your beauty sleep Vinnie,' he laughed.

'Just go and meet him at the gate,' snapped the voice of authority in the background. 'And make sure you search both of them.' They heard the voice say as the intercom went dead.

'So was it him or not?' asked Sleeper.

'It was and it wasn't,' he replied holding onto the gates staring into the grounds. 'It was all of them that had put out the contact of my old man. And believe me Sleeper.' He turned and stared directly at Sleeper. 'Back then, there was no way that I could have gone up against all of them.'

'You let it go then?'

'Not exactly,' he told him. 'Let's put things this way. Me and O'Leary called a truce that night between the two of us. We've personally had no trouble between me and him since then. But only me and him that is. As for the rest of them,' he smirked. 'Let's just say that it may have taken me a good part of fifteen years to complete. But their ain't none of them lads still running what they were back then. I realised through going to war with O'Leary, that too many bodies were dropping. And that just ain't very wise. The others were becoming stronger and stronger as they let O'Leary take the blame. We realised this, that night. So since then, piece by piece I took a little more away from them. They never even knew what was happening to them. It's also the reason that I left old man O'Leary alone. At the end of the day it was him that made me realise where I was going wrong.'

Sleeper grinned at him, acknowledging the intelligence of the man before him. Liking him more and more as the time passed them by. 'I see why you and Prey got along so well now.'

'He was a good lad,' he smiled. 'I always had the time for Prey. He was one of the best lads that I knew. Chopper too.'

'So what did you mean, if Vinnie had been around?' he asked as they watched the small group of four lads making their way down to the gate.

'Vinnie ain't at all reasonable like his old man was,' he said nodding at the crowd. 'He's the one in the middle. Him and his lads just loves this gangster shit. He feels, even though, he'd never admit to the old man that is. But he thinks that the old man

166

was soft back then. He thinks that if the old man had taken care of me back then. Then it would have left the way open for him.'

'He looks nice,' smirked Sleeper at the man approaching with the large scar running the length of his left hand side of his face.

Tony smiled broadly. 'Well I had to put an end to all the malarkey he was causing when the old man was doing his bird,' he said running his finger down his cheek to tell Sleeper that it was he that had put it there. 'Like I said, me and he old man called a truce. That little fuck just wouldn't listen and tried against his father's knowledge whilst he was on the inside to have a go at taking some of my business for himself. So I showed him just why that would never happen.'

They both smiled knowingly at one another as Vinnie approached the gate with a small black box in his hand. Pressing the button, the gates began to electronically open themselves.

Vinnie was quite short in height. But in no way did that deny him his size. He was a big lad, who obviously worked out. Although, Sleeper imagined that it was mainly steroid abuse. He was dressed in black trousers and a matching black shirt. Sleeper recognised the clothes as being Moshino, and despite his large physique, they fitted him well. He noticed that the other three with him were dressed similar and he heard Tony's words of 'they just love this gangster shit.'

He couldn't help but smile at the man before him. Taking in the other three. Sleeper could see that beneath their shirts, were bulges at the waist bands of their trousers. Indicating that they were certainly armed.

'What the fuck are you doing here at this time of the day Henessy?' asked Vinnie stood before him. He looked slightly comical against the size and bulk of Tony, although it was clear that he showed no fear to the other mans size.

'We need to speak with your old man,' he answered staring down at Vinnie. 'We've got some important shit that we're looking into. Possibly the old man could help us.'

'Why the fuck would he want to do that?' he sneered.

'Because he ain't a complete arsehole like you Vinnie,' he answered, smirking right back in his face.

Ignoring the insult he glanced at Sleeper. 'And just what the fuck are you doing bringing niggers to my father's door Henessy. You know just how he feels about them.'

Sleeper smiled nonchalantly at the man, ignoring the blatant attempt to rattle him.

'Just take us to the old man kid,' said Tony, adding the little insult of his own. Holding his arms wide, in order to let himself

be searched he nodded at Sleeper, who staring coldly at one of the other men stood before him.

'No need for that,' said Sleeper reaching into his Armani suit jacket. 'You'll only this.' He produced his Glock Model 21 .45 ACP. The silencer had been removed. But it still looked deadly.

The guy took the handgun and looked at Vinnie. 'Whilst you're at it,' Sleeper continued bending down to his ankle. 'You better take this as well.' Handing over switchblade with a little smile upon his face.

'Anything else we should know about?' asked Vinnie, staring coldly at him then back to Tony. 'Just who the fuck have you brought here?'

'Someone who is obviously very cautious Vinnie,' he laughed then looked at the other three stood there, fingers twitching at the bottom of their shirts nervously. 'Just cautious like you guys are here.'

'Just let them the fuck in will you Vincent,' called the voice from the intercom. 'I becoming tired of this macho bullshit. Just bring them up here... Oh and Tony, if your little Negro friend,' he said the word as if it was pure dirt. 'Even tries anything remotely funny, we'll be eating his eyeballs as appetisers for dinner tonight.' The intercom went dead once again as Vinnie signalled for them to come with him.

'Delightful sounding character,' said Sleeper, glancing at Tony.

'I told you so,' he replied not even looking at him.

'What is it that you want?' asked Dominic O'Leary as they walked into the dining room, where he was sat eating a full English breakfast with all the trimmings included.

He was clearly the father to his son. They were parallel with one another in every way. He was just an older version, who was a heavier build to his son. Sleeper thought looking at the food before him, that he wasn't at all surprised, eating all that for breakfast every morning.

The interior of the house was of obvious expense. Although it was far from being to Sleeper's taste. All the furniture looked to be antique and the house smelt musty. But the perception was what O'Leary wanted, it basically stank of money.

'Just need a chat Dom,' smiled Tony. 'How are you anyway old man?'

'Feeling fine,' he replied tossing a sausage in his mouth.' That was until you turned up to disturb my Sunday morning and I might add, until you refereed to me as an old man,' he smiled at Tony then shook his hand.

'I'm only having you at it old man,' he smirked. 'You don't look a day over sixty five.' He laughed, easing the tension in the room.

'Sit down you cheeky little bastard,' he said, smiling to Tony. 'You want some breakfast?'

Tony noticed that the offer of the seat or the breakfast hadn't been directed at Sleeper also, who up until now hadn't spoke a word. O'Leary merely glaring his unjustified hatred towards him.

'It's alright old man,' said Tony, pulling the chair back, offering it to Sleeper who sat himself down. 'I've had Chinese already.'

Dominic stared from Sleeper unbelievably to Tony then to his son. Who appeared to be a perplexed by the fact Sleeper was sat at their dining room table, 'You had Chinese for breakfast?' asked Dominic, doing his utmost to ignore staring directly at Sleeper.

'Something like that,' he smiled, then turned and glared at the three men stood by Vinnie.

'You stay,' Dominic said to his son, realising what Tony was doing. 'Tell your goons to leave now.'

Vinnie did as he was told then seated himself, beside his father at the head of the table. 'So what brings you out 'ere Tony?'

'Everybody knows that you're the king of smut Dom,' he said. 'But we want to know of you know anything of smut with children in it?'

'Not my game,' he replied casually. 'You should know better than that Tony.'

'I said that to my man here,' he said. 'But he insisted that I still bring him here to ask you himself.'

'You looking to buy kiddy smut pervert?' asked Vinnie, glaring at Sleeper.

'No,' he replied coldly. 'I'm looking for the man who's heading the operation. I want the one who is responsible for using and abusing these children in such a fucked up way.'

'What for?' asked Dominic, still stuffing the greasy food into his mouth.

'That's my business,' he answered.

'Look Dom,' said Tony. 'All we want to know is whether or not you know anything or anybody in that department who may be able to help us here.'

'What's your interest here Tony?' he asked, scooping his piece of toast through the runny yolk before him.

'It's to do with those kids that have been going missing,' he told him.

'What about them?' he asked, pausing with a sausage stuck to the end of his fork.

'We heard that they were being used in some paedophile ring Dom,' he said.

'How do you know that Tony?' he asked throwing the sausage into his mouth. 'From what I've heard on the news. Is that they haven't even found them kids yet.'

'Let's just say that my guy here,' he said glancing at Sleeper, 'found it out and it's led him to travelling up here to look for the one responsible. I happen to agree with his beliefs on finding this pervert. Therefore I have made it my business to help him in every possible way that I can. And that old man is why I am here this morning.'

'So who is it you're looking for?' asked Vinnie curiously.

'Some creep known as the Pied Piper,' said Tony.

Both Dom and Vinnie stared at one another. 'Never heard of anybody called that before. Is that the name of the guy or is it the name of whatever thing he's running?' asked Dominic staring at the two of curiously.

'We're not to sure,' said Tony. 'All that we know is that there was a bunch of other kids that went missing in London. Only somehow it kept its way out of the papers. Now the guy, who was taking them, has been taken care of. Only before he was he said that the one responsible was known as the Pied Piper. He also said that he was from Manchester.'

'You know anything about anybody known as the Pied Piper, Vinnie?' Dominic asked his son who dropped his head and shrugged.

'Do you know something or don't you kid? Was that a yes?' asked Sleeper, 'Or was it a no?'

'Fuck you nigger,' he snapped. 'No ones talks to me like that. Especially in my own home.'

'Vincent,' warned his father. 'Do you or don't you?'

'No,' he replied staring coldly at Sleeper. 'Why the fuck would I know anything about kiddy porn.'

'What about any of our more less than savoury associates Vincent?' he then asked.

'I don't know,' he told him.

Dominic stared back at Tony who sat there patiently waiting. He smiled at him and nodded at him knowingly. Then looking to Vincent.

'What!' exclaimed Vinnie.

'I want you to look into this matter for me Vincent,' he told him.

'Fuck that,' he snapped. 'Why the fuck should I do anything to help these two here.'

'Because I'm telling you too,' Dominic snarled back viciously at him, making him wince nervously.

Sleeper saw in that instant, the rage that was still boiling just beneath the old mans surface. Knowing why years ago, and probably still today, that he was a force to be reckoned with. Vinnie pushed his chair back violently and stormed off out of the room, leaving the three of them alone.

'You have to ignore him,' he said looking at Tony. 'Although you're the last person I have to tell that to Tony.'

'Will you look into things for me please Dominic?' he asked. 'For old times sake eh.'

The old man laughed. 'For old times sake my arse,' he scoffed. 'But don't worry Tony. Vincent will look into it, whether he wants to or not.'

'Thanks a lot old man,' said Tony rising from the chair, indicating to Sleeper that it was time to leave.

'Thank you,' said Sleeper.

'I ain't doing it for you,' he snapped back at Sleeper who merely smiled back at him. 'I'll be in touch of I can find anything out for you Tony.'

'Thank again old man. Sorry to have disturbed you on a Sunday,' he said.

'Sure you are,' he replied without looking up from his plate. With that the two of them turned and left the dining room.

Sleeper was returned his belongings at the front door. The bullet cartridge handed to him separately as he smiled at the guy. Then they were left alone, to walk back down the driveway, with just one of Vinnie's sidekicks watching them as they did so.

'What do you think?' asked Tony as they came upon the gates that were automatically opening.

'Delightful character,' smirked Sleeper, as the two of them laughed.

SEVENTEEN

'You alright Rachel?' asked Tony, as he walked into his living room with Sleeper and Eazy trailing in behind him.

He'd taken both of them back to his house after their meeting with O'Leary. And was shocked to see his sister sat there, visibly upset.

'What's happened?' he asked concerned, as he bent down to her, placing his hands on her thighs. Looking into her dark bloodshot eyes, it was evident that she'd been crying. 'What's wrong kidda?'

Rachel stared from Tony to the two other men, of whom she had never seen before. The big one matched, no that was wrong, he was in fact bigger than even her brother. But despite his size and obvious strength, she tell that he had a friendly nature about himself.

As for the other one stood in the doorway. He was tall, dark, with a slight Oriental appearance. She could tell by the way his dark, inquisitive eyes constantly darted about, taking everything in that there was something very dangerous about the man.

She wasn't quite sure what it was, but there was something about him that sent a chill through her. Not that it worried her though. Because despite his mysterious appearance, there was something also, as strange as it may sound, very endearing about him. She found herself immediately curious about him, and wasn't quite sure why that was.

'It's alright Rach,' said Tony, following her eyes and glancing at Sleeper and Eazy. 'This is Sleeper and Eazy. They're good friends of mine from London. They're looking into the missing kids also. In fact we've got alot to tell you Rach. But first things first Rach, what's got you so upset?'

'Maybe we should...' said Sleeper, indicating that they were about to leave.

'No, it's alright. Please stay,' said Rachel. 'I'm sorry. You'll have to excuse me.'

'What the hell has happened Rachel?' asked Tony.

'I got a phone call from Hunter last night,' she said staring blankly at him. 'She asked me to come and take a look at a crime scene for her.'

'What for?' he asked. 'I thought that you was going to leave all of that alone for now. I thought that you helping Hunter with the Cartwright girl was going to be enough.'

'It's Gabriel,' she told him as his face dropped.

'He's back,' he said, sitting himself on the floor before her, dropping his head into his hands.

'Who's Gabriel?' asked Eazy, sitting himself down on the sofa.

'Gabriel is the killer who took the lives of my husband and daughter last year,' she said looking from him to Sleeper.

Sleeper was taking in every detail about the woman before him. She was extremely attractive, with her mane of red hair that was tied casually away from her face. Her clear blue eyes, which even though they looked tired and sore, were beautiful to look at. Her pale skin suited her overall appearance. Sleeper could tell that, even though she was sat down, she was easily six foot in height.

'That's completely fucked up,' sighed Sleeper. 'I don't quite know what to...'

'It's alright,' she smiled at him. 'I think that I've heard enough apologies to last me a life time. I wouldn't mind, but half the time, people ain't even sure what they're sorry for.'

'You heard what happened last year?' asked Tony. 'Didn't you Sleeper. You know about this fucking psycho, who killed my little niece and brother-in-law.'

'Chan told us about it,' he replied, sitting himself down at the dining room table by the door. 'We'd heard about it anyway though. I think that just about everybody heard about it. Chan said that they still hadn't caught the killer. Is this the first time that he has struck again?'

Rachel nodded her head at him. 'It was just so awful Tony. He's killed all of them this time round. The husband, the wife and their little boy.'

'Jesus,' he shook his head. 'Who were they Rach?'

'It was Otis Fairchild and his family,' she replied.

'Fairchild the brief,' he was shook by the news. 'I can't believe it.'

'You knew him?' asked Eazy.

'He represented a few lads that I know,' he answered. 'Let's just say that I put work his way over the years.'

'Have they any idea just who this killer is?' asked Sleeper.

Rachel shook her head at him. 'Both Tony and I have been investigating into it ourselves over the past twelve months. The closest we got, was a lead telling us that the killer's name was Gabriel. The lead, as it turned out. Was not to be our killer. Although it would appear that the name Gabriel was significant. He signs what he considers to be his works of art Gabriel. He'd signed his so called work of art again last night.'

'What do you mean by,' asked Eazy, 'he signs his work of art?'

'Just that,' she sighed deeply. 'He's not just killing these people. He's presenting them too us in such a way that he considers it to be a work of art.'

'Did he...' Tony hand went to his heart as Rachel nodded.

'He took their hearts again, yes,' she shook her head as the images came back to her. 'He left the doves behind too.'

'Why's he taking their hearts?' asked Sleeper curiously. 'And why is he leaving doves behind?'

'He's a trophy taker,' she told him. 'He feels that he needs to take something from the murder itself. Something that he can keep close by to remind him of what he did that night. By leaving the doves behind he feels that he's made some kind of trade. The doves are some kind of angelic reference.'

'Why angelic?' asked Sleeper, curious to know more.

'The work of art that he's presenting to us, has angelic references,' she said. 'Also his name Gabriel is another reference to his beliefs.'

'Which are?' asked Sleeper.

'This may sound a little crazy to you,' she said.

'Believe me,' he smiled at her. 'After all that I've heard or witnessed this week. It shouldn't be that crazy sounding.'

'He seems to believe for whatever reason,' she said, whilst shaking her head, 'that he is the archangel Gabriel.'

'The one that fell from grace?' he asked.

'That's the one,' she answered. 'Gabriel was one of the first angel's to be tempted by Satan. It would therefore appear that he's carrying out Satan's work here on earth. There were biblical references at both crime scenes. I recognised some of his scrawlings last night as references to the devil himself.'

'What other angelic references are there?' asked Sleeper.

'Using the victim's hearts as a substitute for a paint brush. He writes brief references from the scripture. Old and New

Testament. Plus he draws illustrations on the wall,' she told him. 'He paints wings spreading from the male victim who in both cases were positioned against the wall. In the first murders. He bound and gagged my husband, Peter, against the wall. Binding him to the wooden bed frame. His arms were outstretched as if he'd been crucified. Then after sexually violating the victims, he slices them open and removes their hearts.'

'What kind of sick fuck is this?' exclaimed Eazy, shaking his head at the news.

'He also positioned my daughter,' she let the tears roll down her face as she spoke, 'as if she was praying for forgiveness.'

'And he did the same last night?' asked Tony.

'He took his time last night,' she wiped her eyes, as Sleeper handed her some tissue from the coffee table. 'Thank you. He's trying to perfect his crime. He'd nailed the husband to the wall. Once again as if he'd crucified the victim in some kind of perverted twisted ritual. Again the wings had been drawn on the wall.'

'What about the wife and child?' asked Tony, still sat on the floor.

'He sliced open the wife's back,' she said. 'More than likely whilst he was sodomising her at the same time. Then he positioned her, at the feet of her husband. He had her holding onto his legs as if begging that he take her with him. The doves wings were protruding from her back, as if she did indeed, have wings like the ones he'd illustrated on Otis Fairchild.'

'Don't tell me that this sick puppy does the same to the kids?' asked Eazy, the obvious look of disgust on his face.

Rachel sniffed, wiping her nose, as she nodded her answer.

'He also rapes the children, in the same way?' asked Sleeper. 'Jesus Rachel, I know you said that you was sick of apologies. But I'm so – so sorry.'

'Where was the child?' asked Tony.

Rachel had more tears rolling freely as she thought to the image of the child. 'He positioned the boy on top of the wardrobe. Nailed his hands to the wall and drew what was obviously supposed to be a bow and arrow in his hands. He even drew arrows coming from the bow.'

'Like cupid?' asked Sleeper, baffled by what he was hearing. 'And all of this is against one wall. Almost as if he considers the wall to be a piece of canvas. That is some fucked up shit.'

'Tell me about it,' said Tony.

'Is there some connection between the victims Rachel?' asked Sleeper.

'Possibly,' she nodded. 'They both practised law. Even though my Peter was a prosecutor and the other a defence attorney. They worked within the same field. In fact they went up against one another a few times in the past.'

'What's wrong Sleeper?' asked Eazy noticing his friends face drop.

'My Carol,' he replied as recognition dawned on Eazy.

'Who's Carol?' asked Tony.

'My sister,' he told them. 'She moved up here from London a couple of years ago with my ten year old nephew, Kyle. It's just when Rachel said that there may be a connection between them practising law, it sent a chill down my spine. She's works as an investigator and researcher for one of the larger law firms up this way. It's a good job; she did similar work down in London for years. But after she broke up with this prick of a husband, she wanted to make a fresh start.'

'The law connection may be nothing,' said Rachel staring at him.

'I know,' he said. 'It's just that when you said there may be a connection and from what you've just described, well, obviously it got me thinking.'

'What sort of research does she do Sleeper?' asked Rachel.

'Whatever they ask her to look into basically,' he replied. 'Why?'

'Maybe she'll be able to help us,' she told him. 'It's just a thought. She might have better resources for this kind of thing than we have.'

'True,' he agreed nodding. 'I'll give her a call. Both me and Eazy wanted to drop in on my nephew anyway. So we'll put it to her then. Alright?'

'Sounds good to me,' she told him.

'So are you back on the investigation Rach?' asked Tony changing the subject.

She shook her head at him. 'You know what I want to do to this freak Tony. I told Hunter last night that we would continue to look into the missing girl. But that I didn't want back on the case.'

'I bet that pleased her,' smiled Tony.

'She started tripping out, about why the hell had I agreed to go there in the first place,' she said, 'if I wasn't going to go back on the case.'

'Why did you?' asked Sleeper. 'If you don't mind me asking that is.'

'I wanted to see the crime scene first hand,' she replied. 'I could have gotten hold of the crime scene photographs. But to be honest. To actually be there. To be able to smell the crime itself. To witness first hand the atrocities that have taken place. I know it sounds morbid. Especially with what has happened to my Peter and Becky. But I have every intention of finding this Gabriel. So that meant facing my demons last night. He's not only committed another crime. He's also handed me another chance of finding him.'

'Handed us,' said Tony placing his hand over hers.

'We'll make a trade,' said Sleeper looking to Eazy. 'Tony here has agreed to help us track down the guy that is responsible for the kids that have been going missing. And we always repay favours. So count us in on helping you out in the search for this Gabriel.'

'You don't have to...' began Rachel. 'I mean that's the last thing tha...'

'Yes we do,' said Eazy. 'Sleeper's right. Count us both in.'

'I don't know what to sa...' Rachel began to say again.

'You don't have to say anything Rachel. Besides,' said Sleeper. 'It would appear that your interests in this missing girl might be our only lead in discovering the identity of the Pied Piper.'

'Who?' asked Rachel confused?

'It turns out, that kids from down in London have been going missing lately also,' Tony told her. 'And these lads discovered who was taking them. Only that was just part of the story. It would appear that this guy was using the kids to make films and take pictures whilst he abused them.'

'He told us that the real one that was responsible and behind all of this was known as the Pied Piper,' said Sleeper. 'He said that the kids followed him and his magic flute all the way back to Manchester. That's what brought us up here.'

Sleeper then proceeded to explain all the details of what they had discovered so far. Telling her all about Colin Spencer. Going into graphic detail on what they discovered at his house. In fact telling her just about everything, only leaving out the part of what they did to the guy. Although, he got the feeling the Rachel knew exactly what had happened, only chose not to question his judgement in the matter. When he'd finished he stared at Rachel, who appeared to be deep in thought.

'What's up Rach?' asked Tony.

'That name, the Pied Piper,' she answered.

'What about it?' asked Sleeper.

She glared at Tony. 'You remember what Williamson said about the last time that Charlotte disappeared.'

'Yes,' he nodded. 'Something about her imagining that her prince charming had taken her to a fancy dress ball.'

'Think about what he said though,' she stared at him. 'He said that he dressed her up in a dress for the ball. That she loved it, because they could been seen together as no one would recognise her or know her age. But that's not the bit that had got me thinking. What has, is that she told him that he wore a red and green costume with feathers in his hat. Suppose that he wasn't dressed as a prince at all Tony.'

'You think that she may have been talking about this guy,' said Sleeper, realising where she was coming from. 'That he was dressed as the Pied Piper.'

'But the doc said that it was all in her mind,' said Tony. 'He said that she was a pathological liar.'

'You saw for yourself Tony,' she said sighing deeply, before continuing. 'Just how pathetic a doctor he was. He just let her babble on as he put it. But what if she was actually reaching out for someone to listen to what was happening to her. If you remember, she apparently said that she wasn't to tell anybody his name, because he'd warned her not too. Maybe because he didn't want anybody finding out about him.'

'How many times has she gone missing before?' asked Sleeper.

'According to her psychiatrist,' she said. 'Four or five that he knew of. But that's not to say that she didn't run away before she started going to him. She may have been doing this sort of thing down in London.'

'So this could have been going on for years?' asked Sleeper shaking his head.

'I don't know,' she sighed. 'To be honest about it. It's all a bit of a mystery with the girl.'

'So you think that she could be with this guy right now?' asked Eazy.

'It's a possibility that she's with this guy that she told her psychiatrist about,' she said. 'Whether or not it's the guy that you're looking for I don't know. All that I know is that Hunter claims that whoever called her, told her that if she found Charlotte then she'd find the link to the missing kids. So, let's just imagine that all those other times that the girl disappeared. That it was in fact, this Pied Piper character that she was with.'

'What do you know about this girl?' asked Sleeper.

Rachel then proceeded over the next fifteen minutes to explain just what it was that they had learnt so far. Explaining about the

parents. What it was that they did. What they were like. About how they kept information from them both. Even dropping in the bit about Anabella Cartwright and Tony flirting with one another. Sleeper had smirked at her brother knowingly as he merely shrugged his response. She then told them about Caroline Massey and the harddrive that they needed to gain access to. Finishing off with what Williamson had told them.

'I would say from what the parents obviously kept from you,' said Sleeper. 'And what this wacky doctor told you. That we need to start looking into the family itself.'

'You think that there could be a connection?' asked Tony.

'I'd say that we've got nothing to lose,' he smiled at Rachel. 'Have we now.'

'So you'll work with us on finding the girl then?' she asked.

'I say that if we work together,' he said. 'Then we have got a better chance of locating her whereabouts. I'll have one of my guys look into the London angle for me. See what he can find out for me.'

'It's interesting that the parents kept so much from you,' said Eazy. 'It's almost as if they're trying to hide something.'

'So it's a deal then?' said Sleeper. 'We help one another with finding this Pied Piper. And whilst we're at it, we are at your disposal in whatever help you may need in tracking down this twisted fuck, Gabriel.'

EIGHTEEN

As darkness beckoned, Rachel had left her brother with Sleeper and Eazy at his house in Ordsall. Telling the three of them, that she was going to be all right. That she had needed to do some work with the computer anyway. Further research on what she had witnessed the previous night.

She thought over the events of what had happened the week. Twisting her hair absentmindedly so, as she stood drawing circles into the condensation on the window.

She found herself smiling, as she began thinking about Tony's new associates. The mysterious Sleeper and the huge Eazy. Despite her beliefs that the two of them were extremely disreputable and notorious in ways that didn't bare thinking about. She had found herself, liking both of them immensely.

They had spent the afternoon at Tony's just talking over a whole array of different topics, becoming more aquatinted with one another. She had found them, to be both humorous and intelligent as they bounced wit off of one another, almost like a double act. She could also tell that her brother, who was normally evasive when it came to meeting new people, had struck up an immediate friendship with them both.

Finally dragging herself away from the window, she went to her small bureau. Sitting herself down, she switched her PC on. As she watched the computer going through the motions of booting itself up, she was suddenly startled by the telephone ringing. Pushing her chair back, sighing deeply in frustration of the disturbance, she went to the phone by the window.

'Hello,' she answered abruptly.

'I hope that I didn't disturb you Rachel,' said the voice on the other end of the line. Only the voice was like that of a young boy, although there was an electronic hum to the sound. Almost

as if it was synthesised, programmed, so to speak. She knew in that instant that the voice had been disguised from her.

'Who is this?' she asked, although the chill that ran straight through her, told her what she already knew.

'I think that you know who this is Rachel,' said the voice. 'I think that you've become aquatinted with some of my work. Did you enjoy my presentation to you last night? I bet that it brought back fond memories eh, Rachel. I've waited for you to return home tonight. In fact you've kept me waiting bitch. But no matter. You're here now for me. Just like you'll always be here for me.'

'Gabriel,' she said, her voice almost a whisper.

'Very clever Rachel,' said Gabriel, the child like voice not matching the dark image she'd built within her mind. 'It was about time that the world knew my name. All this Dark Angel nonsense didn't do me justice at all. I had hoped that my name would have been picked up, along with my initial piece of dexterity. It would somehow appear that none of you picked up on it. I had rather hoped that the great name of Gabriel would have been up there with the rest of my kind. But of course it wasn't. Because I am the best of them. The mere fact that none of you so called specialist's caught onto my name is further evidence of just how superior I am to all of you mere mortals.'

'And you believe that you immortal, do you?' asked Rachel shakily.

'I don't think anything bitch,' snapped Gabriel. 'I know, because I therefore am from the all mighty himself. Or at least that's how it used to be. Nowadays, I carry out the work of and for the host of heaven himself. And let me say, that the host of heaven worships you Rachel. But just remember that as much as he worships you, or even spared you your life bitch. That the serpent was always the most cunning of all beasts in which the all mighty made. More cunning the all mighty lord himself even. So you remember just who it was that taught me my ingeniously. For it was the all mighty serpent himself that swooped down and showed Gabriel the true way forward.'

'What is it that you want with me?'

'Oh, I think that you know the answer to that.'

'I don't know,' she cried down the phone line. 'Why did you leave me alive? Why didn't you take my soul, the same way that you took my husbands and daughters so relentlessly that night?'

'I want you to try and find me Rachel,' Gabriel began laughing and the electronic devise that was being used, made a demented intonation to her ears.

'Why me?' she asked again, gaining more confidence from the initial shock of hearing her husband and daughter's killer speaking to her. As she absorbed every detail of what was being said, she asked. 'Why is it that you've chosen me to search for you? Why do you challenge me so boldly? When you know Gabriel that I will find you. And when I do. I will have my vengeance.'

'Because you'll never succeed in doing so,' Gabriel laughed again, ignoring her threats.

'What makes you so certain Gabriel?' she asked. 'You think that because you've waited a year and the police haven't succeeded in finding you that somehow, that means that I will fail in doing so. I don't think so Gabriel. You know why?'

'What the fuck do you know bitch,' snarled Gabriel.

'Because I want it so much more than they do,' she whispered the words down the phone. 'I know what it is, to feel the utmost desire to go out and achieve your twisted fantasies Gabriel. For you have become my fantasy Gabriel. And I will have my vengeance against you, in this life or the next Gabriel. You can never escape my desire, because my desire is so much stronger than yours. My desire will carry me through until the day we finally meet. You think that you have patience, you freak,' she laughed viciously down the line. 'I'm going to give a whole new meaning to patience. Especially when it comes to finding you.'

Gabriel began to laugh at her again. 'You still haven't worked it out have you. I bet that you've waited a long time to say those words to me, haven't you?'

'You bet your fucking life on it Gabriel,' she said. 'And it will be your life that you will pay your marker with, you son of a bitch. I await the day when we will meet face to face Gabriel.'

'Don't you realise that, that is the true challenge for me bitch. Because if it had not been, I would therefore not have spared you that night.' Gabriel began to snigger, taunting her with the cackle. 'That night, you must remember it so well Rachel. For I still hear your screams as I had a waited for your return in anticipation of what you would be confronted with. You remember don't you, it was the night that I fucked your beloved husband. The night I took your little girl's innocence away.'

'Why?' she cried out loudly, allowing the words to get to her as she recalled the images of her husband and Becky.

'Because I could,' Gabriel replied nonchalantly. 'And because they deserved it.'

'How the hell could they have deserved it?' she snapped, regaining composure once again. Infuried at Gabriel's

nonchalance to taking the life's of her Peter and Becky so brutally, without remorse.

'That's what you have to work out bitch,' Gabriel taunted her. 'She screamed for you that night. Little Becky screamed out for her mummy. Only you weren't there. Were you Rachel? The great criminal shrink wasn't there to protect her own family. You were only left to suffer for all eternity in the aftermath of my victorious glory.'

'What about the Fairchild's last night?' she asked. 'Just how did they fit into your warped plan? How did they deserve it?'

'Are you kidding me Rachel! The police are secretly thanking me for that one,' laughed Gabriel. 'They're thanking me for ridding them of the scum that made there jobs, that so much more difficult to do. I have to admit though Rachel. I kind of admired the man. He was almost the like great master himself. As he was your enemy. Prowling around like a roaring lion, just looking for someone to devour.'

'What do you expect them to do,' she said. 'Thank you for doing it.'

'We can't be beaten. We will have our day. The police in general are pathetic. I have to do their jobs for them. But you....' Gabriel paused and she could hear the breathing intensified by the device being used. 'You are my true adversary out there. Not the police. It's why you were spared Rachel. I had to make things a little more interesting for me. I couldn't let things become too boring, could I now?'

'So that's why you chose my family as your first victims,' she said. 'So that you could use me as a pawn in your sick little game Gabriel. If that was the case. Then why have you waited so long to resurface?'

'Like you said bitch, patience is one of life's great virtues,' Gabriel told her. 'Or so they say. But you have not to worry about me waiting so long next time. I have my next lot of victims picked out. Another lot of condemned souls that are to be cleansed by me. A fresh set of hearts, to join my growing collection.'

'Who's the family going to be next time Gabriel?'

'Come now Rachel,' Gabriel laughed sadistically at her. 'You don't think that I'll make things that easy for you, do you?'

'So why have you phoned me you twisted sick fuck?' she snapped impatiently down the phone line.

'I have a gift for you,' said Gabriel. 'In fact Rachel, I have a couple of gifts for you. Just to make sure that I keep you from

losing interest in me. I wouldn't want for that to happen now. So I present two gifts to you.'

'What the fuck...' began Rachel as her computer suddenly chirped out. *"You've got mail!"*

'Ah, I hear that you have received my first gift to you.'

'What's the second thing?' she asked staring at the envelope on her screen, sent through to her e-mail address.

'I'm sure that you'll find it soon enough Rachel,' said Gabriel. 'Let me just say how much of pleasure it's been talking with you at long last. I look forward to the day when we could possibly meet with one another. Only that day, isn't going to be any day soon. Because, believe me bitch. You ain't no where near as clever as you think you are. And all that standing by your window, twisting your hair like the circles you were drawing on the window. Lost in your own thoughts, like tonight. Ain't any way in succeeding to find me. Is it now bitch?'

In that moment, Rachel realised that Gabriel had been watching her from outside. Hidden away by the night's darkness. Pressing her face against the window, so to hide her own reflection, in order to try and see into the blackness.

'Now that ain't going to work,' Gabriel told her as she struggled to try and see someone down below. 'Now it's time for me to leave. I hope that you appreciate the gifts I sent you bitch.'

Suddenly the line went dead. Running to her computer, she accessed her e-mail account. A package appeared on the screen. Computer generated graphics, showed a box wrapped in Christmas wrapping paper. The graphics before her began to unwrap themselves as if indeed it was a present to her.

Rachel dropped into her seat as the screen suddenly filled with a close up of her daughter, Becky, her face taking up most of the screen space. Her mouth covered in black duct tape. Her eyes swollen from the tears that she shed. Her face of innocence broken, as her desperate eyes pleaded with Gabriel who was obviously filming the crime itself through some kind of digital camcorder.

Suddenly the camera zoomed out as Gabriel, using a digital camcorder presented Rachel wit a view of the entire bedroom, where the murders had taken place. Rachel began to sob as she shook her head in disbelief at the images. There, before her was the face of her daughter and the sight of her husband bound and gagged in the background. Their faces in sheer anguish to the torment and agony of the ordeal that Gabriel was punishing them with. The camera zoomed in on Peter. His eyes bulging, as if screaming out for Rachel's help. His head twisting violently

from side to side as the camera zoomed back out. Struggling to set himself free, in order to save the life of their little girl and himself.

Becky's face filled the screen once again. Only as Gabriel had zoomed in on Peter, the duct tape had been removed. Becky suddenly shrieked out piercingly, 'mummy, I want my mummy, please, mummy, help me,' she screamed the words in tribulation at Rachel, as she sat there helplessly watching the sick home movie. The movie that Gabriel had no doubt pleasured himself in self gratification at their tortured souls, that he now presented so banefully to Rachel.

Then just as suddenly as the image had appeared before her, it suddenly disappeared from her view. As twisted as it had been. And as difficult as it was for her to witness, she desperately needed to retrieve the images. If only for one last manifestation.

'No, no, where are you,' she wailed audibly at the screen, that had now returned to the main Windows backdrop. Clicking keys frantically, trying in sheer desperation to retrieve the image that had just been there so tauntingly.

Suddenly, the only sound to be heard from her computer was the demented laughing of Gabriel. The same electronic synthesised laugh she'd heard down the phone line. He was somehow gaining access to her computer through the modem. And in doing so, Gabriel was blatantly laughing right back at her.

She hadn't had a drink in long time. It wasn't that she had been an alcoholic before. But there had been a period after the deaths when she came to rely heavily on booze to numb her senses. Only none of that mattered right now, for right this moment, as the laughing continued to taunt her. She so desperately needed that drink.

Dashing through to the kitchen, Rachel grabbed the freezer door below her fridge. Knowing that she'd saved a bottle of Absolute Vodka in there.

Yanking the door, almost from its hinges. She abruptly stopped herself, as she spotted something along side of the bottle. A strange commodity, which had not been there before.

It was a clear plastic freezer bag. She could tell that it hadn't been placed in there that long as there was steam rising from the bag. She also knew two other things. One she hadn't placed the bag there. And two – whatever was inside of the bag, was an organ of some kind. The demented laughing from the living room was still there. She hadn't dared switching the computer

off, for fear of losing the filmed documentation, which had been sent to her by Gabriel.

Staring at the bag, she could hear Gabriel's voice inside of her head saying *'two gifts for you.'* Knowing in that instant, that was what Gabriel had meant by, *'I'm sure that you'll discover the second gift shortly.'*

Pulling open the kitchen draw, she rooted through the utensils until she came to an old pair of rubber gloves. Slipping them on, she reached into the freezer as carefully as possible, doing her best to ignore the laughing. She carefully removed the bag.

Setting it down on the kitchen table. She sat herself down and let the tears tumble down her cheeks, as she stared at the heart within the bag. And she knew in that instant, without there having to be any kind of medical examination in order to prove it so, that it was Becky's heart the Gabriel had sent to her.

It had been Gabriel's sick idea, of a gift. Gabriel said that it been in order to make sure she didn't lose interest in the case. That, by sending her the digital images she longed to see again. And, sending her, her daughter's heart. That she would keep looking for Gabriel.

But what Gabriel should have realised. Was that she would never lose interest in discovering the identity of Gabriel. That she would continue to seek out the one who believed them self to be the archangel, Gabriel. Even if it took her to the end of her days. Only that wasn't part of her plan either. He'd fuck up soon enough, and she would be the one who would recognise the mistake when it happened. And she'd be ready to strike back with sheer vengeance, parallel to what had been taken from her.

She hadn't even realised that the laughing had now stopped. She been lost in thought, as she'd sat there staring at Becky's heart before her.

Rachel had immediately put the call through to Hunter on her mobile. Explaining what had occurred. Hunter had arrived within half an hour. Andrews and a team of forensics were not far behind her. They took to the heart to be examined. And Hunter and Andrews took Rachel down to the station whilst forensics began the task of going over her apartment with a fine tooth comb.

Sitting in Hunter's office in the city centre. Rachel stared blankly at her friend behind the desk. Shaking her head at what had taken place as she explained in detail what he'd said to her. Explaining once again about some of the biblical references that Gabriel made. Very subtle in the way he slipped them into

conversation. Andrews appeared in the office, with three coffees for them. Handing the steaming mug to Rachel. Then sitting himself down on the edge of the desk.

'Thanks,' mumbled Rachel.

'What the hell is going on kid?' asked Hunter. 'Why has the killer seemingly chosen you to interact with?'

'Gabriel said that I was his true adversary,' she told them both.

'So he does consider himself to be Gabriel?' asked Andrews, as Rachel nodded.

'The voice was electronic, computer generated,' she told them sipping the coffee. 'It was a high pitched voice. Almost like it was a child speaking to me. He told me that the police would never discover his true identity. But he must have disguised his voice for a reason. Or maybe he just did it, because it was taunting to me to have a child's voice tell me things that he'd done. The crimes he'd committed, so gloatingly so. Plus he kept switching from referring to me as Rachel, then as Bitch almost as if he wasn't sure whether or not he actually liked me or not.'

'We need to put a trace on your line at the apartment kid,' said Hunter lighting a cigarette, tossing the packet to Rachel who shook her head. 'Also on your mobile kid. When this freak calls back. We will get a trace on him.'

'He won't call back,' she said. 'Especially when he knows that you've put a trace on it.'

'How the hell is he going to know that we put a trace on it?' asked Hunter.

'Possibly the same way he knew about me stood by my window tonight,' she sighed. 'Possibly the same way he waltzed into my apartment and left my daughter's heart behind for me to discover. Or possibly the same way that I very much doubt that you'll find a trace to the images he sent through to my e-mail address.'

'Back up there for a sec kid,' said Hunter, staring at her. 'What did you mean by the way he saw you by the window tonight? Did you see him outside of your place tonight?'

Rachel shook her head at Hunter. 'But he was there alright. He described what I'd been doing. Just subtle enough hints for me to know that he was out there watching me. He's obviously been watching me for a while. He knowledgeable of my movement's. Enough for him to have broken into to my apartment. And to have done what he achieved tonight.'

'Then we're putting you under twenty four hour police protection,' said Andrews.

'Not a chance,' replied Rachel.

'It makes sense kid,' said Hunter, pulling thoughtfully on her cigarette. 'Plus it may give us a better chance at catching this guy.'

'Fuck that Hunter,' she snapped. 'I ain't going to be your bait for this psycho.'

'What,' she snapped back at her. 'And you think that you're going to be safe out there on your own?'

'I won't be on my own,' she stated.

'Oh that's great kid,' sighed Hunter shaking her head at her. 'So now you're going to rely on your Tony to protect you eh?'

'It would appear, that it has kept Gabriel at bay so far,' she smiled.

'You don't honestly believe that Tony could protect you better we can,' she said, raising an eyebrow at her. 'Do you now?'

Rachel thought to, not only her brother, or the huge black guy that called himself Eazy, but to the dangerous looking one, that was known as Sleeper. The thought made her smile at Hunter knowingly so. 'I'd say that I've got my back covered Hunter.'

'What the fuck does that mean kid?' she snapped. 'And what the fuck are you smiling at kid. This ain't a fucking joke, you know. This is fucking serious. This psycho is still out there and for some deranged reason he's taken an interest in you.'

'I think that I am the one person involved here Hunter,' she shook her head in disbelief at her friend. 'That realises that this isn't some kind of a joke. I mean just what the fuck has this Gabriel taken from you? Or you Mike?'

'That's not what I...' Hunter began.

'I don't give a fuck what you meant Hunter,' she snapped back at her. 'All that I know is that if you should be certain to find this killer first. Before... well... before. All I'll say is that I can't be held responsible for any action taken, if I find him first.'

'There you go with that vigilante bullshit again kid,' said Hunter. 'I've already told you that if you do anything stupid here. Then I won't, as much as I'd like to kid, but I won't be able to help you out of what ever mess you get yourself into.'

'And I've already told you Hunter,' she said. 'That, that's the last thing that I'd expect you to do. Like you've said. He's picked me out for some purpose. He told me that he believes that I am the only one who stands a chance of finding him. And that is exactly what I intend to do. And the last thing I want is to scare him away with you guy's trailing along for the ride. You do your job. And I will do mine.'

'You ain't officially working this case,' snapped Hunter. 'I could have you nicked for obstruction of justice if you get in our way kid.'

'I don't know what you're talking about Hunter,' she smiled cockily at her sat behind the desk. 'I was taking about the job you unofficially asked me to look into.'

Hunter grinned at her. She knew that Rachel had just turned things around on her. 'Touché kid,' she said. 'Just don't start getting to big for your boots kid. If I find you obstructing or holding out on me in any way with this Gabriel character. Then I will have you nicked. And I will not hesitate. No matter how good a friend you are.'

'Will that be all,' she said rising from her chair. 'Because if it is. I'll be going now.'

'You can't go back to your apartment until they've finished in there,' said Andrews.

She tossed her keys at him. 'Just make sure that they lock up when they are done, will you,' she opened the office door and tuned to face them both. 'Just make sure that you catch him first Hunter. Before he kills again. Because believe me. He's getting a taste for this kind of thing now. And he will strike again. He told me so in his very own words that he'd already chosen his next targets.'

With that she was gone, the door slamming behind her as she strode down the deserted corridor towards the elevator.

NINETEEN

As Rachel sat there all alone at her brother's house. She thought back to some of the happier times with Becky and Peter. Remembering the simple days out to the park with Becky, screaming with joy, to be pushed higher and higher on the swings or faster and faster on the roundabouts.

Or even the time they had spent a bank holiday Monday at Chester Zoo. How Becky's face had literally been alight with the joy she felt at witnessing first hand, all the animals she'd seen so many times in her many books.

Question after question. Unrelenting in her enthusiasm for further knowledge to fill her expanding mind with. Wanting to know the differences between the male and the females. Demanding to know how they made the baby ones. Shrieking in delight as her Daddy teased her near the lion's cages. Playfully, pretending to throw her to them.

Rachel smiled as she remembered the holiday in Portugal, the year before all had been lost. The two weeks of not having to worry about anything related to work. Only Peter never quite letting go completely of his office. Constantly keeping in touch, whenever he thought that the two of them weren't watching him. The break had not only been for Becky, it had been for the two of them also. They had both been becoming more and more distant as work demanded so much from the two of them. Or at least, that was the happy medium that they both preferred to place the blame.

But they hadn't really achieved anything over those two weeks. In fact as she remembered it. They had only slept with one another, once over the two week period. But she hadn't minded at the time, as Peter appeared to be spending quality time with

Becky. And she loved to see the two of them playing together so joyfully.

As her thoughts drifted, she let her mind fill with images of Becky and her alone together.

Times spent at Saturday afternoon matinees. The latest Disney movies or Robin William's ones, like Flubber. She loved watching movies. She also loved playing games with one another at home. Always games where she could learn something new. Rachel had been so proud of her daughter's enthusiasm for knowledge.

It had been parallel to hers as a child. Maybe even more so, as Rachel's always went unnoticed to everyone, even her own mother. It had gained the same encouragement that Becky's had. Not that she had blamed anyone for this. In fact, after the deaths of her mother and father, it had probably been her one true salvation. She'd always been a natural achiever, much to the dismay of her teachers, who hated the way she didn't appear to be paying attention. Whilst all the while she silently absorbed any information sent her way. Surpassing fellow students, with her grades always around the A region. Enough to keep her interested and enough to annoy her teacher's all the same.

Tony had always pushed for her do better for herself. Especially after the deaths of their parents. He'd taken it upon himself. Even though, he lacked any real high school education himself. He'd been destined, for the life they he had led. And as much as they were opposites in about every way. They both couldn't deny, the unconditional love that they felt for one another. She owed her entire life to Tony, and yet, he would never ask anything of her.

Although, her other brother, Chris, and Tony didn't get along. She loved him just as   much. She knew that Tony didn't really hate his brother. He just found his rejection, since the deaths of their parents, extremely hard to deal with. Well, that and the fact that Chris, was a leading Police Inspector, out in Hong Kong.

She had fond memories of them being close as children. Even if they were constantly fighting with one another. She knew that there was never any true malice in their squabbles. She remembers that Tony was always on the look out for anybody daring to mess with his younger brother. And very few dared to even think about it.

But all of this had been the reasons for Chris moving away as soon as he had done so. He couldn't bare to live in his brother's shadow. Not with the way things were heading for Tony. He would have had to live the same way as Tony was living.

Knowing that Tony was bound to step into the father's shoes. And she knew better than anybody that, that just wasn't her brother Chris. So, within months of completing school, the army became his second family. And he'd done himself proud. Moving through the ranks, eventually finding himself in the Special Air Service. Something of a dream for him. Only an injury at the hands of the IRA, when he worked undercover in Belfast, left him unable to continue with them.

Broken hearted at the prospect of having to leave the armed forces. He was in a real dilemma as to what exactly he was going to do. As soon as Tony had heard about his brother. He'd done his best to make a mends with him. Therefore on leaving the military, she knew that Tony had been the first to offer him a place along side of him. Further acknowledgement that he didn't hate his brother. Only he had refused. Taking up an offer from an old army associate in Hong Kong, to join him out there.

She stayed in contact with Chris. And knew that he was settled out there, and that he would never return to the United Kingdom. The last time that she had seen him, had been at the funeral of Becky and Peter.

Her two brother's hadn't spoke a single word to one another. Both, way to stubborn to give into the next. In fact, he'd only stayed for two days, before flying straight back out to Hong Kong. She missed him, but she also acknowledged that they didn't have the same kind of relationship that her and Tony had between them.

Basically in Tony, she had someone who would stand by her side through whatever torment she underwent. Like those few months back now, that Hunter had referred to in her office that day. When she questioned Rachel on the rumour she'd heard about them tracking down the killer.

It had been true, in one sense. They had learned about this guy in the search for the killer of her husband and child. And they hadn't intended for what happened to him, or at least that is what they told themselves at the time. Only it was not quite what Hunter thought it had been, for he hadn't been the killer that they were in search of.

Brendan McCarthy, had indeed fed her the information on one of his old patients, Joseph O'Reilly. And the address he'd supplied, had in fact led them to Wythenshawe. Where they had found him to have been living in one of their many council houses. Only, as she sat there thinking back those few months, she clearly perceived all of the events, as if they were happening right there and then before her...

They had sat outside of his house in Wythenshawe. 'Are you sure, about what you found out about this O'Reilly, Tony?' asked Rachel. The house was in complete darkness, as the time was still relatively early at nine o'clock.

'My guy at the station run the check for us,' he smirked. 'Seeing as you didn't want to use your resources ar'kid.'

'We need to make sure that this is our guy,' she said lighting a cigarette. 'If it turns out to be him, then...' she trailed off.

Tony knew exactly what it was, that Rachel thought she wanted to do to the killer of her family. But it was also the reason that he was sticking by her side throughout of this. For if it did indeed, turned out to be the killer, then there was not a chance in hell that he was going to allow his little sister to carry out, what it was, that she thought she wanted to carry out.

He wasn't about to allow Rachel to throw her whole life away if things got fucked up. But, that's not to say that he intended to pay for the crime he would commit. It just meant that he was a lot more experienced in this area, than Rachel would ever be.

'Tell me again,' said Rachel, glancing at Tony. 'I want to hear what you told me on the way up here. I need to absorb the details again.'

'It seems that it had been true. This O'Reilly had been an old patient of McCarthy's for quite some time.' Tony took the packet of cigarettes, and lit one whilst all the while, not taking his eyes from the front door of the house they had under surveillance. 'My guy has done some checking into his background. He says that this O'Reilly is a real wacko. Complete fruitcake. He remembers back then they brought him in for the murders of those two women that he pulled. Anyway, he says that it was like he was talking in tongue or some religious shit. Didn't make a whole lot of sense to anybody. It seems that what the doc said was true. He kept blaming a third party for the murders themselves. But they figured that they had him, bang to rights, as they discovered his blood all over the place. But he claimed that he'd cut his foreskin. Something that a doctor later confirmed to have been also true. But they were still convinced that they had their man. No matter what the doc had said. You see, the police had nicked him several times before. My guy says that he'd been suspected of several other murders before the police had finally nicked him for the killings of the two women in the city centre.'

'He appears to fit the profile of what they were looking for,' said Rachel. 'For us also. Or at least I should say, especially after the information that Brendan McCarthy had told me.'

'He apparently cut the girls up real bad Rach,' sighed Tony. 'My guy says that he didn't remove anything. But that he certainly had himself a good look about inside of them.'

'Like he practising his art,' said Rachel, nodding at the man walking towards the gate. 'You think that that could be him?'

'Looks like it,' replied Tony as they both watched the cautious man enter through his gate.

'Shall we take him at the door?' asked Tony.

'No,' she answered. 'I'm sure that you will be able to get us inside, once he's safely in there.'

He nodded his answer as they watched him disappear inside of his home. The lights to the upstairs bedroom were the first to alight. They could see his silhouette through the drawn curtains. His arms were swinging around, as if he was in anger at something. But they hadn't seen him with anybody as he'd returned home. And the house had been in darkness the entire time he'd been away. They could clearly see him shedding his clothing through the shadows.

'What the fuck is he doing Rach?' asked Tony, bemused by O'Reilly's actions.

Lowering his window, Tony could clearly hear shouting from the house. Observing more ranting and raving, he stared at Rachel in confusion as he shook his head at her.

'Let's go take a look,' she told him, exiting the vehicle.

As the two of them approached the house. The could hear O'Reilly more clearly. He was shouting abuse, but at what or who was of total bewilderment to them.

Walking down the side of the house to the side door. Tony removed a screwdriver and popped the lock easily. Walking through into the kitchen from where the door led them they heard him screaming out, 'you fucking bitch, you fucking slag, try and fuck with me, you...'

Tony sprinted through to the stairway and taking three steps at a time, had reached the landing in three moves. Rachel was trailing as quickly as possible behind him.

Crashing through the bedroom door, they were faced with O'Reilly standing there completely naked with a belt wrapped around his neck, attached to the curtain rail, whilst he masturbated himself frantically.

'What the fuck!' exclaimed Tony, in disbelief.

But it had been Rachel who had spotted just what it was he was masturbating over. For handcuffed to the bed was a young girl, of possibly only sixteen or seventeen. She had been beaten badly, and her naked body was covered in both bruises and what

appeared to be cigarette burns. Her mouth had been gagged with silver duct tape. And from the swelling around her eyes she'd been crying for a long time. Rushing to the girl, Rachel had to force herself from holding her nose. By the smell rising from the bed where he'd kept her hostage, it was apparent to Rachel he'd held her there for quite some time. The young girl had not been set free for any reason it would appear, and that include when the need arose for the bathroom.

'Oh Jesus,' she said, struggling with the handcuffs, as O'Reilly stared in disbelief at what he was witnessing.

She could see Tony eyes darting back and fourth from the naked, beaten girl to the man stood before him. Strangling himself as he masturbated, witnessing his own atrocities. As Rachel stroked the girl's damp hair, carefully removing the duct tape she saw the sudden flash from Tony as his fist, crashed violently into O'Reilly's face. His nose crumpling like paper as he shrieked out loudly.

The second shot, landing flush with his solar plexus as he collapsed to the floor, taking the curtain rail and curtains with him as they both went crashing to the floor. Tony immediately looked outside to make sure that there were no witnesses. Grabbing O'Reilly by his hair, he vigorously dragged the man kicking and screaming as Tony flung him down the stairs as violently as he possibly could.

Rachel quickly searched the room for the keys to the handcuffs. 'How long has he had you here?' she asked concerned voice.

'What day is it?' the girl sobbed.

'Thursday,' she relied, finding the keys in the bedside draw as they both heard the crashes from downstairs.

'I came here with him last Thursday,' she sobbed. 'I thought he was going to kill me.'

Rachel quickly set the girl free and hugged her tightly. 'What's your name?'

'Wendy,' she sobbed, clutching tightly to Rachel. 'He hurt me badly. He raped me and hurt me so badly. Why, why me?'

'It's going to be alright now love,' said Rachel stroking the girls hair.

'I want to get out of here,' she sobbed as Rachel helped her with her clothes. 'Now – quickly, in case...' She trailed off as they both stared at each other.

The banging and crashing had stopped. Wendy had a look of pure panic on her face as they clearly heard footsteps on the stairs.

'Am I alright to come in?' asked Tony from the doorway.

'Yes,' said Rachel. 'It's alright. He's my brother.'

Tony appeared in the doorway. His fists were red and slightly swollen. But apart from that he appeared to be absolutely fine.

'What've you done with him?' asked Rachel as the girl stared in panic at them both. 'This is Wendy,' said added, avoiding using either of their names.

'He's downstairs unconscious,' he replied. Then staring at the girl, 'Now there is two ways we can go about this Wendy. Either, we call the police now who will arrest this freak. He'll probably be out on bail in the morning. Then by the time it gets to court. We'll your guess is about as good as mine.'

'Or we can?' asked the girl still hugging Rachel. 'I don't want anybody to ever know about what has happened to me. I don't want you to call the police. What can you do? You said that there was two ways.'

'Or you can let me take care of him,' Tony said. 'But you have to realise that this can never go any further than the three of us, right here in this room.'

Rachel couldn't believe what she was hearing. Although she knew it to be right. They didn't have any idea just who the girl was. This could cause real problems for them. Looking directly at the girl she said. 'If you let us take care of it Wendy. Then we'll make sure that he never hurts anyone again, ever. But if tell anyone how we helped you then you realise what will happen to us. Don't you?'

She nodded at them both. 'I swear,' she sniffed hugging Rachel tighter then staring at the bed. 'I never want anybody to ever know about this. And I mean ever as well. Just don't let him do this to any other girl.'

'Where do you live?' asked Tony.

'In Cheadle,' she answered. They both knew the journey to be about half an hour there and back maximum.

'Take her home,' said Tony.

Rachel helped the girl to the car. Driving her home, and against her better judgement, she gave her one of her cards, revealing her name. But after what the girl had been through, she knew better than anybody the torment that she would no doubt suffer. Therefore, telling her her she was there if needed to speak about what happened to her. That her door would always be open to her. Wendy had thanked her and gave her kiss on the cheek. Looking as she was, battered and bruised, Rachel watched the girl let herself in through her own front door.

On arriving back at the house she had found Tony, with O'Reilly handcuffed to a dining room chair in the back room. It

was the first time since Tony had dragged him down the stairs, that she had seen O'Reilly. His entire face was twice the size it had been as the swelling from the beating he'd received, had taken hold of him. His eyes were already darkening into blackness and his nose looked have been broken in a least three places. Tony had gagged the man, who looked barely conscious to her.

'Is he capable of talking?' asked Rachel.

'Oh I,' he smiled. 'He's got himself a right foul mouth on him too. As soon as he came too he started with the back chat.'

'If I remove the tape will you answer some questions?' asked Rachel as the O'Reilly nodded frantically at her.

As she removed the duct tape, he spat at her. 'Fuck you bitch.'

The right hook form Tony sent both him and the chair toppling to the floor.

'Just sit him upright,' she instructed as he winced at the sight of Tony lowering himself down to retrieve him.

'Just answer the questions you twisted son of a bitch,' he snapped.

'I know you bitch,' he sneered. 'Your the one who...'

Tony had knocked him to the floor once again as Rachel shook her head at him. Retrieving him from the floor once more she stared at him again.

'I want to know whether or not you're the one who killed my husband and daughter?' she asked calmly staring deeply into his eyes. 'A simple yes or no,' she pushed, as he now winced at her.

'I only wish that it had been me,' he seethed back at her. 'That fucker cost me time. Caged up like some fucking budgie as you all roamed freely.'

Rachel observed the nervous twitching in his eyes as he stared back at her. She wasn't convinced that they had their man. 'O'Reilly... I want to know who calls himself Gabriel?' she said staring directly into his eyes.

'I don't know what the fuck you are talking about bitch,' he spat the words at her.

Tony grabbed the man by his ear and lifted him from the floor as he screamed out in agony at the pain he felt. Even Rachel had to look away.

'They poisoned my mind,' he said in desperation, as Tony dropped him back down to the floor. 'They're the ones you're searching for. But they're not of this world.'

'Where are they from?' she asked.

'They are the taker of lost souls,' he said, now smirking at her.

'Who are they?' she asked.

'They are the voices that instruct me,' he smiled knowingly at her. 'For it is not me that am in control of my actions. I am their puppet, in their sick twisted realm.'

'Who are they,' she snapped at him. 'I demand, that you tell who you believe they are.'

'They are the taker...'

The punch lifted him clean into the air as he crashed into the floor loudly.

'Answer the questions or I will finish you,' scowled Tony, dragging him back up. His eyes were now obviously terrified at the sight of Tony. Adding more doubt to Rachel as to whether or not this was in fact the one they searched for.

'I want to know, why it is that you told McCarthy that their was third person who instructs you to carry out your crimes?'

'They will punish me,' he cried. 'They will seek vengeance for my betrayal.'

'I'll kill you,' said Tony in anger. 'If you don't tell us what it is that we need to know.'

'Don't you realise though,' he said. 'That, that is where they await me anyway. There will be no escaping them.'

'Why do keep saying they?' asked Rachel.

'All of them,' he said, staring at her. 'They are powerful. They are allowed to do what ever it is that they please.'

'I'll ask you one more time,' she sighed. 'Who are they?'

'They are the but one entity,' he smiled. 'For they are all around us, but they are as one. They make me do the things I do. Gabriel says that if I carry out good work then my soul won't be condemned to Heaven. That I will buy my place at the table in the abyss of fiery damnation. Just like your husband and child bought themselves there place along side of Gabriel. For Gabriel is the true one that you search. Only Gabriel will not be found, for Gabriel is the master's favourite.'

'What do you know about my husband and daughter?' snapped Rachel, grabbing hold of him by the face. 'Did you kill them that night?' She wasn't convinced that he had done so. She believed that he knew something of this Gabriel, but was almost certain that it was not his hands that had carried out the final act itself that night.

'I only wish I'd been a free man, to have done so,' he sneered. 'But I was locked up in Altrincham that night for a drink driving charge. But I know who it is that you search for.'

'Who is it?' demanded Tony, grabbing his hair and yanking his head back forcefully.

'I've already told you both,' he smirked; blood was visible on his teeth. 'They are all around you. They are just waiting for the instructions to swoop down and take the souls that they so desire.'

'Enough of this mumbo jumbo crap, you freak,' said Tony. 'I want to know, who the fuck it is, that calls himself Gabriel.'

'I tell you who it is,' he said as Tony let him go.

He sat there staring, from one to the other. 'Go on,' said Tony impatiently.

'Gabriel is,' he stared directly at Rachel, 'the one who fucked your family where they deserved it. And as a reward, they had their souls cleansed as Gabriel took their rotten hearts away with them. But by telling you this, I have condemned myself and they will now search me out, in order to seek their vengen...'

This time he didn't get to finish the words, as Tony lost all patience. Hitting him with a right hook that caught him so hard, both he and the chair flew from the ground into mid air. 'They'll find you in hell first,' sneered Tony.

In the moment, Rachel still swears that everything went into slow motion. Almost as is he hung there in mid air as her mind photographed each expression as he too seemed to realise his fate. Crashing into the wall. The chair exploded away from him, as his head smashed into the solid block behind him.

They both heard the snap as clear as day as his vertebrae shattered. Staring at her brother as they both witnessed O'Reilly slide down the wall, almost cartoon like. Only they both knew in that instant, that it hadn't been any kind of a cartoon. For in that moment, they knew that Tony had killed the man.

'It wasn't him,' she gasped. 'He knew something. But he did not kill them.'

'How can you be sure?' he asked casually, as he stared at the limp form of O'Reilly. Seemingly oblivious to what he'd done, as she stared at him. Feeling the heat of her eyes on him he said. 'No matter what he did or didn't do that night Rach. He deserved to die after what we witnessed tonight.'

Rachel shook her head. 'We shouldn't have been the judge and jury rolled into one,' she told him.

'Whatever,' he sighed, pulling his mobile for his pocket.

'Who you calling,' she asked as he moved her towards the front door.

'Waste disposal,' he'd replied, taking her back to the car...

Rachel suddenly felt that she wasn't alone and looked up. 'You alright there Rachel?' asked Sleeper, who had suddenly appeared at the door to the living room.

She smiled back at him. 'Yeah,' she said. 'Just thinking over old times, happier times. Well some of them were anyway.'

'You know that we're on you, twenty-four-seven,' he said. 'You just give the word Rachel. I know that we've only just met. But I got a lot respect for both you and your Tony. I have the ability to tell whether or not I like or dislike someone within sixty seconds of meeting them. And I also know, that you were trying to work me out earlier on today. And I don't know what you came up with. But, let me just tell you this though. I am one of the best at what I do. It's not necessarily something that I'm proud of Rachel. But right now. I am the best one to have in your corner.'

'I know,' she smiled at him as he turned to leave. 'Sleeper.'

'Yes,' he said, his back still to her, not turning to face her.

'I just wanted...'

He stopped her in her tracks. 'You'll know yourself Rachel, when the time will be necessary for that. And even then you don't need to say the words, for me to know that you mean them.'

With that, he was gone. Only she swore that she could not hear any movement from the hallway. Almost as if it was a cat out there. She smiled to herself at the thought of Sleeper, one of life's true enigmas, she thought to herself.

Her mind drifted briefly back to her thoughts before she'd been disturbed. Rachel had been torn between right and wrong with O'Leary. But if truth was known then she had to admit to finding that it was a relief, to have rid society from scum like O'Leary.

She knows that his death was justified in the eyes of them both. But, for all the relief she felt what she wouldn't admit to anybody but herself, was that she had to live each day with the knowledge of his blood being spilt on her hands. As she stood by, and watched him die at the hands of her brother.

TWENTY

'**H**ello Rachel,' said Brendan stood before her in the very same coffee shop in St. Ann's Square where they had previously met. 'You're looking well, all things considered. You do realise that I've been warned from coming here today.'

She smiled warmly at him, confused at his comment but ignoring it as she gazed into those mesmerising, deep blue eyes of his. Once again, she immediately felt attracted to him. And instantly the remorse washed over her. But, there was no denying that Brendan McCarthy was very good looking indeed. As Rachel noticed the other female's eyes, dining within the coffee shop casually wandering over to him, only confirmed what she saw herself.

'Thank you for coming Brendan,' she said holding out her hand as he shook it. 'I realise things are a little awkward. Are you alright?'

'I'm fine,' he replied sitting himself opposite her, signalling for the waitress. 'But how are you Rachel? How's everything been since we last met?'

'Up and down, as you can imagine,' she smiled at him. 'Everything has been all over the place to be totally honest with you. First off, Hunter asked me to look into a missing girl that she somehow thinks is connected to all those missing kids recently. Both my brother and I began looking into that last week. I was just beginning to immerse my time along with the help of Tony in looking into the girl's disappearance. But, then, well, I'm sure that you've heard. I realise that Hunter has probably contacted you over seeing me. She's probably more than a little pissed with me at the moment.'

'Two coffees,' said Brendan smiling at the waitress, his eyes immediately back on Rachel. 'I know she is. Although she

wasn't too clear as to why. Although, also, I have heard about the second lot of murders at the weekend.'

'Hunter had me evaluate the crime scene on Saturday night,' she said.

'What did you make of it?'

'It was alot worse this time round.'

'In what way?' he asked. 'Sorry, if you don't mind me asking that is. In what way was it worse Rachel?'

'He was a lot more methodical with this slaying than he was with Peter and Becky,' she replied. 'He's beginning to take pride in his work.'

'What makes you say that?'

'By the way he displayed the victims of the family would have taken a lot longer to portray than when he murdered my husband and daughter,' she told him, thanking the waitress for the coffee's that had arrived. 'You should have seen it Brendan. He displayed the entire family in such a way that would have had to have taken a lot of planning. His portrayal bares some significance to his motivation.'

'Before you go any further Rachel,' he sighed deeply. 'The reason I was warned not to be here today. Not that anybody knows that I'm here that is. It was more of a general warning to stay away from you.'

'Why's that?'

'Well... well, you should know that I'm back on the case.'

'I thought that you might be,' she told him. 'It's also one of the reasons I called you. But I don't understand why Hunter has warned you away from me.'

'Well, you see, Hunter says that you freaked out completely the other night. She says that you were her first choice for the investigation. Although I have to honestly say that I still can't believe that she even called you up there. No offence meant at all there Rachel. But well, you know anyway what I'm getting at. So Hunter called me straight in after you'd left the crime scene. Like I said, she told me that the whole thing freaked you out and...' he reached over and touched her hand.

She allowed the contact, even allowed herself to enjoy the contact whilst he held both her hands within his as she thought about the lies that Hunter had told. She wasn't bothered by it. But why she had said those things about her freaking out, was out and out lies. Rachel had assessed the crime scene professionally.

She had been honest and truthful with Hunter. She hadn't let her personal feelings towards the crime become involved in her

assessment. And she didn't blame her for one bringing in Brendan. He was good, even she knew that. In fact it was the reason that she had called and asked to meet with him.

'Don't believe everything that Hunter tells you,' she said as she let his fingers stroke her hand. Suddenly feeling a little awkward she gently pulled her hand free. 'So then, you know that the killer took his time. You saw for yourself first hand, the massacre of the family. And you witnessed first hand the atrocity of the display in which Gabriel presented to us?'

He nodded his response as he sipped his coffee. 'I'm glad that you mentioned the name Gabriel.'

'Why's that?'

'I feel that I must tell you Rachel,' he began, 'that seeing as Hunter brought me back in on the case. Well, that I was forced professionally to tell her of Joseph O'Reilly. I felt I had no choice in the matter you understand.'

'I understand Brendan,' she smiled. She couldn't have expected him not to have said anything. Her only worry was what they may have discovered in looking for him. She was unclear as to what exactly happened after they left that night, only that, as Tony had put it to her that he was going to call waste disposal. After that comment, she had chosen not to prey further into the matter. She found herself silently praying that his waste disposal had been effective enough not to have raised any unwanted issues. 'Have they brought him in?' she asked in a non-committal way.

'Look Rachel,' he said staring directly at her. 'I have no idea what you did with the information I gave you on O'Reilly. And I had no idea, as to whether or not he was still at the address that I had supplied you with.'

'And now?' she asked inquisitively.

'And now,' he smirked knowingly at her. 'Now, all I know is that Hunter has issued a warrant for his arrest. Also that he wasn't and still isn't at the address in Wythenshawe that I gave you. It would appear that his neighbours haven't seen him for quite some time. It would also appear that he hasn't collected any of his social security cheques that he was due. And, it would also seem that according to his neighbours, he was by all means quite a loner. None of them really knew him. They said that he pretty much kept himself to himself.'

'And that's it?' asked Rachel, watching for his reaction carefully.

'Not quite,' he answered. 'It would also appear that one of the neighbours, his next door in fact. Well, he heard alot of funny

noises over a one week period, a few months back now. In fact, he says it was just around the time that this O'Reilly seems to have disappeared. He says that he wasn't quite sure what the hell was going on. But that on one particular night in question he recalls that there was a hell of a lot of shouting and screaming coming from the house. But that it was none of his business. Therefore he never checked if O'Reilly was alright or not. If I remember rightly, he seemed more concerned with the fact that the noise had kept him awake.'

'And what does Hunter think?'

'She can think what ever the hell she wants to think Rachel,' he said. 'To be honest with you. I wasn't going to reveal to anybody that I supplied you with information to that guy. I did what I did that day because of how I acted with you when we first met Rachel. I felt somewhat of the bad guy after that meeting that day.' He suddenly reached over again and took her hands into his. 'If truth be told. And I don't want you take any of this the wrong way here Rachel. But I really like you. Both professionally and, well, and well from what I've seen of you outside of work. I like that side too. That's not to say that I'm hitting on you. And well, it's not to say that I'm not. I kinda feel like some sort teenage idiot that doesn't know what to say here.'

Rachel felt herself blushing. Apart from the fact that she found Brendan McCarthy extremely attractive, he had in not so many words told her that he felt the same way abut her too. She gently released her hands, so not to insult him she smiled pleasantly, trying her best to remain as neutral as possible.

'Hunter asked me what I thought to O'Reilly,' he suddenly said, changing the subject. She could see that he was observing her blatantly flushed. And she was grateful that he'd returned to the issue in question.

'What did you tell her Brendan?'

'That I thought that this guy's fantasy system operated in some perverse way in which he thought that the third party controlling his fantasies was named Gabriel. The only thing is Rachel. I was the one to associate the reference to angels. O'Reilly himself never actually told me that he thought that it was an angel or more to the point, the archangel, Gabriel was the one he was talking about.'

'What made you think that then?'

'The more I studied the crime scene photos. The more I was drawn to the wings and the name in the bottom corner,' he sighed. 'The thing was. I was looking for some kind of a connection with the victims, sorry. With your husband Peter and

the killer. Obviously the police would have been following up on this. But I wanted to cross check everything myself. I'm not quite sure what it was that set it off in my mind. But I had somehow forgotten about the case that your husband had worked against O'Reilly. In fact, and I am sorry to admit this. But I'd been trying my damnedest to figure out just where it was that I knew your husband from. I've worked a lot of cases and given alot of evidence in court before. Because the case had been so long ago, I had forgotten about it.'

'So what set it off then?'

'I worked out what the name was,' he stated proudly. 'I mean, if you think about it. It was obvious. It was right there in our faces for god's sake.'

'What sort of stuff did O'Reilly tell you in your sessions together?'

'He'd tell me that in order to cleanse ones soul you had to remove their heart,' he told her. 'But like I said. He always spoke of these sadistic fantasies through a third party. This Gabriel character. Do you think that it was O'Reilly?'

'No,' she replied abruptly. 'But I do believe that he somehow knew this Gabriel.'

'So you don't think that it was all in his imagination then?' he looked at her like she was the crazy one.

'Not so much that,' she said. 'I believe that through him knowing or acknowledging Gabriel in some way led to his fantasies becoming all that more visual to him. I think that this Gabriel may have even used O'Reilly as an instrument to carry out his own earlier fantasies as part of his build up to carrying them out himself. You said that they found evidence to prove or at least throw doubt into the equation as to whether or not he killed those two women.'

'That is correct,' he said. 'Blood, I believe it was blood that they discovered. It would appear that the police and the prosecution knew of this and chose not to present it at the time of the trial.'

'Well, what if that blood actually belonged to Gabriel,' she proposed. 'But, what if it was O'Reilly that carried out the murders. But it wasn't him that carried out the mutilation after they were dead.'

'What are you getting at Rachel?'

'I now believe that Gabriel was present at those murders. Only he acted as part of the instructive tool that led O'Reilly to killing those two women. But possibly the act of slicing them up was on Gabriel's behalf. The cuts were post-mortem after-all. So that

does not mean that O'Reilly necessarily carried out the mutilation after he'd finished with them.'

'What makes you think all of this?' he asked curiously. 'What exactly did he tell you Rachel?'

She realised that he had said too much regarding O'Reilly. 'I only wish that I'd gotten to ask him,' she replied in best poker face. 'I never tracked him down. I only wish that we'd been able too. Then possibly he'd be able to answer some of my theories himself.'

'How do know so much concerning O'Reilly then Rachel?' he asked suspiciously.

'Let's just say that I called in some old favours from your old hospital in Sheffield and pulled his records.' This wasn't necessary a lie, but it did bend the truth somewhat. For she had in fact had his records pulled for her before they had visited with him. But obviously their visiting with him had led to his demise before they could find out anything more positive than his disillusioned, schizophrenic fantasy that he had been left with of Gabriel.

'So you think that if we find O'Reilly, he could tell us who Gabriel is?' he asked staring at her. She could tell that he hadn't bought the fact that she'd had no contact with O'Reilly, but then he'd never be able to prove anything, so she kept stum on the matter. 'You think that O'Reilly played some part in all of this?'

'Not in relation to the Gabriel's last pieces of work,' she said. 'I believe that they are solely down to him. He works alone now. Or at least that is what I believe.'

'What about the references that O'Reilly mentioned to Gabriel though?' he then asked. 'You think that bares some reference to what you told Hunter on Saturday night?'

'What was that then?' she smiled, knowing exactly what he getting at.

'The stuff on angels,' he said sipping his coffee.

'What do you think Brendan?'

'I think that there is definitely something in what you told her,' he nodded. 'Or I at least think more so now that you've crossed referenced your beliefs on O'Reilly.'

'So you believe that this guy thinks he's an archangel then?' she asked cautiously.

'Hunter told me your entire theory on Saturday when I was at the crime scene in Whitefield.' He laughed a little, and she wasn't sure whether or not he was mocking her.

'And you think that it is a crock of shit,' she said.

'Not exactly,' he shook his head at her. 'I'm sorry. I was laughing at the image of Hunter's disbelieving face from Saturday night.'

'What do you honestly think then Brendan?'

'There has to be some sort of a connection to the illustrations he's left us. Also the fact that he considers himself to be Gabriel bares significant reference to him believing that he's an angel.'

'I've spoken to him,' she admitted.

'I know,' he told her. 'Hunter also told me about what happened on Sunday night.'

She sighed deeply, slouching involuntarily in her seat. 'That fucker is really messing with my head here,' she suddenly snapped in anger as other customers looked in her direction.

'Why do think that he has spared you Rachel?' he asked staring at her. 'I mean, it is now very obvious that you are part of his plan.'

'He said that I am his only true adversary,' she pushed herself up in her seat. 'He says that I will be the only one who stands any chance at finding him. It's basically a direct challenge from him to me.'

'But why?'

'That, I don't know,' she admitted. 'If it was indeed a direct challenge, then why has he waited so long to strike again? Also my husband and Fairchild worked the opposite sides of their game. Peter prosecuted the criminals and Fairchild defended them. It makes no sense. But on Sunday night he was outside of my apartment watching me by my window. He told me subtle enough things for me to have realised that he was there. He told me that he wanted for me not to lose interest in him. He also told me, that he sent the gifts, the first was images of my husband and daughter bound and gagged the night he murdered them. He used some form of a digital camera to capture the images then send them to me in such a taunting way. I can't shake the screams of Becky from my mind. No matter what I try to do.'

'It's exactly what he wanted,' he told her. 'You've become part of his sadistic fantasy system. Your anguish only feeds his desires more.'

'That wasn't the worst part of it,' she sighed deeply, wiping her eyes as she thought back to Sunday night. 'The second gift, well, I'm sure that Hunter no doubt told you about what he sent me as his sick idea of being his gift to me.'

'She did,' he replied. 'Says the results came back as the heart belonging to your daughter Becky, I'm so sorry Rachel.'

He reached over and began stroking her hands. She closed her eyes and allowed the contact. It felt so nice. But at the same time she knew that it was wrong. At the present time anyway, at least that's what she told herself as she pulled her hands away gently so not to offend him, again.

'Just what the hell do you make of all this Brendan?' she asked. 'I mean I seem to be banging my head against a brick wall. I just can't seem to think straight at all. That's why I called you.'

'You realise that I'm not supposed to be talking to you though,' he looked deeply into her eyes. 'Don't you?'

'I know,' she smiled. 'I do appreciate it though. I imagine that Hunter gave you the third degree over me eh? I don't think that she was at all happy about me agreeing to see the crime scene and then not wanting any part of the case. Despite what she may have told you. I evaluated the scene professionally. Only I did it more for myself than for Hunter's benefit. I want to know if I'm heading in the right direction with what I've got so far. Because I've made a promise to myself, that I won't rest until I find this sick fucker and he's made to pay for all the...' She let the words trail away.

'Why don't you tell me what it is that you come up with so far,' he finally said after observing her silently for well over a minute. 'And then we'll bounce it back and fourth with what I've come up with so far.'

'The first thing that is baffling is the true motivation.' She sipped her coffee. 'At both crime scenes there was no jewellery removed from the victims or the house. No cash that was lying around had been taken. I mean Fairchild was wearing a friggin' gold Rolex watch. The wife must have been wearing at least a few grand's worth of jewellery, including rings, bracelets and necklaces. Now obviously this indicates that the motivation wasn't robbery motivated. But I think that there is more to it than that. I mean, I think that Gabriel wants us to know that material possession's have no meaning to him.'

'I have to agree with you there,' he nodded. 'I've gone over this with Hunter. It also adds to the theory of him believing he is an angel. If that is his true belief then he obviously wouldn't need material possessions.'

'Which brings me to the wings that he has illustrated at both murders,' she sighed. 'I know that he signs his name. At least that's what has become apparent to us now. Especially after his phone call. He admitted at being disappointed at the fact that we hadn't picked up on the name and released it to the press. But that is not his signature. I guarantee that if there are more

murders that there will be more wings drawn in the victim's blood. That is his signature that he wants to be known by.'

'So you agree that the way he leaves the scene is his true motivation then?'

'Not exactly,' she said. 'But it is definitely one of his motivations.'

'I agree with you so far,' he said. 'But here is one other thing that appears to have been over looked some what. How do you think he's getting so close to the families?'

'Now that is baffling isn't it,' she shook her head at him. 'No sign of a struggle. No sign of the victims fighting back. And no forced entry.'

'Almost as if he waltzed straight through their front doors eh,' he nodded. 'I've been having trouble with that myself.'

'It's almost as if the victims know who he is.'

'You don't think that that is possible do you?'

'Let's just say that I'm not ruling it out at this point.'

'What about the connection to them both being lawyers?' he asked. 'It must have crossed your mind.'

'It has,' she admitted. 'Although like I said before. They both worked opposite sides of the fence. Gabriel told me that we wouldn't have to wait so long for the next murders. He says that he's already got them picked out.'

'And he obviously didn't supply you with a name and address,' he shrugged sarcastically at her.

'Obviously not,' she smiled, trying her best to see the funny side of what he had said.

'And it's not as if we can keep an eye on all of the lawyers in and around Manchester now, is it?'

'You think that that is where this could be heading?'

'I really don't know for sure Brendan,' she shook her tired head, 'Maybe this entire matter wasn't suppose to go any further than Peter and Becky. But, maybe he's savoured what happened the first time around and has now got himself a taste for this kind of thing now. Maybe that first lot of murders have inspired him to go out and kill more.'

'Do you think that this is spiritual killings,' he sighed. 'Or do you think that there is some kind of ritual going on.'

'Maybe a bit of both,' she shrugged. 'He said that he carrying out the all mighty's work. But I don't think that he was referring to God. So maybe he was referring to Satan instead. In which case. Maybe he's trying to consume people's souls. Some believe if they consume ones soul they will become more powerful. Maybe part of his motivation is to become so powerful

that he can open the gates of hell for Satan to once again rise for the abyss in which he was banished.'

'I need to do some more research into this side of things Rachel,' he admitted. 'What plans have you got?'

'Charlotte Cartwright,' she said.

'The missing girl I presume,' he said.

'The very one,' she replied. 'I need something other than all of this to take my mind from going completely demented on itself. Well, either that or I'm just trying my best to combat the feeling of failure for not being there for my own family.'

'Don't do that to yourself Rachel,' he said rising from his seat. Taking her hands in his he smiled at her. 'I'll keep you informed. No matter what anybody tells me to do or not to do.'

'I truly appreciate that Brendan,' she said holding his gaze.

'Anytime, and I mean anytime,' he squeezed her hands gently, 'that you need someone to talk to, feel free.'

And without another word, he was once again gone, leaving Rachel sat there with her cold cup of coffee and her even colder thoughts, which continued to torment her mind.

TWENTY ONE

'You alright sis?' asked Sleeper, as the extremely attractive olive skinned woman opened the door to the house in Cheadle where they'd just arrived. Tony noticed that it was only her eyes that resembled her brother's, but that all the same there was no denying it was his sister.

'Sleeper... Eazy my big man,' shrieked the woman before them, as Tony wondered whether or not anybody actually used their real names, that when he came to think about it, he hadn't a clue what they were. 'What are you doing up here? Why didn't you call me first? Kyle... Kyle, come and has a look who's here.'

'This is Tony,' said Sleeper introducing him.

'You alright there,' she smiled warmly at him, as her eyes darted back to Eazy. 'Eazy, come and give me a big hug, you bearman.'

Eazy did as he was told, scooping her straight out of Sleeper's arms. 'How's it going sis?' he asked her as he planted a kiss straight upon her lips.

'Still the charmer, I see,' she laughed.

'Uncle Sleeper,' screamed the little boy that ran through the hall, leaping straight up and into Sleeper's arms. 'And Uncle Eazy. Yes, yes, yes. What are you both doing here?'

'We came to see you of course,' laughed Sleeper at the boy's obvious excitement. 'This is our good friend from around your way, Tony.'

'I know you,' said Carol. 'Don't I?'

'Very possibly,' laughed Eazy carrying her through the front door.

'Hello Tony,' said the young lad, Kyle.

'You alright there Kyle?' he asked, as he suddenly felt the loss of little Becky hit him hard; as he observed they way they all were with one another.

'Where do I know you from Tony?' asked Carol inquisitively as they made their way through into the living room that was scattered with toys everywhere.

'I don't know,' he replied sitting down.

'His sister was the criminal investigator or profiler,' said Sleeper, 'whichever one you want to call it.'

'Who?' asked his sister confused.

'The one from last year, involved in the dark angel case,' added Eazy noticing Tony's discomfort.

'Rachel Murphy?' she asked. 'Jeez, I'm sorry.'

'We all are,' he smiled at her.

'It's not where I know you from though,' she smirked at him. 'You've come up in a couple of investigations at work.'

'Sis,' said Sleeper.

'Oh it's alright,' she laughed. 'It was never directly Tony Henessy.'

'I'm glad to hear that,' he smirked back at her.

'What's that in your hand uncle Sleep?' asked Kyle all excited.

'What,' teased Sleeper.

'That package there,' he replied trying to reach for it.

'Oh this you mean,' laughed Sleeper. 'This must be for you,' he told the lad, as he handed the box over to him.

'Ahhh yes uncle,' screamed the young lad as he began tearing at the package. 'Oh yes, oh yes, look mum. Uncle Sleep bought me the new Play-Station.'

'I don't know Sleeper,' she sighed smiling at her son. 'You spoil him too much. He's never off that computer that you got for him earlier this year.'

'He needed that for school,' protested Sleeper.

'Tell him that,' she responded as she cocked an eyebrow.

'Come on Kyle,' said Eazy dropping down to his height. 'Let's you and me set this thing up whilst your uncle and Tony have a chat with your mother. And believe me son; there ain't no way that you're beating me at any of those fighting games.'

'Yeah right,' laughed Kyle tearing open the box. 'You ain't got a chance in hell against me Eazy you big oaf.'

They left the two of them setting up the console, as they made their way through to the kitchen. Tony noticed that it was nicely furnished in a dark pine. It looked very cosy and homely.

'What's wrong Sleeper?' asked his sister as soon as they were out of ears way of young Kyle. 'What's happened?'

'Don't worry yourself,' he laughed.

'What is it Tony?' she then asked staring directly at him.

'We just wanted to ask you for your help,' he told her.

'Oh Christ,' she sighed deeply. 'For a minute there I though that you'd gone and got yourself into trouble Sleeper.'

'Not yet,' he smirked. 'But listen, there is a reason that we are up this way.'

'What is it?' she asked switching the kettle on.

'A couple of things actually,' he told her sitting down at the dining table.

'Whatever I can do,' she told him as she glanced at Tony. 'How'd you like your coffee Tony?'

'Black is fine,' he replied.

'You've heard all about the kids that have been going missing right?' asked Sleeper.

'Jesus,' she shook her head. 'I've been worried sick for the past year with Kyle. He thinks that I'm being over protective, but...'

'No,' agreed Sleeper. 'You're doing the right thing by him sis.'

'He's not in any danger, is he?' she asked looking terrified as she glared at them both.

'Not at all,' smiled Sleeper. 'It's just that we were asked to look into some kids that were going missing from our old estate down in Lewisham.'

'I heard about that,' she nodded. 'Are you saying that the two things are connected?'

'It would appear so sis,' he told her.

'It has something to do with either someone, or something,' said Tony, 'known as the Pied Piper.'

'Pied Piper!' exclaimed Carol looking confused. 'As in the kid's story, Pied Piper?'

'Only this one, ain't just taking the kids away from the town in some story,' Sleeper told her. 'From what we've discovered so far, is that the kid's appear to have been or are being used in sort of paedophile operation.'

'What's your interest in all of this?' she asked him as the kettle clicked off and steam rose wistfully away from its spout.

'I better tell you the entire story,' he sighed, as both him and Tony then proceeded over the next hour, whilst they drank more than a few cups of coffee between them, the story and how everything they had discovered related, including the missing Cartwright girl.

'So how can I help you both?' she asked enthusiastically. 'I want to be able to do anything that I can to help you.'

'We just need for you to discreetly snoop around,' Sleeper told her. 'Also I want you to look into the O'Leary's that we told you about for me.'

'Nice family,' she said shaking her head at him.

Tony stared at Sleeper questionably. 'More the son, Vinnie. He's who I really want you to look into,' he said nodding at Tony. 'The old man seemed to be straight with us Tony. But there was something about that creep Vincent that I felt uneasy about.'

'Fair play,' answered Tony. 'Can you help us Carol?'

'No problem,' she replied taking her brother's hand into hers. 'Anything for the kid here.'

'One more thing then,' he said winking at her.

'What's that then?' she asked as they heard the screaming and laughing filtering through from the living room.

'I want you try and find out what you can on this killer of Tony's sister for me,' he said glaring at her.

'I'll see what I can do,' she shrugged. 'But from I know already, the police ain't even got themselves close to this freak.'

'We'd appreciate it,' added Tony smiling from Carol to Sleeper, as he nodded his appreciation.

'No problem,' she said getting up from her seat. 'But that's enough business for today. Now the two of you make your way through to the living room, so that you can spend some time with Kyle whilst I prepare us all some dinner.'

'Did I hear that you were preparing dinner?' shouted Eazy from the living room as they all laughed. 'About bleedin' time, I'm starving in here as I'm thrashing the little butt off Kyle.'

'Yeah right Eazy,' they heard the young lad laugh right at him as they all shook their heads.

TWENTY TWO

'Hello,' said the quiet voice on the other end of the line to Rachel's mobile phone. 'Is that Rachel?'

'It is,' she replied, recognising the voice immediately. 'Is that Caroline?'

'Yes,' she said, 'I'm sorry that I've called you so late. It's just I couldn't sleep and I've not been able to stop thinking about Charlotte lately.'

'It's alright,' said Rachel glancing at her watch. 'I'm still up anyway. What's on your mind Caroline, apart from Charlotte that is?'

'Nothing to be honest with you. I just miss her so much. It know it sounds a bit soft. But I never even realised how close we were until now. For all her faults, I'd give anything to have her back,' she sighed. 'I was just wondering. Have you had any joy yet Rachel?'

'Not yet,' she admitted. 'Although, I'm actually waiting on seeing someone tonight that may be able to help in some way.' She didn't want to say any more, as she didn't want the Cartwright's finding that she had their daughter's harddrive.

She then found herself glancing over to the far table where her brother was sat with Chan, Sleeper and Eazy drinking and playing cards, and she found herself smiling.

'We've got ourselves some extra help also Caroline,' she told her. 'It seems that there has been kids going missing down in London too. Now we don't know whether or not there is a connection to Charlotte. But that mystery caller seemed to think so. So it seems to be the best angle for us to work with.'

'London?' she questioned.

'That's right,' she replied. 'Why?'

'That's where Charlotte was originally from,' she said.

'Yes,' she replied, 'we know.'

'It's weird though that you mentioned London.'

'Why's that Caroline?'

'I never thought to mention it to you before,' she said. 'It's nothing really. She never really mentioned it before.'

'What, living down in London?'

'Yeah, she was always really quiet if I asked what it was like living down there,' she said. 'But then there was this one time she really opened up about the place. It was this weekend that we spent down there with school last year. You know, going to museums, theatre and shit like that. She really came alive with the place. She seemed to know everywhere down there. Telling all the girls the sights. What everything was. Where everything was. Including some really good clubs that she snuck us out to at night.   Although one of them was a little weird for our tastes. It was this fetish kind of place down in Soho. She just made a joke of it when she took us there. All in all it was a really cool weekend. Then one night when she wouldn't stop talking, all excited, she told me all about this big house that they owned down there in Chelsea. She made the place sound almost magical. But there was something sad there also.'

'What do you mean Caroline?'

'She would be non stop talking about her life down there one minute,' she sighed deeply. 'Then it was as if she'd gone to far with what she was saying and would abruptly stop herself.'

'Did she ever mention any friends or relations from down there Caroline?' Rachel didn't want to reveal that Charlotte did have a twin sister at one time. She's obviously chose to keep that private from her friend and Rachel didn't intend revealing it to her.

'Not really,' she said. 'Everything she said about that place seemed like a fairy tale almost.'

'How so?'

'Big parties that her parents would throw for all the rich,' she laughed. 'She particularly became excited about the fancy dress balls that they held.'

'Really?' asked Rachel thinking about Williamson had told them.

'Yeah,' she sighed. 'You know what Rachel. I never really thought about this before now. But thinking about it now. It was right after we returned from London that Charlotte became a lot more distant with things. It was also around the time that all the stories about her old man being up to no good and shit like that started. I never put two and two together. But maybe that's it

216

Rachel. Maybe she missed living in London. She may have returned back there.'

'That's very possible you know,' said Rachel thinking about everything that the girl had told her. As she thought about things, she thought about the character whose name seemed to keep surfacing, and asked. 'Did Charlotte ever mention anybody called the Pied Piper Caroline?'

The line went quiet for a few moments. 'Once,' she said quietly. 'But it kind of just popped out in conversation. She was telling me about this one time that she ran away before I met her. She said it was with this guy who called himself the Pied Piper and that they went to her old house in London. But then she cursed and swore at herself for revealing his name. She said that she'd been sworn to secrecy over ever revealing who he was or what his name was. To be honest I thought it was just one of her fantasy stories. She was quite the story teller. But I never minded. She was good at telling them... But why do you ask? Who the hell is this Pied Piper, Rachel?'

'I don't know Caroline,' she said. 'I honestly don't know for sure. But his name seems to popping up more and more.'

'You think that this guy is for real then?'

'It's certainly beginning to look that way Caroline,' she sighed. 'But you can't tell anybody about any of this.'

'I won't,' she told her.

'Caroline,' she said as an afterthought. 'I don't suppose you know if they still own that house down in London do you?'

'No idea,' she said. 'It wouldn't surprise me though. I know they all used to take off for weekends away and that Charlotte was always real secretive about where it was that they going. But then again, I just put it down to Charlotte being Charlotte.'

'Thanks alot Caroline,' said Rachel. 'You've been a big help. And if you ever need to talk, just give me a call, alright.'

'Alright Rachel,' she said as it went quiet again. 'Just find her will you. I'm starting to become worried now. She should be back by now.'

'We will,' she told the girl as the line went dead. Although she was thinking to herself, whether they found her dead or alive was another matter all together.

TWENTY THREE

'**M**ind if I join you? You alright there?' asked Sleeper as he walked over to her by the window in Chan's restaurant as she flipped her mobile phone shut

'How did it go today Rachel?' he added, sitting himself down opposite her. The time was close to one in the morning. Chan, Tony and Eazy were relentlessly playing more card games to keep the old man entertained.

But, their main purpose for being there, was a meeting had been set up by Chan, for them to meet this computer guy named Robert, that was to be brought here by Jonah and Kezlo. The only thing was, this guy refused to meet during daylight hours. It was either late at night like this or not at all.

Sleeper had been playing cards with the others. But he'd also been silently observing Rachel sat by the window, absorbed with her own thoughts. He couldn't comprehend what she was going through at the moment with this killer that was known as Gabriel. His only certainty was that for whatever reason, he felt compelled to help her in anyway he could.

'I think that Brendan had pretty much come up with the same as what I had,' she told Sleeper.

'If I can help in any way,' he smiled, 'then you just have to ask.'

'Thanks,' she returned his smile. 'Your help with Charlotte and the missing kids means alot already. How'd it go with your sister today? Tony says that they're a real nice family. I'm sorry that I couldn't make it.'

'Carol and Kyle are fine Rachel. And yes, she is going to help us. She's going to check into the missing kids for us, and also she's going to see if she can find out anything else on the one

who was responsible for killing your... well you know,' he cut himself short feeling a little awkward.

'I appreciate that Sleeper,' she smiled. 'I really do you know. I can't wait until I get chance to meet and thank your sister myself.'

'You will do soon enough. But that's not what I meant, by if you needed help in any way Rachel,' he sighed. 'I've come across some real sick people in life. From all walks of life as well. I've come to know, that you can never take people at face value. But I also have developed a natural ability to be able to work those people out within sixty-seconds of meeting with them. It's become like a sixth sense almost. Some of the things in life that I have done have been really messed up. But sometimes they have been a necessity to do those things. And through that I have this sixth sense where people are concerned.'

'I know you have,' she said staring at him. 'I can see that sixth sense in your eyes Sleeper. The only thing is your eyes don't reveal anything of yourself to anybody else.'

He laughed at her. 'Still trying to work me out eh?'

'Oh I think I've made a pretty good assessment so far,' she laughed back at him.

'And what have you come up with so far Doc?'

'What,' she raised her eyebrows at him mockingly. 'You mean, apart from very dark and very mysterious.'

'Yeah,' he smiled, 'I mean other than dark and mysterious.'

'All I'll say is that you have two sides to you Sleeper,' she told him, holding direct eye contact with him. 'On the one hand, below your cold exterior. You have a very intellectual person. Someone who is constantly aware of his surroundings, no matter where he may be. You're very considerate, as long as it is something you believe in. And if it is something that you believe in, then, well then, you'd give it your one-hundred-and-one-percent. Not a percentage less. Like with these missing kids. You've become involved in something that you wasn't directly involved in, yet it was something that you believed was wrong. Therefore you agreed to help these people. And I know you won't quit until you discover who the Pied Piper really is. I also know that I have you here until this whole thing with Gabriel is over. And I also know that, that makes me feel a whole lot safer.'

He smirked at her. 'And on the other hand?'

Staring at him, taking everything in she said in a very serious tone. 'There is a very dangerous and very lethal side to you that I feel sorry for.'

'Sorry for?'

' Not you, Sleeper. That is not what I meant,' she smiled at him.'I'm sorry for the people who eventually cross one hand into the other.'

'Is that it?' he asked smirking at her knowingly.

'Can I ask you something?'

'Sure,' he replied.

'Aren't you lonely Sleeper?'

'Not at all,' he said. 'I'm not some vampire that only comes out at night Rachel.'

'That's not what I meant,' she shook her head. 'I mean, have you got someone that you're close to? Apart from Eazy over there that is.'

'I have,' he told her. 'We've been together for a very long time now. Since our early twenties. Her name is Lisa.'

He caught her looking at his finger for a wedding band and laughed. 'We've never felt the need. The thought of constituting our relationship with an official arrangement of marriage scares both of us. We both enjoy what we've got and what we've had. The thought of something coming along and ruining that is a little scary to deal with.'

'Do you have children of your own?' she asked.

His face clouded over slightly and he looked a little sad to her. 'She contracted ovarian cancer a few years back. Right around the time we were thinking seriously about it. Almost like God's sick joke on us. Maybe for all my wrong doing. Whatever the reason, she beat the cancer. But, but it left her unable to ever have kids.'

'I'm so sorry,' she told him honestly.

'Yeah well,' he sighed. 'Now I just get to spoil my nephew who now lives up her with my sister that I told you about. And at least I didn't lose Lisa. I don't think that I would have been able to cope with that.'

'Does she know what you do?' she asked. 'Sorry, if you don't mind me asking that is.'

'Even you don't know what I do Rachel,' he grinned knowingly at her.

'You know what I mean,' she said shaking her head. 'Why don't you tell me what it is that you do Sleeper? I think that you should have realised by now through Tony, that I am by far the last person to judge you.'

'I like you Rachel,' he admitted to her. 'There is no bullshit in you. If you feel that you have to say something the there is nothing that would stop you from doing so. So let me tell you

this much of what I did, and still do, kind of. A few years back now a lot of business's that I ran were illegal. Very illegal. And don't get me wrong here either. I'm not trying to justify any of it. There weren't any moral issues back then. Only cash issues. But through that side of business, I or I should say we,' he glanced over at Eazy laughing and joking around with Tony and Chan. 'We lost some very close friends to the business. We can't complain, as it went hand in hand with the business in which we dealt. But when we lost those friends, well, that was the day that I made the decision to seek vengeance for their deaths. I also made the decision to finally get out of that side of business. It opened my eyes a little further than they had been. Made me put things into perspective more.'

'What about the other side of your business?' she asked as he glared at her. 'I'm not stupid Sleeper. I can see beyond the dark and mysterious you, remember. I'm not asking for your admittance here, I'm just wondering how what you just told me affected other things.'

He nodded his understanding at her. 'Let's just say that I became a lot choosier than I had been. On moral grounds that is. I don't want to make myself out here to be some kind of a saint or some other shit. But there is something that you must understand Rachel.' He stopped and stared deeply into her eyes and she involuntarily felt a chill run through her. 'It was the one thing that I was always good at. It was something that I showed a real skill for. If I'd been in the military, I'd of been a bloody hero. Only I wasn't. And that neither makes it right nor wrong. I don't care how you perceive any of this. I'm not justifying any of it to you here. I'm merely laying it out as it is. I don't want you to think that I have no conscience here. Because I do Rachel.'

'I know you do,' she said reaching over and touching his hand to let him know that she understood and was also grateful for sincerity that he was showing her.

'It's just that I have the ability to shut my conscience off when I want to,' he shook his head at her. 'I don't even know why I'm telling you all this shit. I think that it is maybe because I've watched the way your eyes are constantly puzzled when I'm around.'

'True,' she laughed sitting back in her seat. 'Although this piece's together some of the puzzle for me, thank you Sleeper.'

'What about you Rachel?' he asked. 'What made you become involved in the work that you did?'

'As I think you've worked out for yourself, I was always trying to work people out,' she admitted. 'Or more to the point. I was always trying to fathom out why people did the things that they did. It kind of became an obsession. Tony told you what happened to our parents, right?'

Sleeper nodded at her as she lit herself a cigarette and exhaled the smoke. Then taking a deep breath, she smiled.

'I think that it was a major turning point in my life,' she sighed.

'I imagine it was for both of you,' he told her.

'You could say that,' she smiled at him. 'Tony followed my father's footsteps. He also brought me up, which wasn't easy. As curious as I was, I had an uncanny ability to lose myself along the way somewhat. Let's just say that Tony constantly had to step in and put me back on the right track. We have another brother, although it's best not to mention him in front of Tony.'

'Why's that?'

'Because he left for the army soon after the deaths of our parents,' she said. 'Worked his way through into the SAS. But was injured whilst working in Belfast. On being forced to leave the military he left for Hong Kong.'

'Really?' he asked surprised.

'Why do you look so surprised?'

'It's nothing,' he waved her off. 'I've got a really good friend who lives out there.' She could see the smile on his face as he recalled this so called friend. She decided not to question him further.

'What does he do?' asked Sleeper.

'This is why it's a touchy subject with ar'kid,' she grinned glancing over to her Tony. 'He's a leading police inspector out there.'

'You're kidding,' laughed Sleeper seeing the irony in it.

'I wish I was,' she told him smiling. 'So he has one brother working directly for them and me, his sister, also working hand in hand with them. Considering what he does, or did I should say could make him liable for becoming very paranoid.'

'You work a different side of things though,' he said. 'Don't you?'

'I do,' she nodded. 'I'm more involved in helping the police to track down say serial rapists. Taking in all the evidence in a psychological way to try helping the police narrow down their resources in searching for the offender or killer. Obviously I do the same with murder investigations. I've worked with Hunter for a long time now. We have an excellent success rate together.

Much to the annoyance of Chief Mackenzie who for whatever reason can't seem to stand me.'

'Why do you think that she asked you to look onto this missing kid?' he asked curiously.   'That's always confused me somewhat.'

'It has me also,' she shrugged. 'I think in her own way she just wanted me to be actively involved in something. Whether it was official or not.'

'Fair comment,' he said as his eyes suddenly drifted to the top of the stairs. A huge smiled appeared on his face as three lads walked onto the top floor of the restaurant where they all awaited them.

Rachel began to take in the way they looked. One of them, was white, yet had this huge head of dreadlocks that he'd obviously been growing for a long time as they reached their way right down his back to the base of his spine. He was dressed casually in combats and a heavy looking fleece. He had the appearance of a new age traveller, well, maybe no where as near as scruffy or dirty looking that is.

The one next to him looked no older than nineteen, only when he approached them, she could tell that wasn't much younger than her. His boyish school boy looks were deceiving to the eye. Also the neat scar along the bridge of his nose took away some of his innocent looks. He was very good looking, and constantly appeared to be grinning at them, giving him a cheeky, knowing appearance that she liked.

The other one trailing in behind them looked so pale; he appeared to Rachel to be ill looking. His shaved head and black clothing gave him the appearance of Keanu Reeves from the *Matrix*, only not quite so good looking she thought as she glanced at the huge metallic silver case he was carrying with him. This had to be the computer guy that refused to seen in daylight she thought to herself.

'You alright lads?' asked Sleeper warmly, glancing at Rachel. 'Meet a couple of good friends Rachel.'

'This scruffy merchant here...' he laughed at the one with dreadlocks who grinned sheepishly back to him.

'Kezlo,' shouted Eazy making his way over, his face full of glee at the sight of his friends.

'Is obviously Kezlo,' laughed Sleeper as Eazy grabbed hold of him lifting him into the air.

'You alright Sleeper,' nodded the one who had the boyish looks. 'It's been a long time brother.'

'This here,' he grabbed his shoulder and pulled him close, hugging him and taking Rachel by surprise at his show of open affection. 'This is a very good friend of ours, this is Jonah.'

'Hello Jonah,' she said, and then looked to the one still held in the air by Eazy. 'You alright up there Kezlo?'

'This is Rachel,' Sleeper introduced them.

'You alright Rachel. How's it going Tony? Chan?' he nodded at them casually then glanced at the third guy. 'This ill looking mother fucker,' smirked Jonah helping him with his metallic case, 'is the best computer guy in the business. This is Robert.'

Everybody spent the next half an hour getting to know one another whilst Robert set up his extensive array of computer equipment. Once he'd completed setting the equipment up over two of Chan's tables, they then explained to Robert about what it was that they required with the hard-drive and the laptop that had been brought from London.

Robert had gone to work on the laptop first of all and had accessed the laptop's files in no time whatsoever. As both he and Sleeper began to work their way through the files they came upon an assortment of different photographs and even short movies featuring Spencer and so many different children in sexual poses or films that they lost count. Only Rachel couldn't bare to look through what he had stored in the files and found herself walking back over to the window as Sleeper quickly accessed the files looking for clues to the Pied Piper.

At this point, Robert left Sleeper to it and began work on the hard-drive that appeared to proving quite difficult. But then stopping and staring at them all he said. 'Look, things may be a lot easier and a hell of a lot quicker if you tell me what it is that you're searching for. I know it's obviously something to do with these kids that are being abused. And has something, what ever that may be to do with this Pied Piper you've mentioned. But why don't you lay it on the line for me. I'll start to do some of my own searches for whatever it is you're looking for.'

Sleeper briefly explained where it was that they had gotten the computer from and the possible links to the Pied Piper and what they suspected the Pied Piper of. Whilst Rachel did pretty much the same as he did, only explaining that there may be some more sensitive, private material relating to diary's and so forth. She asked him kindly to print that sort of stuff off for her eyes only. She felt that Charlotte should retain her privacy as much as was possible.

'The problem with this hard-drive Rachel,' he said. 'It's not that you can't gain access to the files. The password system here isn't the problem. It's a very simple one. The problem is that someone has tried clear the entire memory of what was inside of those files from the computer.'

'Why would somebody do that?' she asked him

'You tell me,' he shrugged. 'Do you think that it is at all possible that the girl did this before she either ran away or disappeared.'

'I couldn't tell you to be honest,' she admitted. 'Is it possible that her parents did it?'

'Anybody could have done it,' he told her. 'Give me a few minutes to search for where all the files have been deleted to.'

'You can do that?' she asked as he nodded nonchalantly at her.

'It shouldn't be at all difficult,' he told her.

'I'm all but out of leads here,' yawned Sleeper. 'I'm going to join the lads. I need a break from this shit.' He rose, stretching his limbs and went to join the others enjoying one anothers company. All of them were in boisterous moods and it was obvious that they hadn't seen one another for quite some time.

'What exactly is going on here Rachel?' asked Robert after Sleeper had left them both alone.

'We're not entirely sure yet,' she told him. 'All I know is that I was asked to look into this girl's disappearance. And that is, if we found the girl, we would find a connection to these missing kids. Also that they were being used in some paedophile ring. Through all of that, we met Sleeper who had found some connection to this Pied Piper character who we are not even sure exists. So as you can see, we're not entirely sure what the hell is going on.'

'Well let's see what we can find out for you then,' he said and went back to tapping away at the keys skilfully.

'I hope you didn't think that I was being rude by saying that I didn't want you looking at the girls personal files Robert,' she said looking at him.

'It makes no difference to me either way,' he shrugged. 'I ain't interested in the girl's personal goings on. But can I ask you something?'

'Of course,' she replied.

'I've done a lot of work for these lads in the past,' he said and she saw that he was staring directly at Sleeper. 'I don't know exactly what your involvement is here. And it's been a while since I've done any documents for that guy.'

She knew that he was referring to Sleeper. 'He's not going to be a problem,' she told him.

'He never was for me,' he smirked at her. 'But from what you've told me already. If this Sleeper guy, is involved then it will not end happily, and that is a guarantee.'

'From what we've told you,' she returned his smirk. 'Would you want it too?'

He shook his head at her. 'That's not what I meant Rachel,' he sighed. 'I know who you are. And I know who he is. And I may not look as though I am part of the group. But through Kezlo and Jonah I know a lot of lads from around town. And I've done a lot of work for them all. All I'm saying is that I'm quite willing to help you guys out in anyway that I possibly can do. Not only with this Pied Piper shit. But on anything else. The only thing that I ask Rachel is...'

'What?' she shrugged.

'I know that you've got connections to the police. And because of what I do, well, I can't take any chances you know. You may think that I'm some paranoid shit-head here Rachel. And I am after last time. That's why I will only do work through the night nowadays. You see, I can't ever go back inside,' he admitted to her. 'I may know these guys like brothers and I know that they would do anything for me. But I also know that I could never do anymore bird, ever. The first time was bad, but the last time almost killed me.'

'And you consider me to be a liability?'

'Like I said Rachel, I know who you are and that you have close involvements with the coppers,' he told her still tapping away on the keyboard before him.

'Then you also know who my brother is then,' she said shaking her head at him. 'You think if I was bothered at all about things like that my brother would be still walking the streets.'

He realised that he had offended her and immediately ceased typing and stared at her. 'I'm sorry. I never meant to offend you in any way. I'm just still paranoid as hell about prison. It's the reason that I refuse to do any their work through daylight hours. It scared me so much that you'll never see me in the daytime. I wouldn't do it at all, apart from the fact that they pay me top dollar. It also allows me to do whatever the fuck I want, I can stay hidden away from the world. So please, I'm sorry Rachel.' He held out his hand for her as she smiled and shook it. 'No offence.'

'None taken,' she told him. 'Now let's see what the hell we can from these computers.'

Rachel had stayed sat beside Robert as he tapped away frantically on an array of different keyboards before him. They'd been sat there for well over an hour as the lads sat reminiscing over old times spent together. Alot of which, Rachel truly did not want to hear. But she left them to it, as the six of them looked happier than they ever had.

Robert had accessed Charlotte's deleted files almost straight away. She had spent the time reading over an array of different documents that appeared to be constantly spewing out of the printer. Most of it was just school work or old e-mails to friends. Nothing much of interest.

They had finally hit upon the file that had accessed her diary. It had spanned back over the last five years. Rachel had skimmed over the notes that she had typed. She soon discovered that there were chunks missing. That could mean anything from her not bothering to type or the fact that she hadn't been present to type at the time.

Either way it was an assortment of different tales. Rachel now realised what both Caroline and Williamson had meant about her imagination. The diary consisted of all kinds of stories and without even meeting the girl, Rachel was convinced that a lot of them were pure make believe.

The only thing that was bothering her was that there was nothing in there on the Pied Piper. She was beginnings to wonder if he actually existed or not when suddenly Robert sat back and smiled at her.

'What is it?' she asked.

'Look at this,' he told her nodding at the computer screen.

'Oh shit,' she exclaimed as Sleeper was immediately upon them.

'What have you got?' he asked.

'Bingo,' said Tony staring at the screen.

'Pied mother fucking Piper Productions,' gasped Eazy. 'This is it. This is the mother fucker. How the fuck did you find that?'

For before them on the screen was a visual display, elaborately designed with even a logo and motif of the Pied Piper with a winding road full of children following him and his magic flute. Only this wasn't any web site for the nursery tale. This was advertising an array of child pornography to those accessing the web site. The only problem was it was also requesting a password to gain access further.

'How the hell did you find this Robert?' asked Rachel still sat next to him as the rest of them gathered around.

'Through this computer that Sleeper gave me,' he told them. 'I accessed old internet files that had already been accessed. But now that I know how to, I could have accessed it from any system fitted with a modem. Watch this.'

He began tapping away at the keys and suddenly an advert for children's books came up. A whole set of classic children's stories. The website was advertising antique books for collectors. Not just children's books, but an assortment of different reading material.

'This is it?' asked Tony

'Not exactly,' he said. 'This I would imagine is a legit website. Only some cheeky bastard, no doubt the one you are looking for has accessed it and done this.' Punching some more keys brought up the book Pied Piper.

'Watch what this guy has done,' he said as the cursor went to the left hand corner of the page. 'You see that large pixels in this picture look too big.'

'I can't see shit,' said Jonah.

'That's exactly what he wants,' said Robert. 'It's called stagenography. Basically it's what is used to hide encrypted files.'

'What the fuck is it?' asked Kezlo leaning in, to take a better look at the screen.

'Basically if you were not looking for it then you would never have been able to have found it.' Clicking the mouse the screen suddenly shot away, almost like it went was the Millennium Falcon from *Star Wars* going into light speed.

Suddenly the Pied Piper Productions was before them again, along with the small screen in the centre requiring the password.

'Can you access the password?' asked Rachel.

'It'll take some time,' he admitted reaching over to the computer that had Charlotte's hard-drive in it. 'I want to try something else first though.' Tapping away at the keyboard as they were all transfixed on the screen before them. 'There you go.'

The looked to the other screen that he had accessed. 'Where was that?' asked Tony.

'On the girl's computer,' he told them as the same window featuring the Pied Piper had appeared.

'You mean that she had accessed the same thing?' asked Sleeper.

'It would appear so,' he said. 'And from the amount of time spent on the website, I'd say that she had access to the password.'

'You need to find the password Robert,' said Rachel turning to stare at the others.

'It may take me longer than tonight to break it,' he said sitting back. 'In fact if you let me take all of this shit back to mine I can set up a couple of things for you. The first will be a program that will run through the passwords. I use it to hack into other systems sometimes. Only it can take up to a week sometimes. Saying that,' he smirked at them. 'It's never failed me yet.'

'What's the other thing that you can do? asked Chan curiously looking at the lad.

'I can run a trace through the program,' he smiled. 'Only I need my system back at my place to do these things.'

'Where will the trace lead us?' asked Rachel.

'Hopefully to wherever the website is being run from,' he shrugged. 'Although, looking at what we have here. We are dealing with someone who knows exactly what they're doing. There is a lot of security surrounding this set up.'

'You think that it's going to be at all possible though?' asked Kezlo.

'I reckon so,' he replied.

'Alright then,' said Rachel. 'You get yourself packed up.'

'What are we going to do?' asked Tony.

'We are,' she stared at Sleeper and Eazy, 'going to take in the sights down in London with our new esteemed friends here.' They all looked at her puzzled as she smiled at them.

TWENTY FOUR

R achel explained to Liberian at the local library in Chelsea, what it was that she was searching for. They had arrived in London late that afternoon, after catching few hours sleep from leaving Chan's in the early hours of the morning. They had left Robert back in Manchester with all of the computer equipment, to try his best to break into the Pied Piper system.

Rachel had explained what Caroline Massey had told her the night before. And they had agreed to travel straight back down to London to see whether or not there was a connection with what was going on right now and the Cartwright's, from all them years ago.

Sleeper had made some discreet calls on the way down there from his mobile phone. He soon discovered not only the address, but also the fact that they did indeed still own the property down there. Therefore Sleeper left Rachel on her own at the library, whilst he, Eazy and Tony went in search of the address.

As Rachel sat at the computer which held all of the newspapers clippings from the last ten years belonging to Kensington & Chelsea Times, the areas local paper. She began her extensive and laborious task of searching for any articles relating to the Cartwright's. And there were plenty of them. Mainly articles to do with the lifestyle of the family. Covering stories to once again, the charity events that they had held in the past.

It was the one thing that was bothering Rachel. She had met the Cartwright's and for whatever reason, they just didn't come across as very charitable. Maybe it was just the party side of the events that Anabella enjoyed, with Luther just going along for the ride. Whatever it was, she just didn't see the two of them as holding the events merely for raising money for whatever causes were flavour of the month.

After searching through the clippings, she came across the article in which she was searching. It told of the death of Bethany, and just like they had been told by Williamson. It said that she had, had heart trouble. It listed a long list of illnesses the poor girl had suffered as a child.

'Find anything?' asked Tony as he and the others appeared behind her.

'Not really,' she sighed. 'Pretty much what we've been told already.'

'Well, I've set up a meeting for us tomorrow lunch time,' said Sleeper as Rachel rose from her seat, stretching wearily, looking tired.

'Who with?' she asked.

'A detective I know down here,' he told her. 'He used to work this area back then. Claims to have known the family in some sort of way. He was a little cagey if truth be known. In fact he was rather reluctant to meet with us,' he smirked.

'What's with the grin?' asked Rachel.

'I just reminded him of a little job we helped him out with some time back now,' he replied.

'And that seemed to do the trick,' laughed Eazy.

'Come on anyway,' said Sleeper. 'Time to meet the missus. She's got you two set up at my gaff in Marleybone.'

As they pulled up outside of the large town house in Marleybone, she could see that Tony looked impressed. It was centre to a row of identical white houses, black iron railing running around the building. Marble steps ran up to each front door belonging to each house. Although, Rachel could clearly see that they were no longer single houses. They had been converted into apartments. Sleeper led them down some stairs to where the came upon the basement apartment.

'Jesus, Sleeper,' laughed Tony. 'I thought that you owned the whole place.'

'I do,' he smiled. 'In fact, I own the entire block.'

'Serious?' asked Tony nodding his approval.

'Me and Lisa always rented this basement apartment,' he told them sliding the key into the lock. 'They were going through renovations a few years back now. The investors lost a lot of money. At the time we were looking into buying the place anyway. When I discovered that the investors were going through a bad patch. I saw an opening for myself. I just bought in for a higher percentage, and then eventually bought them out all together. They make me a small fortune each month.'

'Christ,' whistled Tony. 'I'm impressed mate.'

'You would be if I told what I ended up paying for them,' he grinned.

'And I wouldn't ask just how he got them down in the price,' laughed Eazy as Rachel shook her head.

'You alright babe,' said Sleeper walking through the door as he scooped his woman into the air lovingly. 'God, I missed you,' he added kissing her passionately.

Rachel observed Lisa curiously. She had both the looks and the figure to have been a world class model. She looked to have an Oriental background. Although her colouring was a lot darker than that. Her skin looked like smooth chocolate milk. Rachel found herself in awe at the way she came across. She also felt their warmth and closeness and despite herself, felt a little jealous. Sleeper made the introductions. And Lisa showed Rachel and Tony to their separate rooms.

'I take it,' said Lisa staring at Eazy who was already making his way through to the kitchen, 'you're staying for dinner Eazy?'

'With your cooking,' he said. 'I'd be the fool not to.'

She'd already shown Tony to his room. 'Have you ever known anybody who can put so much food away,' she smiled as she stood in the doorway to the Rachel was to be staying in.

'He's got the size for it,' she said. 'He's definitely got the size for it,' she added laughing.

'Ain't no denying that,' smiled Lisa. 'Sleeper told me who you are Rachel.'

'Oh, I hope this isn't going to be...'

'It's not a problem,' she shook her head at her. 'He also told me about the fact that you and your brother have become mixed up with these missing kids. He told me all about the connection with this missing girl that used to live down this way.'

'He's been a big help so far,' she said sitting herself down on the bed. 'We seem to be searching for the same goals.'

'He also told me about what it is that you do,' she said. 'He told me about last year. Although I couldn't have forgotten about that. Sleeper was real sickened by what happened to your family. He's no angel but he's got morals when it comes to things like that Rachel.'

'I know that he has,' she replied.

Lisa began to smile at Rachel for no apparent reason then said. 'He's really smitten with you... you know that don't you?'

'You what?' asked Rachel, taken by surprise at the comment.

'Oh, don't worry,' she laughed. 'Me and him are solid. But I could tell over the phone when he told me about you. You

interest him. You're all he talked about on the phone when he was up there. If I was the jealous kind I think I might have suspected that something was going on.'

'But you know it's not,' said Rachel. 'Right?'

'Of course I know there is not,' she laughed. 'It was a compliment Rachel. He very rarely lets himself get close to anybody nowadays. He's happy living in his own little world with all of his old mates. To be honest it's just nice to see him open up a little more. Just keep an eye on him though Rachel. He has a habit of becoming over involved in things that he really shouldn't. But no one, not even me, could stop him if he believes in whatever he gets himself involved with. Like these missing kids. He has his own reasons for that.'

'I know that he has,' she said. 'I think that he has own demons that he's trying to do battle with.'

'I think that you could be right there Rachel,' she smiled. 'Listen, I heard about what happened last weekend in Manchester. I know that the guy that murdered your... well. I'm sorry.'

'It's alright,' she told her.

'Well I know that he has returned,' she shook her head sorrowfully.

'It would be hard not to have,' sighed Rachel as she thought back to witnessing the Fairchild's after they had been slaughtered.

'And I know Sleeper,' she added. 'He's told me that you and Tony are searching for this guy yourselves.'

'We have been,' she admitted. 'And we will continue until either us or the police catch him first. I won't lie to you Lisa.'

'I appreciate that Rachel,' she glanced behind her. 'It's just this guy scares me. It's not normal what he's done and is still doing. I know better than most, what Sleeper is like. And because of that I know that he's going to help you and your brother to find this guy.'

'I've not asked him to,' said Rachel.

'You wouldn't have had too,' she replied. 'It's just the way he is. I know better than most that he can look after himself, and if that fails he always has Eazy as his back up,' she laughed a little nervously. 'But this guy...'

'I don't know what to tell you Lisa.'

'Just tell me that you won't let him do anything stupid.'

'I won't,' she answered.

'Won't what?' asked Sleeper sliding his arms around Lisa's waist.

233

'Do anything stupid,' said Lisa allowing him to kiss her neck.

He kissed his teeth and grinned at Rachel. 'Now what makes you think I'll do something stupid?'

'Because she knows you better than anybody else,' Rachel told him.

'And I know that we're starving,' he replied tickling Lisa. 'So let's eat. What have you cooked for us anyway?'

'Typical,' she sighed breaking free from him. 'Always changing the subject.'

'What's this sauce Lisa?' asked Eazy from the kitchen door, holding a wooden spoon to his mouth. 'This tastes fantastic girl.'

'Oi!' shouted Lisa. 'Get your mitts out of my pans Eazy.'

'Just testing Lisa,' he said returning to the kitchen laughing at her.

'Why don't you rest up for a while Rachel. Dinner will be a couple of hours anyway. When you're cleaned up,' she smiled at Rachel, 'just come on through.'

'Thanks,' she replied letting herself fall back onto the bed in exhaustion.

'A couple of hours,' moaned Eazy.

Rachel had to force herself awake after only an hour, she showered and changed into some fresh clothing. Then she joined the others in the kitchen. Sleeper, Eazy and her brother were all sat around the large wooden table, that had been stained a shade of blue to match the overall colouring of the kitchen.

'Smells good,' she said as she walked to Lisa by the hobs. 'What is it?'

'I hope you like spicy food Rachel?' asked Lisa as Rachel nodded. 'I've gone with a range of Cajun dishes.'

'Really,' asked Rachel looking into the pans. 'What's this?'

'That's for starters,' she told her. 'One of them anyway. It's a crab and prawn gumbo. Along with Oysters Rockefeller - I hope you like oysters?'

'I've never tried them,' she admitted. 'But I'm already looking forward to it.'

'What's this here in these pans?' she asked.

'Now that's the main course,' she stated proudly.

'It's one of Lisa's specialities,' said Sleeper.

'How long is it going to be Lisa?' groaned Eazy as if he hadn't eaten for a week. 'I'm wasting away here girl.'

'You'll be getting nothing at all if you keep on asking me Eazy,' she smiled at him. 'And wasting away my arse. You've got that much stocked up inside of you to last you a lifetime.'

'So what is it?' asked Rachel. 'It smells absolutely gorgeous.'

'It Beef en Daube a la Creole served with Irish Channel roast potatoes and dirty rice,' she began to stir the sauce that the pot roast was cooking in. 'It's basically beef that I've spiced and stuffed with garlic. It cooks in this sauce here to marinate the flavour completely.'

'What sauce is it?' asked Rachel seeing an array of peppers, onions, herbs in the thick sauce.

'It's a special whiskey pepper gravy,' she held some of the sauce on the spoon for Rachel to try.

'Oh my God,' sighed Rachel. 'That is so nice. It's really whiskey?'

'Jack himself is the main ingredient,' she said tasting the sauce herself. 'Now why down you join the others whilst I start serving everything up.'

'About bleedin' time,' sighed Eazy grinning at the others as Lisa scowled at him.

TWENTY FIVE

'You sure that you don't want anything to eat?' asked Eazy as the four of them sat in The Dog and Duck in Fulham, where they had arranged to meet with Sleeper's detective.

'Jesus Eazy,' laughed Tony. 'We've only just finished that mammoth breakfast that Lisa cooked for us.'

'I'm not sure how I even managed that,' sighed Rachel. 'After last night's feast. She'd cooked so much food. And those Spiced Peach Crepes for dessert was probably the most delicious dessert that I have ever tasted. How the hell does she stay so slim cooking food like that Sleeper?'

'She's always been like that,' he told them. 'Unlike some people,' he laughed jabbing Eazy in the stomach.

'I'm a growing lad,' he smiled at them whilst not taking his eyes from the menu before him.

'About twenty years ago,' laughed Sleeper. 'Now it's just your belly that's doing any kind of growth.'

They all began laughing as Eazy ignored them and went to bar to put his food order in.

'Here he is now,' said Sleeper all serious as the overweight, balding man came towards them. He was puffing hungrily on his cigarette as if it was to be his very last one. He appeared to be in his late forties, and his dress sense was extremely messy. A mix and match of different clothing, despite all of this he had, copper, written all over him.

'You alright fat boy?' asked Sleeper as the man sat down. 'This is Detective Jimmy Jenkins folks.'

'Alright Tucker,' laughed Eazy sitting himself back down and referring to him by the nick-name they'd given him of a character from *Grange Hill*, that they used to watch as kids.

236

'Whatever,' he sighed lighting another cigarette from the butt of the other one. 'What is it you lads want to know?'

'The Cartwright's,' said Sleeper.

'What about them?' he shrugged.

'You knew them right,' said Eazy. 'We want to know what you know about them.'

'They were high society,' he sniffed. 'But they were always in there with us copper's.'

'What do you mean by that?' asked Rachel.

'I mean that when ever they threw them big parties,' he said. 'They always made sure that we got invites at the station.'

'Why would they want you lot there?' asked Sleeper.

'Image,' he said. 'They wanted people to know that there was nothing wrong with them.'

'In what way?' asked Rachel.

'Them charity balls and all that other crap was just to hide the fact that the Luther and Anabella were a couple of freaks.'

'Freaks in what way?' asked Tony.

'Does this relate to the little girl that died?' asked Rachel.

'Why do you ask about her?' he wanted to know.

'Did she die from a bad heart?' asked Rachel.

'That's what they say,' he shrugged.

'What do you say though?' asked Rachel staring at him intensely.

'I say that the old man was abusing the kid,' he sighed. 'Probably both of them to be honest with you. Not that we could ever prove any of it. Or more to the point. Didn't want to prove it.'

'Why's that?' asked Sleeper.

'We were called in by social services after the hospital reported the girl to be covered in bruising. We checked it out. The girl seemed real scared to me. Both of them did. And all we got was the usual bullshit story of her falling down stairs or some other crap.'

'You didn't believe it then?' asked Rachel.

'Fucking couple of rich cunts,' he snorted loudly as he sipped his pint of lager.

'Sounds like you didn't get along with them,' said Sleeper.

'It's just the shit that I found out about them afterwards that got under my skin,' he sighed deeply. 'They just used their money and power as an influence to do whatever the fuck they wanted to.'

'So what happened with the kid?' asked Tony.

'That was the problem. That's another reason I can't stand the fucker. But it's also the reason I got to be careful talking to you about them.'

'Why's that?' asked Eazy. 'They ain't even living down this way anymore.'

'Makes no difference,' he said. 'You see, back then. The only reason we couldn't investigate properly was that we got word from upstairs that the Cartwright's weren't to be bothered.'

'Who gave the orders?' asked Rachel.

'No idea,' he told her. 'All that I know is that we got word and backed away. That's what I meant by bullshit charities. Surrounding themselves with coppers. And even holding an event to raise funds for us. Total bullshit. But it obviously worked.'

'You think that it was sexual abuse also?' asked Rachel.

'The abuse?' he stared at her. 'Most definitely. I done some checking after we were first called in. It seems that Luther was caught with a minor some years before all of this. But the whole matter was covered up.'

'Who covered it up?' asked Tony.

'Fucked if I know,' he shrugged gulping the pint before him.

'How old was this girl he was with?' asked Rachel.

'Same age as the girls,' he said. 'It was one of their friends. If I remember rightly the family in question moved away with their little girl. Word has it, that they paid them off.'

'Why did they move up north?' asked Rachel.

'After the death of the little girl,' he said, 'a few too many questions were asked. I suppose that they didn't want the bad publicity. They still own the house though.'

'We know,' said Sleeper.

'Is it used?' asked Rachel.

'I think that they occasionally use it at weekends,' he told them. 'At least that's what I've been told. Why they still own it, is beyond me to be honest. It's a huge thing, just to be used for odd weekends anyway.'

'Nobody looks after it?' asked Sleeper. 'What about live in cleaners or staff of some sort?'

'None that I know of,' he shrugged. 'Why?'

'What about security?' asked Sleeper ignoring his question.

'It's belled up to the local nick,' he said. 'But apart from that there is nobody there that I know of.'

'Find out for definite,' said Eazy. 'We want to know by tonight.'

'What the fuck is going on here lads?' he asked.

'That's none of your business Tucker,' said Eazy glaring at him.

'Look,' he sighed. 'If there's going to be troub...'

'All you need to know is that we need to know Tucker,' said Eazy leaning a little closer towards him. 'That is unless you want anybody to know exactly what happened to your last partner.'

'Fine... fine,' he shook his head as Rachel glanced at her brother, wondering what the hell that was in reference to. 'I'll be in touch in a couple of hours then.'

'Just one more thing before you go Jenkins,' said Sleeper. 'Have you ever heard of anybody known as the Pied Piper?'

He began laughing. 'Like in the children's' story?'

Suddenly Eazy grabbed his jaw and pulled him towards him, inches from his face he snarled at the detective. 'This ain't no laughing matter mother fucker.'

Breaking free, he began rubbing his jaw that still had the figure marks from where Eazy had grabbed him. 'No, no, I ain't' got a clue what you're talking about. Jesus Eazy, you almost broke my fuckin' jaw.'

'Consider yourself lucky then,' he smiled at the detective.

'Alright then Jenkins,' sighed Sleeper. 'You can go now. We'll be expecting your call very soon. And if you think of anything else. You be sure to let us know.'

'Whatever,' he grumbled as he climbed from his seat just as a huge plate containing Eazy's mixed grill arrived. 'Speak to you later,' he said as he stared at Eazy's food.

'Got to keep my strength up,' he laughed at the detective who unconsciously rubbed his jaw at those words.

They watched, as the detective made his way out of the door. Eazy dug straight into his food, smiling contentedly as he did so.

'What now?' asked Tony as Sleeper and Eazy looked to one another.

'Only one thing for it,' said Eazy tossing a sausage into his mouth.

'What's that?' asked Rachel.

'Me and Eazy will go and take a look inside that house tonight,' replied Sleeper.

'What about the security system?' asked Rachel. 'I thought he said it was linked to the police station.

'It's alright,' laughed Sleeper. 'It shouldn't be a problem. After all, I have my very own master key here,' he jabbed Eazy in the side as he winked back at him, with his mouth full of food.

TWENTY SIX

'**F**uck me Sleeper,' whistled Eazy looking back down at his friend from the wall he was stood upon, holding his hand out for assistance. Pulling Sleeper up to the top of the wall that stood just beyond the boundaries of the Cartwright's family retreat as they'd named it, he shook his head as he observed Sleeper smile at the home before them. 'This gaff is the bollocks mate.'

'Is it going to be a problem?' asked Sleeper crouching low, his eyes taking in his surroundings.

The house belonged to a row of old Victorian houses, each four floors in height. All of them had their own gardens, and each garden was privately hidden away from the neighbours by the large brick walls that surrounded them.

'Nah mate,' he replied shaking his head, glancing to the telegraph pole to be found at the end of the wall they were both sat upon. 'In fact, with this here wall to help you on your way. You should have no troubles getting yourself up there.'

'Why the fuck is it always me that has to climb the pole?' he laughed, still crouched and now staring at the pole.

'How the hell do you expect me to get up there?' asked Eazy seriously.

'True,' smirked Sleeper stretching to his full height. 'Damn pole looks to be cringing just at the thought of you attempting to climb up there.'

'What!' exclaimed Eazy tutting as he rooted in the bag.

'Best give me the spikes then,' sighed Sleeper.

He was referring to a set of mountaineering spikes that fitted to the back of your boots. It was far less inconspicuous to use these than a set of ladders that would easily be noticed, despite the late hour of the night that they had chosen to visit the house.

Handing the spikes to his friend he grinned knowingly and asked. 'You remember what the kid showed you to do then?'

'It's been a while,' he answered fitting the spikes to his Timberland boots. 'But I reckon that it'll come back to me when I'm up there.' He'd known that Eazy would have needed him climb the wooden telegraph pole outside of the house in order to bypass the alarm system. He also knew that the kid he was referring to, and this exact method of breaking and entering had been shown to them by one of the best burglars that they'd both known. Not that he ever robbed houses though. This guy used to take down large warehouses and the like. In fact he was one of their closest friends, who was now living out in the Far East.

Quickly going to work up the pole he watched from high above as Eazy went about filling the alarm box with insulation foam. The kind that you sprayed into the space required as the foam expanded and hardened within seconds. This was mainly a secondary, precautionary method, which they still did just to remain on the safe side in case of any problems that they'd over looked. It meant if they had done so, then the bell would not be heard by anyone, even if they were activated. Signalling to Eazy, he watched as his friend entered through the patio doors into the darkness of the deserted house.

Climbing back down the pole, Sleeper removed the spikes and took another look around to make sure that they hadn't been spotted. When he was finally satisfied he leapt silently down into the back garden and quickly made his way through the patio doors after his friend.

'Now this is what you call a nice gaff mate,' said Sleeper handing the spikes back to Eazy as the two of them were stood in living room of the Cartwright's London residence.

'In'it mate,' replied Eazy as he put his tools away and eased the patio door closed.

'You sure that we bypassed the alarm?' asked Sleeper. 'I don't want any fuckin' surprises tonight.'

Eazy laughed at him. 'You was the one up the telegraph pole,' he said. 'Not me.'

'I only done what the kid showed me to do,' he frowned at him shining the maglite torch in his face.

'Then there shouldn't be a problem then,' he shrugged. 'They sure have got themselves some nice gear in here, haven't they brother.'

As Sleeper nodded his response he shone his small maglite around the spacious living room he was impressed by the room's decor. There was no denying it, the Cartwright's had style. The

floor itself was polished dark oak floorboards, with an array of different Chinese, Persian or Japanese rugs. He wasn't exactly sure which origin; the only thing he was certain of was that they were extremely expensive.

He noticed that they were original paintings donning the walls; all of the paintings were modern art. The way the colours from the paintings blended gracefully with the warm colouring of the room gave it an overall welcoming feel to it.

All of the furniture had a real contemporary appearance. The sofas were all modern, and appeared to be soft leather. Sleeper found himself stroking them appreciatively as he gazed at the only thing that looked out of place in there. It was the antique fireplace, which was enormous. And considering it was a fire place was the also the one thing that gave the room a cooler climate tan the rest of its furnishings. Considering the home wasn't supposed to be in use, the place was very warm and not all musty smelling as they had imagined that it may have been.

'That them?' asked Eazy gazing above the fireplace.

Sleeper shone the torch above the mantel piece and was surprised that he'd missed the painting that hung there. For there was a large painting of what was quite obviously the Cartwright's years before. It had to have been from some time ago, as there were both the daughters featured in the painting. They both looked to be around seven or eight years old and both appeared to extremely happy. Sleeper wondered if that was the only way the mother and father could present the two of them happily after what they been told. By putting it in a painting instead of a photograph they could present them to outside world anyway they chose to.

'It must be. Happy families eh,' nodded Sleeper. 'The missus looks well groomed.'

'In'it,' laughed Eazy.

'Rachel tells me that she was coming on to Tony when they visited with them,' said Sleeper. 'Apparently the two of them couldn't take their eyes off one another. Blatantly flirting with one another right in front of the old man.'

'Really,' laughed Eazy.

'So Rachel says anyway,' he smirked.

'The two of them are alright you know,' he added.

'I know they are,' said Sleeper. 'You know that you don't have to stand by me on this one Eazy. It's just that I really like both of them. And I just want to...'

'When have I never stood by you on any decision you've made,' he said cutting him off.   'Now enough of this

sentimentality bollocks. Let's do what we came here to do. You take the upstairs and I'll take downstairs.'

'That's good,' smiled Sleeper.

'What is?' shrugged Eazy.

'I get three floors and you get one,' he laughed.

'Ah, come on,' groaned Eazy rubbing the base of his back. 'My backs been playing up like mad recently.'

'It didn't seem to have any bother climbing over that wall just now,' he smirked as he shone the light into his face.

'Best not to take any chances then eh,' he laughed. 'Now come on brother, or we are going to be here all night and you know that we've still got to get some supper before the night is out.'

'Never mind your back,' said Sleeper shaking his head at his friend. 'You carry on eating like you are and you won't be able to fit through these doors.'

They both laughed as Sleeper took off up the stairs. Making his way around the house, Sleeper noticed nothing out of place. The bedrooms were all obviously still in use. Clothes hung in wardrobe and draws. What was obviously the children's room looked untouched from when Charlotte had been a young girl. It didn't resemble a teenager's room at all. But Sleeper just put it down to the fact that they were not supposed to use the place that often.

Sleeper took his time searching the bottom of the wardrobes for false panelling like he'd discovered at Spencer's home. But had no such luck. He then began the laborious task of checking the floorboards around the edges of the carpet for any indication to further hiding places.

Feeling disappointed with the lack of finding anything conclusive he made his way back downstairs. Eazy was sat on the sofa in front of the fireplace. He appeared to be almost sleeping as he stared the picture above the mantel piece.

'Any joy?' asked Sleeper.

'Nada,' he shook his head.

'Cellar?'

'There isn't one,' he replied. 'I checked everywhere and couldn't find anything whatsoever that was incriminating towards the family. Except a few dodgy paintings that they probably paid a fortune for that is,' he laughed.

'Same here,' Sleeper sighed deeply. 'It appears to be what it is. An empty house.'

'Tucker was right about one thing though,' said Eazy.

'What's that then?'

'Why the fuck would anybody want to keep such an enormous gaff like this if they weren't going to live here.'

'God knows mate,' he sighed. 'It's got to be worth a few million easily.'

'That's just the house alone,' replied Eazy. 'The gear in here has got to be worth around the same or even more.'

Shining his light at the painting of the family. 'Just what the fuck are you hiding from us?' he asked the painting, the light directly on Luther Cartwright's face.

'And there was nothing upstairs at all?' Eazy asked turning his head to look at Sleeper.

'Absolutely nothing incriminating towards the old man,' he shook his head.

'You reckon that Tucker was having us at it?'

'There is no reason for him to have,' he replied.

'Oh well,' said Eazy pushing himself from the sofa. 'Let's get the fuck out of here then. You'll have to do the honours with the phone lines mate. We'll reset everything so that no ones any the wiser to us being here.'

'Alright,' he said making his way towards the door as Eazy walked to the fireplace once again shining his torch at the painting of the family. 'We ain't finished with you yet Cartwright,' he said as Sleeper suddenly swivelled around and stared at Eazy.

'What!' exclaimed Eazy. 'What's with that look?'

'Tap your foot,' he commanded.

As Eazy did so unquestionably, he looked up at Sleeper. 'Shit, how the hell did you hear that over there?' For undoubtedly there was a hollow sound, disguised by the thick Japanese rug that had been placed there.

Sleeper and Eazy pulled the rug back revealing the wooden floorboards and they both stared at one another. For they were not staring at a few false wooden slats, but an entire trapdoor that was at least four foot by four foot.

'I knew there had to be a basement to this gaff,' said Eazy bending to take a closer look at the door. Quickly removing his tools he picked the lock on the door, hooking his finger around the small brass loop that acted as a handle he eased the door open. A rush of heat escaped from the basement.

'You hear that?' asked Sleeper.

'Whatever it is,' said Eazy listening to the hum coming from darkness. 'It's electrical.'

'Best take a look then,' said Sleeper shining his torch down the steep wooden steps. 'After you Eazy. At least if you fall, I'll have something to soften the blow.'

'Cheers mate,' he laughed as he began to climb down the steps carefully. Shining his light in order that Sleeper could see more clearly, he watched as his friend leaped silently through the hole, landing as quietly as cat would, next to him. 'Show off,' he said smirking as he shone his light into Sleeper's face.

'What have we got then?' asked Sleeper shining his torch at their surroundings.

'Jesus Christ, Sleeper,' whispered Eazy as he was afraid of disturbing someone. 'What the fuck is this place. It looks like some kind of an all exclusive dungeon or something.'

'That is exactly what it could be mate.'

As they stood at the base of the steps, Sleeper found the string hanging from the ceiling and gave it a slight tug. Suddenly the whole place lit up brightly, dazzling them, white spots tracing before their eyes as they tried their best to focus on their surroundings.

'What the fuck...' said Sleeper, for surrounding them in a perfect circle was a row of around ten wooden doors. All of them appeared too heavy in weight and matched the oak floorboards from upstairs that were also mirrored here in the basement. Each door had a small window, and without even having to take a closer look, Sleeper could tell that it wasn't glass, but unbreakable perspex.

'I don't get a good feeling about this brother,' sighed Eazy staring in disbelief at what they had discovered below the Cartwright's living room.

'To anybody else,' said Sleeper, 'this place could resemble some sort of a plush health club or gymnasium.'

'Tell me about it,' replied Eazy. 'Only I get the feeling that isn't the reason they built this place.'

'It's as if each door could take you to a sauna or training room,' said Sleeper walking towards one of the doors. Only as he approached the door, he feared that none of the rooms would be used for such uses. Peering through the perspex into the concealment of the room he could see exactly what it had bee set up for.

Trying the handle, he realised it was locked. Glancing at Eazy, who already had his small leather bag of tools out they soon entered the room.

'What the fuck is this?' asked Eazy staring into the room.

The room was around a weird shape accounting for circular shape to the cellar. But it was a large room and had been painted with pastel colours that gave it a deceiving look. There was a single bed in the centre of the room that was covered in some sort of children's quilt coverings. A few toys lay scattered around the bed and it did indeed have the overall appearance of being a child's bedroom.

'You seen this?' asked Eazy as Sleeper stared sadly around the room. Observing what Eazy was staring at, he noticed the small, minute, almost invisible to the eye black dot. 'What is it?'

'This is high tech surveillance. Fibre-optics mate. They use this shit when they don't want anybody to know that it is here. Like when trying to set someone up. My guess is, that this is hooked up to a camera somewhere. Look,' he said pointing around the room at the walls. 'There are four all together.'

'This is fucked up,' said Sleeper. 'Let's check the other rooms out.'

As they checked the rooms, they found an assortment of different fantasies arranged into each room. Everything from children's fairy tales and Disney films, to more sadistic looking rooms, filled with S&M gear. They also knew that from the size of some of the leather straps and binding in these rooms, that the chances were, that they had been used with children.

'Best check this out Sleeper,' said Eazy as he opened the last door they came upon at the back of the steps from where they had entered. 'Just look at all this shit. This is what the electrical hum was mate.'

The room, in which they now stood, was full of monitors and computer equipment. They could see that the monitors were all connected to an array of different recording equipment from video recorders to recordable DVD systems.

'This is just so fucking messed up,' said Eazy as Sleeper began flipping switches.

They soon realised that each transmission from each room was sent to this room where it was recorded on the devise before them. Clicking away at the keys, Sleeper realised that the cameras had a range of features from zooming in close on the bed to gaining a range of different angles. The whole process was making him feel sick as he sat there examining the control deck before him.

Eazy now sat himself down as Sleeper pushed himself away from the console board in disgust.

'Just what the fuck are we dealing with here Eazy?'

'Pure evil,' sighed Eazy now concentrating on the computers before him.

'You think this could be it?' asked Sleeper looking around the room.

'Whoa, check this out,' said Eazy, bringing up a recording with them inside one of the rooms only moments before. 'The cameras are set up with motion sensors to go off whenever anybody enters those rooms.'

'What about the computers?' asked Sleeper as Eazy began tapping away at the keys.

'Let me take a closer look at them,' said Eazy.

As Sleeper began to search the room he soon realised that it was lot bigger than the others they had been in. At least three times larger than the others they had entered. The walls were covered in an embankment of shelves. Each shelve stuffed with video tapes and DVD's with a range of boys and girls names scribbled on them with their ages ranging from as young as three months old to eleven years old. In fact, some of the tapes were that old, they were betamax video cassettes, which were no longer in use.

'Christ Eazy,' he sighed holding the old tape up for him to see. 'Just how long do you think this shit has been gong on?'

'This is some real fucked up shit brother,' he said.

'This is some serious shit that they've got set up here though,' said Sleeper. 'Just how the hell has he got away with all of this for so long without anybody finding out about it?'

'You reckon that the wife is in on it?' asked Eazy.

'How the hell could she not know about something like this?'

'You reckon that they have had something to do with their daughter going missing Sleeper?'

'After witnessing this lot,' he shook his head. 'What do you think?'

'I think that Cartwright has got some serious questions to be answered.'

'That's a fucking understatement ain't it,' he said. 'Any joy with the computer?'

'This system is well protected,' he said shaking his head.

'We need to get these tapes checked out,' said Sleeper as he inspected the tapes closely.

'Be my guest,' said Eazy. 'You're not getting me to look at the shit on them things.'

'You think that this Cartwright is the Pied Piper?' asked Sleeper.

'If he's not, then he knows who the mother fucker is,' he sighed as he continued to tap away at the keys. 'What do we do with all this shit Sleeper?'

'We need to talk to Rachel first,' he replied.

'Then what?' he asked. 'What if this is the Pied Piper though?'

'Then we'll have to decide what we are going to do,' he shook his head. 'I'm not sure yet where Rachel's loyalties lay here.'

'What do mean?'

'She might want to bring this freak in through her copper friend.'

'And you?'

'No question about it,' he said. 'If this is our guy, he's a dead man walking.'

Eazy grinned at his friend and nodded his approval.

TWENTY SEVEN

William Morgan's heart still felt warm in Gabriel's hands, holding the organ as an offering to Michael, who Gabriel believed was looking down from high above. Gabriel had come fiercely, at precisely the same time the heart was removed. Morgan's eyes were still bulging from their sockets as Gabriel climbed from his bloody torso and stared down at the latest victim.

To feel the power of life and death literally in the grasp of your hands excited Gabriel beyond belief.

The family had been picked as a direct challenge for Gabriel. Knowing that William Morgan and his family had been still grieving for the loss of his partner and their close friends, the Fairchild's. Otis Fairchild's partner at the firm which they had both owned, William Morgan and his wife and four year old child were always to be slayed, only Gabriel had decided upon bringing forward the previous date, allotting the Morgan's to the top of the now compiled list.

Also knowing that the police had them under close guard after the previous week's events. Not that the twenty-four police protection that had been granted them would bother Gabriel any.

In fact, Gabriel savoured the challenge of slaying the Morgan's almost immediately after killing the Fairchild's. Gabriel already had, had the family under surveillance at the same time as the Fairchild's had been under surveillance.

That's not to say that they were picked at random because of the surveillance, because they had not been. William Morgan, his wife Patricia Morgan, and their little girl of four years old, Suzy, had been carefully chosen, like the list that Gabriel had now accumulated over the past twelve months. Although it was a list that had been amassed deep within Gabriel's mind unwittingly for a lot longer than that.

Only neither the police, nor Rachel had made the connection yet. Only Michael had made that connection for Gabriel after the slaying of Peter and Becky, pointing out how right it was to now go forth and continue the slaying of those who they believed deserved it.

Gabriel had watched time and time again as William Morgan walked criminal's free to continue with their destined lives of crime. Just as Otis Fairchild had been doing the same with his very own clients. But history stretched further than that, and only Gabriel and Michael seemed to be aware of that. What made things all that worse to witness, was that both families appeared not to hold any morals whatsoever within in their field of work or away from it.

From watching the family, Gabriel knew that William was, just like his partner, also having a extra marital affair with a defence attorney from another firm within Manchester. And the wife was also having an affair with her personal gym instructor at the local gym in Altrincham. Not so far from their family home where Gabriel now stood within, that he couldn't pop back to the house during the day as Gabriel had observed on many occasions.

Only this time around, the police and Rachel hadn't had to wait so long in order for Gabriel strike fear into their lives once again. No twelve months gap in between the murders, in fact it had only just been a week to the very night, since the last lot of murders took place. They were still trying their best to gather evidence from that lot of murders, when Gabriel had made the decision to strike again.

It was part of Gabriel's plan, not keep any set time scale, making it all that much harder for the police and Rachel to fathom out what exactly was going through Gabriel's mind. Gabriel had been so careful this time around, knowing that their were police stationed right outside of the house. Gently pushing the curtain to one side, Gabriel observed the two policemen half asleep in their car. Obviously not suspecting that the killer would dare to strike again so soon after the last murders.

But that was what also made it so right, as Gabriel knew that by striking now, right under their noses, was not only laughing in their faces, but it was also the best course of action to take. Not to mention the added excitement of it all that Gabriel felt. Standing over the latest crime scene, Gabriel took in the latest creation and thought back over what had just taken place.

Gaining access was more than easy enough. Even with the police stationed right outside of the house. As they had no doubt

discovered by now, the Fairchild's had been drugged with the very drug that Otis Fairchild had been defending his client with – Royphnol.

In drugging the Morgan's, Gabriel had studied their patterns. Knowing that around ten o'clock at night, both the husband and wife settled in for drinks as they watched television. Breaking into their house earlier that day, Gabriel had managed to drug his bottle of Bushmills malt whiskey and her bottle of Gordon's gin.

Therefore drugging the family before entering their home through the back entrance had been of pure genius in ones mind. Gabriel also knew that the police did their check on the family at ten o'clock, just before they settled down for the night, and wouldn't bother the family again until the morning.

As for the child, well she hadn't needed drugging, as little Suzy had been sleeping when Gabriel had struck.

Discovering William and Patricia Morgan in their drug induced state of mind in the living room, Gabriel had smiled knowingly at them, stood there donned in the black full length rubber outfit that was part of the disguise worn. Not that it mattered now anyway, for even in his drug induced state, Gabriel saw the recognition in William Morgan's eyes as the silver duct tape was placed over their mouths as a precaution. Gabriel then hoisted him over the right shoulder and took him upstairs.

Placing him against the wall, Gabriel had instructed William to stretch his arms out wide. Doing as he instructed, still dazed and confused by the potency of the drug he'd been spiked with. Removing the nail gun from the black duffel bag, grinning at Morgan intentionally. Gabriel shot the nails through both of his hands, and his feet as only William Morgan's eyes gave recognition to the pain he felt. Tearing his clothes from him violently, Gabriel caressed William Morgan's chest teasingly as he stared wildly back into Gabriel's eyes.

Quickly setting up the digital camera on the extendible tripod, and setting the lens to wide angle shot in order to take in the entire room in one shot. Gabriel then left the husband entrapped to the wall, and went to retrieve the wife. Dragging her upstairs by her hair, Gabriel threw her onto the floor at the foot of the bed as she stared vacantly at the sight of her husband now naked at the nailed to the wall.

Smiling menacingly at the two of them, disappearing from the room to awaken the little girl, as she was to be the first to die. Gagging her, Gabriel taped the little girl's mouth with silver duct tape as she awoke, so not to alarm the police outside. Panicking at the sight before her, she instantly began struggling and

viciously; choking her in between muffled screams that only Gabriel could silently hear. Sliding the knife around the next victim, teasing the surface of her skin with the point of the blade.

William Morgan's eyes pleaded with Gabriel as the knife suddenly struck through the flesh as the wife's blood sprayed wildly form the arteries surrounding the heart. Flipping the wife over, her face a mask of sheer terror as her last breath had been taken from her, and she was already dead from the knife wound inflicted. Gabriel then began the task of removing the heart, whist all the while still penetrating the now deceased corpse of Patricia Morgan.

The sounds of what just took place are still with Gabriel as strong as they had been as their life's had been taken so brutally from them. Sounds touching flesh like an electric current, energising. Her fear gives Gabriel control of the fear felt deep inside. And control is power, and power is the ultimate aphrodisiac pleasure. The clarity of vision, to act upon their fantasies and release the dark power from within the dark, internal abyss.

William Morgan was struggling as best as he could from his imprisoned position as Gabriel climbed away from the bloodied corpse of his wife. The knife dripping with the crimson tide that had flooded from within the now mutilated body. William also covered in not only the blood of his wife, but that of his deceased child.

Stood before him, Gabriel teased Morgan with the very knife that had taken the lives of both his wife and child, and would no doubt take his. Grabbing hold of his cock, Gabriel squeezed hard, and was surprised to see that Morgan began to become aroused. Smirking at the man, Gabriel taunted him teasingly.

Tightening the fingers around Morgan's throat, Gabriel observed as the life began to drain away form the last victim. Just at the point where Gabriel thought that the man was about to pass out, the knife was plunged deeply into his chest. Tearing the flesh wide open, as Morgan's frenzied eyes stared wildly into the eyes of his killer.

Observing the eyes closely as the shock of what was happening took hold. Feeling the pain of Morgan as the knife slid its way into his chest as he gasped the pain showing clearly through his eyes as he shuddered away to the next life. Gabriel continued to smile as the heart was removed; feeling heightened pleasure of what was taking place.

Thinking of Rachel, knowing that she didn't know anything about the ultimate power and euphoria of taking a life. Never

considering the exquisite music of pain and fear, or how that music elevated the musician.

Elevation, ecstasy, arousal. These are the things Gabriel feels in triumph, stirred into the darker emotions of anger and hatred and frustration to burn constantly inside of oneself. Manipulation, domination, control, Gabriel's powers extending beyond the victims themselves. Reminding oneself of the fact, these very same powers are being excised over the police and Rachel.

Gabriel then went to work with his latest master piece. Taking as much time as was necessary with placing the victims how they should be discovered. Gabriel then went to work on the walls, leaving the trade mark wings and also leaving more clues with the references that would surely confuse them even further than they already were.

The standing back and staring admiringly at the work of art created, wondering if they would truly appreciated what had been achieved her that night. For still attached to the wall, completely stripped naked, his arms out stretched as the wings protruded from his arms was William Morgan.

His chest had been torn open, the heart removed with the trade made by leaving the white dove. Gabriel had become even more creative, using the white sheets in order to create the affect of the wings stretching out from where he lay.

Using the blood that had dripped from the victim's heart to illustrate the details of the wings in greater detail. In fact, Gabriel was quite proud of the achievement.

The wife was at the foot of the bed, also stripped naked. Holding onto her husband's bloody legs as Gabriel had sadistically placed her mouth over the flaccid penis of her dead husband. Her life taken from her as Gabriel raped the woman, who in her drugged state of conciseness gave no resistance.

Leaving the child still positioned at the top of the book shelf with a few alterations made to suit the work of art being created. Gabriel then dismantled the video camera, placing both that and the nail back inside of the sealed bag, which would be later burned along with the rest of rubber clothing that Gabriel was now removing.

Quickly going over the crime scene with the same precision that would be later attributed to it. Feeling pleased that nothing unnecessary had been forgotten. Looking over victims one final time, breathing the beloved stench of death in deeply, Gabriel then walked to the bedroom door. Glancing back, pleased with the nights work, feeling the warmth of their hearts in the small bag strapped across the chest area. Gabriel then fled into the

darkness of night, and waited for this next masterpiece to be discovered.

TWENTY EIGHT

'**W**hat the hell is all this?' asked Tony as Sleeper opened the trunk to his Mercedes, revealing the cardboard boxes they had retrieved the night before.

It was Sunday morning, Both Sleeper and Eazy had not long since arrived back to Marleybone. They had both agreed to stay until first light, in order to review some of tapes they had discovered in order to try and locate whether or not their was any connection to not only the Pied Piper, but also Charlotte Cartwright. They were trying to find tapes featuring the two daughters they'd observed in the painting, but had so far been unsuccessful.

Sleeper had contacted Robert whilst they were there. He explained where it was that they were and about the system before them that was protected. Robert had explained a series of different processes in order to try and gain access to the programs held within there. They had eventually gained access, but only so far as the basic set up of the system itself. With Robert acting as a guide on the other end of the line, Eazy had managed to open a series of files that bore some of the same reputation to what they had discovered in Manchester.

Realising that without Robert here to do the work himself, they were hitting their heads against a brick wall. Robert had also told them that he'd broken the codes last night to the systems that they had left him, but that it didn't necessarily mean the two were linked. Pointing out that it was best that they didn't access the Pied Piper system from down there until he'd had chance to see the computers himself.

'Are they what I think they are?' asked Rachel peering into the trunk, reading what was obviously the child's name and age featured on the video cassettes found in there.

'We didn't wake you last night,' said Sleeper closing the trunk, 'as it took a lot longer than we thought. We've not been back that long. And we couldn't spend any longer in there, as we had to reset the alarms without being seen.'

'You found these tapes at the house?' asked Tony glancing to Rachel.

'Yeah,' sighed Eazy. 'And believe me. We only took a fraction of what was stocked up down there.'

'Down there?' asked Rachel.

'You should have seen this shit Rach,' said Sleeper shaking his head at her sadly. 'If this guy ain't the Pied Piper he certainly has knowledge of another paedophile ring that is being run. They had this, well, what can only be described as a kind of dungeon or some other shit beneath their living room.'

'We wouldn't have even discovered it,' said Eazy, 'if it hadn't been for the brother's bat like ears here.'

'I don't understand,' said Rachel. 'What do you mean by dungeon or some other shit?'

'Exactly that,' replied Sleeper. 'Basically, we'd about given up at the house. We weren't getting anywhere with finding anything whatsoever incriminating towards the family. The only thing that we couldn't understand was why they owned this huge house down here. I mean, it's not just the gaff itself that's worth a mint. It's the contents to the place as well. And don't get us wrong by thinking that it was a walk in the park to get in there last night, because it wasn't. They've got themselves state of the art security. No common burglar is finding his way in there. And even if a professional does the job, he wouldn't be looking for we were last night.'

'What's this dungeon you're on about?' asked Tony lighting a cigarette.

'It's what had been built into the basement of the house,' he replied.

'We thought that it was weird that a place as big and as old as that didn't have one basically,' Eazy told them.

'So where was it?' asked Rachel.

'We discovered this trap door that was concealed beneath this rug in front of the fireplace.'

'And this is where it took you?' asked Tony nodding at the rear of the car.

'We're talking about a proper set up here,' said Sleeper leading them back to the apartment. 'They'd spent some serious dough on setting the basement up like they had done. As you reach the bottom of the stairs, you're surrounded by a circumference of

different doors. Each door taking you through to different room. The entire area is made up of oak. They got it looking real classy until you realise what its purpose actually is.'

'Like it's some sort of plush gymnasium,' said Eazy shaking his head at the thought of the place. 'They have it set up with eleven rooms in all.'

'What kind of rooms?' asked Tony.

'Sick ones,' sighed Sleeper staring back at him. 'They also have this one room. It's bigger than the rest of the rooms. About three times as big easily. It's stocked up with videos, DVD's and a whole array of computer shit.'

'What for?' asked Tony.

'It's where they make those tapes,' sighed Rachel realising what they were telling them both.

'Exactly,' said Eazy staring directly at her. 'It's like Sleeper says, they set the place up like their own personal dungeon.'

'Each room has been designed different to the next one,' said Sleeper opening his front door. 'An array of different fantasies have built into these rooms. Everything from school class rooms to nursery rooms all the way through to very sick looking S&M rooms. There is some real perverse shit down there.'

'But that's not all of it,' said Eazy as they made their way through to the kitchen.

'What else is there?' asked Rachel.

'The only thing that was the same with each room,' said Sleeper, 'was that they had high tech surveillance cameras in the walls. The type that you don't see unless you're looking for them known as fibre-optics.'

'That's what the last room is set up for. The one with all the computers and recording equipment in there,' said Eazy. 'They have motion sensors set up to trip as someone enters the rooms.'

'Have you watched any of the tapes yet?' asked Rachel.

Both of them looked sick to their stomachs. 'It ain't at all pretty,' said Eazy.

'We couldn't find anything on Charlotte though,' added Sleeper. 'In fact the only reason we took any of the tapes, was to see if you recognised any of the people in the tapes.'

'What!' exclaimed Tony. 'You can see these sick fucks in there?'

'They're masked up or disguised in ways that doesn't reveal them fully,' said Eazy.

'We just thought that maybe you'd be able to spot something that would give it away as being Luther Cartwright,' said

Sleeper looking to Rachel. 'Maybe even the missus also, Anabella,' he added glancing to Tony.

'You what,' he shook his head. 'You're not telling me, that she's involved in this as well?'

'She had to have known,' said Sleeper. 'It's not at all possible to have set something of this size up without her having full knowledge of what the husband was doing.'

'Nah,' sighed Tony at the mere prospect. 'Shit... really?' he stared at his sister who shrugged her answer at him.

'I said that there was something weird about them,' said Rachel.

'Oh shit,' shuddered Tony at the thought of the wife being caught up in this whole mess. 'Oh man, that makes me feel sick.'

'There's a woman in those tapes Tony,' said Sleeper. 'Whether or not it's this woman, is another matter all together.' He could clearly see that the thought of this woman who Tony had been attracted to, and now the prospect that she'd been abusing kids had visibly shaken Tony.

'What about the Pied Piper?' asked Rachel. 'Did you find anything on him down there?'

'The systems were protected,' said Eazy. 'We spoke to Robert who explained how to break through the basic set up. But he also pointed out that it was best if we didn't take things further.'

'Why's that?' asked Tony, still shaking his head in disbelief.

'When we spoke with Robert this morning,' said Sleeper. 'He told us that he's got some serious shit for us to look at. He also pointed out that he only just managed to avoid losing everything all together. He said that the Pied Piper system was set up to somehow shut down completely through unauthorised access. He reckons that whoever we're dealing with certainly knows his shit alright.'

'We've to get back up to Manchester today,' added Eazy.

'Why?' she asked. 'What's he found?'

'He wouldn't go into details,' said Sleeper. 'Just that he'd cracked the system and that we should see what he's got for us in person.'

'What do we do now then?' asked Rachel. 'I mean apart from heading back to Manchester that is.'

'That's what we were going to ask you,' said Sleeper as the four of them now sat down at the kitchen table.

'What do you mean?'

'What I mean Rach,' he said. 'Is that I need to know where you stand in all of this.'

'If Luther Cartwright is the Pied Piper, then we have to let Hunter know,' she replied as the three of them stared at her. 'What?'

'If he's the guy,' said Sleeper. 'Then we can't let you do that.'

'You can't be serious,' she said staring at him.

'He's right,' said Tony taking her hand.

'You've said it yourselves though. We don't even know whether or not it is him though,' sighed Rachel. 'What if you go after this guy and it's not even him, or them.'

'It makes no difference to us,' said Eazy. 'Not after what we saw last night.'

'So what,' she snapped at them. 'You're going to act as the judge and jury against the family then?'

'This shit has been going on for years Rachel,' said Sleeper. 'There was tape's that old down there that they don't even use the videos anymore.'

'They've also stepped things up for the new era,' added Eazy. 'Recordable DVD's for Christ sake. And with the computers that they had set up down there and internet links, God knows what's been sent directly through to be aired on the internet as they abused these kids.'

'But we need to be sure that this guy is the Pied Piper,' she told them. 'Even you must realise that Sleeper.'

'It's him,' he replied coldly. 'I just know that it is him.'

'You don't know that for sure,' she said. 'What if it's not him and all we do, is alert the real Pied Piper to go into hiding. What if we scare him away?'

'She's right in one sense,' said Tony.

'We need to go and see Robert then,' said Eazy. 'See if we can find anything more substantial against this freak.'

'Let's see what he's got for us first then,' said Rachel. 'Then we'll make any sort of decisions after that, alright.'

'That's alright with us,' said Sleeper. 'But then if it turns out to be him, then you have to let us handle it.'

'I'll make you a deal,' she said rising from her seat. 'First we see what Robert has for us.   Then if it's conclusive that Luther Cartwright is the guy, then you let me go and see them first.'

'Why?' asked Eazy. 'Why not just let us handle things Rachel?'

'Because I was asked to look into the missing girl only,' she told them. 'The fact that we've stumbled upon one another. And the fact that it all now appears to tie in with this Pied Piper shit wasn't our main concern. Charlotte was my concern in all of this. And I won't rest until I find out what has happened to her.

If you go and do whatever it is that you're going to do, then we'll never find out.'

'Fair enough,' said Sleeper.

'Only I go with you,' said Tony.

'Fine,' replied Rachel, thinking that she wasn't going to let her brother anywhere near the family if it did indeed turn out to be the Cartwright's behind this entire mess. She knew him too well to let him get personally involved. Whatever Sleeper and Eazy decided to do was down to them.

It wasn't that she disagreed with what they were saying, for she'd be the hypocrite if she did. But this battle hadn't been theirs in the first place. They'd only strayed from the path in discovering the identity of Gabriel into the path of now discovering the identity of this Pied Piper character.

'Best get your gear together then,' said Sleeper. 'Traffic shouldn't be at all bad today with it being Sunday.'

'Good,' smiled Eazy. 'Then we can stop and get some food before we leave then.'

'Rachel?' asked a panicky sounding Hunter on the other end of the line to Rachel's mobile, as they were about half way back to Manchester.

'What's wrong?' asked Rachel as the others glanced at her.

'Where the hell are you? What's all that noise?' asked Hunter as Rachel glanced at all the traffic that was speeding past loudly in the opposite direction to them

'I've been looking for Charlotte Cartwright,' answered Rachel.

'Never mind that for now,' she snapped, and then suddenly asked. 'Sorry, what have you found out?'

'I'll get to that later,' said Rachel realising the friend was all flustered. 'Now what the hell is wrong Hunter?'

'It's best that you hear this from me first,' sighed Hunter deeply.

'What, what is it?'

'It's him again,' she replied quietly. 'He's killed again already Rachel.'

'Gabriel... Jesus... already,' said Rachel shaking her head as Sleeper pulled across the line of traffic behind them as he eased the car to a standstill on the hard shoulder. 'When did it take place?'

'Last night,' replied Hunter.

'Who were they this time?'

'Fairchild's partner,' she sighed even deeper. 'William Morgan and his wife Patricia. And their little girl, Suzy. He's done it

again. Just like the others kid. He's raped and mutilated them once again. He's taken their hearts and left us with pretty much the same as he already has with the previous lots of murders.'

'For fucks sake Hunter,' snapped Rachel. 'Surely you had them protected for Christ's sake.'

'We did,' she replied quietly.

'Then how the hell did he get to them?'

'We don't know,' she admitted.

'What the hell do you mean, that you don't know for fucks sake,' screamed Rachel taking everybody by surprise. 'I told you that he had next set of victims picked out. He told me that himself. Surely you had to have considered the family to have been at risk after telling you that.'

'We did,' she said. 'They were being watched around the clock. Against their protests I might add.'

'And you wanted me to have police protection,' said Rachel sarcastically.

'That's below the belt kid,' said Hunter.

'How the fuck is it below the belt for fucks sake Hunter,' snapped Rachel. 'You've just let the killer walk straight through you as if you weren't there.'

'I know,' she answered quietly.

'How the hell could he have gotten past your so called police protection and murdered another family right under your noses?'

'We're looking into it kid.'

'Well you're doing a bang up job so far Hunter,' sighed Rachel. 'You do realise that the press are going to have a field day with this shit.'

'Tell me about it kid,' she sighed.

'What's your next move then?'

'I need you're help here Rachel.'

'What about Brendan?'

'He's still on it,' she told her. 'But I want your input also. It's so fucked up kid. I mean if the things you say are right about the killer's visual fantasy fading. And him feeling the need to kill again to feel the same euphoria he felt on the night he murdered them. Then just who the hell are we dealing with Rachel?'

'I just don't know Hunter,' she admitted.

'Will you come in?' she asked. 'Please kid.' This had to be the first time that Rachel had heard Hunter plead in anyway whatsoever.

'Not in any official capacity though,' she told her.

'Anyway that you'll agree is fine by me.'

'Brendan is more than capable enough,' she said.

'I know that he is kid,' she replied. 'But I figure that two heads will be better than one. You may pick up on something he misses and vice versa.'

'It'll have to be later on tonight now Hunter,' she said thinking about where they were travelling back to. 'I'll come to see you then if that's alright with you.'

'Why?' asked Hunter. 'Why not come in now. Where are you?'

Rachel looked around the car at the three other staring questionably at her. 'I'll just see you later on Hunter.'

Clicking the phone shut without saying good-bye she stared vacantly at the others, Tony was the first to speak next to her. 'He's killed again?'

'Fairchild's partner and his family. He's killed them all again in the same way he's killed them before.' she said wiping her eyes. 'Jesus fucking Christ, just who the fuck is this twisted arsehole.'

'Morgan?' asked Tony putting his arm around her pulling her close. 'William Morgan?'

'That's not the best of it,' she told them. 'He killed them right under their very noses last night.'

'What do you mean?' asked Sleeper.

'Exactly that,' she shook her head at him. 'They had the family under police protection.   Gabriel slipped right through them as if they didn't exist to him as they sat outside the house watching the family, killing all of them.'

'Jesus, he'd got some balls on him,' said Sleeper. 'I'm sorry. I didn't mean for that sound like it did Rachel.'

'I know you didn't,' she answered. 'But you're so right anyway. I mean to strike only a week after killing the Fairchild's, takes balls. To kill Fairchild's partner at the firm, takes even bigger balls. But to kill the family as the police are sat outside, well that just takes the piss completely. He must have water fucking melons as a set of balls.'

'How the hell did he get past them?' asked Tony.

'Maybe he really is an archangel,' said Eazy looking confused by the whole matter.

'You know,' sighed Rachel. 'I'm beginning to think you could be right there.'

'So what's next then?' asked Sleeper.

'What time have we got to meet Robert?' she asked.

'Jonah and Kezlo are to take us to him after midnight,' Eazy told her.

'Then I'll go and see Hunter first then,' she said. 'That way I can meet up with you guys after that.'

263

'So you're going to go back to working the case?' asked Eazy.

She shook her head. 'But I want to see the crime scene photos,' she told him. 'I need to learn first hand what I can about the investigation.'

'Will that help?' asked Sleeper.

'This guy just has to fuck up along the way somehow,' she sighed. 'And I want to be the one whose spots the mistake. Because when I do, it means that I can get to him first.'

'Amen to that,' smiled Sleeper as he slid the car in gear, easing them back out onto the busy motorway.

TWENTY NINE

'Thanks for coming Rachel,' said Hunter as she walked into her office at head-quarters in Manchester's city centre, where both Mike Andrews and Brendan McCarthy were looking over the crime scene photographs.

The office stank of cold coffee and stale cigarette smoke. Hunter was sat behind her desk puffing hungrily on her cigarette, treating the stick of nicotine as if it was a gourmet meal. She looked exhausted to Rachel, as if she hadn't slept a wink in weeks. But despite this fact, it was true to say that it wasn't the worst that Rachel had ever seen her friend. She almost seemed to thrive on these dire situations, which had become Rachel's nightmares recently.

'Alright guys,' said Rachel pulling a chair back.

'What are you doing here Rachel?' asked Brendan staring at her.

'I asked her to come,' said Hunter waving him off.

'You sure that you're up to this Rachel?' asked Andrews. 'You know that you don't have to be here.' He added as Hunter scowled at him, and he avoided her eye contact. Rachel thought that there had been possibly some kind of argument over Hunter calling Rachel, requesting that she be here for this, but she let it go all the same.

'Two heads could be better than one, right,' she said glancing to Hunter and smiling as best as she could under the circumstances.

'My sentiments exactly,' replied Hunter.

'What have we got then?' asked Rachel sitting herself next to Brendan McCarthy and looking over at the colour photographs in his hand.

'Pretty much the same as last time,' he told her. 'Have a look for yourself.'

'And the angels, the children of heaven, saw and lusted after them,' said Rachel reading the bloody scriptures that had been written on the walls from the photographs she held.   'That's from Enoch, The Apocrypha and Peeudepigrapha of the Old Testament.

'They took themselves wives of all whom they chose,' she added. 'Nephilm refers to the offspring that the angels produced by marrying human women. Consume, devoured mankind, all of this is scriptures. Yeshua is very interesting as it is mentioned both in the old and the new testaments. Yeshua spoke of the situation of the Nephilm, which would exist on earth just before his second coming.

'Chains of darkness, the spirits in prison, Appollyon right there,' she said pointing to the photograph. 'And Abaddon are references the word destroyer. The angelic ruler of the abyss.

'Whoa,' she suddenly said. 'Look here at this.' She held the picture up for them all to see as she pointed the top right hand corner of the picture. The opposite sides of where Gabriel had signed his name.

'What is it?' asked Brendan.

'It spells Michael,' she smiled.

'Who's Michael?' asked Hunter.

'For there were seven angels in all, under Satan's rule,' she smiled as she held up her fingers one at a time. 'Metraton, supposedly one of the top ruling angels, Seraphiel, Jehoel, Uriel, Shemuel, Natanael and Michael.'

'So where does Gabriel come into it?' asked Andrews.

'There is an entire army of these angels,' she told him.

'Like what?' asked Brendan looking somewhat unconvinced along with Hunter.

'Seraphim are the angels that act as overseers of the satanic world,' she said. 'Cherubim is Satanic wisdom and knowledge. Thornes have an interest in human doings and also have demons and fallen angels deal with them. Dominions carry out those three and also channel satanic wisdom to those on earth. Virtues try to influence in leadership areas. Powers act as a spiritual guide but are very rebellious. Pricipalities give guidance to world leaders and try to persuade them to hold one world government headed by Satan or by a possessed soul. Many believe that these angels were the angels that possessed Adolf Hitler and Gengas Khan to name but a couple. Then you have

Archangels and Demons that carry out Satan's decrees and work at all levels.'

'Jesus,' whistled Andrews.

'So which does Gabriel come under?' asked Hunter.

'Cherubim, virtue, powers and obviously the most famous he's renowned for,' she said staring back their disbelieving faces. 'Archangel.'

'How's this Michael fit into all of this?' asked Brendan.

'Through being one of Satan's seven archangels,' she said. 'We'll get to all of that in a moment. But basically I think that Gabriel believes that Michael is watching over him as he carries out his work.

'God was angry at the rebellion of The Watchers, who by the way are angels,' she told them. 'He therefore decreed that these wayward angels would be locked underneath the earth. In a prison designed for spirits until the day of judgement. The book of Jubilees and the book of Enoch both speak of this punishment.'

'What does all that mean in English Rachel?' asked Hunter.

'Gabriel for whatever reason wants us to believe that he's this archangel,' she sighed and started the photograph of the latest crime scene. 'He thinks that he's carrying out Satan's work here on earth, with the archangel Michael watching over him. The taking of the hearts is an offering to Satan. If you believe all of that, that is.'

'So you don't believe that he truly thinks he's an angel then?' asked Brendan.

'Let's just say that I don't think we should channel all of our resources into it, no,' she replied. 'Tell me what else we've got. Then let's go over things again without trying to focus on the archangel bit to much eh.'

'We know that he drugged the Fairchild's now,' he told her. 'You were right in thinking that he'd drugged them. He'd used the drug rophynol.'

'You brought Nigel Collin's in?' asked Rachel referring to the defendant of Otis Fairchild's.

'Alibied up for both nights,' replied Andrews.

'Solid as well,' shrugged Hunter. 'In fact, so solid that he happened to be drinking in the same boozer that Chief Mackenzie himself was drinking in on both occasions.'

'I bet he's happy at the moment,' smirked Rachel sarcastically.

'Don't even go there kid,' said Hunter shaking her head.

'So he managed to drug the family again?' asked Rachel. 'I presume that's why you told me about the Fairchild's.'

'We're still awaiting the reports for the autopsy,' replied Brendan.

'But we are presuming that's what he did here,' said Rachel staring at the photograph showing William Morgan nailed to the wall, mutilated and violated.

'It would appear so,' said Brendan. 'Yes.'

'Have you figured out,' sighed Rachel, 'just how the hell Gabriel got in there last night with your guys sat right outside Hunter?'

'He entered through the rear of the house.' She lit herself another cigarette from the butt of the other that had been smoked right the way down to its filter. 'We've managed to pull boot prints from the garden. Size ten.'

'Well at least that's something then,' said Rachel. 'But it doesn't explain how he got past your officers at the rear of the house.'

She watched as both Hunter and Andrews dropped there heads. 'There wasn't any back there kid.'

'Jesus Hunter,' she snapped. 'What the fuck were you playing at? Especially as it would appear that he gained access through the rear of the house last weekend at the Fairchild's place.'

'We didn't consider them to be at real risk from this guy,' offered Andrews.

'How the hell do you figure that one?' snapped Rachel.

'Because I told them so,' said Brendan.

'You serious?' she asked in disbelief whilst staring at him, holding eye contact.

'Come on Rachel,' he shrugged pulling his eyes away. 'You can't tell me honestly, that you'd have thought he was going to strike so soon after the killings last week.' He added this with his head dropped.

'Well he obviously thought that it was the best time strike back at you,' she said abruptly. 'How could you possibly not think that he'd strike again?'

'A week!' exclaimed Brendan, taking offence. 'It took him a year last time to strike again.'

'And what was he doing for that year Brendan?' asked Rachel. 'Because whatever it was, it wasn't remaining satisfied with his first lot of murders... was it?'

'He told you that he'd picked out his next lot of victims,' said Andrews. 'Right Rachel?'

'That's what he said,' she took a deep breath. 'He blatantly said that we wouldn't have to wait so long this time around.'

'You think that he's got more victims lined up?' asked Hunter.

'Most definitely,' she replied. 'You have to investigate the victims here. Because believe me, he hasn't done any of this just because he gets off on it. There has to be a connection between the victims. Peter may have worked as a prosecutor. But he went up against both Morgan and Fairchild in the past. Maybe there is some kind of a connection there. There has to be. We just need to find out what the hell it is.'

'Were they working any of the same cases?' asked Brendan.

'You'll have to look into that,' she replied. 'With every victim, and I mean every victim.   That includes the wife and the children. We have to consider the very possibility that some part of their lives may have a link to their death. Here it would appear that our killer has something against lawyers. So that doesn't narrow the field down all that much. But it may be something else, the wife's, the kid's, although it's more than likely the husbands that are his true motive here. It may be the thinnest thread that we are looking for here. It very well could be something that we don't consider relevant to the case. But sometimes, that's all we need to catch our break.'

'So you think that the killer knows his victims before hand then?' asked Andrews.

'Most definitely so,' answered Brendan. 'Just how close he is to them, is a completely different matter all together.'

'I think that this killer is a master manipulator,' said Rachel. 'I believe that what we are dealing with here is someone who obviously blends in well. He can probably read people in a heartbeat. And he can obviously change colours like a chameleon.'

'He's definitely becoming bolder with his crimes,' added Brendan enthusiastically.

'That's a fucking understatement ain't it,' said Rachel sighing deeply. 'His crimes have progressively become much more bolder with each murder carried out and much more flamboyant each time. Just look at the way he's improvising using the white bed sheets here.' She pointed the crime scene photograph showing Morgan stretched out against the wall. 'He's using the sheets as if they are in fact wings. Using the blood from their hearts in order illustrate the detail more graphically.'

'Away from the angelic references,' said Brendan glancing at her. 'That's what you said.'

'You're right,' she sighed. 'What we also need to start looking at, is the type of background that the killer has more than likely come from.'

'Like what?' asked Hunter.

'Like this guy could be extremely intelligent for starters,' Brendan answered for her.

'It would certainly seem that way,' added Rachel. 'As a child he could have been bright.　But he was probably always in trouble. Probably felt all alone at school. Couldn't relate to the other kids because he considered himself to be different.'

'He's certainly fucking different,' said Andrews. 'You mean to say that the killer could have been thinking about doing this shit as a kid.'

'He probably had trouble concentrating at school because his mind was filled with thoughts of domination and control of his peers at school,' said Rachel. 'Possibly even fantasising about what he would do to them given the chance. He probably became a pathological liar at an early age, which helped develop the way he can blend in so masterfully.'

'His trouble concentrating could have been because of an early addiction to these sexual fantasies that we are seeing here today,' said Brendan. 'The fantasies could have already been becoming a lot more violent. They may have been provoked as early as five or six years old. Especially in a house where there was abuse taking place or open sexual promiscuity going on.'

'You're kidding!' exclaimed Hunter.

'It may boil down to having been forced to watch his mother at some point,' said Rachel. 'The serial rapist we brought down last time became a patient of mine. So I could study why it was that he carried out such horrific acts. He told me all about his mother who used to lock him in a closet and he was forced to watch her have sex with strange men. He became aroused intensively, only because he knew that it was wrong and he was forbidden to watch. Only the more it was forbidden, the more irrepressible it became at the same time.'

'What goes through his mind as he's carrying out the murders then?' asked Andrews.

'Any number of things,' sighed Rachel. 'By the killer knowing these thoughts to have been wrong for so long. They have in fact become part of his sustained internal processing and cognitive operation. They are therefore in effect natural to him. In effect, by becoming natural to him he doesn't see his murders as being deviant in anyway whatsoever.

'Also, killers that I have spoken to in the past, describe the instant in which their victims were dying at their hands.' She paused and took a deep breath. 'Well, some serial killers described an insight that was so intense to them that it was like an emotional quasar, blinding in its revelation of the truth.'

'Revelation of the unenlightened,' added Brendan.

'That's what they say,' she shrugged.

'You believe that this guy thinks he's an archangel then?' asked Hunter. 'Gabriel as he calls himself.'

'Never expect for a serial killer to openly admit that they were responsible,' said Rachel. 'Gabriel more than likely believes and will speak of his crimes through a third person. Michael I believe in this case. It's what I said I'd come back to. Like many others, probably still after they have been found guilty beyond any doubt. Many killers will talk about that side of them which is capable of committing murder as a separate entity. The evil twin syndrome they will call it. I think that by the fact the he's leaving the doves behind as some kind of trade, he feels he's justifying in his own mind what he's doing. It is his small scrap of conscience to rationalise, to push the guilt away from him and onto their darkside.'

'How do you come up with all of this?' asked Andrews.

'You have to focus not on the emotions of their crimes,' she replied. 'Instead, you have individual components of their crimes. Trying all the while to eliminate the human factor and your own human reaction to the crime. Reliving their crimes is a crucial component in dealing with a serial killer's life cycle. Fantasy, violent fantasy, facilitators through to murder back through to fantasy, to murder to violent fantasy, leading you to step over the line into murder and on and on and around and around.'

'Another thing,' said Brendan. 'Going back to the bit about him being able to blend in. I just want to point out that through experience I have learnt that people can have more than one side. And a dark side that is capable of killing in the same way this killer is doing so, proves that he capable of anything.'

'Including,' added Rachel. 'Disguising himself from us very well, right?'

'Right,' he answered. 'This guy for whatever reason has so far eluded us. Now everything that Rachel and I have told you about the profile on this guy so far is more than likely to be correct. But don't go and make the mistake of then thinking that he'll be easy to spot. He could very well be someone that you all know in some way, no matter how small a way that may appear to be.'

'What about the scene itself?' asked Hunter as Rachel began looking through the photos.

'How the hell didn't your guys see or hear anything Hunter?' asked Rachel. 'He's obviously taken his time here... once again I might add. Have you seen the way he's positioned the arms of

271

the male victim for Christ sake. It's almost as if he's looking for his own heart with his arms positioned like they are. And after rigour-mortis set in over night, he probably looks just like that still. How could they not have noticed anything was going on Hunter? This isn't as if he's waltzed in here and executed them with a bullet to the back of the heads. I mean he's taken his time with each victim. There has to have been noise made. How did he get into the house and subdue the victims so quietly, if your lot were outside. How's he...'

'What?' asked Hunter. 'What is it kid?'

'Did you have the house under surveillance that day?'

'They weren't at the house,' said Andrews. 'They'd spent the day out shopping in Wilmslow. We had two non uniforms watch them the entire time.'

'Why?' asked Brendan.

'He knows your routines and he knows when you're at the house and when you're not there.'

'What makes you say that?' asked Andrews.

'I want their autopsy reports asap,' she told them. 'What was the last time that your guys saw them last night?'

'Ten o'clock,' said Hunter. 'Same time it's been all week.'

'Same time?' asked Rachel shaking her head. 'He knew this.'

'How?' asked Andrews.

'He's had you under surveillance at the same time that you've had the family under guard,' said Brendan realising where Rachel was going with this. 'Possibly even longer than that. He may have followed the family at the same time he followed the Fairchild's.'

'I still don't follow,' said Andrews.

'You think that he went into the house during the day and somehow drugged them?' added Hunter as things became clearer to herself.

'Phone Lucy,' said Rachel abruptly. 'I want to know if it's possibly to tell how and what time they were drugged last night.'

'He's completely taking the piss with us here,' said Hunter picking the phone up and dialling the number for the mortuary.

'Tell me about it,' said Rachel. 'Not only has this guy deceived you in sneaking past you last night. But if I'm correct he's done the same in broad daylight.'

'This is Lucy,' said the voice through the speaker phone that lay upon Hunter's desk.

'Lucy, it's Hunter,' she said outloud.

'You alright girl,' she said as they heard her yawn straight after. 'What can I do for you Hunter?'

'Have you carried out the autopsies yet?' she asked her.

'I'm about to start on the male victim right now,' she replied. 'I've already done the child and female victims already.'

'Hold on will you,' said Hunter as they stared at her. 'We'll be right down there. And will you check into whether or not they were drugged Lucy.'

'I already have done so,' she told them. 'I'm just waiting on the results to come back now.'

'See you soon,' said Hunter as they all made their way to the door.

Stepping out into the corridor they were suddenly confronted with an angry looking Chief of Police staring coldly at the four of them. 'What the hell is she doing here?' screamed Chief Superintendent Tom Mackenzie as they were all now stood outside the office.

'She's with me,' said Hunter casually pulling her door shut.

'I thought she wanted no part of this,' he snapped.

'I don't think that I have much choice in that department Mackenzie,' Rachel shot right back at him. 'If you haven't forgotten, it was my family that were the first victims.'

'But...' he began.

'Please,' said Hunter calmly. 'Let's talk over here chief.'

'Whatever,' he sighed deeply taking hold of Hunter's arm leading her away from the group stood by the office door.

'Just list...' began Hunter.

'I want to know what the hell she is do...'

'She was just here to give me an update on the Charlotte Cartwright situation Chief,' said Hunter calmly trying to smooth over things. 'That's all she's here for. So why don't you calm down.'

'How the hell do you expect me to calm down Detective Hunter,' he replied, as he tried to keep his voice down. 'When it's me that has to face the music with the reporters as to why we let this killer not only slip right through our fingers...' he gritted his teeth as he glared directly at Rachel, before shaking his head in frustration as he suddenly shouted outloud, 'But also go and kill the entire family whilst your officers were outside I might add.'

'We're working on an answer for you right at this very moment,' she replied nonchalantly.

Frustrated and angry at Hunter's response, realising just how unprofessional he'd just acted, he therefore turned his attention to Rachel. 'Well,' he said abruptly staring at her. 'Have you found the missing girl yet or not?'

'That's just what she was about to go over,' added Hunter trying her best to drive the attention away from Rachel. 'Right after we've solved the murders from last night that is,' she added sarcastically.

'No I haven't,' replied Rachel angry at Mackenzie's attitude whilst stepping towards the man before her, 'I haven't succeeded in doing your job for you yet.'

'What the hell does that mean?' he snarled straight back at her. 'And I'll remind you Detective Hunter that I am your boss and refuse to be spoken to like that from members of the publ....'

'Yes sir,' said Hunter mockingly as Rachel suddenly stepped forward and poked him.

'Interesting people the Cartwright's,' she said staring at him as he looked at her disgusted by the invasion of his space. 'Especially seeing as you appear to be such good friends with them Chief Mackenzie.'

'What's that supposed to mean Murphy?'

'Never mind,' she sighed turning away from him, realising that she should tread carefully here.

'I want to know what the hell that was in reference to you little...'

'That enough Mackenzie,' interrupted Hunter stepping between the two of them.

'I want a report on my desk first thing in the morning Hunter,' he snapped back at her, realising that he was outnumbered here, he turned away from Rachel, staring at Hunter coldly as he then began to walk away. 'On both matters,' he added with his back still turned to them as he stormed down the corridor.

'What a complete dickhead,' sighed Hunter as all four of them watched him leave. 'What was that all about anyway kid?' she added, looking in her direction.

Realising that she may have said too much already and the fact the fact she'd promised the others that they would discover what they could themselves first, she smiled and said. 'I'll tell you about it in a couple of days. I need to look into things further. Let's just concentrate on this lot first eh.'

'We best get a move on then,' said Andrews.

'We'll get back to this matter,' said Hunter staring suspiciously at Rachel.

'What've you got Lucy?' asked Hunter walking through to the mortuary where the autopsy was to be carried out.

But as Rachel witnessed the corpse of the male victim upon the table shook her. It was almost surreal, with the body on the examination table away from the dark and horrific crime scene.

The whiteness of the room engulfing the bloody torso of the victim. Enhancing the horrors more vividly against its pureness. William Morgan's entire torso sliced wide open and the rib cage pulled back with his left hand placed with the fingers folding around the stripped flesh and bone as though it was holding it open for the entire world to see. His right hand placed open handed where the very heart had once belonged. Almost as though it was searching for what was once there.

The voices around her sounded far away as she felt the blood drain from her head. Her legs buckled and gave way beneath her. She went down on one knee, unconsciously holding onto Brendan's arm next to her. Scrambling like mad to stand again, just as quickly as she did her best to regain composure. Emotions swirling through her like a cyclone, shock, horror, embarrassment and confusion.

'You alright?' asked Brendan helping her to her feet.

'Just give me a minute,' she said.

'You sure you want to be here for this?' asked Lucy shaking her head. 'I still think it's too soon Rach.'

'I'll be fine,' she said blowing air out and taking deep breaths. Immediately regretting it as all she inhaled was the smell of the death presented to them before her.

'Any news on whether or not they were drugged?' asked Hunter ignoring Rachel.

Lucy nodded to her as she looked back down at the corpse. 'Same as last time.' She looked to some kind of chart in her hands. 'Rophynol.'

'What about the kid?' asked Hunter.

'He didn't drug the child. And just the small amounts of the drug that we found in the male and female victims blood would have killed the little girl if he'd given it to her.'

'You have any idea just how it was given to them?' asked Rachel.

'Their stomach lining was damaged where the killer tore them open,' she replied. 'Although I still found traces of alcohol in their system. It's possible that he gave it them that way. Although there are no signs of them being forced to do so.'

'Is it possible to find out what time they were drinking?' asked Hunter as she glanced to Rachel.

'Possibly,' she said. 'It won't be easy but I'll see what I can do for you.'

'Thanks,' replied Rachel walking closer to the table.

Behind Lucy, hung the X-rays and photographs that had been taken earlier. 'What are all those?' asked Andrews.

'Everything that we've gathered so far from the bodies that I've examined,' she told him. 'They're his charts and X-rays there.' She added pointing to the right hand side where all of the evidence was assembled.

She then proceeded to tell them in detail, what it was that she discovered with the wife and the child. Details that Rachel found hard to digest, with images still so strong of that night, just over twelve months ago.

'I've already weighed and measured this body.' She indicated to the corpse on the examining table. 'It weighed in at one hundred and ninety six pounds. That's with internal organs included that had come away from his stomach as he hung from that position on the wall. Mainly intestines and stomach linings,' she said. 'His height measures in at five foot ten inches.

'I've already gone over the body with the laser to illustrate and collect evidence for you,' she told them. 'Although my guess is that you won't find any trace of anything that belongs to the killer.'

'Why's that?' asked Brendan. 'Surely that's not at all possible in this day and age.'

'Normally I'd say you were correct,' she said. 'But I've carried out all the autopsies so far and have found nothing, and I mean nothing.'

Lucy then took her time as she went over every square inch of the body visually; describing in detail everything she saw, every wound, every mark, new and old. The full examination took a little over an hour to complete.

'In my opinion he died from severe trauma,' she told them. 'That's speculation at this point. Although you'd be safe to put money on me. You see here where the serrated edge to the knife has torn open the victim's chest as the heart was removed. 'Well that to me is clear indication to the victim dying this way,' she added.

'You think that it was carried out post mortem?' asked Brendan.

'No one could have stood the pain of their chests cut open and their hearts removed and remained alive through the process,' she said. 'Plus I need to check. But it would appear that the killer was still sexually violating the victims post mortem.'

'What about those marks again?' asked Rachel pointing to the victim's neck.

'There are several tales of ligature marks around the neck on all the victims,' she said taking a closer look. 'It would also appear that the cord or belt was loosened and tightened throughout the ordeal as there is one single red furrow, but several.

'Normally I would have put the cause of death down to asphyxiation,' she sighed. 'Due to ligature strangulation. But it appears from the way the cord was tightened and loosened, that the killer wanted to merely punish them further.'

'Nice,' said Andrews sarcastically.

'Also the most common indicator of this is that the thyroid bone had been crushed on all the victims at the base of the tongue in the upper part of the trachea.' Pointing to the eyes she glanced at them to make sure they were taking notice. 'The eyes also showed signs of peechial haemorrhaging.'

Rachel took in the appearance of the wound in the victim's hands and feet area. The binding of the nails that the killer used as the victim had struggled frantically had only cut and tore into the skin further. His hand and feet had swelled like balloons.

As Lucy spoke to them she continued to catalogue and measure different areas of the corpse.

'What's this on the back of the ankle?' asked Rachel observing the slices there.

'I found that on all the victims,' said Lucy. 'My guess is that the killer sliced the achilles tendons so that the victims never stood a chance of escaping anyway.'

'As if all this wasn't enough,' said Rachel.

'Have you any idea who he's got in mind as his next lot of victims?' asked Lucy staring at Rachel.

'Your guess would be as good as mine at the moment Lucy,' she sighed, glancing to the others.

'What's your next move going to be Hunter?' asked Brendan.

'We've still got a lot to cover,' she replied.

'What about his next lot of victims?' asked Rachel. 'There has to be some sort of connection to them working in law. You need to look into that first. Because if it only took this guy a week to strike again, then it leaves things wide open to you. God only knows when he'll decide it's time for him to kill again.'

'What would you suggest?' asked Andrews. 'That we lock all of the lawyers away in their homes.'

'Well it didn't work this weekend,' snapped Rachel, feeling the exhaustion of everything happening around her. Trying to sort through the tangle in her head in order to take her attention away from the tight feeling in her throat. She found herself thinking, concentrate on the issue at hand, not the problem inside. Trying

to evaluate the situation in hand she shook her head. 'Sorry Mike, christ, just when we thought that he'd given us a second chance at catching him and that we could actually make some progress he goes and kills again. This really is like something straight out of a terrible nightmare that you can't wake up from.'

'So what do you suggest we do then kid?' asked Hunter ignoring her little outburst.

'That's for you to decide, not me Hunter,' she said. 'Thanks again Lucy.' She turned away from the table.

'Where are you going kid?' asked Hunter.

'I need to get out of here,' she said, her back still turned to them.

'But...' started Hunter.

'Let her go,' said Brendan as she glared at him. 'Just leave it for now eh.'

'I'll be in touch in a couple of days over Charlotte Cartwright,' said Rachel as she pushed the doors before her open, and with that she was gone.

THIRTY

'**W**hat time did she say she'd meet us Tony?' asked Jonah sat next to him in the passenger seat as they sat outside Chan's restaurant, that had long since closed for the night as it was gone two in the morning. Jonah was referring to Rachel who'd agreed to meet them at twelve at Chan's place in order to go and see Robert.

'I know he keeps late hours Tony,' said Kezlo from the back seat. 'But we said we be there just after twelve.'

'Still no joy with her mobile?' asked Sleeper suddenly appearing at Tony's open window. 'You want to go and check it out?'

'Nah, she just said that she'd be running lat...' he smiled and nodded to the end of the road where headlights had just appeared. 'That's her Explorer now.'

'We taking all three motors?' asked Jonah.

'Is that going to be a problem?' asked Tony. 'I just don't want to leave any of these motor's out in the open, in the city centre when there's still scallies like you two running about the streets, Jonah.'

They all laughed as Rachel eased over to the curb. 'I'll go with Rachel,' announced Sleeper as Tony looked suspiciously at him. He signalled for Eazy to follow them, and then walked over to Rachel's Ford Explorer climbing into the passenger side.

'You alright Rach?' he asked as he smiled at her.

She looked extremely tired; he could tell the week's events were beginning to take a hold of her. 'I just needed to go home and shower after being at the mortuary,' she told him rubbing her eyes. 'My clothes stank of, well... well, what can only be described as death clinging to them.'

'What were you doing there?' he asked as they pulled out after the others.

'Observing the autopsy of the male victim from last night,' she sighed.

'This is definitely this Gabriel character again, right?'

'It's him alright,' she replied. 'The fuckin' freak is draining me of all my resources. This and the whole scenario over the last couple of weeks have been multilayered like a bad onion.'

'What do you mean by that?'

'You peal one layer away and it smells worse with the next layer,' she shook her head. 'Everything seemed average enough when we became involved in all of this. Missing teenager, that was it. I hadn't looked into anything over the last twelve months, apart from searching for the killer of my husband and daughter that is. It's as if Gabriel waited patiently all year, waited for the commemoration of the night he took my family away from me so viciously to pass. Waited for me to become involved in something else entirely. Just so he could fuck with my head completely. It sounds paranoid, but it's as if he knew that everything would escalate into the chaos that has happened. So that's what I meant by it all appeared average enough, then as each layer as been peeled away, it's like, oh, this has now happened, and oh shit, now it's this, and so forth, and so forth.'

'It has become like that,' agreed Sleeper.

'It's like everything is beginning to crowd in on me,' she said glancing at him, his dark mysterious eyes penetrating right through her as she looked away. I can't seem to get a clear perspective on things. There are too many players becoming involved here. Their sick ideas, their twisted emotions are beginning to bleed into one, which is bleeding into the cold facts. The cold facts that I need in order to analyse the situation at hand.'

'None of us expected things to escalate like they have done Rachel,' he told her. 'Not me, not Eazy, nor you or your brother. That's just the way it has gone and we're now left with the aftermath of dealing with it.'

'I know,' she sighed deeply, resting her head against the steering wheel as they pulled up behind the others at the traffic lights. 'It's just the way my mind works Sleeper. It's like a computer sometimes. It overloads and I have to empty the trash out from it. I just haven't realised how much junk has logged itself in there. I've got strategies and theories' running through my head like it's a rat maze. Each rat is desperate for a way out.'

'You'd be very lucky to go through life,' he smiled at her, 'and not feel like that at some point,'

'Can I ask you something personal?' She glanced at him as they pulled away.

He gave a little laugh. 'It ain't stopped you yet girl.'

'If this turns out to be Cartwright tonight,' she began. 'Then what are you going to do to him, to the family for that matter. As it would now appear that the wife was also involved.'

'It depends on what Robert has found out,' he said. 'The main goal here is to discover who it is running this paedophile operation. If he isn't the Pied Piper, he's got to know who is. I'll just ask him nicely to tell me the true identity if it ain't him.' He smirked at her through the darkness of the vehicle.

'You're going to kill him,' she said dropping her head slightly. 'Aren't you Sleeper?'

'And let me ask you this Rachel,' he said quietly. 'What is it of Gabriel that you seek? Is it to bring him to justice through the letter of the law? I think not Rachel.'

'That's...'

'That's the same thing girl,' he cut her off. 'But I would never judge you on the matter.'

'I'm sorry,' she sighed.

'Never apologise for that,' he said. 'I'm not leaving your side until we've found both our guys.'

'And if that takes forever,' she looked at him. 'Because that's how long I've committed myself to finding Gabriel, Sleeper.'

'Then you better start getting used to having me around,' he said as he pushed himself back in the seat and made himself comfortable.

She knew that was the end of the conversation, and also knew the feeling of undiminished invulnerability with this person by her side.

'Tony?' asked the voice on the other end of the mobile phone that had just startled everybody in the vehicle.

'Who's this?' he asked anxiously.

'It's Paul mate,' said the voice. 'No need to bite my head off Tony.'

'Sorry mate, it's been a long day and night,' he sighed as Jonah indicated that they turn right at the next lot of traffic lights. 'What's up brother?'

'I know this may sound a little odd mate,' he said. 'But have you any idea where ar'Caroline may be?'

'No,' he replied confused. 'Why would you ask me Paul?'

'Because she's been missing since Friday night Tony,' he told him. 'I wouldn't normally be bothered, as I know that she can look after herself. Plus her and Charlotte always used to spend weekends at one anothers. But she hasn't done this sort of thing since Charlotte went missing.'

'No joy with her mobile?' asked Tony thinking about Charlotte.

'It's switched off,' he told him. 'I've even called the coppers, and y'know that I'd never do that. But only because Jackie was on me case about it. They just laughed me off though. They couldn't give a fuck mate'

'You tried her friends?'

'She's become quite the recluse since Charlotte disappeared,' he admitted. 'She's become obsessed as to what's happened to her friend since you both came around to see her. She was determined to find out what happened to the girl.'

'Do you know whether or not she's been round to the Cartwright's mate?'

'I reckon so,' he said. 'That fuckin' wanker Cartwright.'

'What about the Cartwright's, Paul?' asked Tony.

'That wanker just had a go at me on the phone,' he said. 'Because he says that Caroline has been mithering him.'

'Mithering him how?' asked Tony.

'Jackie tells me that she became convinced of the old man having something to do with the girl going missing,' he told him. 'Why? You don't think that he has something to do with her going... I'll strap that mother fucker...'

'I don't know nothing mate,' lied Tony, calming the man down. He knew Paul's temper. He also knew that he'd only have to suspect that Luther Cartwright had something to do with his daughter going missing, in order to do some serious bodily harm to the man. And that was the last thing they needed right now... well until they'd found out more for themselves that is.

'I've probably got to go and see the Cartwright's with ar'kid tomorrow mate,' he told him the truth. He just didn't reveal all of it to him. 'We'll go and see them. Then we'll come and see you at the club mate. Alright?'

'Alright,' he sighed. 'I'm just worried about her mate.'

'I know you are,' he replied. 'Like you said though. She's probably just stayed away for the weekend. She'll show up. Just wait and see,' he added, although he was not convinced by his own words as he said them.

'Cheers Tony, laters,' he said as the line went dead and Jonah signalled to the side of the road.

'What is this place?' asked Tony as they pulled up outside of what appeared to be an abandoned warehouse in Stretford. All of the lights were out and some of the windows had been shattered. The old faded sign that hung over the top floor window, read Boardman's Furniture Factory.

'It's where Robert lives,' laughed Kezlo from the back seat.

'We told you he was paranoid,' smiled Jonah.

'What the hell is he doing living here though?' asked Tony, easing the car to a halt outside of the building.

'It was shut down years ago now,' said Kezlo. 'The company was only a small set up. It went bust through the mid nineties.'

'How come he ended up with the place then?' asked Tony. 'Or does he just squat here lads?'

'Nah man,' laughed Kezlo. 'His uncle owned the building. Past away whilst Robert was serving a five stretch for all the gear he was producing for us back then. He left the building to him. In all honesty. He could make himself a nice bundle if he rented or sold the place off.'

'He makes a nice bundle anyway,' said Jonah. 'You just wouldn't think it to look at him or to see this gaff from the outside. Just wait until you see the shit he's got set up in there though.'

'What now then?' asked Tony as he noticed Eazy and Rachel's headlights pull up behind him. 'Shall we get out and ring the bell, or what lads.'

'Just pull in through there,' instructed Kezlo as the large steel shutters, about the only new looking thing about the building automatically began to open.

'How's he know that we're here?' asked Tony

'He has sensors that tell him when someone stops outside of here,' said Jonah. 'Up there, look.' He added pointing the top of the three story building. 'He knows who's here before they even realise it.'

'Jeez,' laughed Tony easing the car forward. 'Just how paranoid is this guy!'

Climbing from the car into the deserted shell of what had probably once been a prospering business years ago. Tony then looked around himself, taking in the details of what could only be described as an abandoned warehouse. There was no sign of life, apart from the pigeons that had struggled to escape through the busted skylight as their peace had been disturbed so abruptly. He could see that the skylight's window pane's had been broken, making the interiors decor. Although he could also see a range of different sized satellite dishes stationed on the roof in the

darkness. In fact there was that many he couldn't count them all. 'Just what sort of work is he involved in?' he asked staring at Kezlo and Jonah.

'He works mainly with the internet these days,' replied Kezlo as the others approached.

'What exactly does he do?' asked Rachel.

'Gathers information,' said Jonah shrugging.

'What sort of information?' she asked.

'Anything you want pretty much,' replied Jonah. 'Illegal information if that's what you require. Which we do in most cases,' he laughed and his boyish looks really stood out. 'Also a lot of legal shit that keeps him covered where the authorities are concerned,' added Kezlo.

'Where's this guy Kezlo?' asked Eazy walking over to them.

'You sure that there is anybody even here?' asked Sleeper glancing to Tony who nodded to the skylights.

'I take it there not just for Sky sports lads,' he laughed.

'Come on,' said Kezlo. 'This way, follow me and watch your step.'

'I still don't understand what you mean by he gathers information Jonah,' said Rachel as they followed the others.

'He hacks into other peoples systems and delivers the information to whoever wants it,' he told her.

'What kind of information though?' she was real curious now. 'And how the hell do people even know about him for Christ sake, hiding away in here.'

'Believe me,' he laughed. 'People know of his services. Although, most of his communication is done right here. Hardly ever leaves the place. Plus me and Kezlo get him a lot of business. It's good for us actually. We get to merely sell off his information on certain scores that he comes up with.'

'Scores!'

'You sure you want to know this?' he asked glancing at Tony's back as he helped Rachel up the steps towards the door they were heading.

'Not really,' she smirked. 'But tell me anyway.'

'He'll give out guaranteed scores to say someone who wants to deprive somewhere or someone of whatever it is that they are holding,' he said. 'But say that particular person wants a guarantee, of say what the bank will be carrying on a certain day. Or what stock they'll be holding, at say a certain warehouse, well he can find the information for you. Excellent commission for him, me and Kezlo.'

'Oh,' she said. 'That's not just it though, is it?'

'Nah,' he replied as a large metal door slid to one side revealing industrial metal steps that ran down into a well lit basement where the heavy bass of Eminiem's new album pumped its way through to them.

'What else then?' she asked curiously as they made their way down the metal steps.

Rachel was taken back by the sheer magnitude of the room that they came to. Not only by its vastness, by the by the way he had set the place up. It looked like the control deck of something out of *Star Trek, The Next Generation*, not the original series. The room covered the entire size of the building above it. All for walls were covered from floor to ceiling with electrical equipment. 'He helps a lot of legit businesses as well with anything they have problems with. Whether it's legal problems or illegal problems he's their man,' said Jonah as he saw Rachel's expression.

'Look at this place,' said Rachel as she stared in disbelief at the high tech room found within the old shell of a building.

'You're privileged to have been invited here,' said Kezlo, as Robert approached them tapping away at a palm sized computer. 'I reckon that only me and Jonah have seen this place outside of hyper space where he now appears to live.'

'You all alright?' asked Robert taking his eyes from the small computer screen before him.

'This is some gaff you've got set up here Robert,' said Eazy looking around.

Around the four walls, were banks and banks of computer, stereo, television and all the latest DVD and video equipment. It was unreal to look at. Floor to ceiling was covered in all the latest equipment range of gizmos and high tech toys. There appeared to be endless monitors and televisions screens, all of them turned on showing an array of different images and programs that were in the process of running various programs.

'Thanks,' he smiled at them, as he watched their astonished looks. 'You best come on through and have a look at what I've got for you.'

'We've got these as well with us,' said Sleeper showing him the box with the tapes in them. 'We took them from the house in London.'

'They belonged to the Cartwright's?' asked Robert.

'That's where we got them from,' said Eazy.

'Then I don't want to see them then,' he told Sleeper nodding at the box. 'And make sure that you take it with you when you go, will you.'

'What've you found?' asked Rachel.

'You best all make yourselves comfortable,' he said signalling to the black leather embankment of sofa's that formed a circle in the centre of the room. 'I can bring it all up on the monitors right next to where you're sitting.'

As they sat themselves down they couldn't help but notice the four computer screens at each end of the seats. Robert went to the main frame computer before them, sitting himself down as he began tapping away at the keys.

'First off, is what you got from the guy in London,' he said as the Pied Piper Productions suddenly came up on the screen that they'd all already seen at Chan's that night.

'What happened when you broke the code?' asked Sleeper.

'I ran it through this programme here,' he said tapping away on a separate keyboard. 'It's capable of breaking most systems.'

'Can you break into any of these systems?' asked Tony impressed.

'There's a lot that I can't access to be honest,' he told them. 'But you'll be surprised at just what is easy and what's not these days. Like police files are relatively easy to access considering who they are. They have quite a basic system set up. Don't get me wrong here either. They are well protected. You're not going to have some spotty teenager accessing the system and wiping out or adding to any criminal records or anything like that. I just mean that they are easy for me to access.'

'So what was so difficult about the Pied Piper system?' asked Rachel.

'It took over forty eight hours to access the system,' he said. 'The password wasn't as simple as just a word. It used a series of higher and lower casing along with numbers. I ran a random program and just got lucky to be honest. Only when I got through to their system they appeared to be waiting for me.'

'What's that mean?' asked Sleeper.

'They immediately put a trace on me,' he said. 'Their system was set up, so that they know just who it is that is accessing them. The program would have automatically shut down taking a lot of my files with it if I hadn't realised what was happening. It was designed so that if the police try and break into their system. Then they are going to get burnt badly. They'll probably lose a lot of shit from their systems. It will also leave behind a lot of virus's that will take them pure time to get rid off.'

'What did you do then?' asked Eazy.

'I bypassed the trace and on a hunch that I had. I ran it straight back to the Cartwright's residence in Prestbury,' he smiled. 'I

had already accessed their home computer through the files that I opened on the young girl's harddrive.'

'What happened?' asked Rachel.

'It automatically allowed me in the system through the password and the trace at the Cartwright's residence,' he began tapping away at keys again. 'Whoever set this shit up though, is most definitely in the know. I've come across banking and security system's that would have been easier to break than this would have been.'

'What did you find though?' asked Jonah.

'This,' he announced, as the screen suddenly accessed through to a menu screen. 'You merely use the cursor to access which ever sick show it is that you want to watch. Watch this,' he said as the screen suddenly filled with pictures of young girls in different poses.

'This is there selection of six years old girls,' he said shaking his head. 'But you have age ranges from six months to eleven years. Boys and girls. You are charged for the amount of time that you spend on the website. Whoever set this up is making a mint from it, believe me. It's real fucked up shit that they've got on there. Be my guest if you want to access any of it. But I would just take my word on it if I was you. That's only the tip of it as well guys. But we'll get to that.'

'What about Cartwright?' asked Rachel. 'What did you find on Luther Cartwright?'

'As I searched their system, I came across a secret menu that regular normal every day Joey's wouldn't have known about.'

'What do you mean by that?' asked Tony.

'It was a system within a system,' he told him. 'I crossed referenced with what the Cartwright girl had accessed on her lap top and found that she had somehow found her way into these files.'

'What was in there?' asked Sleeper.

'I don't know whether or not the shit in there was for real,' he sighed deeply. 'But this was kids being beaten badly. In some cases... well, I'm sure that they very well may...'

'What?' asked Rachel. 'What is it Robert?'

'This is what the girl discovered,' he said tapping away at a few more keys.

Suddenly the screen filled with a young girl tied to a bed. Immediately Rachel recognised that the girl was a young version of the photo's that she's seen of Charlotte. Although she wasn't sure whether or not it was Charlotte or Bethany on the screen. It was an old film, you could tell by the quality of the print.

'What the fuck is this shit?' asked Eazy gringing at the image on the screen.

'Is that Charlotte?' asked Tony.

'It's either Charlotte or it's the younger sister Bethany,' replied Rachel as they all observed the young girl who looked scared out of her wits.

Suddenly another figure entered the frame. He was dressed in a fancy dress outfit, almost like he was royalty. A king maybe, but not the Pied Piper. They couldn't tell who it was, because he was disguised by the mask he wore. Walking over to the bed where the young girl lay trapped, he began to molest the girl as they all looked away from the screens.

'Turn this shit off,' snapped Tony.

'You need to see the end of it,' said Robert as he clicked a few more keys taking it to the end of the film.

'Oh my God,' said Rachel as she and the others witnessed the girl at the end of a severe beating with what looked like a rubber hose of some kind. The sight before them was so horrific to watch, that it sickened them to their stomachs.

'Turn it off now,' demanded Tony rising from his seat.

'There,' said Robert as he paused the film. 'You can see who that is now.'

The mask had pulled slightly away from the face and Rachel covered her mouth. 'Oh sweet Jesus. It's him Tony.'

'It's fucking Cartwright,' snarled Tony.

'I may hide away in here,' said Robert, 'but even I recognised the face.'

'What else is in these restricted files?' asked Sleeper.

'More of the same kind of thing,' he said. 'There are other films with what appears to be kids dying in them. But like I said. You can't be certain if they live or not. It may even be an act.'

'Why's that?' asked Eazy.

'Because if it's not, well then, it's putting it in snuff movie territory,' he replied. 'And that my friends, is the stuff of urban legends. It supposed to exist but no one knows for sure whether it does or doesn't. It's just one of them things.'

'Oh shit,' sighed Tony.

'What?' asked Rachel

'Paul Massey phoned me tonight. When we were on our way over here,' he stared at her. 'He says that Caroline is missing, since Friday night.'

'We go and see them now then,' said Sleeper grabbing his jacket.

'No,' snapped Rachel. 'We agreed that I would see them first.'

'This changes everything Rach,' said Sleeper.

'He's right,' nodded Tony. 'And you know it ar'kid.'

'I see them first,' she said. 'We still don't know where Charlotte is. And we don't know for sure if they've had anything to do with Caroline going missing or not.'

'I'm coming with you then,' said Tony.

'They ain't going anywhere,' said Rachel. 'Now I suggest that we all get some rest tonight. It's been a fucker of day for all of us.'

'But...' began Tony.

'But fuck all Tony,' she said abruptly at him. 'I need a clear head to question them and believe me. After the past two week's events, it ain't even close to clear. So we do this my way or not at all. I swear to God, I'll phone Hunter with the information right now lads.'

'First thing in the morning,' said Sleeper watching her closely. 'Alright Rach.'

She nodded her response as they all stared at her, not quite sure what to make of her response to what had just been revealed to them.

THIRTY ONE

Rachel found that her vision was impaired by the early morning haze that appeared to levitate eerily all around her, like the ghost's that always seemed to be by her side these days. The reoccurring nightmare had woken her as she drifted in and out of restless sleep, if that's what you could call it. She often dreamt about the night that she arrived home to find her husband and daughter slaughtered by the mad man that was still forever taunting her. Only this time was different, for not only were her Peter and Becky there, but also Charlotte and Caroline.

As she arrived home in the dream, she was drawn to the upstairs bedroom, just as she always was in the dream. Only this time as she arrived, Gabriel was also there, only it wasn't Gabriel, it was the Pied Piper, or was it the same entity. She wasn't sure of anything as she couldn't see the killer's face as he positioned his victims in the way that he wanted them depicted in his latest work of deranged art.

As Rachel screamed out to help them, her voice became muted like that of an old silent movie. With this failing to prevent what was happening, she ran at the killer before her. Determined to stop him, determined to kill him herself. Only it was no use as the floor beneath her turned to quick sand, the more she struggled, the harder it became. Sinking deeper and deeper into the abyss, as she screamed her muted pleas at the killer who blatantly kept his back to her.

She had awoken startled and dazed at what had happened. Drenched in cold sweat, seepage from very possible pore, she psychically shivered as the images of the dream remained strong in her mind and the perspiration intermingled. Climbing from the settee where she had been dozing, she went straight to the

bathroom where she began to take an extremely cold shower in order to wake herself completely.

It also prompted her to make the decision that she'd already made at the back of her mind anyway. And that was to get to the Cartwright's before the others, including her brother. It wasn't that she believed what they were going to do was that wrong. It was to do with the fact that she wanted to know the truth about what had not only happened to Bethany.

But also as to the whereabouts of Charlotte, whom she was now convinced had either ran away because of what she'd discovered or more than likely in Rachel's mind, had been taken care of by her very own parents, so not to spill the beans on them.

There was also Caroline now included in all of this, if they indeed had something to do with her disappearance, then Rachel wanted to find out. She also felt that by confronting them herself, she would achieve a lot more than she would with any of the others there, including her Tony.

She felt bad that she hadn't told the others what she'd planned to do. Feeling that she'd somehow deceived them the night before in some way. But saying that, she hadn't gone to Hunter with any of this yet. Although that was also something that she felt extremely divided about.

Something that Sleeper had questioned her about, kept running back and forth through her mind. Why had Hunter really asked her to look into the missing girl? She's believed that she was doing Hunter a favour in finding out what had happened to Charlotte Cartwright. But two things kept bothering her.

The first was the mysterious phone call that Hunter had claimed to have received, telling her about the missing girl and the connection to the paedophile ring. Rachel honestly believed that if Caroline had in fact made that call, then she would have admitted it to her. So who made that call to Hunter?

The second thing that was bothering her was that Hunter didn't appear to be over anxious in discussing anything with Rachel that they had discovered in the past two weeks. In fact, she'd only really questioned her when she herself had brought the subject up. She realised that Hunter's mind was elsewhere at the moment with the return of Gabriel. But still, after asking for her help, she hadn't really shown much interest in the girl. Why?

Both these things and more bothered Rachel. Had Hunter somehow known where this was all going to lead them? Had she been warned off the Cartwright's like the detective down in London had said that they had? Had she used Rachel as some

kind of a pawn in her investigation that went a lot deeper than Charlotte Cartwright? Did she already have knowledge of the Pied Piper?

Whatever it was, she had made the decision that she was going to be the to confront the Cartwright's before she made her decision on what it was that she was going to do about them.

It was just gone five thirty in the morning as she tackled the winding lane towards her destination. She didn't care what time it was or the fact that her body felt as if it needed a weeks worth of sleep to catch up on itself. She didn't even care that she was about to wake the Cartwright's from their beauty sleep. All she cared about right now was getting to the bottom of this thing. And she therefore believed that after what they were made to witness, only hours before at Robert's place, that the Cartwright's had the answers that she searched for.

Pulling into the driveway, hearing the sound of gravel crunching loudly beneath her tyres in the stillness of dawn, she instantly saw the upstairs bedroom light come on. Easing the Explorer around to the rear of the house, she climbed down from the vehicle.

'Who's there?' called the woman's voice from the back door.

'It's Rachel,' she replied walking towards the door. She could see the Anabella Cartwright was wearing only a small black silk slip that barely covered her.

'You realise just what time it is for crying out loud,' she sighed.

'About quarter-to-six I think,' she answered sarcastically pushing her way past Anabella Cartwright in the kitchen.

'What the...' she began.

'Where's your husband?' demanded Rachel making her way through to the hallway looking up the stairs.

'What's this about?' asked Anabella wrapping her arms around herself as she shut the back door. 'Have you found something out about where Charlotte is?'

'Something like that,' she said staring coldly at the woman. 'Now where's your husband?'

'I'm right here,' he replied casually walking down the stairs tying a silk dressing gown at the waist. 'Hello Ms. Murphy,' he smirked at her.

'We need to talk,' she said abruptly making her way through to the living room without being offered.

Sitting herself down in exactly the same spot that she had sat in before, she watched as the two of them sauntered into the living room, glancing questionably at one another as they did so.

'Have you found where Charlotte is?' asked Luther making his way straight over to the drinks cabinet despite the extremely early hour of the morning.

'I was going to ask you two the very same thing,' said Rachel as she watched the man pour himself a large measure of Glenfidich malt whiskey.

'It was you who was hired to look for her,' he said smiling at her as he smelt the aroma of the malt whiskey within the tumbler. 'So why would we know where she is.'

'What happened to your other daughter Bethany?' asked Rachel casually.

'That's none of your damn business,' said Anabella as she sat opposite Rachel switching on the antique gold side lamp next to her, holding her hand out without even looking at her husband as he now prepared her a drink.

'How did you find out about Bethany?' asked Luther as he handed his wife the drink he'd been preparing.

'How could you have not expected me to,' she said shaking her head at them.

'It wasn't at all relevant,' said Anabella.

'How so?' asked Rachel.

'Because our daughter dying,' said Luther, 'and the other running away for a few weeks, are two completely separate issues.'

'We'll see,' said Rachel staring inquisitively at the two of them.

'And just what the hell is that supposed to mean Ms Murphy?' asked Anabella abruptly. 'Why didn't you also tell me that Charlotte was in therapy?' asked Rachel ignoring the woman's question.

'Because it wasn't and still isn't any of your business,' said Anabella sipping her drink as she pulled her legs up onto the sofa, making herself comfortable. 'Just as Bethany isn't any of your business either.'

'What really happened to Bethany?' she asked them.

'She had a weak heart,' sighed Luther without any real compassion. 'Poor thing.'

'And that weak heart didn't have anything to do with maybe the fact the little girl was being abused in any sort of way?' asked Rachel casually, who then added 'Would it now Luther?'

'I haven't the foggiest what the hell you're going on about,' he replied nonchalantly at her. 'Why would you even think such a God awful thought woman? Bethany was well looked after. She received the best care that money could buy. Only in the end it

293

wasn't enough. Now what is this about? Where did you get such nonsense about our daughter being abused in any way whatsoever?'

'Alright then,' said Rachel. 'Do either of you have any idea just who the Pied Piper might be?'

She immediately saw the two of the glance nervously at one another. 'We don't know what you're talking about,' he said less confidently as she noticed that he'd answered for the both of them.

'You mean like in the fairy tale?' asked Anabella.

'Possibly,' replied Rachel. 'Or possibly someone who was in close contact with your daughter over the years.'

'We don't know what it is that you're talking about,' said Luther not able to hold eye contact with her. 'What is all this Pied Piper rubbish that you are talking about? You're not making any sense here.'

'Nice house you've got down in London,' said Rachel smiling at them.

'What house?' asked Anabella.

'The one that you still own in Chelsea,' she replied.

'How'd you know about that?' asked Luther staring at her.

'If you didn't want any of this to be discovered,' sighed Rachel dropping her head. 'Then why did you let me investigate the disappearance of your daughter.'

'Because you were only supposed to look into my daughter that has run away from home,' Anabella told her. 'Not to go snooping into any of our other affairs.'

'That's why we didn't want the police involved here,' said Luther. 'Besides, what the hell has our home in London got to do with anything?'

'I'll get to that,' said Rachel. 'Have either of you seen Caroline Massey recently, you remember the girl don't you? The one that your daughter was very close to.'

'That silly little bitch...' began Anabella.

'We haven't seen her,' said Luther cutting her off.

'Are you sure that you don't have any idea where the girl may be?' asked Rachel. 'It would appear that she has also gone on the missing list now. A bit of a coincidence, don't you think?'

'Just what is that you are getting at Ms Murphy?' he asked.

'You don't think that we know where that girl is,' asked Anabella. 'Do you?'

'Do you?' responded Rachel.

'We have no ide...'

'What about your own daughter then?' asked Rachel cutting him off abruptly.

'Are you suggesting like that fruitcake of a detective that came around here,' laughed Luther. 'That we had something to do with the disappearance of our Charlotte?'

'Oh, I'm not suggesting,' she smirked. 'I'm accusing.'

'Do you actually realise just how ridiculous you sound?' said Anabella.

'Not at all,' said Rachel. 'Or at least I shouldn't do. Not to the two of you, that is.'

'This is completely insane,' sad Luther.

'Bethany, Charlotte, Caroline,' said Rachel slowly. 'And God knows who else is on the list.'

'That's it,' snapped Luther. 'I want you out of here now, or I'm calling to police to have you removed.' He began to make his way over to the phone.

'Do you recognise this?' asked Rachel holding the small black box up for them to see.

'What the hell is that?' asked Luther turning to her as Anabella stared at the object and then smiled.

'That couldn't have been of any use to you,' said Anabella smugly.

'What is it?' asked Luther walking back to the sofa.

'Your daughter's harddrive that belongs to her computer upstairs.'

'That's what's known as stealing Ms Murphy,' snapped Luther.

'The memory has been deleted anyway,' added Anabella casually sipping her drink.

'And why would you have deleted the memory from your daughter's computer Anabella?' asked Rachel. 'Unless there was something on there that you didn't want anybody else to see that is.'

'My daughter's personal thoughts in her diary were nobody's business but her own,' she said. 'Besides, you couldn't have read anything that was in there.'

'Why's that?' asked Rachel smirking at the two of them knowingly.

'Because, like my wife said,' replied Luther. 'The files had been deleted from that computer.'

'You'll be amazed at what's possible these days,' she replied. 'Especially if you know the right people that is.'

'Okay,' said Luther sitting on the back of the sofa. 'So you found someone who could access the deleted files. Very clever. But so what?'

'I saw what your daughter had hidden away,' she told them both.

'So you saw my daughter's diary then,' he laughed.

'It was quite entertaining,' smiled Anabella. 'Wasn't it Rachel? She has quite the imagination doesn't she?'

'Oh she did indeed,' agreed Rachel nodding, whilst at the same timewaiting...hoping he would slip up. 'Or maybe she used her imagination to hide away from what was and what had been going on for years.'

'What are you suggesting?' asked Luther.

'If you'd read her diary,' said Anabella. 'Then you'd know that it was full of mumbo jumbo. Only it was our daughter's mumbo jumbo, so we did what we thought was right and deleted the files so that nobody could go nosing around through her private life.'

'That's not the only thing that you can find on these harddrives,' she said. 'You'd be amazed at what the harddrive will keep stored away, even though you think that you've deleted it.'

'Look Ms Murphy,' said Luther. 'I'm becoming bored with this entire matter. Now I'll ask you one more tim...'

'Where did your daughter use to go, when she ran away from home?' asked Rachel cutting him off as she lit a cigarette and sat back in the sofa observing them very carefully.

'How are we supposed to know that,' said Luther. 'She ran away, and then came back and that's all we know.'

'Who's the Pied Piper?' she asked again.

'A guy in the fairy tale that used his magic flute to take away the town's kids,' replied Luther sarcastically.

'Was it the Pied Piper who used to take your daughter away?' Rachel asked. 'You know, when she supposedly ran away all those times before.'

'What is this crap?' asked Anabella.

'Did he use his magic flute on her Luther,' she asked staring coldly at him. 'Or was that not the only flute he used on your daughter Anabella?'

'I demand that you leave right now,' screamed Anabella.

'I ain't going anywhere until I get some straight answers,' she told them. 'Now, who is the Pied Piper? Is it you Luther?'

'This is becoming ridiculous Rachel,' he sighed. 'Now you're upsetting the both of us, so I'm asking you one more time to leave this house, this very instant.'

'If it's not you,' she said ignoring his request. 'Then you better tell me who it is.'

'If you don't leave right this minute,' said Luther walking toward her. 'Then I'll be forced to call the police.'

'And you're so very close to them,' she smiled. 'Aren't you Luther? All those money raising events were a good cover to have.'

'I don't know what it is that you are insinuating,' he said coming around the sofa, and standing directly before her.

'Paying people off in high places,' she said. 'Even if it was as subtle as doing it through your many charities. You had them all convinced that you were such a good family. Holding these events to raise money for the police, and other charities that could make you look good. All so that no one would bother you.'

'Just what has this got to do with Charlotte?' asked Luther shaking his head at her.

'How close are you both to the Pied Piper?' she asked.

'We're not standin...' began Anabella.

'I know about the paedophile ring that is run by this guy calling himself the Pied Piper,' she told them. 'What I want to know is whether or not it is you Luther?'

'That's absurd,' he replied a little shakily she noticed.

'Are you the ones who're been abducting the kids recently?' she asked them. 'Is that what Charlotte discovered about both of you?'

'What!' exclaimed Luther.

'Or did she know all along?' she added. 'Or did she suspect what had been always happening.'

'This is ridicu...' began Anabella.

'Kids need love,' said Rachel. 'And because of that they can be easily manipulated by that need. What happened to Charlotte? Was she abused like her sister? Or was she feeling jealous because you only gave her twin sister the attention. Only she didn't realise what kind off attention you was showing her. Did she Cartwright? And she so desperately needed to feel loved in from both of you? Or so she thought anyway Cartwright. You're a sick man. And you, you fucking bitch!'

'Don't you dare talk to me like...' said Anabella.

'Did you just like to watch Mrs. Cartwright?' she asked. 'Or did you like to join in with your husband?'

'We never laid a finger on Charl...' began Luther.

'So was she already being abused by someone else other than yourself? Is that it? Was she the Pied Piper's property and not yours?'

'I've heard just about enough of this cra...' he was suddenly before Rachel as he grabbed for her. Rachel merely pushed his hand away.

'I know all about the basement that you've got set up in Chelsea,' she told them as Anabella instantly looked panicked at her husband.

'You know nothing,' he said stepping away from her. 'How could you?'

'A couple of very good friends paid your little pad a visit whilst we were down there,' she admitted.

'They couldn't have,' said Luther. 'It would have been...'

'Impossible,' she laughed. 'You've obviously not met some of my friends, have you? They can make impossible, very possible when they want to.'

'You still don't know...' started Luther.

'I know all about the website that's known as Pied Piper Productions,' she added. 'I know all about the website that's found within the website. The one that features kids being beaten, tortured, and possibly even killed you sick fucks. I also know that you're featured in one of their twisted sick movies. The one involving your daughter Bethany and a rubber hose pipe that is being used to beat the girl half to death, maybe all the way. Is that how you little Bethany really died Cartwright.'

'You don...' he began again.

'I know that Charlotte somehow managed to see that movie herself,' she told them. 'She somehow found her way into that website. Maybe found the password to access it in one of your hiding places. I honestly don't know how she managed it. But somehow she did and all I know is that is what probably set all of this into motion.'

'I don't know what you're talking...' he started to say as he stepped further away form her.

Rachel couldn't see Anabella as Luther was now stood directly in front of her. But she imagined that she was squirming more and more with what was being said. She enjoyed the thought of getting to them as their masks had been finally removed and their true banefulness was being revealed.

'Give yourselves up to me,' said Rachel. 'Tell us where Charlotte is, and Caroline,' she added, although still unsure as to whether or not they knew where the other girl was.

'No,' snapped Luther. 'Fuck you bitch!'

'No what Luther,' said Rachel. 'Agree or you'll have to face the consequences against a force that is a lot worse than the police, and you better believe me on that one. And I want to

know right here, right this moment just who the fuck the Pied Pip...'

She didn't even see Anabella move, as she was that quick. All Rachel saw was the light from the lamp become extremely bright as it crashed into her head knocking from the sofa to the floor. As she looked up all she could remember was the silhouette of Anabella and the outline of the lamp as it crashed down viciously at her again slamming into her face as she felt the glass shatter. The lights of both the lamp and the inside of her head fell into complete darkness as she was knocked unconscious.

THIRTY TWO

'**Y**ou sure that she's going to be here Tony?' asked Sleeper as they tackled the winding road that was taking them towards Prestbury. It was still early and the last strands of early morning mist drifted by as Sleeper steered the silver Mercedes whilst glancing at Tony. 'Why'd you think that she dumped us to come here on her own brother?'

'It's this one here,' said Tony pointing the long driveway that led to the Cartwright's home in Prestbury. 'Where the fuck else is she going to be?' added Tony, all apprehensive as they pulled the vehicle around to the rear of the house.

'What made you certain that she'd be here already?' asked Eazy from the rear seat as he glanced at his watch. 'For starters, it's only just coming up to eight in the morning.'

'I thought it was a little weird last night, when she insisted that she go home by herself,' said Tony. 'I guess that I didn't think much to it because of how everything went last night. Her head's been fucked since that fucking psycho killed her... well you know.'

'We know,' said Eazy. 'But why'd she leave you behind? Fair enough if she'd wanted to leave me and Sleeper behind. But I mean, she said that the two of you would go and see the Cartwright's.'

'She obviously didn't want me here for this either,' he replied.

'I wouldn't take it too personally if I was you,' Sleeper told him. 'I think for the first real time since all this began, she feels herself being pulled in two different directions. One side of her agrees with the three of us. The other has worked too closely with the law for her not to be thinking that way, you know what I mean.'

'Something else is bothering me though. I had trouble sleeping last night after we got in. Then when I finally managed to get me head down, well something woke me,' he told them both. 'I'm not even sure what it was, I know this sounds crazy lads. But somebody's scream woke me, and well, I'm positive that it was ar'kid's scream.'

'A dream,' said Eazy staring at him like he'd already gone crazy on them.

'Plus she wasn't at home Eazy,' added Sleeper, defending what Tony had just told them, as he pulled the over to the garages. 'She's definitely taken off somewhere. And I agree with Tony here. This place is odds on favourite.'

'Hey,' protested Eazy, 'I ain't arguing here lads. I want to find her just as much as the two of you. You tried her phone again?'

'It's still switched off,' said Tony climbing from the vehicle replacing his mobile in his back pocket. 'I just know that she's gone and come here on her own.'

'But why would she do that brother?' asked Eazy as his mammoth frame climbed out from the rear seat. 'Especially now that we've discovered what we have done.'

'That's precisely why she'll have come alone,' said Tony. 'Rachel would have wanted to question the Cartwright's without feeling the pressure of us being there. She knew what would have happened if we'd been the ones to question them.'

'That brings us to another point in question,' said Sleeper staring at the silent house before them.

'What's that?' asked Tony heading straight for the back door.

'What if she ain't here and those two fuckers are?' he asked.

'Then we do it the professional way lads,' said Tony. 'At the end of the day I know the reason why ar'kid didn't want us to be here when she questioned them. She'll be hell bent on trying to find out what has happened to the daughter, Charlotte and possibly her friend Caroline... my pal's daughter.'

'You think that she could have called her friend into to help her with this one brother?' asked Sleeper as they made their way to the kitchen door. 'The copper... what's her name... Hunter?'

'I just don't know lads,' replied Tony as he began banging on the back door. 'I don't think that she would have done in all honesty.'

'But they've got to have had something to do with all this shit that has gone down,' said Eazy. 'No question about it. After what we found in London and with what Robert discovered on those websites. It's just got to be this mother fucker and his deranged wife.'

'The problem is though,' began Tony banging louder on the door. 'We certainly know that they are guilty of the shit we discovered. But what we're not certain of is whether or not they've had anything to do with both the two missing girls.'

'Why didn't you tell your mate about what we'd discovered, when he phoned you about his girl missing?' asked Eazy as Tony ceased banging and began looking through the windows into what appeared to be an empty house.

'Paul Massey and me go back pure time,' he told them as he began trying the patio doors that led through to the living room. 'I still remember him as a little scally running about the estates causing mayhem as he went. But I also remember thinking to myself back then that he'd be a force to be reckoned with, in years to come. And he was and very much still is. Luckily for me though, ar'paths never crossed when it came to any trouble as he was making his name for himself. Let's just put it this way lads, no questions would have been asked until they were asked in intensive care. He's got quite a wild temper.'

'It doesn't appear as if anybody is home,' said Sleeper nodding to Eazy, who immediately understood and began to walk around the house in order to check the security out.

'What if they've done something bad to her Sleeper?' asked Tony.

'They get their kicks from hurting and sexually abusing little kids brother,' he told him.

'I know,' he replied. 'But...'

'We'll find where she is,' he said cutting him off. 'We still don't know for sure that she was even here,' he added.

'You think that they've killed their daughter?' asked Tony.

'I definitely think that they killed or at least contributed greatly towards the death of the little girl we saw in that film last night,' he replied. 'As for the other, then we'll just have to ask them politely to tell us the truth. I can be very persuasive when I want to be Tony.'

'They have to pay for what they've done,' said Tony trying to force the patio doors open.

'They will brother,' replied Sleeper as he pulled Tony's hand gently away from the door. 'Wait for Eazy.'

'Where the fuck could they possibly be at this time of the morning?' asked Tony anxiously as Eazy suddenly appeared pulling his small leather bag from the front of his trousers where he kept it hidden.

'The house is belled up. Nothing like down in London. No where near as good a system. It's just your usual bog standard

set up. Not that any of that matters anyway though,' he said slipping the two thin pieces of metal into the patio locks as he masterfully adjusted them as they all heard the door unlock.

'Why's that then? asked Tony.

'Because either they're in or they're just not answering the door,' he held the door open for Tony. 'Or they seem to have forgotten to set the alarm before they went out.'

'Why would they have done that?' asked Tony walking through into the living room. 'Hello, is anybody home?' he called out loudly to no response.

'Maybe they were in some kind of a hurry,' said Sleeper carefully pulling a pair of black leather gloves on. 'Give Tony some of the plastic ones we've got,' he then instructed as Eazy began wiping down the patio door.

'Here,' said Eazy handing the surgical gloves to Tony. 'Sleeper, you and Tony take the upstairs and I'll check down here.'

'Looks they were either having a late drink,' said Sleeper holding the whiskey tumbler up for them to see as he nodded at the other tall glass set on side of table. 'Or an extremely early one.'

'What's this?' asked Tony bending down and picking up a long shard of glass.

'That could be anything,' replied Sleeper not wanting worry him as he silently observed where the lamp had once been on the table with the second glass. 'Why don't we head upstairs,' he suggested.

Tony nodded his response, but just as they were making there way to the living room door he suddenly stopped. Turning around he bent down and picked up a very plain looking gold chain. 'Oh shit,' he sighed staring intensely at the piece of jewellery.

'What's that?' asked Eazy.

'Rachel's,' he replied quietly. 'It was Becky's. I know because I bought it for her christening. I also know that Rachel wore it wrapped around her wrist as a keep sake of Becky's.'

Without another word, Sleeper quickly ran upstairs and began checking the bedrooms as Tony followed suit. They found the house to be completely empty. The bed was still unmade in the main bedroom. The wardrobes were full, and basically there wasn't any clues left for them. Running straight back downstairs, they found Eazy was already outside by the stables.

'Anything?' asked Sleeper.

'She's definitely been here,' he told them as he opened the barn door.

'What you got?' asked Tony rushing over to him.

'Fuck!' exclaimed Sleeper, for before them was Rachel's Ford Explorer.

'I'm going to kill the moth...' began Tony.

'Think first Tony,' said Sleeper as Eazy began checking the other stables out. 'We need to find them. We need to find Rachel. Where could they be? You know this family better than we do. Now where could they have taken her?'

'I don't know,' he replied. 'I just don't know.'

'They stables are clean,' said Eazy walking back over to them. 'Apart from all the horse shit that's in there that is.'

As he said this, Tony suddenly stared at them both. 'This is just their private stables at their house. It ain't their main business. They've got themselves a stud farm someplace else,' he said.

'Where's the stud farm?' asked Sleeper as they all ran towards Sleeper's Mercedes. 'Come on Tony think brother. Where the fuck is it?'

'I'm trying to think what that cocksucker told me that day,' he replied.

'Is it near her...' began Eazy.

'I got it... it's over in Knutsford some place,' he told them as they jumped into the vehicle. 'I'm not sure where though.'

Sleeper pulled his mobile from his pocket as he started the car. 'I know a man who'll definitely know,' he said as he eased the car back out onto the country lane hitting speed dial on his phone. 'When it comes to horses or any kind of gambling for that matter, who'd you call?'

Tony nodded and smiled.

Struggling to open her eyes, Rachel tried to focus on her darkened surroundings. She could stench the undeniable smell of horses all around her and immediately thought that she was still at the Cartwright's place in Prestbury. As she tried to sit up, Rachel discovered that she was in fact strapped to a heavy wooden table top of some kind.

Looking around herself as she eventually came around a little more, she realised that her clothes had been torn, but not taken away from her completely. Just hanging off her like she was some kind of Egyptian slave girl. Rachel immediately noticed that the lighting had changed all around her as she shook her head to try and clear it in order to focus better.

They had replaced the electric lighting with candles as part of their sick fantasy. The candles flickered through the slight breeze that found its way into the room or barn where they held her captive. Rachel was immediately reminded of Gabriel as she suddenly focused in and saw that the Cartwright's. Both Luther and Anabella were stood at the foot of the table.

It was almost like she was seeing them clearly for the first time. Neither of them held any of the gracefulness they had before. Both were dressed all in black, including Anabella Cartwright's make up. Giving her an all together more sinister appearance. He wore his hair long, and it covered his shoulders as they whispered to one another like secretive children would.

'The bitch is awake,' she heard Anabella say. She could clearly see that the woman was becoming aroused by the flames, the flickering light becoming very sensual, exciting, and erotic. Anabella's excitement heightened by the helpless image before her, of Rachel strapped to the table.

As Rachel twisted her head to try and clear her head some more, she was faced with the tip of a hunting knife. Still struggling to focus, the blade was pressed against the right hand side of her face. She realised that Luther was beside her and that Anabella was at the bottom of the table where they had arranged her to their satisfaction. She was bound at the hand and feet with the plastic twine that merely tore deeper into your skin if you struggled.

'This is madness,' said Rachel as calmly as she possibly could.

'Not even close Ms Murphy,' said Luther Cartwright in a quietly spoken voice.

'You can't expect to get away with all of this,' said Rachel pulling her face away from the sharp piece of metal.

'And we're not about to let you get in the way of what we've getting away with for years,' he added.

'So you are the Pied Piper?' she said glaring at him as he smirked at her. 'Where's Charlotte?'

'Rachel,' called out a voice that was full of fear.

'Caroline,' she called back to her. But from her position, strapped to the table in such a crude way, she couldn't see the girl properly.

'Shut it you little whore,' screamed Anabella as she strode over to where they held Caroline captive. Slapping the girl hard, her nails drawing blood across Caroline's left cheek. From what Rachel could make out, Caroline was chained to some kind of pipe in the far corner of the wall, her clothes torn from her.

'What the hell do you want with Caroline?' asked Rachel staring directly at Luther.

'We didn't want anything with her,' he said smiling at her. 'It's just that she wouldn't leave it alone about Charlotte.'

'But now that she's here,' said Anabella as she caressed the girl's breasts that were fully exposed. 'We might as well have some fun with her,' she added as Rachel saw her bite down on Caroline's right nipple hard enough to draw blood as the poor girl screamed out in agony. Anabella wrapped the piece black duct tape that had come loose and hung down from Caroline's face back over her mouth.

'Leave her the fuck alone you sick fucking bitch or I'll...' began Rachel as she felt Luther suddenly grab her hair viciously.

'Or you'll what?' sneered Luther, his breath warm against Rachel face as she still smelt the stench of the whiskey he'd been drinking.

'The girl's done nothing to you two,' said Rachel as Luther let her hair go free and Anabella still molested the helpless girl as she struggled to free herself from the hands of the sick twisted pervert before her.

'Leave her the fuck alone,' cried Rachel towards Anabella as Luther merely watched on.

'You want some bitch?' said Anabella finally leaving the poor girl who appeared to be terrified. 'Do you... you fucking little good for nothing nosy bitch.'

'I'd have thought that we were both too old for you,' said Rachel defiantly. 'I thought that little kids were more in line with your sick perversions.'

'You'd be surprised at what gets me off these days bitch,' she replied walking over to the table top.

'Where is....' began Rachel.

'She had to be taken care of,' smirked Anabella. 'Just like the two of you are to be taken care of.'

'None of you could leave it the fuck alone,' snapped Luther as he put down the knife and picked up what appeared to a large set of pliers. Only they didn't look to be the kind a mechanic or electrician would use, more like what they used on horse's shoes.

'What did you do with Charlotte?' asked Rachel again as she tried her best not to stare at the pliers as he walked over to her.

'She joined the others,' said Luther.

'What do you mean?' asked Rachel. 'Joined the others?'

'You know exactly what we mean,' said Anabella. 'Not that, that's our area of pleasure of course.'

'What's that mean?' asked Rachel as Luther opened the pliers.

'She finally came up against the one that she thought she could trust,' said Luther. 'Even more so than her very own mother and father. The truth crippled her, even though she'd known him all along.'

'Only when she found out the truth,' said Anabella. 'She just couldn't take it.'

'Take what?' asked Rachel confused at what was being said to her. 'Watching that movie of your husband more than likely killing his very own daughter.'

'That was just the tip of the iceberg. She only got what she deserved,' smirked Luther as he teased Rachel's nipple with the pliers. 'Besides, little Bethany had served her purpose. And she was becoming too old for us anyway.'

'Why her?' asked Rachel, desperate for answers. 'Why her and not Charlotte?'

'Charlotte belonged to him from day one,' he screamed at her. 'Now enough questions, time for some serious pain, whilst we ask you a few questions of our own.'

Grabbing the tip of Rachel's breast, squeezing the pliers as hard as he possibly could. Brutally enforcing the pliers tightly against her nipple.

Sharp excruciating pain making her want to scream out loudly, but not wanting to give him the satisfaction. It seemed like an eternity passed before the white noise that rang through her head faded. She was breathing like she just sprinted a four-hundred yard dash.

Sweating, shaking, the haze clearing from her vision as she became face to face with Anabella and Luther Cartwright and their demented smiles at her anguish.

'We want to know exactly who it is that knows what's been going on,' said Luther as he opened the pliers around her other nipple. 'He needs to know.'

'Who's he?' gasped Rachel trying her best to concentrate.

'Him of course,' he laughed at her.

'Are you the Pied Piper?' asked Rachel as tears streamed down her face. 'Yes or no you sick fuck?'

'Just tell us who else knows about the operation?' asked Luther ignoring her question.

'We take it that your brother is one of them,' said Anabella stroking Rachel's legs, her hand rising around her thigh. 'I kinda liked him as well.' She added smiling.

'You sick fucking bitch,' snapped Rachel. 'What is it? Your head is so fucked up, that you like both kids and...'

'I fuck whatever I like to fuck,' she cut Rachel off. 'You'd be amazed at what can get me off sexually.' She grabbed Rachel between her legs and began probing with her thumb as Luther bent down and licked her face.

'Get the fuck away from me you couple of freaks,' screamed Rachel as she squirmed and struggled to break free from them.

'I think she likes it,' said Anabella not letting go.

'Just like they all do dear,' added Luther. 'Now tell us who the fuck else knows about Pied Piper Productions.'

'Even if I told you,' said Rachel. 'You couldn't stop them from coming to kill the two of you.'

'Oh don't be so ridiculous girl,' sighed Luther as he began to apply the pressure of the pliers. 'Just how the hell do you think we've got away with what we have for so long?'

'You can't hide behind your police friends,' said Rachel, still struggling to free herself from Anabella's grip between her legs.

'You have no idea of just where this would have taken you,' he said as his mouth brushed against her ear image her cringe.

'Why don't you tell me then,' she said trying her best to keep them talking. 'I mean you're going to kill me anyway. So why don't you just go ahead and tell me anyway, what the fuck have you got to lose Cartwright?'

Suddenly the white flash of extreme pain shot through her once again. Only this time she screamed out in sheer agony as the pain rippled throughout her entire body as he squeezed the pliers against her left nipple so hard she thought he'd actually sliced the nipple away from the flesh. All the while he laughed sadistically at her, as his wife continued to feel and fondle Rachel. It all became too much for Rachel to deal with. She felt herself losing consciousness as darkness greeted her once again.

She didn't know how long she was unconscious for. It was the loud grunting noise that brought her around. Her hair felt matted and stuck to the side of he face as she twisted her head around to where Caroline was.

'Nooooo,' screamed Rachel as she watched in horror as both Luther and Anabella groped and molested the girl who barely appeared to be conscious anymore. 'Leave her the fuck alone.'

'Oh,' smirked Anabella walking back over to her. 'You're back with us, are you?' She stroked Rachel's wet hair away from her face as Luther came over and joined them.

'Just tell me why?' said Rachel, her voice was horse and not sounding at all like hers to her own ears.

'We'll trade,' said Luther as Anabella came around the table and began rubbing Rachel's breasts.

'Ahhh,' smiled Anabella tauntingly at her. 'There, there. I'll make your sore nipples feel all better.'

'Get your hands off me you sadistic bitch,' snapped Rachel pulling herself away as best as she could.

'Tell us the names of knows about this,' said Luther pulling out what could only be described as pruning clippers used on roses and such like other flowers. 'Or next time you'll begin to feel what real pain is Ms Murphy.'

'I can't,' she cried.

'Obviously you're enjoying the real pleasure that comes with the pain,' smirked Luther grabbing her breast viciously. Squeezing the breast so that the sore nipple reddened as he bit down hard on the exposed flesh. Rachel squealed out as the pain took hold of once again. Spitting the blood from his mouth as he stared down a Rachel. The blood making him look even more deranged than he already did.

'They all like it in the end,' he laughed at her. 'The pain becomes their one comfort in life.'

'Don't talk crap,' Rachel screamed in sheer anger through gritted teeth. 'You pick defenceless little children to become your puppets of pleasure before you kill them.'

'Whatever,' sighed Luther. 'Now why don't you be a good little girl and tell us what we need to know.'

'And if you're a good girl,' smirked Anabella, who hadn't removed her hands from Rachel's naked flesh yet. 'We may just tell you who killed your husband and child.'

'How the fuck do you know who the killer is?' screamed Rachel as she then wondered whether or not it was at all possible that they were connected in some sick twisted way.

'We all share the same vices in life,' smirked Luther. 'No matter how different they appear to be. We have the ability to sniff one another out. It's like our own special little club.'

'Tell me?' said Rachel.

'Tell us first who knows,' said Luther as he began clipping the pruning sheers tauntingly at her.

Rachel was divided by what she should do here. Why had she decided to come on her own, what should she tell them, they already knew about Tony, what if there was someone a lot higher that could get to her brother and friends before they could finish this thing.

Luther suddenly grabbed her left nipple in the pruning sheers and all that Rachel remembered was screaming out loudly as she past out into the blackness once again.

THIRTY THREE

'**R**ight, Susan,' said Chief Superintendent Tom Mackenzie as he strode into her office like a whirlwind that wasn't about to be stopped. She immediately saw Detective Inspector Stephen Halenbrook trailing in behind him, as the two men sat themselves down on the opposite of the desk to Hunter and Mark Andrews who were going over evidence that they had gathered from the weekend.

'Now I know that we don't always see eye to eye Hunter,' he began to loosen his tie, stretching his neck from side to side making cracking noises. 'But I've just had my balls and my arsehole chewed off in the press conference that we've just held.'

'I bet that was nice,' replied Hunter sitting back and pulling deeply on her cigarette. 'Balls and an arsehole, all in one session chief.'

'Enough of your sarcastic nonsense Hunter,' he sighed. 'Now, I know that you are more than capable out of everyone right here on the force, to catch this guy.'

'Why,' she looked at him with mock amazement in her eyes. 'Compliments first thing in the morning, I don't quite know wha...'

'You know Detective Halenbrook here right?' he said cutting her off abruptly.

'We've met,' she responded glaring at the man who always reminded her of a weasel in his skinny rat like appearance. He was also very rarely away from the chief's side these days. That was the truth, but the truth was also that she hated the man, as it was well known fact that he was the chief's true brown nose kid. He always worked the jobs that made him look good to the superiors, and it was always Chief Mackenzie that gave him the jobs. The only thing was, she wasn't quite sure what he was

311

doing sat here in her office, along side of the chief at just gone nine o'clock Monday morning. 'So chief, are you going to cut straight to the getting fucked in one way or another, so we can forget all this tedious foreplay bollocks or what?'

'I want this killer found Hunter,' said Mackenzie glaring at her. 'He's taking the piss out of not only us but the victims as well.'

'I'm glad that you've noticed chief,' she sighed.

'Are you any closer to discovering just who this guy is yet?' asked Halenbrook in is weasel like voice.

'I'm just on my way to arrest him now,' she answered mockingly staring at him.

'What about the criminal investigators?' asked Mackenzie. 'You've still got Brendan McCarthy helping you right?'

'Right,' she replied.

'I'd like a report with what he's come up with so far,' said Mackenzie. 'I've got to be able to give the press something a little more solid than we've given them this morning or we'll be crucified in the papers. Now my superiors are chewing on my arse, so I'm chewing on yours Hunter.'

'Look,' said Hunter shaking her head at the two of them. 'Let's cut the crap out here lads. Just what the fuck is it that you both want? And I mean, besides what we all want. As in catching this stone cold killer before he strikes again.'

'Your still handling the case load on the missing kids, right?' asked Halenbrook.

'I am,' she nodded.

'We are,' added Mark Andrews defensively.

'Not anymore,' Mackenzie told them. 'I'm putting Stephen here, back on it.'

'What!' exclaimed Mark Andrews. 'We've made a lot of progress from when he was working the case. And we're handling both case loads more than sufficiently.'

'But you're not making any real progress with either of them,' added Halenbrook.

'We never expected this killer to...' began Andrews.

'It's not open to discussion,' said Mackenzie cutting him off. 'You should be pleased that I'm lightening your load Hunter.'

'What is it that you want then?' she asked cautiously.

She didn't trust either of the men opposite her. And she didn't believe for a minute that they merely wanted to lighten her work load. But she wasn't displeased to burden the missing kid's case back over to Halenbrook who was originally on the case anyway. Although she also knew from the amount of work both her and Mark had, had to do, that he hadn't got as far as they

had. And the last thing she needed was him to fuck all of their research up. So she decided right there and then, that she'd play ball with the two of them. Besides it could possibly work towards her favour if she played them correctly.

So, smiling as best as she could at them both she said. 'I could certainly do with putting all my resources back into the original case chief. So, fair play. What can we both do for you?'

'I want you to update Stephen here on everything that you've come up with so far,' Mackenzie told her. 'I want all your theories laid out as to what you think has happened with the kids. Then Stephen here will take it from there. Alright?'

'Alright Mackenzie,' said Hunter sighing deeply, as she shook her head at them. Slowly opening her desk draw, she began pulling the files relating to the case on the missing children. 'You want the entire story?'

'Everything,' said Halenbrook smiling at her, his weasel teeth making her gringe slightly as he rubbed his chin thoughtfully.

'We believe that the kids that have been taken,' she told them, 'have been used in some kind of a paedophile ring that has been set up.'

'What makes you think that?' asked Mackenzie.

'A trace that led us to a website that had been set up for this kind of thing,' she said. 'We couldn't be certain before we lost the trace. But we were almost certain that is was the little boy, Dougy Robins from Lacey Green in Wilmslow, who was being abused on the live transmission.'

'Why the hell didn't I hear anything on this?' asked Mackenzie livid at her as his face began to darken to a crimson shade.

'Because we one, wasn't certain it was the boy,' she replied calmly. 'And two, we lost the transmission almost immediately. Simon Forester in the computer resources department hasn't even come close to tracing where the transmission was being aired from.'

'I still should have been told about it,' he said glaring at her.

'And if it wasn't the little boy that was being abused,' she sighed. 'We didn't want the story to leak and the family to grieve unnecessarily for Christ sake.'

'You think that is what the kids are being used for?' asked Halenbrook. 'I never came up with that angle.' He admitted to them as Hunter found herself wondering just what angle he'd come up with at all.

Keeping her mouth shut, she decided it was best to relay all the information they had researched on the angle they had covered.

Let Halenbrook see just where it was going to take him when he investigated the case.

'Okay then, listen up,' she said sitting back in her seat as she lit another cigarette, exhaling the smoke above her head. 'We'll give you all the background details on what it is that you could be looking for.'

'Go ahead then,' said Halenbrook making himself more comfortable, placing his hands before him in a very feminine way Hunter thought as she silently observed the weasel before her.

'Because of the age of the children that have been going missing,' she said, 'it would put them in the age scale of pre-pubescent children. Which makes it more than likely that they were in fact taken to be used by paedophiles for use in paedophilia material in possibly one format or another? Maybe even several formats that we'll come too. Or they could have even have been taken to be molested in some way or another. This doesn't always mean that the act has to sexual. It's a good possibility that these kids after all this time are in fact dead. That could also have been the main reason for their abduction I don't mean to sound callous in any way. But I would say that, that is our safest bet at the moment to presume this. Our only hope is to discover who is responsible.

'Because of the wide age range between the paedophiles and the children that have been taken. The abductors would have had to try and find a way into their lives that wouldn't have aroused suspicion. These people try and find ways to legitimise their contact with kids. They are also very adept at locating both troubled and withdrawn kids. They will have acquired this skill through years of practise. Trial and error so to speak.'

'You think there could have been others then?' asked Halenbrook.

'Most definitely,' replied Andrews. 'Whoever we're dealing with here, has had a lot of practise for the kids to have disappeared in the way that they have, without a trace so to speak.'

'How do you think they achieved this?' asked Halenbrook.

'It would have been very much like a dating process between and boy and a girl,' answered Hunter glaring at the weasel. 'What would have taken place with the paedophile and the child in question, would have been pretty much the same approach, as say a boy maybe buying flowers or chocolates to try and win him the heart of the girl he desires.'

314

'That doesn't appear to have been the case here though Hunter,' said Halenbrook. 'The kids seem to have been taken in pure daylight. Right from under their parents noses. So there doesn't appear to have been any...'

'It's the same difference,' she said cutting him short. 'Basically the guy or woman for that matter that is taking the kids has probably seduced the child by lavishing gifts upon them Halenbrook. The technique would have no doubt been followed through after the kid was taken in order to obtain sex from the child.'

'We know that the children all came from parents who were addicts of one form or another,' said Andrews.

'You think that there is a link there?' asked Mackenzie.

'Possibly,' said Andrews. 'But if the abductor knew this, he or she could have also used this as a method in taking the kids. We're not saying that the kids were definitely being abused at home already. But if they were, it could have a wide range of abuse, including neglect.'

'Like Cathy Morris from Levenshulme,' said Hunter. 'Her parents didn't even realise that she was missing. In fact it was a concerned neighbour that called that one in two days after she had been abducted. So basically if the paedophile had prior knowledge to this and the family.'

'Then he or she for that matter could have been sympathetic with either boy or girl,' said Andrews. 'For as you know, both sexes of children have been taken so far.'

'That's also another scenario that you've got right there,' said Hunter lighting yet another cigarette. 'As twisted as it sounds, the abducted children may also start to develop feelings towards the offender. Apparently, according to Rachel this is a well known process of dynamics at work here. It's a process of sympathising that has become known as *The Stockholm Syndrome*.'

'What's that then?' asked Halenbrook.

'For instance, let's say hostages in a bank raid or even a hijacking,' began Hunter. 'Well, they will begin to develop feelings of attachment to there captors. Therefore it works in the same way with children who are victimised in this very same way. It could also be the reason that these particular kids were picked in the first place. You have remember that paedophiles are masters of manipulation when it comes to children. It's only as an abused child grows older, does he or she see that these benevolent feelings towards their abusers, begins to dissipate as the painful truth begins to set in.'

'You said that there was a difference between paedophiles and molesters earlier,' said Halenbrook. 'How so?'

'Paedophilia is a psychological disorder,' replied Andrews. 'It is a distinct sexual preference for pre-pubescent children. Rachel has told us, that they will have recurrent, intense, sexual urges and sexual arousing fantasies through a duration of at least a six month period each year. This will usually stem from them being involved in some kind of sexual activity with a minor.'

'It generally means that the child will be below twelve years old,' added Hunter. 'This matches the profiles so far with the kids that have been taken from the estates. Another thing that you have to understand is that because this is a psychological disorder, it means that they don't necessarily have to actually engage in the sexual act.'

'What the hell does that mean?' asked Halenbrook.

'That the paedophile might keep his or her life a secret from the rest of the world,' she told them. 'Not sharing, not going public with it. Although still feeling the necessity to stay involved with children. Through work maybe. Through maybe even marrying a single parent in order to gain that access to a child. Maintaining access to children at all times has become a defining trademark in paedophiles.'

'And the molester's?' asked Halenbrook taking hold of the file from the desk, glancing through it.

'They can have different motivations for their crimes,' she replied. 'And quite surprisingly, those motives can sometimes not be at all sexual.'

'What about the use of the internet?' asked Halenbrook.

'There are a number of different sites which are usually protected,' answered Andrews. 'Websites like a collection of internet links of special interest to boy lovers, encyclopaedic collections of boy love articles, absolutely uncensored sex pics from around the globe, teens sucking dicks pics. The list is enormous,' he added.

'Modern technology eh,' said Hunter staring directly at Mackenzie. 'It would appear that by introducing the internet to these freaks. It has become their biggest ever achievement in finding one another. And not just within the same country, but world wide at the simple click, click, click of a mouse cursor.'

'What else have you got?' asked Halenbrook.

'You'll find that a lot of these freaks will try and justify or legitimise their actions in their behaviour,' replied Andrews. 'As in claiming that sex between adults and the young is somehow alright. That it is in someway pure or kind or even innocent in

some twisted way. They will also use these words as part of the utilisation that they are indeed referring to some saintly behaviour taking place instead of what it actually is.'

'Precisely, rather than the plain and simple fact,' continued Hunter, 'that they are sexually exploiting children. It is a common trait between these people who believe that since the attraction to minors is indeed a compulsion, that they are doing nothing wrong. So they therefore seek out methods to try and reinforce their beliefs.'

'That's right,' added Andrews. 'In fact, some of them even believe that they are being persecuted by the rest of society. We've seen on certain websites material such as "to end the oppression of men and boys". Almost as if they're trying to make themselves sound like a political party rather than a bunch of freaks that like to molest young boys and girls. Even to the stage in America, where they already have society's set up. One of which I might add, has a shocking brazen attitude towards this lifestyle. One of these society's mottos is "sex before eight or it's too late".'

'And you really think that these kids are being used for the internet?' asked Halenbrook.

'Yes, we believe that the kids have been used on one or more of these websites that we've told you about,' said Hunter.

'Just how big is this internet set up?' he then asked her.

'WWW... dot is what it is. What do you think that shit stands for? World Wide Web of course,' she replied shaking her head at his ignorance. 'You've got access to a computer that's hooked up, and then you've got access all over the world. What the internet also provides the child molester's and peodophile's with is a range of unique opportunities. Basically he or she cannot hang around schools or playgrounds for very long, before they will begin to arouse suspicion to themselves. But what he or she can easily do nowadays is hang around chat rooms on the internet where children are speaking to one another through cyber space or whatever the fuck you call it. All they have to do is conceal their age and chat away quite freely.'

'Without being detected?' asked Halenbrook.

'Pretty much yes,' replied Hunter. 'Before the internet age they could only dream about such unlimited access to vulnerable kids. With the use of the computer and the internet, they use these chat rooms. This makes it much easier and a lot less riskier than before to interact with children, going totally unknown to the parents.'

'Surely the police or law enforcement agency's can stop known offenders in some way,' said Halenbrook.

'Rachel tells us, that what they've discovered over the years, is that paedophiles have very predictable patterns which they tend to stick by,' answered Andrews. 'As in they will keep meticulous records of their collections and victims. They often write detailed logs and diaries that will cover their sexual conquests unlike any other criminal.'

'What do you mean by that?' asked Mackenzie.

'That unlike say burglars, muggers, car thieves,' said Hunter. 'Well, you see hardly any of them collecting artefacts. So why do these people?'

'Also the police are well aware of a lot of known offenders,' said Andrews. 'And in a lot of cases they will obtain search warrants for there properties and seize any computer equipment they may find.'

'But, the internet has also opened up the world of pornography to kids as well,' said Hunter. 'Before the internet, kids couldn't say easily look at that sort of material in corner shops. But with the internet it's become a very simple activity which has a lot of parents worried.'

'Surely they must be fighting all of this,' said Halenbrook.

'Of course,' tutted Hunter. 'Back in '98, the US customs officials cracked an organisation known as *The Wonderland Club* whose name had derived from *Alice in Wonderland*. This alone is a long symbolic reference in the paedophiliac world. This website peddled some of the worst and most vile filth that you've ever seen. Including the raping of children and live shows showing sexual abuse to children. A lot of which was being carried out by family members live. Through this one investigation that led them to *The Wonderland Club*, it led them all the way over here to England and onto Western Europe. Like I said before, this is a world wide problem.'

'How did they avoid the authorities for so long?' asked Halenbrook.

'They were a secret society that hid themselves away,' Andrews told him. 'They tried on numerous occasions to break them. But the members used secret passwords to meet in private chatrooms, that they constantly changed to avoid being tracked down.'

'In the end,' said Hunter. 'There were a total of forty seven additional countries that were also involved.'

'No shit!' sighed Halenbrook. 'So is there anything that can indicate that a person is a paedophile?'

'According to Rachel, they will usually exhibit a series of personality characteristics,' said Andrews. 'Even though these can be quite common characteristics, so it doesn't mean they are immediately a paedophile. But there are indicators.'

'They will often have what become known as a special relationship with his wife,' said Hunter. 'They often have failed marriages due to their sexual interests. But they will remain married in order to disguise this fact. Often the wife will know. But very often she will choose not to say anything for fear of social stigma or disgrace.

'Displays a fascination or unusual interest in pre-pubescent kids is another trait,' continued Hunter. 'But that doesn't immediately make them a paedophile, although it should at least arose suspicion. Along with exaggerated term he or she would also use, such as blissful, innocent, God sent or pure or any other descriptive labels that seem inappropriate or excessive. You have to remember that they cannot help themselves and will therefore reveal themselves through their figures of speech.'

'Another thing to look at is their hobbies,' said Andrews. 'Hobbies such as toy collecting, building models or any such other hobby that you associate more with children than adults. Possibly even one of his or her rooms will be decorated like that of a child's theme. This can often reveal the preferred age bracket of their victims.'

'They'll usually be over thirty years old,' said Hunter. 'With no real friends of his or her own age. He possibly changes his home address frequently without wanting to reveal why to anybody.'

'Also their collections of pornography will be considered to be their most valued possessions,' Andrews told them. 'They will have collected this collection over the years and it will reflect their most inner fantasies and thoughts.'

'What would the collection consist of?' asked Halenbrook.

'Slides, commercial photographs, souvenirs, toys, Polaroids,' said Hunter. 'And virtually any other type of material that relates to child sex. No matter how minute it may appear.'

'The paedophile collector falls into three categories,' said Andrews.

'Which are?' asked Halenbrook.

'Closet collector is one of them,' replied Hunter. 'This guy maintains and views his material in private. And usually, will not molest children. He can often build up his material over the years in secret, without say, even a life in spouse even knowing about it.'

'Isolated is another kind,' said Andrews. 'This kind of collector is actually engaged in molestation and likes to display his or her collection to the victim whilst molesting them.'

'What's the third?' asked Halenbrook.'

'The third is the Sharer collector,' answered Hunter. 'They basically trade and display their material. Usually a profit will be made by the collector. He or she will also keep the company of other peodophile's.'

'What else do these collections mean?' asked Mackenzie in a wearied manner.

'Collections serve as a crucial need to a paedophile,' said Andrews irritated by the chief's nonchalant attitude. 'Firstly, the pornography will be used in their crimes. Using the material to try and persuade or lower a youngster's inhibition in order for them to have sex with the adult. It is an important step in their seduction process.'

'Secondly,' said Hunter abruptly. 'These fucko's will use the shit as a means to self gratification.' She moved her hand as if she was masturbating extravagantly, enjoying the chief's uncomforted appearance. 'Plus it can be used as an arousal faze prior to any sexual activity that is to take place. They can also use the photographs as further blackmail in order to get victims to perform in further sexual acts that the do not want to.'

'And the victims?' asked Halenbrook.

'The victims, after engaging in such acts of depravity against their own will,' said Hunter, 'will go through a complex set of emotions, according to Rachel that is. Who's obviously dealt with victims in the past. The emotions can include humiliation, attachment to the offender and fear of exposure. Their fear that a family member or friend may discover what has going on and they will suffer harsh consequences. The peodophile's know this and use against the victims. But going back to the collections, that is the biggest pivotal role in a sex offender's life. They will use this tool as a trade to induct the victims into there sexual fantasies. It is also why we the police and other law enforcement's are constantly on the alert to the onslaught of pornography on the web.'

'And what has Rachel had to say about all this?' asked Mackenzie.

'It was her, that we got most of this stuff from,' replied Hunter.

'And the missing girl,' he said. 'What of the missing Cartwright girl? Has she had any progress there yet?'

'I don't know,' shrugged Hunter. 'All I know is that she is going to come and see me in the couple of days over it.'

'Fine,' he sighed rising from his seat and walking to the door with the weasel two steps behind him. 'Now I want this killer caught before he strikes again, you hear me.'

'You're not the only one,' replied Andrews just out of ears breath as the two of them disappeared through the door.

THIRTY FOUR

*I*t was their old family home in Wilmslow. She knew that it was there home instantly, why wouldn't she know? Only it appeared to be different, she wasn't quite sure what it was, that was different as she approached the silent house. Maybe it was the purple haze surrounding the perimeter of the house that made it stand out from the rest of the street.   Or maybe it was because she knew what awaited her within the dark confines of the domicile. But whatever it was, one thing was for certain; the house was drawing her towards it like some unnatural magnetic force.

It was only then as she approached, did she realise that she wasn't in fact walking. She appeared to be levitating towards the house, with everything passing her by in surreal time lapse frames. Only as she looked down towards her feet, she couldn't she them for the early morning mist that hovered and glowed with the effluence of the purple obscurity that surrounded her home. But that wasn't right either, as it appeared to be the dead of night and not the early morning. So what was this early morning mist doing all around her?

Or was it, that it wasn't in fact mist at all. Was that bodies that she could make out. Bodies that were floating through the smog. Was in fact more lost, paralysed souls searching, longing for a way home all around her? But why was she there with all those misplaced souls. Unless maybe, possibly, they were reaching out for her help in some way. But how could she help, if she didn't even know the reason for her own presence there.

As the heavens opened up all around her, she suddenly remembered where she'd been. She had been held captive along with Caroline Massey by the demented double act of Anabella and Luther Cartwright.

She abruptly heard the thunder roar throughout the night's sky as she simultaneously witnessed the rapid sheets of tempestuous lightening, that illuminated the stratosphere in fluorescent shades of purples and pinks against what appeared to be an old black and white movie of some kind, and although the movie appeared to be familiar, she still couldn't quite place where she knew it from. Before she even realised it, she was upon her front door, her old front door she reminded herself.

Feeling the infection that shook her body violently at the mere thought of what awaited her beyond the sanctuary of the front doorway. Although at the same time, knowing that no matter what, she would pass through and beyond the passage into the abyss of what had now become more of an asylum than the family home that it had once been. Pushing against the door, that was already open, she felt the warmth of the interior. Only as she entered this time, everything appeared to be different. She didn't feel the instant terror that usually followed her through the entrance into the anticipated insanity, it felt almost ubiquitous like.

Immediately feeling as though she was at peace with everything around her, she called out for her husband and daughter as though nothing had ever changed. Only no words left her mouth. She called again. But still no words came. They just refused to be audible. What was happening? Something caught her eye ahead of her, where the kitchen was to be found.

It was Joseph O'Reilly who her and her brother had tracked down earlier that year, or at least it was what was left of Joseph O'Reilly. His body was black and charred, almost as if he been burnt alive as the smoke drifted away from him. But that wasn't correct; at least she thought that she knew in her mind that wasn't correct. He began to grin at her, his teeth as white as the purest snow against his charred exterior, only the white of his eyes matching in any way whatsoever. She suddenly saw his hand as it disappeared from sight and he grabbed at something, Jesus, what the fuck was going on?

Suddenly a scared and helpless Caroline was in his possession. How had he found her? How did he even know about Caroline? Was this her fault? Had Caroline followed Rachel to this place? It just wasn't possible that he should have hold of her. Suddenly wrapping a black leather belt around Caroline's neck as she offered no resistance, merely allowing the tears to roll down her face as she stared despairingly, her eyes pleading, begging for her help.

But then, it was as if she finally caved in and gave herself up to the inevitable of what was about to happen. Turning and raising her arms as a gesture, offering herself up to him, as though she had indeed given up on both herself and the one before her.

Trying to scream for the madness to stop, as she attempted to make a move towards the two of them she realised that another force was in fact moving her towards the stairs. Just as that was happening the kitchen door began to close on the other two. Her last image was of Joseph O'Reilly forcing the poor girl down onto her knees as he rose what looked like a large old rusty pair of scissors, high above his head. Smirking, grinning knowingly, as the door slammed shut, almost as if a great squall of zephyr had forced it closed.

Turning her attention to the upstairs landing, as she still floated involuntarily towards it. Still not able to see her own feet as she glided mysteriously around what she still believed to be the lost souls. Souls belonging to all of the victims of these twisted sick minds she had encountered recently.

That's when she heard it, she was sure of it. It was the sound of her daughter singing joylessly. She so desperately wanted to see her. Willing herself towards her daughter's bedroom door. But the more she willed herself the more everything seemed to reverse on her, making it almost impossible, as if playing a cruel joke upon her.

Then suddenly the door opened, swinging back with so much force it appeared to float away from its very hinges, and she was upon it in that very instant.

She couldn't help but smile at the sight before her. For it was one of the many pathways that they were both so familiar with at Alderley Edge. The red and golden leaves glistening from the shards of sunlight that broke through the branches above where she could clearly see her daughter. Singing, laughing, tossing leaves into the air. Calling out her daughter's name as loud as she could, she soon came to realise that she still couldn't be heard. Not even to herself.

Then she saw her husband further ahead, towards where the pathway ended. It was the two of them hand in hand. Was it? She couldn't be certain. She was certain that it was her husband though, as he called out for their daughter to join them further on up ahead.

But the image of her next to him wasn't right, it just wasn't right at all. In fact it wasn't her. Or was it? If it wasn't her, then just who was it, and why was she holding her husband's hand so lovingly? Suddenly their daughter squealed with joy as she took

*off after them both. Just as she always had done so with her and
Peter.*

*Willing herself with everything that she had, to follow them, she
realised that once again, she couldn't move from the very spot in
the open doorway. Just then, her daughter stopped running and
stared to the end of the pathway shaking her head at something.
Only it wasn't light up there any more. There were no shards of
sunlight breaking through any of the branches. And she could
feel the damp draft that washed its way over the pathway like a
trail of death ablutioning its fear over the sanctified,
unblemished land that surrounded the woods. Witnessing her
daughter shiver, as she suddenly noticed her mother in the
doorway.*

*Smiling, waving, and then responding to her father's voice
behind her. But as Rachel turned her attention to the end of the
pathway, she screamed out loud involuntarily. For stretched
between the trees at the end of the pathway, with actual white
wings sprouting gloriously from his arms, was her husband, who
also appeared to now be floating like that of what he was
depicted, an angel.*

*He was awaiting their daughter, who was drawn between the
two of them. Only now he was alone. Now the image of the other
woman, or maybe it been the image of herself, as she had in her
own mind, abandoned them both. Whatever or whoever it been,
had now disappeared from sight.*

*She suddenly heard a flute, or a whistle of some kind from
beyond where her husband floated so gracefully. Their daughter
merely stood there, staring in disbelief at her mother and then
back to her father. But then her daughter was drawn to towards
the fanfare that penetrated through the woods as if it was a
magical orchestra operating on a single instrument. How was
that so? Surely one instrument, especially a whistle or a flute
couldn't produce the compelling sound that they could all
clearly hear.*

*Then, suddenly turning, her daughter began to run towards the
music, as she then noticed that it was in fact the Pied Piper. He
was dancing around her husband who still floated high above
them both now. His magical flute whistling it hypnotic tune,
drawing their daughter in closer and closer to the both as he
continued to circle her husband.*

*This wasn't happening she kept telling herself. Not now, not the
Pied Piper as well. Struggling to see his face that was hidden
beyond the green and red mask that matched his entire outfit.*

She then saw her daughter abruptly turn and stare directly into her eyes, as her hand reached out for the Pied Piper's.

Screaming for them stop. Screaming for her husband to swoop down and stop them both from leaving. She felt tears begin to roll down her face as she realised that she was paralysed to help either of them. Her daughter's mouth began to move as she began to speak. And although she couldn't hear the words that she said to her. She knew exactly what they were.

'Why Mummy? Why didn't you help us Mummy?'

Then just like that, they were gone from both hers, and her husband's sights. Her husband began to lower towards the ground. Was he approaching her? It appeared like he was in his angelic like appearance. Swooping gracefully from side to side as he moved in towards her. She imagined that it was in fact, only possible for an angel, to achieve such an act of defied gravity.

Stopping only a few feet away from her, he then smiled at her. No words, nothing, just a smile that suddenly dropped and changed everything. His body suddenly began to shake, as if he was having some kind of a seizure. Convulsion after convulsion as if was over- dosing on some kind of demented drug. It was then that she noticed the extra set of almost black, filthy wings rising from behind him. Only these wings weren't just filthy, they were saturated in blood that dripped away from their feathers towards the woodland surrounding them. It was also in that same instant that she heard Gabriel's deranged laugh directed at her.

Reaching out to help her husband, her finger only inches from his as she desperately tried to save him. Only she was helpless to do so as his chest suddenly tore open. His blood spraying wildly as she felt its warmth covering her from head to toe. There was so much blood, that she couldn't comprehend it at all.

Screaming, screaming louder as she felt the warm liquid hit her face, and also realising that she could now hear the sound of her own screams. She then also realised, that she was in fact no longer in that place. In fact she appeared to have travelled at a thousand miles an hour, as she was sucked out of what was now transparent to her. Her nightmare was abruptly brought to an end as she heard the words screech out at her.

'So you want to know why bitch?' sneered Luther Cartwright. Splashing filthy water, this was no doubt used for cleaning the stables out with, all over Rachel's face as she began to once again regain consciencness.

Or was she wrong? Had her nightmare in fact, just begun?

THIRTY FIVE

Rachel immediately noticed the leering face of Anabella Cartwright over in the far corner of the room, where it appeared that Caroline was also unconscious, or at least that's what Rachel prayed for. Bringing her attention back to Luther, as she struggled to focus, shaking her head, the water piercing her eyes intensely.

'Just tell me why?' she asked; as Anabella walked casually back over to the table. Her make-up had run through what appeared to be sweat, making her features to be perceived as even more maniacal, than she had looked before. 'Why children?' added Rachel.

'Because we could,' he replied nonchalantly back at her. 'And because we were shown the way by him of course.'

'Who's the hell is him you keep referring to?' asked Rachel. 'Is that the Pied Piper?'

'Bethany was a hindrance to us,' said Anabella. 'They both fucking were. Well, that was until he showed us how she could benefit are needs and desires. Needs and desires that we hadn't even realised existed.'

'So it began with Bethany?' said Rachel.

'It began long before that for me,' smirked Luther. 'I could have had any woman that I wanted. I mean just look at Anabella here. Any man would give just about anything to be able to fuck a woman like Anabella every night. But that just became monotamous for the both of us. We wanted to experience different things. Different heights of unbelievable pleasure. Forbidden pleasures. That's was all until the night he introduced us to the slaughter of innocence.'

'We were always adventurous,' laughed Anabella viscously. 'But we bored of everything. Just like Luther here told you bitch.

328

That was until the first time he showed us just what it could be like. To feel the power. To feel the innocence of the flesh in your hands. To watch as they respond to your every move.'

Rachel listened as they told her what they had done, gloating about it. But she couldn't help but wonder whether or not the he, whom they kept referring to, actually existed. Or whether it was just them merely talking through a third party to justify their crimes deep within their own minds.

'What's Pied Piper Productions?' asked Rachel.

'You wouldn't believe the way that modern technology opened things up to us,' said Luther enthusiastically as if talking about a new hobby and not the molestation, and God only knew what else, of children.

'I know just how it opened things up for you,' sneered Rachel. 'I've researched just how big things have become for the likes of you. I know all about the way you have and your kind have managed to dodge the authorities.'

'Us and our kind,' snapped Anabella. 'Fuck me, if only you knew. We're the new breed of our kind. You people think that you've seen so called peodophile's or child molester's as you call them? You haven't seen anything that even comes close to the so called horrors of that yet. We were never as common as that. Even you should have realised that one bitch.'

'So just what the fuck are you then?' screamed Rachel. 'You ain't anything special. You are just like the rest of the demented freaks out there.'

'But no we are not,' laughed Luther. 'For we are the new dimension of cruelty and abuse Ms Murphy.'

'How fucking so?' demanded Rachel.

'For we become one with the...' began Anabella.

'Enough,' shouted Luther with piercing eyes directed at his wife. 'She needs to know nothing further.'

'But,' said Anabella, 'I was just going to explain about the collection of innocent sou...'

'I said enough woman,' he screamed at her.

'You're nothing special, the two of you,' taunted Rachel trying her best to bring them out some more. 'You just used the kids over the internet. Just like the rest of them did. Maybe you took things one step further with your website that was hidden within the other website, but...'

'What you found down in London is just the tip of the iceberg,' laughed Anabella cutting her short. 'That was merely an expansion of what he already had set up.'

'Whose he?' asked Rachel persistently.

'London was our private club,' smiled Luther, ignoring her question. 'But only a handful of us knew about it. That was until you stuck your nose in. He helped us to build it. He helped us to keep it a secret.'

'What about the other kids that were taken in London though?' asked Rachel. 'I know that you didn't take the kids from down that way.'

'What the fuck do you know?' sneered Anabella.

'You said that only a handful knew of the house in London,' smiled Rachel. 'What's odds on favourite, that a certain guy that has disappeared on you all recently from down that way, goes by the name of Spencer,' she smirked at them as she saw the recognition hit both of them. 'In fact, let's go one further. And please, correct me if I'm wrong here.   But wasn't it Colin Spencer who resided in Guildford that was taking the children from down that way?'

'How the fuck do you know about him?' screamed Anabella as her husband glared at her with madness stirring deep within his eyes.

'Through investigating this whole fucking mess,' sighed Rachel. 'That's the fuck how I know,' she added shaking her head at them both.

'He wasn't important,' said Luther. 'In fact, if you and your brother have gotten ridden of him, you did us both a favour.'

'I didn't,' said Rachel through gritted teeth, 'and wouldn't ever do shit for the two of you.'

'The twins were unexpected you know,' said Anabella unexpectantly. 'We hadn't planned on having children of our own. But when they arrived. They became ours to do with what we pleased. Bethany became ours and Charlotte was an offering to him.'

'Who do you keep talking about?' asked Rachel becoming more and more confused by the proceedings of what was happening.

'Yes,' pondered Luther ignoring her question. 'The twins. You know, Charlotte was always head strong from an early age. It was best that she was passed over. But Bethany, well sweet dear little Bethany. She merely became ours,' he laughed.

'So you abused and tortured that poor little defensivless girl all those years?' asked Rachel closing her eyes. 'People like you make me so fucking sick. There's good, decent people like me who go and have their child ripped from them. And, and then there are people like the tw...'

'Oh give it a rest,' laughed Anabella. 'Don't you realise just how much money this whole thing...'

'So that's what it comes dow...' began Rachel.

'Enough,' screamed Luther.

'It's all your set up,' said Rachel taking a different angle. 'Right?'

'No, it's not our set up,' laughed Luther as he picked up what appeared to be a surgical blade used in operations.

'So who else is involved?' she asked them again.

'Let me indulge you in a brief history first,' said Luther.

'Just get to the fucking point,' snapped Rachel becoming restless with the entire situation in hand. 'And no more bullshit. You're going to kill me anyway. So just get to...'

'Oh,' sighed Luther extravagantly. 'You're right about two things there Ms Murphy. One. Getting to the point is exactly what I intend to do,' he suddenly drew the tip of the blade just below her neck line, piercing the flesh as the blood trickled down, around the white flesh surrounding her breasts, that were still showing through where the wife had ripped open her white blouse.

'Please,' said Rachel without any pleading in her voice whatsoever, as she struggled not to scream out from the severe searing pain that followed the blade. 'Just tell me whatever it is that you're going to tell me.'

'When the internet was invented, they didn't realise that they were opening the doors so unwittingly. Welcoming in people like us. It was our true Godsend. It was his gift to us,' said Luther, apparently lost in his own thoughts as he now paraded about like some kind of college lecturer. 'Before then in the shadowy world of child worship. We had to rely on newspaper ads, sex clubs that we visited anyway and even prison contacts that could help us. Before all of this, we had to cruise streets or visit parks, where children played in order to locate our next lot of victims. Now we can hide behind the anonymous shield of the internet. We can find validation through communication with others just like ourselves, in the anonymous corridors of cyber space. We're all just a few clicks away from one another.'

'I'm so happy for you,' answered Rachel sarcastically, appalled at the way he described what they were doing without any remorse at all.

'But then we found another lot of victims that were awaiting us anyway,' gloated Anabella. 'He was the one to point it out to us, for his needs and desires as well, you understand.'

'All that I understand is that you both took children to be used in your sadistic and cruel games that eventually led them to...' Rachel trailed off, not actually wanting to say the words.

'The children of the abused,' laughed Luther. 'Are you serious? They were the ones who longed for us to come and take them away from their abusers. What could we do, but oblige the little buggers.'

'You're obviously talking about the missing children,' said Rachel. 'Where are they now?'

'He took them,' smiled Anabella. 'Once we had finished with them.'

'Who the fuck is he?' screamed Rachel.

'For he is the all-mighty,' laughed Anabella. 'He gets his kicks in very different ways to most of us. And believe me; we get ours in very strange ways.'

'What does he do with them?' asked Rachel, although she feared she already knew the answer to the question.

'He cleanses their poor little souls,' said Luther with a smile that condoned whatever it was that happened to them.

'Is he Gabriel?' asked Rachel suddenly releasing that the killer of her family and the Pied Piper could very well be the same person. 'You said that you knew who the person was that killed my family.'

'Oh dear God,' laughed Luther. 'No. But Gabriel has passed through our world.'

'Who is he?' asked Rachel as calmly as possible.

'Not even Gabriel knows the answer to that,' said Anabella.

'How do you know about these kind people?' asked Rachel. 'Just how the hell do you sick fucks, seek one another out?'

'Tell us who knows Rachel?' asked Luther smiling at her. Enjoying her tortured suffering of disclosed knowledge. 'We'll finish you off quickly. I will not even try to lie to you Ms Murphy. We are going to kill you, no matter what else happens. That I promise you. But if you don't do as you're asked to, well then, we'll...'

'We'll take great pleasure in keeping you alive as long as possible whilst we torture the information out of you,' cackled Anabella.

'Just my brother,' she lied as best as she possibly could under the circumstances. She figured that Tony would be able to look out for himself. Especially with the help of Sleeper and Eazy by his side. Only those two names were names that she didn't intend revealing to anyone. Especially these two demented fucks before her. 'Only me and him know what was going on,' she

added calmly staring Luther directly in the eyes. 'We weren't even sure. That's why I came to see you both by myself.'

'I don't think that even your brother was capable of breaking through into our system,' said Luther stroking her face, as if actually cared for her. 'You had to have had some outside help of some kind. And we want to know just who and where we can find that outside help. You see Ms Murphy. We've been that busy covering our tracks this last couple of weeks, that we didn't even realise that there was somebody sneaking around inside our website.'

'It's just me and him,' she told them again.

Luther suddenly grabbed her ears on either side and pulled them violently making her scream as his spittle made contact with her face. 'Don't fucking lie to us. We want... no, we fucking demand, that you tell us who the fuck else knows.'

'Just me and him,' she cried out loud. 'I swear I haven't told anybody else.'

Luther walked around the table so that he was at her feet. 'Anabella, go and get the jump leads from the Range Rover.' He smirked at Rachel as he stroked the bare soles of her feet. 'If you don't want to talk, that's alright Ms Murphy. But we will know everything that we need to know. He taught me this little trick. He uses it himself sometimes on the little bleeder's.'

'You want the bucket of water as well?' asked Anabella all excited.

'Of course,' he grinned, as he walked over to the far table where his large bag lay. She could only see his back from where she lay. She could also see that he was pulling something onto his hands as he rolled his shirt sleeves up.

As he turned back towards her, she could clearly see that he was wearing a pair of heavy duty rubber gloves and she immediately knew what they had in store for her.

'Now,' he said smiling as he made his way back over to the table as if he was about perform an operation. 'When Anabella returns, we'll begin again.'

'Fuck you Cartwright,' she spat the words at him.

'No,' he snapped. 'Fuck you – you fucking little bitch.' And with that, he punched her straight between the legs into her crotch.

Screaming out in agony. Rachel felt herself losing consciencness again. Shaking her head frantically to stray from passing out, everything began to turn surreal on her. Struggling like mad to focus she saw Cartwright grinning like an idiot at her from where he still stood.

'Fuck you' began Rachel. 'Fuck you and your demented whore of a wife.' She finally got the words out in one defying moment.

'No young lady,' he smirked at her. 'It will only be us, that does any of the fucking around here today.'

'Fuck you' she began but suddenly stopped. For she abruptly witnessed Luther Cartwright go up on his toes. Almost as if somebody had suddenly drawn an invisable noose tightly around his neck and wrenched it severely.

'What the...' began Rachel as she saw his eyes suddenly bulge. She could make out what was happening. Was he having some kind of a seizure? She didn't know. His psychotic eyes just glared in what could only be described as equivocal trauma.

'You alright, Rachel?' she suddenly heard from behind Cartwright, as his limp body slumped to the floor.

For stood there, still holding the lethal looking blade covered in Cartwright's blood was Sleeper. She hadn't even heard him enter the room. Nor had Cartwright for that matter. He had walked through the room silently and killed the man silently, without a single word or a moment's hesitation. Sliding the blade into the base of the Luther Cartwright's skull and straight through into his brain.

'Nooooo,' she suddenly heard, as Anabella was marched into the room with Tony rushing over to her.

'Jesus ar'kid,' he sighed as he struggled with one hand to set her free, and the other to cover the parts of her body that were exposed in a brotherly way that couldn't help but make her smile wearily. 'Just what the fuck were you thinki...'

'You killed him,' screamed Anabella as Eazy batted her to floor with one swift movement. Hitting the stone floor harshly, Eazy sneered his hatred at her as he began to untie Caroline who was still dazed and confused, but appeared to coming round some what.

'You alright Rach?' asked Sleeper untying her feet as Tony glared at him to make sure he wasn't looking at his sister inappropriately.

'Where am I? she asked them.

'Their stud farm over in Knutsford,' replied Sleeper. 'We had a hell of job findi...'

'Chan told us where this place wa...' began Tony as he scooped her up into his arms.

'You fuckers,' screamed Anabella cutting him short, crawling up from the floor. 'You know nothing at all. It's wasn't us that you sought out.'

'Then just who the fuck was it?' boomed Eazy's treble bass voice shaking her.

'Why don't you just tell us what we...' began Sleeper.

'Fuck all of you,' she screamed as she grabbed for the holdall where Luther had kept producing his tools from. 'You think that you're all good enough to fuck with us? To fuck with him. You're the fucking crazy ones if you think that you can fuck with the Pied Piper.' She screamed even louder as she suddenly turned on them all with what appeared to be one of the shotguns that Tony and Luther had been firing at clay pigeons with that very first day they had all met.

'Whoa,' said Rachel stepping forward. 'This isn't the way that this one has to play out Anabella. Put the gun down.'

'Fuck you, you psycho babbling bitch,' she sneered and glared past her at Tony. 'Why don't you come over here lover boy,' she added smirking at her brother.

'Take me,' offered Rachel.

'I fucked you already,' she laughed. 'Now I want to fuck your brother.'

'It's alright Rach,' said Tony stepping towards the woman who held the shotgun directly at his head.

Sleeper stepped forward at the same time so that he was positioned just in front of Rachel.

'Your gun hotshot,' snarled Anabella glaring at Sleeper with deranged, wild eyes. But all the while, not taking the shotgun away from Tony. 'And any other little weapons that you've got hidden away.'

'No problem lady,' smiled Sleeper casually dropping the knife he'd killed her husband with. Then slowly, carefully reaching behind himself, he lifted his shirt tails up and removing only one of his guns Rachel noticed. 'Here,' he smiled tossing the handgun over to her. 'There is just this as well,' he added, as he slowly reached down to his ankle and produced a long knife. 'That's all I'm holding.'

'Is that fucking right you fuck?' laughed Anabella inching the shotgun towards Tony. 'Somehow I just don't believe you, so, I guess this fucker dies just to make su...' screamed Anabella as there was suddenly a blast of white light from behind Sleeper.

'No,' screamed Rachel as the recoil from the gun pushed her backwards, as she continued emptying the entire cartridge from Sleeper's handgun into the woman before her. 'That's what you call getting fucked you bitch.'

'Rachel,' said Tony rushing over to her as he scooped her into his arms. Sleeper smiled at them both glancing casually back at

the bloodied corpse of Anabella half sprawled over the back table filled with bullets from his spare Glock model .25.

Then nodding at the second corpse by the foot of the table centre of the room was the body of Luther Cartwright. 'Well that takes care of that doesn't it?' he smirked at her as he saw Tony grab for the gun. 'No, don't touch it. Not until we know what the fuck we're going to do here.'

'It's alright,' replied Rachel pulling the gun away from him. 'You alright Caroline?'

'I just want to go home Rachel,' she sobbed as Eazy wrapped his mammoth arms around her to comfort her.

'In that case,' said Rachel taking in her surroundings, 'you lot get out of here. Including Caroline. Tony take her home to her mother and father. Explain to them what has happened. Tell Paul that justice has been served; she was never here, alright?'

'But...' began Tony.

'But nothing Tony,' said Rachel staring at the corpse of Anabella Cartwright. 'This will be my statement and my statement alone.'

'But Rach...' began Tony once again.

'Sleeper,' said Rachel ignoring Tony. 'Contact Jenkins down in London. Get him to have a search warrant issued for their home in Chelsea. I'll have Hunter contact him. Tell him to be expecting the call from her. I'll let Hunter deal with this mess any way she sees fit to. You all have to trust me here one-hundred percent.'

'You got my backing,' said Eazy with his arm still protectively around Caroline.

'But what abou...' began Tony one more time, unsure what to do, but knowing he didn't want to leave his sister alone.

'But nothing Tony,' said Sleeper cutting him off and taking his shoulder. Winking at Rachel with what could only be described as a satisfied grin upon his face, he then said. 'We do as Rachel says without any further questions.'

'What the fuck does that mean?' asked Tony rising turning to Sleeper as Eazy walked over with Caroline.

'It means that we are out of here,' he smiled nodding at Rachel as he led the others away from the room with her left to deal with the aftermath.

THIRTY SIX

'**H**ow are you feeling kid?' asked Hunter, as they sat in her office. Hunter and a team of investigator's had arrived at the Cartwright's stud farm in Knutsford within half an hour of Rachel calling them. Rachel had explained very briefly to Hunter about what had happened and had also said that she'd appreciate it if Hunter could keep it as quiet as possible until she'd had time to explain. Hunter had readily agreed.

Rachel felt extremely sore all over. Her body ached liked she never thought that it possibly could. Her nipple's felt as if they still had a hot poker from a live fire-place pressed against them. The stitches she'd required just below her neckline, stung as the pain killer they had shot her with began to wear off.

But none of that, felt anywhere near as bad as she felt violated in the very same way, a rape or molest victim would have. What made it all the worst, was that everything was still clouded within her mind. Because of the amount of time she had spent unconscious, everything floated around her mind in surreal flashes that made her literally shudder at their formidable images.

But despite all of that, she realised that she had to give the performance of her life before her friend and associate, Hunter. Because no mater what, she had to provide them both with the necessary proof about the Cartwright's, to avoid being convicted with their murder's herself. Not only that, but she also had to convince them, that it was in fact her, that killed both of them.

Not just Anabella, whose death still hadn't quite hit her yet, or more to the point, the death at the very hands before her, hadn't hit home yet. Yet another thing she felt confused about, why didn't she feel, at least a little more than relief at the taking of one's life, or two for that matter. For it was still down to her that Luther Cartwright's life had been taken. And all that she felt on

337

behalf of them both was what could only be described as sheer gratification at the fact they could never hurt or even lay their filthy hands upon another child again.

Staring at Hunter vacantly, she finally smiled weakly and said. 'I'll be alright,' she shook her head, at her own words. 'I still can't quite believe what has happened. What will happen with me now Hunter? Am I going to be charged with their murder's Hunter?' she asked, wrapping her arms around herself as she drew her legs up to herself. Despite the fact that she had showered and changed into some of Hunter's spare clothing, she still couldn't rid herself of feeling Anabella's or Luther's mauling hands upon her.

'Everything should work out kid,' smiled Hunter. 'Especially after you've been over looked by Lucy, who will no doubt confirm, all of the horror's you've already told us. We'll look at what they're going to do about any charges later.'

It was true that Rachel had spent the last couple of hours not only being examined, but also cared for by Lucy as she explained what had happened to her. Lucy had been sure to collect any evidence that she could, before allowing Rachel to go any where near water. But that still hadn't helped her, no matter how hot she'd allowed the water, she could still free the violation that had taken place.

'Don't worry about that at the moment kid,' said Hunter. 'But, just tell me exactly what the hell happened there this morning?'

'Through investigating the missing daughter,' sighed Rachel. 'We, sorry, I, discovered about the Cartwright's, and, well...'

'Just how the hell did you discover that the Cartwright's were the one's who were behind this whole mess though?' asked Andrews as he passed her the hot mug of black coffee. 'I mean the Cartwright's for fucks sake Rach. You do know just how bad all of this looks. I mean the Car...'

'She knows,' said Hunter cutting him off. 'But you better start at the beginning of this whole mess kid. I've only got so long before Mackenzie starts to demand his own answers. And it'll be better if I have the whole stor...'

'Who was that mysterious caller?' asked Rachel before she could finish. She glared at Hunter as she sipped the hot liquid, feeling its warmth taking control.

'What mysterious caller?' asked Hunter, leaning forward.

'The anonymous one that you told me about,' replied Rachel. 'The one that you claimed told you that, when you discovered the missing girl, as in Charlotte. That you would also discover a connection to the missing kids.'

'It was anonymous,' shrugged Hunter. 'How the hell should I know?'

'I just find it a little weird that you never knew who made that call.' Rachel sat back in the chair and took a deep breath. There were holes missing everywhere. And despite how bad she felt, she was determined to find some of those answers out for herself. So she added to Hunter. 'Especially seeing as you then went ahead and followed up on it.'

'What's that supposed to mean kid?' asked Hunter. 'I followed up on it because I was working the missing children case and that was about the only lead whatsoever that we'd had. What's it matter now anyway kid?'

'Because without even finding the girl' began Rachel staring at her friend, 'I found the connection.'

'But how?' asked Andrews.

'Are you absolutely positive that they are responsible?' asked Hunter. 'I mean we've got forensics down there right there excavating the entire area surrounding their stud farm. They will have about started digging right now. We need to be certain that they are the one's responsible. I mean if the press get a hold of...'

'It's them alright,' said Rachel cutting her short again.

'What does Tony know?' asked Hunter. 'We'll have to bring him in for his...'

'You will get my statement,' said Rachel. 'And that will be the only statement you're gonna get out of either of us.'

'But what if...' said Andrews.

'You two listen to me now,' said Rachel. 'I don't know exactly why I was brought into this whole fucking predicament. The only thing that I do know is that this morning I put a stop to those two miserable fucks ever hurting anymore children, ever again. I also know that I'm even more confused about everything that has evolved. And especially since before I got involved on your behalf Hunter.'

'What's that supposed to mean kid?' asked Hunter. 'I only asked you to help because...'

'I don't even want to know why anymore,' she sighed. 'Just answer me this, did you have any idea at all, about the possibility of the Cartwright's being involved in the paedophile ring Hunter? I mean did you know what kind of people these were, that you was sending me to see? On your behalf I might add?'

'I didn't know,' said Hunter. 'I swear kid, if I had...'

'They claimed to know who Gabriel was,' she said dropping her head.

'They were just fucking with your head kid,' said Hunter smiling at her. 'I mean, just how the hell are they going to know who he is?'

'They said that Gabriel had passed through their world.'

'What the fuck is that supposed to mean though?' asked Hunter. 'Forget about it kid, they were just fucking with your head. Because of knowing who you were.'

'I don't know,' sighed Rachel shaking her head. 'They still seemed to know more than they should have on Gabriel. Why taunt me like that if they didn't?'

'Because they were just trying get inside of your head,' said Hunter. 'Instead of you getting inside of theirs.'

'But...'

'But fuck all kid,' said Hunter. 'They knew shit where it came to the other fruit-cake that we're dealing with. But what they obviously did have knowledge of was what you have told us about. So why don't we start there.'

'She's right Rach,' said Andrews smiling. 'Why don't you start again with what happened there this morning?'

'Yeah kid,' began Hunter, 'just how the hell did you manage to kill both of them?'

'Just how did you manage to free yourself?' asked Andrews inquisitively. 'I mean, if you were fastened to the table like you say you were.'

'I'll get to that,' replied Rachel glaring at him.

'You better get to it pretty quickly kid. Like I said before, I'll have Mackenzie all over me on this one. And I don't want any fucking surprises.' Hunter paused, opening her packet of cigarettes, lighting one and tossing the pack onto the desk as a sign of offerance. 'So what I suggest to you, is that you start with just how did you manage to kill the both of them, like you did?' added Hunter, cocking an eyebrow at her.

'They questioned me over and over as they fucked with my head. They wanted to know about what I knew and just how I knew so much,' said Rachel. 'That fucking bitch mauled me with her filthy fucking hands. I passed out at least a couple of times. So God only knows what she did to me then.' She physically shook at the thought of this, as she remembered her words of *"I've already fucked you bitch"*. 'He did most of the torturing. He seemed really to get off on it. He used the pliers on me. He beat me. Punched me. Had that freak molest me. And

when all of that failed, he ordered his wife to get the jump leads and a bucket of water.'

'Jesus,' said Andrews. 'What the fuck was he going to do with them?

'What the hell do you think Mike,' snapped Hunter. 'He was hardly going to wash down his car that had broken down, was he now?'

'As he was putting his rubber gloves on. I managed to free myself,' lied Rachel. 'The knife was by the table. I didn't know what else to do. I panicked as he was turning. It was just a reflective reaction to the fear I felt. I struck out at him.' She paused and took a deep breath shaking her head. 'I struck out and, well, I hit the base of his neck.'

'Where was the wife?' asked Hunter. 'I mean at this point, when you killed the husband?'

'Outside still,' replied Rachel.

'Then what happened?' asked Andrews staring at her with eye's of disbelief.

'She came running in with the shotgun,' she told them. 'I'd already found the handgun in the back of his trousers. She aimed and I guess I fired first. I didn't stop until the gun clicked over, and over again, and again. And well, the rest you know.'

'And that's it?' asked Hunter suspiciously.

'That's it,' she sighed.

'You're telling me that there was nobody else involved?'

'Like whom?' she shrugged.

'Oh I don't know,' said Hunter holding her arms in the air. 'Maybe your Tony for starters. Or maybe it could have been the two black guys that you seem to have been hanging around with recently kid. One of which I'll add has himself quite a reputation as a hit...'

'You been keeping tabs on me Hunter?' asked Rachel stopping her in her tracks. 'Have you?' she added, trying her best to mask her surprised recognition to her friend's knowledge.

'I'm a copper,' replied Hunter nonchalantly. 'It's my fucking job to know what the fuck is going on kid,' she snapped.

'So you have been follow...'

'I just know kid,' said Hunter waving her off. 'If you tell me that's the way it went down. Then hey kid, that's the way it went down.'

'It was,' said Rachel holding eye contact with Hunter.

'Then so be it,' sighed Hunter.

'But how did you trace all of the missing kids back to the Cartwright's?' asked Andrews. 'And where the hell are they Rachel.'

'That I don't know,' she shook her head at him. 'But I do know that they one part of the responsibility for the kids that went missing. I have the proof. I also have proof that they were also responsible to some affect if not all for a certain website that I'll show you both.'

'Whoa,' sighed Hunter. 'What do you mean one part responsibility?'

'I'll come to that. But first off let me tell you both, that the Cartwright's are or were behind, or are somehow directly involved in a peodophile operation that is known as Pied Piper Productions,' she told them both. 'I think that this character that is known as the Pied Piper well he actually exists as well.'

'What do you mean by that?' asked Hunter.

'I mean that there is a website that has been set up featuring kids of all ages actively involved with adults or portrayed in various sexual positions or by themselves,' she answered. 'The website has to be secretly accessed, and its name is Pied Piper Productions.'

'Are the kids the ones that have taken from the estates?' asked Andrews.

'They are featured in another part of the website,' she told him.

'What do you mean by that?' asked Hunter. 'And just what or who the hell is this Pied Piper? Was it Luther Cartwright?'

'I can't be sure,' replied Rachel dropping her head. 'I think it was.'

'What the hell do you mean kid?' asked Hunter. 'Think!'

'I can't be certain,' she replied. 'Basically the investigation into Charlotte led us down to London, where the Cartwright's used to live.'

'And?' asked Hunter impatiently.

'And it also led us to discover, that the reason the family had moved up north in the first place, was that their other daughter had died under mysterious circumstances.'

'What other daughter?' asked Andrews.

'Charlotte was the one sister, belonging to identical twins,' she told him. 'The other girl was known as Bethany. She died when he was only ten years old.'

'From what?' asked Hunter.

'Allegedly a weak heart,' she replied. 'But I'll show you something in a minute, which will throw a hell of a lot of questions at that theory.'

'What else did you discover whilst you was down in London?' asked Hunter.

'That they still own their home down there in Chelsea.'

'So what?' shrugged Hunter. 'Ain't no crime against owning two homes. Especially when you were as rich and as arrogant as the pair of them was.'

'Did you know that there has been children going missing in London also, over the last year or so?' asked Rachel

'You what!' exclaimed Andrews as he stared from Rachel you Hunter.

'That's right,' said Rachel. 'Kids just like the ones up here also. From estates, from homes where the parents are either abusers themselves or addicts of some kind. Don't you find it strange that there wasn't a connection by your lot made? I mean come on for Christ sake. Think about it. Something just ain't right here Hunter.'

'I don't know wha...' she began as Rachel cut her off again.

'And the other thing that I know is that is what led us to the Pied Piper connection. Apparently the guy who was responsible for the kids that went missing in London, was a guy known as Colin Spencer. Don't ask me where he is now, as I honestly don't have a fucking clue, nor do I wish to know. But, this Spencer character spilt the beans on the Pied Piper. Or least part of what he knew. He said the guy was protected. Just like Luther Cartwright believed he was protected, by raising money for the police. He figured he had connections. Also this Spencer character claims that the Pied Piper used his magic flute, on the kids he took, all the way back to Manchester. This would also tie in with Luther Cartwright, as he owned the house down there, but lived up here. Maybe he brought the kids back up this way, when they'd finished with them down there.'

'How the hell did you discover all that out kid?' asked Hunter.

'Jesus Hunter,' sighed Rachel. 'What were you expecting? If you didn't feel that I was capable of looking into this case successfully, then why the hell did you ask me to get involved at all?'

'I asked you to look into the disappearance of a missing girl,' hissed Hunter. 'Now we've got all of this fucking mess. Including – one – the still missing girl, and – two – the dead parents of the said still missing girl.'

'Now you listen to me Hunter,' replied Rachel through gritted teeth. 'What you asked me to look into, was a missing girl that had some kind of a connection to the missing children. One thing led me to the other. And like you just said yourself, I still

don't know where Charlotte is, or if she's still alive for that matter.'

'Okay kid. Fair play,' answered Hunter shaking her head back at her. 'But apart from what this Spencer guy, whoever the fuck he is, apparently told you. I'm still a little lost on just how all of this led you back to the Cartwright's.'

'First off,' said Rachel tossing a phone number scribbled upon the piece of paper, across the desk that lay between them. 'That number there is to a detective Jenkins down in London.'

'So,' shrugged Hunter as she picked up the piece of paper. 'Who the fuck is that?'

'These people claim that they were protected in some kind of way. I'm not entirely sure how. But I want you to contact that man. He has already been tipped off to get a search warrant first thing this morning to their home in Chelsea. He knows exactly where he has to look. And when he finds what he will, he'll know that his suspicions on the Cartwright's were correct all along.'

'Why this guy though?' asked Hunter.

'Because I trust that he was never involved personally with the family,' she replied. 'He had his own personal distaste for them, when he told us his suspicions.'

'What's he going to find at the house kid?'

'A trapdoor that will lead him into a secret basement,' she replied.

'What's behind the trapdoor?' asked Andrews.

'It leads straight to hell,' replied Rachel as she glared at them both.

'What the fuck is that supposed to mean?' asked Hunter.

'The Cartwright's have got the basement set up as their private prison, where they use and abuse children in a variety of different ways whilst they film their sadistic escapades.'

'You're joking?' said Andrews.

'Do I look like I'm joking about here,' she snapped, as she hugged herself tighter, drawing her knees up onto the chair further for personal comfort. 'Sorry Mike,' she added.

'Go on kid,' pushed Hunter.

'They've got the whole thing set up to film and record what they do to these kids,' she said. 'But it goes much further than all of that. It's all connected in some way to the website I mentioned. They've been at it for years. But they kept repeatedly talking through a third party for their crimes. As in he or the all-mighty.'

'Do you think that there was somebody else involved?' asked Hunter. 'Do you think that this Pied Piper, or whoever he claims to be, is still at large?'

'I'm not sure,' she shook her head. 'I've seen that behaviour before in serial killers or serial rapists, where they shift the blame to ease their own consciences. But let me show you this,' she said rising from her seat, and walking around the desk to Hunter's computer.

'What you doing?' asked Hunter as Rachel began tapping away at the keys.

'This thing is hooked on line, right?' asked Rachel as she glanced to Andrews. 'You better come around here and take a look also.'

'What is it?' asked Hunter as her partner came around the desk and they both stared in fascination at the screen before them.

'What's that?' asked Andrews as he stared at the advert for some old antique nursery rhyme book.

Accessing the page advertising the Pied Piper, Rachel quickly accessed her way through into the website known as Pied Piper Productions.

'Where did that just come from?' asked Hunter leaning forward.

'They've got it set up so that you have to know what it is that you are looking for,' she replied. 'You need to get your computer department to take a look at it.'

'What's the password?' asked Andrews. 'Do you know it Rachel?'

'I do,' she replied. 'But it's more complicated than that.'

'What do you mean,' asked Hunter impatiently. 'Just put the password in for God's sake. I want to see...'

'It's been set up so that they know whose accessing them,' she cut Hunter off. 'But I know from a friend of mine just how to do this,' she said as she began tapping away at the keys, bypassing the trace straight back into the Cartwright's home.

'How'd you just do that?' asked Andrews impressed.

'The Cartwright's were obviously registered users of the site,' she told him. 'Not just users either. I think that is was them, who either set it up or had help in setting the whole thing up.'

'So he was the Pied Piper?' asked Andrews amazed at what he was being told.

'I'm still not certain,' she shook her head. 'Possibly, very possibly.'

'Just how did you find all of this out kid?' asked Hunter siting back in her seat.

'I stole Charlotte's harddrive from her computer,' she admitted.

'You did what?' asked Hunter seemingly appalled.

'I wanted to access the girl's secret files to gain more information on her,' she said still tapping away at the keys. 'I didn't realise that it was going to lead me where it did. Jesus Hunter. You think that I invited all of this fucking mess. You think that I invited myself to be tortured and fucking molested by those couple of freaks this morning, whilst tied to that table. Well I fucking didn't, All that I did, was what you aske...' she broke down, as the tears began to flow.

Hunter suddenly rose from her seat and embraced her. 'I'm sorry kid, shush now, I'm a fucking idiot at times. You should know that better than anybody else.'

'It's just such a mess,' sobbed Rachel. 'How could they do these things?'

'What's this?' asked Andrews staring the image on the computer screen.

'That's what I was on about earlier,' sighed Rachel composing herself and then wiping her eyes and nose with a tissue from the desk. As she freed herself from Hunter's embrace. 'It's the website within the website.'

'What's on here?' asked Hunter.

'This for starters,' she replied as she clicked the keys.

The next image that came up was of Bethany tied to the bed. They all sat there silently as they watched in horror at the events taking place. Nobody spoke a single word as their eyes remained glued to the screen. Transfixed at the horrors taking place.

'There,' snapped Rachel as she paused the film. 'Who's that?'

'That's Luther Cartwright,' said Hunter in astonishment as she suddenly realised who she been watching beat the girl half to death.

'And that is Bethany,' sighed Rachel. 'The other twin sister.'

'Oh my God,' sighed Andrews. 'What else is in these files?'

'I've not seen any of the other ones,' she replied. 'But I'm told that there is much worse ones than that. Ones that even feature, what appear to be the children actually being killed.'

'No,' said Hunter glaring at her. 'Are you fucking serious?'

'You need to check all of this out yourselves,' said Rachel turning away from the computer.

'Why didn't you come to me with this first kid?' asked Hunter still looking astonished.

'I wanted to be certain before I did so,' she replied as she walked back around the desk.

Suddenly the door crashed open loudly startling the three of them. 'What the fucking hell has happened this morning Detective Hunter?' screamed Chief Mackenzie as he tore into the office with Stephen Halenbrook following behind. 'And what the hell happened to the Cartwright's?'

'I killed them both,' replied Rachel without any remorse whatsoever.

'Arrest this woman now,' he screamed at her, and then glared at Hunter awaiting her response.

'What for?' shrugged Hunter, as Mackenzie stood over Rachel glaring his hatred at her. 'You want me to arrest the kid here. Rachel Murphy? Our very own Rachel Murphy I might add Chief Mackenzie? What the hell for? For self defence against those couple of freaks?'

'What the fuck is that supposed to mean Hunter?' asked Mackenzie calming slightly as he recognised one of her many outbursts that he appeared to have trouble dealing with. 'The Cartwright's were pillars of society. And I don't care what this woman has told you. They were...'

'You better hear what she has to say,' said Hunter cutting him off.

'And what she has to show you,' added Andrews still staring at the computer screen.

'The were up to their necks in this missing kids case chief,' said Hunter. 'We've got the London branch going into there home in Chelsea as we speak.'

'You can't do tha...' began Mackenzie.

'It's where they had everything set up,' said Rachel. 'This has been going on for years.'

'You were asked to look into their missing daughter Murphy,' he snapped. 'Not to go sniffing around their private li...'

'I'm warning you now chief,' said Hunter. 'You better sit down and listen before you put your foot in your mouth.'

'Let's hear it then?' he said sighing deeply as he nodded at Halenbrook to also take a seat.

Rachel then took the next couple of hours to fill them in on everything she'd learnt about the Cartwright family, leaving not only her brother completely out of the story, but also Sleeper and Eazy. Finishing off with how she killed them both herself.

'Right,' sighed Mackenzie, shaking his head. 'I just can't believe that the family was messed up in all of this. Just how is all this going to look?'

'It'll look exactly how it was,' said Hunter. 'That the Cartwright's manipulated and used the police to go about what they did.'

'This could work in our favour,' he suddenly responded chirping up.

'What the hell is that supposed to mean?' asked Hunter.

'For starter's Detective Hunter,' he raised his eyebrows at her, 'It might just be what you need to cover the lack of success you're having with your other case.'

'Fuck you Mackenzie,' she snapped.

'No Detective Hunter,' he smirked. 'I think that it is more like fuck you. Now Rachel. Listen to me. I want you to make your statement to Detective Inspector Halenbrook here.'

'But chief,' protested Hunter.

'It's his case now,' he snapped smirking at her. 'Remember Detective Hunter. You gave the case to him this morning. And you will do as I say for a change. Now, Ms Murphy, if you'll come with the two of us.'

As the three of them left the office, with Rachel shrugging at Hunter who was clearly seething, she then said. 'You ain't heard the last of this Chief.'

THIRTY SEVEN

As Rachel soaked in the hot bath tub at home, she let the tears roll at will as she sponged herself over and over. She'd been at the station all that day, going over and over the case involving the Cartwright's. By the time Hunter had dropped her off at the apartment in Salford, she'd fully felt the events of the last few weeks come tumbling down upon her like a ton of bricks.

Before they'd left the station, word had come back from the stud farm in Knutsford that they still hadn't found any bodies buried there yet. The next step was obviously the house in Prestbury and along with the joint investigation being headed by Jenkins down in London, at their home in Chelsea. But Rachel had a feeling that they were not to discover any of the bodies at either of those.

There was still a lot about the case that bothered Rachel. Some of the things that the Cartwright's had said were playing on her mind like twisted riddles she couldn't fathom out for herself, no matter how hard she tried. Both Halenbrook, whom she had taken an instant dislike to, although she wasn't quite sure of the reason why, and the Chief Superintendent Mackenzie, had kept her locked away in the chief's office whilst they went over and over everything with a fine tooth comb.

It was as if they both didn't believe her, or just didn't want to believe that these so called pillars of society as Mackenzie had described the Cartwright's had carried out such atrocities. But it was as if they were having trouble coming to terms with the fact that the family had been behind, not only the missing children, but were also actively involved in this whole Pied Piper set up. She had shown them both the way into the system, not revealing just how it was that they had managed to break into the system,

despite the fact they kept pushing her on the matter. They just didn't seem to believe that she had managed all of what she had on her own. And of course they were right in doing so, because without the help of Tony, Sleeper, Eazy or Robert, she'd have never have even got close to any of the evidence against the family from hell.

They had wanted to know in detail how she had killed the two of them. Over and over they asked her. Almost as if they were doing their best to trip her up, or trick her in some way into revealing that it wasn't her that was there all alone. It was as if they were possessed in bringing someone to justice for ridding society of these couple of freaks. They hadn't looked too pleased when it was confirmed by Lucy, that Rachel had indeed fired the gun, which as yet, was still untraceable.

Nor the added fact that there was only Luther Cartwright's and Rachel's prints to found on the knife that had been responsible for the slaying of her captor. They knew with the statement and the evidence that Rachel had supplied, that they didn't have a hope in hell of charging Rachel with the murders of the Cartwright's. They could possibly go for manslaughter charges against her, but she didn't think that would happen. Especially with Hunter backing her all the way, even if it was no longer her case.

She then began to think about poor Caroline at the hands of the deranged pair that had mauled and violated her also, leaving her feeling the way she did right now. Really feeling for the girl, knowing that she had to visit with her to make sure that she was going to be alright. Knowing exactly what the girl felt. Scrubbing the sponge all over herself, doing her best to rid the condemned empathy that riddled throughout her body. Watching as the water cascaded over her bruised naked flesh back into the bathtub. Red streaks running away from the wound below her neck line tainting the water into different blemishes of scarlet and cherry.

But the worst feeling of all was the fact that she hadn't accomplished what she had set out for in the first place. To find the missing girl, Charlotte Cartwright. And that bothered her more than anything else. They way her mother and father spoke of her, was as if she hadn't been their daughter or hadn't been theirs in some way. Things like *"she was an offering to him"* or *"she belonged to the all-mighty"*, all of those words still playing on her mind. And just where was the girl. In fact, not only the girl, but the missing children that had been featured in the films found on the website.

Climbing from the bathtub, feeling like the weight of the world still sat upon her shoulder's as the hot water had failed to ease any of the stiffness she had felt when finally released from the station. Stretching her limbs as she used the soft white bath towel against her naked flesh, she then pulled her white terry bathrobe over herself. Hugging herself tightly she made her way from the bathroom.

Just as she stepped out into the hallway, there was frantic banging at her front door.

'Who is it?' she called out.

'It's me,' called Tony in the same frantic tones he'd banged on her door with. 'Open the door... where have you been? Why have taken the phone off the hook? Why is your mobile still swit...'

'Calm down,' she said opening the front door as his mouth was still working overtime.

He suddenly grabbed hold of her and pulled her tightly towards her. She let herself go and felt his immediate love, affection and concern. She enjoyed the feeling, and realised just what had been missing in her life.

'You three alright?' she asked Sleeper, Eazy and Chan who were stood in the shadows behind Tony.

'We're fine,' replied Sleeper stepping forward into the light. 'Your brother here has been driving us mad all day though.' He smirked at her as she gave him a little smile.

'We bring him here,' said Chan. 'So he stop hurting our heads.'

'You better come in then,' she told them stepping away from the door and her brother's embrace. She saw the emotion her brother felt at that precise moment and hugged him tightly again. 'Thanks,' was all she said to him as she kissed his cheek.

'I'll put the kettle on,' announced Eazy as his huge frame disappeared into the kitchen, and they all made their way into the living room.

'I just had to get into a hot bath,' she told them as she replaced the headset to the phone. 'I'm sorry if I worried you. I should have called. But I just...'

'Don't worry about it,' said Sleeper sitting himself down next to Chan. 'So is everything cool or have got problems?'

'Yeah, what'd they say ar'kid?' asked Tony sitting on the arm of the chair to remain close to her.

'Before any of that,' said Rachel. 'How's Caroline? Did you get her home alright?'

'She was real shook up you know,' answered Sleeper.

'Paul went ape,' added Tony. 'It took the two of us to calm him down as we explained what had happened. Jackie was with Caroline upstairs knowing all too well what he's like.'

'Once we calmed him down,' said Sleeper, 'and explained that the Cartwright's had been dealt with appropriately, only then did he seem to come around.'

'It hit him hard,' said Tony shaking his head. 'I don't think that he could quite believe what had happen...'

'I'll have to go and see her,' said Rachel.

'I'd leave it a few days first,' Tony told her. 'They had the doc in there with her as we were leaving. He said that she'd be heavily sedated over the next week or so.'

'She'll be alright,' nodded Sleeper. 'She's a tough little girl. I think she'll pull through this.'

'I hope so,' sighed Rachel really feeling for the girl.

'So what has Hunter had to say about everything Rach?' asked Tony.

'Let's put it this way,' she sighed deeply, shaking her head. 'It ain't no longer Hunter's case.'

'Why's that?' asked Sleeper.

'Because Mackenzie, that's the chief at the station has handed it over to his right hand man, Halenbrook,' she replied.

'Who's he?' asked Eazy.

'A complete dick,' answered Chan.

'Ain't that the truth,' smiled Rachel at Chan.

'I almost forgot. My chef stay late for you tonight Rachel,' he told her holding up the brown paper bag. 'I have him prepare food for you. I would take it from me now, before Eazy spots it.'

'Thanks a lot Chan,' she said. 'I'm absolutely starving.' She lied about the last bit, but didn't want to hurt the old man's feelings.

'What the fuck is Halenbrook doing working Hunter's case?' asked Tony.

'You know this guy as well?' asked Sleeper.

'Most people do,' he laughed. 'The chief at head quarters is one hell of prick. But Halenbrook. Now he's a complete fucking idiot. I remember back when he was just a street copper. He was afraid of his own shadow. But that's not to say that he wasn't as bent as a two-bob note. He not so much taxed the lads that I knew back then. More of turned a blind eye for a kick back.'

'That was until Mackenzie turned up on the scene a few years back now,' said Chan. 'Mackenzie soon takes him under wing. Was not long before he becomes a detective right along side of Chief.'

'So who's this Mackenzie?' asked Eazy. 'That name is familiar you know.'

'Maybe,' answered Tony. 'I'm not absolutely positive. But I'm sure that he is from down your way.'

'He is,' Chan told them. 'He used to work closely with Anderson.'

'Who's Anderson?' asked Rachel as she saw the looks of recognition dawn upon Sleeper and Eazy's faces. 'I'm sure that I know that name.'

'What the fuck ever happened to that guy?' asked Tony staring at Chan and also glancing suspiciously at the other two.

'No idea,' replied Chan nonchalantly. 'I think maybe he returned to London.'

'Nah man,' said Tony shaking his head. 'I sure that something else happened to him. He nicked some heavy crews back in the day if I remem...'

'Anyway,' said Sleeper cutting him short. 'This Mackenzie was at Scotland Yard. He was one of their top boys. He was originally from Congleton, or some area around Cheshire. I can't quite remember now. But he was transferred down south back in the eighties. I only remember it so well, because straight away he began to make a name for himself. Although I don't think that he managed things himself. But he was good with the top people; therefore with them liking him, he rose through the ranks pretty quickly.'

'So you know who he is?' asked Rachel.

'All that I remember of him,' said Sleeper, 'was that he seemed to ride the backs of others quite successfully.'

'What do you mean by that?' asked Tony.

'Basically,' he laughed. 'He claimed other people's achievement's to be his own. I know a lot of other copper's hated him. But he did it successfully enough, to win him promotion as governor up here.'

'I remember that guy now,' said Eazy. 'He was always in the papers down our way back then. I knew that his name was familiar. When did he turn up here?'

'About seven or eight years back now,' said Rachel. 'I only remember it because it wasn't long after that, that I took time off because off with expecting Becky. He never liked me for some reason. I still don't reckon that he does.'

'Yeah, yeah,' said Tony. 'Wasn't Anderson supposed to step into the old chief's place after he retired? You must remember Chan. But something happened to him. I'm sure that Mackenzie

turned up here within a couple of years of Anderson going walkabouts. He ended up as the chief instead.'

'What do mean, he went walkabouts?' asked Rachel. 'And just who was this Anderson?' She directed the question at Sleeper.

'Just some copper that worked both up here in Manchester and down our way in London,' he shrugged.

'Fucking bent copper,' snapped Tony. 'He used to tax all the crew's back then. Word has it that he set things up with some lad's from over Salford way, so that they were running things for him. I was working the Canary Islands a lot back then so didn't really have any run ins with the man. But I'm sure that he running around like a one man army. And then he just seemed to disappear from the scene. Even the police didn't give a straight answer or reason for...'

'I don't know anything about that,' said Chan. 'Anyway Rachel...'

'You must remember that Chan,' said Tony. 'That was back in the day with Prey and Chopper, and that old geezer they knocked about with. What was his name now?'

'Steve,' replied Sleeper.

'That was him,' replied Tony.

'So what about this Mackenzie character?' asked Eazy changing the subject. 'Is he bent as well? And what about this other guy who's now running the case Rachel?'

'All I know of Mackenzie is pretty much what you've just said,' she replied eyeing the three of them suspiciously over the conversation that had just taken place. 'Hunter say's that they carry him nicely along as it goes. Although I reckon that he's feeling the pressure at the moment with Gabriel striking not only a week after the last lot of murder's, but also right under their very noses.'

'So why's he put this other guy on the case?' asked Sleeper.

'It's his golden boy,' she replied. 'I'd say that he's got Halenbrook lined up for promotion. And let's face it, with this in his back pocket. It's going to do very nicely indeed.'

'What about Hunter though?' asked Tony.

'She's pissed off alright,' she sighed. 'She only handed the case over to them this morning. Mackenzie told her that he wanted her to put everything that she could into this case against Gabriel. I tell you though. I reckon if it wasn't for Mackenzie and the fact the top brass love him so much. Then I'd say that it'd be Hunter as chief. She's worked hard enough for it. She's about the best detective that they've got.'

'I bet she's got the hump though,' said Tony. 'Imagine handing the case over and then within hour's it appears to have been solved.'

'She is,' she told them shaking her head. 'I would have kicked up more of a fuss to keep her on the case. But we were already treading lightly on dodgy ground. I didn't think that I should push it.'

'So what happened then?' asked Sleeper. 'Is everything cool like I asked?'

'As far as I know,' she replied. 'It took a lot of convincing, that it was in fact me had killed the two of them. But they seemed to buy it, in the end. Especially as the forensics came back with the gun's residue all over my hands. Plus both Luther Cartwright's and my prints were found all over the knife they discovered at the scene,' she added staring at Sleeper who smiled at her.

'Thanks,' was all he said.

'You think that they will find any other evidence?' asked Eazy as he walked through into the living with a tray full of mugs.

'If they do... Thanks,' said Rachel taking the hot mug into her hands. 'Then I can't see how they'll trace it back to any of you guys. Although...' She stared at Sleeper then Eazy.

'What is it?' asked Sleeper.

'Not that it should matter,' she paused. 'But Hunter somehow knew about the two of you hanging around with us recently.'

'How the hell did she know that?' asked Eazy sitting at her bureau where the computer could be found.

'I'm not quite sure,' shrugged Rachel. 'She didn't question me further, other than to point out that she knew the two of you had been seen with the two of us recently.'

'How'd you reckon that she knows that though?' asked Sleeper.

'Through her many grasses of course,' Chan told him. 'It's how coppers know most of the things that they do.'

'True,' replied Tony. 'Is it going to be a problem? Do you two want to leave the area for a while?'

'Fuck that,' replied Sleeper. 'We're here to stay, just like we promised you we would. Besides, she ain't got anything on us.'

'The brother's right,' agreed Eazy. 'If things look like they may be becoming a little too hot then we'll reconsider. But for now, don't worry about it.'

'Thank you,' said Rachel, admitting to herself that she felt a whole lot safer with the two of them still around.

'So have they charged you with anything?' asked Tony concerned.

'Not yet,' she told him. 'Mackenzie wanted me arrested for their murders at first. Only once Hunter had managed to clam him down somewhat and I then went on to explain in detail everything that I knew of the Cartwright's, well, he certainly seemed to change his tune after that.'

'It was clear cut self defence,' said Tony. 'I mean what the fuck else was you supposed to do?'

'Plus Jenkins, down in London came through for us,' she told them. 'Hunter contacted him. They got the search warrant for their home in Chelsea. Hunter had him explain to Mackenzie over the speaker phone as I was giving my statement to Halenbrook and him. He basically told him of all the shit that they discovered down there. They are running a joint investigation into the family now.'

'So is it Jenkins running the investigation down our way?' asked Eazy.

'Yeah I reckon so.'

'That'll be cool then,' he replied. 'At least we will be kept informed on anything that they discover.'

'He also said that they he had some hassle at first getting the search warrant to the Cartwright's place. They weren't going to allow the warrant at first,' she told them. 'Well that was until Hunter phoned them and explained that the two of them were dead. And also the fact their was still missing kids involved here. They soon enough received the warrant.'

'So have they found the bodies yet?' asked Eazy.

'Were they out at the farm?' asked Sleeper hopefully.

Rachel shook her head at them both. 'Not so far,' she told them. 'But they owned a lot of land surrounding that area in Knutsford. It'll take some time to excavate the entire area. Plus they will begin pulling apart the homes in Prestbury and Chelsea now. Hopefully...'

'But they know everything about the missing kids?' asked Tony. 'They've got to know now that it was the Cartwright's that were responsible, right?'

'I accessed the Pied Piper Productions for them,' she said. 'I showed them the film with Luther Cartwright in it. There was also a lot of other stuff that their computer guy kept on coming up with. There was also a lot of other material on the website involving Luther and Anabella. Other adult's were also actively involved with children in those films and photograph's. Several were already well known offender's to them. But...'

'But what?' asked Tony. 'It had to be hi...'

'I couldn't say conclusively that he was the Pied Piper,' said Rachel cutting him short. 'I wish to fuck that I could have.' She sighed deeply.

'You don't reckon that it was him,' said Sleeper. 'Do you Rachel?'

'It was all the twisted shit that Anabella said whilst you was there,' she replied. 'Plus before you turned up... whilst they had their filthy hands all over me.'

'They what!' exclaimed Tony.

'They kept talking through the all-mighty or he,' she said ignoring Tony. 'It was as if there was someone else involved.'

'Who though?' asked Sleeper. 'Cartwright not only fitted the profile of what we was looking for. But also had the access to being both down in London and here in Manchester where both the kids disappeared from.'

'I know,' she shrugged. 'You're right. But what if this creep is still at large. What if we killed the wrong guy?'

'He deserved to die anyway,' said Tony staring at her with hurt eyes.

She knew that he felt he somehow let her down in not being able to protect her. Not that it was true. She had made the decision herself to go and see the Cartwright's alone she obviously hadn't expected for what happened to have happened. But it had done and now she was the one who had to live with the aftermath.

'I not saying that he didn't' she said shaking her head. 'But if this wasn't the guy and this Pied fucking Piper is still out th...'

'Maybe the investigation into the case will reveal something further,' said Chan.

'That's true,' agreed Rachel. 'Now that the police are fully involved, they may indeed find more out than we were able to do.'

'But if he wasn't the guy,' said Eazy shaking his head. 'Then what about what we set out to do?'

'So what do want to do?' asked Sleeper. 'If he wasn't the guy. Then I'd say that we just killed our only true lead in the case.'

'So what now then?' asked Tony.

'We leave it to the police to sort out,' said Rachel.

'Maybe my Carol will be able to help in some way,' he told them. 'I still haven't contacted her since we saw her last week. But she'd told us that it could take her a couple of weeks to find anything out. And I didn't think that we'd have discovered as much as we had done without her help.'

'You think she may have discovered anything that we may have missed?' asked Rachel

Glancing at his watch, seeing that it was only just gone twelve thirty. 'It's a little late,' he said. 'But she tends stay up late. I'll give her a call now.'

Pulling the mobile from his pocket he hit speed dial. 'You alright sis,' he said smiling as he'd obviously just got through to the other line.

'So what about the case against Gabriel?' asked Tony as they suddenly all saw Sleeper's face drop.

'What is it?' asked Rachel immediately concerned as Sleeper darted straight out of his seat.

'Somebody else just answered the phone,' he said grabbing his jacket. 'It was some demented fuck laughing straight back at me, he said that he'd just put my sister out of her misery.'

'Oh fuck,' said Eazy who was already at the door.

'What the...' began Tony.

'I'm outta here,' snapped Sleeper as he shot through the door with Eazy directly behind him.

'We'll follow you there,' said Rachel running for the door to get changed. 'I don't believe this shit.'

THIRTY EIGHT

'**H**er name's just Carol, what the fuck does it matter right now,' cracked Rachel at the phone with all the annoyance she could muster. This was as both she and Tony sped through Manchester's city centre towards Cheadle, breaking just about very possible speed limit to get to where Sleeper's sister resided.

They were literally only four or five minutes behind Sleeper and Eazy. Streaks of yellow from the street lights past them in a blur, as if they had been past through a slow shutter speed of high quality camera. Tony was driving as fast as a cheetah in pursuit of his prey, in order to catch up with the others. Rachel had made the decision to phone Hunter, against Tony's protests. She had a bad a feeling about all of this. She couldn't quite place the fear she felt, she only acknowledged that it was very real. Nobody knew quite what to expect, but deep down, Rachel just knew this wasn't going to have a happy ending. That was the reason for calling Hunter immediately.

She knew if things were how she imagined them to be, then Sleeper was going to be all out for blood. That she could relate to, better than most. But she also had to acknowledge the fact that she'd kept Hunter in the dark over most of the Pied Piper and the Cartwright incident. She couldn't take a chance in leaving her out of this, without allowing herself to become to caught up on other people's behalf's, as much as she hated too.

'What's her surname?' asked Hunter, as Rachel heard the sound of car horns in the background of wherever Hunter was resonancing their anger at her for reasons Rachel didn't know of. 'Fuck-you!' She suddenly screamed, startling Rachel. 'Sorry kid, not you. It's just this damn... anyway, now what's her last na...'

'Stop asking me pointless fucking questions Hunter,' she screamed back at her. 'All that I know is what I've just told you

for Christ sake. She lives at that address that I've just given you. He's there right now.'

'Who is?' asked Hunter. 'Damn fucking impatient fuckers. I'm just at the entrance to the M56 kid. There is fucking cars everywhere screaming at me. Now start agai...'

'For fucks sake Hunter, are you even listening to me or what,' she said shaking her head at the phone. 'It's Gabriel, I think,' she said as Tony ran a red light, cars all around sounding their aggravation at them for the delirious and dangerous driving taking place.

'What the hell do mean... *think* kid?' Hunter said impatiently.

'Will you just...'

'I'm already on my way,' said Hunter cutting her off. 'I've just turned around. It ain't far from here; I can be there in fifteen minutes or so.'

'Thank God,' she sighed. 'The only thing is, I fear that we may already be too late.'

'There is one thing that I don't understand though kid,' said Hunter. 'Who the hell is this woman, I mean why her for fucks sake kid?'

'It may not be Gabriel,' Rachel told her, as they skidded around the roundabout, taking them towards The Parkway. 'She was looking into the Pied Piper for us as well.'

'You what kid!' exclaimed Hunter. 'What the fuck was she...'

'She's our friend's sisters,' explained Rachel, as she grabbed the dashboard, with Tony zooming past several of the cars ahead of them. The row of deserted, closed shops through Moss Side, a mere haze to her as she continued to try and talk to Hunter.

'Let me guess,' she screamed. 'It's one of those two black guys', it's their sister. Am I right or what kid?'

'It is,' replied Rachel sighing. 'She's an investigator for some law firm up this way Hunter. We thought that she may be able to help us in some way. Look Hunter, none of that is important right now... is it for fucks sake. All that is important is that she's got a young boy living with her. Now are you going to call this in or no...'

Tony suddenly grabbed her arm startling her. 'Just her for now,' he said. 'We don't know how Sleeper is going to react to...'

'But Ton...'

'I heard,' said Hunter down the line. 'I'll call it in after we get there. It may be nothing yet kid.'

'Just hurry the fuck up Hunter,' Rachel told her as they pulled off The Parkway, towards Cheadle.

'Jesus Tony,' she said. 'This ain't time for your fucking code of the street. We're talking about real liv...'

'I know what we're talking about Rach,' he said. 'But like you said, we don't know who or what is responsible yet. Hell, we ain't even sure that anything has happened. Either way, I don't think that Sleeper is going to be too pleased that you've just gone and called Hunter in on this one.'

'We had to for fucks sake Tony,' she said glaring at him as he concentrated on the road and traffic ahead of them. 'If this freak has somehow got to Sleeper's sister. Then they would have had to have been brought in anyway.'

'We should have waited,' he told her, turning down one of the side streets from the main drag where numerous pubs, restaurants, supermarkets and seemingly endless amounts of take-aways that had already past them by.

'This can't be happening Tony,' she sighed deeply as tears swelled within the rims of her eyes. 'Oh Jesus, what if he has somehow got to Sleeper's sister. What if... oh my God, what if... I'll never forgive myse...'

'We'll soon find out, one way or the other,' replied Tony. 'This is the house.' He pointed to the house belonging to row of what appeared to be both houses and flats all in the same street of exact buildings. The front door wide open as light spilt out onto the street where Sleeper's silver Mercedes was parked half on, and half off the curb, skew-whiffed onto the road with the engine still running.

As they skidded to a halt directly behind Sleeper's vehicle, they both bolted straight towards the front door.

Gabriel had observed silently as the one who called himself Sleeper driving the silver Mercedes had almost run the vehicle straight into the house itself. They had jumped up the curb in a hurry to witness Gabriel's latest creation without the knowledge of the killer's presence so close.

Although even Gabriel had to admit, that this latest creation wasn't by far the greatest of work that had already been carried out for Michael.

For starters, Carol Sillverone hadn't ever been part of Gabriel's or Michael's plans. Only through her work at Daniel's law firm in the city centre, where she was as an investigator, had she become known to both of them. Yet still, she hadn't been an initial problem, for neither of them had known her as one of the condemned souls that had gathered over the years. In fact, if

truth be known, she hadn't even been within the perimeters of Manchester for all that long.

But all of this was up until the last week or so, when she had decided it would seem, on her brother's behalf, to look, not only into the missing children, but to also to snoop around and see just what it was, that she could discover about Gabriel.

And that, she shouldn't have done. Because when she had gone poking her nose in where she shouldn't have been, and not just in one place, but two places. Gabriel knew, through the knowledge that Gabriel had, that she had already pissed another lot of people off with her nosing around in their business. The thing was, she was very good at her job indeed. Gabriel had known this from the beginning and had kept a close eye upon the victim, for that very reason. And it had been a good job that Gabriel had kept an eye on Ms Sillverone. For she had got closer than the others in discovering the truth, on both behalf's.

And for this very reason, Gabriel had known that if the situation had been anticipated any longer, then it wouldn't have been Gabriel visiting her home that very night. Only, that chance couldn't be taken, not now, not ever. So taking it upon oneself, Gabriel decided that it was best, to dispose of Carol Sillverone before she became an even greater threat to them both.

Smiling sadistically as Rachel and her brother pulled up behind the other vehicle, knowing what it was that awaited them all inside. Gabriel watched, savoured the moment where Rachel looked up to the top bedroom window, shaking her head as it was clearly visible, she was already shaking herself. Knowing far better that the others, what it was that awaited their arrival

Then as the two of them ran through open front door, Gabriel heard the screams of anguish. Relishing the initial screams, like a mother would hold deeply onto the memory of the first noises, no matter how slight they may be, of a new born child. Eyes closed, imagining the look of sheer terror on the faces that walked through the gates of hell into that bedroom. Gabriel began to laugh out quietly so not to alert anybody, as lights began to appear throughout bedroom windows, at the noises disturbing their now sleepless night.

'Nnnnoooooooooo.' They heard the cry from upstairs as they both entered through the front entrance to the house. Quickly observing her surroundings, doing her best to contain as much information as possible about what she witnessed, before they ran two steps at a time towards the upper level of the home.

As they reached the top of the stairs, Rachel could see the bloody footsteps that trailed from where they could now see Eazy slumped against the open bedroom doorway. Observing the detail of what appeared to be large boot prints, Rachel realised what she had dreaded. Although deep down, and as much as she regretted it, she had known that it come to this all along.

'Eazy,' Rachel called out as he turned towards her slowly, his face revealed everything she needed to initially know.

'Oh noooo sis, nooooo Carolllll, what has he done to you, nooooo,' cried Sleeper from within the confines of the darkly lit room, where he anticipated their imitate arrival, that was already too late for any of them.

Rachel pushed her way past Eazy's mammoth frame to gain access to the bedroom. He had tears streaming down his face without any shame associated to them. As she entered the darkly lighted chamber, she covered her mouth involuntarily with the shock of witnessing yet another of Gabriel's sadistic creations.

The bedroom was ablaze with only the several candles that had been strategically assembled around the room by Gabriel, for the best effect to his prevailing conception. The night she had arrived home the year before, came flooding back to her, and threatened to wash her away, as she grabbed onto the arm of Tony despairingly as she struggled to regain composure.

'Oh, fuck me,' exclaimed Tony holding his sister up with ease, as he wrapped his arm around her tenderly, suddenly breaking the emotion with. 'Just what the fuck...' As he failed to find his own words, shaking his head.

Examining the room around her, she noticed that Sleeper had hold of his sister, as he struggled to ease her away from the wall where she was remained entrapped. He also wanted her far away from the deranged artwork that covered, it's once pale colouring that was too hard to decipher through the candle light.

His sister looked as if she had been flayed of all her skin. But Rachel didn't believe this too be so. But she had lost a lot of blood that much was certain for sure. So much in fact, that she appeared to have been drained of it, as her bloodstained posterior hung there against what had once nothing more than a painted wall. She was fully naked and exposed for them all to bare witness to, as their were drawn back towards the horror's displayed before them, like some deranged dark force field, drawing them back in to recite the image over, and over again, again.

'I need to help him for Christ sake,' said Tony, as he let go of Rachel and grabbed hold of the mutilated corpse next to Sleeper.

Her chest had been torn open so viciously, that Gabriel had ripped straight through the main arteries, hence the amount of blood that appeared to cover not only her body, every surface, but also every inch of the room through the diminished light. But as gruesome as it all was portrayed to them, there was something just not quite right about what was before them.

Gabriel had then used the blood from the victim to create his latest master piece. That was the same as before, but what was different? Their were the trademark wings so gloriously spreading away from the victims arms, onto the wall so lavishly, again the same, so that was wasn't different, so what was it?

Not only that, but his artwork was becoming better and better, and as much as Rachel hated to familiarise herself with the scene so unemotionally, she knew that was going to be the only way to get through this nightmare. Also, there was the usual scrawling; only she didn't recognise them as being as familiar as the rest had been. What the hell was bothering her so much about this crime scene? What was different about this than the others?

That's when it hit her about what wrong this time around. For this time it was different, she swore it was, as she stared at the victim. Stepping closer as both her brother and Sleeper struggled to lift the body away from the wall. She reached out, and touched the still warm flesh of the victim.

'What the hell are you doing Rachel' snapped Sleeper.

'Just wait one sec...'

'Leave her be,' said Sleeper staring at her with cold eyes.

'He's not taken her heart,' replied Rachel staring directly back at him.

'What the hell has that got...'

'He's left her heart in place,' Rachel pointed out. 'He never made the trade, he's just...'

'We can all see what he's done,' sneered Sleeper as he then took a deep breath. 'I'm sorry Rach, I know what it is that you are...'

Suddenly the silent Eazy was before her as he gently, yet forcefully eased her hands out of the walls where they had been nailed. Her bloodied, mutilated corpse slumped against him as she fell away from the wall. Easing her body to the floor with the same care and consideration you would place a child into its cot at night. Eazy then stared with pure anguish at Rachel, as he shook his head in disbelief.

Rachel was rooted to the spot as she silently watched Sleeper crouch down to the floor where his sister lay. Sleeper then looked up powerlessly at Rachel, as if searching through her soul

for the answers to the questions that were racing throughout his mind. His eyes no longer dark, nor mysterious, as he openly shed tears for his sister.

'Why... why the fuck has he killed my sister Rachel.'

Rachel stood there at a loss for words, as she shook her head at him. She honestly didn't know the answer to the question.

'How could anybody do this?' asked Eazy, as he stared vacantly at the woman he'd loved like as sister also.

Suddenly Rachel heard something from another room. Catching Eazy's attention as the other two stared helplessly at the body before them, she mouthed the word's "Where is the boy?" Eazy quickly looked around the room, just as Rachel had already done so, as the delayed recognition dawned upon his face.

Walking back out into the hallway quietly, as she noticed his huge frame block what little light came from within there. She listened carefully trying her best to trace where the noise was coming from. It was a small whimper. But where was its location, she couldn't decipher the sound clearly enough to find its location.

'Kyle,' called Eazy in hushed tones, so not to disturb Sleeper still in the bedroom. 'It's me Kyle.'

'Shush one sec,' said Rachel. 'Listen carefully. You hear that?' The both heard muffled scuffling, like crazed rats trying to escape a doomed situation.

'Kyle... It's your uncle Eazy, Kyle,' he called out a little louder, still not wanting to disturb Sleeper, as he grieved for his sister. 'Where are you Kyle?'

They heard the noise again. 'There,' said Rachel still trying her best to focus her hearing on a bearing.

'Downstairs,' said Eazy as he ran in that direction.

Rachel remained standing right where she was, she heard the noise again. Only there was a slight echo to it. And it did appear to come from downstairs, where she could now hear Eazy tearing the house apart searching for the boy.

Glancing back into the bedroom, she saw that Tony had dropped to his knees beside Sleeper and had wrapped his arm around him affectionately, as he felt his friend's loss also. Looking back down at the bloodied footsteps that stopped short of the stairs by a couple of feet at least, she realised that the killer had either changed or cleaned themselves, before venturing out of the house.

Then there it was again, the noise. Heading through into the bathroom, she noticed that the bath was still full of water.

Dipping her hand into it, she noticed that the soapy suds were still warm. She found her mind continually wandering between the guilt she felt and the questions that kept evolving around and around her head like the waltzes at the fun fair that didn't roll straight at all.

What had happened here tonight? Why was Sleeper's sister picked? What had she found out about Gabriel? What had she discovered about the Pied Piper? Who had Gabriel known about her in the first place? Why didn't Gabriel take the heart? And where the hell was the boy? Had he been spared? All these questions and more refused to cease coming at her like a speeding train. For she knew that the answers to them, would be demanded shortly, not only from Sleeper himself, but also Hunter when she final arrived.

That's when she heard the noise again. It was coming from below the bathtub itself. But how was that so? Kneeling down on the floor she pushed the bath panel towards their corners. Realising that it was loose, she did her best to slip her fingers into the tiny, almost minute gap, failing to do so all the same. Looking around the bathroom for something to help ease the panel away she couldn't anything of use. Grabbing for the toothbrushes that lay beside the sink, she began to prey away the panel as one of the toothbrushes snapped. But it was just enough to open up the gap for her to fit her fingers through.

Pulling the entire piece of finished pine away, she suddenly jumped back in voluntarily with fright, 'Ahhhhhhhhhhh, leave me alone, go away,' was all she heard as the high pitched scream come straight for her.

'It's alright Kyle,' said Rachel recovering from the initial shock. Easing herself forward towards the frightened boy wearing patterned pyjama's, and was hidden in the extremely confined amplitude, below the bath tub. 'I'm a friend of your uncle Sleeper and Eazy.'

'Leave me al...'

'Kyle,' said Eazy as he bent down to the floor. 'Come here Kyle. It's me; it's your uncle Eazy.' His voice had dropped all of its density, and sounded strange coming from him.

'Eazy... Eazy... where's Mummy,' screamed the little boy in a high pitched, panic stricken tones as he scrambled out from under the bath tub, looking filthy from all the dust that had settled beneath there. Leaping straight into Eazy's arms, he began with a barrage of his own questions. 'Where's Uncle Sleeper? Where's my Mummy? What happened? What happened to my Mummy?' Where's the dark man? The man in

the funny shiny outfit, the one that grabbed hold of my mummy downstairs? Where's...'

It suddenly became too much for him as alleviation and consternation worked side by side, taking control, as the boy suddenly collapsed against Eazy and passed out. 'We need to get him the hell out of here.'

'Kyle, oh thank God,' said Sleeper as both him and Tony appeared from the bedroom. He stroked the boy's damp hair in Eazy's arms. 'Thank God. Thank fucking God. This is a nightmare. Where was he?'

'I found him beneath the bath tub,' Rachel told him. 'I think that he must have been in there as his mother was attacked downstairs. He was clever enough to hide beneath there. I had trouble removing the panel. But his hands must have been small enough to...' She stopped in her tracks as she observed Sleeper taking in the fact that the boy had hadn't been slayed and was still with them.

Without saying a word, she walked back to the bedroom door, looking at the body that had been covered by Sleeper. The bedding they had used was already a dark shade of red as the blood continued to seep its way through. Shaking her head, she stepped towards the room for a closer inspection as Sleeper touched her shoulder.

As she turned she realised that he hadn't even turned back towards the room. 'This freak of nature doesn't realise what he's come up against Rachel.'

Placing her hands on top of his she said. 'I know, I truly know Sleeper,' she bowed her head as she closed her eyes. 'I'm so sorr...'

'Don't,' he said as he squeezed her hand.

'But I truly am,' said Rachel.

'What now?' asked Eazy as he continued to cuddle to young boy who had allowed sheer exhaustion to take over and who now appeared to be fast asleep in his arms.

'I've already called Hunter in,' Rachel told them.

'You've what,' he suddenly snapped at her.

'They would have got involved anyway, Eazy,' she told him.

'I don't give a fuck...'

'It makes sense Eazy,' she said. 'Right Sleeper? They needed to know. It was better that I called her in than...'

'She right brother,' said Tony placing his hand on his friend's shoulder as Sleeper appeared to be drawn in every possible direction.

'What the hell?' said Hunter as she came darting up the stairs. 'Jesus kid, what the fuck is going on? What the hell are all these...'

'It's him again Hunter,' screamed Rachel, cutting her short. 'He's gone and killed again. And why? Because he's still at large to do so.'

'What have we got then?' she asked ignoring those stood around her, walking through to the bedroom. 'What the fuck has gone on in here? Why has she been removed from...'

'What the fuck did you expect me to do?' sneered Sleeper viciously, as even Rachel stepped away from him, as he got right in Hunter's face. 'Leave my kid sister up there like tha...'

'I know who you are,' said Hunter before he could finish. 'And you'll stay away from this. This is my investigat...'

'We've got ourselves a witness,' said Rachel trying to calm things down. 'The boy saw who it was.'

'What the... Where the hell was he?' asked Hunter staring at the boy unbelievably, as she noticed him for the first time.

'He was clever enough to hide away when he saw his mother being attacked,' said Eazy as he stroked the boy's hair, refusing to let go.

'Where?' asked Hunter.

'Beneath there,' answered Rachel pointing to the bathtub.

'We're going to need to question him,' said Hunter as a matter of simple fact. 'We'll need to know what he...'

'Like fuck you will,' snarled Sleeper viciously.

'He's the key witness to a murde...' began Hunter.

'I don't give a fuck,' said Sleeper as he took a step further towards Hunter. 'His mother has just been butchered by some fucking physco that you still haven't managed to catch yet...' He lowered his tone of voice as he was only inches from her face.

'And why did he pick her?' asked Hunter.

'Because we asked her to help us,' sneered Sleeper pressing his forehead against hers. 'Because you were fucking incompetent to do your job in putting a stop to all this madness.'

'You'll get the fuck outta of my fa...' Hunter pushed him away, as he stepped forward again at her.

'Believe me when I tell you this, detective or no fucking detective,' he whispered the words to her, as the three of them watched on silently. 'I was always going to help Rachel track this fucking psychopath down, but you know what. This Gabriel fuck has just made his first mistake.'

'And what's that?' asked Hunter just as quietly, 'What mistake?' she added, backing away from Sleeper as his eyes

literally turned as black as charcoal and all life ceased to exist within them. So much so, that it even sent a chill straight through Rachel as she involuntarily stepped away further herself.

'This Gabriel or whatever the fuck he wants to call himself,' he said stepping away himself from her as she stood within the bedroom doorway, 'has just gone and made it personal.'

'There'll be no vigilant...'

'Then either you find him first,' said Sleeper before she could finish. 'Or believe me when I say, I will find him.'

'How do you know Kyle saw him Rachel?' asked Tony, doing his best to draw Sleeper away from Hunter, who at the present seemed hell bent on taking this thing out on her.

'He asked what happened to the dark man that grabbed his mother downstairs,' Rachel told them. 'He said the man in the shiny suit, whatever that meant. I'm not too sur...'

'We need to get a descrip...' began Hunter.

'You'll leave him be for now,' said Sleeper, taking the boy into his arms from Eazy. 'We're outta of here.'

'You just can't...' began Hunter again.

'It's alright,' said Rachel. 'Let them go for now. You go with them Tony. Take them all back to yours. Get the doctor to overlook the boy.'

'What about you?'

'I'll stay here with Hunter,' she told him. 'I'll come straight to yours once I'm finished here, alright.'

'If you say so,' he sighed as he took off after the other's down the stairs.

'Jesus kid,' sighed Hunter glancing from her to the blood stained bedsheet. 'Who the fuck are associating with? He's a...'

'True friend,' said Rachel before she had chance to finish. 'Now come and take a look at this. He's changed his pattern.'

'Now hang on a minute kid,' said Hunter as she followed her into the bedroom. 'I want some answers relating to that guy and I want them...'

'You'll get them,' she replied not even looking to her as she dropped to the floor. 'Look here for yourself.'

Hunter was staring at the scrawlings on the wall, as she lowered her eyes to the bloody corpse. 'Oh shit,' she shook her head. 'So it's definitely him again. Just what the...'

'What's that?' asked Rachel cutting her short.

'Where?' asked Hunter as she bent lower for a closer inspection of what Rachel was showing her. 'Is that what I think it is? Is that still the victim's heart?'

'It is,' nodded Rachel. 'He's changed his pattern for some reason and I haven't got a clue why. I think the boy was over looked. I'm still not quite sure how Gabriel missed the boy. But that isn't really what I mean here. Why is there no dove? And why has he gone to the trouble of tearing her torso open like that, if he didn't intend to take the heart like the rest of them Hunter?'

'That's yours and Brendan's department kid. I'm calling him right now,' she replied stretching to her full height, removing her mobile phone. Looking through the curtains and out into the street she saw Sleeper climbing into his car as the big one, Eazy climbed into the back of the car with the boy in his arms. Watching the vehicle reverse, into the crowd that had gathered, as they all dispersed away from the speeding motor. She shook her head. 'I'm also calling the team down here right now kid. I've got what appears to be half of Cheadle stationed in the street outside. As they all eagerly await to discover what all the commotion is about.'

'I'd say you've got more on your hands here Hunter,' said Rachel as she continued to examine the body, 'than mere fucking commotion.'

The street was bustling with the community, despite the early hour of only six o'clock in the morning, Gabriel was still there along side of the crowd that had formed and refused to disappear. All of them eager to discover a little more about the events that had taken place within the confines of the once quiet home. But only Gabriel knew exactly what had taken place, and at the moment, was feeling as though the emotions that were swirling around inside, were being pulled in two different directions.

The police had done their job and had cut the area off surrounding the house where Gabriel's latest victim remained inside to be removed. They had all been inside of the house for hours. Forensics was still collecting what evidence they could. The medical examiner was now leaving the house with the corpse of Carol Sillverone wrapped in the body bag, the sister to one of Rachel's new associates, the one who called himself Sleeper.

Gabriel knew of the man. Knew of his work even. Because even though it wasn't any where near as creative or flamboyant as Gabriel's was. It was never the less in the same field. No matter what Sleeper thought of himself, he took the lives of others, just like Gabriel did.

Only not for the same reason that Gabriel did either. Only now, the stakes of the game had been upped, as Gabriel knew fully well that Sleeper would try and discover the true identity to Gabriel along with the rest of them.

It was true that Carol Sillverone hadn't been part of Gabriel's plan, but she had become a necessity. Gabriel was disappointed that the little boy had avoided being killed. But he had been no where to be found as Gabriel had searched everywhere. Eventually giving up, having to give up as time was running out. Especially when the phone beside the bed had rang loudly startling Gabriel. And when Gabriel had recognised the voice immediately as that of Sleeper, there had been no alternative but to flee the scene as soon as possible. But what Gabriel or anybody else could have never imagined was just how perfect that would have turned out. Not that anybody, but Gabriel knew this right now. Gabriel had needed to flee the scene, in order to be able return, now going unnoticed to everyone around the scene itself.

Gabriel wondered whether or not the boy was going to be a problem. The boy was part of the reason that Gabriel's emotions felt as if they were being pulled in different directions. Elevation at the victory of another death, but trepidation at the thought of a possible witness. Not that the boy would have recognised Gabriel wearing the disguise that was always worn. Gabriel would have to wait that one out, to see just how much the boy knew, for Gabriel now knew that the boy would now be well protected by Sleeper.

Gabriel shook the thoughts away, watching from the side of the crowd that had gathered. There were reporter's gathered everywhere trying to catch a break with the story. Gabriel observed as Rachel walked from the interior of the house and slumped to the pavement. Police and forensic experts were still everywhere as she sat there all alone ignoring everyone as they scurried around her engrossed in their jobs. Gabriel smiled, knowing that Rachel was doing her job right there and then on the pavement, as her mind had probably gone into overtime trying to fathom this one out.

Gabriel wondered exactly what was going through Rachel's mind, right at this precise moment, after spending hours inside the house going over and over the crime scene. Knowing for certain, that this murder had baffled them all beyond belief.

Although Gabriel had confidence in her, knowing that she would soon be able to fathom out why the victim had been chosen.

Smirking dogmatically as Gabriel continued to observe the surrounding of the crowd and house. If only she knew, if only they all knew that Gabriel was right here, right now, watching them all run around like headless chickens. It pleased Gabriel; in fact, it turned Gabriel on, just to think how close the one they searched for, was there, right now, right this very minute. If only they realised that the taker of condemned souls, was within their grasp.

But they didn't know. Gabriel was far too superior to these mere mortals.

Rachel had her head in her hands as she rubbed her face, trying to wake herself from the nightmare within. Rubbing the red, sore looking eyes. Gabriel knew what had happened with Cartwright's the morning before. It had also been one of the reasons that Carol Sillverone would have had to have died anyway. In had just been a case of who would get to her first.

Gabriel smiled, observing Rachel. She looked tired. She looked as though she needed to rest. This is what made it so much better to carry out what had been planned. The sister had merely been a bonus to Gabriel. Yet a further puzzle for them all to try and piece together.

Reporters were all shouting out to the officer's trying their best to get a quote. Oh how Gabriel would love to give them a quote. But Gabriel wasn't stupid. Besides, why give the game away when there was still more to be accomplished.

Especially after the gratitude shown by Michael, after the last couple of slayings. Gabriel had felt Michael's pride in the work that had been carried out. He was proud of the way Gabriel continued to baffle them all.

But he was proud of the way Gabriel had begun to take more pride in the work being carried out. It would only take a few more souls to finish the job that would set them all free.

But there was other thing that needed taking care of first. It was already supposed to have been taken care of. But it hadn't quite worked out that way. Oh well, Gabriel thought stood there. They would all just need another little shove in right direction.

And what they were all to discover after they had checked the evidence, was their clue that had no doubt been left for them. Gabriel hadn't even planned it. It was just one of those things that had worked out so perfectly after Gabriel had fled from the scene, to hide within the darkness of shadows in the alleyway across the street.

Once that little problem had been taken care of, it would leave the way open for Gabriel and Michael to once again rule. They

would be untouchable to anybody ever again. Just as the problem had always remained untouchable. Everything was going to work out just fine, and Gabriel almost could contain the perturbation that was felt stirring from deep within.

THIRTY NINE

'**Y**ou look shattered Rachel,' said Brendan sitting down next to her in Hunter's office as she struggled to open her eyes. The brightness shining through the window, blinding her eyes momentarily, as she tried her best to focus. The time was just gone eleven o'clock Tuesday morning. Rachel had been dozing restlessly since all of them had returned from the house in Cheadle only a couple of hours before.

As soon as Rachel had sat in the chair, exhaustion had hit her. She hadn't even realised that she'd fallen into unsettled sleep. At first she was convinced that she could still clearly hear Hunter and Brendan talking with one another, even believed she was talking with them. It was only with her mind still working overtime, had she realised that the dreams that wandered aimlessly around her head, were in fact, actual dreams and not reality. But as she awoke, she realised that were in fact very much reality and not that far off base, from the twisted images that had just haunted her sleep.

'I feel more than just shattered,' replied Rachel, stretching as she yawned at the same time. 'After everything that has happened over the last few weeks, my body feels as though I've just gone twelve rounds with Mike Tyson.'

'You still sore?' he asked, as he handed her a steaming mug of coffee.

'Thanks a lot. Like you wouldn't believe,' she answered accepting the coffee gratefully. 'Those sadistic fucks not only abused me physically, but mentally they almost drained me of what little sanity I've got left. And just when I think that it is over, Gabriel goes and kills again. But not only does he just go and kill. But he goes and kills the sister of someone who has not only devoted himself to getting to the bottom of the missing kids

from London that led him all the way up here to Manchester. This in effect, led him to meeting me and my brother.

'Through which we searched for the missing daughter Hunter asked us to look for. That in effect led us to the Cartwright's. And that led us to something none of us expected, this whole God forsaken nightmare, involving someone known as the Pied Piper. And as if all of that wasn't enough Brendan, he also committed himself to helping me also, and this he just didn't have to do. And I shouldn't have allowed for it, but...'

'He agreed to help you find the killer of your family,' said Brendan finishing her sentence. 'Right?'

'Right,' she shook her head. 'He'd asked his sister to not only look into the missing kids. But also to look into Gabriel for us. Both he and Tony had explained what they knew. She worked as an investigator as you now know. She had agreed to help us... And she didn't have to. I feel so bad; I never even got the chance to meet her.'

'What had his sister found out?'

'That we don't even know,' she said rubbing her weary eyes with the palms of her hands. 'And I think that makes it even worse. I mean just how the hell did this freak know about her Brendan?'

'Maybe she got closer than any of us had, in discovering just who the killer really is,' he suggested.

'Possibly,' she agreed. 'She was looking into the missing kids also though. In fact it was that, which Sleeper had originally asked her help with. She had said that it could take her a couple of weeks to come up with anything. I would have thought that the missing kids would have prioritised anything to do with Gabriel. So how the hell had Gabriel discovered she was investigating him also?'

'Maybe she only looked into Gabriel and not the missing kids Rachel,' he shrugged.

'Or maybe we're all missing something here,' she sighed deeply as she sipped the hot liquid. 'I wonder what it was that she discovered that had her killed so sadistically. Sleeper never contacted her, as we never imagined that we'd have got as far as we did over such a short period of time.'

'That's it though Rachel. I mean, you seem to have done a pretty good job there without her help,' he told her. 'It seems that the computer guys here are singing your praises about the Pied Piper case, as it's now been renamed.'

'They shouldn't,' she shook her head. 'Don't say fuck all to Hunter. But I had a lot of help to get as far as we got. Like I said,

we could never have imagined that we'd have stumbled across all the things that we did. It's just that I had to leave a lot of people's names out of my statement.'

'Either way,' he smiled. 'I know that Hunter is real proud of what you...'

'Where is Hunter by the way?' she asked cutting him short.

'She's down at the lab still,' he said. 'They've pulled a lot of evidence from the house, including those bloody foot prints that matched those we found at the back of the Morgan's home at the weekend.'

'Jesus,' said Rachel shaking her head. 'What a fucking nightmare this whole thing is Brendan. What the hell did I ever do to deserve all of this? As if it wasn't enough that this guy decided to pick my family as his first lot of victims. But now, now it seems as if he wasn't content with that. Now he's decided that he's going to return to forever haunt me and all of those around me. Jesus Christ...'

'We'll catch him,' he said smiling reassuringly at her. 'It's just a matter of time before he...'

'We ain't got a matter of time though Brendan,' she cut him short again. 'I mean just how many have to die, before enough is going to be enough?'

'That's not what I...'

'I know it wasn't,' she shook her head. 'I'm sorry... It's just my head at the moment is...'

'I think all our heads are working over-time Rachel,' he reached out and touched her cheek affectionately.

The skin surrounding his thick fingers, felt warm and soft as she allowed the contact. His fingers gently stoked her cheek as he smiled at her. He stroked her hair away from her face, sliding it behind her ears, as she gazed into his mesmerising blue eyes. She began to feel the strong attraction to him that she always felt when she was around him, as the guilt began to creep it's way back in. Pulling her face away, but smiling so not to offend him, she quickly reached for Hunter's packet of cigarettes, lighting one.

Rachel hated this. She felt as if all she wanted to do, was lose herself in Brendan's arms. Feel his warmth and allow the comfort of another human's contact against her. She missed the loving feel of flesh against flesh so dearly. But she also knew that it wasn't right... not yet anyway. She exhaled the smoke as Brendan continued to stare at her as he shook his head. She made a decision right there and then that she wouldn't allow anything to happen. Not until the killer of her husband and child

had been sought out first. Then, and only then, could she allow for anything to happen.

'Hunter is still pissed at the fact that the crime scene had been messed with,' he told her changing the subject, as he witnessed her discomfort. 'The print lab has come up with several sets of prints from the house.'

'There was nothing I could do to stop Sleeper entering the house first,' she sighed, as she pulled deeply on the cigarette. 'I mean it was his sister for fucks sake Brendan. I still don't have any idea how Gabriel found out about her.'

'Just how is it that you've come into contact with this guy Rachel? I mean I know you said it was through looking for the missing girl, Charlotte Cartwright' he asked sipping his own mug of coffee. 'Or guy's as I should put it. Hunter tells me that there are two of them,' he added.

'Like I said. It was through Hunter asking for me to look into the missing girl for her, Charlotte Cartwright,' she replied shaking her head. 'All that Hunter wanted me to do was try and get a better perspective about the girl herself. Hoping that it would lead us to finding the girl. She even agreed that Tony could help me. She told us that some mysterious anonymous phone call that she received had told her that if she found the girl, then she'd find some connection to the missing kids. Only what we didn't know was that there had kids of a similar situation to the ones up here had also been going missing in London. Our friends were led all the way up here with the evidence that they discovered. But you know what Brendan.'

'What?' he smiled at her.

'The one thing that I feel so bad about,' she shook her head. 'Is that we're still no closer to finding the girl. Charlotte is still missing. All I was asked to do was look for the girl Brendan. And I've still not been able to do that successfully. Instead, all I did was open a bigger can of worms.'

'Oh don't beat yourself up like that Rachel,' he smiled. 'Like I said, Hunter is real proud of what you achieved. We all are. I mean, from what Hunter has already told me. If it wasn't for you, then the Cartwright's would still be abusing those kids.'

'I know,' she sighed. 'It's just that I can't keep my mind from the fact that I wasn't one-hundred percent about whether or not Luther Cartwright was the Pied Piper.'

'You still think that this guy is out there then?'

'Yes, I think that he is,' she told him. 'I mean, don't get me wrong here. Luther Cartwright was the perfect match for this guy. He fitted any profile that you could come up with. Only...'

377

'Only what?'

'Only the two of them kept talking through a third party.'

'But that's common in any of these kind of offenders,' he told her. 'You know that better than most Rachel. It's their way of...'

'I know,' she agreed. 'But something just wasn't right. There was something that didn't quite fit. I just know that we've missed something along the way. Including the Pied Piper himself. Who, if still out there, has no doubt been alerted to the fact that we are, not only onto him. But also the Pied Piper Productions website that had been set up. I don't know what else Halenbrook has come up with. Hell, I still don't know if they've found any of the bodies or not.'

'Not yet, I hear they'll be finished with the family home in Prestbury first,' he told her. 'I hear it's quite a place they've got themselves up there. Hunter told me that it was the perfect hideaway.'

'It is,' she nodded. 'Very secluded from the rest of the homes in that area. You've even got your own plot of woodland at the back. You could stay hidden away there without anybody knowing about it for quite some time.'

'I hear they're going to block the house off once they've finished with it,' he added. 'God knows what they'll end up doing with it. From what I hear, that and the one in London will be just like another Cromwell Street. Nobody in their right minds would want to live there. The place will probably just become deserted, a place where kids will dare each other to enter the place.'

'I know what you mean,' she sighed deeply, not really listening to him go on about the house, that was the last thing on her mind right now. 'I bet Hunter is pissed at me over Halenbrook, right?' she said, changing the subject.

'Hunter is pissed off about a lot of things,' he said. 'Not just the fact that they haven't located any of the bodies Rachel. But also the fact that Halenbrook is receiving all the praise on the case.'

'I feel real shit about all of that,' said Rachel. 'I know how it must have looked to Hunter. I really wish that I had protested more. But, well to be honest. I thought that I was skating on pretty thin ice as it was.'

'From killing them both, is that what you mean?'

She nodded slowly. 'You want to know the worst thing about that Brendan,' she dropped her head to avoid eye contact. 'I still don't know whether or not, it's just the fact that it hasn't hit me properly yet. But I feel absolutely no remorse whatsoever

towards the fact I've taken another human... in fact I've taken two human lives. I can't believe that I actually killed with these very hands and don't feel bad about doing it.' She held her hands up to her face. 'If anything I feel...' She didn't continue with the words, for fear of what he would think of her feeling good, about the fact she'd killed and now had blood on her hands.

'And you feel that somehow...'

'Don't physco analyse me Brendan,' she stared at him. 'I don't know what it is. Maybe the night Gabriel took my family from me. Maybe he stole my soul at the same time he paralysed my Peter's and Becky's souls.'

'What do you mean,' said Brendan gazing at her, 'paralysed their souls?'

'I believe that until Gabriel is brought to justice. Either, with my very own hands,' she said. 'Or at the hands of the law. Then their souls are still left hanging paralysed, waiting for justice to be sought out before they can be truly released, to rest in peace for all eternity.' She could see that Brendan was watching her, questioning her own sanity.

'Pretty lame eh,' she shrugged.

'Not at all,' he smiled. 'But what did you mean by; he stole your soul also?'

'So much so, that I've lost my emotions to react to the crime I committed. That I've become the same as he has,' she replied. 'Maybe that's how I'm part of his plan. This is what he want...'

'Don't talk so much crap,' he said reaching out and taking her hands into his. 'How the hell could you have become like Gabriel. All that you did was what you had to do. You defended yourself from any further anguish and torture at the hands of the Cartwright's. You did exactly what any other strong person would have done.'

'Where is my guilt then?' she asked allowing him to caress her hands. 'Why don't I feel anything at the fact I killed those people.'

'What you are feeling is that you have rid society of the evi...'

'But what...'

'But nothing Rachel,' he cut her off as she stared helplessly into his eyes. She suddenly felt his presence as he entered her personal space.

Leaning back in the chair as he moved to kiss her, she couldn't believe that she was actually allowing this. When suddenly, the door opened.

'What a fucking day,' snapped Hunter as she entered looking over the paperwork in her hands, not noticing the two of them so

close, as Brendan pushed himself away and Rachel whistled a sigh of relief.

'In fact, what a fucking couple of weeks,' she added as Andrews followed her into the office.

'What've you got?' asked Rachel as she looked sheepishly away from Brendan as he sat down in the chair next to her also avoiding eye contact.

'Good news,' she smiled as she sat down and immediately reached for the cigarettes. 'And bad news of course.'

'Of course,' said Rachel sarcastically.

'We sent the prints we found through the system. I had the prints sent via the computer down to London. We've eliminated your two friend's sets of prints from the crime scene with Jenkins down in London,' she told her shaking her head. 'I still want to interview the boy though. I'll want the three of them to come in kid.'

'I'll see what I can do,' she said. 'But I ain't promising anything. You guys ain't exactly top of his list of favourites at the moment.'

'I don't give fuck, whether we are or we ain't,' she said blowing the smoke out extravagantly. 'I want...'

'We don't always get what we want Hunter,' Rachel pointed out. 'I said that I'll see what I can do.'

'Where are they now?' asked Andrews leaning against the wall with his arms folded across his chest.

'I don't know,' she lied, knowing full well, that they were either at her brother's house or Chan's place in Worsley.

'What's the bad news?' asked Brendan. 'I always say it's best to start with the bad, never the good.'

'We're missing a lap-top computer from the house,' she said.

'How do you know that?' asked Rachel.

'Everything was set up at home,' said Hunter. 'She had everything there. Printer, disks, files of work. But no computer. So we're missing the computer. It makes sense that it is a lap-top because the killer isn't going to take an entire PC is he. Plus if he was going to take the computer and it was a PC then he'd have just taken the harddrive. Not the damn monitor or keyboards. Besides, we've checked at Daniel's where she worked and they have confirmed that she worked with a Dell lap-top.'

'Fair comment,' agreed Rachel. 'But why is it so important at the moment?'

'Because we could have done with looking at what she had researched over the past week for you,' said Andrews.

'There could have been incriminating evidence on there,' said Hunter. 'Evidence that would have help us when we finally nail this freak.'

'You think that the killer took it?' asked Rachel.

'Possibly,' said Hunter. 'But there is something else that you should know. It was something else that you said about the fact she was looking into the O'Leary's.'

'What about them?' asked Rachel.

'They had come up in the investigation when Mike and I were working it,' she told her. 'As soon as you mentioned their name, or more to the point, Vincent or Vinnie as he prefers himself to be known. We knew that there had to some kind of a connection with what we had come up with.'

'I'm not sure what it was though,' admitted Rachel. 'All I know is that Tony and Sleeper went to see the O'Leary's as they are the main ones who run the porn this way.'

'But we had Vinnie suspected of involvement with kiddie porn,' Andrews told her.

'Really?' asked Rachel.

'We couldn't get anything positive on him though,' added Hunter. 'Well, that was until this morning that is.'

'Why's that then?' asked Brendan.

'Because this morning,' she winked at Rachel. 'We found something very interesting at the house.'

'What?' asked Rachel intrigued.

'I think that we've just caught our first real break,' she told her smiling.

'The other prints?' asked Rachel hopefully.

'That's part of the good news,' smiled Hunter. 'I took into account what you told us about the fact that the victim had been helping them with the missing kid's case.'

'You think that there is a connection?' asked Rachel a little confused.

'Have you heard of Freddy *Fingers* Marshall?' asked Andrews.

'No,' replied Rachel looking to Brendan who shrugged. 'Should I have?'

'Probably not kid,' said Hunter. 'But he's a real nasty piece of work. He also works closely for Vinnie O'Leary. We know of several professional hits that he carried out for him. He does his dirty laundry so to speak. He's very good at his job also. That's why we have always had trouble making charges stick against him.'

'And you're telling us this, because...'

'Because we found his palm print at the house this morning,' smiled Andrews nodding.

'Honestly?' asked Rachel feeling a little light headed at the news.

'Honestly kid,' said Hunter. 'And this mother fucker has a jacket so thick that he fits the profile without a doubt. Check it out,' she added tossing the large file onto the desk.

Rachel began reading through the numerous accounts of arrests and suspected crimes this man had committed. Heading straight for his greatest hits, she soon realised that this guy had a lot of sexually related crimes tried against him. But it didn't end there, armed robbery charges, four failed manslaughter charges that prosecution had dropped against him at crown court. There were so many prohibited weapon charges against him; Rachel couldn't believe that he was still walking the streets.

It would also appear that his favourite weapon of choice was the use of a knife, now that certainly fitted the profile. He'd not always been so lucky to avoid conviction either. He had served two jail sentences for his crimes relating to ABH, actual bodily harm, where he'd left his victim sliced so badly that he'd almost bled to death. And the last conviction was back in 1996 when he'd been convicted of rape of a minor. A girl of eleven years old who had been left blinded when he allegedly poured acid into her eyes. But that's when Rachel suddenly noticed something else that caught her eye.

'Whoa,' said Rachel staring straight at Hunter. 'You have seen this here?'

'What?' asked Brendan looking through the other sheets that Rachel had discarded to the table.

'You couldn't possibly mean who his brief was back in '96?' asked Hunter grinning.

'Fairchild defended him back then unsuccessfully,' she said smiling.

'Exactly,' she said. 'I was waiting for you to make the connection.'

'What was the case?' asked Brendan.

'Rape of a minor,' said Rachel as she continued to read. 'He apparently blinded the poor girl with acid before he raped her.'

'You're kidding!' exclaimed Brendan.

'If he's not our guy,' said Andrews, 'then...'

'Have you issued the warrant?' asked Rachel not taking her eyes from the material before her.

'We have,' said Hunter. 'Although we've got no current address for him.'

'Hang on a minute,' said Brendan. 'If this guy was sent down in '96 for rape and blinding this girl. Then what is he doing out?'

'His new brief had the charges over turned against him,' she said. 'New DNA evidence proved it wasn't him that had raped her. They immediately dropped the charges against him for the now alleged blinding of the girl. But there is something else that you should know.'

'What's that?' asked Rachel glancing at her.

'Vinnie was a suspect in the case back then,' said Hunter. 'But we never had enough to even bring him in for questioning.'

'So, what has this to do with...' began Brendan.

'You think that the reason Sleeper's sister was picked,' said Rachel, 'was because she got too close to something on the O'Leary's?'

'A very good possibility,' said Hunter. 'And we've got a current address for that sleaze bag. So I had a warrant issued for him also. He's being picked up as we speak.'

'This is all starting to turn pear shaped,' said Rachel. 'Where the hell, does either of these guys fit into the puzzle against my Peter or Becky.'

'Peter had worked cases against both of them in the past,' said Hunter as Rachel shook her head.

'You think that there are two of them doing the killings?' asked Rachel.

'Do you not think that, that is possibility?' asked Andrews.

'It's something that we've not considered,' said Brendan.

'Jesus,' sighed Rachel. 'Just when we thought that it couldn't get any worse. It looks as if we may have two killers on our hands.'

'I thought that the lead with the O'Leary's was to do with the missing kids though,' said Brendan looking confused.

'It was,' said Rachel. 'But what if the two are somehow connected.'

'How do you mean?' asked Andrews.

'I mean that this is exactly what we've been missing all along,' she said. 'I told you that the Cartwright's talked of the all-mighty and referred to another party as that or he or him even.'

'So?' he shrugged.

'And they also said that Gabriel had passed through their world,' she added. 'They told me things like they didn't get their kicks from killing the kids; it wasn't their department as they put it.'

'So what?' asked Hunter.

'What if,' she stared at the three of them. 'What if... what if the Pied Piper and Gabriel are the same person?'

'You reckon that's possible?' asked Hunter.

'Hear me out here,' she said. 'This will sound crazy, but just hear me out. Since everything last year, I've had these dreams...'

'Dreams?' Hunter raised her eyebrows at her.

'Just lately,' said Rachel ignoring her, 'both the Pied Piper and Gabriel have appeared side by side through the course of the dreams.'

'And we're supposed to work off your dreams kid?' smiled Hunter shaking her head.

'I'm not saying that,' she said. 'But let's look at it this way. Let's just say that Gabriel or the Pied Piper took things one step further from when ever he or they started out.'

'You mean from when he killed your family?' asked Andrews looking confused.

'Maybe he started long before that,' Rachel told him. 'Maybe he started out killing the children. What we also have to take into account here is that the children are also being raped at the time of the murders.'

'We never looked at it that way,' said Hunter nodding her agreement. 'You're right kid. What if all of this started with the kids and evolved for whatever reason into the killer taking things one step further and killing not just children, but also...'

'This is one hell of coincidence,' said Brendan, not looking as if he believed what he was hearing.

'It may be fuck all,' said Rachel. 'But I think that we need to question this Vinnie O'Leary on what it is that he knows.'

Just then the phone on Hunter's desk rang. 'What is it?' she barked down at the phone, annoyed at the interruption. 'Alright, fine, we'll be there in a couple of minutes.' She replaced the headset.

'Who was that?' asked Rachel.

'Well it looks as though you'll get to ask those questions kid,' she said standing. 'We've got Vinnie downstairs in the interview room right now. I say that just you and I question him. If I remember what the cocky little shit is like. Then he'll probably get off on the fact that he's got a couple of women in there questioning him. He'll think that we're giving him the soft touch. Are you up for it or what kid?'

'Let's go,' smiled Rachel pushing herself out of her seat, determined to get to the bottom of this thing.

FORTY

'**S**o how come the O'Leary's came up in your investigation Hunter?' asked Rachel as the two of them made their way through the corridor's, that would lead them to the interrogation rooms found in the basement of the building, where the holding cells were also to be found.

'Not a lot people know this Rachel,' she said. 'But little Vinnie down there, has himself a weakness for young girls.'

'How young are we talking?'

'The younger,' replied Hunter, 'the better as far as he is concerned.'

'How come he's not been caught before then?'

'Oh he has,' said Hunter as she stopped and stared at Hunter. 'His old man Dominic O'Leary knows all about it. That's why it's not common knowledge. All I know is that he was brought in, a few years back now, over allegations of underage sex with a group of girls at a nearby school in Hale, when the family had just moved over that way.'

'How old were the girl's?'

'Thirteen, fourteen if I remember correctly,' she told her. 'But that was the only time that charges were brought against him.'

'What had they had him in before for?'

'When he was only a young lad still living in Salford,' she said. 'If I remember rightly, he was only young himself. About twelve, possibly thirteen. I don't quite remember as it was a while back now. But anyway, some old man caught Vinnie playing about with his daughter. She was only five or six. He went ape about it. Called the police straight in. The only thing was, and we could never prove this. The family just upped and moved away from the area. Word had it, that the old man stepped in once again, and warned the family off.'

385

'So he's been at this sort of thing for a while then?'

'Oh yes. From what one of my grasses tells me,' she shook her head. 'Nobody dares to speak about it. But apparently it's a private little joke behind his back as too how he can only get it up with kids, the sick fucks. They apparently all laugh, because he still tries to give it the large one with the girls whilst he out. But it's just all for show.'

'So what happened then?' asked Rachel. 'I mean with the girls from the school.'

'His old man had the whole thing covered up.'

'But why?' asked Rachel. 'I mean that's twice now that you know about, he's not that way inclined is he?'

'Far from it,' she shook her head. 'He's ashamed of what the little prick had been accused of. He's like your Tony in that department. Can't stand the nonces. But at the end of the day, it's still his flesh and blood. And with no wife around any more. He seems to rely on Vinnie more and more these days.'

'How did he manage to have it covered up though?'

'I ain't too sure kid,' she sighed. 'Because I also remember at the time, because of where the school is situated in Hale. You know, a lot of rich kids and all that. Well the parents were outraged when they found out.'

'So what was Vinnie's excuse?'

'He said that the girl's had been gagging for it,' she told her. 'Said that they had consented to the sex taking place.'

'He didn't even deny it,' asked Rachel shocked.

'Gloated over the issue. That's why the parents were outraged,' she said. 'I know that they tried to take things one step further by having Vinnie convicted privately. But once again the old man had the families warned off. And believe me, old man Dominic may be getting on now. But if he gives the word, a lot of heads will turn.'

'This guy sounds unbelievable.'

'You should ask your brother about him,' she said. 'I hear that they've had a few run ins over the years.'

'I will do,' she replied.

'Don't get me wrong either kid,' she said. 'By saying that he's into kids and shit, don't go getting the wrong impression before you walk in there. Because as your Tony will tell you. He's still very much one of the main lads about town. And he is considered by many, to be one of the main heads. But that's also what I meant, by he'll think that we're giving him the soft touch, you know, with the two of us going to see him.'

'Alright, but I'm still a little confused Hunter.'

'Why's that kid?'

'Just because he's suspected of molesting girls,' said Rachel. 'That doesn't explain how it led you to him.'

'You know what his old man does?' asked Hunter. 'Right?'

'Right,' nodded Rachel. 'From what Tony tells me, he's the heavy hitter of the porn industry up this way. Tony says that he's not only distributing the gear, but he's also manufacturing it.'

'He's dead right there kid,' agreed Hunter. 'The only thing is, some time ago, before these kids went missing. Mike and I were investigating this outfit that was running live shows over the internet, with what was supposed to be school girls having sex with older men. We'd received complaints from some local politician. Can't remember who now. But anyway, he claimed that his daughter had told him about this website featuring the girls. Apparently the girl claimed that some of her school friends from some private boarding school some place, actually starred in these live shows.'

'And Vinnie was involved in that?'

'He was,' she said. 'Only it turned out to be faked.'

'What do you mean by that Hunter?' asked Rachel. 'How was it fake?'

'The girls were just made to look younger than they actually were,' she said. 'It was a scam basically. The daughter was full of shit. None of her mates were in those movies. We thought that she'd basically wasted our time. But we were also intrigued by what had been set up. So the two of us stayed with the case for a while. Perverted curiosity, I supposed you could call it.' She laughed at herself.

'I always knew you were a twisted fuck Hunter,' smiled Rachel.

'Oh I don't know,' she smirked. 'I think both me and Mike picked ourselves a couple of tips up from some of the other shows.'

'Now I definitely know that you're a sick little puppy Hunter,' said Rachel shaking her head at her friend.

'Anyway, the one thing that we did discover through this,' said Hunter, 'was that Vinnie was running a lot of other enterprises without his father's knowledge. His old man doesn't have a clue that his son runs these separate little ventures. He's completely in the dark, or chooses to be anyway.'

'Like what though?'

'A whole array of these shows were being aired at different times of the day and night if you know what you're looking for. You have to register with them, which we managed to bypass

387

through our computer department. Then the one accessing the website is charged by the minute to watch these shows.' she told her. 'So we kept an eye on what was being aired.'

'And...'

'And we came across one show that featured young children.'

'How young are we talking?'

'Around nine or ten years old,' she answered.

'And Vinnie was responsible for that?'

'We couldn't be certain,' she said. 'We know that he was responsible for most of the stuff being aired. But we just couldn't be one-hundred percent that he had anything to do with that. Although I had that gut feeling that told me, that it was definitely him.'

'Well which website did you find it on?'

'That's not important,' she told her. 'You see, the problem with these websites is they can automatically transfer you over to over websites without you realising. You see the ones who set these things up, are clever sons of bitches. But I don't need to tell you that kid. But anyway, if say a customer shows a certain interest in let's say school girl's like we initially did. Then another website can pick the trace out and transmit their stuff over to it. I don't completely understand how it works. But it's both extremely clever and extremely fucked up at the same time.'

'And you weren't able to trace it back to its source?'

'Not at all,' she shook her head. 'Besides, it wasn't an open case anymore. Like I said, it was more to satisfy mine and Mike's curiosity with the way things were heading. We soon moved onto another case and it was soon forgotten.'

'Until now,' said Rachel.

'Until now,' she nodded. 'He was obviously one of our first suspects when we found the link to the internet.'

'Why the hell didn't you tell me any of this?'

'Because I never asked you to look into the missing kid's case,' she replied. 'Did I now kid? You took it upon yourself to get yourselves involved there.'

'Fair comment Hunter,' sighed Hunter. 'But I still don't know how you expected for me to not get involved.'

'You're right kid,' she shrugged. 'I suppose I was a little out of order. I mean, I reckon that I kinda of figured that you'd stumble across something more, than we'd be able to find out for ourselves. Especially after I received that call. And especially with you not being one of us. So yes, you're right I kinda hoped that these people would open up a little more to you than they

had to us. I should have told you more, and I guess I would have kid. But you didn't need for me to. You went and did a cracking job without me having to even give you a helping han...'

'Enough, stop blowing wind my arse Hunter,' said Rachel cutting her off. 'Let's just go and see what this guy has to tell us.'

'This is him,' said Hunter nodding at the door they were now stood before.

'Let's go then,' said Rachel opening the door.

As they entered the room Rachel stared contemptuously at the small, yet large figure sat by the table all alone. She noticed the scar that ran down the left hand side of his face and wondered where he'd received it. She noticed a nervous tick, that refused to stop twitching at the side of his neck, and she knew instantly, that his stocky build was down to steroid abuse.

'What the fuck have you got me down here for Hunter?' he asked in a irritated manner, as Hunter shut the door behind her.

'We've got some questions to ask you Vincent,' she told him sitting opposite him, with Rachel by her side.

'I ain't got shit to say to you couple of delightful looking ladies,' he smirked. 'But hey, I'll shoot the breeze here with you for a while. See which one of you I like more than the other. Oh and please... it's Vinnie.'

'Well Vinnie,' said Rachel. 'We have ourselves an incident that took place last night. And the two of us think that you could very well be the right guy to talk to about it.'

'Don't I know you?' he asked staring inquisitively at her.

'I doub...'

'Your Henessy's sister,' he nodded, as he stroked the scar along his cheek with the backs of his finger nails.

'Yes I am,' she admitted, seeing no reason why she shouldn't.

'Not that, that matters though Vinnie,' added Hunter.

'She ain't no copper,' he said angrily. 'What the fuck is this all about Hunter?'

'I'm not,' agreed Rachel. 'But what we'd like to do is ask you some questions in relation to...'

'I ain't even been read my rights Hunter,' he suddenly protested, before Rachel had finished. 'And you got me sat here with some physco analysing fruit-cake.'

'You haven't been arrested yet Vinnie,' Hunter told him.

'So why have the boys in blue turn up at my door with a warrant then?'

'Because we knew if we'd merely requested that you come down here,' said Hunter, 'that you wouldn't have come at all.'

389

'True,' he laughed and Rachel saw the way the scar moulded into his features, making him uglier than he already appeared. 'Do I need my brief here for this or what Hunter? What the fuck do I know, that you're so interested in?'

'It's only a couple of questions Vinnie,' smiled Rachel.

Kissing his teeth as he leaned back the chair. He folded his wide arms across his chest and then he nodded at her. 'Now why don't we cut to the chase and you get right to the point. What is it that you've got me down here for?'

'Freddy Marshall,' said Hunter glaring at him.

'Fingers,' he shrugged using the guy's nickname. 'What about him?'

'Freddy Fingers Marshall he's known as right?' added Rachel. 'When was the last time that you saw him?'

'Not for a long time now,' he shrugged nonchalantly again.

'How long?' asked Hunter.

'Must be a couple of months at least,' he sniffed as his eyes began to wander, so not to look directly at them.

'You sure about that Vinnie?' asked Hunter cocking her eye brow at him. 'Couple of good friends like the two of you...'

'And you haven't seen him for months,' Rachel finished what Hunter was about to say. 'You sure about that Vinnie?'

'At least that,' he nodded. 'Why?'

'What is your involvement with him?' asked Rachel. 'How is it that you're such good friends Vinnie?'

'He lives on my old estate,' he said. 'Y'know how it is. We just know each other from way back when.'

'What's he up to nowadays?' asked Hunter.

'How the fuck am I...'

'Is he still blinding young girl's with acid,' said Rachel casually. 'You know, before he rapes them.'

'What the...'

'Oh, I'm sorry,' said Rachel holding eye contact with him. 'Or was that you Vinnie? Isn't it you, that has a fondness for the younger se...'

'This is fucking outrageous Hunter,' he sneered viciously at them both. 'You bring me down here like this and...'

'What do you know of the Pied Piper?' asked Rachel as she saw the instant recognition in his eyes.

'Fuck all,' he shook his head. 'Apart from the fact that your Tony and some nigger came to the old man's house a couple of weeks back, also asking about him. The old man said that I had to look into it for your brother,' he sighed deeply then added as an after thought. 'Fucking wanker.'

'Your father or my brother?' She smiled at the way he was becoming rattled.

'Your fucking brother of course,' he snapped.

'And what did you find out Vinnie?' asked Rachel.

'Nowt,' he shrugged. 'I mean why would I know anything about some fucking idiot calling himself the Pied Piper?'

He didn't sound any where near as confident as he had done so a few moments ago, Rachel noticed as she observed him closely. She knew that he was lying; only she wasn't entirely sure what he was lying about.

'We hear that the Pied Piper and you hold similar interests Vinnie,' said Hunter casually lighting a cigarette as she tossed the pack across the table.

'What the fuck is that supposed to mean Hunter?' he snapped at her.

'We hear that this Pied Piper character is into...' began Hunter.

'I don't know what the fuck he's into,' he sneered at her. 'And I don't know what it is that you are insinuating here, but I...'

'Who is the Pied...' started Rachel.

'From what I read this morning,' said Vinnie suddenly smiling with pure arrogance at them both. 'It was someone called Luther Cartwright. Surely you of all people should know that.' He paused and stared at Rachel. 'Some rich geezer right, from Prestbury right. Him and his wife, they were the ones that were behind whatever the fuck it is that you're questioning me about.'

Hunter and Rachel glanced at one another. They hadn't seen the morning papers with being tied up with the murder from the night before. Nor had they seen Mackenzie or Halenbrook to confirm what Vinnie was telling them. They suddenly felt awkward for being put into this position. Rachel could read it all over Hunter's face as she tried her best to regain composure.

'Don't tell me you ain't seen it,' he laughed. 'It's all over the fucking front pages for Christ sake. They say that one of the leading detectives from right here at this station has pretty much solved the missing kid's case. Halenfuck or whatever he's called.'

'What' snapped Hunter infuriated.

'Yeah,' he sniggered. 'It also says that you had some involvement with their deaths Rachel.' He smirked at her, as he reached over the table and grabbed the pack of Hunter's cigarettes and then lit one.

'Don't believe everything that you read,' said Rachel.

'So you didn't kill them bot...'

'Who's Gabriel?' asked Rachel catching him off guard, trying to get the upper hand on him again.

'I, I don't know,' he answered a little shakily.

'What do you know of him?' asked Rachel. 'Come on now Vinnie, surely the likes of you and Freddy Marshall know of...'

'I don't know what the fuck either of you are...'

'Where's Freddy?' asked Hunter.

'I don't...'

'When was the last time that you sa...' began Rachel.

'What the fuck is this,' he snapped. 'What the fuck has Finger's got to do with...'

'We've got him cold,' smiled Hunter getting back into the swing of things.

'You got him cold for what?' He couldn't hold eye contact for more than a couple of seconds at a time.

'So you like little girls?' said Rachel, throwing him off balance again. 'I hear that you get your kicks from little girls Vinnie.'

'Shut the fuck up bitch,' he sneered at her, as he leaned over the table. 'You don't know shit.'

'Sit the fuck down Vinnie,' snarled Hunter. 'Why did you send Freddy Marshall to kill Carol Sillverone?'

'Who?' he looked infuriated at the mere mention of the name.

'Carol Sillverone,' said Rachel. 'You knew her right Vinnie?'

'Why... why would I... Why would I...'

'Did she get close to you both Vinnie?' asked Rachel. 'Did she discover that you and your pathetic little friend are the ones not only behind the Pied Piper? But also the dark angel case that has become known to us as Gabrie...'

'I honestly don't know wha...'

'Yes you do,' said Hunter.

'I want my fucking brief here right now,' he said shaking his head them. 'This ain't fucking right Hunter. What the fuck is it that you think we've, I mean... I've don...'

'Whose we've?' asked Rachel. 'Are you possibly referring to your mate, Fingers?'

'I ain't saying jack shit more until you get me my brief...'

'Does he carry out all your dirty work Vinnie?' asked Rachel.

'I don't know what it...'

'Or do you do the jobs together?' asked Hunter. 'Is that it... do you work as a pair? Who does what Vinnie? Which one does the raping and which one does the slicing open of the chests? Who removes the hearts Vinnie? Come on now Vinnie...'

'This is utter bullshit,' he snapped pushing himself out of the chair.

'Sit the fuck down Vinnie,' sneered Hunter. 'We ain't finished with you yet boy.'

'Fuck you Hunter,' he said casually, as he went for the door.

Rachel had never seen Hunter move so quickly, as she was out of the chair and had grabbed hold of him by the door. 'I said sit the fuck bac...'

Just then the door to the interrogation room opened. Stood there was a perplexed looking Chief Mackenzie standing along side of a very attractive dark haired woman, who looked to be in her early forties. But she certainly held her age well and could have easily passed for early thirties. She had strong looking cheek bones that Rachel imagined would have looked good in a photograph. She was smiling either pleasantly or smugly, the latter Rachel imagined it to be more the case. She was dressed in a fitted Prada suit with matching briefcase that put a smile on Rachel's face. Rachel didn't have a clue who this woman was, but she was beginning to get the feeling that this meant trouble for Hunter.

'I strongly recommend that you release my client now,' said the woman who just walked abruptly through the door into the room.

'Who the fuck are yo...'

'Alright Claire,' smirked Vinnie winking at her.

'I'm Claire Harrison detective Hunter,' she smiled as she handed her card to him. 'And this is my client. So I suggest that you either charge him or release him.'

'He's free to go,' said Chief Mackenzie who was stood in the doorway shaking his head at Hunter.

'What the...' began Hunter.

'I'll deal with you in a minute,' he said through gritted teeth as Vinnie and his brief both grinned at her. 'Good-day Mister O'Leary, Ms Harrison.'

'Thank you chief,' she replied smiling warmly at him, as the two of them left the room.

'Just what the hell were you thinking Hunter?' screamed the chief as he slammed the door so hard that bounced back open.

'You've just let a potential susp...'

'Jesus Christ Hunter,' he sighed. 'You try my patience like you wouldn't believe.'

'But we found Freddy Marshall's print's at last night's crime scene,' she protested.

'I know exactly what it was that you found detective,' he told her glaring his hatred at Rachel. 'But that doesn't give you the right to go dragging...'

'He's a well known associate of the man,' said Hunter still staring through her empty doorway in disbelief.

'That doesn't make him a potenti...'

'Why the fuck don't you just let me do my job and you do yours Chief Mackenzie,' she was right in face and Rachel could see her anger clearly showing through. 'What the hell is it that you've got against my...'

'And what the fuck is she doing interviewing,' snapped Mackenzie walking over to the seat where Rachel was still sat.

'That was my call,' defended Hunter as Rachel rose from her seat easing the chief out of her way.

'I don't give a rat's ass whose call it wa...'

'I'm out of here,' said Rachel pushing past Mackenzie as roughly as she possibly could.

'Good,' he replied staring at her. 'And don't you hurry back now Ms Murphy. Well, that is, until we've decided what it is that we are to do about the Cartwrig...'

'Fuck this shit Hunter,' she said shaking her head sorrowfully at the man. 'Go and work things out for yourselves from now on. I've just about had it up to here with all of you. And Chief, You know where to find me if you want to charge me,' she smiled sarcastically at him as she disappeared through the door leaving the two of them scowling at one another within the confines of the room.

FORTY ONE

'Where's Kyle?' asked Rachel full of concern for the little boy she couldn't get out her mind. 'Is he safe?' she then added, sitting herself down at the table in Chan's restaurant, where the others had gathered.

The night was coming to an end and had his staff clearing away for the night. Rachel looked over at Chan who bowed his head in sorrow for yet another loss at the hands of this killer, who now appeared to be hunting every one of them. Rachel felt her emotions being pulled in every direction. She felt like quitting, just giving up and curling into a ball. Hiding some place where nobody would ever find her. Only she knew that she couldn't that, not just yet anyway.

'I've got him stashed at a safe house with Lisa,' replied Sleeper, who Rachel noticed looked exhausted for the first time since she'd met him. Although as tired as he appeared, there was no denying the holocaust that blazed through his eyes. Only Rachel now knew that, that conflagration was so fierce for different reasons.

'How are the both of you?' asked Rachel placing her hand on top of his.

'I think you know better than most, just how the hell I am Rach,' he placed his other hand over hers and squeezed it. 'I think that you better tell us what it is that you know so far.'

'That way we can plan what it is that we are going to do with this mother fucker,' sighed Eazy.

'Alright,' she nodded. 'But what I want you all to do is listen carefully. Because at the moment, all we've got is a lot of speculation.'

'What have they found out?' asked Tony, smiling sadly at both her and Sleeper.

'Will this help us in any way?' asked Sleeper placing the Dell lap-top on top of the table before them.

'They're looking for that,' she told him. 'They think that the killer took it.'

'My sister was double paranoid about getting it stolen,' he said. 'I knew where she kept it hidden. I figured that she'd maybe have something useful on here that we could use.'

'Have you not had a look at it yet?' she asked him. 'Is it protected?' she added thinking of all the problems that had occurred with the other systems.

'I've no idea Rachel,' he sighed deeply. 'I figured that we'd wait and see what you had to tell us first.'

'Besides, we've not been back that long,' said Eazy. 'We pretty much headed straight back down to London. We figured that the police would want to question us. And that just ain't happening.'

'They do,' said Rachel. 'They want to know what it is that Kyle saw also.'

'They ain't questioning my nephew,' said Sleeper. 'They ain't getting anywhere near him until we've got to the bottom of this ourselves Rachel.'

'I had a feeling that you was going to say that,' she smiled. 'I told Hunter that I would do my best in asking you, but...'

'Only me and Eazy know where they both are, right now,' he told her. 'And that's the way it's going to stay.'

'It ain't that we don't trust you,' Eazy suddenly said.

'It's alright brother,' nodded Tony.

'He's right,' agreed Rachel. 'Right now, I have to say that, that is probably for the best that nobody's knows. We don't want to know.'

'The police ain't exactly been doing a bang up job so far Rachel,' said Sleeper. 'Especially where it comes to protection. I can keep him better protected than they can.'

'Sleeper I'm so sor...' began Rachel.

'It ain't your fault girl,' he said as she was drawn back into his eyes, witnessing the sheer anguish that he felt. 'All we need for you to do now, is help us solve this case before the police do. That way we can seek out this guy before they do. That's all I ask of you now Rachel, just help me to avenge all of the wrong this freak has done.'

'I will,' she nodded. 'How is Kyle really? Have you spoken with him? Does he know what has happened to his mother?'

'He's a smart kid,' smiled Sleeper. 'He knew without us having to tell him what had happened.'

'It was the first thing he asked as he came around,' added Eazy. 'He asked us straight out, whether or not his mummy had gone to heaven the night before.'

'We told him straight,' said Sleeper. 'There was no use lying to him.'

'I agree with you,' said Rachel. 'But does he know what happened?'

'He asked us if the man wearing the shiny black outfit had sent her to heaven,' said Eazy shaking his head.

'Did he describe what the man looked like?' she asked them.

'From the way he described him,' said Sleeper. 'Whoever it was, was wearing black leathers... maybe motorcycle leathers.'

'Or PVC or even silicone of some kind,' suggested Rachel.

'Why?' asked Eazy.

'The nature of the crimes suggest, as bad as sounds,' she paused. 'But kinky sex, I know it sounds shitty. But... Also it may be the other reason why we aren't finding any fibres or hair at the crime scenes.'

'Did he see the guy's face?' asked Tony.

'We asked him that,' said Eazy shaking his head at the answer.

'He said the guy wore a black mask,' said Sleeper. 'He said it was the same as the outfit he wore. I just presumed that it was a motorcycle helmet to be honest. But now that you've said that Rachel, well I ain't too sure now.'

'It very well could have been,' said Rachel. 'That's what I said before. There is a lot of speculation in relation to everything. Things may have even taken a turn for the worse. If that's at all possible.'

'How so?' asked Sleeper.

'Everything has either escalated,' she told him. 'Or it's just as it was before. There is still a lot that I need to figure out.'

'There's one thing that we can't figure out,' said Eazy. 'It's how this Gabriel character found out about her Rachel.'

'That's been confusing me also,' she admitted. 'Well, that was until earlier on today. Since then I'm either even more confused or I'm a little more enlightened.'

'What's the supposed to mean Rach?' asked Tony.

'I'm completely off the case now,' she told them. 'I told them both pretty much to go to hell this morning. Mackenzie was ranting and raving. He was also, still threatening me with the Cartwright's murder. So that was it, I told them to shove it.'

'Why though?' asked Sleeper. 'What's happened this morning? What have they found out?'

'I'll tell you in a moment,' she said. 'But I just want to point out, that it doesn't mean that I'm not going to give this whole mess, my one-hundred percent guys. I just want you all to know that. You can't believe how sorry I feel about your...'

'We know that you'll give it your everything,' nodded Sleeper.

'When I got home today,' she told them. 'I began to piece all of the evidence and my theories together. That's what I meant by I'm either more enlightened or even more confused.'

'I think you better explain Rachel,' said Sleeper. 'Because I'm confused as shit, and from the look on Eazy's face, him too.'

'Alright, but listen up,' she said. 'I don't want you jumping any guns here right. Because at the moment we only have one solid bit of incriminating evidence from last night. Only I'm still not completely convinced. Some things fit and other things don't fit at all...'

'What evidence?' asked Sleeper.

'They found a palm print at the crime scene last night,' she told him. 'Actually in the bedroom.'

'What about our prints though?' asked Eazy.

'Yeah,' nodded Tony. 'Surely our prints were discovered there as well.'

'You've all been eliminated with the prints they discovered,' she said. 'Jenkin's cleared the two of you. Although Hunter is still out for...'

'Fuck her,' snapped Sleeper. 'I didn't like that bitch at all.'

Rachel observed the look of Sleeper's face. She could tell that it was something more than just last night that he didn't like about her. But she put it to one side, for a later date. Now wasn't the time to be questioning him.

'Whose print did they find Rachel?' asked Tony.

'Freddy Marshall's,' she told them. 'You must have come across him right Tony?'

'Fingers!' exclaimed Tony looking bewildered.

'Who the fuck is Fingers?' asked Sleeper leaning closer into the table. 'You know this fuck?'

'What's his name Freddy Marshall?' asked Eazy.

'Yeah,' shrugged Tony. 'They call him Fingers because whilst growing up he was right little thief. He's caught up in all sorts of shit these days though. But the name Fingers has just always kinda of stuck. What the fuck was his...'

'Did Dominic O'Leary ever get in touch with you?' asked Rachel as she lit a cigarette, exhaling the smoke. 'You know, from when you both went to see him?'

'He didn't,' replied Tony shaking his head.

'What's he got to do with anything?' asked Sleeper.

'Hang on a minute,' said Tony. 'Fingers and Vinnie are close mates.'

'I know,' she said. 'We need to take a look at that computer once I've told you everything that I know.'

'You think that it was this guy that killed my sister?' asked Sleeper with no emotion whatsoever in his voice.

'He's killed before,' said Tony. 'Several times that even I know of.'

'So we go and see...' began Eazy.

'Hear what I have to say first,' said Rachel cutting him off.

'Isn't he doing bird though?' asked Tony still looking perplexed by discovering the information Rachel had just told them.

'What for?' asked Eazy.

'Something to do with raping some kid,' said Tony shaking his head. 'Apparently he blinded the poor girl with acid at the same time.'

'He's out anyway,' said Rachel. 'Had the conviction overturned by his lawyer. But I bet you didn't know, that Vinnie was also a suspect in that case.'

'Really,' said Tony with a look of disgust on his face.

'Did you also know that Vinnie prefers young girls?' she asked. 'And I mean very young girls lads.'

'I heard rumours,' said Tony. 'But you don't listen to too much of that shit. Why'd you ask?'

'I had a short interview with him this morning. That was before his lawyer kicked us into touch,' she said. 'Hunter filled me in on his past. She also told me to ask you about him.'

'We've just had our share of run ins along the way ar'kid,' he told her. 'What did Hunter tell you about him?'

'To cut a long story short,' she said. 'His old man has covered up to cases that Hunter knew about.'

'What cases?' asked Sleeper absorbing every detail of information.

'One going back to when he was a little kid. He was only around eleven or twelve years old himself at the time of this happening,' she said. 'Apparently he was caught molesting some girl of five or six years old.'

'You're kidding,' said Tony pulling his face at the mere thought of it.

'The girl's old man caught him at it,' she said shaking her head. 'But that's not all. He also was brought in a few year back and

charged with sex with a minor. Although he claims the girls consented to the sex.'

'What kind of a pervert is he?' asked Eazy.

'I knew that there was something not quite right about the guy,' said Sleeper as Tony nodded at him.

'I still don't quite follow what all this has to do with the case though Rachel,' said Tony.

'Nor did I,' she agreed. 'This is where it becomes all a little more than confusing. You see, Hunter traced some internet scam a few years back now, that Vinnie was and probably still very much is, running. Without his father's knowledge I might add.'

'What internet scam?' asked Sleeper.

'It was a website that puts out live sex shows at different times of the day,' she told him. 'Apparently you register with the website and then you are charged by the minute for the use of it.'

'Fuck,' said Tony. 'That little fucker must be making a pure mint from that.'

'That's not all though,' said Rachel. 'You see, the reason Hunter suspected that he had something to do with the website that featured one of the missing kids, is because...'

'Hang on a minute,' said Tony holding his hands up. 'What are you saying here. That Vinnie was a suspect in the Pied Piper case?'

'Apparently so,' she nodded. 'Hunter claims not to have told me, because we were only supposed to look into Charlotte Cartwright, not the missing kids.'

'So you're now saying that it could have been this Vinnie character behind the Pied Piper case?' asked Eazy.

'Hunter came across this website featuring a film with children being abused in it,' she said. 'It was through watching the website that Vinnie had set up that she came into contact with the other website.'

'I don't believe all this,' said Tony shaking his head.

'The thing is,' said Rachel. 'Hunter isn't sure whether not it was him. She just has a gut feeling about it.'

'It must have been his website though,' said Sleeper. 'If she accessed it through his website to come in contact with the other. It must be related.'

'Not necessarily,' she said. 'Apparently, if let's say you access a certain window on his website it could take you through to another without you wanting it to. For instance, the schoolgirl's one that Hunter accessed...'

'School girls?' asked Eazy sighing.

'It was apparently just girl's acting younger than they were. You know dressed in school uniforms and so on.' she told him. 'But if you accessed that window. You obviously showed an interest in that age group right.'

'Right,' agreed Sleeper.

'So another website puts a trace on you,' she told them, 'and sends you some other stuff through, with even younger girls in there.'

'Jesus,' sighed Tony. 'Who the fuck ever invented this bleeding internet.'

'I'm still lost here Rach,' said Sleeper. 'I mean, what the fuck has the Pied Piper got to do with Gabriel?'

'That's the confusing part I was telling you about,' she said. 'But I always said that I wasn't one-hundred percent about Luther Cartwright being the Pied Piper.'

'So now you're thinking that it's Vincent O'Leary?' asked Tony.

'He didn't strike me as the all-mighty, as them pair kept referring to this third party,' she sighed. 'But who knows, looks can be deceiving right.'

'I don't buy it,' said Tony. 'And how the hell is Vinnie connected to Gabriel, Rachel?'

'What if we've over looked all along is that the Pied Piper and Gabriel is the same person,' she said.

'Now that's a bit more than mere coincidence,' said Sleeper.

'Yeah,' smiled Eazy. 'You can't honestly believe that Rach?'

'Alright,' she said sitting up. 'You asked your sister to look into the missing kids for us.'

'I did,' said Sleeper. 'But I also asked her to look into the killer of your family remember.'

'I know that,' she nodded. 'But back in '96 when this Freddy Fingers or whatever the fuck you want to call him. But when he was sent down for raping and blinding that kid. He was represented by Otis Fairchild.'

'Seriously?' asked Tony.

'And it was Peter's office that prosecuted the case,' she added.

'But not Peter directly,' said Sleeper. 'Or was it?'

'No it wasn't,' she admitted. 'That's yet another confusing factor. I mean yes, right you can connect him to Fairchild and obviously he may have been bitter against the partner as well, Morgan. He could have had it for them, because of the firm they owned. But I couldn't find anything that related him directly to Peter or my daughter.'

'What about my sister though?' asked Sleeper.

'She was investigating the Pied Piper,' she said.

'So now you think that Vinnie is the Pied Piper,' said Tony pulling his face. 'And that Fingers is Gabriel? Or maybe Vinnie's Gabriel and Fingers is the Pied Piper, Jesus, what the fuck is going on.'

'I know it sounds crazy,' she admitted holding her hands up. 'That's the other confusing thing. I mean I haven't met this Freddy guy, but I've read his file. But I have met Vincent and if the two are anything like one another. Well I just wouldn't have put them in same category as Gabriel or the type of murders we've seen committed so far.'

'I have to agree with you there ar'kid,' said Tony sipping his whiskey.

'But then again, his palm print was found at the scene last night,' she said. 'He's a reputed killer. Hunter tells me that he's Vinnie's right hand man. That he carries out paid contracts for Vinnie.'

'That is true,' said Tony. 'But...'

'And that he's extremely good at his job also,' she added. 'He apparently is so good, that he doesn't leave them any where near enough evidence to ever convict him of his crimes.'

'And that would fit what has happened so far,' said Sleeper nodding. 'If you are to carry out contracts within the disposal business. Then you cannot be successful, if you don't have prior knowledge to the forensic procedures that take place.'

'Have the police brought this guy in?' asked Eazy.

'They don't know where he is,' she told him. 'They've issued the warrant on him though.'

'Jesus, so you really think, that it is this guy,' said Tony still trying to absorb what was being said at the table. 'But why all the flamboyancy to his crimes?'

'Maybe he began to enjoy his work a little too much,' said Eazy.

'There is something that is bothering me here though Rachel,' said Sleeper.

'What's that then?'

'What you just said about this guy being so careful with his previous crimes,' he said. 'And I ain't just talking about these murders I don't just mean the dark angel, Gabriel, archangel stuff, whatever you want to call it. But you said that he's carried out work for Vincent in the past and they've never been able to make anything stick.'

'That' right,' she agreed with him.

'So why make such a blatant mistake then,' said Sleeper. 'Why after all this time, has he gone and fucked up like he has Rachel?'

'I honestly don't know Sleeper,' she said. 'Like I said, the whole thing has become more confusing than it previously was.'

'He's right though, you know,' said Eazy. 'How has he managed to leave a palm print against the wall?'

'Maybe he was careless,' suggested Tony. 'Maybe he didn't wear any gloves.'

'But the first thing any professional does, is wear gloves brother,' said Eazy. 'Everybody knows that. Whether it's a burglary or taking on a hit. You're always, as a professional, going to wear gloves, right.'

'He's definitely right there,' said Sleeper. 'It would appear that this guy has made one hell of a mistake. But what I can't figure out is why?'

'Unless it wasn't him,' suggested Tony.

'What do you mean by that?' asked Sleeper.

'You see,' he said, 'you're all forgetting that I know this man. And yes, he is a psychopath. But there are psychopaths... and then there are proper psychopaths... right Rach?'

'Correct,' she said. 'But why are you so convinced that it's not him. I mean don't get me wrong here. I'm not saying that it is one-hundred percent this guy. But there are other things that relate the two.'

'Fingers carries out Vinnie's dirty work,' said Tony. 'Now what if that's all this was. I don't want to sound heartless here Sleeper.'

'It's alright,' he said. 'Go on.'

'Well what if he went to carry out the contract on your sister,' said Tony. 'But the job had already been done for him.'

'What about the palm print though?' asked Eazy coming around to his way of thinking.

'I have a theory there too,' he said. 'Like I just said. There are psychopaths and there is pure psychopath's. Imagine you turned up and were faced with what we were last night. Now I don't care how fucked up this guy may be himself. But imagine that you were going to kill somebody. But when you got there, that person had not only already been killed, but had been, well had been killed and portrayed in the way that we...'

'We know,' said Sleeper. 'And you've got a valid point. But the palm print?'

'I don't know,' he shrugged. 'Maybe the sight before him was so much to take in. That, I don't know, maybe he took his glove off to wipe his face.'

'And leaned against the wall with it,' said Eazy. 'Now that's a possibility.'

'There all possibilities,' she smiled at Tony. 'But you could definitely be onto something there Tony.'

'What else have you got that connects them Rachel?' asked Sleeper. 'You said that there were other factors to consider.'

'Yeah, yeah right,' she looked thoughtful as if Tony had set her mind off in a new direction all together. 'The other thing that I thought about, was that the kids were also raped remember,' said Rachel. 'It is something that we not so much overlooked, but didn't connect to the two incidents. The abuse of the children through the Pied Piper. And possibly the deaths at the hands of the Pied Piper could have led this guy, or these guy's to step things up another level right. They took things to a new height by killing those that they hated so much through either being convicted by them, or not defended successfully.'

'You think that Vinnie could be helping him then?' asked Sleeper.

'Now hold on a minute,' she said. 'I'm not saying that either of them are definitely the killers or the abusers, it's just a good possibility at this point.'

'I'd say it's very fucking good possibility,' said Sleeper.

'You need to let me work at all of this some more first,' she told him. 'Remember what happened with the Cartwright's.'

'As I remember it,' he smiled. 'We rid society of a couple of no good pervert's that had terrorised children for years.'

'You were also the one to point out that if Luther Cartwright wasn't the Pied Piper,' she said, 'then we'd just killed our best lead.'

'She's right here brother,' said Eazy nodding in her direction. 'We need to be one-hundred percent certain this time.'

'But what abou...' he began.

'But fuck all brother,' said Eazy not allowing him to finish. 'This time we do it Rachel's way. You don't even have to ask whether or not you've got my backing, because it would be an insult on your behalf to do so brother. But the police are going to be shit hot about this whole fucking nightmare. We can't afford any mistakes or loose ends to be left floating in the wind. We find out for sure first, alright brother?'

'Alright,' agreed Sleeper.

'I'm so glad that you said that,' sighed Rachel. 'Now let's have a look at what it was that your sister had found out.'

Switching the computer on, Rachel shook her head as the password box came up on the screen. 'Looks like we need to pay Robert a visit again,' she said.

'Just what the hell was it that she found out Rachel?' asked Sleeper staring at the screen before them.

'I don't know,' she admitted. 'But whatever it was, could be the proof that we are looking for Sleeper.'

'What do we do in the mean time?' asked Eazy.

'I say that we at least pay little Vincent a visit,' said Sleeper, smirking at Tony.

'It can't do any harm to question him ourselves now,' agreed Tony looking at his sister. 'Right ar'kid?'

'It can't,' she said. 'But just don't go breaking his legs or any other shit that you lads get up to.'

'Ahhh,' smiled Tony. 'You're hurting my feeling now ar'kid,'

'Yeah, right,' she shook her head at him.

FORTY TWO

'This is twice that you've brought one of his kind to my house Tony,' said Dominic with utter disgust written all over his face, as he glared directly at Sleeper. Both him and his son were stood in the open doorway to his home in Hale where Sleeper and Tony had just arrived. It was cool morning, and Tony had to keep blowing in his hands to try and keep warm.

'This had better be good Tony; I don't like it when you bring uninvited guests along to my home like this.'

Sleeper had handed over all his weapons at the gate where the two of them had been searched again by Vinnie's henchmen. Vinnie, the smarmy shit, was grinning foolishly from behind his father, just within the confines of the house. Sleeper eyed him carefully as they approached.

'He insisted on coming though,' laughed Tony, smiling at Sleeper who still hadn't taken his eyes from Vinnie. 'You alright anyway Dom?' he added, smiling warmly at the old man despite the cold weather.

Dominic who was still dressed in his dressing gown despite the fact it was almost midday, and freezing outside, glared unhappily at the two of them. 'You better come on through before we all freeze our bollocks off.'

'What's the matter this time Henessy?' asked Vinnie. 'You lost your leash for that puppy you've brought with you.'

'Oh, he ain't no puppy kid,' he nodded at Sleeper. 'He's a pure thorough bred – fully trained pit bull. So you better fuckin' watch yourself Vincent.'

'Whatever,' shrugged Vinnie glaring right back at Sleeper. 'Just make sure he doesn't shit in the house. The cleaner hates it, when that happens.'

'I got him trained so that he only bites people in their homes –
no shitting is allowed,' smiled Tony winking at Vinnie.

'Come on through,' said Dominic. 'What can we do for you
this time?'

'Can we talk over a few things Dom?' asked Tony, ignoring his
son as he felt Sleeper glaring at Vinnie. Tony smiled as he saw
Vinnie quickly divert his eyes away from   Sleeper, who as yet,
still hadn't spoken a word. 'We need to ask the two of you some
questions if that's alright?'

'They clean?' asked Vinnie to one of the three men stood
behind the two of them.

'Yes boss,' replied the largest of the three, holding out both
hands to show him the two handguns and three knives, two of
which were throwing ones. Sleeper merely smirked at the man
who eyed him cautiously.

'This guy go anywhere without those things?' asked Dominic
nodding his head at the array of different weapons displayed.

'Obviously not,' he laughed.

'You want coffee?' asked Dominic as they all made their way
through back into the dining room.

'Cheers,' replied Tony as one of Vinnie's men wandered
towards the kitchen. 'Make that two coffee's,' he called after the
man who didn't turn around.

'So what can I do for you?' asked Dominic, as the four of them
sat in pairs at the opposite ends of the table.

'You find anything out for us old man?' asked Tony.
He glanced at Vinnie who merely shrugged. 'Well, did you or
didn't you Vincent?'

'Nah pops,' he replied. 'I reckon that the papers got it right
yesterday. You know with all that shit about the Cartwright's.'

'You reckon that it was the Cartwright's that were heading the
paedophile ring Vinnie?' asked Tony. 'Did you happen to know
the two of them Vinnie?' As he asked this, he immediately saw
recognition in the lad's eyes.

'Why would I have known them?' he asked without being as
cocky. 'What would I be associating with those couple of freaks
for?'

'I don't know,' shrugged Tony. 'Funny people can attract
funny people.'

'What the hell is that supposed to mean Henessy?' he asked
looking to his father for support.

'So you're saying that you knew neither of them?'

'That's right.'

'Do you know anything about the website that is known as Pied Piper Productions?' asked Tony.

'Yeah, from what I read yesterday it was this Luther Cartwright geezer, right,' he replied.

'I don't know Vinnie,' he said. 'Was it?'

'Come on now Tony, you should know that better than any of us here,' smirked Vinnie. 'From what I hear, your sister killed the two of them.'

'And I hear that you met with her yesterday,' he smirked.

'Fucking bitch,' he sneered. 'Both her and that...'

'I'd be very careful what you say boy,' sneered Sleeper viciously, defending Rachel and speaking for the first time, as Vinnie looked to his father for backing once again.

'You sure that you didn't find anything out Vinnie?' asked Tony. 'We thought that the task would have been right up your street.'

'And why the fuck would it have been up my street?'

'You seen Freddy Marshall lately?' asked Tony ignoring his question blatantly.

'Why the fuck is everybody so interested in Fingers all of a sudden?' he snapped back at them.

'We've got a few questions for him,' said Sleeper.

'Fingers ain't worked for me for quite some time now,' he said as Tony noticed Dominic look at him questionably without thinking. He knew, right there and then, that Vinnie was lying to them.

'What's that boy gone and done now?' asked Dominic neutrally. 'He was always getting himself into trouble.'

'We ain't sure if he's done anything or not,' shrugged Sleeper noncommittally.

'He's right,' said Tony. 'But we think that he may have some answers for us in relation to something completely different.'

'You don't think that he's caught up in this paedophile shit?' asked Dominic. 'Do you Tony?'

'I don't know,' he replied. 'Maybe you should ask your son about that Dom.'

'Why the fuck should he ask...'

'I think that you're the puppy that needs keeping on a leash,' said Sleeper cutting him short as he glared his hatred at him.

'What do you know about all of this Vincent?' asked Dominic. 'If you know something that you haven't told me, then I want to know boy.'

'I don't know what they are talking about pops,' he said shaking his head.

'What was the last contract that you issued Fingers with Vinnie?' asked Tony.

'As if I'm going to tell you tha...'

'Did you issue a contract on my sister?' asked Sleeper casually picking at his teeth, as the old man glared at his own son. 'Did you have my sister killed kid?' he added unexpectedly.

'How was your sister killed?' asked Dom.

'It would appear that it was the same killer that took the lives of ar'kid's husband and daughter,' added Tony.

'So what has that got to do with my son?'

'Yeah,' protested Vinnie, 'I don't even know who your...'

'Sure you do,' smiled Sleeper. 'She was the one who was investigating you and all the other little perverts out there.'

'Now hold on a minute,' said Dominic. 'You'll show some respect in my home boy,' he added, staring directly at Sleeper and holding eye contact.

Sleeper nodded silently, as Vinnie sneered at him. 'Yeah boy, you better watch yourself around here.'

'Shut up Vincent,' instructed Dominic without even looking in his direction. 'What was your sister investigating?' Was she police?'

'No she wasn't,' he replied. 'She worked as an investigator for Daniel's law firm in town.'

'I know the firm,' replied Dominic. 'But what I don't know, is what it was, that she was investigating.'

'She was looking into the missing kids for us,' he told him. 'Also into the other matter Tony just mentioned, the incident concerning his sister. It would appear that by investigating those incidents, she managed to upset somebody.'

'And why would my son have anything to do with your sister's investigation?'

'Freddy Marshall's prints were found at the crime scene,' said Sleeper.

'That still doesn't mean that my son had anything to do with it,' said Dominic shaking his head. 'And what has one lot of paedophile's that you were just talking about, got to do with this killer that you are now talking about?'

'We know that Fingers carries out your son's dirty work,' said Sleeper kissing his teeth.

'But that doesn't me...'

'We also hear that you covered up at least two incidents up for Vinnie in the past,' said Tony not allowing him time to finish. 'At least two from what we hear old man.'

'What is this bullshit?' said Vinnie.

409

'What incid...' Dominic began to say a little shakily.

'The first that we know about,' said Tony, 'is the molesting of a five or six year old little girl.'

'Fuck you Henes...' snapped Vinnie as Sleeper cut him off.

'And the second is under age sex with some school girls,' he said smiling at the two of them. 'Maybe that's what prompted your idea for the website that you own kid.'

'How the fuck have you found out about those incidents?' asked Dominic staring at the two of them, with shame written all over his face. 'And what fucking website?'

'They don't know what they're talking about,' said Vinnie looking away for them all.

'A little bird told us about the convictions,' said Tony. 'And from the look on you face old man, I'd say that your little nonce of a boy, has shamed you on more than just those two occasions.'

'Watch your mouth Tony,' warned Dominic.

'Why?' he asked. 'Because the truth hurts old man.'

'I said to watch your...'

'Jesus Dom,' sighed Tony as he shook his head in disgrace. 'How the hell could you cover something like that up? Your own son is a nonce. I'd heard the rumours, but Jesus, it was your son. And no matter what I thought of him personally, I never figured you'd let him get away with that.'

'Fuck you Henessy,' screamed Vinnie. 'I ain't no fucking sex case... you... you... what the fuck do you...'

'Getting a bit flustered Vinnie,' smirked Sleeper, still picking at his teeth casually.

'And fuck you too nigg...'

'Now, now Vincent,' warned Sleeper wagging his finger at him, as if scolding a naughty boy. 'I've warned you once today already. Be very careful what you say to me boy.'

'I don't have to take this shit in my own...'

'What website?' asked his father cutting him off with a wave of the hand. 'You said idea for website.'

'Oh don't listen to them pops,' he said placing a hand on his father's shoulder.

Shrugging his hand away. 'I asked you, what website you were talking about Tony?'

'You mean that you don't know about it,' smiled Tony at Vinnie.

'We've got lots of websites,' said Dominic looking to Vinnie who had bowed his head. 'But I want to know which one you were talking about.'

'It would seem that little Vinnie has ventured out on his own,' said Sleeper. 'It seems that he wasn't satisfied with what you supplied him with Dom.'

'What do you mean?'

'I've told you pops,' said Vinnie trying to get his father's attention, as he was ignored by the three of them, like he didn't even exist. 'Don't listen...'

'Apparently a reliable source, tells us that it has been set up for years now,' said Sleeper, bending the truth. 'Apparently you register with the site and the kid there gets paid by the minute for use of it. She tells us that they first came across it, because of suspected school girls that were allegedly being used on there.'

'What's this they're on about Vincent?' asked Dominic turning to face him.

'I ain't got a clue pops,' he shrugged, but still avoiding eye contact.

'It would also appear that when you access this website,' said Sleeper interrupting them. 'That you gain access to further websites featuring children.'

'You little shit,' snapped Dominic. 'Just what the fuck have you been up you...' He suddenly stopped himself and glared at the other two – it was as if time had suddenly stopped as they stared back and forth at one another. 'I think that it's time that you both left... now.'

'But...' began Sleeper.

'We're outta of here old man,' said Tony nudging Sleeper's elbow as Dominic stared at his son.

'What the fuck have you been up to Vincent?' asked his father staring at his son with disgust, as the heard the front door close. Knowing that the other two had left the house, he grabbed Vinnie by the shoulders and shook him. 'What the hell have you been up to behind my back?'

'You shouldn't listen to them two,' he said defensively.

'What is this website they are on about?'

'I honestly don't know.'

'Come on now son,' he said. 'You forgetting how many times I've bailed you out of trouble when you lost yourself to temptation. Did you have any involvement with those Cartwright's that were in the papers yesterday son?'

'Listen pops; I honestly don't know what they are talk...'

'Don't bullshit me,' he said. 'Now I want to know. Did you know them pair of nonce's or not Vincent?'

'No,' he answered vigorously shaking his head. 'Why would I?'

'You tell me,' he said. 'Who else is involved in this mess son?'

'You don't want to know,' he sighed dropping his head.

'Why don't I?' he asked stroking the top of his sons head affectionately, unable to stay mad at him. 'What have you gone and caught yourself up in Vincent?'

'This goes really high pop's,' he said, his head still dropped.

'What goes really high?' he demanded. 'Who is that you're talking about?'

'I can't say,' he sighed. 'It'll create trouble like you wouldn't believe.'

'Who the fuck have you gone and got mixed up with now?'

'All of this goes a lot higher than either you or me,' he told him looking up with tears in his eyes. 'Even I won't cross this...' he let the words slip away.

'What's that supposed mean Vincent?' he asked confused. 'You're not making any sense boy.'

'Don't worry about it pop's,' he suddenly said, regaining composure. 'It's nothing really. There is no trouble.'

'I wouldn't bank on that son,' he sighed rubbing the back of his son's head. 'I think that the trouble has already been caused.'

'What's that supposed to mean?'

'I think it has already been caused,' he replied, 'those two turning up here like they have. I don't know what it is that you've managed to...'

'Don't worry about them two,' he pulled himself away and wiped his eyes. 'I don't know anything about any website. I honestly don't know what it is that they are talking about.'

'So what are they so interested in then?'

'I don't know.'

'And what about Freddy?' he asked. 'I know you lied there. I know you were with him only last week at the house. So what's he got to do with all of this. Did you put a contract out on that nigger's sister or not?'

'No,' he protested. 'I just didn't want them knowing that I'd seen him after the cops questioned me about it also.'

'The last thing we need is that black fucker on our backs,' sighed Dominic. 'There is something about him I don't like son. I'm not even sure what it is about him that spooks me. But I tell you what son, I'm not afraid to admit it, whatever it is; it scares the hell out of me.'

'Don't worry about him pop's,' said Vinnie. 'I'll deal with that fucker.'

'Just be very careful,' said Dominic. 'I don't want us ending up in some damn war over any of this.'

'Just don't worry yourself,' smiled Vinnie, convinced that he's successfully blagged his old man into believing him. Although he left wondering what he was going to do now.   Especially after what he'd heard today.

'What did you make of all that?' asked Tony as they walked through the gate to the main street.

'He's a lying little fucker,' replied Sleeper coldly, as he pressed the key control to unlock his car.

'Apart from that,' smiled Tony.

'He definitely knows more than he's letting on to us.'

'I agree with you there,' said Tony. 'So what do we do now?'

'We keep a close eye on him,' said Sleeper as they climbed into the car. 'I want to know where he goes and who he sees.'

'I know that I've had my share of run ins with the lad,' said Tony, as Sleeper stared at him. 'But I never wanted to believe all that stuff I'd heard about him being a fucking nonce. You just don't want to when you actually know them in person, even if you hate the pricks. It's a horrible thought, especially when you know them personally. You know what I mean?'

'I know what you're saying. Only I find the boy in there, too fucking stupid to actually be involved in anything at all,' said Sleeper shaking his head. 'Even this internet scam he's got going. It just seems beyond that boy's capacity to be involved in such activities.   He doesn't appear to have the brains to run anything without his father's knowledge or backing in it.'

'I know exactly what you mean there,' nodded Tony. 'It's the other thing that is bothering me from what ar'kid said last night.'

'What's that then?' he asked as he started the vehicle.

'He just doesn't fit the profile as ar'kid would put it,' said Tony. 'In either department as far as I'm concerned.'

'Don't worry about it for now,' said Sleeper sliding the gear stick into reverse. 'We'll keep an eye on him for the next few days. Hopefully he'll panic and lead us wherever it is we want to go.'

'And if he doesn't?'

'Then we'll be paying the little fucker and unexpected visit,' smirked Sleeper, as Tony nodded in agreement.

FORTY THREE

'You're not going to believe what I have to tell you,' said Hunter, as Rachel opened her front door. It was freezing outside, and despite the warmth of her apartment, Rachel was wearing a heavy knit sweater with an old battered pair of Levi's. She wore her favourite moccasin slippers upon her feet, yet still found herself wiggling them to keep them warm from the cold exterior.

Hunter on the other hand, was still wearing, only her navy suit with white blouse beneath it, the suit had always reminded Rachel of a bank manager, not that she'd ever told her that. And besides, it looked good on her, like almost everything else that she wore. No matter how casual or business like she dressed, the clothes always complimented her body, as her long blonde hair cascaded freely around her face and shoulders. She was rubbing her hands together like a kid who'd just found the key to the local sweet shop. But Rachel just wasn't in the mood for any of this today.

She planned on spending the day all alone. She wanted time to not only rest, but to go over all of her notes and research, before her brother and Sleeper reported back with whatever they discovered at the O'Leary's that morning. She didn't hold much hope out there. She reckoned that from what she's seen of Vincent O'Leary the day before, he was bound to clam straight up when they both appeared at this door demanding answers to their questions.

'What the hell do you want Hunter?' she asked, as she wrapped her arms around herself to combat the cold weather doing its best to sneak past her and join the warm interior of her apartment. 'I thought that I told you that I wasn't having any further to do with the case.'

'Your problem kid is,' said Hunter smirking away at her, 'that you won't leave the case alone, no matter what you say. So I don't care what you say, I know you're going to want to hear this.'

'If you say so,' she sighed, too tired to argue. 'Go on then,' she added impatiently.

'Grab your jacket kid,' said Hunter, already turning away from the door.

'Why? Jesus Hunter,' said Rachel, annoyed at her friend's demand. 'Where the fuck are you dragging me to now?'

'Just get your jacket and meet me at my car,' she said, walking away with Rachel still stood in the doorway shaking her head and muttering obscenities under her breath at the woman's back.

'What the hell is so important?' she asked climbing into Hunter's black Golf GTI that thankfully already had the heater running, although she still had her hands placed right against the air being blown through the filters. 'That you need me there for it?'

'You'll never guess who Freddy Marshall's brief is?'

'Who,' yawned Rachel, now rubbing her eyes to wake herself some more.

'Claire Harrison,' she smiled at Rachel, as she eased the vehicle into gear and pulled out of the parking lot, which was situated behind the apartments.

'From yesterday!' exclaimed Rachel. 'You mean Vincent O'Leary's brief right?'

'The very one,' she was grinning stupidly at her.

'I suppose we should have figured that out though Hunter,' she said ignoring her exuberance. 'I mean come on, if Freddy and Vinnie are as close as you say they are. Then who do you think it was, that did everything they could to have him freed?'

'I know,' she agreed. 'I was extremely slow off the starting blocks kid. I figured that out after they'd gone. So I have done some checking around.'

'So?' asked Rachel. 'And what's with that stupid grin Hunter?'

'Alright, listen up,' said Hunter. 'Now I bet your gonna guess who his current girlfriend is? But at the same time your not gonna believe it.'

'Noooo,' said Rachel, as it dawned on her why her friend was grinning like she was. 'She's his girlfriend as well! No fucking way Hunter!'

'That's right kid,' she banged, the steering wheel excitedly.

'You're right,' she nodded. 'I can't believe that the woman we saw yesterday has anything to do with the guy that I read the jacket on in your office.'

'I know,' said Hunter. 'I couldn't get my head around it either.'

'She looked so...'

'I know,' laughed Hunter.

'So where are we going to now?'

'To see her of course,' she replied.

'So what are you taking me there for then?' she demanded. 'And where is our back up just in case. I mean if this creep really is the killer, then...'

'After the way she steam rolled in there yesterday,' said Hunter, struggling to get a cigarette from the packet, as Rachel took it from her and lit one for her and one for herself. 'I wanted to talk to her alone first.'

'But what about Mackenzie?'

'Fuck Mackenzie,' she snapped. 'I can hardly ask for her to come down to the station, can I? So I figure that we pay her a little visit.'

'Why me though?'

'Because I want to know, how it is, that this woman's fucking mind works for Christ sake kid,' she told her glancing in her direction. 'I mean she's got to have a couple of screws loose up there, if she got Freddy Fingers Marshall as her boyfriend. Especially seeing as she is also a brief. And a very respectable looking one I might add.'

'Why not Brendan then?'

'Because you'll be able to give me a much better insight to her,' she said. 'You're a woman, so it'll be much better than what he can come up with.'

'Where does she live then?'

'Over Heaton Park way,' she replied.

'I don't know Hunter.' Rachel was tapping her fingers against her nose as she wondered whether or she actually wanted to be here. It was weird, but in a way she felt as though she was betraying Sleeper and the others by not letting them in on this. Not that she'd had chance, or had even known where it was that they were going before she'd got in the car with Hunter.

'What is there to know,' said Hunter, as they pulled to a stop by the traffic lights.

'Mackenzie for starters,' she told her. 'He seems to have really got it in for me at the moment and I don't think this is the right way of winning him over.'

'Fuck him,' she said, as the lights changed and they pulled away. 'He's got it in for everybody but his little bum-chum Halenbrook.'

'What about Brendan then?'

'What about him,' she shrugged.

'Won't he get the arse over the fact that you're taking me there and not him?'

'Fuck him as well,' she said nonchalantly. 'I want you there kid, not him, not Chief Dickhead or Halenfuck who has piss all to do with this anyway. And that's all that matters.'

'Ah but what ab...'

'Ah but fuck all kid,' she smiled, as smoke drifted aimlessly from her mouth. 'If she's there all alone, then she'll open up more with the two of us there. Don't you agr...'

'What like Vinnie did yesterday?' she asked cocking her eyebrow at her.

'Different situation all together,' she said shaking her head. 'If I'd brought along Brendan or Mike even. If I'd taken them with me today, then she just won't open up at all for us.'

'You think she knows about Freddy?'

'She's got to know kid,' she replied. 'Especially after having Vinnie released yesterday. He'll have spilled the beans about Freddy's prints being found. My guess is, he'll be in hiding already. But that's why we need to find out what it is that she knows.'

'Why would she openly stand by someone,' said Rachel, 'who she knew was involve...'

'We don't know for sure yet, what he's involved in,' smiled Hunter winking. She appeared to have already judged him on the basis of what Rachel had said the day before. 'Right kid?'

'You're right,' she sighed. 'But I also have to admit that I'm still being pulled in two different directions over what I think to the two of them being involved. I mean Vinnie was arrogant and obnoxious enough. He's got the sexual motivation. Marshall also has the sexual motivation, even if that charge was overturned against him. And this guy certainly is violent enough. You also have Vinnie in that department. But from what I read and what I saw of O'Leary first hand. Something just ain't right at all about the pair of them.'

'But you do reckon, that the two of them have some kind of involvement though?' said Hunter glaring at her. 'Right kid?'

'I honestly couldn't say at this point Hunter.'

'What about your theory on the two of them starting out with the kids though?'

'That still goes, I think,' she shook her head, totally bewildered at her own thoughts. 'I thought it was bad enough when it was two completely separate cases. Also when we thought that they were separate persons, which they very well could still be. But now that everything has collided, my head feels as though it's about to explode at any given moment.'

'It's a pity that when they searched the house the other night. That they didn't find that computer from there,' she said changing the subject, staring at her, as Rachel turned away and gazed out of the window to avoid eye contact. 'I don't suppose that your friend's know where the computer is, do they kid?'

'I have no idea Hunter,' she lied.

'You have seen them though right?'

'I've seen them.'

'Good, because I want the three of them...'

'Then you'll have to arrest them then Hunter,' said Rachel. 'Because I'm telling you now, they won't be coming in for questioning.'

'They'll have to kid,' she said. 'It's the la...'

'Then you go and explain that to them,' Rachel told her, staring straight back at her.

'But we need to question the young lad,' she added looking none too pleased with what Rachel had just told her.

'I don't know where he is Hunter,' she told her truthfully, as she witnessed the rage bubble over in Hunter's face.

'What the fuck you mean, that you don't know where he is kid?' she screamed at her. 'I only them go that night because of you and your promis...'

'I didn't make you any promises Hunter,' she said in a demeanour fashion. 'You just presumed that they would stick around for you.'

'Where the hell have they got the boy?'

'I honestly don't know,' she replied. 'And to be quite truthful, I don't want to know where he is Hunter.'

'This is outrageous kid,' she sighed. 'He is the material witness in one of our murders. He could very well be the one we need to convict on the grounds of whatever he saw that night. We need to see...'

'You won't find him,' she said cutting her off. 'He's long gone from this area.'

'I can't believe that you let them take...'

'One,' said Rachel holding a finger up. 'I didn't let them do shit, I'm not there keeper's. If they choose, as they did do, to bail the boy away safety, then that is down to them. And Two,' she

held another finger up. 'As Sleeper quite rightly put it Hunter. You lot haven't exactly been too successful in the protection department. Or even for that matter, in getting close to this freak yet. Have you now?'

'That's a little below the belt kid.'

'Is it?' she shrugged. 'I don't think so. And neither did they. Sleeper says and I believe him when he says it. But he says that the boy will be better protected where he's got him stashed away.'

'So he's going to go after this Gabriel himself now,' said Hunter. 'Is that it? Is that what's going to happen now kid. You and your little band of vigilant...'

'Give it a rest,' she said, sighing deeply, before continuing 'will you Hunter.'

'But...'

'I don't know what he's going to do,' she lied once again, and didn't feel any guilt about it whosoever. 'The only thing that I do know is that he helped me, and now his sister has been killed because of it. And not only that, but that poor lad has been left without a natural mother. And why? All because he agreed to help me with my problem. So you see Hunter, where he's concerned, you'll get jack shit from me.'

They didn't speak for several minutes as Hunter silently headed towards Heaton Park in Whitefield. Rachel thought about Sleeper and couldn't rid the anguish that burned deep inside of her. If only they hadn't met. If only he hadn't agreed to help her. If only she hadn't agreed. If only... if only... if fucking only, she thought to herself.

'Freddy's a strong suspect here kid,' said Hunter suddenly breaking the silence inside of the vehicle, that could have been cut with a knife moments before. 'He's got all the trademarks listed. He's got the previous in the right areas. He's definitely got the connections. And if you are correct about the fact that the two of them are involved, then he has the help right there.'

'What about his motivation for committing the crimes though?' she sighed deeply.

'The lawyers for Christ sake,' she said. 'They've either fucked him or freed him. He either hates them or loves them.'

'What with the way he's...'

'Look,' said Hunter. 'All we know for certain, is that at some point Freddy has been in that house. Now the print lab said that it was definitely a recent print that had been left behind.'

'I'm still not convinced Hunter.'

419

'I don't know what it is that you're expecting kid,' said Hunter. 'Not everything requires complicated reasoning for what has taken place.'

'I know that,' she nodded. 'But the mere nature of these crimes committed has taken a creative level of planning meticulously. This is not only premeditated murder that we're talking about here. Whoever the real killer is here, has his own reasons for committing these murders. And those reasons must relate in some way to...'

'Look kid,' sighed Hunter as she over took the vehicle in front of them. 'Maybe you're just looking too deeply into this thing. Because of how personal the case is to you. Maybe that's clouded your perspective somewhat.'

'So what the fuck, have you got me riding along with you for then?'

'Because you're still the best that I know kid,' she smiled. 'Clouded perspective or not, I have every confidence that you'll be able to help me crack this thing wide open. And today's a perfect opportunity for us to start with. This is it, it's that one there,' she added pointing the semi-detached house in the quiet street they'd just parked in.

'Nobody appears to be home,' said Rachel as she watched Hunter bang away at the front door. Looking around herself, Rachel observed the quiet street. It was obviously a street with a lot of employment, as there didn't appear to be anybody else around. Hunter began looking through the windows, doing her best to see through the reflection. Rachel shook her head at her friend's lack of respect for other people's privacy.

'The TV set is on kid,' she told her.

'So maybe she left it when she went out,' she replied. 'Or maybe you should call for back up. Because it could be Marshall that's not answering the door Hunter.'

'Let's try around the back of the house,' suggested Hunter, as Rachel blew warm air into her hands.

As they made their way around the house, Rachel couldn't believe how quiet it was in the street. Apart from a few birds that still hadn't flown south, chirping merrily, she literally could hear any other noise. Approaching the back of the house, Rachel noticed the nicely kept garden that was frozen over with a layer of frost. For some strange reason, she found herself wondering whether or not it was Claire Harrison that looked after the up keep. She very much doubted it was Freddy Marshall, that's if he even resided here at this address with her.

'Looks like someone forgot to shut the door,' said Hunter, who was already pulling plastic gloves over her hands as the silence was broken by the low hum of the television set filtering through to them outside..

'What you doing?' asked Rachel, as steam rose from her mouth. 'What are you giving me those for Hunter?' she asked, as Hunter handed her a pair of the gloves.

'We're going to take a look,' she replied. 'What do you think we're going to do?'

'Call for some assitance Hunter,' said Rachel suddenly getting a bad feeling about entering the house. 'Something ain't right here, call it in first.'

'What for?' she asked. 'We don't even know if there is anything wrong here. Let's just take us a quick pee...'

'What if he's in there though Hunter?' Rachel went off her gut instinct and it told her that it was a mistake to enter the house. 'Please Hunter.'

'You stay here if you like kid,' she said pushing the door open further still. 'And if Fingers is here. Then we'll issue him with his warrant,' she smiled.

'Hunter...'

But she'd already gone through the door. 'Hello... hello... is anybody home?' She called out as Rachel followed her through the door shaking her head at her back.

'Doesn't seem like anybody is here,' she said without turning around.

'Let's go then,' pushed Rachel.

'Let's just take a quick look around first eh kid,' she said heading through the kitchen into the living room. Rachel took in her surroundings. The house was very contemporary. However everything looked like it come straight out of an Ikea catalogue. The house was bright and filled with modern colours, right through from the abstract paintings on the wall to the vase's to the crockery.

The living room was done out exactly the same as the kitchen, colour wise at least. But despite its colourful and warm appearance, Rachel shivered for some unknown reason. There was something in extreme contrast to what she was staring at right now. She wasn't sure what it was, but whatever awaited them, she was sure that it would only be made up of a dark crimson colouring. 'Come on Hunter,' said Rachel. 'Just call...'

'Just a quick look upstairs kid,' she cut her off, as she made a bee line for the stairs, with Rachel reluctantly following her.

As soon as they reached the top of the stairs Rachel saw that there was no light coming from the back bedroom. Breathing deeply as Hunter pushed the door open slowly; she smelt the stench of death before she'd even crossed the threshold into the room.

'Oh fuck,' cried Hunter as Rachel followed her into the room.

'Jesus,' sighed Rachel, for before them was Gabriel's prevailing conception.

Strapped completely naked against the wardrobe was the woman they had seen the day before. Bloodied white sheets hung elaborately behind the victim, just like the trademark wings that had become Gabriel's symbol at the ever mounting crime scenes. Pinned or nailed to the ceiling were the sheets. The torn open torso of the victim against its white back drop extended effulgently the full horrors of his latest creation. There was similar scrawling that Rachel had witnessed at Sleeper's sister's home. She made a mental note of what they said as she stepped closer to the victim.

'He's done it again,' she said.

'You can say that again,' sighed Hunter flipping her mobile phone open.

'No,' said Rachel glancing round at her as she pointed to the open chest. 'He's left the heart once again.'

'What's it mean though kid?'

'I've no idea,' she replied shaking her head as she had to cover her nose from the stench rising from within the corpse. 'But believe me; it bares some relevance to why he no longer feels he's making a trade with these two victims.'

'Well,' said Hunter holding her nose and mouth with her hand as she awaited somebody to answer on the other end of the line. 'I'd say that Freddy has just hit the top spot of our suspect's list.'

Rachel merely nodded her response, thinking that she still wasn't one-hundred percent, that Freddy was their guy. No matter what evidence proved contrary to her beliefs before her, as she continued to examine the body in detail.

FORTY FOUR

'**J**esus Rachel!' exclaimed Tony, walking through into her living room with Sleeper and Eazy trailing in behind him. They had just arrived at her apartment in Salford after eating dinner at Chan's home with him and his wife. Chan's wife Ling had made a fuss over Sleeper. Although it was true to say that they were all worried about him after what he'd gone through. Tony knew better than most what could happen, after all, he witnessed it first hand with his sister. So because of that, he was intent on staying as close as possible to his new friend.

But none of them expected this at the apartment. Rachel had transformed her living room into what looked like one of the investigative rooms to be found at head quarters in the city centre. She had filled every available wall space with crime scene photographs and theory's she had come up with. Her printer appeared to be continually churning out further material that they presumed she required.

She perceived the look on the faces of the others, and knew instantly that they wondered seriously about her sanity at this present moment. But she had a plan, and wanted to test the theory out on the three around her before she took it any further. She wasn't even completely sure, whether or not she was heading in the right direction with this thing. All she knew for certain after today, was their approach so far had not come up anything solid, apart from one hell of a lot of speculation.

Now she had to take another look at the case, only from new angles that she hadn't tried before. She smiled at them pleasantly, just to let them know that she hadn't completely lost the plot.

'We've just heard about the other victim over the radio,' said Sleeper as he began looking closely at the photographs covering the walls, whilst shaking his head.

'It was another lawyer,' commented Eazy, sitting himself at the bureau as he began looking through what was being printed out. 'Right Rachel?'

'Yes,' she nodded. 'You are right Eazy. I was there, when Hunter discovered the body this afternoon. The killer had struck in the early hours of this morning.'

'What the hell were you doing there?' asked Tony glaring at her.

'I didn't think that you were going to help them any more Rachel,' said Sleeper eyeing her carefully.

'I'm not,' she protested. 'But I think that you better sit yourselves down and listen to what I have to say.'

'What's with all this stuff?' asked Eazy, as Tony and Sleeper moved the paperwork from the sofa to make room for themselves.

'Yeah,' said Tony placing the file he'd just picked up and placed it on the coffee table with all the other items Rachel had stacked there. 'What the hell are you surrounding yourself with these nightmares for?' He signalled to the pictures.

'I'm already surrounded by the nightmares,' said Rachel lighting a cigarette and wondering just how many of the damn things she'd smoked that day. From the coppery taste within her mouth, she figured she had to gotten through at least two packs that day alone.

'So how come you had to go with that woman?' asked Sleeper, as she immediately caught onto the fact that he'd not used her name.

'The victim today was Claire Harrison,' she told them, pulling deeply on the cigarette as though her life depended on the stick of nicotine that was probably killing her slowly.

'Who was she then? The radio didn't mention any children. Was there?' asked Tony as he bowed his head in sorrow for yet another victim.

'No, there were no children, Thank god. But you're not going to believe this,' she said looking at each of them to make sure they were listening. 'But she was the brief that   let loose O'Leary yesterday morning.'

'She's O'Leary's brief?' questioned Sleeper.

'But that's not the reason that we went over there this afternoon.'

'What was it then?' asked Eazy, still looking through all of the information from the internet that she'd discovered.

'She was also the brief... that had the conviction against Freddy Marshall over turned,' she told them as she saw the looks of recognition on their faces. 'She was the one that had the man freed on his rape charges. Also the charges against him were dropped in relation to him blinding that poor girl.'

'No shit,' said Sleeper. 'What's wrong with this guy? Why has this prick got it in for...'

'No, wait a minute,' she said. 'That's not all of it. You'll never guess who his girlfriend also was.'

'Who?' asked Tony.

'Claire Harrison.'

'The same woman,' said Sleeper shaking his head at the news.

'Jesus,' said Tony shaking his head. 'What was wrong with her? I mean what the fuck did she see in Fingers?'

'So this is open and shut now,' said Eazy. 'Right Rach? It's got to be this guy right, has to be.'

'I know this will sound crazy,' she sighed. 'But... I still ain't convinced yet.'

'You've got to be though Rachel,' said Sleeper staring at her.

'That's what this all is about,' she told them. 'I tell you, I've not only missed something along the way. But I've also got to work out, why he's now leaving the hearts behind.'

'He didn't take the heart again?' asked Tony as she shook her head.

'So what does all that mean though?' asked Sleeper.

'That's what I'm trying my best to figure out,' she replied. 'I'll get to a theory of mine in a minute. I want to know your reaction to what I've come up with. It may be nothing but...'

'Try us out then,' said Sleeper.

'First things first though,' she said. 'Did you manage to see the O'Leary's?'

'Yeah,' said Tony. 'The old man demanded that we leave after we told him about the website.'

'So he didn't know?' she asked.

'Not from what we could make out,' said Sleeper. 'Vincent knows a hell of a lot more than he's letting on though – that's for sure Rachel.'

'So what are you going to do then?'

'We're going to go back over that way,' he replied. 'Tony says that he doesn't usually head out until later on at night. So we figure we'll follow him and see where it takes us.'

'Did you question him on the Cartwright's?'

'He knew them alright,' said Tony.

'Yeah definitely,' agreed Sleeper. 'The boy would be no good in a poker game. Because he says that he didn't. But it was written all over his face.'

'Also when we questioned him to the whereabouts of Freddy,' said Tony. 'He said that he no longer works for him. Said it had been pure time since he last saw him.'

'But the old man gave him straight away on that score,' added Sleeper.

'How so?' asked Rachel.

'Because as soon as Vinnie denied seeing him for a while,' said Tony. 'The old man looked at him inquisitively. I just knew from the way he looked, that he'd definitely been in contact with him recently.'

'The old man then tried to cover it up with questions about what we wanted with him.'

'What did you tell him?'

'The truth,' said Sleeper. 'That his print was found at the house where my sister was killed.'

'What did he say to that?'

'Just that it wasn't incriminating enough for us to then blame Vinnie,' said Tony.

'It isn't. Yet that is,' she replied. 'What we need to do is we need to gain access to your sister's computer to see what she had found out Sleeper.'

'We've got to go and see Robert tonight,' he replied. 'We figured we'd drop in on him after we've checked Vinnie out.'

'So what else was said at the house?' asked Rachel.

'I kinda felt sorry for old Dominic in the end,' said Tony sighing deeply.

'Why?'

'Because the poor old sod has tried to do right by his son,' he sighed. 'And all that little twat has done, is throw it right back in the old mans face.'

'You should have seen the look on his face, when we told him that we knew about the cover ups that had taken place concerning Vinnie,' said Sleeper. 'I thought that the old bastard was going to start crying on us.'

'The look of disgrace was written so clearly over his face,' said Tony. 'He hated the fact that we had knowledge of what his son had done. He also knows what it'll do to his reputation if word gets out, rather than it remaining merely a rumour.'

'What did he say about it?'

'He denied it of course,' said Tony.

'Got himself into quite a fluster about the whole thing though,' added Sleeper.

'What about the old man?'

'Just wanted to know, how it was that we knew,' said Sleeper.

'But from the look of him,' said Tony. 'I'd say that it wasn't the first or last time that he'd had to bail his son out of trouble for that kind of behaviour.'

'That little fuck certainly has a lot to answer for,' said Sleeper.

'It turns my stomach to think that I've known him for so long. Even if I hated the little prick,' said Tony shaking his head. 'But I've really known him, if you know what I mean.'

'So what happens now?' asked Rachel. 'I mean if he doesn't lead you all anywhere.'

'Then we'll just have to pay him another visit,' said Sleeper.

'And this time,' said Eazy. 'I'm definitely coming along. I don't give a shit what this fucker will think when he sees me knocking at his door.'

They all smiled at him as he looked to Rachel and asked. 'What's all this mean Rachel?' he asked her holding out one of the many sheets that still refused to stop printing off from the machine.

'It's another theory that I've come up with, Eazy,' she told him, whilst looking at the others. 'I just want to sort through that lot to see where he getting most of his information from.'

'How do you mean?' asked Sleeper.

'A few things that have been said recently, I'd not picked up on.'

'Like what?' asked Tony.

'Stuff to do with the internet,' she said. 'Things about how much stuff you can actually find on there these days. Also the way he baffled forensics. Like Sleeper said, you need to have prior knowledge of forensic procedures if you're going to do any kind of a job successfully. The internet is crammed full with all of this kind of thing.'

'You're kidding,' said Tony.

'I swear I never realised just how easy it was to access so much information from it,' she said. 'All the paedophile set ups got me thinking about how big this whole thing has become. So I started surfing through... as they say, just to see exactly what, say, our killer has also surfed his way through.'

'You reckon that this is where he's got most of this kind of thing from Rachel?' asked Eazy holding a couple of the sheets containing information on the archangel Gabriel.

'I think he's fucking with us big time,' she said taking some of the sheets from Eazy and glancing at them as the others glanced at one another not understanding.

'How so?' asked Sleeper.

'Like I said,' she told him. 'He left the heart once again. But that's not all. It was something that Hunter said today, that got me thinking also.'

'What was that?' asked Tony.

'That maybe we looked too deeply into this thing,' she told him. 'But maybe that's exactly what he wanted in the first place. And who better to drag into this mess in the first place... but me.'

'Eh!' exclaimed Eazy.

'You mean that by dragging you into this in the first place,' said Sleeper understanding. 'That he knew, because of the nature of your work as a criminal psychologist, you would give him the acclaim that he wanted.'

'Yes, I reckon so. But that's only part of it though,' she nodded. 'I think that my family were supposed to have been the only ones looking back on it. I mean I would have profiled the killer as definitely striking out again – just like Brendan also suggested. The whole thing had it written all over it. But what if that wasn't the plan at all. I mean I've never been able to work out why it took him a year to strike again. And following the time lapse of one year, we've been hit four more times within such a short space of time. Why not do this in the first place? Last year when he killed my Peter and Becky, I mean why wait a whole year and then go completely off the rails and slaughter so many people in such a short amount of time.'

'I don't follow,' said Eazy.

'Maybe he's got himself him a little taste for this kind of thing now,' suggested Sleeper.

'I think you're definitely right there Sleeper. It's also part of why I think he's taking it to the next level like he has. Let me explain first, a little about what he wants us to believe him to be,' she said lighting yet another cigarette. 'Gabriel in the bible is forever the angel of mercy which doesn't match our guy. I mean Michael was the angel of judgement. Michael apparently took Gabriel under his wing as they fell from grace. So the angel of mercy is not all that Gabriel has become known for. He is the archangel of annunciation, humanity, heavenly mercy to name but a few, but he's also one of the two top ranking angels of vengeance, death, revelation, truth and hope.'

'Who was Michael?' asked Eazy.

Rachel spent the next half hour going over what she had with Hunter, Brendan and Mike Andrews just after the slaying of the Morgan's. Subjects such as Enoch, The Apocrypha and Peeudepigrapha of the Old Testament that the killer had copied parts of, from different scriptures. She discussed the Watchers, explaining that they were angels. She explained how Michael was one of the seven angels' under Satan's rule. She went on to explain about the different groups of angels and which each represented. Finishing with how the killer wanted them to believe that he was carrying out Satan's work under the watchful eye of Michael. By the time she'd finished she could clearly see that they had no idea what it was she was talking about, so she smiled at them and gave out a little laugh.

'What's all this mean though?' asked Sleeper obviously unamused.

Rachel grabbed a handful of the papers from Eazy. 'This, this is what I'm on about,' she laughed waving the papers around. 'Alright, look. From just reading what I have here. He was also considered to be the angel of communication.'

'So what's he trying to communicate to us Rachel?' asked Eazy. 'That he likes the part about being the angel of vengeance and death over the other ones he's apparently renowned for.'

'Quite possibly, yes.'

'I still don't fol...' began Tony.

'He was considered to be the angel of prophecy as well,' she told them. 'He apparently is the angel who told Mary of the saviour. He was also apparently the angel involved in the destruction of Sodom and Gommorah from Paradise Lost. Enoch says that it was Gabriel who was sent to destroy the giant children of the fallen watchers. And he did this by turning them against one another.'

'You think that he considers the victims to be these giant children?' asked Sleeper. 'The children of the watchers as you put it.'

'I think that Gabriel has two lists of victims picked out,' she told him. 'And to answer your question, yes. I do believe that he holds certain beliefs that these victims are the one he should bring vengeance upon. But only because it's what he's read up on. Because there is something a lot more personal about the first lot of victims, my Peter and Becky. Because not only did it then take a year for him to strike again. But he also kept the same pattern. The taking of the hearts with the trade made with him leaving the doves in their place.'

'Why hasn't he left the doves behind the last two times?' asked Tony.

'Because I don't believe that they were part of his plan,' she said. 'Before, there was scriptures scrawled on the walls like I've told you, all baring reference to words like Rekulla for instance, which meant trade. As in he traded the doves for the hearts he's taken.

'But today and the other night I noticed the word dishonest,' she said. 'Now at first I wasn't sure what it referred to. But it's from a passage *"by your many sins and dishonest trade you have desecrated you sanctuaries"*. The word Nachash also appeared. Now that refers to the Hebrew term *"to shine"* or *"to glow"*. Which I believed meant it was how Gabriel perceived himself. But you see the mistake that Satan made, was, by showing God the flaws of the humans; he also revealed his own short comings. This resulted in God placing an age lasting animosity between mankind and Satan. But you see from that point forward *"the shining one"* became *"the adversary"*.'

'This is weird,' responded Eazy.

'Dei gar auton basileuein achri hou the panyas tous echthrous hupo tous podas autou,' she said with more than a little difficulty, as she observed their bewildered faces, smiling at them, this was exactly what she had in mind.

'What the fuck does that mean?' asked Sleeper.

'It's Greek text, something else that he scrawled onto the walls,' she told them smiling. 'It means *"For He must be reigning until He should be placing all His enemies under his feet."* You follow me so far?'

'Not at all,' said Sleeper.

'Eazy?' she asked looking to him as he shrugged that he didn't know.

'What about you Tony?' she smiled at him as he shook his head.

'Exactly,' she laughed crazily.

'What the fuck...' said Sleeper staring at her like she was completely deranged.

'Like I said before, he's fucking with us,' she pointed to the first three lots of murders. 'They all appear to be very clever. They all appear to have a very clever motive. All the scriptures scrawled on the wall. All the biblical references. It's exactly what he wanted us to believe... It's the very reason he's fucking with my head so much. Don't you see it? Yes, very clever, but only in the fact that it's confused the fuck out of all of us since he first killed my husband and daughter.' She was ranting on as

she paced back and forth waving papers in her hands around, as they were all looking at her, like she'd utterly lost it.

'So your theory is?' asked Sleeper totally confused.

'You still don't see it?' she asked him cocking an eye brow as he shook his head at her.

'Neither do I,' said Tony.

'You know where he's fucked up?' she asked.

'Where?' Tony asked totally perplexed.

'The last two murders were not so clever. Oh yes, don't get me wrong. They had all the trademarks of his last murders. The wings portrayed upon the wall. The scriptures, although he used different ones this time around. He's still trying to make us believe what he wants us to believe so, so much. That he is this archangel.'

'I don't see what was so different though,' said Sleeper. 'Not looking at these photo's Rachel.'

'This time around, it was about simple slaying because he considered the victims to have become a liability to him,' she said. 'As in Sleeper's sister was investigating him, so he killed her. The same with Harrison this morning. Not that she was investigating him, but she may have been too close to him. Especially if it is Freddy Fuckfingers. But even if it's not him, maybe Freddy knows something that the real killer was worried about. He's wiping out the people he's now considering to be a liability.'

'And that's why he's not taking their hearts?' asked Sleeper.

'Right,' she nodded. 'He's not taken their hearts because it's personal to him. He's made it clear that he's not sticking to any previous game plan that he had before. He's taking this to the next level. This is frightening, but is also good for us. Because it is where he'll make the mistakes. Believe me on that score,' she said. 'This son of a bitch is basically just out there enjoying himself at our expense. All that I'm certain of right now is if we don't stop this guy soon then he's going to just keep on killing and killing. The power of taking anothers life seems to overpower his real reasons he set out with in the beginning. But that's where he'll fuck up.'

'We ain't got the luxury of time to let him continue to do that though Rachel,' said Sleeper.

'I know we haven't,' she sighed. 'That's why I needed to work through all of this information right here.'

'You really believe that?' asked Sleeper. 'You really think the answers lie within all of this here in this room.'

431

'Yes I do,' she replied. 'Like Hunter said. Sometimes you can just look too deeply into things. And I've realised that's where I've been going wrong with this case. I need to sort through all this crap, take it right back down to the basic structure. He killed my husband and my child. But why?'

'That's what all want to know,' sighed Tony.

'Exactly,' she said. 'We need to work out why the victims have been picked, just like we've worked out the reason he killed the last two. At least there, we can see his true motive. But with the others, the clues lay with them. Not with the reason why he's killing the way he is. We've concentrated on that subject for too long. In fact I believe that we played right into his hands with it.'

'So what are we going to do now then Rachel?' asked Sleeper.

'I'm going to strip this thing bare and start again,' she said. 'I need to look at it all again without the archangel part distracting me along the way. I need to rework it, adding the Cartwright's, O'Leary, Freddy and even the Pied Piper. They may have nothing to do with one another. There may not be a connection at all there. But at the moment there are way too many coincidences for my liking.'

'You honestly think that he's doing all of the elaborate scenes to merely confuse you all?' asked Eazy.

'I think that he fed off the media hype surrounding the situation for a whole year,' she said. 'He had a plan to begin with. But maybe that plan ended with Peter and Becky. Maybe he figured I would make him notorious without having to kill again. I'm not entirely sure. But that's what I need to figure out. I'm not denying that the archangel bit, Gabriel as he wants the world to know him, plays a part in his conjunctive way of thinking. Because obviously it does. But what he's achieved far greater, than I imagine even he imagined, is that we've been running around in circles trying to fathom out the archangel part.'

'So you reckon that he's now just using the whole thing as an excuse to just kill whoever he pleases?' asked Sleeper not looking convinced.

'Yes and no,' she replied. 'You see, I think that he gets such an intense thrill from the actual murders now, that yes, he's killing whoever he feels is a threat. Whether it's personal to him or not. But also no, because I don't honestly believe it was to stop with the Morgan's. Not once he started killing a year later. He has a plan hatched. But he's getting off on the notoriety of managing to evade us like he is. The thrill of evading us, mixed with the sexual exhilaration he gets from both raping and killing his victims probably leaves him as hard as a Louisville baseball bat.'

432

'What!' exclaimed Sleeper.

'Sorry, I didn't mean that to sound the way it did Sleeper.'

'So what about this Freddy Marshall then?' asked Eazy.

'You reckon that he's the one or not Rachel?' asked Sleeper.

'I couldn't answer that honestly,' she replied. 'I need to spend time breaking all of this down and then I need to seriously start again with it.'

'Then we better leave you to it,' said Sleeper pushing himself out of the sofa. 'We'll see what we can kind find out through Vinnie and then we'll report back to you, alright.'

'Alright,' she smiled at all of them as they rose to leave, watching their confused appearances, knowing the questions that roamed throughout their own minds right now.

FORTY FIVE

'**I** thought I'd pop around and see how you are?' said Brendan, more than a little coyly as she opened the front door. He was stood there, wearing a Berghaus navy fleece that was zipped to the neck as his long dark curls hung loosely around his face and shoulder. Wearing a simple pair of old jeans and a pair of Timberland boots, made him seem all that more rugged. In fact the only thing that looked out of place with him was the two bottles, one red, and the other white wine he was holding, from the way he dressed; she would have imaged climbing ropes instead of the wine. The thought made her smile at him.

'What's with the grin? He asked her.

'Nothing,' she laughed. 'Nothing at all, come in.'

'Thanks,' he looked at her questionably.

'What can I do for you?'

'I thought that maybe you could use a little company tonight,' he told her smiling, as she found herself becoming lost in his smile once again. 'No talking shop though, just a nice drink and to talk about anything but the damn case.'

'Sounds alright,' she replied, wondering what the hell she was doing. 'But my living room is kind of a mess right now.'

'How so?' he asked as he stepped through into it. 'Oh!'

'I know what you're thinking,' she sighed. 'But...'

'But nothing,' he smiled, although it was clear in his clear blue eyes that he was also questioning her sanity, along with the others who hadn't long since left her to do her work. 'Have you eaten yet Rachel?'

'I don't feel like going...'

'Well what have you got in your fridge then?' He was already making his way through there, before she had time to answer. Placing the bottle's of wine on the side board he opened the

434

refrigerator and peered inside. 'Now let's see, why don't you make yourself useful and open the wine,' he said without turning as she laughed.

'I don't think that you're gonna find much in there,' she said. 'But I'll open the wine anyway Brendan.'

'Oh I don't know,' he turned his head and smiled at her. 'I'm the master at making something from nothing. I have to be, as my fridge, usually has less in there than this one does.'

'Why don't we just drink the wine,' suggested Rachel, not at all hopeful of him finding anything edible enough in the fridge.

'You must be joking,' he replied as he held up a half pack of chicken breasts and tub of sour cream. 'When was the last time that you ate?'

'I can't remember to tell you the truth,' she shook her head.

'There you go then,' he smiled at her as he removed his fleece. He was wearing a simple plain white tee-shirt, which looked as though he'd shrunken it in the dryer, not that Rachel was complaining, as it clung to his upper torso dramatically.

Rachel couldn't help but stare at his body, which looked fantastic through the tight tee-shirt. Every line and tone showed through his top, and she had never realised that he had such a good body before. Whenever she had seen him before, he'd always been wearing a suit of some kind. She liked the look of him, and it took her just about all of her self will to stop herself from getting up and ripping that tee-shirt straight off his back.

The thought made Rachel feel wicked, as she shook her head to clear away any further conviction. She gave a little chuckle, thinking that, what she really needed was a cold shower, not the simple shake of the head.

'Let's see what else you got in here,' he said rooting through cupboards, oblivious to Rachel's staring at him. 'You've not opened that wine yet?'

'Sorry,' she replied, taking the bottle of wine and sitting at the old pine table, opening the bottle of Sauvignon Blanc. 'There, pass the glasses would you please. They are in the top one there,' she said pointing to the cupboards.

'There you go,' he said handing two long stemmed glasses that had, had more than their fair share of abuse over the last year, as Rachel comforted herself nightly with bottles of wine, or whatever other alcohol she could lay her hands on.

'What are you doing?' she asked cocking an eyebrow at her as he smiled. 'What are you smiling at now?'

'It's they way both you and Hunter do that with your eyebrows,' he laughed. 'You know, neither of you have to say a word when you do that. It just about says it all really.'

'I'm glad that it amuses you,' she told him.

'It's not an insult,' he said seriously thinking he'd offended her. 'I think that it's very attractive actually. It gives you a lot of character.'

She felt herself blushing as he continued to gaze at her. 'What you cooking then?' she quickly asked to change the subject, feeling extremely embarrassed by the fact he'd said that he found some part of her attractive.

'Well I found this,' he said holding a jar of tarragon herbs, 'and this,' he added holding a packet of brown rice.

'And the culinary delight that you plan on making is...'

'Why, chicken in tarragon sauce with fresh, well kinda of fresh anyway, but these mushrooms here,' he laughed. 'I think it was a good job that I came around to use this stuff up. It's all border line, but I think we'll get by... just.'

'Sounds delicious,' she admitted as she suddenly felt the hunger take a grip of her stomach.

'I'm also going to make you my special rice,' he told her smirking.

'Which is?'

'I'll do my best to make sure that it doesn't stick to the pan,' he laughed. 'If I manage that, then it's my special rice.'

'Nice,' she smiled, liking his sense of humour, liking him, to be perfectly honest about.

'You just sit back and relax,' he said. 'Whilst I prepare everything.'

'Sounds good to me,' she replied as she sipped the wine. 'This is real good, very nice indeed.'

'You better give me a glass then,' he said holding out his hand as she passed him the glass. His fingers lightly touched her hand at the same time, and she swore it felt like an electric current running straight through her, as she pulled away.

'Thanks,' he said sipping the wine as he began chopping the onions and mushrooms, expertly crushing the garlic in one go, before moving onto the chicken. She was impressed with his apparent ease around the kitchen. She found herself thinking about how Peter fumbled about without any ease at all, and the thought of her late husband whilst another man was stood in the kitchen, made the guilt return.

'I think you've done this before,' she told him to keep the conversation going.

'I told you,' he said as the onions began to sizzle in the butter. Dropping the pieces of sliced chicken in next, sealing them quickly as the mushrooms followed. Next he added the cream along with some of the white wine and chicken stock he'd found in the cupboard. Finally, the tarragon herb itself was thrown in with the other ingredients. All very quickly done, as he then lowered the heat and turned towards her. 'I told you that I'm the master of making something out of nothing.'

'I think I believe you,' she told him as he sat opposite her.

'So what about Claire Har...'

'No talking shop,' he shook his head at her. 'Tell me something about yourself.'

'Like what?' she shrugged.

'I don't know,' he replied sipping the wine. 'How about your childhood?'

'What is there to tell,' she said, wondering if he knew anything of her past. Worried of how he would judge her if she told him all about her family background. But then also deciding, what the hell, they either accept you for you are or they don't. 'Alright then, but you better make yourself comfortable.'

'I already am,' he replied with utter ease.

'I grew up not to far from here,' she began. 'This was a long time ago, before they put all of this cash into the area. The estate where my family lived and older brother still does, although with the money he's got, I'm not at all sure why. But anyway, it's known as Ordsall. No doubt you've heard of it.'

'I don't think that there are many people, who haven't,' he laughed. 'Must have been tough growing up there.'

'It wasn't as tough as it could have been,' she sighed. 'Not with whom my father was, and then Tony, my brother of course.'

'What happened to your father?' he asked. 'Is he still alive?'

'No, both of parents were killed.'

'I'm sorry.'

'Don't be,' she smiled. 'Believe me, it was a very long time ago. I was only eleven at the time. You see, my father, Thomas Henessey was originally from Belfast. He was a real wild one, which was until he met my mother, who at the time was Katherine Coppershaw. She was so beautiful you know...'

'I can tell, just by looking across the table,' he smiled; as she found herself blush shamelessly again.

'Anyway, my mother calmed old Tommy down,' she laughed. 'Much to the relief of everybody around at the time. Soon after meeting her, Tony arrived into the world and my father started

to, not so much to change his wicked ways. But, well, let's say that he became a lot choosier in his profession...'

'Which was?'

'Armed robberies,' she shook her head. 'And high line burglaries.'

'You serious?' he actually laughed.

'Believe me,' she replied. 'When it comes to my family, I'm always serious.'

'What happened to them Rachel?' he asked in a quiet voice.

'They were both shot to death right outside of their home,' she replied. 'Certain people thought that he was becoming way too big for his own good. He wasn't so much as stepping on other people's toes, as getting under their noses. They knew that Tommy was becoming bigger and stronger as time past. So the best way that they saw fit to end his reign, was to simply kill him.'

'They ever catch the ones respon...'

'I don't know. All that I know for sure is that Tony stepped straight into my father's shoes. Very much to the dismay of others around town I might add,' she cut him off. 'Also, I remember that it was Tony who had to look after me and my other brother.'

'Other brother?'

'Yes, I have two,' she nodded. 'Christopher is my other brother. He's only a few years older than myself. Tony's, ten years older.'

'So he was twenty one when he had to take charge of the family?'

'That's right,' she smiled at the thought of him. 'Although he didn't have to look after Chris for too long. For as soon as he finished school, Chris soon left the family.'

'Why?'

'He didn't want to be part of my brother's world at the time,' she told him. 'So he left for the army as soon as he got out of school. I suppose that became his family of sorts. He did real well for himself. Finally passing the gruelling test at Hereford and achieving his dream...'

'SAS?'

'Yeah,' she said. 'It's funny really, because he then went back to the birth place of my father, Belfast, to help the British fight the IRA.'

'Is he still...'

438

'No,' she replied. 'He was injured whilst out there. To cut a long story short, he was asked to leave on medical grounds. Broke his heart to do so.'

'So where is he now?'

'Hong Kong.'

'Why there?'

'You're not going to believe this when I tell you,' she laughed. 'You know who my older brother is, right?'

'Of course,' he nodded. 'Not that I ever judged him thoug...'

'My brother Chris is a police inspector out in Hong Kong,' she laughed. 'I'm real proud of him,' she added.

'I bet your Tony ain't though,' he smiled. 'Right?'

'Oh I don't know,' she said. 'I think that it was hard at first to come to terms with it. But because they're both as stubborn as one another, they still won't talk to each other. I know for a fact though, that our Tony loves ar'kid to death. Just won't admit it. Prefers the safety net of the world within which he grew up. Why do you think he won't leave that god forsaken estate? It's because it's the only place he still feels safe in.'

'He's quite a character from what Hunter has told me about him,' he told her as he got up and stirred the food and poured the rice into the boiling water.

'He's that alright,' she laughed.

'Hunter seems to like him though,' he said sitting back down at the table. 'She actually seems to have a lot of respect for him.'

'Despite all of his faults,' she answered. 'He's actually one of the fairest guys that you could ever meet. Don't get me wrong here; he ain't no saint, that's for sure. But he's so committed to standing up for what he believes in. Not only that. He'll stand by any friend, like you wouldn't believe. He'll give that person his one-hundred percent.'

'Just like he's giving you his one-hundred percent,' he smiled.

'He's been like a rock for me since last year,' she nodded 'I know it sounds a little cliché. But I seriously don't know what I've have done without him. Going back further than that as well. He's always been there for me. No matter what. No questions asked. He's one of kind. Like when I was going through my teenage years and I'll openly admit I was a nightmare. Always getting into scrapes with other gangs or crews as we used to call them. Even a couple of brushes with the law, believe it or not. But anyway, I started to lose my way on heroin, with the other kids on the estate at the time. He was the one to step in and send me away to college and then university.

He paid my way through, wouldn't let me get a job. Just wanted for me to do well, and so for him that's exactly what I did.'

'Sounds like quite a guy,' said Brendan.

'He's most certainly that.'

'So what about...'

'That's enough on me,' she cut him off. 'So tell me, what about you then?'

'Tell me more about Peter and Becky first,' he said. 'If it's not too painful I mean.'

'You know everything there is to know about them,' she replied.

'Tell me something that I don't know,' he said. 'Only if you want to that is.'

She didn't hesitate, as she thought of her little girl and smiled. 'This used to be our favourite time of the year,' she smiled as memories flooded back. 'Mine and Becky's anyway. We used to love going to Alderley Edge together on a Saturday afternoon. We'd spend all day there. It's so beautiful at this time of the year. All the different shades of auburn and gold shimmering magically. Becky used to love all the caves that are there. She was always climbing deeper and further than I could ever get. She used to worry me so much. But she was so fearless, for such a young innocent child.'

'Did Peter used to go with you?'

'Now and then,' she sighed. 'He was always so busy. He never had time for anything but work. He was obsessed with his job. I used to admire that at first. But towards the en... well anyway. I mean don't get me wrong, he did spend time with us. He absolutely adored and loved Becky unconditionally. But towards the end, we just became so distant. I not really sure why. I suppose we were both victims of our own jobs.'

'But you always made the time for Becky,' he reminded her.

'I did,' she smiled. 'I miss her so much. It's as if I've lost a piece of me. And no matter how hard I try to retrieve that piece, I know I never will. I mean I miss Peter also, I just realised how terrible that must have sounded by not mentioning him also.'

'It was a different kind of love that you felt for Becky,' he told her.

'It was,' she admitted. 'I miss him. And I loved Peter dearly for all he was. But the day that my daughter was born and I held her in my arms for the first time. Well that was they day that I realised exactly what the word love actually meant. And yes, I did love Peter. But I suddenly realised that it was a different kind of love. Sounds stupid eh?'

'Not at all,' he answered. 'How was Peter with Tony?'

'Jesus, now that was a complete nightmare,' she replied. 'They hated each other, almost straight away. And believe me, it wasn't just because of what Peter did on Tony's behalf. They were like the original chalk and cheese. I think Peter actually feared that one day he may have to come up against Tony. Not that they would have ever let that happenforthe simple fact that there would have been conflicts of interest. But that didn't matter to Peter. The arguments that we had abou...'

'Did you argue a lot?'

'A hell of a lot towards the end,' she sighed shaking her head as Brendan poured her some more wine. 'But it was only when he was gone that I realised how pathetic and just how sorry I was for all of the arguments. It was such a waste of time. I think that towards the end, I actually began to prefer the time alone that I had.'

'Why did you have time alone?'

'Because he had to work so much,' she told him. 'He continually had to work late into the night. It really strained our marriage. I hardy ever saw him. But when he was killed, I realised just what it was that I had lost.'

'I'm sorry to hear that,' he said. 'I'm also sorry I asked.'

'It's alright,' she smiled. 'I never mind talking about Becky.'

'I'm not surprised,' he told her as he got up and stirred the creamy sauce some more that had reduced and started to thicken.

Rachel sat there in silence thinking about her lost ones as Brendan finished off the dinner for them both without either of them saying a word to one another. The silence, as long as it was, was very comfortable. She liked that immediately. She watched him as he drained off the rice, spooning heaped mounds onto the plates. Then he spooned the delicious smelling chicken and mushrooms in tarragon sauce over the rice. Placing the plate before her, she took in the aroma of the food before her and smiled at him as he sat back down.

'This smells absolutely delicious, Brendan.'

'You better taste it first, girl,' he laughed. 'Before you comment on it.'

Scooping the food into her mouth, she closed her eyes as the chicken literally melted on her tongue. 'Oh god, that is so nice,' she commented. 'Where did you learn to cook? And whilst you're telling me that, perhaps you could tell me a little about yourself.'

'The cooking part,' he smirked at her. 'Well, that came from soon realising when I went away to university, that if I didn't

learn how to cook fast. Then I was going to spend the rest of my life eating beans on toast or pot noodles of course.'

'Chicken and mushroom was always my favourite,' she laughed.

'Mine too,' he laughed along with ease. 'So anyway, what do you want to know about me?'

'Are you married?'

He burst out laughing. 'What?'

'It's a valid question,' she frowned. 'I don't know anything about you at all.'

'No, I'm not married,' he said. 'Came close once. When I was a lot younger that is.'

'What happened?' she asked as she enjoyed both the food and the company. 'Sorry, if you don't me asking you that is?'

'She was killed in a car accident. Well kind of a car accident anyway,' he told her holding eye contact. 'It was a hit and run basically Rachel.'

'Jesus, I'm sorry,' she sighed. 'I shouldn't have asked.'

'It's okay,' he said. 'It was a long time ago now. I was only twenty-three at the time. We attended the same university in Edinburgh. Her name was Sarah Macaleb, we were madly in love. I imagine that it was the kind of love you can only feel at that age. She was returning home to the dormitory late one night, when it happened. I guess since her, I've never found that same feeling that I had with her.'

'And you've never been close to anybody since?' she asked. 'I find that hard to believe.'

'I was already studying clinical psychology,' he told her. 'Her death was what prompted me to study to be a criminal psychologist. I wanted to understand the minds of someone who could basically do something so awful and leave without having any conscience about what they'd done.'

'Did they ever find the one responsible?'

'Never,' he shook his head. 'And every day that I investigate these god awful crimes that are committed, I'm constantly reminded of her.'

'And you've never laid her to rest?' asked Rachel unbelievably.

He suddenly laughed. 'Christ, don't get me wrong,' he told her. 'I ain't no friggin monk Rachel. I see women, of course I do. I've just never felt the need for marriage. I guess I've just never found the right girl.'

Rachel wanted to get off this subject, so asked. 'What about your family,' she smiled. 'Where are they from? Have any brothers or sisters?'

'We're originally from Glasgow. My father left us when we were really young. Immigrated to the States. We never saw or heard from him again.'

'You've never thought to look him up?'

'Nah,' he shrugged. 'He was a pure no good waster from what little I remember of him. He used to knock my mother about something rotten. I think both me and my mother were glad to see the back of him. I think only my older brother missed him. But he would have, because he was just like him.'

'Where's your mother now?' asked Rachel. 'Is she still in Glasgow?'

'No, my mother died just over a couple of years ago from cancer,' he said. 'It was after her death that I travelled down here to Manchester. There was nothing left for me up there. And I was offered the same kind of work that I was helping the police with up there. Besides, I used to travel about a lot. So I wasn't too distressed about upping and leaving.'

'What about your brother though?' she asked. 'Does he still live up there?'

'Like I said, he was just like our father,' he said. 'Frasier was his name, he's someplace, but I don't know, neither do I care to know where he is. He was the black sheep of our family. I suppose he was a little like your Tony without being anywhere near as considerate. Anyway, like I said, I've no idea where he is nowadays. Or if he's even alive for that matter. He never even showed for mum's funeral.'

'I'm sorry to hear that,' she told him honestly. 'Are you not lonely Brendan?'

'I am alone,' he replied. 'But no, I am not lonely.'

She gazed into his eyes for a moment, and saw the sadness he felt for the loss of his mother. 'Let's change the subject eh,' she suggested. 'No more talk of families.'

'Thank god,' he laughed. 'Let's open the other bottle of wine.'

They remained sat at the dinner table whilst they talked over a variety of issues. None relating at all the case. She enjoyed his company immensely and felt at complete ease with him. She enjoyed the subtle flirting that passed between them. There was no denying the fact that she was attracted to him. And she believed that he was to her. In fact they were sat there enjoying one anothers company for that long, that they hadn't even noticed that it had just gone twelve o'clock. Feeling a little awkward at the time and the fact that he was still sat there. Rachel decided that she needed to make an excuse, before things got out of hand.

'I better get these washed,' said Rachel indicating to the plates. 'It's getting late Brendan.'

'I'll give you a hand,' he said.

'No, you cooked,' she told him. 'So I'll wash.'

'Fair enough,' he smiled at her.

As Rachel began running the hot water into the sink her mind spinning in all directions from the wine and also from the simple fact she wanted Brendan, but wouldn't allow herself that pleasure. She suddenly felt his presence behind her. It was then that she suddenly felt his lips brush her temple lightly as he placed his hands around her waist.

She felt just how strong he could be as she finally let herself go. His lips were soft and warm as he moved down to her cheek. Against the weaker part of her will, she gave into temptation and desire and turned to face him. Staring deeply into his blue eyes, she let his lips find hers. They were warm, firm and just wet enough as they kissed passionately, Rachel felt as if, she just found the perfect match for her mouth.

The feeling that raced throughout her, flooding all of her emotions were equal parts, pain and pleasure, bitter and sweet.

He pressed himself against her, as her back pressed in the sink where the hot water still cascaded. She felt the droplets splashing her back as he leaned over and switched the water to cold, whilst all the while they kissed each other, as if their lives depended on it.

Rachel was tearing at the white tee-shirt, just as she had fantasised about earlier. Brendan eased Rachel up and onto the sink itself as he began to fill the vase by the sink, still not relenting from letting her lips away from him, as his tongue searched the inside of her mouth eagerly. He suddenly poured the cold water down the front of Rachel's chest, as she writhed with excitement at the sensation. Pressing his hips between her legs, she could feel just how hard he already was, as she wrapped her legs around him.

Brendan ripped her soaked wet blouse open, as buttons flew in every direction. He had both her breasts cupped in his hands, as the cold water and the cool air hardened her nipples straight away, as he eagerly squeezed and bit at them. It was all becoming too much for Rachel as she fumbled with his belt and zipper.

Reaching in to his jockey shorts, she immediately felt his hard cock in her hands. As she squeezed it hard, she heard him sigh with pleasure, as he bit and sucked at her nipples even harder, as she encouraged him to so. Holding his head against her chest

tightly, as she felt his hands searching her buttons to the front of her jeans. Freeing them open, as he tore them away from her legs. As she lay there semi naked waiting for him.

His fingers suddenly probing her wetness, as he found the exact spot. She squeezed his huge throbbing cock harder and harder, as he teased her with his strong fingers. She began to push his head down, as he willingly kissed her all over before he was between her legs with his eager tongue. She shamelessly wrapped her legs around his head as she poured more water down the front of her. Watching in awe as the water cascaded down her breasts, separating, running down into Brendan's long hair, which she had wrapped in her fingers.

She could feel herself on the brink of coming, as he went down on her hungrily she was pulling his hair so that he'd return to her. He continued to kiss her all over, the sensation of naked flesh against flesh, felt so good, as she grabbed his cock and directed it towards her. As he entered her, she literally screamed with the sheer pleasure she felt.

Picking her off the sink, holding her in his strong arms, as they began to build a rhythm together. Pumping harder and faster as they worked in sync with one another. Brendan had her against the wall as he fucked her like she'd never been fucked before. Harder, faster, as their lips and tongues searched one anothers mouths.

She began to shake, as he pumped her deeper and deeper, when suddenly, it was as if a flash went off in her head, as they both came in sync with one another. Both screaming so loud, as her nails dug into his back so hard, she knew that she had drawn blood. It was the world's best orgasm in her mind. She had never known it could feel so good.

But just as quickly as she felt the gratification, the guilt washed over like a tidal wave, as she broke down into tears. Without saying a word, Brendan scooped her into his arms and carried her through to the bedroom as she continued to cry, both in indulgence and anguish.

Placing her on the bed, he then continued slowly make love to her. And there they stayed, until dawn, both discovering every inch of one another, as they fitted together slowly in perfection.

FORTY SIX

'**W**hat did you make of Rachel tonight?' asked Sleeper, as they sat waiting just down the road from the O'Leary's house in Hale. It had just gone twelve o'clock and they had been sat there for the past three hours waiting for Vinnie to make a move. They knew he was still in there, as Tony had phoned from a land line in Altrincham, as they'd made their way over there. It had been Vinnie who had answered the phone, even though Tony hadn't spoken a word, he could hear panic in the lads voice. 'I mean I know that it's your kid sister Tony. And you don't need to ask how either of us feels about her. Because you already know that.'

'He's right Tony,' added Eazy from the backseat of the vehicle. 'She seemed a little out there brother, you know what we mean?'

'I know exactly what you mean lads,' he sighed. 'But after last year. I've seen her like this before. She wouldn't even remember it herself some of the times, as she was that wasted. She lost herself in drink quite badly, but understandably of course. I'd find her walking around, ranting and raving, as she spurned out ideas and theories. Then the next day she wouldn't even know what the fuck I was going on about. In the end, whenever I found her like that, I just never told her about it the next day.'

'I ain't ever seen her drink that much,' said Sleeper. 'Not whilst she's been with us that is.'

'She still drinks,' he admitted. 'But she managed to calm herself down somewhat. Don't get me wrong lads. She wasn't an alcoholic. But she was heading that way. I stepped in and made sure that she was going to be alright. It's just the way her mind works sometimes lads. You just have to roll with it. Besides, there may be something in all that she said, anyway. She might not be that far off base lads.'

'True,' nodded Eazy. 'Either way, I found all that shit about Archangels and Satan pretty fucking fascinating to say the least. I think that this freak has definitely probably done just about as much research on the subject, as Rachel has.'

'I think that you could be right there brother,' said Sleeper. 'But I also agree with Rachel in some respects.'

'What do you mean?' asked Tony.

'I think this mother fucker is definitely fucking with our heads like you wouldn't believe.'

'What about her theory concerning Vinnie and Freddy?' asked Tony.

'Whoa,' said Eazy. 'Is that the little weasel there?' He was pointing at the dark coloured Lexus that was pulling out from the electronic gates.

'That's him,' nodded Tony.

'Right,' said Sleeper, switching the ignition over, but leaving the headlights off. 'Is he alone Tony?'

'Yeah,' he replied. 'Well from what I can tell that is.'

'Let's see where this little weasel is going, at this time of the night,' said Eazy.

'It might be no where,' admitted Tony.

'Well,' sighed Sleeper as he took off after the dark colour Lexus. 'That's what we're here to find out.'

'So anyway Tony,' said Eazy, as they followed the car through Hale towards Altrincham. 'You never answered me.'

'On what?'

'Vinnie and this Freddy Fuckfingers, as your kid sister called him,' he laughed. 'You reckon that they are involved or what?'

'Vinnie's a dick,' he said with no respect at all for him. 'But Freddy, he's a different breed all together.'

'What do you mean by that?' asked Sleeper, easing the car to a standstill, several behind the Lexus that was by the traffic lights.

'Freddy was always going to be one of the main lads around town. He just had that wild streak in him. Handy fucker too,' Tony told him. 'The only thing was. He didn't have too many mates to back him. But I suppose, that was also the reason he got himself such a reputation. He's around my age. So if you think about it. He should have already made it. But he was just too much of an outsider, so to speak. That's probably the reason why him and Vinnie became such good mates.'

'You think that he's a sex case too?' asked Sleeper.

'I like to say no,' he said shaking his head. 'But now that we know for certain about Vinnie, well, I just couldn't say that with any true conviction.'

'Is he as good at his job, as Rachel's copper mate says he is?' asked Sleeper interested.

'From what I've heard he is,' replied Tony. 'But I also heard that he tends to take the jobs a little too personally.'

'What do you mean by that?' asked Sleeper.

'He freelances for several crews that I know of,' he replied. 'But his main crew is obviously the O'Leary's. But the way I hear it, I don't think even the old man likes Vinnie using him these days.'

'Why?' asked Eazy. 'How did you mean, he gets personal with the jobs?'

'Because he tends to become over involved with the job,' he told him. 'Like this one time that I know of, when he was brought in to take care of this lad from over in Leeds, who was stepping on everybody's toes big time. This lad lived in the Chapel Town area of the city. The lads over that way were more than capable of taking care of the job themselves. But they wanted outside help. Freddy was recommended. The thing was supposed to be a simple hit, nothing fancy. Just kill the guy and get the hell out of dodge.'

'So what happened?' asked Sleeper.

'He kept the guy alive for two days,' he told them. 'In the guy's house as well. Tortured his scared as fuck arse for two days solid. Taking him to the brink of death, and then reviving him. The guys, who gave him the job, loved it when it all came out later on. But a lot of other crews I know won't use him any more.'

'After two days in the house,' said Sleeper looking puzzled. 'They couldn't find any forensic evidence to prove that he did the job? He must be fucking good.'

Tony suddenly laughed. 'They didn't find shit,' he said. 'Because there was no house left for them to find shit in.'

'How do you mean?' asked Eazy.

'He burnt the fucking thing down with the corpse still inside,' he said. 'Whilst the victim was still alive I might add. It was like the final indignity against the lad. The post mortem showed just how badly he'd been tortured after they discovered his body.'

'They never brought him in over it?' asked Eazy.

'Not from what I remember,' he said.

'What do you think then?' asked Sleeper. 'You think that this cat killed my sister or not Tony?'

'I just don't know,' he shook his head. 'It's a good possibility with the way he handles his work. But I just always imagined when we found the killer of Rachel's husband and little Becky...

well... well that it was going to be really deep. You know, like this guy was actually the devil or some shit.'

'I know what you mean there brother,' sighed Eazy. 'I mean this cat, whoever the fuck he is. No matter who he may be, has definitely got to have a few loose rattling about up there.'

'Well, let's see where this little prick takes us then,' said Sleeper.

'Where's he heading towards?' asked Eazy from the back seat as Vinnie passed straight over the roundabout.

'Wilmslow,' replied Tony.

'Who do you reckon lives over there?' asked Sleeper.

'Fuck knows,' he replied. 'It's not all rich kids and footballers that live over that way. There are your proper rum estates as well. Well, two of them at least. I know some right scallies that live over this way. The little fuck could be visiting with any one.'

'You're a good friend with the old man,' said Eazy. 'So what with all the animosity between the two of you?'

Sleeper glanced at Tony as they both smirked. 'It's a long story,' replied Tony. 'But basically it has to do with when old man O'Leary was banged up. Little Vinnie decided that, it was going to be his time y'know, to make a name for himself.'

'So what happened?' asked Eazy.

'Going back about five years or so,' began Tony. 'I used to still run a fair bit of the charley that was being knocked out that I was bringing into the country whilst based in Spain. I used to work closely with a lad known as Batty from Wythenshawe. Proper top lad...'

'I know him,' added Sleeper, as they entered the long tunnel that ran directly beneath Manchester Airport's runway, as the blue and yellow lights flashed by in succession leading to bright white lights, as they sped through the tunnel at speed. 'He was good friends with Prey... Chopper more I think.'

'Yeah,' replied Tony. 'It used to be Sean Macreedy that dealt with him. That was until Prey had Chopper put in charge of that side of things from what I remember. Back then Batty used to be able to clear any amount of gear that you could throw at him. He was also one of town's leading ticket touts. All the big United Matches, season tickets included. Used to love ripping off the Red's fans cause' he was a proper all out Blues fan. Bang into Man City he was. Also all the big concerts. Proper, proper lad he was. He just thrived off the streets.'

'Didn't he go down though?' asked Sleeper glancing at Tony.

'Yeah,' he replied nodding. 'Batty was one of the first crews to be hit hard by that guy we was talking about the other night. You remember him, Anderson. It got me thinking afterwards about the guy. If I remembered rightly, Prey and Chopper's crew, was one of the few back then that didn't feel this guy's wrath. Like I said, I was in the Canary Islands a lot back then, watching over my investments, as they all battled it out with one another back here in town. But I still had my ear to the street. I still knew all the moves that were being made.'

'So what happened with Batty?' asked Sleeper, wanting to change the subject from Anderson.

'He hadn't been out all that long,' he said. 'We'd stayed close, even when he was doing his bird. I made sure that he'd receive packages on the inside from me. So when he got out. We hooked up again. I hadn't been back in the country all that long. But the one thing I caught onto almost straight away, was the way things had changed. Don't get me wrong 'ere lads. E's and shit were and are very much still out there. But they were for that younger generation that was probably about five or six years old when we were all popping them and making complete tits of ar'selves.'

'Ain't that the truth,' laughed Eazy.

'I know,' agreed Sleeper. 'I remember how I loved the feeling I got from the damn little things. But sometimes my head went completely west on them. They hadn't been like that in the beginning, but when those little doves and other manic ones, started to hit the streets, well that's when it all started to turn to pot. I ain't done them for time and would never pop one of those crazy little fuckers again.'

'That's what I was talking about,' said Tony. 'The timeshare out in the Canary Islands makes me an absolute mint. But as you both know, when you're in the business, no fucker wants you out of it. Although saying that, I just receive the cash from it nowadays. Just have to put in the occasional appearance to keep certain guys or crews in check. Anyway, getting back to the point. When I returned home, the first thing that I got onto, was the fact that every fucker was abusing charley like you wouldn't believe. I mean we'd always done back then. But we were always the guys with the cash right. The only kids doing it were the ones who could afford the occasional gram here and there.'

'I know what you're saying,' agreed Sleeper nodding. 'It was exactly the same down our way.'

'Ain't the fucking truth,' said Eazy. 'Jesus, I know of twelve – thirteen, fourteen, fifteen year old kids that are doing the shit these days.'

'Exactly,' said Tony as they drove past the huge garage on the right hand side of the road that dealt in high class motors such as Ferrari's and Porsche's. The whole place was lit up brightly against an almost white back drop, to show off all of the amazing vehicles in their best possible light. 'That's why when I returned home, I was mithered and mithered for my contacts in the business. Now I didn't really want to get back into it to be truthful. I still had my dough working the streets from before I went away and was happy enough with it. But they mithered and mithered me. So when Batty got out looking to hook up, it seemed like the ideal opportunity. I trusted the guy, and I knew that he was looking for action. So I put him up, introduced my contacts to him. Fronted the cash, and within twelve months we were running just about all of the bugle throughout Manchester. Things were pretty cool for a while.'

'Then what happened?' asked Eazy.

'Then certain people began sticking their noses in,' he said. 'Up until now you see, only me and Batty knew who the key figures were. I was like the silent partner so to speak. Batty was always mob handed, so rarely needed my backing, which was cool with me.'

'So what did you mean by certain people sticking their noses in?' asked Sleeper as they entered the town of Wilmslow, Vinnie's Lexus cutting through one of the main high streets as it came to a stop up ahead at the traffic lights. He was oblivious to the fact that they were following him.

'Vinnie decided that the best way to make his name, whilst his old man was away, was to get the lads what they all wanted.'

'Charley,' sighed Sleeper. 'Right?'

'Right,' he replied. 'Everybody's favourite friend.'

'And worse fucking enemy,' added Sleeper. 'It's why me and Eazy got the fuck out of it. We thought that smack-heads were bad for grassing. But at least most smack heads were from the streets. This lot were high line punters, that didn't want to give up their high life's in the city if things came on top for them. And they wouldn't think twice about turning on you, to get themselves out of the shit.'

'Too fucking right,' agreed Tony. 'Anyway, little Vinnie, like most of town knew that Batty was the guy running the show. You wanted top grade gear, then Batty was the man to see. So Vinnie went to see him, alone the first time. Only he didn't just want to gear, he wanted the contacts and the custom to go with it. Obviously Batty said no way. But the little shit kept insisting that he give him what he wanted. So Batty gave him a kicking

and sent him on his way, simple as that. No need for me to get involved.'

'Then what happened?' asked Eazy as Sleeper turned left towards Alderley Edge.

'The kid took it as an insult,' said Tony. 'He got his crew and his father's crew together and went to work. Set up his own little network, which to be quite honest, wasn't at all that bad. Only the gear he was getting in was no where near as good as ar's. It had been banged way too much with novocaine. Which when a guy wants to cook that shit up into rocks, it just ain't gonna happen.'

'So what difference did it make then?' asked Sleeper as the continued to follow the Lexus through the now almost deserted roads. 'If his gear was shit, then what did it matter to you anyway?'

'He began using his crew to put pressure on our customers,' he said. 'Like I said to Sleeper before Eazy, these kids, and even O'Leary's older heads as well, but they just love this gangstar shit. So they began putting pressure on our guys and we began losing business. Batty tried to deal with it in his own way, but didn't have much luck. Vinnie's crew were out there, weighing people in, left, right, and centre. Batty didn't even tell me anything about it at first. Just told me business was slow, I wasn't arsed really. I felt that it was more in Batty's interest, than it was mine anyway. So I just left him to it. But about three months later, things were getting real bad, that little fuck was actually winning. Although I still didn't have any knowledge of it, as I was spending most of my time travelling back and forth between here and the Canary Islands. Eventually Batty approached me and told me what had happened. Said that this little cunt had taken his crew practically to war over it all. And he had too many men dropping around him, from unwarranted attacks against them.'

'So you got involved then?' asked Eazy smiling for the back seat.

'I merely sent word to Vinnie, to back the fuck off, or I would get personally involved,' he said. 'I pointed out clearly, that it was my business that he was fucking with, not Batty's. I told him that we were taking back what was rightfully ar's to begin with.'

'How did he take that?' asked Sleeper.

'Called for a meeting with Batty,' he told them. 'Batty said that he'd deal with it himself. Didn't want me involved. I think his pride was little hurt that I'd had to step in. He figured this way

he could redeem himself. So I left them to it. I only wish that I...'
He dropped his head as he stopped telling the story.

'What the hell happened?' asked Eazy.

'Vinnie killed him,' said Tony. 'Gutted him like a fish. The whole meeting was a set up. He had three times as many lads there to the meet. So Batty's crew couldn't do fuck all.   Vinnie dealt with Batty himself, sending me a message back, not to try fucking with him ever again.'

'So that's how he got the scar,' stated Sleeper smirking.

'What scar?' asked Eazy.

'You'll see,' replied Sleeper.

'I knew that I was treading on dodgy ground with him being Dominic O'Leary's son and all,' said Tony. 'Me and the old man had been good friends now for some time. But I had to strike back in order to keep face. So I travelled to Durham, where the old man was doing his stretch and laid it out for him. I told him that I'd have to deal with his son personally. He begged me not kill him. He told me that he'd send word for his people to back off. But I knew that wouldn't happen even if he sent word. But for the sake of the old man, I said I'd leave it in his hands.'

'And did you?' asked Eazy.

'I did,' he said shaking his head. 'And he didn't listen. They all thought that they'd become these big time gangstars. So I showed them just how little they really were. I gathered only three of my best men, and we hit back at six of Vinnie's closest associates. Three of his and three of the old man's, just to send him a message also.'

'What did you do to them?' asked Eazy, as Sleeper smiled knowing exactly what had happened.

'Let's just say that they aren't around no more Eazy,' he smiled at the big man who nodded his head.

'Why leave the kid alive then?' he asked.

'Respect for the old man I guess,' he said. 'But I couldn't let it completely go. So I broke into his house as he was sleeping. He only awoke, as I wrapped the duct tape around his mouth. Only I heard his silent scream, which rang throughout his eyes as I sliced him, as deep as I could, right down the left hand side of his face.' He drew his finger right across the cheek to indicate what had happened.

'And he never struck back after that?' asked Eazy intrigued by the story.

'We never heard a dickey-bird after that,' he smiled, as he suddenly pointed out the window. 'He's just taken a right turn down there.'

'I see him,' replied Sleeper, as they then continued for the next five minutes to follow him in silence. The roads, although not country lanes, were just as winding to deal with. Several times they thought they had lost the Lexus and Vinnie. But as the road came out into an open stretch they saw his back light's again.

'Where he going now?' asked Eazy, as they clearly saw him pull into a small secluded street or cul-de-sac of some sort. All the houses looked brand new in the circular street. They pulled to a standstill as they watched him pull up outside of one of the new looking houses in the small privately owned cul-de-sac, which was situated just outside of Alderley Edge.

They watched Vinnie as he climbed from the vehicle, which looked way too big for him. He walked over to the house where he'd parked, as the front door opened before he'd even knocked. The man in the doorway represented a little weasel of sorts, as they observed him rant and rave at Vinnie before signalling him inside.

'Who the fuck was that?' asked Sleeper, glancing to Tony.

Tony kissed his teeth as he began to shake his head. 'I think we may ourselves a problem 'ere lads.'

'Why's that?' asked Eazy.

'Because I know who the fuck that is that he is metting with,' he sighed deeply.

FORTY SEVEN

'You look happier than I've seen you in age's kid? You're almost glowing Rachel,' said Hunter, as she opened her front door to her apartment right in the city centre itself, just off Deansgate. It had never surprised Rachel, that Hunter lived so close to her place of work. She thrived off the job; Rachel had never seen anybody so devoted to the job, like Hunter was. The nefarious exploits of sanity, that were everybody else's nightmares appeared to be Hunter's one authentic sanctuary.

But Rachel understood better than most, that the world needed the likes Hunter. For if they did not exist, the consternation would never cease to end. Although as she stepped in the darkly lit apartment, Rachel saw for the first time since she'd known her friend, the exertion that was being utilised daily. She looked more tired, exhausted even, than Rachel had ever known her to be.

She was wearing black faded jeans, along with a white blouse that Rachel recognised as one she wore for work sometimes. She wore no make-up at all. And her beauty still shone through, despite the extremely dark bags below her bloodshot eyes. She was already smoking as she'd opened the door, and Rachel found herself wondering just who, out of the two of them, was getting through more of the damn things these days, her or Rachel.

'You called me,' said Rachel feeling as Hunter as put it, better than she had in long time. And she knew the very reason for feeling this way. Despite all of the guilt she felt, she couldn't deny that what had taken place the night before had brought her around to feeling this way. She was dying to tell somebody about it, even Hunter, although she wasn't quite sure how her friend would take the news.

Not that her friend had ever shown any interest in the man himself, that wasn't it at all. But because of work ethics, she believed Hunter may frown upon the situation slightly. So decided, right there and then, that she wouldn't let Hunter know until the time was absolutely right. So smiling at her friend she added, 'Remember Hunter. You asked to see me.'

'I know, I know kid,' she said. 'Come on through. I've got something that I want to discuss with you. A kind of favour I suppose.'

'Not more favours Hunter,' she sighed.

'No,' she shook her head with her back still turned to her. 'This favour is one that I'm going to do for you kid, but I just want us to talk over a few things first, alright.'

'Alright,' she replied struggling to see in the hallway where they still were, 'Why am I not surprised you're still working off the clock Hunter?' she added, as she followed Hunter through into the very plain looking apartment, into the even intelligible looking living room. It had been the first time that she ever entered Hunter's domain, although she'd been here before, she realised, that she had never passed further than the hallway before, as they were usually on their way out.

'I'll get us some wine,' she said, leaving Rachel all alone, as she disappeared into the kitchen.

The walls were white, but suited the unadorned apartment. The several candles acted as the rooms only light, as they flickered and burned brightly. There was more than enough light to see, and the candles produced a more relaxing atmosphere, that Rachel thought they both needed right now. The walls were bare; no pictures hung there, which Rachel found a little strange. Although saying that, she soon realised that Hunter probably spent so very little time in the apartment, as she was either always working or out dating the numerous men she allowed herself to sleep with.

There were a couple of white book shelves, which Rachel wandered over to. Rachel didn't have Hunter down as a casual reader. Observing the books on the shelves she noticed that they were work books, or research books anyway. There was a variety of topics listed there, from murder to rape to an assortment of old non-fiction crime stories from Victorian times. Some of which Rachel recognised as reading herself. Books like Dealing with the Aftermath of Violation by Donahoe, Seductions of Crime by Katz, Inside the Criminal Mind by Somenow, Without Conscience by Hare and Sexual Homicide:

Patterns and Motives by Ressler, Burgess and Douglas, to name but only a mere selection of what filled the shelves.

Rachel had recommended most of the books to Hunter. Only, she had never realised that she had actually looked them up, and had actually gone out and bought them. She had to admit to being quite surprised.

'Here you go kid,' said Hunter, walking back through to the living and handing her the glass of deep red wine. 'You look a little surprised there kid.'

'I never knew that you had read any of these.'

'Why,' she smiled. 'What reading material did you have me down for, Catherine Cookson, Linda La Plante or some other shit kid.'

'No,' she laughed. 'I don't suppose I had you down as any kind of reader apart from your numerous reports that you are constantly poring over. Well that's if I came to think about it.'

'I just wanted to apologise for the other day,' said Hunter, as Rachel sat herself down on the sofa, as Hunter took the armchair by the oval window that over looked the back end of the city centre.

'Why?'

'Because I, one, shouldn't have dragged you there with me,' she sighed, as she sipped the wine. 'And two, should have listened to you, when you said to call for back up. It was irresponsible of me.'

'It's alright Hunter,' she told her with a little smile, to let her know that she shouldn't burden herself with any more guilt. 'So do you have any leads yet?'

'Only that there is a nation wide alert on Freddy Marshall,' she told her. 'We've everybody looking for him.'

'You really think that it is him Hunter?' she asked as she sipped the wine.

'We've got his prints, we've got his semen on the bed sheets, we've got motive,' Hunter was counting them off on her fingers as she said this. 'I say that we've got him cold, without a moments doubt in my mind.'

'Why would he have gone to all the trouble of...'

'You looking into this, too deeply again kid?'

'I did some checking myself last night,' she said. 'It turns out that you were right about Freddy being prosecuted by husband's office, the CPS. Peter actually went up against him also, years back that is.'

'What for?'

'Just some embezzlement case back in the mid eighties,' she told her. 'It was one of Peter's first cases. I found it when I was going through all of the old files that Peter had kept. The case got thrown out of court, on grounds of, lack of evidence against Frederick Marshall.'

'And you're still not convinced that it's him then?'

'I'm not sure of anything anymore more,' she said rubbing the tiredness she felt in her eyes. 'To tell you the truth that is.'

'I know what you mean there kid,' she agreed. 'It's been one hell of a case, hasn't it? I mean I honestly have to admit, that I've never seen anything like this before in my life. And I thought I'd seen just about everything I possibly could, when it came to the depths of depravity that society reaped upon one another.'

'You don't need to tell me that Hunter.'

'I know I don't kid,' she smiled. 'But it'll soon be over Rachel. We'll find where he is soon enough. I can guarantee you that for certain.'

'What if it's not him though?'

'It's him kid,' she said. 'I told you that you looked way too deeply into all of this. That's all it was.'

'But what makes you so certain.'

'You mean apart from all of the evidence we've got against him right now,' she cocked her eye-brow at her, as Rachel smiled at what Brendan had said the pervious night. 'Alright, you read his greatest hits the other day, right?'

'Right,' she replied still smiling.

'So what wasn't in those files was the jobs we've suspected him of all along kid.'

'Like what?'

'He's a contract man,' she said. 'We've known that for a while. Just as we've known about your new associate for a while too kid. I know all about Sleeper's history. Although he's good, in fact he's very good; one of the best, any of us has ever come across. You remember a guy called Robert, or Bob Anderson from back in the eighties, early nineties.'

'Maybe,' she said thinking back to the conversation a few nights before. 'What about him though?'

'Well Anderson was one of ours, but he was a mean son of a bitch kid,' she said. 'He was just before your time. I was still working my way through the ranks. But this Anderson used to work with Stephenson years ago. You know him, used work Serious Crime Squad. Headed it in fact. Became involved in the

uprising drug scene at the end of the eighties and early nineties with a detective called Walsh.'

'I know both of them,' she said. 'I've worked separate cases with them in the past. They're good guys; I like the both of them. I didn't know that Stephenson worked with this Anderson though. Just who was he then?'

'We had to send him packing down south after he nearly killed some guy through a routine interrogation,' she said. 'To cut a long story short, we brought him back as the violence associated with the on going turf wars, that were related to drugs escalated. They had hit Manchester badly. But rumour had it, that he became a little too caught up in his work.'

'What do you mean?'

'He was bringing different crews down all over the boroughs, just like he had done before we booted him south,' she lit a cigarette and tossed the pack to Rachel who declined. 'Nobody knew quite how he was managing it. He had no partner, but he consistently brought these crews down like no one else seemed able to.'

'So what was wrong with that?'

'He began running his own crew,' she said. 'Or so they say at least.'

'You're kidding,' said Rachel shocked. 'What the hell happened to him?'

'He just disappeared.'

'Just like that,' Rachel shook her head.

'Another rumour I heard, was that the station received a package containing all of the relevant information that proved he's been working both sides for years. But it was just a rumour as far as everyone was concerned. But from what I hear...'

'Hang on a sec,' said Rachel. 'What has any of this got to do with Freddy or Sleeper for that matter?'

'I heard that it was your friend, the one that calls himself Sleeper,' she smiled, 'that he was the one that disposed of the body... permanently.'

'Well I don't know shit about that Hunter,' she said, knowing that something had happened, just from the looks on their faces the other night. 'And what about Freddy Fuckfingers?'

'Fuckfingers,' laughed Hunter. 'I like that... Fuckfingers... anyway. He's also a contract killer, kid. But unlike your friend who apparently is inactive as far as we know. He's remained very active over the years.'

'It doesn't make him the killer of...'

'Freddy takes real pride in the work he does,' she said. 'And I don't just mean killing them kid.'

'What do you mean then?'

'He likes to capture his targets,' she said. 'Usually within the confines of there own homes. And rather then simply put a bullet through back of the skull professionally. He prefers to torture the victims. He likes to keep them alive for as long as possible. We've found his victims in some right states.'

'How the hell, if you know all this,' said Rachel, 'Let him get away with it for so long? I mean, if he's such a cold killer. Then what the hell are you doing, letting him walk the streets, for fucks sake Hunter.'

'He's managed to evade us so far,' she shrugged.

'So far,' said Rachel. 'I can't believe that you've never been able to make any of this stick against him. Who contracted the hits?'

'He's part of O'Leary's crew,' she said. 'But he also freelances a lot of work out of town. That's what makes it so much harder to...'

'Jesus Hunter,' she sighed. 'I still can't believe...'

'Oi, don't start with any of your moral standards here kid,' she snapped, cutting her short as Rachel stared at her shaking her head. 'Especially when you're running about town with a reputed killer yourself,' she added with a little smirk.

'That's differ...'

'There ain't no difference here kid,' she said, as her phone suddenly rang out in the hallway. 'Damn thing! Just give us a sec, will you kid.' She got up and left the living room.

Rachel sat there wondering over what Hunter had just told her. Not only about Freddy, but also about Sleeper. She'd known all along what it was that Sleeper had been. I mean she'd witnessed him kill first hand. But she wondered just what it was, that this Anderson character that Hunter spoke of, had done to Sleeper and if he had indeed been the one responsible for the man's extinction. As her mind wandered freely, she remembered back to the first time both her and Hunter had met...

'I just want to know how somebody's mind would have worked when going about this kind of murder,' Hunter had said, as she sat opposite in her private office, situated in St. Ann's square.

It had been the first time that Rachel had met Hunter. She had worked with the police from several towns and city's in the past few years, handling work loads between her private patients and the work they had asked her help in. And she had heard all

about the woman detective before her, but this was the first time she'd ever met her.

She was taken back at the detective's sheer beauty. She was so striking that Rachel had, had trouble believing she as actually a police officer or detective for that matter. Especially knowing that she had been involved some horrific cases that Rachel had studied in her own private time. The woman had all the features of model, deep cheek bones, long lush blonde hair that flowed with apparent ease down her back. And a body that most women, models included, would have literally died for.

Hunter was asking for help with a serial rapist that was not only raping his victims. But also killing them by stabbing them repeatedly through the face as the rape was taking place. They had found no semen or any other forensic evidence at any of the scenes, and so far, no witnesses that could help them.

The killer was also shaving the victims of all hair, post mortem. And this not only included their hair upon their heads, or just their pubic region, it also included all bodily hair. The police and forensic team, also never found any of the body hair within the vicinity of the bodies. This was one of the reasons she was sat before her right now.

'Why all the hair?' asked Hunter.

'He's either taking the hair to rid all forensic evidence, which at the moment appears to have worked,' she said. 'But my opinion is that he's taking the hair as a trophy for his crime committed.'

'Trophy!'

'Yes trophy,' she told her. 'The hair has some personal meaning to him. It reminds him of what took place on the night of the murders.'

'Jesus!' she exclaimed. 'What kind of a freak are we dealing with here?'

'Have you got the crime scene photos with you?' she asked as Hunter as she'd asked Rachel to simply refer to her, handed her the A4 manila envelope.

Emptying the contents onto the desk before her, she began to examine each photo carefully. The first few pages, relating to each case that had taken place, were area-establishing shots leading to the bodies. Such as the hallways or landings out side of the bedrooms. Gradually each photograph focused down onto the body. Picture's taken from every conceivable angle. There was a lot of blood at each scene where the killer had stabbed to victims through their faces. Another thing that Rachel noticed

was the way limbs had locked, this sometimes happens through the victims trying to protect themselves through violent deaths.

The post-mortem pictures had been excluded. But Rachel knew that the pathologist would have washed and cleaned the body. She also knew that these bodies then resemble statues upon the examination tables. Very often like the work of art, displayed to the world by a vandal of sorts.

She soon realised that this was all three victims shown in the photographs. Each victim had been discarded as if the were nothing the killer after he'd finished with them. Strewn on their living room floors or beds, stripped completely naked, including all hair, made them appear ghostly like, even alien like.

'Tell me more about the case,' said Rachel as she continued to look through the photographs.

'He's breaking into the victims homes late at night,' she said. 'All of the victims have been single mothers so far. It has been the children that have discovered the bodies on each occurrence as well. Poor little sods,' she had sighed shaking her heads. 'It was bad enough for us to enter those scenes. Never mind them. Anyway, each of the victims were from different parts of town. Levenshulme, Ardwick and Hulme.'

'But all of these areas are relatively close,' Rachel pointed out.

'We know,' she nodded.

'Have you chased up any old leads from that area?' she asked. 'Or any area surrounding the city for that matter. This guy will definitely have built his way up to this stage. He will have priors for maybe minor sexual offences such as exposing himself in public maybe. You need to work that angle against any other cases with sexual offenders in the area. He will also have been watching the victims before hand. He may have even known them personally at so point. Or followed them from school. He will have watched the victims late at night and have gotten to know their patterns. I believe that it is roughly a month between each case so far, am I right?'

'Right,' she nodded. 'Before we go any further, can I admit something to you?'

'Sure,' she smiled, almost immediately knowing what the detective was about to say.

'I'm a little sceptical as to just how you can help us here,' she admitted. 'Now I know that you've helped the police in the past and I know that you've got quite the success rate with them. But I'm still a little...'

'Alright,' she said. 'The questions we first have to ask ourselves are this. What sort of knife did he use? Does he work

with knives as a profession? Is that why he's comfortable with them? Is he right handed? 95% of people are. If so, is it possible to then tell where he was standing or in this case the position he was in just before he stabbed the victims? You see these here?' She pointed to the marks around the wrists and ankles.

'Yes,' she replied.

'The victim had been bound and no doubt gagged as well, so not to alert the child,' she said. 'We have to ask, was this before or even after?'

'Why after?'

'Because that could be part of his fantasy system.'

'How do you mean, part of his fantasy system?'

'His fantasies would have led him up to this point,' she replied. 'Further questions like how long the victim was conscious, how quickly did they die? All these answers are important as they will influence the larger question of the killer's motivation. That is what I meant by his fantasy system within his mind.'

'I still don't follow,' she said.

'What is the killer achieving from the murder itself? It will help us to perpetrate what motivates the killer's mind and shape his personality functioning,' she told her. 'My job would be to take a psychological approach to analyse the crime committed. I will not be doing your job for you. All that I will be doing, will be helping to narrow your resources so to effectively help break down the necessary information.'

'I don't know,' sighed Hunter, shaking her head still not convinced.

'What is there to know,' smiled Rachel. 'You're here asking me for the help, not the other way around Detective Hunter.'

'True,' she smiled aback at her.

'Alright then,' she said. 'Tell me everything, and I mean everything that you know so far on the case. Then leave the information and the crime scene photographs with me. See what I can come up with.'

'Fair enough,' she agreed, as she sat back in the chair and began to tell Rachel everything, all the while Rachel continued make notes and to look at the photographs before her, as she tried to get inside the mind of the one responsible.

They had been the start of their association, and within a week they had brought in their first real suspect in the case. A guy by the name of Lincoln Holdings, aged thirty-two years old. He was from Eccles, and he worked as a gardener for the city council, around the city. His jobs took him to different parts of the city, including the schools of the children whose mothers had been

463

brutally raped and murdered. He fitted Rachel's profile down to a tee. Although Hunter still hadn't been convinced by Rachel's methods. The guy had all he trademarks of what Rachel had pointed out. The minor sexual offences against him were just part of what Rachel had pointed out to them.

Rachel had also advised the Hunter and her partner, Mike Andrews on questioning the man, on how best to approach the interview, in order to draw him out. She knew that Hunter also frowned upon this. But she told them, to make him feel good about them both first of all. That way he'd feel safe. He'll still know that there may be a consequence, but he wouldn't think, that they'll suddenly turn on him. Or that they'd think him a monster or some kind of an animal for what he'd done. Instead she had explained, he'll think that they'd want to understand, how it came about.

She told them to explain to him such things, as saying, that by being a sexual deviant he wasn't alone in the world. That there were other people who would understand him. But that they understood how hard it was for him, but that they had heard of such things before.

Rachel pointed out that as they came closer to the truth, breaking down a barrier at a time. They would eventually reach a point when they could go straight for the heart. She said that very often, it would come in a rush, almost like a sense of relief to the guy. She told them to let him spill everything out without interrupting him. Then when they had finished, and only then, should they go back over everything and fill in all of the details with the case.

Rachel had seen the doubt in Hunter's eyes as she explained all of this to them. She was not only an arrogant woman; she was slightly stuck in her ways. But she had given way to Rachel, as they hadn't been getting anywhere with the case. Rachel knew that the woman considered her to be a last resort.

That was until he did exactly as she said he would in the interview, breaking down like a little child, as he told them everything they had wanted to know. And then they found the jars buried in a playing field at the back of Lincoln Holdings house. Each jar, containing the hairs of all the victims. It was from then on, that Hunter had seen the light so to speak and had remained in a close working relationship with her, Rachel Henessey as she was still known back then...

'Sorry about that,' said Hunter, as she walked back into the living room. 'It was work, Lucy to be precise.'

'Has she got anything?'

'They've just confirmed the semen they've found in the victims anal area as being Freddy Marshall's,' she said sitting down. 'That and a shit load more evidence to indicate that he's definitely our killer.'

'So it looks like he's made his first real mistake then,' she sighed, wanting so much to believe it was this guy. 'Eh Hunter?'

'It looks that way kid,' she said staring at her. 'Look, I know that you thought that it was going to a lot deeper than all of this kid. But that's just the way it sometimes pans out for us.'

'I know it is,' she nodded. 'One of the theories I was working on last night, was that this guy was fucking with us all along.'

'He may not have been,' said Hunter. 'He may have certain believes that he is this archangel or whatever the fuck you want to call it. But either way, we ain't going to know until we find where the son of a bitch is hiding.'

'And you still have no idea where he is?'

'No,' she said. 'But, that's the favour I was talking about kid, I owe you big time. And I don't just mean over this case. I mean from when we first met and all the help you've provided me with over the years.'

'That was my job to help you,' she replied not at all sure where Hunter was leading with this.

'I know it was,' she nodded. 'But you always gave it a little more than ever had to. You remember just what I was like when I first met you?' she asked this and saw Rachel smile broadly. 'What's with the grin kid?'

'I was just thinking back to that case against Lincoln Holdings,' she told. 'And the first time you sat opposite me. I can't believe you just mentioned it.'

'I was a bit of an arrogant bitch back then,' she said. 'Eh kid?'

'What do you mean back then?' she cocked her eye-brow at Hunter, as she laughed. 'You still are an arrogant bitch Hunter.'

'Fair comment,' she replied. 'Hopefully this will redeem some of that then kid.'

'What will?' asked Rachel.

'I tell you, what I going to do for you kid,' she began. 'I mean, now that we're pretty certain that it's Freddy Marshall behind all of this mess. When I find him, I'm going to let you know at the same time. It'll be then down to you, what you decide to do with the information.'

'Why would you do that Hunter?' she asked cautiously.

'Because, like I said,' she smiled warmly at her. 'I feel that I owe you. I also feel that I've let you down on some ways, by not

465

catching this guy sooner. When I think back on it now, he should have been a suspect back then for us. I guess I overlooked...'

'But what will happen when you find him Hunter?' She wanted to know exactly what it was that Hunter was offering her.

'I won't lie to you kid,' she said. 'We're going to arrest him. He's going to go down for all his crimes. But I'll give you half an hour head start. I can't get any fairer than that kid. Alright?'

'Thanks,' she replied, smiling at her friend, who she realised was not only putting herself on the line for Rachel, but also her distinguished career she built over the years as one of the city's leading detectives.

FORTY EIGHT

'I feel as if I'm being pulled in so many directions Brendan,' sighed Rachel, as she lay naked next to him in her bed. He'd been waiting for her that night, when she had returned home from Hunter's. They had practically been at each other immediately, tearing at one anothers clothes, as they entered the apartment allowing the passion they felt for one another take control.

Struggling to remove each others clothes in their eagerness, as they made their way to the bedroom at the same time. Eventually Brendan had picked her up and carried her through to the bedroom, where he completed the task of removing both their clothes.

They had just finished making love for the fourth time; Rachel couldn't believe how insatiable he was. It felt as if they had just finished, when he was already caressing her, teasing her, before once again, making love to her passionately. She loved the close contact they had with one another, the touching and susceptible discovery of one anothers bodies. It felt as they she had missed so much since Peter had been killed. She had promised, and promised herself, that this wasn't going to happen. But when it did, she was powerless to prevent it from happening.

'What do you mean by that?' he asked, as he stroked her back lightly, his fingers wandering aimlessly as his eyes smiled at her.

'I'm not going to deny the attraction I felt for you,' she said. 'Although I have to admit that I didn't feel that way when I had first met you,' she laughed.

'I was a bit of a tosser,' he smiled at her. 'Wasn't I?'

'A bit of one,' she cocked her eyebrow at him as he laughed, leaning forward and kissing her. 'But I couldn't deny what I felt.

Although I told myself that I wasn't going to let anything happen, well, at least not until I'd laid Peter and Becky to rest.'

'You already have done,' he told her.

'No,' she sighed deeply. 'I won't have done that until Gabriel is found.'

'And then what?'

'What do you mean?'

'I mean, what will you when discover Ganriel's true identity?'

'I don't think that you want to know that,' she told him as she dropped her eyes.

'What you're talking about won't be like when you killed the Cartwright's Rachel,' he said lifting her face so he could look into her eyes. 'You're talking about cold hearted revenge. What is the expression, an eye for an eye?'

'How about a heartless heart for the two loving ones I lost.'

'What you're actually talking about is not that different fro...'

'It's completely different,' she snapped.

'So you are going to kill him then?' he shook his head at her.

'If that's what it comes down to,' she said defiantly. 'Then yes, I'm going to ki...'

'I don't want to know Rachel,' he said before she could finish, and the phone in the living room interrupted the both of them.

'I best get that,' she said.

'Who the hell is that going to be Rachel?' he asked glancing to the bedside clock. 'It's three-twenty in the morning.'

'So,' she shrugged as she got out of bed and grabbed her dressing gown.

Walking through to the living room, as the phone refused to relent its loud shrill, she shivered slightly from the cool night's air, as she switched the light on. Rubbing her head and eyes, tired, she grabbed the headset.

'Hello,' she said in a tired voice, to let whoever had phoned her know that they had disturbed her.

'Rachel,' said Tony. 'You alright?'

'I was,' she yawned.

'Sorry kid,' he said sincerely.

'What the hell you phoning me at this time for?' she asked without malice.

'I know it's late,' he sighed; she could hear Sleeper and Eazy in the background. 'But I figured you'd still be awake.'

'I was,' she smiled to herself. 'Kind of, anyway.'

'Can we come around?' he asked, a mix of excitement and trepidation in his voice.

A shadow suddenly filled the living room as she turned and smiled at Brendan who was stood there completely naked as she eyed him thoughtfully. She nodded that everything was alright, as he stepped through the doorway and kissed her forehead.

'What was that noise? Are you still there Rachel?' asked Tony, bringing her back to her senses as Brendan continued to smile at her.

'Yes, it was nothing,' she replied defensively. 'Sorry Tony, yes I'm here. What is that you wan...'

'So can we?'

'Can you what?'

'Come around for Christ sake girl,' he sighed, annoyed with her.

'It's not a good time,' she told him, as Brendan smiled back at her, turning to return to the bedroom.

'You're never going to guess what we've found out though,' he said. 'And what do you mean this ain't a good ti...'

'It's nearly three-thirty in the morning,' she reminded him. 'We're not all night-owls ar'kid. What's so important?'

'I can't say over the phone.'

'Why?' she asked, then remembering the laptop added quietly, so the Brendan couldn't hear. 'Have you found something on Carol's computer?'

'Not yet,' he told her. 'Fucking Robert is out of town for a few days.'

'I thought that he never went anywhere.'

'He doesn't usually,' he sighed. 'Or that's what Jonah and Kezlo told us anyway. Seemingly someone had a problem in Germany. He couldn't do the job from here, so he flew out there a couple of days ago.'

'When is he going to be back?'

'They're not too sure yet,' he said. 'Jonah says they'll contact us as soon as he arrives back to town.'

'That's a shame,' she said. 'We could have really done with seeing what was on that computer you know.'

'I know,' he agreed. 'Look Rach...'

'What is it Tony?' she asked concerned. 'Is it really important? Do you really need to come here now?'

'Forget about it,' he told her. 'It'll probably be better if we just come around after we've finished later on tonight.'

'What do mean?' she asked. 'Why later on tonight? Why not in the morning?'

'We've got some shit to sort out first,' he told her. 'Sleeper's got to pick some shit up from Chan's in the afternoon so we'll

just head back to mine now and get our heads down. Then we've got to pay someone a little visit in the evening. In fact, thinking about it. It'll be much better if we come and see you then.'

'You're not making any sense Tony,' she told him, wondering if she just let them come around now. 'You better come aroun...'

'Nah,' he said before she could finish. 'Sorry, I shouldn't have called. We'll see you later on tonight. It might be late though. So make sure you're...'

'Doesn't matter what time,' she told him. 'And Tony...'

'Yeah.'

'Just be careful,' she told him as she wondered what it was that they were up to.

'Aren't I always,' he said with a little laugh. 'Laters.'

'Goodnight,' she replied, as she replaced the headset.

Now she was wishing that she'd just agreed to them coming around. She didn't know what had been so important, but she realised that for the first time in a long time she had shut Tony out herself. Making her way back through to the bedroom she found Brendan stretched out on his back, still naked as she smiled at him.

'It was just Tony.'

'I figured that,' he told her as she climbed back in to bed beside him.

'Ain't you forgetting something,' he said.

'What?'

'Your dressing gown,' he laughed grabbing her waist, as he pulled the gown away.

She giggled stupidly, feeling like a naughty teenager as she fell into his arms. 'This is crazy,' she told him shaking her head as he kissed her.

'What is?'

'All of this.'

'Why is it Rachel,' he asked he caressed her body. 'You had to move on at some point. What were you going to do, stay alone forever?'

'No,' she dropped her eyes. 'But it still shouldn't have happened so quickly.'

'It's been over a year now,' he reminded her.

'I know,' she said. 'But...'

'But nothing Rachel,' he said as he kissed her shoulders and neck. 'I've waited a long time for this.'

'You only met me last year,' she giggled.

'I've waited since last year then,' he laughed as he continued to kiss and caress her.

'What's going to happen afterwards?' she asked as he stopped kissing her and stared at her.

'After what?'

'After we've found Gabriel I mean.'

'You mean after you've killed him?'

'That's not what I said.'

'But it's what you meant,' he told her shaking his head slowly. 'Isn't it?'

'It's just something that I have to do Brendan.'

'And what if the police catch him first?'

'They won't,' she replied dropping her eyes again.

'What makes you so sure of that though?'

'They just won't,' she sighed.

'Do you know something that you've kept from us?'

'Who's us?' she asked.

'The police and me,' he said lifting her face, so he was able to see her eyes.

'No,' she shook her head at him convincingly, as she smiled. 'All I meant was that I have more determination than the rest of you, to catch this freak.'

'Let's not talk about it any more,' he said as he kissed her forehead.

'What do you suggest we do then?' she asked, as her hand was already lowering towards his groin, he groaned quietly as she took him in her hand.

'Well,' he said as he kissed her neck and then her mouth. 'I'd say that your suggestion is probably better than mine.' He rolled his body over and onto her as she gazed into his mesmerising eyes.

'Will I see you later?' asked Brendan as she saw him out of the front door. They were both fully dressed and it had just gone ten in the morning.

'I don't know,' she told him.

'Can't I come around when I'm finished at the station?'

She remembered the conversation with Tony, but at the same time wanted to see the man before her. 'Early on,' she smiled as she kissed him. 'But you can't stay over tonight.'

'Spoil sport,' he grinned at her.

'You have to be out of here by ten o'clock,' she said pushing him away.

'Like this ten o'clock?' he asked her hopefully.

'No,' she laughed. 'You can cook me dinner, then you can be on you're way.'

'Thanks,' he laughed at her shaking his head. 'That sounds like a good deal, I get to cook dinner and then...'

'And then we'll see just how grateful I am,' she said kissing him again.

'I'd better buy the food then,' he said. 'Because I doubt that you've got anything edible left in that fridge of yours.'

'You're probably right,' she agreed. 'See you later.'

'See you...' he suddenly stopped as Hunter appeared.

'Morning,' she said eyeing the pair of them. She had an armful of files with her. 'A bit early for a visit, ain't it McCarthy.'

'See you then Brendan,' said Rachel. 'Thanks for popping round.'

'No problem,' he said as he turned to leave, giving a slight nod at the detective. 'Detective Hunter.'

'I'll see you at the station,' she said with a cold stare.

They both watched him walk along the balcony as Hunter turned to face Rachel at the door. 'What the hell is going on kid?'

'Nothing,' she shrugged, surprised at her little outburst. 'He came by this morning, just to see how I was. That's all Hunter.' She wasn't even sure why she just lied to her. Maybe it was the disgusted look upon her face.

'It's a bit early though kid,' she said as she glanced around to see if the man had disappeared.

'You're here,' Rachel reminded her. 'Aren't you?'

'I never realised that the two of you were so close?'

'We're not,' said Rachel. 'You coming in or not?'

Hunter stepped through the door as she continued to glare at Rachel. 'You fucking him?' she asked abruptly.

'Hunter!'

'Well,' she said staring at her with questionable eyes. 'Are you kid?'

'No I'm not,' she snapped. 'But even if I was, it'd be none of your business. You'd better come on through.'

'What the hell is all of this?' asked Hunter, as she stepped into the living room which Rachel had, in her confusion discussing Brendan, forgotten about the state of the living room. 'What's going on in here kid? Why have you...'

'It's just research.'

'Research my arse.'

'Look Hunter,' said Rachel, annoyed with both herself and her friend. 'What is it that you want?'

'I brought you these,' she told her, handing her the files whilst all the while staring the walls.

'What are they?'

'By the look of this room kid, it looks like I did you a favour,' she said. 'It's the copies of the case files so far. I had Mike copy them for you.'

'Why?' she asked. 'Why now?'

'Because I figured that you'd be conducting your own investigation,' she sighed. 'I just hadn't figured it'd be anything quite like this. I didn't even know that you had all of this stuff.'

'Well now you know,' she said. 'And thanks for these. Do you want a coff...'

'No,' she said abruptly. 'I've got to get out of here. I'll see myself out. I need to be at the station. See you later kid.'

'See you later,' she said as she watched her friend walk back out of the living room. Rachel was left wondering why she had lied to her friend about Brendan.

FORTY NINE

'**W**hoa!' exclaimed Tony, as Sleeper opened the metallic silver case containing a small arsenal of weapons that he owned. 'You sure you've got enough shit in there mate?'

'I told you the brother likes his toys,' laughed Eazy.

'Nice hardware,' commented Chan. 'But you sure that you're going to need all of that just for the O'Leary's Sleeper?'

'I figure after the last two times that we've been there,' he said glancing at Tony, 'that the little prick Vinnie had three of his lads with him. I figure that they're his own crew, right?'

'Right,' agreed Tony. 'The three that have frisked us on both occasions are part of Vinnie's crew.'

'So therefore,' he replied. 'I figure that the old man must have at least three, but hopefully only two inside of the house. He's that paranoid, he probably keeps them inside of the house, out of sight.'

'Possibly more, I'm not too sure,' he nodded. 'But listen, why don't we just do what we have the last couple of times and just go and ring the bell. I got you in there on both occasions mate. This is over the top brother. You're practically talking about going to war with them. And we're not even sure that...'

'That's exactly it though,' he said cutting Tony short. 'We don't know. And after the other day when we went there, they clammed right up as soon as we mentioned anything that they considered to be out of order. The old man may love his son enough to cover all of his shit away from the realities of the world. But I ain't prepared to let them get away it. I want to know the answers to the questions that I've got to ask him. Now if you don't want any part of this Tony. That's alright. I understand'

'I never said that,' he protested holding up his hands. 'You know that I'll back you here. All I'm saying is that what we are about to do is a little...'

'The brother's right here,' said Eazy nodding at Tony. 'Believe me, when it comes to this kind of shit. It's always best to have Sleeper in your corner. Honestly Tony, this we do Sleeper's way and I guarantee that we'll be walking out of there with whatever answers we require.'

'Alright,' agreed Tony, still a little wary. 'So like I said though, I ain't too sure of how many the old man keeps inside of the house. But I say you're definitely right in presuming that he'll have himself covered. His own men will be protecting him. They have been since he got out.'

'How good are they?' asked Sleeper.

'They are old timers like me and the old man,' laughed Chan. 'But there is one that is known as Ryan Donnelly. His son is also part of Vinnie's crew. But he's the one who watches the old man's back. He was good in his day. Bare knuckle fighter. Used to take on the gypsy's. Good fights they were.'

'Good odds as well old man,' laughed Eazy.

'Not so good in the end,' he smirked. 'He beat everybody.'

'So we need to keep an eye out for him,' said Sleeper.

'Like Chan says though,' said Tony. 'He's getting on a little. But that won't be our main concern. Our main concern will be how heavily armed they'll be. I know that all of Vinnie's crew carries. The same will go for the old man's boys. So we either go in there blasting or...'

'Or we do it my way and there won't be too many casualties,' he smiled. 'At the end of the day, I'm not even interested in the old man, or any of his crew. All I want is some straight answers from the kid. The old man is merely an obstacle. So let's say worse case scenario, there'll be three of us against possibly nine or ten of them,' as he said this, he looked back down at the case.

'I can get some lads together,' said Tony. 'We can make things a little more even if you like Sleeper.'

'Me too,' added Chan enthusiastically, desperately wanting to have more involvement than playing host to his guests.

'That won't be necessary,' replied Sleeper shaking his head. 'It'll be better if just the three of us head up there. Besides, it wouldn't be any where as much fun if we made it odds on even, would it,' he smirked at them.

'So what do you suggest then?' asked Tony as Sleeper began removing the pieces to the automatic rifle together. 'And what the fuck is that?'

'This here is a modified Springfield Incorporated M1A,' he smiled. 'It's a modification of the M14 that has been around for almost forty years now. Obviously it's gone through several changes. But the basic structure is the same. I had my guy down in London dismantle it and add the specifics that I requested. The scope is a Bushnell 3-9X, usually used with the Remington all-new bolt action. The model 710, both me and Eazy have used it before up in Scotland. Excellent rifle. And to answer your question on what we'll do Tony. I'll put it this way, from observing the house on both occasions, I seen the high walls with the razor wire. That will not be a problem. The problem will be when the two of us are over the wall and into the grounds itself...'

'Hey, hang on a minute there,' protested Eazy. 'I already told you. The next time that you go in there. Then I'm coming with you.'

'You are doing,' he smiled tossing the M1A assault rifle to him. 'You'll be positioned out of sight at the far wall. There is a tree that will act as cover for you. I've brought the night scopes along with me. So you'll be able to see alright. All I want for you to do until we get inside of the house is act as our eyes. Just make sure that you take care of anyone that you don't think we'll be able to handle or is about to get in our way. Try not to kill them though – just do your best anyway. Just be sure to take their legs out, if that's possible with your damn shooting skills. You remember how that one works don't you?' He smiled at Eazy thinking about the last time he'd let him use a rifle.

'I do,' he said confidently. 'Although I found the Remington a little easier to handle.'

'Yeah,' said Sleeper. 'But one, we ain't got the Remington with us. And two brother, you ain't that good a shot anyway,' he laughed.

'Ahhh come on,' smiled Eazy. 'Me can shoot an elephant at fift...'

'Precisely,' smiled Sleeper. 'We ain't shooting at any damn elephants. These will be much smaller targets. Not that you've ever shot at elephants for that matter! Anyway, that one will be better. If all hell breaks loose, which we're hoping to avoid. But if it does, then at least you can switch it over to automatic fire, instead of single shot. Just spray them if things get a little out of hand.'

'Oh great,' said Tony staring at Sleeper. 'So whilst he's spraying them with bullets. Just where the fuck will we be in terms of the line of fire.'

'We'll be alright,' he winked at Tony, although it didn't make him feel all that much better.

'You really think you need all of this?' asked Chan holding one of the handguns in the palm of his hand.

'I think that the kid is paranoid at the moment,' said Sleeper. 'And I don't care who his new friends are. If this fucker is close with that guy we seen him with last night, then he knows a lot more than he let on the other day.'

'You reckon this guy is somehow involved for sure?' asked Chan.

'That's exactly the reason I want the lad questioned,' said Sleeper, still defending his beliefs. 'If he's close to this guy then he's a liability to us. If we botch a snatch job up, and the old man is in with this guy as well. Then we'll just be sending a fore warning to them. They'll have everybody alerted and on to us in no time at all.'

'So that's why you want us to hit the house,' said Tony. 'Kill two birds with one stone, so to speak of course.'

'Something like that,' he nodded as he removed one of the handguns. 'I want them all in one place. After I've got what I need from Vinnie then we'll be on our way.'

'Are you going to kill him?' asked Tony seriously watching for Sleeper's reaction to the question

'Why?' asked Sleeper without any emotion, as he handed the small Beretta Model 8045 Cougar .45 ACP. over to him, holding eye contact at all times. 'Would that cause you problems if I had too?'

'It would,' he said. 'Not that I've got any time for the kid. And if it turns out that he's involved deeply in all of this. Then we'll do it. But at the moment we're not sure of anything positive. But if it remains all speculation, then I'll have to go to war with the old man again.'

'Then we'll dispose of the problem before it becomes one for you. Like I said, the old man isn't my concern. But if the old man becomes a problem. Then I'll kill him as well,' replied Sleeper casually, taking the small black handgun back from Tony who was staring wildly back at him. 'That's going to be no use to you,' he added, laughing with ease.

'I never agreed to popping the old man,' he protested.

'You don't have to agree to either brother,' said Sleeper, examining another handgun from the case. 'Because if I feel that it's the right thing to do, then believe me brother. I will not hesitate in doing so.'

'But what abo...'

'Let's just see what he can tell us first eh,' he said smiling, as he handed him a Springfield TRP and also a Les Baer Thunder Ranch Special .45 ACP. They're better suited to your size. Plus you'll handle the recoil better with those two. How do they feel?'

Tony sighed deeply giving in to him. He handled to two guns separately, and then began to unload and reload the clips looking down over the tops of the handguns, until he smiled and said. 'These will be fine,' he said shaking his head. 'But just do me one favour Sleeper. Wait until the kid tells you everything that he's got to tell you before you go making any rash decisions. Alright?'

'Alright,' he nodded, as he pulled a lethal looking blade form the sheepskin sheath. It was hooked at the tip of the sharp looking blade, and had what appeared to be a bone handle, that was intricately carved into a dragon's head. 'I've got one or two methods of making someone talk,' he winked at Tony.

'I see that you still have the present then,' smiled Chan.

'Of course old man,' he said.

'What present?' asked Tony.

'Nothing mate. Don't worry about it,' answered Eazy. 'So what time tonight then?'

Tony eyed them suspiciously. 'It's gets pretty dark early these nights,' he said. 'So I figure that we hit them early enough to avoid missing Vinnie. Yet late enough so not to arose any suspicions. I mean the last thing we want to do is have copper's crawling all over us, if all hell breaks out up there.'

'These should help with that then,' smiled Sleeper, as he handed each of them different suppressers to their weapons.

'What about them though?' asked Eazy as Sleeper handed him a Glock model 21 .45 ACP.

'I want you to aim for their legs if possible Eazy,' he said. 'We only want the men wounded. Me and Tony will deal with them after that.'

'I meant what about the noise they'll make?'

'The house pretty much stands all alone,' said Tony. 'You saw that for yourself last night Eazy.'

'I know,' he agreed. 'But it's still a little too close to other homes in that area for my liking.'

'We'll be alright,' said Sleeper. 'I usually like a hell of a lot more time to plan something like this. But I've got a gut feeling that's telling me that we need to take of this before we venture any further. We need to find out for sure if Vinnie's sent this Marshall character to kill my sister or not. And if so, then we

need to find out the reason for him doing so. It has to be tonight.'

'Fuck it!' nodded Tony screwing the suppresser onto the gun. 'Let's do this shit and get it over with then.'

FIFTY

Darkness had fallen quickly as it always did through the winter months that were fast approaching. They had taken two separate vehicles, Sleeper's Mercedes where he had stored the small arsenal of weapons they were taking with them and also one of Tony's other vehicles, a brand new Cherokee jeep.

Tony eased his vehicle over behind Sleeper and Eazy, switching his headlights off. They had parked the vehicles at the back of where the house was situated and were pleased to discover that it was a lot more secluded than the posterior. As they departed from their vehicles, the cool night air sent a chill through each of them.

The sounds that could be heard all around them was the sound of nature restlessly moving around. Either an owl or pigeons were close by. The low cooing sound could be heard in the distance as Tony approached the others.

'We'll go in over there,' said Sleeper, pointing to the far right hand side. The wall was around nine or ten feet in height. The razor wire sparkled in the moonlight, and appeared to be what it was, deadly. 'The tree will act as our cover. You sure that you'll be able to climb up there Eazy.'

'That tree looks scared to death already,' smiled Tony. 'Listen lads, you sure that this is the only way to go?'

'What do you mean?' asked Eazy.

'I mean,' he sighed, staring at the two of them. 'Why the fuck have we got to go in there like some commando assault team. I've got us in there the last couple of times. I'm sure that...'

'You better stay out here,' said Sleeper bluntly. 'Because I've already told you once today. I ain't coming away without any answers tonight. I understand your predicament, so why don't yo...'

'No, no, that's fair play brother,' he told him, nodding with a smile to tell him that everything was alright. 'But still, we could just take the kid when he hits the streets.' He tried one more time.

'You're right,' he agreed, but shaking his head at the same time. 'We could. But like I said earlier Tony. The only problem with that, is that the problem won't remain isolated. What I need first Eazy, is for you to check the perimeter. You have the old alarm system laid out for you that Tony here gave you, right?'

'Right,' he said taking off.

'What makes you so certain that they won't just be using the same system?' asked Tony as Eazy took off.

'Because I've seen the kids scar close up,' he grinned. 'And believe me, he'd have been pissed that you got past his men that night with the basic set up you told us about. He won't have kept the same system installed. Give Eazy a few minutes; he'll have the security wired for us so that we can pretty much sneak in there.' He walked back over the vehicle and began removing the false panel.

Tony was left stood there wondering if what he'd said made any sense. No matter what Vinnie had done, or what he was responsible for, he just couldn't shake the fact that he still liked the old man. He knew that if they went ahead with this tonight, then there was a good possibility that there was going to be repercussions in the long run. Watching Sleeper remove the case, he wondered also about his two new friends. Despite the short space of time that they had known each other, he considered the two of them to be true friends.

He began to think of his sister. Rachel had seemed a little weird on the phone the night before. Even if it was as late as it was. She still acted strange, although he couldn't put this finger on it. He knew better than anyone else that she'd been through so much over the past year. He'd witnessed first hand the way the brutal murders of her husband and daughter had torn her apart. She always enjoyed life. She always appeared to be happy with Peter, even if he didn't like the man.

Although, even the marriage appeared to be strained towards the end. She wouldn't open up to him about it, because she knew how he felt about the man. But he knew that they were having troubles. And he knew that was one of the reasons that she felt the guilt that she did now. Somehow thinking that if things had been right between them, all of this would not have happened.

But he knew that Rachel's deepest loss lay with Becky. She had become everything to her, and him also. He'd loved the little girl like he would have loved having his very own daughter. The hole that was left gaping when this sick freak took their lives wouldn't be filled until they had found the killer... or was it killers... responsible.

That's why he was being pulled in so many directions where it concerned the man before him. Glancing back down at Sleeper who was now removing the array of different handguns and the assault rifle. Professionally checking over the weapons with precision. Sleeper was a lot harder than anybody he knew to fathom out. He truly liked he man, but there was something more than just dark or mysterious about him.

He thought that the night his sister had been slayed, he'd seen the other side of him where the darkness lay in wait to resurface. But the only clear side of him that had been revealed was his ability to shut off all of his emotions. He knew that the man would not grieve fully for the death of his sister until he'd got to the bottom of al this mess. That's what reminded him of his sister.

He'd seen the look in his eyes before that night, but he didn't tell either of them that he'd seen it. But that night, all life that seized to exist within the depths of his eyes, was the same look he'd seen within his sister's eyes. The two of them couldn't be more opposite to one another, yet at the same time, couldn't be more alike.

Eazy was already making his way back over to them, smiling. Now he was a lot more open than his friend. He was easier to fathom out. Tony thought that Eazy, despite his enormous imposing size, was like a gentle giant. The image of him had remained in his mind of that night earlier in the week. Holding onto the young boy, as the anguish and sorrow raced through his eyes. He knew the big mans strength must be immense, even more so than his own. But he considered his heart to be even bigger still. He was generous in his ways, and no matter what, you couldn't help but like the guy.

'What we got?' asked Sleeper as Eazy wandered back over to them.

'I've disabled the cameras which if they are being monitored will arose suspicion,' he said. 'But I figured you'd want them disabled anyway.'

'You're right there,' he said glancing at the wall. 'What about those?'

He was looking at the security lights that would no doubt be fitted with motion sensors. 'Disabled those from the ones that were by the gate.' he smiled. 'It's typical really. It's supposed to be security. So what do these firms do, they fit everything together in one place.'

'Why?' asked Tony.

'Makes it easier for them I suppose,' he shrugged. 'Maintenance wise that is.'

'What about visually?' asked Sleeper. 'How many men did you see?'

'They've got three men patrolling the grounds,' he replied. 'Although they ain't got a clue about how to go about things. They are all bunched together just making the rounds. I wouldn't say that they are expecting serious trouble. Although they are armed, but judging from their size they could handle themselves anyway. Because I might add, they are three big lumps.'

'Youngish?' asked Tony, as Eazy nodded. 'They're Vinnie's lads.'

'We've seen them both times we were here,' said Sleeper handing them their designated weapons. 'But if what you've said about the old man being paranoid, then I don't believe that he's going to not have his own men by his side.'

'True,' he agreed. 'Like I said, he's got Ryan Donnelly. His son is the one that searched you last time. He also still uses some of the old crew on the streets. So the chances are he's pulled some of them back so that he's got them by his side in the house.'

'You're probably right,' said Eazy. 'They're two others that I could see by the upstairs windows. One is that end and the other is over there.' He pointed in each direction.

'So how many all together?' asked Sleeper.

'I seen five like I just said,' he told them. 'So let's presume that there is at least eight, possibly worse case scenario is that there are ten of them protecting the two of them inside the house.'

'And just three of us,' smirked Tony, not liking the odds at all. 'Just how messy is this going to get?'

'Just watch your back,' smiled Sleeper as he nodded at Eazy who then without another word, made his way over to the tree.

Eazy climbed the tree as the two of them made their way over to the wall. Sleeper used Tony to shoulder him up onto the wall as he went to work with the razor wire, clipping it away with ease. Within seconds he was through the wire and over the wall.

He suddenly appeared again, holding his arm out to pull Tony over. As he grabbed and yanked Tony up and over the wall, Tony literally couldn't believe the mans strength. It was almost

unbelievable; Tony felt as if a tremendous giant had just scooped down and picked him from the ground. He stared in awe through the darkness at the man.

'Ready?' asked Sleeper without looking at him.

'Sweet,' he smiled as the two of them separated as planned.

Making their way through the nightfall in opposite directions, they weren't but a few feet from one another. When they suddenly heard the unmistakable pop, pop, pops from the tree. It sounded almost like a small paper bag popping quietly. But the white streaks from the tree indicated that it was no bag as Tony looked to Sleeper, who now nodded that he should follow him.

Screams could be heard clearly from at least two men by the house. Heading towards the noise they saw the two men, lying on the ground in agony as the Eazy had tore through both of their legs with the large calibre bullets.

Quickly taping their mouths with duct tape, Sleeper signalled to Tony to see what he could. Giving him a quick nod to let him know that he understood, he didn't even hear the shot ring out, as he suddenly cried out in anguish, as the bullet that caught him though the left shoulder sent him spinning like a rag doll tossed through the air despite his size.

Suddenly all hell broke loose, as all that could be heard was the sound of gun fire. Diving towards Tony, Sleeper pulled him towards the shelter of the house, as bullets exploded around them, grass and gravel exploded with them.

'So much for the surprise attack,' said Tony through gritted teeth as Sleeper actually smiled at him.

'You alright?' he asked Tony, who was clearly in pain.

'Felt better,' he smirked, as he grabbed his shoulder and saw the panic in the eyes of the two men left where they were.

More flashes could be seen from the tree as more screams rang out. 'Wait here,' instructed Sleeper as he suddenly pulled the two men free from the onslaught. Dumping them next to Tony who struggled to get up, but as he got to his feet, Sleeper was no where to be seen.

The next thing he saw, was Eazy running across the lawn, assault rifle spraying wildly as he continued to shoot at the men protecting the house.

'Fuck me, this shit feels good,' he laughed wildly like a crazed lunatic. 'Where's the brother? Whoa, you alright. I seen you hit the ground. It was the guy upstairs. I took care of him,' he grinned at Tony as he continued to look around him.

'What now?' asked Tony.

'That shoulder going to be alright?'

'It's alright,' he replied. 'We need to get out of here, or at least where we're not sitting ducks.'

Eazy nodded that he understood, as he couched down to the two men removing one of the duct tapes. 'How many is there in the house?'

'I ain't got a clue where Sleeper went,' said Tony, as Eazy grabbed the man's face and pulled it close to his. 'He just disappeared on me.'

'Yeah,' he smirked, glancing at Tony then back at the man. 'I asked you a question boy. How many more than the four, not including you two that I've just dropped, is there?' he asked the scared looking man that Tony recognised as Donnelly's son. 'Come on, I've got six of you, but I want to know how many more boy?'

'Another four,' he answered shakily, his face contorted in the pain he felt. 'Not including the old man or Vinnie.'

Placing the tape back over his mouth, he nodded at Tony. 'Let's make a move. We need to get inside of the house.'

'What about Sleeper?' he asked.

'He'll be taking care of business,' he replied. 'Now, can you move with that shoulder? Or are you just going to sit there feeling sorry for yourself.' He grinned stupidly at Tony as he struggled to get to his feet, the pain burning deeply in his shoulder.

But as soon as they stepped out of the cover of darkness, bullets tore up the ground around them. The shots were coming from an upstairs window at both ends of the house. Eazy cursed. 'I thought I'd taken care of both of them. I figured that others up there had both joined the other ones downstairs.'

'Obviously not,' said Tony. 'So what now?'

'Henessy,' they heard the old man shout from upstairs window as light spilled out onto the lawn, his shadow cast along with it. 'What the fuck do you thin...'

'That's what I'm talking about,' said Eazy suddenly laughing as the old man stopped in mid sentence and another shadow joined the old mans on the lawn.

'What's happened?' asked Tony, as Eazy casually walked out on the lawn and looked up at the window where he saw the back of Sleeper move away from the window with the old man.

'Come on,' he smiled as Tony confused and in pain followed the big man.

'Why's no one firing at us?'

'You'll see,' he said as he casually walked through the back door, where Tony could see five men, one was Ryan Donnelly

who didn't look at all impressed. The other included Vinnie who looked absolutely livid, backing into the kitchen unaware that they were heading through the door with guns already trained on them. They all had their arms in the air, as they watched what ever was before them.

'You just fucked yourself Nigger,' snarled Vinnie, through gritted teeth as the Eazy casually removed the handgun from the back of jeans startling him. 'What the...'

'I think I better take this,' laughed Eazy. 'That is before you go and shoot yourself in the arse boy.'

'You alright kid,' smiled Tony, as he realised what had happened.

'You just fucked yourself big time Henessy,' sneered Vinnie.

'I said to remain quiet,' said Sleeper, from the open doorway, as Tony smiled at him.

He was well protected with Dominic O'Leary before him, the lethal looking hooked blade held close to the old man's throat.

'Tony,' pleaded Dominic.

'I said quiet,' said Sleeper in a menacing voice.

'What the fuck is all this ab...' began Vinnie, as he suddenly screamed out in agony, the bullet that had been silently fired from Sleeper's Glock handgun, shooting him through his right kneecap.

'I said quiet,' he smiled shaking his head, as he nodded at Eazy.

Eazy pushed past the other men in the room, and grabbed Vinnie by his hair, dragging him through the open doorway towards the stairs. Releasing the old man, as he grabbed Vinnie from Eazy, the gun still trained towards the kitchen where Tony also had them covered.

'Me and you are going to go for a little chat boy,' he said as he turned to leave.

'No wait,' pleaded Dominic. 'Take me instead.'

'This ain't personal old man,' said Sleeper, as he kept his back turned to the kitchen where Eazy had just returned to. 'Believe me, if I thought you had the answers to the questions I wanted, then it'd be you that I'd be takin...'

'Get your fucking hands off me nigger,' screamed Vinnie, his face demented looking, as the pain became worse.

'Tony,' said Dominic, dropping to his knees. 'Don't let him do this. He doesn't know anything, honest Tony. You'd know that I'd tell you if he did. Please Ton...'

'He should have just answered the questions the other day then,' he told the man, who he helped up into a kitchen chair as

his men looked on, not quite sure what to make of the old man on the verge of tears.

'You lot come with me,' said Eazy leading them outside.

'Why Tony?' asked Dominic, as they were left alone and they saw Sleeper dragging Vinnie up the stairs as he screamed a string of venomous insults at him. 'What the fuck have you gone and don...'

'What the fuck are you protecting that prick for?' asked Tony before he could finish.

'He's all I've got left,' he replied, as Tony couldn't help but feel for the man before him.   'What's he going to do to him Tony?'

'I ain't even going to bother trying to lie to you Dominic,' he shook his head at him.   'He's going to put him through some serious pain old man. It has to be done. We need to know...'

'But he doesn't kno...'

'Where's Fingers Dom?'

'I don't know,' he said dropping his head.

'He was here though,' he said. 'Wasn't he old man?'

He nodded slowly. 'But I don't know if it had anything to do with that mans sister Tony. I swear it.'

'Then why is Vinnie so reluctant to tell us?'

'I don't know,' he shook his head.

'You know where your son was last night?' he asked. 'For well over two hours I might add?'

'No,' he replied slowly.

Tony proceeded to tell him where they had followed his to the previous evening whilst he sat there in a state of complete shock as he explained just whom it was he'd been visiting with.

Suddenly the others appeared, carrying what appeared to be wounded men. Their eyes in agony at the pain they felt, but the cries of anguish muted through the tape Eazy had placed over their mouths. Next was Eazy, he was dragging what appeared to be two dead guys into the house.

'Where's the cellar?' he demanded as one of the other men nodded the way and they all disappeared out of the kitchen. 'Right then, let's get you lads down there. You can wait this thing out or we can battle it out right now.' He smirked at the men as they shook their heads, glancing back and forth at the bulk of Tony and the mammoth frame of Eazy.

'Stop this madness Tony, please I beg you to. Remember just how far back we go,' he pleaded as the others disappeared. 'Please Tony, tell me... tell me... tell me what he's going to do with my...' Dominic began to say, as the intense screams

suddenly filled the interior of the house as the old man dropped his head in sorrow.

The three of them had waited in the kitchen as the screams continued throughout the duration. The old man kept his hands over his ears for most of that time, as Eazy and Tony drank cups of coffee, neither of them saying much. Only looking to their watches wondering just what it was that was taking place up them stairs.

Finally, Sleeper had called down to Tony, telling him that the old man could see his son now. He'd taken the old man up there as they then made their way, away from the house towards the main gates.

'So what's he say?' Eazy finally asked, breaking the silence hanging between them.

'You don't want to know,' replied Sleeper coldly, his first words since shouting Tony. 'I need to go and see Rachel alone.'

'Why?' asked Tony, confused and a little shaken by the sight he'd just witnessed through the open door of the bedroom where Sleeper had been.

'Then I need to call Chan,' he added ignoring his question.

'What the fuck is going on Sleeper?' demanded Tony.

'Yeah brother,' added Eazy also looking a little confused. 'What did the kid tell you? Was it this Fuckfingers or not?'

'I just need to see Rachel,' he repeated.

'Now hang on a minut...' began Tony.

'Just let me see her first,' he said without looking at either of them. 'Eazy, you go with Tony. Tell Chan to wait by the phone. He'll know which one.'

'But...'

'Just do as I say,' he snapped, walking ahead of them as they looked to one another confused.

Tony just stared at the back of him, wondering what the hell had happened up those stairs. All he knew for certain was that he'd spared Vinnie O'Leary his life. What little was left of it anyway. After he'd finished punishing him over and over again, he had spared him. Why?

Tony didn't know the reason why. And he'd only caught a quick glance at Vinnie as he'd taken the old man upstairs to him, but it had been enough.

Vinnie had been strapped naked to a chair, and although he couldn't be positive, he was almost certain that although he had spared him his life, he had taken away his manhood. The last

image he had was Dominic rushing into the room towards a bloody and delirious Vincent.

FIFTY ONE

'**W**here the hell are the others Sleeper?' asked Rachel annoyed, as Sleeper eased the already running Mercedes into gear. It was just gone four-thirty in the morning; Rachel had been waiting for Tony to arrive the night before as planned. Only when he hadn't shown by twelve and Brendan had still not left, she had succumb to temptation and ended up sleeping with him again.

When Sleeper had arrived all alone at her doorstep, looking flustered and a little wired at the same time, she had panicked. Sleeper told her abruptly to get dressed and meet him downstairs, which was when Brendan had appeared in the hallway, with only the bed sheet wrapped around him. She wasn't quite sure what Sleeper had made of the situation, only that he didn't look too impressed. Merely shaking his head, he instructed that she better hurry as they both had to go somewhere.

'Answer me Sleeper,' she demanded as he pulled out into the main road.

'Who was he?'

'Who?' she shrugged, knowing full well who he had meant.

He kissed his teeth as he started at her. 'Is that the other one?'

'Other what?'

'Other one like you?' he asked her. 'You know crim' shrink or whatever you want to call it Rachel.'

'Yes,' she nodded, as she sighed deeply. 'I don't quite know how I'm supposed to feel about it all though. I feel as if I doing something wrong, yet at the same time, well, you know what I...'

'It's your life Rach,' he told her. 'What were you going to do? Become a friggin nun or what girl?'

'I suppose not,' she said, tapping her lips thoughtfully. 'I won't deny that I was always a little attracted to him Sleeper. Only, I also promised myself that I wouldn't get involved with anybody until we'd caught the killer. Gabriel or whatever the fuck calls himself. I knew that he was attracted to me, or at least I thought I did. It had been so long with no other than Peter, that I kinda...'

'So what's the problem?'

'Never mind that for now,' she said changing the subject, and looking to him as she wrapped her Berghaus jacket tighter around herself to try and get a little warmer. 'You going to answer my question or not?'

'They're with Chan.' he said. 'I needed to see you alone.'

'Why though?'

'Because of what I was told a couple of hours ago.'

'Let's back track a little here Sleeper,' she said. 'Why don't you first tell me what happened the night before that.'

'To cut a long story short,' he said shaking his head, 'we followed Vinnie...'

'And,' she added as he stopped in mid sentence.

'And he led us to Halenbrook's over Alderley Edge way.'

'You what? Detective Halenbrook? Are you for real?' she was shocked. 'So now you think that Halenbrook is somehow involved?'

'Just bare with me,' he said as they pulled up at the traffic lights.

'Maybe he's on his payroll,' she snapped, thinking that this was becoming more and more confusing by the day. 'Surely he's not involved in this whole mess.'

'What conclusions did you come to?' he asked her. 'I mean did you find any connection to the O'Leary's, Freddy Marshall, the Pied Piper and Gabriel.'

'There were connections all over the place,' she sighed. 'But whether or not the connections are relevant to one another, is another matter completely. Why?'

'We visited with the O'Leary's a few hours back,' he told her as they took off again.

'And they just let you in?' she asked cocking her eyebrow at him.

'Not quite,' he smirked. 'Your brother was shot when we...'

'You what?' she screamed at him.

'Calm down, he's alright,' he told her realising how bad what he just said sounded. 'He was shot through his left shoulder. But Chan's got some doctor with him right no...'

'How the fuck did he manage to get shot?'

He could tell that she was annoyed. 'We figured, no that's a little unfair. I figured that it would be best if we just dropped in on them unexpected like. I figured after the other day when we questioned the lad and his old man kicked us out, that this time around we wouldn't be welcomed with open arms.'

'How badly wounded is he?'

'He'll be alright. The bullet went straight through luckily,' he said nodding. 'I knew that he wouldn't make this trip. And I didn't want Eazy here for it either. The way I figured this...'

'Hang on a minute Sleeper,' she said. 'What the hell happened there last night that my brother ended up taking a bullet?'

'We try to sneak in on them,' eh told her. 'Only they must have expected it. Anyway, whilst your brother and Eazy kept them busy I managed to get to the old man upstairs. I held him hostage 'till I got hold of Vinnie.'

'Did anybody die?'

'Maybe,' he shrugged.

'That's it,' she frowned at him. 'Maybe?'

'That's all I can tell you for now,' he said. 'Your Tony and Eazy would know more on that score than me. I took the kid upstairs and left the others to them.'

'Did you kill Vincent?'

'No,' he shook his head. 'But he came extremely close to death.'

'What did you d...' she stopped herself. 'On second thoughts, I don't want to know what you did to him.'

'I don't take pleasure in it,' he said defensively. 'I did what I had to, to make him talk.' He dropped is head as he began shaking it slowly back and forth. 'I also made sure that he would never be able to abuse or touch any more little kids or innocent victims. But it's not like I... you know what I'm trying to say... don't you Rachel?'

'I know,' she told him, without looking into his eyes. 'So what did he tell you? Is it Freddy Marshall or no...'

'He wouldn't cough to anything at first,' he told her. 'He was scared, and I don't just mean of me Rachel.'

'What do you mean then?'

'He was scared of the person he eventually told me about?'

'So he was involved then,' she said. 'He did know who the Pied Piper was?'

'He was involved.'

'So what...'

'Listen,' he said cutting her short. 'I'll get to all that. I'm still waiting to hear from Chan before I can even go there. But we're

going to an address he gave me. He says that we'll find Freddy there.'

'Did he send Freddy to kill your sister? she asked. 'Is Freddy, Gabriel? Where are we going to find him?'

'Hold up,' he sighed. 'Like I said. He's involved in the missing kids or more to the point. He's involved with the one he claims to be the Pied Piper. Apparently Freddy knows nothing of that side of things.'

'So why did he send him to kill Carol?'

'He's says that my Carol, got to close to the truth,' he said. 'He says that the ones responsible couldn't deal with it themselves. He said that he was ordered to find someone to carry out the hit against my sister, but definitely one-hundred percent as he put it, not Kyle.'

'So he ordered the...'

'He didn't order it,' he told her. 'He merely carried out someone else's orders.'

'And you believe him?'

'After what I put him through Rachel,' he sighed shaking his head at the same time, 'I believe that he was more scared of what they would do to him, than me.'

'Who's they?' she asked. 'You mean Halenbrook?'

'That's not all he told me about,' he said, ignoring her question. 'He told me that Freddy definitely isn't the killer, that he wasn't the one who killed your family or my mine.'

'But surely he...'

'He says that Freddy is scared for his life,' he told her. 'Says that Freddy went to carry out the hit, no questions asked. But when he got there he saw the killer leaving the house. He knows who the real killer is.'

'Who is it?' she snapped.

'The kid said that whoever it is, must have scared him real bad,' he said. 'Because whoever it was, he wouldn't even tell his best mate. Just said that he had to go into hiding until this whole thing blew over.'

'You sure that you believe all of this?' she asked a little frustrated. 'And what did   Vincent tell you the relation to the Pied Pi...'

Just then there was a loud shrill from a mobile phone. As Sleeper removed the phone from beside the seat she noticed that it was an old Motorola phone. One of the first ones that were so big and bulky, that they were more hassle than they were worth. But what she couldn't understand was why Sleeper had this phone.

'You alright Chan,' he said into the mouth piece. 'You got that information for me...' There was a pause as he nodded at whatever Chan was telling him. 'Yes I'm sure that's what he told me old man.' Another pause. 'Well that's what we're trying to find out.' Another pause as he glanced at Rachel. 'We'll go and see after we've visited with Freddy. Cheers for that old man. We'll see you later.' He switched the phone off and replaced it under his seat.

'What was all that about?' she asked. 'And what are doing with such an old phone Sleeper?'

'It's untraceable,' he told her. 'I've got the thing chipped so that it scrambles all calls. Nobody can scan it or pick it up by accident or any other means through the airways.'

'So what about the other thing?'

'Let's see what Freddy has to say first eh.'

'Why?' she asked. 'I'm so fucking confused here Sleeper, that I don't know if I'm coming or going.'

'Because you'll not believe me,' he said as he glared at her, 'if I just tell you.'

'Try me.'

'I want us to see with our own eyes if what the kid told me is true,' he said. 'So first we'll drop in on...'

'Where is he?' she asked as her mobile phone began to ring. Annoyed at the interruption she yanked the phone free from her jacket glancing at her watch. It had to be Brendan seeing how she was. She'd left him there, but he'd said that he'd be leaving soon if she wasn't going to stick around.

'What? It doesn't mater where I am. What? Whatever Hunter. You called me remember,' she said into the phone impatiently as Sleeper saw her begin to nod at whatever she was being told. 'He's where? Macclesfield? Are you sure that's the right address?' There was some time in between as Sleeper observed her absorb the information. 'You're one-hundred percent about this Hunter? We're on our way, and thanks,' she added as she switched the phone off.

'Don't tell me,' said Sleeper. 'The address you've just received is 376 Peter Street in Macclesfield.'

'That's where we was heading anyway right?'

'Why did she tell you first?' he asked, wanting to know why the police would inform her before they went after the man themselves.

'She said she'd give us half an hour on him.'

'But why?'

'Because she claims that she feels...'

'She's full of shit,' he snapped. 'And how did she find out where he is?' he demanded, not at all happy.

'She said that one of her snitches just gave the address,' she told him. 'She also says that the lab came up with his semen at your sister's house.'

'When?'

'Just last night.'

'And they never found it before?' he shook his head.

'This isn't...'

'Something is a miss here Rachel.'

'What do you mean by that?'

'This is why I needed you here for this,' he told her. 'If what the kid told me is true, then I want you question him. I don't want to have to resort to what I did with Vinnie. I want the right answers from him. If he provides them, then I'll kill him quickly. But I need you tell me whether or not he's lyi...'

'Whoa,' she said. 'You can't just go around kill...'

'And if he is the one?' he asked her. 'If he is the one that killed your family Rachel? What then? Or have you got a different set of morals on that score. You seem to forget that this guy would have killed my sister if she hadn't already been killed.'

They sat there in silence as she thought over what he said, and he speeded towards the town of Macclesfield.

'Why don't you like Hunter?' she asked him.

'I don't trust her.'

'Simple as that?'

'Simple as that,' he replied. 'I've told you before Rachel. I have an uncanny ability to work people out. And she gives off some bad vibes. And believe me; I've been in the vicinity of some very...'

'Maybe your signal a little haywire,' she told him. 'If she didn't care, she wouldn't have supplied me with...'

'Listen Rachel,' he said. 'If Freddy's whereabouts are available to the police from the streets, then believe me girl. They're available to the killer also.'

'Oh shit,' she sighed, 'I never thought about that. How long will it take us to get there?'

'About another ten minutes if I floor it,' he said, as they speeded through the deserted roads towards their destination.

'You sure that's the house?' asked Rachel, as they climbed from the car in the quiet residential street. There was nobody around and the house they were stood outside was one of the larger ones on that street of miscellaneous looking houses. It

looked to be three stories high, either that or they'd converted the loft into another floor. The house looked, not so much deserted, but that all its residents were, as they should be at this time of the morning, asleep.

'It's 376 ain't it,' he said, passing her a set of clear gloves. Gloves like that of a surgeon, as she pulled them over her hands he nodded towards the side of the house. 'Let's check around the back of the house. Apparently Freddy knows the owner of the house. They did time together a few years back in Strangeways. Apparently the guy's straight, he just got stitched on some job a few years back at Manchester Airport. Freddy took a liking to him and watched his back whilst he was inside. Because the guy's clean so to speak, no one apparently knows about him.'

'There's a gate,' she said, as they made their way down the alleyway at the side of the house. 'There is a light on up there,' she pointed to the top floor. 'Look, it's flickering I think.'

'The gates locked,' said Sleeper staring at the top floor. 'Just give me a minute. Eazy's got all of the tools,' he told her as he went to work on the door. Although using a switchblade to try and force the lock open.

As the door finally gave way, with a loud crack, they both stood silently still. Paranoid that they had just disturbed someone. Hearing no alarms or anything to indicate they had been discovered, they walked through into a large conservatory. The air was cool and they could see their breath in clouds of white whispers.

The place stank of flowers and plants that appeared to be hanging and surrounding them everywhere. The conservatory led through the house's back door and into the garden. The door led through into the kitchen, but was locked. Sleeper didn't want to chance busting the lock without his tools, so walked out into the garden, where there was another door to be found.

'Check this out,' said Sleeper quietly, indicating for her to look at the door. 'Someone has already forced this.'

'Is it open?'

He nodded as he pushed the door open, his Glock already pulled, as Rachel noticed the extension on the end, knowing full well that it was a silencer or suppresser, whatever they called it. Walking through into the cold dining room that looked as if it had never been decorated. The walls were cream or even white; it was hard to tell in the light that they had. Family photographs donned the walls; some very old ones were beside some more up to date ones. The table and chairs were old looking, but they suited the room. Walking towards the door they found the

hallway that led through to the front door. They could see the outline of Sleeper's silver Mercedes through the frosted glass.

From what they could see in the diminished light, the rest of the house looked nothing like the dining room. It was decorated conservatively, but it complimented the homes interior. They made their way towards the stairs in the darkly lit house, as Sleeper suddenly looked at Rachel.

'You hear that?' he asked her quietly.

'What,' she said confused.

'Someone is up there,' he said in hushed tones.

'You sure?' she asked, as she couldn't hear a thing.

'Positive,' he said.

'What are we...'

'This way,' he said as he headed up the stairs.

'Shit,' she sighed following him.

But as they came to the landing they noticed a pine spiral staircase that led them to another level. They could also see the light that they had seen from downstairs. Before Rachel could say anything Sleeper was already making his way towards them. He was only two steps up, when suddenly the light from upstairs darkened as a shadow filled its void.

Before they knew what had happened, a completely head to toe, black clad figure leapt directly at Sleeper, before he could aim his gun at the target. Their was a high pitched scream, like that of a child from the figure as it knocked Sleeper flying into Rachel who involuntarily screamed out loud as the three of them tumbled towards the other set of stairs. Everything was happening so quickly, Rachel couldn't focus her mind or her vision on anything.

Rachel stopped just short of the top stair as the other two tumbled straight down them. The wooden banister snapping in several places as Sleeper struggled to grab a hold of whomever it was he was fighting with. Spotting something shiny, Rachel saw Sleeper's handgun by the landings banister. As she grabbed for it, totally confused at what was happening, she heard them both hit the floor as Sleeper groaned loudly.

Gun in hand, Rachel leapt for the stairs as she saw Sleeper lay there all alone grabbing his right leg. She just caught sight of the black clad figure running for the dining room door as she ran down the stairs.

'Shoot the fucker Rachel,' cried Sleeper in agony as blood seeped from his leg.

'Jesus,' she screamed. 'What the...'

'The mother fucker stabbed me,' cried Sleeper, as he struggled to remove the large hunting knife that was protruding from his leg. 'Go on Rachel,' he cried out in agony as he pulled the knife from his leg.

Leaving him there, she ran for the dining room door, straight through the dining room itself and into the back garden that's only light was from the moon. But no matter how little light she had, she saw the silhouette of the black figure running across the neighbour's wall. Tall, slim, athletic looking, almost reminding Rachel of a cat or more to the point, *Catwoman* played by *Michelle Pfeiffer* in *Batman Returns*.

Rachel aimed the suppressed handgun at the target as it sped along the wall with ease; she aimed and fired the gun as it exploded in her hand. The suppresser, restraining the loud roar that should have followed the shots as she continued to empty the pistol at the target. The recoil from each shot, sending her arms forcibly back into her chest, as the figure turned and nodded at her before jumping down out of sight. Sprinting across the lawn she leapt at the wall grabbing the top brick, pulling herself up onto the top, she took pursuit of the one she'd searched so long for.

Leaping down from the wall into another garden, she saw another street ahead as yellow street lights left the opening hazy. She ran through an alleyway belonging to the house leading out into the opposite street. But as she got out into the deserted street, she heard the tumultuous reverberation of a motorbike, as its wheels screeched and spun wildly. Looking to the top of the street, she saw the black clad figure zooming away into the night.

Admitting defeat to herself she turned, and ran as fast as she could back over the wall and into the garden belonging to 376 Peter Street. As she got through the dining room into the hallway, Sleeper was no where to be seen. But there was a trail of blood leading back up the stairs. She ran towards the pine staircase two at a time and then pulled her way up the spiral case. The whole floor was made of pine floorboards; she saw that the trail led into the bedroom on the left hand side where the light spilled from.

As she entered the room, she saw the back of Sleeper shaking his head. Immediately looking at the wound where the knife had struck she saw that he'd tied a tea-towel around his leg, to stem the flow of blood that had seeped everywhere.

'You alright?' she asked, the handgun burning slightly in her hand as it began to throb from the guns ferocious discharge.

He merely nodded his answer as he stared at the sight before him. Because the blood he'd lost was nothing compared to the latest creation Gabriel had left for them. For hung from the wooden curtain rail naked, with his chest torn open, was Freddy Marshall. Rachel recognised him immediately as the man from the photographs she'd seen in his file.

The curtains had been pulled up and over his arms, nailed into the corners of the sloping ceiling that was part of the roof. The way he'd portrayed his victim in the room that had been built into the roof of the house, actually made him look as if he was swooping down towards you. Blood still dripped from him as Rachel once again observed the fact that Gabriel hadn't taken the victims heart.

Just what was going through his mind as he carried out these horrific acts of the depraved. She noticed something else though, as she bent to take a closer look at his face. His eyes were missing from there sockets. Only they hadn't been popped from them. Gabriel had literally cut them out as an act of vengeance for what his victim had seen.

'Is that him?' asked Sleeper without turning towards her.

'It's him,' she said.

'Looks like the kid was telling the truth then,' he sighed.

'He must have been,' she said. 'Because Gabriel has cut his eyes out of their sockets.'

'Why?'

'Why do you think?'

'He saw something that he wasn't supposed to.'

'Exactly.'

'Whoever the fuck it was, was one strong son of a bitch Rachel,' he said in disbelief. 'But there was something weird about him.'

'What do you mean?'

'I'm not sure yet,' he said looking at her. 'It was like he wasn't real almost. I know it sounds strange, but there was something not right about him. I just can't put my finger on what it was though.'

'So what now?'

'We get the fuck out of here,' he said turning. 'After your little display outside, I've already clocked six or seven lights come on in the neighbouring area. Even with the silencer fitted, there was some commotion.'

'You going to be alright with that leg?'

'I will be, once we get the hell out of here Rachel,' he said, making his way towards the door as he turned and looked at the

corpse once more. 'We're getting closer to the truth Rachel. We have to be, you know why?'

'Why?'

'Because he's only one step ahead of us now.'

'I know,' she said, but wasn't at all sure why.

FIFTY TWO

'**Y**ou sure that you're up to this?' asked Rachel concerned, as she drove Sleeper's Mercedes across the town of Knutsford, towards the address Sleeper had provided for her. The night's sky had turned to early morning mist, which floated in a surreal demeanour, which seemed aware of the temperament that had been set. Rachel's head hurt like you wouldn't believe.

She couldn't quite comprehend the fact she had, had Gabriel within her grasp, so close and yet as always, so far away.

Concepts and notions raced through her head like a speeding bullet that wasn't to be stopped, about how close they had been only hours before. Thoughts about what Gabriel had gone and done once again. Sleeper had been right in what he said about them getting closer to the truth. But what she feared more than anything was that they may have scared him away in hiding once again.

Because for whatever reason Gabriel had set out killing innocent people for, it had now changed. His motivation for his crimes now was a lot simpler to fathom out. It would appear that he was killing to cover his tracks along the way. Anybody who was considered a threat was merely being disposed of in what he obviously perceived as acts of vengeance.

But then when the police, not so much her, thought that they had worked out just who the killer was, it takes yet another twist as the killer kills their suspected killer. She shook her head at all of the thoughts racing through them and stared at Sleeper who hadn't answered her and was clearly in a lot of pain. 'You still haven't told me what else Vinnie told you.'

'Christ, this hurts,' he said ignoring her more recent question and answering her old one, grabbing his leg, looking at her as he smiled. 'Don't worry about it, I'll be alright. Look, what Vinnie told me, well I'm not hiding anything... well I suppose I am. But

501

it's only because I want to show you first what he told me. I think only before even I've seen it with my own eyes, will I truly believe it myself. What time is it?'

'Seven twenty,' she replied. 'Why?'

'I just wanted to know. I'm wondering if this cat is still going to be at home or not,' he told her. 'So Rach, you really like this guy or what?'

'You what!' she exclaimed. 'Why you so interested?'

'I just am. That and the fact I'm trying to keep my mind off this bleeding pain,' he said. 'What do you know about him?'

'What's with the thousand and one questions Sleeper?'

'I just wondered what the guy was like,' he smiled warmly at her, although she could see that he was in so much pain that the smile was little strained. 'I just wondered what it was that you liked about him.'

'We should get you to a hospital,' she said, wanting to change the subject on Brendan. She still wasn't sure of what it was that she felt for Brendan McCarthy. And questions about what she knew about him, just made her realise that basically she knew nothing, apart from what he'd told her the other night that was. She knew she was attracted to him, she even knew she liked his company, but what else did she really know about him.

'I ain't going to no hospital,' he said breaking her thoughts.

'But it won't stop bleeding Sleeper,' she shook her head. 'You look a little a pale as well.'

'I've always looked a little pale girl,' he smirked at her. 'Or so the brothers keep telling me anyway.'

They both laughed, as she couldn't believe he was joking about with her in such a casual manner. 'Are you sure that you're going to get through this?'

'I will,' he said. 'I don't want to chance putting this off. If what the kid told me about this Pied Piper is right, and let's face it. What he told us about Freddy Marshall was right. So if he's right, and I pray to god that he's actually wrong for all our sakes. But if he's right then we can't waste any time on it.'

'You're starting to scare me here Sleeper,' she said honestly.

'That's because it scares me,' he said.

'But I don't believe that you're scared of anything...'

'There,' he said ignoring her, and pointing to a opening through what appeared to be a dirt track of some kind, taking them away from all residential areas. 'Pull in down that road over there.'

Just who the hell had Vinnie told him about, that it scared the man beside her? The man who she thought wasn't scared of

anybody, although, she thought possibly it was different kind of fear that he felt.

'Where does this lead us?' she asked, as they were suddenly surrounded by over grown fields and trees.

'To a farmhouse,' he told her.

'Who's farmhouse?'

He didn't answer her. He just sat there lay as far back in the seat as possible, as he continued to stare out of the window at the countryside surrounding them. Her mind was filled with confused convictions. Thoughts and concepts about what Sleeper was keeping from her. What was Halenbrook's involvement in all of this? Was he the Pied Piper? At this point she thought that she'd believe just about anything.

She wondered why it was that she hadn't heard from Hunter. She supposed that she was tied up with the house in Macclesfield, where they had no doubt found the body of Frederick Marshall in the upstairs bedroom. Rachel also wondered if anybody had spotted the two of them. And what would happen when they discovered Sleeper's blood at the scene.

And just how had Gabriel found out about Marshall's whereabouts? Just who the hell was Gabriel she wondered? For that must have been him only hours before. Why had he stopped on top of that wall and nodded at her, taunting her even more than he already was doing.

And what had Sleeper meant by saying the he seemed almost unreal. A strange entity of some kind. He hadn't said anything further, and she could tell that something about the killer they searched baffled him. It had all happened so quickly that Rachel didn't get a good enough look at the masked figure. The only images that remained were like those that haunted her dreams, only that hadn't been a dream, for that had very much been reality. They had stood within the same confines of the house that the killer who had taken their families had stood at the very same time he'd been there.

'You need to pull in over there,' said Sleeper. 'We need to check whether there is anybody at home or not.'

'And how are we going to do that?' she asked, pulling the car behind a embankment of trees that took them away from the dirt road they had travelled down for the last ten minutes. She could just about see the farmhouse up ahead. It looked more like a cottage than a farmhouse, there certainly didn't appear to be any animals running around.

'I'll make a call,' he said struggling to turn so he was able get to the phone.

Rachel leaned over his body to retrieve the phone and felt his presence a little more than she should have, as he smiled at her. There was nothing sexual about it, but she felt something else, as she stared into his black eyes.

'Here,' she said handing him the phone, a little embarrassed without knowing why. 'Let me take a look at that leg whilst you do what ever you've got to do.'

As Sleeper began to punch in the numbers from memory, Rachel untied the bloody tea-towel. Tearing at his black trousers, revealing the pale brown flesh that was now a dark tide of wet sticky blood. She touched the outer part of the gaping gash in his leg as he flinched and couldn't help but smile at him as he laughed at her. But saying that, it was very serious. There was no denying that it was a bad laceration. It looked deep; in fact it looked as if it could have slightly severed through an artery, hence the amount of blood that was still flowing from there.

'No ones ho...' he suddenly stopped what he was saying, as she looked at him. He was staring out of the driver's window as she looked out she saw the Maroon Ford Granada zoom past, totally unaware of them being there. 'That was him.'

'Who?' she asked impatiently, becoming tired of all his evasiveness. 'Who the fuck was it Sleeper?'

'Let's go,' he said wrapping the bloody tea-towel back around his leg as they departed from the car.

Considering the severity of the gash, Sleeper appeared to be able to walk along with only a slight indication of a limp as they headed for the house.

'Why won't you tell me who it is Sleeper?'

'Because I want to be certain first,' he told her.

'And how you going to do that?'

'Two things that I know about. First thing we need to do is check the cellar out. Once I have the confirmation of what Vinnie told me, then I'll know...'

'How will you be certain of it though?'

'Because after that...' he stopped and looked at her then replied. 'I know where the children are buried Rachel. If what he told me was correct that is.'

'Shouldn't we bring the police into this Sleeper?' she asked. 'I know how you feel about them. But if what you're saying is...'

'Let's take a look first,' he told her. 'Then we'll decide what it is that we are going to do. Alright Rach?'

'Alright,' she replied a little warily. 'You better take this hadn't you.' she added handing him the silver Glock handgun that she still had in her possession.

'No,' he shook his head, as he reached around the back of him. 'You better take this. I think you emptied the other already.' He handed her another bullet clip for the gun as she reloaded it professionally, loading one bullet into the chamber.

'I think you've done that before,' he said nodding at her as he couldn't help but smirk at the same time.

'What do you think, with growing up around Tony,' she smiled at him as they entered the gate into the small yet very plain looking garden that surrounded the farmhouse or cottage, whatever it was. It looked like something straight out of an old painting, although the house hadn't received its full potential

'Just not much practise firing them,' added Sleeper indicating to the gun as Rachel shook her head at him.

'Yeah,' she shrugged. 'I've not got much experience in that department, as you well know after my pathetic attempt to...'

'Don't worry about it,' he said. 'But I feel a lot better if you kept hold of it for now.'

'What about you?' she asked, as he reached down into the left hand side of his black jacket and produced another handgun of similar appearance.

'I think I'll be alright,' he told her.

'Who the hell lives here,' she said, more as a statement now than a question, as they stood before the large house. It looked deserted. No lights were on and only the sound of nature could be heard all around them.

'Let's take a look in this guy's cellar,' said Sleeper, as he pulled his switchblade and jammed it into the door where the lock was located.

The door gave surprisingly easily and they were standing before an open doorway almost immediately. 'Whoever it is, sure isn't concerned about security,' said Rachel staring into the darkly lit home. 'No alarms either.'

'I know,' shrugged Sleeper. 'But who'd hear them all the way out here though.'

'True,' she replied, stepping through the doorway into the nicely furnished house.

The house was both warm and very conformable looking as Rachel pulled the gloves over her hands, that Sleeper once again gave her. Although the house appeared to look very nice and comfortable, although it didn't feel lived in. She immediately suspected that whoever lived here, lived all alone.

Sleeper walked straight for the stairs and around the back of them where the kitchen could be found, they discovered a wooden door. It was locked and appeared more secure than the front door was. He used the blade once again to gain access, taking a little longer than he did with the front door. As soon as the door opened, they felt the warm air rise up and out through the door.

'Follow me,' said Sleeper hitting the light switch, as he made his way down the steep wooden steps in the now brightly lit cellar.

'What's down here?' she asked, as they both were now stood in one of the rooms that was spacious, but was nothing out of the ordinary. 'It just looks like a laundry room Sleeper. Washer, dryer, dirty clothes.'

'Wait a minute,' he said, as he stepped towards a large metal cabinet that looked like one of the cabinets that Hunter had in her office, the ones that contained all of the many files, relating to old cases. 'Here, feel this.' He was moving his hand around the side of the cabinet.

Taking Rachel's hand he placed it against the side of the door. 'Is that a draft?'

'Help me to move this will you,' he said, grabbing the heavy cabinet as they both eased it away from the wall.

'What the hell is this?' asked Rachel, staring at the large hole that had been professionally cut through into another room that was completely in the dark.

'Well there is only one way to find out,' said Sleeper, crouching low enough to step through into the room. Fumbling about, it was Rachel who found the light switch as they were suddenly engulfed in array of different magical colours.

'Check this shit out,' said Sleeper looking around himself, as he stepped to the entrance and took a good look at the painting shaking his head. He then walked over to the far side with there was electrical equipment, with his back to Rachel as he asked her. 'You worked out what the theme is yet?'

She didn't answer, as she stared in a mixture of awe and horror at the room. It was about twenty five – by twenty five foot in diameter. There was computer equipment everywhere to be seen. Shelves were stacked with endless amounts of video cassettes and DVD covers. Very much like what Sleeper and Eazy had discovered down in London.

But that wasn't the main thing you noticed, for the entire room, including the ceilings had been painted with a colourful mural. It reminded Rachel of a children's nursery or bedroom filled with

magical colours that flowed into one another. As Rachel stared in disbelief at the main concept of the painting, she realised that she was looking at pictures of kids that had been painted, all of them dancing along happily around the walls back towards to entrance they had stepped through.

But as she stepped closer she realised that the kid's faces that had been painted, were in fact the children that had been taken from the estates. Some faces she didn't recognise, but she presumed that they were from London. She suddenly stopped in her tracks as she stared at the doorway where the picture of the Pied Piper had been painted gloriously. As she walked over to the door, with Sleeper now sat at the bureau with all of the computer equipment as he tapped away at the keys, there was one face belonging to the children that really stood out to her, it was the face of the girl that had hold of the man's waist, the man being the Pied Piper playing his flute for all the kids that followed him.

'What the...' she began to say, as she stared at the picture and Sleeper tapped away at the computer bringing an array of new and more perverse material than they had already discovered. 'Sleeper, Sleeper, look. That's Charlotte Cartwright that he's painted on the wall.'

'Probably,' he answered not moving away from the desk.

'What do mean probably Sleeper?' she snapped.

'The other kids faces are those of the ones that have gone missing, right Rachel?'

'Right,' she replied angrily again. She was becoming agitated by his attitude, as Sleeper got up and walked over to her. 'But what abou...'

'Take a good look at the Pied Piper's face Rachel,' he said, taking her face gently in his hands and turning it, holding it towards the painting as her jaw literally dropped. 'Charlotte belonged to him. The Cartwright's had known him for years. They gave her to him when she was only a baby. I just can't work out why he never killed her earlier. Vinnie told me all about it last night.'

'No, no, this can't be him,' she said in true disbelief.

'Why do you think he's got away with for so long?'

'But he's... no this can't be...'

'Can't be what Ms. Murphy,' said the voice from the doorway that she instantly recognised. 'I can't be the Pied Piper. Why not? He was always my favourite hero when I was growing up. Around these parts I might add. I just loved the way he was able

to entice the kids away so easily. It just made my spine tingle when I th...'

Sleeper went for gun as he realised he left it at the desk with the computer. 'Don't you move another step,' screamed Halenbrook, at him as he pointed a large looking handgun at him.

But Rachel wasn't even looking at him; she stared in utter disbelief at the man beside him. 'Mackenzie,' cried Rachel in pure undiluted stupefaction, as she stared at both him and also Halenbrook as they stepped further into the room.

'So now you know,' he smiled at her, with his arms folded across his fully uniformed chest. Dressed to the hilt in his chief of police uniform that he wore so proudly, as Halenbrook pointed the gun at the two of them.

'I'll take that Rachel,' said the weasel, Halenbrook, as she handed the gun over to him and he retrieved Sleepers as well.

'Why?' she asked. 'Why Mackenzie? How could you kill children? For what? They were so innocen...'

'Because I could. Because to take a life that hasn't really lived yet gave me great pleasure Murphy,' he was smirking at her as and she realised that he looked nothing more than a child himself as he recounted what he had done without any remorse towards his victims as he then added, 'Besides, they begged me to kill them in the end. They had been abused so badly by my associates that they always came so willingly with me. Especially when they saw the uniform. I mean after all, what do you always tell your children. If you get in trouble or lost now kids, always find yourself a nice policeman to help you.' He roared with laughter as Halenbrook smiled cruelly at them as they shook their heads as at one another.

'Why Charlotte Cartwright though?'

'Because she went and discovered the truth about not only her family,' he said. 'But also about me. She found out about the website. You may not believe this, but I really loved the girl. But she should have been killed along with her sister all those years ago. She was becoming older and more knowledgeable. The plan all along had been to stage an accident where they would both be killed at the same time. Only Luther fucked it up with one of his drunken sessions with the girl. I had to do everything I could to cover the whole issue up and have it written off as an accident. So it made things harder for us, we was just setting the website up and the last thing we needed was people snooping too closely into the death of the girl.

'So we couldn't kill Charlotte back then, as there had already been too many questions asked about her sister's death. So we did the opposite, she got anything and everything she wanted. But it was never enough. The girl was fucked in the head. She had come to think of me as her lover, but as she got older she didn't pleasure me anymore. But she wouldn't take no for an answer. She always wanted me at the end of the day. That's why I used to have to sneak her away for a few days at a time. Whenever she started to get a little too hyper. She was like a time-bomb waiting to go off. But then started getting suspicious about her mother and father. She told me all about it. She thought what we had done, had been out of love for her.

'But she thought what her father and mother were doing with the stable girls at the house was somehow wrong. That's what I mean by she was fucked in the head. She went and did what you did. Snooped around without even me knowing about it. That's why we didn't want you snooping around her disappearance. She was too much of a liability, just as you've now become too much of a liabi...'

'You're fucking sick Mackenzie,' said Sleeper.

'Oh come on now,' he said. 'How can you of all people say something like that about me? Especially when you're much more of a cold killer than I'll ever be.'

'Never put us in the same league.'

'So what would you call what you did to Vinnie last night then?' asked Halenbrook. 'That poor lad won't even be able t...'

'He got what he deserved,' said Sleeper, as Rachel just stood there staring at the three of them still in a state of utter disbelief.

'You cut his damn balls off for Christ sake,' said Mackenzie, with apparent disgust upon his face.

'And if that wasn't enough,' added Halenbrook, 'you broke all of his fingers so badly I don't think he'll be able to use them properly again.'

'I should have cut them off as well,' said Sleeper coldly. 'But don't worry, I won't make that mistake with the two of you.'

Rachel was shaking her head; this was all just too much. 'Why did you even let me look into the case?'

'Hunter the silly cow threatened to go to the press about the disappearance of the girl,' said Mackenzie. 'And you were only then supposed to provide her with a better picture of the girl. Not conduct your own fucking investigation. It all began spiralling out of control and we just couldn't stop it from doing so. We thought that it all ended with the Cartwright's. We couldn't have

planned a better ending, well, that was until we found out about your sister. She had found the connection between the O'Leary kid and me from years ago. I was the one who helped have his charges dropped. Without the old man knowing of course. But it was soon after that, that I recruited the lad for my own uses. So your sister was to be the last chapter in the story, no more loose ends. But she obviously not only pissed us off, she obviously pissed the killer of your husband and child off.'

'Do you know who Gabriel is?' asked Rachel. 'Anabella and Luther claimed they knew who he wa...'

'They told me they knew also,' he said shaking his head. 'They were both full of shit though. They knew fuck all. I tell you, if I knew who this mother fucker was I'd bring him in. It'd be just the thing we need to get the support we need from the public.'

'Where are the children?' asked Rachel believing he didn't know who Gabriel was.

'Dead and buried,' he laughed. 'I had some fun with them before they suffered. I can see the questions racing through your eyes Rachel. You're doing your best to try and analyse me. Aren't you? You want to know why I did it. What makes me do the things that I do? Just how did he turn out the way he did? It's all a viscous circle Rachel. My great-great grandfather did his kids, that led to my great grandfather, doing my granddad, that led to him doing my dad, that led all the way down to me and my sister, who I ended up killing when I played the games that my granddad and my dad used to play with me. They all suffered, just like my sister suffered at the hands of...,' he stopped himself, as they could clearly see that he had became aroused at what he'd told them.

'What do you want me to do with them?' asked Halenbrook.

'Take them both to the burial site,' he smiled. 'We'll bury them with the others.' He saw Rachel's look.

'You have them her...'

'Of course I have them buried here at my house,' he smiled as he straightened his tie. 'I mean what better place to bury their little bodies. I mean who the fuck is going to actually come and dig up the grounds of the chief of police? You should just never have gone sticking your nose in where it wasn't wanted.'

'Now come on,' said the little weasel next to him.

'You taking us to the greenhouse?' asked Sleeper.

'Bravo,' laughed Mackenzie clapping his hands at him. 'That's right; we're taking you to the greenhouse.'

Halenbrook stepped closer to Sleeper. 'Bad cut you've got there,' he smirked as he slammed the handgun into his leg, and

he gritted his teeth to drive out the pain collapsing to the hard concrete floor. 'I'll be taking all of these as well,' he added as he removed all of Sleeper's knives, including the throwing ones and the hooked one with the carved bone handle.

'Leave him be,' said Rachel, as she helped Sleeper to his feet.

'Thanks,' he mumbled as Halenbrook stepped away from them.

'Come now,' said Mackenzie, as they all walked up the wooden steps and out into the kitchen.

Mackenzie led them out in to the garden that looked just as plain as the front garden had. Leading them down and into the huge greenhouse he had at the far end of the garden. Rachel was instantly reminded of the aroma of what she had smelt in the conservatory

'Why did you set up the website?' asked Rachel. 'Why would you do something like that, you sick pervert?'

'Believe me,' he smirked, as he followed them through the door into the greenhouse. 'If you only knew just how many times the site is accessed each day, you wouldn't even ask me something so ridiculous. I make so much money from it it's untrue.'

'So that's what it all comes down to,' said Sleeper. 'Fucking money?'

'Oh that's only a small part of it,' he said. 'I just figured that I might as well earn from my pleasures so to speak.'

'How can you keep something so big from so many peop...' began Rachel.

'Oh believe me Ms Murphy,' he sighed as Halenbrook pushed them deeper into the greenhouse. 'After your involvement we've got to rearrange everything. We'll shut the website down and open it again. It's easy enough to do when you know how. Our security will have to be tighter than ever before. But I will say one thing, from all of the information you supplied Hunter with, you actually provided us with some good ideas,' he laughed. 'Ironic really, you tried to help Hunter and in doing so, you helped us inadvertently.'

'Fuck both of you,' sneered Rachel.

'Like I said before,' laughed Mackenzie sadistically. 'I think it's more like fuck you. Now I think it would be quite appropriate if you began digging over there Ms Murphy.' He pointed to the far right corner of the green house.

'If you dig deep enough, which we want you to do, as we'll be burying you both there,' said Halenbrook. 'But seeing as the last one that was buried there was Charlotte, it'll be quite fitting really, don't you think.' He laughed sadistically at her.

'Go fuck yourself,' said Sleeper, grabbing the shovel as Rachel took it from him shaking her head.

She knew there was no way that he could manage that with his leg, as she began shovelling the hard frozen soil away.

She lost track of how long it before she was almost five foot down, her arms aching as she felt the hot sweat mingle with the cool air making her shiver, when she hit something soft. Bending down she wiped way the dirt and realised that she was staring at the face of Charlotte Cartwright through the thick blue plastic bag, where she had been placed before burial. The frozen ground had preserved her well. She could see that her throat had been slit wide open. She continued with her hands to brush away the cold wet soil. Brushing away as much as she could, as she stared at the naked body of the girl that was covered in an array of different bruises. It was clear that she had been psychically abused before her life had been finally taken from her.

Rachel felt tears escaping for the girl she had never even met, yet felt as she had known so well. Her face looked so innocent, although Rachel now knew that all of that innocence had been lost years before at the hands of the sick pervert behind her. Covered in dirt and filth that appeared to be everywhere, she shook her head at Sleeper as he held his hand out to help her out of the hole.

'Now then,' said Mackenzie aiming one of Sleeper's guns at them. 'I believe that we've just about come to end of any more uses for you.'

As she stood before Mackenzie and Halenbrook, staring at the man she now realised had always loathed. And the weasel of a man beside him, who she had taken an immediate dislike to. Shaking her head at them as they grinned stupidly at the two of them, she knew that she was about to die at the hands of these sick freaks of nature.

The thought only angered her further still; they couldn't be allowed to get away with this. This couldn't be happening. People had to know the truth about what they had been doing. She felt a rage building from deep within. She felt as if her head was about to explode, everything that had happened just boiling and boiling towards the surface, as she suddenly without thinking of any consequences, swung out with the spade as hard as she could, aiming straight for Halenbrook who was the closer of the two.

She caught Halenbrook square in the face as he squealed in agony, dropping to the floor like a sack of potatoes. Suddenly

shots rang out, as Sleeper ran, ignoring the pain he felt in his leg straight for Mackenzie. Leaping at him, as Halenbrook jumped for Rachel, only she swung again at his head, the spade slipping side ways in her grip, slicing a gash straight across his face with the side of the spades funnel, more screams as Mackenzie and Sleeper fell to the ground and he struggled to get the gun that Mackenzie refused to relinquish.

Halenbrook was screaming in agony, as Rachel raised the spade above her head and hit him flush in the face with the flat side of the spade as he was knocked fully unconscious.

Suddenly she saw Mackenzie hit Sleeper in his bad leg, as he screamed out loud and Mackenzie freed himself. He was already on his feet as he did not hesitate in pointing the gun directly at Sleeper who was rolling around grabbing his leg.

'Fuck yo...' he began to say.

'No Mackenzie,' said Rachel suddenly behind him without his knowledge, 'I think it's more like fuck you!' She squeezed the trigger the Glock that Sleeper had given her, point blank range at the base of his skull as his face exploded and skin and brain matter mixed with bone covered the glass to the greenhouse.

Rachel stood there in shock as Sleeper stared at her nodding to tell her that she had done the right thing, as she began to shake uncontrollably. And as she let all the tears she felt for the children buried beneath her feet flow freely, as Sleeper took her in his arms and held her as tightly as he could whispering that everything was going to be all right.

FIFTY THREE

Rachel head was spinning out of control as she did her best to try and stay focused on all the issues clouding her mind like the early mist they'd perceived earlier. Nothing made sense anymore. Nothing at all, it was just like when they turned one brick over, a heavier one appears in its place.

Just how had Mackenzie been able to do the things he'd been doing? But the answer had been right before them. It had been exactly as Sleeper had put it, *"how do you think he's got away with it for so long?"* I mean who in their right mind would have believed that the chief of police, who was supposed to protect and serve the public, would betray them all at the highest level deceit.

She felt drained of all life as she tried to comprehend all of the madness that surrounded her. And so, she had told Sleeper, who had insisted on driving after witnessing the state Rachel had been left in, that she wanted to be left all alone. After they'd left the farmhouse in Knutsford, she simply requested that he take her home. They were almost back in Manchester, when Sleeper called Chan, instructing him to make two phone calls. First he was to phone Detective Hunter with an anonymous phone call, at Rachel's request, which hadn't pleased Sleeper at all.

Chan was to inform her as to what she'd find at the house in Knutsford. Rachel wondered what Hunter was going to make of all this. She knew that she hated the man, but she didn't think for one minute that Hunter would have believed that he could have possibly been involved at the highest level of the operation. Rachel felt as if she was being pulled all over the place as Sleeper eased the car over to the curb.

It was almost eleven o'clock in the morning and she just didn't know where the time had gone. It seemed they done so much

since Sleeper had picked her up the night before. He was to travel straight over to Chan's from dropping her off in Salford. Chan had already arranged for a doctor to be there after he'd explained what had happened. Chan also told him to tell Rachel that Tony was doing fine, but that he was worried about her. She had told him to explain to Tony that she'd see him later that night, for right now she had to be isolated from everyone with her own thoughts. She didn't want anybody around right now. Her head had completely gone west and the latest turn of events had knocked her for six.

Walking through her front door, her head dropped as she felt the weight of the world pushing her further towards the ground. As she looked up, she was shocked to see Brendan standing there.

'What you doing here?' she asked wearily.

'I never left,' he told her. 'You look awful.'

'Thanks,' she replied, shutting the door and right now, just wanting him to disappear. 'Shouldn't you be some place else Brendan. I'd have thought that Hunter would have...'

'I guess after listening to your calls that came through to your answer machine, that I should have been someplace else,' he told her as he took her in his arms, but she shrugged him away as he stared at her. 'I switched my mobile off. I've no doubt that Hunter tried contacting me. But when I heard about Freddy Marshall. What I mean to say is that Hunter left several messages for you, that's how I found out. Well, I just figured that after that man picked you up last night. Well I figured that you were already... Oh fuck, I don't know what I'm trying to say, apart from, that... I just wanted to be here when you got back.'

'I think it's maybe best if you just left.' She appreciated what he had said, or tried to say anyway. But she just needed space right now.

'Not until we've got you into a hot bath,' he told her walking through to the bathroom, reluctant to leave, as he began running the water. 'Now are you going to tell me what happened or not?'

She walked through to the bathroom as he was bent over the tub rinsing his hands in the water to see how hot it was. 'I don't think you want to know what I know.'

'Why don't you try me,' he smiled at her, as she felt herself being drawn to him once again.

He began pouring the moisturising suds into the water as the water began to froth wildly. She was staring vacantly at him. She didn't know what to say; she still hadn't fully comprehended the

facts of what they had discovered or what she had done. Halenbrook was also dead; she killed him when she had slammed the spade into his face. She hadn't realised just how hard she'd hit him, not that she had cared at the time. Only now, she had both their deaths on her hands. And that she was having some trouble dealing with right now.

Sleeper offered to take care of the corpses of Halenbrook and of his superior, the chief of police, who had abused not only his position, but the innocence of so many. God only know how long he'd been killing children, maybe it went back a lot further than they could even imagine. How could someone do the things they did. She didn't buy all this viscous circle crap.

She knew people who had been abused and would never think of laying there hands on another child in such a way. But what Mackenzie did was try and justify what he'd done by saying it was genetic almost. What a crock of complete shite. All that he had done was reveal himself to be what he always was, a true coward. Why take the lives of the innocent so brutally.

And the bit about the children trusting police officers. He couldn't have been more right. It was what all parents told their children. And he had known this. He had wormed his way through the ranks on the police force for this very reason. It had taken him years to achieve, but he had finally got what he wanted. And in such a position, he was untouchable. Especially when all of the higher brass thought so much of him.

It was also the very reason why she hadn't allowed for Sleeper to dispose of the bodies. She couldn't let him hide the evidence, no matter what the consequences may be to her. This made her wonder what would happen now. She knew that Hunter would head the investigation into the chief and through the investigation they would discover Rachel's involvement. She just didn't care anymore.

But what she didn't know was how far they would allow Hunter to get with the investigation. She feared that because of Mackenzie's position, they would do everything in their power to cover it up. So to help matters along the way, she knew that Sleeper had also instructed Chan to make a second phone call to inform somebody at the Manchester Evening News that they knew of what had not only taken place, but where he could also find the police that very morning.

He was a reporter by the name of Andrew Radcliffe, who had won awards for his many reports over the years, yet had always remained right here in Manchester. They knew him to be one of the straightest reporters around. She didn't want anything

covered up, and Sleeper agreed with her. They wanted the world to know what had happened.

'It's ready,' said Brendan, breaking her thoughts as she shook her head slowly at him.

'Sorry.'

'Don't be,' he said, as he stretched to his full height and came to her. Walking around to the back of her, he kissed her neck as he began removing her filthy clothes slowly, until she was fully naked. Moving her towards the bath, he helped her into the hot soapy water, as she felt it take control of her tension.

After about five minutes of neither of them saying a word, as he continued to sponge her down as if she was a helpless child. She stared at him, tears inter-mingled with the water dripping through her hair. Could she trust him enough to tell him? Everybody would know about Mackenzie by the end of the day. But would he understand what she had done to the man? She liked to hope that he would. And there was going to be only one way to find out, so sighing deeply she suddenly broke the silence and said. 'I know who the Pied Piper was.'

'What do you mean was?' he asked, not looking at all shocked at what she had just said, as he continued to sponge her down.

'Why don't you look surprised at what I just told you?' She asked as she searched his eyes for recognition of what she had just told him.

'I'm just listening Rachel,' he told her smiling, as she wondered if it was at all possible that he already knew that it was Mackenzie. 'You'll tell me who it is if you want to. Do you? Do you want to tell me who he is?'

'You're not going to believe me,' she said, dropping her head.

'Why?'

'Because he wasn't the all-mighty,' she said. 'But he was the chief of police himself. We found out that it was Ma...'

'Mackenzie,' his face looked astonished, although she thought he didn't actually seemed that surprised... but she let it go, putting it down for now to her state of mind at the present time. 'You're telling me that it was Chief Mackenzie that was taking the kids?'

'No,' she said. 'He was taking the kids from the ones who took the kids. The Cartwright's took the kids from up this way, just like the guy in London took the kids from down that way. Plus the O'Leary'sand god only knows who else. But it would have been Mackenzie who supplied them with the information as to which parents were addicts or which children came from abusive

homes. After all he had access to that kind of information. He used and abused his...'

'How the hell have you discovered all of thi...'

'Just listen,' she said, before he could finish. 'He was the one who Charlotte used to run away with. The Cartwright's gave Charlotte to him as a gift, to show the loyalty to the freak, all those years ago in London. She was supposed to have been killed in an accident along with her sister Bethany, but Luther Cartwright fucked it up. They couldn't chance killing her after that. But Charlotte had just got too close to the truth in the last year, just like I got too close. She discovered what her parents had been doing over the website. She discovered the film. She then ran away to Mackenzie, thinking in her confused state of inclination, that he was somehow going to protect her. Only when she realised just who he really was, the one thing that had been right in front of her for so many years without her realising. Well, then it just was too late for her.'

'You're saying that Mackenzie killed her?'

She nodded slowly. 'But not just her.'

'All the kids?'

'All of them,' she said. 'God knows how many others that we don't know about. But none of that will matter.'

'Why?'

'Because the police are going to find the bodies.'

'Where?'

'In Knutsford,' she sighed deeply. 'At Mackenzie's home.'

'Is he there now?'

She nodded as she looked deeply into his eyes. 'He's there alright, but he won't be going anywhere. Nor will that little weasel Halenbrook. They'll find their bodies in the greenhouse where the children are bur...'

'Halenbrook is involved as well, and what the hell do you mean,' he looked at her searching her eyes for truth, 'their bodies? What have you gone and done Rachel?'

'I killed them both,' she said bluntly as he fell backwards into the toilet.

'You killed the chief of police,' he was shaking his head at her, his eyes wild in despair as he continued to shake in head, as if trying to rid his mind of what he'd just been informed.

'Yes,' she said defiantly. 'And I'd do it all again if I thought that it prevent...'

'It's the chief though... And it's another police officer, a detective for Christ sake. You killed the chief and a detec...' he trailed away lost for words as they sat there in silence. 'What the

hell did you go and do Rachel? Do you actually realise what you've just told me for Christ sake.'

'I just told you that he killed dozens, probably more in fact, of kids,' she said staring at him as he continued to shake his head. 'I killed Halenbrook with a spade and I shot that wanker Mackenzie through the back of his head. As he was about to kill a friend of mine I might add. I had no choice. I did what I had to...'

'Not this time you didn't,' he said getting to his feet.

'What do you mean Brendan?' she said. 'They made me dig my own grave. It's how I know the bodies are there. I found Charlotte. They were going to kill the two of us. It was them or u...'

'I mean, that this time it was different,' he told her, as he walked to the door. 'I can see it in your eyes as clear as day Rachel. This time you enjoyed it.'

'How can you even say something like...'

'I can say it,' he said, 'because I can see it so clearly Rachel. You liked what you did, you enjoyed the fact you took someone's life this time. This wasn't like the Cartwright's Rachel. This time you took real pleasure from killing those men.'

'How can you say something like that to me,' she screamed at him, as he turned his back on her.

'I can't be around you right now,' he said without looking at her.

'What!' she exclaimed.

'I always knew that if you came face to face with this Gabriel that you would...' He sighed as he stopped, closing his eyes as if he was deep in thought. 'But I kinda of figured that we'd have caught him before you did that. That way, I would never have to bare witness to what I just have in this very room.'

'It wasn't like that...'

'Yes it was,' he said turning towards her.

'What the fuck do you know?' she sneered at him, as he came back to the bathtub and bent down.

'I... like you Rachel,' he pointed to his right eye, 'have stared real killers in the eye.'

'So fucking what?' he responded defiantly.

'So,' he shook his head. 'I never thought I'd be staring into the eyes of one as she arrived home today.'

'You're full of shit Brendan,' she screamed at him. 'Get the fuck out of my face and get the fuck out of my...'

'Don't worry,' he said pushing himself away from the bath. 'I'm out of here.'

She watched as he walked straight out of the bathroom and then she heard the front door slam. She broke down right there in the bathtub. Why had he said such things to her? Why had he called her what he had? Made out that she was the one in the wrong? What had he seen that she hadn't? Why had he just left like that? Had she become the monster that she feared so much? Did she really enjoy what had taken place?

She didn't know how long she was lay there, all she knew was that the water had gone cold as she suddenly jumped at the banging at the door. Leaping from the bath she grabbed a towel and ran to the door, convinced it was Brendan that had returned to see her.

'Brendan...' she called out as she yanked the door open.

'No it's not' snapped Hunter, pushing her back into the apartment. 'Was he fucking here kid?' For the first time ever, Rachel witnessed panic in her friends eyes.

'What the fuck is going on Hun...'

'Was he here or not kid?'

'Yes.'

'How long ago?'

'I don't know,' she said panicking, as she saw her friends face and sheer look of horror upon it. 'Maybe fifteen minutes or more. Hunter suddenly crackled into the radio she was holding. 'McCarthy is in the area everybody, find him now, and I mean now. Mike...'

'I'm here,' came back over the airways as Rachel stared at Hunter.

'I want the son of a bitch found immediately,' she screamed at the radio.

'What the fuck is going on Hunter?' asked Rachel, wondering what it was that she wanted so desperately with Brendan.

'It's him.'

'What the fuck do you mean it's him Hunter?'

'He's Gabriel,' she said, as the news shook Rachel so badly, that she collapsed against the wall as Hunter grabbed her.

'What the...'

'We've got witnesses from last night who identified him from pictures we showed them,' said Hunter.

'Why would you show them his picture?' She refused to believe what she was being told. 'Why Hunter?'

'Because of the description they gave us,' she said. 'One said that she was sure that she'd seen him in the newspapers. They positively id'ed him as the one getting off a motorbike in the opposite street to the one where we found Marshall. It's him alright. He's been playing us all like fools all along kid.'

'No, no, no I don't believe it,' cried Rachel as tears resurfaced. 'You can't just believe what some witnesses told you Hunter. Surely at the hour that they saw him and in the dark light. And what about... No, this just can't be right Hunter.'

'Listen kid,' sighed Hunter, 'I didn't want to believe it either. I know you liked him, we all liked him kid. But I think that he was infatuated with you Rachel. Have you asked yourself why you were spared that night? We all questioned why it took him so long to resurface. Maybe it was his way of gaining contact to you kid. Maybe by continuing the killings he knew that he'd be close to you again. And hey, it worked. Maybe this is all the motivation we've searched for. You, all along, was the motivation, you was his motivation. He was trying to get close to you. I've heard him sing your praises in the past, but I never thought anything of it.'

'Alright then,' she said not believing any of it. 'What about the others? What about Morgan and Fairchild? What about them Hunter?'

'They both ripped him apart in court over the last couple of years,' she said. 'Made a mockery of what it was that he did. Maybe he perceived them as heartless lawyer's kid. Hence taking their hearts with him. Maybe all of what he did was just a way of fucking with all of our heads. You said that yourself. He's done everything that he has merely to baffle and confuse us. Fuck, can't you see it all now kid?'

'It still doesn't prove...'

'Listen, I know you were at the house last night,' she sighed. 'I gave you the fucking address for Christ sake. I also found these by the back door.' She held her hand out with the used brass bullet casings.

'What do you want me to say?'

'I know you're pissed off here kid,' she said holding her shoulders and staring at her face. 'But listen to me, we've got his prints all over the knife that we found there along with what we presume is his blood over the smashed banister.'

'It's Sleeper's,' she said.

'There are two blood types though,' she said. 'He must have been hurt somehow. We found traces of blood out back going over the back wall and down the alleyway. It's come up as the

same blood type that we found on the banister. Lucy has rushed all of the tests through because we didn't want to just take the word of the witnesses into account. That's how we know it's his prints kid. We're just waiting on the tests to come through.'

'It can't be him,' she was shaking her head uncontrollably as her wet hair swung back and forth when it all suddenly came tumbling down upon her as it appeared to fit into place. Running through to the bathroom, she spewed the lining from her stomach as the yellow bile stung her mouth. She could not comprehend that a man she had shared her bed with was the one who was responsible for the deaths of her husband and daughter... it just couldn't be.

'Lucy got semen all over the place,' added Hunter, standing over her as she rubbed her back like a mother would. 'And I betting odds on favourite that it belongs to him kid.'

'No, no, no,' wailed Rachel, still on her knees. 'He can't be Hunter, Nooooo. He can't be the one. Nooooo, he shared my...'

Hunter grabbed hold of her, as she pulled her up from the floor. Grabbing her arms she held her close and hugged her tightly. 'I'm so sorry kid, I really am.'

'How can he be the one,' sobbed Rachel, as she held so tightly to her friend.

'That's what we need to find out kid.'

'He was just here with me,' she sobbed. 'We argued about...'

'About what?' she asked as she stroked Rachel's wet hair.

'About what I did to...'

'Mackenzie,' she finished her sentence. 'I know what you did already.'

'Have you been to the house?'

'We have,' she said. 'We got confirmation on Brendan's prints whilst we were there. I came straight over and left a team of...' She led her through to the kitchen. 'Look we don't have to talk about that for now. Let's go through here.'

'What now Hunter?' asked Rachel, shaking physically as she thought of Brendan touching her in this very room.

'Why don't you start by telling me whatever it is that he's told you kid,' she said, as Rachel sat down at the table. 'It looks as if he's being playing with us all, like we was a bunch of puppets, here only for his own sick perverted amusement.'

Rachel sighed deeply as shook her head and just stared out of the window, tears rolling down her face as if they were never going to stop themselves.

FIFTY FOUR

Almost a week had past and they had heard nothing more of Brendan McCarthy. He seemed to have disappeared from the face of the earth. The case into him was dragging and Rachel knew better than most, just how frustrating this must be for the police. They had no leads and Hunter appeared to be so wrapped up in both cases that she hadn't really had time to visit with Rachel, whom for the time being was staying with Tony on her old estate of Ordsall.

Rachel was sat in living room, lost in her own thoughts, pretty much as she had been all week. The fact that Brendan was the prime suspect as Gabriel changed so many things. She had shared time with this man; she had even shared her bed with him. She never imagined that it would have been someone that she would have known so closely. And the simple fact muddled everything within her head. Rachel had barely slept that week. Even surrounded by the three who had sworn not only to protect her, but to also seek vengeance. She found herself constantly drifting in and out of restless sleep. Never quite sure what was reality and what wasn't.

Then to top all of that was the case against Mackenzie that was all over the national and local media outlet from the press to just about every news station on the television. It was also why she was hiding away at her brothers. The Sky news program that she watched, though it was muted, covered the two stories.

She was in the headlines again, and she hated the publicity she was receiving. She had been linked to the Mackenzie case through someone leaking her name to the press and the fact that she was looking into the missing girl, Charlotte Cartwright. She knew that they would hound her until they got a story. But luckily for her, they dared not to enter the confines of the estate

whose reputation preceded most of the other well known estates in the area.

Also so far, only she, Sleeper and Hunter knew that she had been intimate with the man. Sleeper had never said a word about what had happened between her and McCarthy to the others. She hadn't wanted for them know, she knew that she'd tell Tony when the time was right.

But the last thing she needed right now was her brother or the press over reacting to the issue. The issue that she was having enough trouble dealing with it herself, without anybody else interfering. How had she of all people, been so blind to him. She had lost count of the number of times she had been sat so close to the man, the man who was now the main suspect in the slaying of so many people.

But worst of all, how had she let herself give in to the temptation of the man who had taken the lives of her husband and daughter so viciously. She just couldn't forgive herself. She had set out to kill the killer of her family and along the way become side-tracked into issues that didn't concern her directly. Everything had become so clouded that she believed that she had lost her edge. She still couldn't believe that she'd been so blinded by all the facts that when she thought about them had been right there in front of her.

If she thought that she had felt guilt before, then she had been mistaken. She had not only let the killer of her family lay his hands upon her, she had let him enter her, become one with her. She shuddered at the thought of it, and what it worse was there was no denying that she had enjoyed the contact of him... at the time anyway. Now she was merely left with the repulsion of what taken place.

She had tried to work things out in her own mind. Unravel the puzzle where most of the pieces had been lost along the way and fit it back together again.

Things like the case against Joseph O'Reilly that Peter had tried. When Brendan claimed he first met her husband, but hadn't realised it was him. The fact he'd given O'Reilly to them on a platter. O'Reilly had said that he wasn't Gabriel, but that he knew of him. Is that what he meant, that McCarthy was in fact Gabriel? And if he believed that he was Gabriel, then who was Michael. Or were both characters, acting out the same fantasy through the same entity.

She'd been blinded by too much already to even contemplate thinking straight. And to think, he'd actually told her with his very own mouth, that he'd been O'Reilly's shrink to start with,

but he'd said over in Sheffield. And then he'd told her that he'd moved straight from Glasgow, why hadn't she picked up on his blatant mistake… or was it a mistake? Thinking about it, it was like he was constantly testing her to see if she was falling hook, line and sinker with everything that he fed her. He was testing to see if he could get away with it all. Knowing he could, because of the attraction she'd felt towards him. It had clouded all of her judgement, as he played mind games with her.

'Someone is here to see you Rachel,' said Tony, interrupting her thoughts as he stood in the doorway with Hunter just behind him.

She looked exhausted, completely drained as walked through into the living room with Sleeper and Eazy trailing behind her. Her hair was tied up, but Rachel could tell it was because she hadn't washed it. It looked greasy to the eye and her clothes looked like she had worn them over and over for the last few days. But still, no matter what, she couldn't hide her natural beauty.

'You alright kid?' she asked glancing at the two behind her then back to Rachel.

Rachel sighed shaking her head. 'I just… well… you know… I still can't believe it Hunter.'

'I know,' she replied.

'Have you found where he is yet?' asked Sleeper, sitting at the dining room table with Eazy as Tony sat right beside Rachel.

'Not yet,' she replied without looking at him.

'Have you've nothing to indicate where he could be?' asked Eazy.

'Nada,' she replied, as she sat down in the armchair and immediately lit a cigarette.

'What have you got then?' asked Tony.

'We searched the address that he was registered to in Walkden,' she said. 'We found all kinds of shit there. Nothing that you could call solid evidence. But one hell of a lot of incriminating evidence.'

'Like what?' asked Sleeper.

'We found all kinds of paraphernalia to do with archangels and so forth,' she answered still refusing to look at him. 'But not that it mattered anyway.'

'Why?' asked Rachel.

'Not after all the checking we've done into him,' she said, pulling deeply on her cigarette as she exhaled the smoke. 'He attended Edinburgh University like he told you kid. Only one of his final papers that he submitted was all about archangels. He

apparently researched how the mind of an archangel would work in relation to the scriptures you can all read in the bible. He was, from what we've been told, kind of an obsessed with them. Especially the one known as Gabriel. He believed that he knew exactly how their minds worked. He also completed another paper on the mind of Lucifer himself. And how Satan got into the minds of the archangels and made them carry out his work. Very much as he probably believes he's been carrying out his work lately. He was obsessed that these archangel's were all around us. And that the demons worked side by side with them. We spoke with an old girlfriend who told us all about his obsessions. She stayed on at the university and became a lecturer herself. She used to see him just before he started dating the girl he told you about kid.'

'The one that died in a hit and run accident?'

'Oh no Rach. She didn't die in no hit and run accident kid,' she said. 'She was found butchered and raped to death in her halls of residence. The body had been mutilated so badly that it was him that had to identify her remains.'

'And he was never a suspect?' she asked in disbelief.

'He had a solid alibi for the night. He was out with some friends who all claimed they had been drinking in the student's union bar up there. There were too many people that cleared him for the time of the girl's murder,' she told him. 'Although looking back on this now...'

'Well what about his mother or brother then for that matter?' she asked. 'Is is mother dead? Is the brother still up that way?'

'Mother, brother and the so called father who he told you went to America,' she said 'all died in a suspicious house fire when he was only nine years old. The house burnt down with them all asleep in their rooms.'

'You're kidding,' said Tony.

'Not at all,' she said. 'It was his aunty who brought him up. She still lives up that way. The girl remembered her and we looked her up. And you're never going to guess what it was that she did for a living back then.'

'I think I'll believe about anything at this point,' sighed Rachel.

'She was a local brass, a well known hooker,' she said. 'Like I said, we've been up there and spoken with her. She openly admits it, quite a looker too to be honest. I imagine she must have been busy in her day. Anyway, she says that little Brendan was always such a shy lad when he was a boy. That all he ever did was read books. But she also remembers that he was kinda obsessed with these angels. She had explained to him that his

parents and brother had been taken to heaven by the angels, but she said he turned around and said that they hadn't...'

'What do you mean?' asked Rachel.

'She says that he told her that the angels from heaven didn't take them,' she shook her head. 'But the archangel's of hell took them.'

'Why would he say such a thing?' asked Rachel.

'I'll get to that,' she said. 'But the other thing she told us was that he was always sneaking up on her.'

'What do you mean?' asked Rachel. 'Do you mean she used to bring her clients home with her?'

'All the time,' she said. 'She says that she knows he used to always watch her. But in the end she just let him get on with it. Said that she didn't care, as she figured he was getting an education out of it.'

'When was the last time that she saw him?' asked Sleeper. 'Are they still close to one another?'

'No,' said Hunter. 'She says that after he left university she never saw him again. No letters, no visits, nothing. Said she'd heard what it was that he had become through him being on the news and so forth, but that was about it.'

'What she say about the house burning down?' asked Sleeper.

'That's what I was getting to. She told us that the kid was being abused by the father and the brother. Both sexually and mentally,' she said finally looking at him. 'The aunty says that the boy still loved his mother, but because she turned a blind eye to what was happening he turned on her as well. That's why...'

'Hold on a minute,' said Tony. 'So you're telling us that he did burn the house down.'

'It was a gas explosion according to the report,' she told him. 'But the authorities and the aunty found it a little strange that they found Brendan in the back garden after the house had nearly burnt down. He claimed that he'd been sleep walking. Lame as fuck I know. But they just didn't push the matter. And besides which, the aunty had said she'd take him in. I think she was actually a little scared of the boy back then, she just didn't want to admit it.'

'No wonder he was so evasive about taking about his family,' said Rachel. 'In fact when I think about it, he told me next to nothing about himself. I think now, looking back on it, he kept testing me to see just ho much he could get away with. I think that the fact he worked so closely with the investigation must have been one hell of an arousal for him. To be able to walk

around the crimes scenes after he'd committed the crimes. Jesus Christ, this is...'

'What about staff over in Sheffield where he used to work?' asked Tony.

'Have they said anything about what he was like?' added Rachel.

'Just that he kept himself pretty much to himself,' she said. 'Although he did have a numerous amount of girlfriends. He was quite the ladies man. I think he lost his shyness along the way. He just never settled down.'

'Why did he come to Manchester?' asked Eazy.

'We now think it was because of his obsession with Rachel,' she said. 'It seems that he'd been watching her for some time.'

'What do you mean by that?' asked Sleeper.

'Old newspaper cuttings, documented scrapbooks on her,' she said. 'All that sort of thing was at the house. Photographs of Rachel and Becky at Alderley Edge. Pictures of Peter. Although I have to admit we didn't find anything on Morgan or Fairchild. Or the other victims for that matter. But none of that matters. If he wasn't the killer he wouldn't have run like he has done.'

'What about the hearts?' asked Rachel.

'We've not found them yet kid,' she told her.

'What about the evidence you found?' asked Sleeper. 'Rachel says that you found blood and semen at the house with Marshall.'

'We still haven't discovered whose the other blood type that we found in Macclesfield belonged to,' she stared at him. 'I doubt that we will either. Not that it's important now anyway. All that's important is that we find him.'

'Was the semen his though?' asked Rachel.

'Yes it was kid,' she said. 'He obviously found some way to plant the evidence against Marshall when he paid is girlfriend a visit. Either that or she just had anal sex with Fuckfingers. And that wouldn't have been at all surprising considering the amount of semen and other sex toys we found all over the house. They must have been at it night and day.'

'How did he find out where these people were?' asked Eazy.

'He used our resources,' she replied. 'They were available to him. We had no reason to question anything he did.'

'So what moves do you make now?' asked Sleeper, not at all happy about the lack of progress they had all made.

'We're all over it, we'll find him,' she told him. 'I swear that we will, don't you worry about it.'

528

'How do you know that he's not already left the country?' asked Eazy.

'We've got airports covered and we've got...'

'None of that will matter,' said Sleeper.

'He hasn't left yet,' said Rachel.

'What makes you so certain though?' asked Hunter.

'He's still got me to contend with.'

'You really think that he's that stupid kid?'

'He wants to finish his little game,' she told them. 'If what you're saying is true then he'll want me dead now.'

'Well that just isn't going to happen,' said Tony.

'I can't stay shacked up here forever, can I now?' she said.

'You can stay here as long as...'

'You know what I mean Tony,' she sighed. 'I need to get back on my own two feet. If I don't then he'll have won.'

'But no matter,' he said. 'You're staying put until we...'

'What's happening with the other case?' asked Sleeper, not allowing him time to finish as he thought about what Rachel had just said.

'You mean Mackenzie and Halenbrook,' she laughed, staring at him. 'That's like the biggest thing that has happened in years. The higher brass have all got their tales between there legs at the moment. They can't believe any of it. I can't believe it myself. I always knew that he was up to no good. But nothing like this. Jesus, I mean he was so far gone it's uncomprehendable.'

'What did you find up at the house?' asked Sleeper.

'You mean besides the mess you and the kid left us,' she actually smirked at him as he eyed her coldly. 'Don't worry about it. The gun was untraceable as far as we know. They certainly didn't match these,' she tossed the brass shell casing to him that Rachel had discharged when shooting at Gabriel or Brendan as that's who it would now appear to be.

'Where'd you get these?' he asked her.

'She took them from the house that night,' said Rachel.

'But neither those nor the fact you two were there, made it into any reports,' she added. 'I also left out the fact, that I would place safe bets on these casing belonging to the same gun. Seeing as the same size bullet was used to kill Mackenzie was fired from exactly the same sort of gun.'

'So what do you do with me now?' asked Rachel.

'Fuck all kid,' she smiled. 'I've written it off as a burglary gone wrong.'

'You'll never make that stick,' said Tony.

'I already have,' she said. 'Obviously someone was robbing Mackenzie's house when they discovered that fucking cellar of his. They saw the tapes featuring him actually killing these kids...'

'That's what was on those tapes?' asked Sleeper shaking his head.

'It was his very own private collection of snuff movies,' she said. 'We figure that Mackenzie comes home with Halenbrook and discover the burglar. They take him out to kill and bury him in the garden where they've been burying kids over the years. He somehow got the better of them and killed them. He was obviously the one who put the call through to me. Albeit we were all a little confused how he might have found my mobile number...'

'What conclusion did you come to?' asked Rachel.

'Well obviously Mackenzie had it in his mobile phone,' she grinned.

'Thanks Hunter,' said Rachel as Sleeper continued to eye her suspiciously.

'No... thank you kid,' she said climbing out of the chair. 'All I can do now is catch this fuck before he decides he wants to strike again. I'll keep in touch, alright.'

'Alright,' smiled Rachel, although now a little more enlightened, she still felt as confused as she had before.

FIFTY FIVE

Rachel had decided two nights later, that enough was enough. She wasn't going to let Gabriel or Brendan McCarthy, if in fact they were the same person, either way; she wasn't going to allow him to dictate her life any longer. She'd spent enough time locked away like a prisoner, as if it was her that had done wrong. She talked it over with Sleeper who had agreed, that maybe she needed her own space, or at the very least, that they both needed to get out of there for a while.

Sleeper explained how he'd watched her closely over the last week, and how he could tell that she was being driven close to dementia, if she stayed cooped up any longer. But she also knew that what he was saying wasn't only for her benefit. Because he too, was feeling as if they weren't achieving anything beneficial either by staying locked away from the world.

'Can't you think of anything that might indicate to us where he may be hiding Rachel?' he asked her, as the two of them sat there all alone. It had just gone one-fifteen in the morning and both Tony and Eazy had retired to bed leaving the two of them still talking about a number of issues. But no matter what they spoke about, it always led straight back to Brendan or the case.

'We barely talked about him,' she sighed, after a little while of thinking over what he'd asked. 'I only wish that I knew more Sleeper.'

'There must be something though,' he said, still pushing her to try and remember more about the one they all searched for. 'Something that you can remember. No matter how small or irrelevant it may appear Rach. Something he let slip without thinking about it. What about when you weren't alone? I mean, what about if he played all of you side by side, in his twisted sick little game. Didn't actually say it to you, but maybe to

531

someone else in the room. You know, like gave away little clues along the way somehow. I don't know what I'm saying to be honest. I know that this is your department. But I mean all the evidence points to this guy. So what do you think? I mean honestly Rach, you knew him pretty well. You think we've got our guy or not?'

'I know I knew him,' she said, blowing air out in an exaggerated manner as she thought about how close she had known him. 'But it's like before, when you asked me about what I knew about him...'

'And you conveniently changed the subject you mean,' he smiled at her.

'Yeah,' she shook her head, 'I guess I did. But only because I was so embarrassed about the simple fact that I didn't really know him at all. And because of that, I didn't know what you might think of me.'

'And why would that have mattered anyway?'

'It just would Sleeper.'

'But why?' he asked. 'I mean we've only just met. And don't get me wrong there Rach; you know how much you mean to both me and Eazy.'

'But with you Sleeper,' she said holding eye contact with him. 'I feel some sort of a connection that I haven't felt in a long time. And you know that I don't mean anything sexual either Sleeper.'

'I know you don't Rachel,' he said grinning at her.

'So that's why it matters what you think of me,' she added.

'Listen Rach,' he said. 'I know I just said that we may not have known each other all that long, but you know me better than most of my closest friends know me. And that's only because of how I feel about you. There is an honesty in you that doesn't hide away, like it does in most people. You say whatever you're thinking. That I like. I also like the fact you've probably got bigger balls than most people that I know,' he laughed at this, as she smiled at him.

'Thanks for that,' she laughed.

'It's the bleeding truth girl,' he winked at her as she shook her head, and then went all quiet on him.

'Just one other thing Sleeper,' she said looking around to make sure that they were all alone, then dropping her head in compunction, 'I want to say how grateful I am to you, for not mentioning what happened between me and him,' she couldn't even bring herself to say his name, as she thought of him in that way.

'It wasn't, and still isn't my business,' he stated. 'Can I ask you something though?'

'Of course you can.'

'Well now that everybody appears to have already judged this cat,' he said. 'And the fact you never answered me before, what do you really think Rach?'

'You mean do I believe he's the one?'

'That's exactly what I mean Rachel,' he told her. 'I mean I can relate some of what he's done, but there's bit's I don't understand.'

'I know exactly what you mean there,' she agreed. 'There are bits missing all over this damn case. It's like one of those old puzzles that you find in an old attic someplace. You think that it'll still be good to put back together, only along the way you discover that there is just too many pieces missing for you to piece the whole bleedin' thing into one whole picture.'

'You're starting to lose me again.'

'Well, it's like with Peter and Becky.' She sighed as she gathered her thoughts before continuing. 'I still can't find a clear connection towards his true motive. I mean, he told me all about Peter trying this case that he had only remembered afterwards. It was an old case with some guy that used to live right here in Manchester.'

'What was that then?'

'It was this case against this guy called Joseph O'Reilly,' she said. 'I don't think that I ever told you about this. But he arranged to meet with me months after the murders. The case was going nowhere and the police had no new leads. Nor me or ar'kid for that matter. But anyway, he called me out of the blue and told me to meet him in St. Ann's Square. When I met him, he told me that he felt guilty for the way he'd treated me when we had first met.'

'Treated you how?' he asked confused. 'I thought that the guy was supposed to be obsessed with you.'

'That's Hunter's theory, not mine,' she said. 'The first time we met, I shouldn't have even been in the room. Obviously they weren't allowing me work the case, and through work he'd done for them before, they brought him in instead. I kinda guilt tripped Hunter into letting me in on it. I was out of order really. I knew just how bad it was going to be, and it was bad having to listen to the mechanical way that he described what had happened as he gave out his theories and ideas as to what happened that night. But no matter, I was still insistent on them allowing me to be there. He was extremely rude and arrogant

about me being there. He said bluntly that I shouldn't be allowed anywhere near the case. He told me afterwards, that he felt threatened by my presence. How much truth was in that now, I honestly don't know. Although thinking about it now, he actually said that he was in awe at the work I'd achieved in the past.'

'So who was this guy he gave you?'

'This O'Reilly had come up against my husband who was working the CPS case against him,' she said. 'He was a real nasty piece of work. He was accused of rape and murder. He'd mutilated the bodies of the victims after he'd killed them. Anyway, it was all very similar to what had happened to my Peter and Becky. Only he conveniently remembers this afterwards. Says that the guy used to be a patient of his years ago. He said that the O'Reilly guy talked through a third party, one known as Gabriel.'

'Hadn't your husband put him away though?'

'He had,' she said. 'But the conviction had been overturned as they'd kept evidence from the defence. They had found another blood type at the scene. One that hadn't belonged to the victims or O'Reilly. And one the CPS had conveniently forgotten to mention. So anyway, when this guy was set free, he returned to Manchester where like I said, he'd apparently had lived before. He met me, and told me all about him. Explained all about his background and the work he had done with him. He said that I could do whatever I wanted with the information he was providing me with. And then he gave me the address to O'Reilly, who at the time was living over in Wythenshawe. I don't know if you know the...'

'I know the place. My Nan used to live over that way,' he told her. 'But what I don't understand is why did he do that for you if he was working the case at the same time? You know, give you the address that is?'

'Like I told you,' she shrugged. 'He said back then, that he felt guilty for what had happened.'

'So did you find this guy?'

'Me and Tony found him,' she said. 'Only when we did, he had himself another victim already at the house.'

'What happened?' he asked as she just shook her head at him, telling him what he needed to know. 'Oh right, I see. Your Tony right?'

She nodded that he was correct, as he smiled at the news. 'Maybe that was some kind of a test though,' she then said.

'Test in what way though?'

'He wanted to see what I was capable of killing another human being.'

'But you didn't kill the guy Rach.'

'I let it happen,' she stated. 'So I as good as killed him.'

'No you didn't,' he told her shaking his head. 'Believe me when I tell you it isn't the same thing at all.'

'What about the Cartwright's then?' she asked him. 'Or Halenbrook, or the chief of police, Mackenzie? What if what he said about me was right? What if I've become what he wanted for me to beco...'

'You're just psycho-analysing yourself Rach,' he said. 'You're nothing like any of those people.'

'But what ab...'

'But fuck all Rach,' he told her. 'Listen though; you're getting side-tracked here. Because what I don't understand is how would any of that, that you've just explained, would have led him to kill Peter or Becky.'

'That's the bit that I can't work out either,' she said. 'Look at it this way, if Morgan and Fairchild destroyed him in court, then fine. You've got yourselves a connection and motivation right there. The taking of their hearts could relate to him perceiving them as being heartless, right. You know, like in, heartless defence lawyers right?'

'Right,' he nodded.

'And then he kills your sister,' she said dropping her head.

'Right,' he pushed her, wanting to know more from her.

'There, we presume that she got to close to him,' she said. 'Just like she got to close to the Pied Piper. That reminds me, have you had the laptop accessed yet?'

'Robert is back from Germany tomorrow night,' he said. 'But I still don't follow you here Rach.'

'Your sister was an act of vengeance, so to speak,' she said. 'Or more to the point... she was killed because of whatever knowledge she had right.'

'And the other lawyer,' he said. 'Marshall's girlfriend.'

'She possibly knew too much as well,' she said. 'Or maybe she knew fuck all. But Gabriel wasn't taking any chances by this point. He'd strayed from his path into another path. So whether or not Marshall had spilled the beans to his girlfriend didn't matter to him. So he just takes it upon himself, and kills her anyway. Because by this time he's getting a real taste for the work he's carrying out. But once again, like your sister, it was because she got in the way.'

'The same with Freddy,' he said, following where she was leading with this. 'He was killed because of what he had seen. He could identify the killer, so the killer struck first, right?'

'Right,' she nodded. 'So now go back over it and who is the odd one out?'

'Your Peter and Becky,' he said.

'Precisely,' she said. 'They just don't fit into the equation. Especially when it took the killer a year to strike again.'

'But there you go, it still ends up, back in his court though,' he said shaking his head at what she had told him.

'How so?'

'Alright... Here's another one for you then,' he kissed his teeth, as he thought for a moment. 'Why when he's killed all the families including the wife's and the children, would he have spared you? I know you've said things like he wanted you to make his name and all that other stuff Rach. But seriously, why do you think he spared you your life. There has to be something else in why he's continued to leave you be.'

'I just don't know what it is though,' she said.

'Then we're back to McCarthy and you, aren't we Rach,' he said. 'It's got to be him. Think about it. He wanted you alive throughout all of this madness. I mean he could have killed you at any time, especially when you welcomed him into your home and your bed... Sorry – you know what I mean. But he didn't do anything, did he Rach?'

'Maybe he's not the killer then,' she told him. 'I mean you should have seen the look in his eyes when I told him I killed Halenbrook and Mackenzie. He completely freaked out about it. Said that he couldn't be around me anymore. He was repulsed by what I had done. I mean he literally freaked out on me. Said all kinds of things, told me what I'd done, was nothing like when I'd killed the Cartwright's. He said that this time I'd enjoyed killing them. It wasn't an act of doing what I had to, like when I was put in that position with the Cartwrig...' She suddenly trailed off as she stared at him.

'What?' he asked. 'What is it Rachel?'

'You want to take a drive somewhere?' she asked. 'I've just had a thought. It may be nothing but you never know.'

'Let's go,' he said, already out of his chair.

FIFTY SIX

'**W**hy we heading towards Prestbury?' asked Sleeper, as they tackled the winding long country roads through the darkness of the countryside surrounding them.

It had just gone 2:26 in the early hours of the morning. The night was dark and cold; although it had been raining earlier it had stopped for the time being. But the roads were still wet, and Sleeper was having difficulty with the damp leaves scattered about everywhere. The wind had also picked up, and even within the confines of the car, they could hear the high pitched whistle, which sounded like a demented witch circling high above the vehicle.

'Just talking about McCarthy, got me thinking about all the other times I been sat there with him,' she said. 'You know, whether it was at home or at the station or even the crime scenes.'

'And?'

'And there was this one time that we was all alone in Hunter's office, it was the night after you sister had been...' she suddenly stopped herself. 'Well anyway... He kept asking me pointless questions about the Cartwright's home in Prestbury. About what it was like up here. And that he'd heard that you could hide away up here without anybody knowing you was there. That kind of thing. I remember it so well, because I remember thinking how stupid the questions sounded. Stuff like they would never be able to sell the house, it would be another Cromwell Street, all that kind of shit.'

'I still don't follow though,' he said. 'What's that got to do with anything?'

'That's exactly what I thought at the time,' she said. 'I changed the subject and began speaking about something else. But

thinking back, he was a little over interested in the house. Like he had some morbid fascination in the place. Or like...'

'Or like he wanted to know of a safe house he could use, if things came on top for him,' he added before she could finish. 'Think about it...'

'Why do you think we're heading out this way?'

'You think he might be here?'

'Well I don't know do I!' she said. 'But I don't believe that he has left the area just yet. I not even sure why I'm left with this feeling. But after everything that has happened. And with the bodies now found at Mackenzie's in Knutsford. This place is going to be sealed off right.'

'And he's going to know this,' said Sleeper, nodding as she continued to stare out of the window. 'I think that you could be onto something here Rach.'

'Or I could be onto fuck all,' she stated glancing around at him.

'Either way,' smiled Sleeper half laughing, 'at least it's got us out of the friggin house.'

'That's true,' she nodded as they could see the house in the distance. 'Park up over there Sleeper. We'll walk the rest of the way.'

'Alright,' he said, easing the car to a halt, as they both climbed out into the cold night air, the wind whipped around them viciously. It was so powerful that they could barely hear themselves think. Whistling even louder and much more demented than it had sounded within the confines of the vehicle, they hadn't realised just how bad it was outside of the car.

The sky was as black as the ace of spades, as bright white and silver stars sparkled brightly against its morbid backdrop. As they looked to the house, they were not at all hopeful, as it stood upon the hill in total darkness. They could clearly see the crime scene tape as it whipped back and forth in the bluster.

'Come on then,' said Sleeper. 'No point in hanging around here.'

As they made their way across the road, Rachel began to think about McCarthy again. Could it be that he was the one. He had to be really, thinking about it. You couldn't have a better suspect, if you painted one yourself. Everything pointed towards him and like Hunter said, if he was innocent then why has he run like he has. It still hurt so much though, to honestly believe that he was the one, when she had allowed him to get so close to her.

They came to the long gravel driveway, as they began the long walk towards the deserted house. They gravel shifted and moved about like loose sand beneath their feet and the weather wasn't

helping matters. She just thanked god that it had ceased raining earlier. Wrapping her coat around her face she strode on defiantly. Only they hadn't realised just how far it was on foot, as they had always driven before now. Climbing under the crime scene tape they both walked around to the posterior of the house. Looking through all the windows into the house, they could see that it had been torn apart by the police whilst they had conducted their search of the premises.

Sleeper checked all the doors, the double glass patio ones, the kitchen one, even the front door, but they were all locked. Quickly checking the windows at floor level, he finally gave up on that idea.

He smiled at Rachel as he produced the small lack leather case that belonged to Eazy. As he removed the small silver pick locks, she shook her head at him with a little smile. Within seconds he'd picked the lock to the kitchen door. Entering the cold and now damp smelling interior, Rachel felt a chill run through her. The kitchen stank of stale food and even staler coffee, and Rachel found herself wondering about the stable girls for no real reason at all. She felt guilty that she hadn't picked up on the fact they too were being abused by Anabella and Luther. Without thinking, she made a mental note to look the girls up. Sleeper was already through into the hallway, as he switched his small maglite torch on. It's small yet intense beam bounced back and forth, as they began checking all of the rooms.

They found nothing at all to indicate that anybody but the police had been there. Rachel wondered what would become of the place now. Wondering if Brendan was right in what he said about them never being able to sell it. But as she took in her surroundings, she doubted they'd have too much trouble selling the place.

It was only as they walked up the winding staircase, did she begin to feel like they were truly intruding on the house. And not because of Anabella or Luther, but because of Charlotte. As she approached the girl's bedroom where she had sat before, she stood at the open doorway, and felt the sorrow of how all this nightmare had begun. Sleeper was already checking out the other bedrooms as she crossed the threshold into the girl's room. Walking to the bed, where the sheets had been stripped away so brutally, she sat down and scanned her surroundings.

Looking to the dresser where the photograph of her and Caroline still sat, she suddenly began to cry. Allowing the tears to tumble down her cheeks, she felt Sleeper's presence at the door as she smiled at him through her tears.

He simply nodded at her and said. 'I'll check out by the stables.' He had known full well, that she wanted to be alone, as she sat on the dead girl's bed. He left her to her own thoughts as he made his way back down the stairs in the deserted house.

Standing in the kitchen, Sleeper looked out towards the stables. He didn't relish the thought of combating the northern exposure, as he had come to name the weather up this way. But he knew that Rachel was safe enough upstairs, so he made his way out the door within which they had entered.

Making his way over towards the stables as the wind did its best to penetrate through his clothes, and did a damn good job of it, he shivered as he blew into his hands to try and regain a little warmth. He could tell that the stables were pretty much the same as the house... totally deserted.

But at the same time, he didn't want to be in there with Rachel as she grieved for the girl, Charlotte Cartwright. Even if the two cases now looked to be separate, they still would never have met if it hadn't been for the simple fact that she had agreed to look into her disappearance.

All he knew was he trusted his instincts and they told him not to trust her. This in all honesty, in his line of work, was probably for the best. He wasn't at all hopeful about being out here at this ridiculous hour. He still wasn't sure as to why Rachel had thought he could be here. Nobody in their right minds would be out here in this weather. He was sure that no one had been here since the police had searched the place. But still, it had been worth a shot anyway.

Opening the large wooden gate, very much like one you'd find in a farmyard, he stepped through into the court yard that doubled as the stables. Everything was in darkness as he approached the fist stable. Looking around he spotted nothing a miss, as he realised all of this was totally pointless being out here. Quickly checking the other stables, he figured that it was time for them to leave, as he turned to make his way back inside of the house.

Just then he spotted something out of place on the floor. It was a single tyre track that had obviously been recently left there. He could see that the track had indented into soil just between the gravel and the courtyard. As it had stopped raining only shortly before they had arrived it would have made the track a fresh one. Bending to take a closer look he realised that he was looking at what appeared to be motorcycle tracks. Several in fact, although they all appeared to have been made by the same bike. As he touched the floor, lost in his own thoughts about whom or what

left the tracks, he suddenly felt somebody else's presence behind him.

Quickly turning, trying his best to regain composure and balance in one go, he saw a large black object swing at him, as he felt it make contact with his face. He immediately felt his nose break, and the right hand side cheek crush like paper, as he hit the floor with force. Struggling to scramble to his feet, he felt the object hit the back of his skull with serious force. That's when he lost consciencness as everything turned into blackness.

Rachel sat there staring at the photograph of Charlotte and Caroline together. She reached out and removed the photo from its frame, as she thought of the two girls in happier times. She felt saddened by the thought of how much Caroline was going to miss her best friend. Knowing how close the two of them had been, made her feel her own loneliness in life. She could hear Sleeper walking back up the stairs as she put the photograph in her pocket, ready to leave the house as they had been unsuccessful in discovering anything worthwhile. She sighed deeply as she saw a shadow by the door. Smiling to Sleeper as she pushed herself off the bed, when she suddenly screamed out loud.

'Scream as loud as you want Rachel,' smiled Brendan, stood in the doorway dressed from head to toe in black motorcycle leathers, his long hair now gone – his skull shaved totally bald as she almost didn't recognise him. 'Ain't nobody gonna hear you all the way out here.'

'Where's Sleeper?' she demanded.

'Oh he's taking a little nap... permanently' he said, as he dropped the large baseball-bat to the floor allowing it to bounce as he grinned at her. 'He's joined the others in the depths of the fiery abyss... for he now sleeps in hell.'

'You've killed him,' she gasped. 'No... no... I don't bel...'

'Believe whatever you want,' he smirked at her, looking demented with his new hair style. 'I knew you of all people would work things out, I knew you'd come and find me.'

'So it's true then,' she said, watching him pulled a large, extremely sharp kitchen knife from the back of his trousers. 'You are Gabriel?'

'No,' he smiled at her. 'I am Michael. Have you still not worked it out Rachel? Oh, you do disappoint me girl.'

'What the fuck is that supposed to mean Brendan?' she snapped, angered by his nonchalant attitude. 'Or are you just so fucked up, that can't tell the difference nowadays.'

'For I am Michael the great archangel...'

'Stop talking nonsense,' she said abruptly, doing her best to hide her fear. 'You're nothing... you're nobody. You're no fucking all-mighty... or any great archangel. You're just human like the rest of us Brendan. Only you've lost your soul somewhere along the way.'

'But you don't understand Rachel,' he said stepping into the room, the knife by his side. 'Can't you see it with your eyes, what is happening to me? What it is that they're trying to do to me – to you – It wasn't what you've been led to... '

'All I see is the deranged freak that killed my family,' she snapped at him, stepping further away.

'But you are wrong.'

'Oh that's right,' she said, staring coldly at him as her eyes scanned for something to grab hold of. 'Never expect a serial a killer to admit to the murders he has committed. Right Brendan?'

'But it isn't so,' he said, stepping towards her.

'Get the fuck away from me you sick fucking...'

'How can you say those things,' he smiled at her. 'After the time we shared together,
Rachel. The good times we had. The sex that was so goo...'

'Time we shared through you deceiving me,' she said defiantly, as he stepped closer still, and she still hadn't spotted anything of use to grab hold of.

'But I made Gabriel do it for us,' he said, as she shook her head at him. 'For the two of us Rachel. So that we could be toge...'

'What the fuck are you talking about Brendan,' she said, frustrated and becoming more confused with him. 'You are fucking Gabriel. What the fuck is the matter with you? Are you that fucked in the head that you think you're three people?'

'You have to belie...'

'I don't have to do anything Brendan,' she snapped, pushing him away, as she backed towards the bedroom window. 'I know all about you. I know all about your past Brendan. You lied to me about everything, you fucking monster. You raped and abused my child like she was nothing. Then you killed the one man that I lov...'

'But you didn't love him. And he never loved you. If he did then he wouldn't have been...' he stopped what he saying, as he shook his head at her and she wondered what he was talking about. 'Not the way I loved yo...'

'Wouldn't have been what? Oh just shut the fuck up, just shut the fuck up with all your fucking lies,' she screamed at him. 'I

know what you did to your family. I know you burnt them alive whilst they slept. Was that the beginning of it? Was that what started all of this in motion Brendan. Or was it watching your aunty get fucked by a range of different men, when you was just a little boy and not capable of fucking anything but your right hand!' Rachel was taunting him, as she tried to move her way around the room towards the door where she could escape.

'It wasn't like you think...'

'And the girlfriend that was killed in a hit and run accident,' she said, still moving. 'I suppose you had nothing to do with her death either, right. You didn't rape and butcher her either eh? Don't you realise that I know everything...'

'But you know nothing,' he said, grabbing for her as she tried to push him away, but he grabbed her arm tightly.

'What was I to you?' she asked as he stood there.

'I thought you were different Rachel,' he said, not relinquishing his grip on her arm. 'I thought you understood me.'

'Well I don't,' she cried, he applied pressure. 'The only thing I understand is what it is, that you are responsible for...'

'Don't say things like that to me,' he was still talking to her in such soft tones, almost like a mother talking to a child

'Why,' she screamed at him. 'Because the truth hurts Brendan.'

'No because it's not true,' he said pulling her close as she felt his arousal against her and felt the repulsion rise once again. 'I'll tell you the truth if you want to hear it,' he suddenly smirked at her.

'Tell me,' she cried as he wrapped his arms around her. 'Tell me the truth if it wasn't you Brendan.' She was sobbing tears as she wanted so desperately to believe he wasn't the one responsible.

'But can you handle the truth?'

'I can,' she said, as he pulled her close and placed his lips against hers as she struggled to break free from his grip. Suddenly stepping away from her he smiled as she wiped her lips frantically, as he suddenly hit her hard with his open palm, knocking her to the floor as he then grabbed her hair and dragged her to the bed screaming.

'You can't handle the truth,' he sneered at her unzipping the leathers, as she stared despairingly at him. 'After everything that I did for you, even if you never realised it. Well If I can't have you for myself then no one can ever have you ever again bitch.'

He was tearing at her clothes as she did her best to fight him off, but he was just way too strong for her. He kept trying to kiss her as she continually moved her face away from him. Not

wanting him anywhere near her, as he struggled to remove his leather trousers. She had tears rolling down her face, 'Stop... please stop – stop it – please Brendan... don't do this,' she cried the words to him as he refused to stop.

'You brought all of this on yourself,' he said actually smiling at her as he managed to tear her knickers to one side and she felt his hard penis against her. 'You should have taken better care of your husband Rachel, that way I wouldn't of had to send Gabriel round to see them both.'

'Tell me who he is?' she cried, totally confused and now beginning to believe what he was saying. 'Please...'

'Oh you don't have to say please,' he smiled sadistically at her, as she felt him begin to enter her and she screamed as loud as she possibly could, as suddenly his face contorted in agony, and he fell unexpectantly backwards from the bed, straight through the doorway, as if pulled by some unknown spiritual force.

But it was no spiritual force at work, for it was Sleeper who had hold of him from behind. She could see that he was hurt as she scrambled from the bed half naked and fell to the floor, twisting her ankle as she cried out in agony. Sleeper's face looked bruised, and swollen as blood dripped all over him. Only the whites of his eyes could be seen clearly as she witnessed him, wrapping his arm around Brendan's throat as the man screamed in pain. The two of them began to struggle with one another, as Brendan swung his elbow straight into Sleeper's chest and he winded him.

Breaking free, he turned and punched Sleeper in the face as he winced at the pain added to what he felt already. As Brendan swung at him again, Sleeper ducked out of the way as he brought his fist up into his stomach, literally lifting him off the floor as Rachel crawled towards the door, unable to get up with her ankle, and drained of all her energy, but desperate to help Sleeper in some way.

As the two of them continued to knock one another about, Rachel felt totally confused, as she suddenly remembered his words of Brendan promising her the truth. Realising that he was her only hope in ever discovering... but before she could even think another thought everything fell into slow motion like a bad Chinese movie that tried to capture too much in one shot as she witnessed Sleeper wrap his arm around Brendan's neck from behind, and he tightened his grip on the man who still continued to struggle. She saw the blade suddenly appear as if by magic from nowhere as Sleeper, then drove the hooked blade through Brendan's back, and tore straight through his heart, as Rachel

544

screamed out loud, as the blade burst through his chest and the two of them collapsed into a heap on the landing.

'Nnnooooo Sleeper,' cried Rachel. 'He's the only one who kno...' She trailed off in total confusion.

Brendan's eyes bulged from his face, as Sleeper pushed the bloodied body away from him. She stared in disbelief at the two of them as it all came tumbling down on her. She couldn't believe what had just taken place. She couldn't believe that Sleeper had killed him. Even as he lay there with blood seeping through his clothes, she still couldn't fully comprehend what had just taken place.

What had he meant by, *"I'll tell you the truth, if you want me to,"* was he the killer or not? Or was he still playing games right up until the end? She suddenly came back to reality as she noticed that Sleeper was breathing fast and hard, wounded and hurt, as she clambered over to him and put her head against his chest as he stroked her hair, as he still held the hooked blade in his hands protectively, as Brendan's blood trickled over his hand and fingers.

She turned her head and stared into the whites of the manic eyes, staring right back at her from Brendan McCarthy or was it Gabriel or even Michael for that matter? Either way, it didn't matter any longer, as he lay dead within feet of the two of them.

'It's over Rach,' he sighed exhausted, as he kicked Brendan's bloodied corpse away from them both and he continued to stroke her hair as she cried like she hadn't cried in such a long time. 'It's finally over Rach.'

FIFTY SEVEN

'**D**amn!' exclaimed Eazy laughing. 'You is one ugly mother fucker brother.' He was referring to Sleeper's face, which had swelled badly from being whacked with the baseball bat the night before.

The four of them were stood outside of Tony's house in Ordsall, as the dark heavy looking clouds did all they could to break out into a downpour. It was extremely cold and blustery, but still they stood there talking away. And despite the late hour of eleven o'clock at night, young kids still roamed the streets looking to cause havoc and mayhem along the way.

Most of them shouted out to catch Tony's attention as they past. All wanting him to acknowledge them in some way, no matter how small. It was still cold outside, but they were stood there waiting for Sleeper and Eazy to leave; only they had started chatting again, once outside the house.

After the last few weeks, they had formed a real bond between the four of them. And none of them felt like breaking it, although after spending most of the day at the head quarters in the city centre, Sleeper had thought it best, if he left the area as soon as possible, so not to take any chances with the law, over the killing of Brendan McCarthy, whose body had been discovered when the police had arrived at the house.

They had both given statements to the police about the turn of events the night before. Rachel had explained to Hunter just why it was, that the two of them had been there in the first place. She wasn't quite sure what Hunter made of it all, she knew that she wasn't pleased that they had found Brendan themselves and that they hadn't informed her of his whereabouts also. Even though Rachel had explained that it been just a hunch from something that he'd said one time. Although she thought that she was far

from pleased at the fact he'd been killed, and killed by Sleeper for that matter.

She told Rachel that she had acted wrong in going after him herself, even if she did have the help of Sleeper with her. Hunter said that she'd given her way too much freedom with the case in the first place. But at the same time she knew that her friend was saying most of this for the higher brass's benefit.

But still, she hadn't been over pleased when she had arrived on the scene with her team of investigator's trailing behind her. All of this been much to Sleeper's dismay who had just wanted to dispose of the body himself. He had practically begged that Rachel let him deal with the situation, but she hadn't allowed for that to happen.

She said that this time round, the police had to be involved, and that they couldn't walk away from it like last time. She wanted Hunter to know everything, including what he'd said to her, about not believing he was Gabriel. It had made everything all that more confusing for Rachel. So much so that she still wasn't one-hundred percent that Brendan was the killer they had searched so long and hard for. Despite what the rest of them kept saying, that he was definitely the one.

He had to be really, when she thought about it, but still, she just wished he hadn't laid the seeds of doubt within her mind. But maybe that's what he wanted all along, to keep her guessing right up until the very end. And there was still the missing hearts that they had failed to find; maybe if they had them, maybe then she would be more convinced as to the facts that were so neatly laid out for everybody else.

She stared at Sleeper who was shaking his head at Eazy as he continued to wind him up about the state of his face. It was yet another issue for Rachel to feel guilty for. He had once again, laid his life on the line for her, only this time he'd come off far worse than before.

Sleeper had told her, that he truly believed he was a dead man, when the bat hit him for the second time. He said that the sheer force that he'd been hit with, felt like he'd been hit by a speeding train. He'd also added that he believed that they were chasing their own tails out there at the Cartwright home. He hadn't believed that there was anyone else in the vicinity. Even when he discovered the motorcycle tracks, he still had felt that they were all alone. Right up until the very last second. But by then it was too late.

His face was a right mess. His nose had been broken in two places and his cheek bone had been shattered along with a gash

that had required eighteen stitches leaving him scared for the rest of his life. The wound to the head, where the bat had hit him had needed several stitches, yet refused to stop bleeding through the bandage that he'd been made to wear. She knew that he must have had one hell of a headache, although he hadn't complained to her about it. He just, like everybody else, appeared to be relieved that it was all over.

'Thanks a lot Eazy,' he smiled, though his mouth was swollen along with his nose. 'I knew I could count on you to make me feel so much better than I already did.'

'Well that's what goes and happens when you leave me behind,' he said. 'You see, if you'd taken me along then none of this have happened brother. But no, you both had to be the heroes once again and save the day.'

'Make that both of us that you shouldn't have left behind,' said Tony, smiling at Rachel who hooked her arm around his in a sisterly way. 'Just what were you both thinking last night? That's three times that you left us behind now.'

'We knew you both needed your beauty sleep,' said Rachel laughing as she poked him in the ribs.

'Ain't that the truth,' added Sleeper, rubbing his aching jaw.

'Well you better take a week's nap then brother,' roared Eazy. 'It'll take at least that much beauty sleep to get you looking any near like normal again. Shit, I'd say that you give that thing from *The Goonies* a run for his money looking like that. Damn – you're almost scary looking.'

'I don't know what I'd do if I didn't have you around for moral support Eazy,' he said still shaking his head at him. 'So what's your friend say Rach? You know... the copper.'

She smiled at the fact he still refused to say Hunter's name. 'You know what she said,' she told him. 'She says that they won't be pressing any charges against you. That's why I can't understand why you're both shooting straight off.'

'I know what she said,' he nodded. 'I mean what were they going to charge me with anyway? That freak just got what he deserved. But still, I don't trust no copper's when it comes to shit like this Rach.'

'She's alright you know,' defended Rachel. 'She ain't like other...'

'Whatever,' he shrugged. 'At least we can all sleep safer tonight anyway. Fuck what the police think about what happened. They couldn't do it, and we just made sure that he's never going to kill again. Right Rach?'

'I know, but...' She trailed off.

'You're still not convinced are you?' said Sleeper staring her.

'Oh come on Rach,' added Eazy. 'You're not still having doubts as to whether or it was him or not?'

'I wouldn't be,' she said sighing. 'I just wish he hadn't said he'd tell me the truth, you know.'

'He was just doing what he'd doing all along Rach,' said Sleeper. 'Fucking about with your already over active mind. You need to give your brain a damn holiday girl.'

'I know,' she smiled. 'But it's just he said that he was going to tel...'

'When,' said Sleeper annoyed with her. 'After he'd finished raping you. Come on for Christ sake, it was him.'

'Sleeper's right Rach,' said Tony. 'He got what he deserved. You were lucky that the brother was there.'

'I know that I was,' she agreed, but then added. 'But he also said that he was Michael and not Gabriel.'

'He'd have told you he was Jesus Christ or even the Devil himself! He'd have told you anything you wanted to hear, just to be able to deny what he'd done,' said Sleeper. 'In fact he probably was more like Satan than any of the freaks that he believed he was.'

'He's right kid,' said Hunter, appearing from no where, as she walked up the street towards them. 'There is no two ways about this. He played us all for fools. We walked side by side all the way with this lunatic, and he let us tag along for his own amusement. You alright lads? Tony?'

'You alright Hunter,' said Tony, nodding at her as kids from the estate eyed her suspiciously.

They weren't the only ones eyeing her like that either, for both Sleeper and Eazy stared their distaste at her. Totally blanking that the fact she had acknowledged them. Not that it bothered her though as she merely ignored them back.

'You alright?' asked Rachel, smiling at her friend who looked better than she had in a long time. She looked almost vibrant, and so much more dynamic, than she had in the past year of dealing with all the absurdity, that had surrounded every one of them.

'I'm just glad that it's all over,' she said, hugging Rachel affectionately, taking her by astonishment. 'How you holding up kid? You need anything? Is there anything that I can do for you?'

'I've had better days,' she admitted. 'But thanks for asking anyway. And I think that I'll be fine for the time being.'

'Haven't we all had better days,' she laughed out loud, taking them all by surprise at her exuberance. 'But I have to admit, that

I'm so glad that we've finally put a stop to all the insanity. Finally we, no sorry, you found the one that was...'

'If indeed he was...' began Rachel.

'Why do you keep doing this to yourself kid?' she asked.

'She's right,' added Sleeper, looking at her, doing his utmost to not even look in Hunter's direction. 'You're beating yourself up further than you already have been Rach. We got the guy, clear cut; it was him without a doubt.'

'But how do you know for sure?'

'Because that's what I came to tell you,' said Hunter smiling. 'We've found the hearts buried out back in a shallow grave, at the Cartwright's place kid. They were in freezer bags. He must have kept them at his place all along. Knowing that we never suspected him, he kept them right under our noses.'

'Really?' asked Rachel finally starting to truly believe.

'Really kid,' said Hunter.

'It looks like the work he was involved in finally got to him,' said Tony.

'That's it,' said Hunter. 'He was always a fruitcake kid. From what it looks like now, he started the killings with his parents and brother. Then escalated from there. Only he wasn't stupid. Because he studied the one subject, where he knew he'd always have close access to these kinds of crimes. Like Tony said, it all just became too much for him to contain. He finally had to go out there and start committing the crimes he'd sworn to help solve. He knew crime scenes and forensics better than most of the copper's I've got working for me. He used people like that O'Reilly character, who we never found by the way. But he used him as a pawn in his little game. We've also identified his blood, as the blood they found all those years ago. He was at this sort of thing for a long time, just maybe using others to carry out his dirty work, until he finally stepped into their shoes to do the work himself. We're investigating more of his old patients now. We think that he may have brainwashed them in some way. Possibly using them to carry out killings for him, just to see what he could get away with and what he couldn't.'

'But why me?'

'Because you were the real challenge for him,' she replied. 'He knew that you were his true adversary within the world he lived. He wanted to prove that he could get away with the crimes he planned on committing, by not just fooling us, but fooling you at the same time. We're also looking into how close he was with Mackenzie now. We know that he'd worked other cases with

him. And considering what Mackenzie thought of your methods, it's questionable as to why he'd employ his services.'

'Unless they were actually working side by side,' said Tony.

'I don't know about that,' said Rachel.

'Mackenzie said that if he knew who was responsible,' said Sleeper, 'he'd bring him in for the publicity alone. I can't see that he knew. But then again we'll never really know for sure now anyway, will we?'

'Well either way,' said Hunter, her back to him as he watched the kids run about the estate. 'We're going to look into it. It may be nothing.'

'Or he may have just known the Cartwright's,' added Rachel. 'Remember they said that he'd past through their world and that...'

'Just let it be eh kid,' said Hunter. 'Just be happy that it's over.'

'I am,' she sighed, finally accepting the truth of what everybody was telling her. 'So who'll be taking the Chief's job then?'

'Oh didn't I say,' she smiled broadly winking at her.

'What's with the grin then?' asked Rachel, playing along. 'Don't tell me they gave the job to a lazy cow like you?'

'They gave you Mackenzie's job?' asked Tony, laughing at what Rachel said.

'They certainly did,' she said, overjoyed.

'You deserve it,' said Rachel. 'Congratulations Hunter.'

'Thanks,' she said. 'So anyway, what will you do now?'

'I haven't thought about it,' she replied.

'Well you know that you're always welc...'

'I think I've seen enough horrors to last me a lifetime Hunter,' she said before she could finish.

'I reckon you have,' she said. 'Anyway, I only came by to give you the news about what we'd found at the house, before you heard it from somewhere else. And to see how you were of course. But anyway, I better get back to the station.'

'Thanks again,' said Rachel.

'No,' she said, holding her hand warmly. 'Thank you kid, for everything.'

'See you later, Chief,' laughed Tony.

'Yeah... See you later Tony... Rach,' she looked at Sleeper and didn't say anything, as he stared coldly at her. 'I guess I'll be seeing you then as well.'

'I guess you will,' he replied, as she walked off. 'I still don't like that bitch.'

'Don't let her bother you brother,' said Eazy smiling.

'I don't even know what it is to be honest,' he said looking to Rachel. 'But there is just something about her that gets my back up.'

'What,' said Rachel, grinning at him. 'You mean besides the fact that she's a copper.'

'Yeah,' he laughed. 'I suppose you're right.'

'So are Kyle and Lisa both alright?' she asked him.

'They are,' he said, smiling at the thought of them both. 'They've returned back the apartment in Marylebone.'

'How's the boy?' asked Tony.

'Lisa says that he's been pretty quiet,' he said. 'She finds him crying in his sleep and has to stay with him until he stops.'

'What will you do with him?' asked Rachel.

'Adopt him as my own,' he said without hesitation. 'There shouldn't be too much trouble in doing so.'

'What about Carol?' asked Tony.

'They release her body in a couple of days,' he said. 'I having her buried with my Nan down our way.'

'Let us know when,' said Rach.

'I will,' he replied.

'So what are you going to do?' asked Eazy.

'The only thing that I know for certain, is that I'm going visit Peter and Becky's graves tonight,' she said. 'Besides that, I couldn't tell you.'

'That reminds me,' said Sleeper. 'We need to stop in on Robert before we leave.'

'Is he back from Germany then?' asked Rachel.

'Kezlo phoned before,' said Eazy. 'Said he arrived back this morning. Told us that we could see him later on.'

'Not that it's of any use now,' said Sleeper. 'But Carol might have had some things on that laptop for Kyle. Or legal documents, either way I'd like to take a look at it now.'

'I sorry Sleeper,' she said. 'I know you say you don't want hear it from me but I am.'

'What's done is done,' he sighed.

'Oh shit, I almost forgot,' she said, reaching into the hidden map pockets, that came with all Berghaus jackets and removing the handgun. 'I think you better take this back now. I don't think I'll need it any longer.'

'Keep hold of it,' he smiled. 'As a little keep sake of everything that has happened.'

'Thanks... I think,' she said, shaking her head. 'You have a safe journey then.'

'You take care girl,' he said hugging her. 'And thanks for everything.'

'I think that you've got things a little mixed up there Sleeper,' she said, holding him tightly. 'It's me that should be thanking you for everything.'

'You be sure to stay in touch big man,' said Eazy hugging Tony affectionately.

'We will,' he said.

'You take care Sleeper,' he said, as the two hugged one another, surprising Rachel at their openness.

They were both still stood on the pavement, as they watched the two friends climb into the vehicle, with a squashed looking Eazy behind the wheel, as Sleeper merely laughed at him, before they finally took off back down to London.

FIFTY EIGHT

As Rachel made her way over towards Macclesfield, taking the same route she always preferred to take, she allowed her mind to wander. She had always assumed that this time right now, after the killer had finally been killed himself, would feel a lot different than it actually did.

It was weird, she felt the sense of relief, which she knew she should feel, but at the same time, she felt as if she should be more susceptible to what had taken place at the Cartwright's residence the night before.

Shaking the uneasy feeling away, she stared straight ahead of her at the dismal weather. The climate all day, had followed the previous night, and had not relented whatsoever. Both day, and now night, had been threatening the imminent catastrophe. Only as yet, it still hadn't arrived.

Rachel was praying that it would hold off, at least until she'd visited the graves of Peter and Becky, and with that in mind she sped towards her destination.

Smiling, as she past Alderley Edge, watching, as the trees swung about wildly in the dramatic gale. Despite their capacity and significance, even they struggled with the realities of nature in the acrimonious world, within which we all did our best to survive each day as best as we could. She found herself thinking once again, back to the times she spent there with Becky.

As she thought of Becky's joyful little face, she felt the tears begin to swell within the rims of her eyes, as she pictured her daughter, laughing and screaming with without a care in the world. Just as it should have been for her at that age.

She had been, just like they had all been, so innocent. Why would anyone want to take away a child's life so willingly? They hadn't even had the chance to live life before it had been

554

so brutally ripped from them in such a violent way. But the conviction only angered her deeply, so deep in fact that the rage, that by now should have subsided, began once again to boil to the brink, testing even her own sanity.

She could feel her grip on the steering wheel tightening, as she thought of the killer, Gabriel... Brendan, alone with her husband and daughter enjoying, even relishing as he'd watched them suffer, at the hands of his psychotic mind.

How Brendan McCarthy could have done what he did, and not just to her family, but to all the people who he had decided within the confines of his own inclination, that they had somehow wronged him. What drove anybody to commit such acts of depraved consternation?

She thought about how close she had allowed herself to become to the man who was responsible for the deaths of those closest to her. She was still having difficulty with discovering that he was the killer. He had fooled everybody, but what was worst of all, was that he had succeeded in convincingly deceiving Rachel into, not only concealing the fact he was the killer, but also that he had cared enough about her, that he had wanted to be close to her. He had blatantly flirted, and used his good looks to seduce and deceive her further still and she had fallen hook, line and sinker for it.

God only knew how many times he'd done this kind of thing in the past. It would be part of Hunter's investigation now, to dig deep into his past, to try and fathom out what else he'd been responsible for. Motivations and incentives on Brendan's behalf to Rachel were still clouded like a thick layer of smog that refused to be penetrated.

She couldn't help herself with these thoughts. If only she concentrated more in the first place, then maybe the madness wouldn't have escalated to the height's within which they had. Brendan or Gabriel as he wanted the world to know him had strayed from his path whilst committing the crimes he did so gruesomely. He had set out with a plan in mind, but had taken the lives of others without any remorse shown towards his victims. Killing, merely to avoid taking any chances of being captured, so that he could go on killing more and more innocent people along the way.

But when would it have concluded, when would have all the insanity ceased to continue. When would enough, had been enough. She thought that it would never have been enough for him in the end, because he was enjoying the murders way too much, losing sight of his own goals. But that's where he made

his mistakes and he just made too many mistakes in the end. He let his guard drop, in the process of taking too much pleasure in the murders himself.

And then there were the sexual acts of nefarious sadism, where he had raped the victims anally. What had been the motivation or the reasoning behind that? Had he merely done it to disturb and shock the public, because if had been, he had succeeded doing exactly that. But that couldn't have been the only objective behind it; he had to have been extremely sexually aroused, to have carried out up to three successive rapes, one after another, with each of the victims.

But she had slept with the man; she knew that his sexual capabilities had been some what excessive. But not to the extremes of what had taken place with the victims. She hadn't known any serial killer or rapist that got his kicks from having, what she considered a prevalent sexual relationship, to then going out and achieving sexual arousal at such levels of amoral prominence.

Usually the person would have been sexually incapable of being able to achieve any kind of normal sexual relationship. She knew better than anybody, for a fact, that hadn't been the case. As she thought about this, she began to feel the great depths of guilt she kept trying to bury away, only it kept resurfacing again... and again... and again. She had nobody to blame, but herself for allowing what happened to happen. But that notion alone, just made it all the worse to deal with.

All these thoughts bled back into images of Peter and some of the happier times that they had, had. Her relationship with Peter to begin with, was the best thing that had happened to her in years. He offered her the stability she had so longed for. He had been the opposite, to just about anybody she had really known. And that was the one thing she truly liked about him, despite the fact he was also extremely good looking. She would always catch other women staring at him whist they were out. And she had to admit, she liked that, favouring the fact, that she was the one who was with him.

But she truly regretted the way things had been between them in the end. All the magic that they had been between them in the beginning, had been lost along the way somewhere, and all that appeared to be left was the endless and pointless arguments. They would bicker and squabble over the slightest of issues. Sometimes, Rachel believed they did this, merely to acknowledge the fact that they still existed within each others lives.

What a waste it had all been, and had Brendan somehow known about all of this? He told her before he died, that Peter hadn't loved her. What had he meant by that? She knew that he could have just been saying these things, to try and get inside her head more than he already had done. But he said it with such conviction, as if he had truly known the man as a friend.

She couldn't remember Peter ever mentioning him before. But maybe they had known each other through work. It would also have made sense, where it came to the fact they had not found any forced entry into the house that night. Had Peter welcomed his killer into the house so willingly, that it led to the murders of both him and Becky?

Questions after even more questions ran throughout her mind, as if it was a maze they couldn't escape from. Only the answers she searched for, were now long gone. She would probably never learn the truth about why or how.

They were questions that were no doubt, destined to haunt her, for the rest of her life. If only she and Peter had spoken with each other more, instead of shouting or ignoring each other. She wished more than anything in the world, that she could turn back time, if only to make times happier between them.

The last year had been a difficult one. There was no denying it. They had both blamed work for the difficulties, but that was merely the easy option for them both to take. She knew that if they had both tried hard enough, they could have made things better than they had been. Like the holiday they had taken in Portugal.

There, where they weren't surrounded by work, had shown just how far apart they had now drifted. Realising that they were only staying together at that time, for the sake of Becky, who meant the world to the both of them. But no matter what, no matter how many arguments they had, had, or however many times they had fallen out, she had always loved him, despite both their faults.

As she pulled up to the locked and bolted, double gates belonging to West Park cemetery in Macclesfield, she thought back to the last time she had been there. It had been only weeks before. It had in fact been the night before she had been dragged into the depths of unbelievable trepidation, that people believed only happened to others in today's society. It had also been one year, to the night, that their lives had been stripped so incisively from the two of them.

Exiting the vehicle, she felt the freezing, brusque bluster, scourge past her and back again, whistling loud as it weaved in

and out of the gates and railings. It was almost as if the wind was like forfeited spirits searching their way around the boundaries of the mausoleum, trying to find their way home. And as they searched, the long eerie branches from the trees, whose outlines were the only thing visible to her, through her limited vision as they swooped down in the gale, as if doing their best to recapture the lost souls, imprisoning them to the cemetery where they had been condemned to spend eternity.

But not her, Peter or Becky, as their souls would no longer remain incarcerated to the confines beyond the wall and gate before her. For that was the reason that she was here tonight. For tonight, she could finally tell them that she had come to release their essences free to be at peace within the world they now lived. Tonight was the night that she could finally set free, Peter's and Becky's souls, that had been desensitised for way too long now, as she sought out the justice for their slayings.

Staring through the heavy iron gates, into the deserted cemetery she shivered. Pulling the jacket around her, zipping her Berghaus jacket to the top, so that it covered half of her face from the brutal gale force winds all around her. Quickly climbing the gates structure, as she pulled her way over the top railing. But just as she jumped down from the iron gates, into the cemetery itself, she felt the first drops of rainwater, as sheets of lightening suddenly without warning enlightened the darkened sky, followed by loud, rumbling cracks of thunder.

Ignoring the weather as it pounded against her, she soon found the path that led to rear of the cemetery. Walking through the pitch black darkness, she easily found the graves she searched for. It was almost like she had a homing beacon fitted. Standing before the grave stone, she closed her eyes and said a little prayer for the two of them.

Opening her eyes, she smiled down at the names of her dead husband and daughter, as the heavens finally opened up fully, with the threatened downpour. But the rain didn't bother her at all, as she finally began to savour the relief she had waited so long to experience. Finally accepting the truth she had denied herself. Bending low to the ground she touched the moistened headstone affectionately, as she lay, two single white roses down onto the graves of Peter and Becky Murphy.

Closing her eyes tightly, Rachel's mind filled with glorious images of all the happier times that had passed her by. She clearly saw within the confines of her mind, both Peter and Becky; laughing and smiling, waving to her from afar as she felt the weight finally, at long last, unburden itself. As the rain

continued to drench her, she opened her eyes to darkened night skies and smiled like she hadn't allowed herself to smile for such a long time.

For she now knew, that, the paralysed souls of her loved ones, had finally been set free.

EPILOGUE

'I know what you're thinking,' said Gabriel quietly, almost as if speaking to oneself and who, was crouched like a cat perched precariously at the foot of the four poster bed. Knees were bent almost to a forty five degree angle, fingers interlocked with the chin latently in position.

It was almost as if Gabriel was indeed a great scholar pondering over the day's events. No longer disguised, or shrouded away from the world as the next and the last victim lay before Gabriel. He was half dressed with his dark trousers unzipped exposing his lack of any underwear whatsoever. His expensive black designer silk shirt unbuttoned and casually exposing his large well defined torso. His muscles convulsing and twitching every so often as the drug continued to take effect.

The last victim's mouth was concealed with silver duct tape. And his feet and wrists were bound tightly to the bed. Not that it would have mattered with the amount of rohypnol he'd consumed. As Gabriel continued to stare down silently, making the entire scenario all that worse for the victim who was trying very hard to focus through the powerful effects of the rohypnol that had spiked his drink earlier that evening. Earlier that evening as he'd sat there enjoying the company of whom they had spent so long in searching for, and whom they had been convinced they had put a stop to.

But how wrong they had been thought Tony strapped there so vulnerably. So incapable to do anything as the drug endeavoured its way through his blood stream as he continued to stare back in what can only be described as utter dismay at Gabriel.

'I couldn't believe it myself Tony,' Gabriel smirked at him, almost as if reading the thoughts racing at a completely different pace to how his body felt at this precise moment. Gabriel

appeared to be suspended there at the foot of the bed, very much like an angel observing the situation in hand.

'I've been wondering and wondering just when, finally, all this fucking madness that has reigned for so long would cease to exist Tony? Or would I be forced to take care of the final piece of the puzzle. Does that piece need taking out of the equation eh Tony? That piece belonging to your sister of course, one Rachel Murphy. What do you think eh Tony?' asked Gabriel as Tony's eyes seemingly pleaded for his sister to be sacrificed, all the while his eyes still desperately searching for the answers. Gabriel then began quietly thinking about Rachel, who as far as Gabriel was concerned, was still to be considered a possible liability. But what would Gabriel do? Did she really need slaying like the others – or should she be left to live another day? After all – wasn't this really the point of everything that had taken place in the first place?

'So many questions that you're eyes are almost begging me for the answers,' Gabriel's head was shaking back and forth. 'But hey Tony... You know what? You don't need to worry about Rachel. Because you are to be the last one... not her. Of course... you know it was to be her. But where would the fun be in that eh Tony? Especially now that she thinks that she's going to lay it all to rest. Put the past behind her and finally get on with her life. But you know what? That does exactly why I'm leaving her be. The not knowing... the not ever knowing will torment her for the rest of her days. And she'll never work it out. I mean surely now you realise why she's never gotten close before. And that's just how it's going to end Tony. No matter how hard she tries she will never discover the truth. I mean how could she?' laughed Gabriel.

Stretching to full height, Gabriel stood over the immobilized Tony Henessey whilst still grinning and experiencing the ascendancy one always felt at this precise moment. Feeling auxiliary gratification from the fact Gabriel was abundantly exposed for the very first, and the very last time this ritual would take place.

Stepping down from the bed in one smooth motion like that of a cat stretching from slumber. Feet touching down lightly onto the warm carpet of the darkened room encasing the bedroom. The bedroom that over looked one of the cities worse crime ridden estates. A mere candle presented the only visible illumination within the boundaries of the vicinity. As the downpour continued its onslaught beyond the converted house its shimmering flame flickering back and forth from the night's

breeze that swept throughout the cities miserable skyline, Gabriel began looking back in retrospect at the event's of the past year. Ignoring Tony who remained too drugged to even resist the confines of the bed.

Looking back at the events that had now taken place, and despite the undeniable fact that Gabriel had taken deep unadulterated enchantment in the sadistic acts that had been carried out. Rachel Murphy had always been at the forefront of everything that had taken place, even if Gabriel hadn't realised so to begin with.

'You know Michael… actually Brendan MaCarthy as his true identity was Tony… either way though; he sure hadn't expected things to have turned out the way they have. We had both had gone into this thing as a way of me seeking out a way to release all the hurt and abuse that I had suffered throughout life. Brendan MaCarthy had come into my life initially as a means of psychotherapy to help me to understand the way my mind was working. But he was there for more than just that. He was a means of support in more ways than one. He'd helped me to distinguish things more clearly than they had previously been perceived. Beliefs that I had kept buried deeply away. But that were always just bubbling over beneath the surface of it all.'

'You still want the answers to all those questions that must be swimming around your murky mind eh Tony,' said Gabriel smiling, whilst still staring out of the window, only glancing back casually towards him.

'You still don't understand do you? I don't expect you to in all honestly. I'm not even sure that I totally understand it all myself. You see, things just began to plummet way out of control. And that's only because I had finally wised up to what it was that MaCarthy had really been up to all along. I knew that if I didn't let him take control of things completely that I stood a better chance than he did of seeing this thing through to the very end. I knew that at any given moment the tables could have been turned on me. It was why things had to change… everything had begun to become more and more blurred within my mind. There was no clear definition to the acts of depravity that were being committed by my hands with Michael's – *no not Michael* – Brendan MaCarthy's guidance and support. That was why the game plan had changed so dramatically and without MaCarthy's knowledge to the change of direction. He merely believed that his disciple… his great archangel Gabriel as he believed me to be. Great fallen archangels as he believed us both to be. Well he believed that the great Gabriel who had at one point worshipped

the very ground that crazy fucker walked on was just taking care of loose ends so they could continue with his original plan. But that hadn't been the case at all and MaCarthy should have given me a lot more credit than he did.'

Wandering back towards the bed Gabriel climbed back onto the bed and actually straddling over Tony's lower waist whilst all the while smiling sadistically. 'Towards the conclusion it hadn't been like the initiation when the psychotherapy sessions that had first begun with MaCarthy all those years ago Tony. For MaCarthy had abused his position and taken things to the next level, allowing me to feel that MaCarthy was the only genuine support out there, both physically and mentally.'

Thinking silently about this fact Gabriel now knew that the mind bending sessions that MaCarthy had used and abused had been for his own perverted goals and gains in life. It had after all been him who had burrowed so deeply into the recesses of Gabriel's psyche with assurances of aiding Gabriel to deal with past history. History that had been intensely dormant for so many years. In fact it had been at one time Gabriel's true resource in the chosen profession to get through each day and thinking all around oneself was normality... when in fact the acts of depravity surrounding Gabriel weren't customary in any kind of way.

'Brendan MaCarthy had taken my past history, and he had used it, used along with contemporary day and age to twist and turn events so that all this shit about fallen archangels began to make some kind of sense. So much so that all that crap really clouded my judgement on things. They became so imbedded within my own mind. So much so in fact that the beliefs of what should have been, were now in fact contorted and deranged into what Michael... *no not Michael...* not Michael at all,' sneered Gabriel through gritted teeth.

'That's just what he would have wanted... for the world to believe that he was in fact the first angel to have fallen from heaven into the fiery abyss along with Satan. The first of the archangels who carried out the work of Satan right here on earth. You really believe that I of all people fell hook, line and sinker for all that bullshit Tony?'

'But anyway... that wasn't the case at all... and I just had stop thinking that way. McCarthy was just a mere mortal – *nothing else* – he was just fucking Brendan McCarthy, that's all he was. A man like any other man in body... just not within his own warped mind or blemished soul. But that was the point of the man, for he had used all of his perverse and misrepresented

knowledge to his advantage. God knows how many more were out there that he'd left abused so mentally that you were left grasping at the reality left surrounding you Tony.'

Reaching over the side of the bed whilst still straddled across Tony's waist, Gabriel reached down and grabbed for the large hunting knife that had been used with the first lot of victims, the Murphy's and was so fundamental within this present scenario, impeccably so when you thought about it. Teasingly stroking Tony's open chest with the knife, grinning dementedly as Gabriel continued to explain.

'It was his one true talent in life though. For he had a gift like ability to sniff out and use other people's nightmares that they tried so hard to shield away. And I had been doing a fucking good job of doing just that over the years… keeping the nightmares suppressed at the back of my mind. Well that was until the sessions had begun with Brendan. For he'd then take these nightmares and as he talked me through them trying to make me understand them deeper than I'd looked at them before. The whole time he'd be using his seductive soothing words to convince you that you had done no wrong. Whilst in fact the entire time he'd be using the information to his advantage. Using it in the same way an abuser would go on to abusing victims themselves.'

'The truth is Tony,' sighed Gabriel, 'he'd somehow discovered the truth behind the abuse that I had suffered as a child. Suffered at the hands of an even more twisted and perverted father that I had been brought into this fucked up world by. A fucking police officer as well Tony. Can you believe that shit? He was both sexually violent to me, not to mention the fucking mental abuse I was made to suffer on a day to day fucking basis. So much so that I had begun to believe was normality for a child to be abused in such a way. You wouldn't believe the pain and suffering I was made to go through Tony.

'All this had continued for years,' Gabriel actually had tear filled eyes as Tony glared back helplessly. 'That was until the day that the authorities had come and taken me into care. And that of all things, MaCarthy was so able to relate to. Especially after what he'd gone through himself at the hands of not only his father, but also his brother. The having to deal with the guilty feeling of the abuse we had both suffered. Abuse made all that worse by the ignorance of both our mother's who turned a blind eye to what was happening through fear and embarrassment of the discovery of what was happening within the confines of their homes.'

Thinking about this fact, Gabriel realised that in fact, even though they had both gone in separate directions through their professions and their lives. But there was no denying the links they both kept within the dark and sadistic world of the abuse they'd suffered. Realising the very question that Tony would now be asking himself Gabriel laughed out loud, filling the silence of the room with the possessed cackle. 'You're asking yourself why the children then eh? Aren't you Tony? Well to answer you, it was the very reason why the children had also been made to suffer this time round. They had to be punished for the mistakes and wrong doing of our so called guardians in our lives. Made to suffer in exactly the same way perverted way. Made to pay the same price we had been made to suffer all those years ago. Albeit we took things a step further with our victims. But hey... we... sorry I couldn't leave any chance of witnesses floating around. Could I now Tony?'

'But that's also where there was a difference between me and MaCarthy though,' said Gabriel still stroking the knife back and forth aimlessly. 'You see that sick little puppy had taken the first steps all them years ago now... in fact he had still been a child himself back when he'd taken his first steps towards becoming what I had recently become. You know what that is Tony? That's right... a cold bloodied killer born out of relentless exploitation endured at the hands of those you were led to believe cared most about you. And born out of that we sought vengeance and sheer retribution in knowing that you had succeeded where others had failed you.'

'Others out there, other people like the lawyers that roamed so freely with their guises of good will that would reach out and help you in your hour of need. But they had failed me as a child. My father being a police officer all those years ago had seen quite nicely to that Tony.'

But Gabriel knew that personal strengths and ambitions had grown from this life, and by using all of the neglectgence and pessimism Gabriel was able to channel it in a new direction towards the goals that were so desired in life. Only Brendan MaCarthy had primed those dreams, desires and goals all that much more translucently... well in the beginning anyway.

For that's when realisation had dawned upon Gabriel of just what was actually possible in this contemporary day and age where the facades of society which were deemed so respectable, allowing them to hide away from suspicion of not only the law, but also the public eye which judged you so much more than anybody else.

'You're wondering about Mackenzie now aren't you?' said Gabriel. 'I had known about Mackenzie years ago you know. I just needed your sister to go after him. And I knew after MaCarthy informing your sister about O'Reilly and one of you two taking care of him. I knew right there and then that when she discovered the truth out about Mackenzie that one of you would go after him for certain. Even more so after the events that unfolded with the Cartwright's. No matter what exactly happened there that day.'

Gabriel had known all about the information on O'Reilly that MaCarthy had fed to Rachel. Knowing that either Rachel or Tony had killed the man for sure is why it had been necessary for her to be the one who discovered the true identity of the Pied Piper. For Gabriel had known what would happen when the truth was discovered. Especially with the help and aid of Sleeper from London. In fact Sleeper was never part of any equation. It had been a case of mere coincidence that he had become involved in any way whatsoever. And it had been a major risk slaying his sister. For Gabriel knew of his capabilities and just what would be set into motion given killing somebody so close to the man.

But the sister had gotten close... but just how close Gabriel wasn't entirely sure of at the time. And she could have been left to the hands of Freddy Marshall, because in that department she had discovered the truth out about Vinnie and the O'Leary's involvement in the paedophile ring. But by that point there were to be no chances to be left floating in the wind. Freddy had been a case of wrong place at the wrong time. For Gabriel knew that there had been way too good of a chance that he had witnessed Gabriel leaving the house that night. Chances couldn't be taken anymore. It was true that one path had strayed wildly into another. But that was what was keeping everybody off balance – the police – Rachel – everybody.

There was no apparent reasoning or motives that they could fathom out to the slaying of the others in the aftermath following the slayings of the Murphy's, or the Morgan and Fairchild families. But all this played into Gabriel's favour with suspicions and motives shifting balance continuously without ever landing back at Gabriel's doorstep.

'But you see Tony,' said Gabriel continuing once again, 'the thing with Mackenzie that I found out about, that nobody knew. This was through his corrupted family of more so called law abiding members of the police force. Was the secret that they had brushed nicely under the carpet years and years ago now. It

was the truth about the fucking pervert killing of his younger sister. That's right... she was but a child... and so was he. All of which had no doubt set him along the path he had followed as the Pied Piper the sick fuck. But that's not the real reason that Mackenzie had been so important an issue to me. It was his authority and supremacy that he held over people that I so dearly longed for. For I knew that with that kind of influence I would be untouchable. Just as Mackenzie had remained so influential over the years.'

Thoughts of Mackenzie brought Rachel back to Gabriel's attention... poor old Rachel Murphy, Gabriel thought sat there staring at the eerie shadow that was produced upon the bedroom wall from the candle flame still shimmering back and forth as Gabriel laughed out loud in a sadistic way with Tony stirring slightly down below. She had been used so much more than she would ever realise... for she would never discover the truth she had so extraordinarily searched for all along. She had merely been a pawn to be used in MaCarthy's game. Only looking back on it, that's exactly what Gabriel had also been used for. Well that was until Gabriel turned the tables on the great Michael – *MaCarthy* – whatever the fuck he wanted himself to be known as.

Thinking back to Rachel, Gabriel knew full well that in her search for the killer of her husband and daughter – precious Peter and Becky – precious fucking Peter who had betrayed his wife more than she'd ever know. Peter Murphy who Gabriel had known for years – and, who Gabriel had been so, so close to.

Now Gabriel wondered if Rachel or even Tony would have searched so long and hard to seek out vengeance if she had known just how bad her husband was betraying her for years now and seriously doubted it. She may have searched long and hard for the child. But not for him if she had known the truth behind his betrayals that only MaCarthy and Gabriel had known about.

'Still more questions eh Tony?' smirked Gabriel. 'All I say about Peter was that you had more than good reason to hate the man. And not just because of his profession. But because he'd been betraying your sister for years. And by doing so he had hurt me so badly in the process of staying loyal to that fucking child. You do realise just what it is that I am saying here don't you Tony?'

Tony somehow managed to slowly nod his head slowly as he dropped his eyes from Gabriel's demented stare that appeared to penetrate straight through to his soul.

'It's also why MaCarthy had poisoned my mind into believing that it was the right thing to do... to slay them so brutally that night over a year ago now. Although I have to say Tony, I never realised before that night the sheer depths of unadulterated pleasure I would feel so intensely in carrying out the depraved acts that Michael had taught so well. There was a perverted – *kinky* – sexual side to MaCarthy that both sexes had experienced over the years. It was also the one thing that had thrown everybody off my trail all along. Ingenious... I think at the thought of the masquerade that had been paraded right before their very eyes. They couldn't have got that side of things more wrong if they'd tried. In fact Lucy had been the only one who actually got close on that one. But I don't think that anybody actually bought into her theory one little bit.'

'For all three families it had been personal to me Tony, and there was reasoning and purpose behind Peter and Becky as I just mentioned. Although looking back on that... it was probably more for MaCarthy's gain than mine in the long run. For he had wanted to get closer to Rachel all along. Only back then, it hadn't been part of the now clearer, bigger picture.'

Spotting the recognition of confusion awash within the recesses of Tony's bewildered looked Gabriel smiled broadly. 'She never told you about him? Did she Tony?' Gabriel began laughing wildly. 'Oh yeah... he had a thing for her and he'd used me as a tool towards gaining access to her. Fucking ironic isn't it eh?'

Tony was shaking his head in what he probably imagined was quick motions... but which in his still succumbed state of mind looked more like slow motion from an old dated black and white movie to Gabriel.

'So now you're wondering about those couple of cocksucker's aren't you. Well let me tell you that here was also good reasoning for the slaying of Morgan and Fairchild. Only it was reasoning that I had kept concealed away through sheer embarrassment of my profession. Embarrassment that stemmed and was suffered through the abuse that I had been violently forced through. It had been just like the abuse suffered at the hands of my father all those years ago. It had happened one drunken night when both Morgan and Fairchild had drugged me with exactly the same thing that I have drugged you with Tony. And that's when they abused me in that same perverse manner that I hadn't experienced since childhood.'

'And once again MaCarthy had used his sessions to delve into to secreted abyss of my mind. He kept reminding me over and over again just how much pleasure derived from the slaying of

Peter and Becky and just how much more pleasure could be gained by taking it to the next level with more carnage. But once again... I had become brain washed with MaCarthy's soothing sessions and was once again I was led down the immoral path towards commiting more sadistic massacres that had begun to fuel my own depraved fantasy system. And what for? Just so that the great Rachel Murphy would once again become involved in helping not only the police... but also helping him as well.

'Only by this point I had really had become blinded with all this nonsense of archangels and vengeance and the game that they were playing as MaCarthy continued to put it.' Gabriel sighed deeply as in thought, the tip of the blade drawing blood from around the area surrounding Tony's heart. 'Only this game was beginning to get out of hand. For this was no game at all... this was for real and we both knew it with the slain lives that had suffered abuse and brutality and horrific murders that I left trailing more and more frequently as time passed.'

'But once it dawned upon me that Brendan never cared whatsoever and that he was in fact merely using me as his pawn in his own demented little world was when I decided to take things to the next level.'

'And the next level consisted of taking the game out of MaCarthy's hands and taking hold of the reigns to work things towards my own advantage before things were beyond my grasp. I knew that in order to get away with all of the slaying, it would have to be MaCarthy who would take the fall for everything. And I knew that over time, I had more than enough corroborating evidence that I had collected to be able to lay the blame solely at his door.

'For it would be the great, Gabriel... fucking Gabriel, eh Tony?' Gabriel continued to laugh as the knife was penetrated slightly further into Tony's chest, his eyes the only acknowledgement of the pain he felt. 'For it will be I who will conquer all and when MaCarthy finally realised what was taking place it had become too late. Because no one would believe him now anyway. For he had been involved from the very beginning. So much so that he truly believed that it was him that was in charge of the game. That it was him in control of the game... that it really should be him taking the praise for the game they played and not me. Well so be it I figured. Why not? He could take all of the credit and all of the blame and no matter what he'd say in the aftermath; if I had indeed allowed him to live he wouldn't have mattered... because I mean who the hell was

going to believe the freak anyway? Especially with the story he'd have to tell them.

'For Christ sake Tony,' sniggered Gabriel like a naughty school child. 'Even I can't believe it.'

But none of that had mattered anyway because Rachel had discovered his whereabouts before anybody else had. And with the assistance of Sleeper had taken care of MaCarthy before Gabriel had even gotten chance to get near Brendan.'

What if? What if thought Gabriel as suddenly all dark thoughts of the past began to forward. 'And so now you know Tony,' smirked Gabriel pushing the sharpened blade deeper as Tony's eyes bulged. 'One last heart to claim and then the game will finally cease to exist anymore. And best of all... they'll never know because I will see to it that they never get close to the last of the fallen archangels... for I am truly the one,' laughed Gabriel riotously as the blood began to spray vehemently and the sensation of complete euphoria began to once again to take possession forcefully.

As Gabriel observed all the police running around the estate that was usually off limits to even them, scampering in all directions like headless chickens, as they searched hopelessly for the killer they thought had finally been stopped. But who had yet once again returned to haunt them all. Gabriel's consciousness was teeming with what could only be described as pure tranquillity. The madness of the scene before Gabriel seemed like a distant delusion as Gabriel had become lost within the confines of one's mind.

Just how long Gabriel had been stood there was beyond Gabriel's comprehension that had been completely and utterly forlorn in ones thoughts over what had just taken place. And here it was finally.

The vehicle that Gabriel had been waiting so patiently to finally arrive at the scene. For it was Rachel's Ford Explorer that was making its way through the masses that had gathered, towards the concealed house that had been taped off. The frenzied assembly of inhabitants to Ordsall were keeping the police too busy for them to even notice Gabriel before them. They had gathered and things looked threatened enough to abrupt at any given moment around Gabriel.

Studying, observing even as a shell shocked perceived Rachel climbed down from the vehicle and walked slowly towards the house. One of the officers who were trying to keep the crowd at

bay immediately recognised her and allowed her through the crime scene tape.

Just then the door to the brightly lit hallway opened towards her, as Gabriel was immersed flamboyantly from behind with the luminosity from the hallway behind her. Rachel was struggling to adjust to the illumination before her; when she suddenly focused through tear filled eyes and dropped her head in total anguish of what she knew awaited her beyond those doors, as her long time friend opened the door entirely to allow her to re-enter the nightmare all over again... and that's when Gabriel couldn't help but actually smile back beneath the poker face that she had kept so hidden away for so long now.

'I'm so sorry kid,' said Gabriel.

'Jesus Hunter,' was all she said as she fell to her knees.

www.ingramcontent.com/pod-product-compliance
Lightning Source LLC
Chambersburg PA
CBHW030742030726
47497CB00001B/98